BEYOND THE WOODS

Other Anthologies Edited by Paula Guran

BEYOND THE WOODS

FAIRY TALES RETOLD

EDITED BY PAULA GURAN

Night Shade Books
New York

Night Shade books may be purchased in bulk at special discounts for sales promotion, corporate gifts, fund-raising, or educational purposes. Special editions can also be created to specifications. For details, contact the Special Sales Department, Night Shade Books, 307 West 36th Street, 11th Floor, New York, NY 10018 or info@skyhorsepublishing.com.

Night Shade Books® is a registered trademark of Skyhorse Publishing, Inc.®, a Delaware corporation.

Visit our website at www.nightshadebooks.com.

10 9 8 7 6 5 4 3 2 1

Library of Congress Cataloging-in-Publication Data is available on file.

ISBN: 978–1–59780–838–5

Cover illustration by Marta Sokolowska
Cover design by Claudia Noble

An extension of this copyright page can be found on page 526.

Printed in the United States of America

For Tanith Lee
19 September 1947–24 May 2015

Long before Tanith's passing, I'd decided to dedicate this anthology to her. Angela Carter may be the mother of the modern fairy tale, but Tanith Lee was one of its closest aunts. You'll find Carter rightly revered in most every academic exploration of fairy tales; Lee is seldom mentioned. Carter has always been considered "literary," while Lee is labeled as "genre."

Ultimately, I think Tanith Lee is probably as influential among today's fairy tale *writers*—whether they are aware of it or not—as Angela Carter.

But Lee did not write only fairy tales; she was a prolific creator of many varieties of fiction. She deserves appreciation from more than just the fairy tale corner. Being honored with a World Fantasy Life Achievement Award at least acknowledged the importance of her body of work.

Two of her stories grace this volume, the first—"Red as Blood"—and the last, "Beauty." That, too, had been decided before her passing.

Tanith touched a multitude of lives and I treasured my own long-distance friendship with her. She was—and, I suspect, remains—a magical being. You see, I finished the copyedit of "Beauty" for this tome and checked my email. I found a note from Tanith's much-beloved husband John Kaiine. He had been kind enough to email me the details of the ceremony that celebrated her life.

Read the last two sentences of "Beauty" yourself.

You decide if the timing was sheer coincidence . . .

Or if her magic remains.

CONTENTS

Introduction: Throwing In

Paula Guran

"The way to read a fairy tale is to throw yourself in." — W. H. Auden

Marina Warner's wonderful little book, *Once Upon a Time: A Short History of Fairy Tale*, was published in late 2014. Delightfully readable, concise yet detailed, it provides the general reader with an excellent and up-to-date introduction to the evolution of the fairy tale as "a valued and profound creation of human history and culture."

The book also reminded me of the term "wonder tale." I think it is really more appropriate, if not as familiar, nomenclature.

But I fear, if I were to attempt anything like a comprehensive introduction here, I would wind up quoting far too much of it. So I've taken a very informal approach.

It is not that I feel *Once Upon a Time: A Short History of Fairy Tale* is devoid of debatable points. I'll leave all such discussion to the more academic except for a single point I will dare to address in my most unscholarly fashion. Warner writes:

The most difficult task has now become how to make a story of child abandonment and cannibal witches bearable for children at Christmas, as well as for those older and more knowing, in order to keep the truth-telling inside the stories. Increasingly, the tendency now is to leave them to us, the grown-ups.

I think Warner missed something. Actually, quite a few somethings.

This anthology collects previously published stories primarily suitable for adults—both retold tales and new wonder stories.

Ellen Datlow and Terri Windling's anthology series of *Snow White, Blood Red; Black Thorn, White Rose; Ruby Slippers, Golden Tears; Black Swan, White Raven; Silver Birch, Blood Moon;* and *Black Heart, Ivory Bones* is comprised of original fiction by authors who retold or invented new fairy tales. So did my own *Once Upon a Time: New Fairy Tales.*

Kate Bernheimer's "literary" anthology, *My Mother She Killed Me, My Father He Ate Me: Forty New Fairy Tales,* was also for adult readers.

But—

Datlow and Windling have also edited books for children: *A Wolf at the Door, Swan Sister,* and *A Troll's Eye View: A Book of Villainous Tales,* as well as those for slightly older readers: *The Green Man: Tales from the Mythic Forest, The Faery Reel: Tales from the Twilight Realm, The Coyote Road: Trickster Tales, The Faery Reel: Tales from the Twilight Realm.*

Although called "speculative fiction," many of the stories for young adults in *Firebirds, Firebirds Rising,* and *Firebirds Soaring,* all edited by Sharyn November, are wonder tales.

More recently there have been the Gavin Grant and Kelly Link-edited *Monstrous Affections: An Anthology of Beastly Tales; Rags and Bones: New Twists on Timeless Tales,* edited by Melissa Marr and Tim Pratt; and *Unnatural Creatures: Stories Selected by Neil Gaiman* (and Maria Dahvana Headly).

And that's just off the top of my head and personal bookshelves.

As for recent fantasy novels intended for young adults and teens that could be recognized as extended wonder tales—the list is far too long to even begin.

Truth-telling stories are not just told in books these days. I'm not even considering dance, drama, music, art, cinema, or television.

Introduction: Throwing In

What new stories will become classic "guides" and repositories of human culture can only be determined with time. But they *are* being produced.

On a similar note . . .

There is a learned professor, Armando Maggi, who believes fairy tales have lost their magic. That, even though we need new myths to guide us through reality, we aren't capable of inventing them; we just keep going back to the old tales and reinterpreting them. Since the complexities, moral ambiguities, and raw unpolished shock and violence of the original narratives have been simplified into stories suitable for children, we can no longer dream.

Evidently, Professor Maggi believes we have no new stories to replace the old and that no one is "saving" fairy tales by writing new ones.

Poppycock!

Professor Maggi must not read much fiction (or explore other arts and media). A myriad of fairy tales are being marvelously reinterpreted or retold or newly invented. And far from being sanitized for the kiddies, many of these narratives are just as gritty, transformative, subversive, weird, and powerful as what came before. Some are inventive and adventurous while maintaining a certain fidelity to their antecedents. Others, as Angela Carter sought to do, put new wine in old bottles so the pressure of the new wine explodes the old bottles.

And authors are also using the "wine" of non-Western cultures to broaden the basis of our dreams.

Gee whiz, Professor Maggi, this has been going on for about forty years!

You've never heard of (to name only a few) Holly Black, Susannah Clarke, Lev Grossman, Gregory MacGuire, Robin McKinley, Marissa Meyer, Catherynne M. Valente, or Jane Yolen? Not even *Neil Gaiman?*

That we have lost some of the "morals," essential elements, and characters from the earliest tales is, no doubt, true. And one cannot argue with the good professor when he states the first step to rediscovering the power of fairy tales is to fully comprehend their roots, to explore the history of oral and written storytelling.

At least I *think* these are points he espouses in the 448 pages of his book, *Preserving the Spell: Basile's "The Tale of Tales" and Its Afterlife in the Fairy-Tale Tradition*. Admittedly, I gained my impressions from reading

3

interviews and excerpts and the like. As of this writing, the book has yet to be published. Since the excerpts I've read are stultifying and the book costs $55.00, I doubt I'll be reading it any time soon.

But when the *University of Chicago Magazine* relates how Maggi is invariably asked, when giving talks on the subject, "So, where are the new stories?" he can't answer the question except with, "It has to be a cultural change. It can't be one person who saves fairy tales," and he implies this is not being done by anyone—one feels one's perceptions are probably valid.

As for exploration, understanding, and rediscovery—I also see this is currently being accomplished and has been for decades. I'm sure his book is another valuable contribution to the study of fairy tales. But it's not as if Maria Tatar, Marina Warner, Ruth B. Bottigheimer, Jack Zipes, and so many others have been *sitting on their hands* since Max Lüthi's simple examination of fairy tale plot, structure, style, and meaning in *Es war einmal: Vom Wesen des Volksmärchens* (1962) or Bruno Bettelheim stirred the cauldron by analyzing fairy tales in terms of Freudian psychology in *The Uses of Enchantment* (1976) . . . or all the scholars before.

As for non-experts, there seem to be a lot of folks interested in finding out more about the beginnings of the old stories they now know in several forms. They are finding free sources online and reading. Example: Jack Zipes's *The Original Folk and Fairy Tales of the Brothers Grimm* made all 156 stories from the Grimms' 1812 and 1815 editions available in English for the first time. The pricey hardcover (or ebook or audio book) published in 1914 by Princeton University Press is selling quite well, and not just to libraries.

They are also reading "new" old tales. Published by Penguin in 2015, *The Turnip Princess and Other Newly Discovered Fairy Tales*, authored by Franz Xaver Von Schönwerth, and compiled by Erika Eichenseer, reveals 500 fairy tales that were locked away in a German archive for over 150 years. For a "social science" book it has gained considerable attention and decent sales.

Ahem.

I'm not sure I was ever on a track here, but if I was, I've probably derailed. In sum: Fairy tales are transformative and human beings need them. But the stories themselves transform and evolve even as new ones are invented. Not all of them are going to please everyone or fulfill what they see as cultural needs or even entertainment. But since nowadays they seem to go in so *many* directions, chances are that some of them are taking whatever one feels is the proper path. The roots of wonder stories are vast and extend all over the world; those rhizomes don't result in a single vertical stem. They branch out and wind about and weave here and there; they diversify, multiply, mutate, and sprout in infinite variety and fresh new fictional flora.

And they aren't at all hard to find.

In fact, there are thirty of them right here in your hands!*

Paula Guran
July 2015

*You might check out the acknowledgments page at the end of this book. You'll find the original sources for the stories selected are both numerous and diverse: seven different print or online magazines, fifteen different anthologies from three countries, four different single-author collections, and a photo book.

Twists on "Snow White" are now common, but Tanith Lee's "Red as Blood" (1979) was probably the first to so profoundly invert and subvert the traditional. The intersection of fairy tale and a certain horror trope was also a significant innovation. Lee's use of Christian mythology recalls the Brothers Grimm, but unsettles fantasy readers accustomed to more secular symbolism. The story was nominated for both the Nebula and World Fantasy Awards.

Red as Blood

Tanith Lee

The beautiful Witch Queen flung open the ivory case of the magic mirror. Of dark gold the mirror was, dark gold as the hair of the Witch Queen that poured down her back. Dark gold the mirror was, and ancient as the seven stunted black trees growing beyond the pale blue glass of the window.

"*Speculum, speculum,*" said the Witch Queen to the magic mirror. "*Dei gratia.*"

"*Volente Deo. Audio.*"

"Mirror," said the Witch Queen. "Whom do you see?"

"I see you, mistress," replied the mirror. "And all in the land. But one."

"Mirror, mirror, who is it you do not see?"

"I do not see Bianca."

The Witch Queen crossed herself. She shut the case of the mirror and, walking slowly to the window, looked out at the old trees through the panes of pale blue glass.

Fourteen years ago, another woman had stood at this window, but she was not like the Witch Queen. The woman had black hair that fell to her ankles; she had a crimson gown, the girdle worn high beneath her breasts, for she was far gone with child. And this woman had thrust open the glass casement on the winter garden, where the old trees crouched in the snow. Then, taking a sharp bone needle, she had thrust it into her finger and shaken three bright drops on the ground. "Let my daughter have," said the woman, "hair black as mine, black as the wood of these warped and arcane trees. Let her have skin like mine, white as this snow. And let her have my mouth, red as my blood." And the woman had smiled and licked at her finger. She had a crown on her head; it shone in the dusk like a star. She never came to the window before dusk; she did not like the day. She was the first Queen, and she did not possess a mirror.

The second Queen, the Witch Queen, knew all this. She knew how, in giving birth, the first Queen had died. Her coffin had been carried into the cathedral and masses had been said. There was an ugly rumor—that a splash of holy water had fallen on the corpse and the dead flesh had smoked. But the first Queen had been reckoned unlucky for the kingdom. There had been a strange plague in the land since she came there, a wasting disease for which there was no cure.

Seven years went by. The King married the second Queen, as unlike the first as frankincense to myrrh.

"And this is my daughter," said the King to his second Queen.

There stood a little girl child, nearly seven years of age. Her black hair hung to her ankles, her skin was white as snow. Her mouth was red as blood, and she smiled with it.

"Bianca," said the King, "you must love your new mother."

Bianca smiled radiantly. Her teeth were bright as sharp bone needles.

"Come," said the Witch Queen, "come, Bianca. I will show you my magic mirror."

"Please, Mama," said Bianca softly, "I do not like mirrors."

"She is modest," said the King. "And delicate. She never goes out by day. The sun distresses her."

That night, the Witch Queen opened the case of her mirror.

"Mirror, whom do you see?"

"I see you, mistress. And all in the land. But one."

"Mirror, mirror, who is it you do not see?"

"I do not see Bianca."

The second Queen gave Bianca a tiny crucifix of golden filigree. Bianca would not accept it. She ran to her father and whispered: "I am

8

afraid. I do not like to think of Our Lord dying in agony on His cross. She means to frighten me. Tell her to take it away."

The second Queen grew wild white roses in her garden and invited Bianca to walk there after sundown. But Bianca shrank away.

She whispered to her father: "The thorns will tear me. She means me to be hurt."

When Bianca was twelve years old, the Witch Queen said to the King, "Bianca should be confirmed so that she may take Communion with us."

"This may not be," said the King. "I will tell you, she has not even been christened, for the dying word of my first wife was against it. She begged me, for her religion was different from ours. The wishes of the dying must be respected."

"Should you not like to be blessed by the church," said the Witch Queen to Bianca. "To kneel at the golden rail before the marble altar. To sing to God, to taste the ritual bread and sip the ritual wine."

"She means me to betray my true mother," said Bianca to the King. "When will she cease tormenting me?"

The day she was thirteen, Bianca rose from her bed, and there was a red stain there, like a red, red flower.

"Now you are a woman," said her nurse.

"Yes," said Bianca. And she went to her true mother's jewel box, and out of it she took her mother's crown and set it on her head.

When she walked under the old black trees in the dusk, the crown shone like a star.

The wasting sickness, which had left the land in peace for thirteen years, suddenly began again, and there was no cure.

The Witch Queen sat in a tall chair before a window of pale green and dark white glass, and in her hands she held a Bible bound in rosy silk.

"Majesty," said the huntsman, bowing very low.

He was a man, forty years old, strong and handsome, and wise in the hidden lore of the forests, the occult lore of the earth. He would kill too, for it was his trade, without faltering. The slender fragile deer he could kill, and the moon-winged birds, and the velvet hares with their sad, fore-knowing eyes. He pitied them, but pitying, he killed them. Pity could not stop him. It was his trade.

"Look in the garden," said the Witch Queen.

The hunter looked through a dark white pane. The sun had sunk, and a maiden walked under a tree.

"The Princess Bianca," said the huntsman.

"What else?" asked the Witch Queen.

The huntsman crossed himself.

"By Our Lord, Madam, I will not say."

"But you know."

"Who does not?"

"The King does not."

"Or he does."

"Are you a brave man?" asked the Witch Queen.

"In the summer, I have hunted and slain boar. I have slaughtered wolves in winter."

"But are you brave enough?"

"If you command it, Lady," said the huntsman, "I will try my best."

The Witch Queen opened the Bible at a certain place, and out of it she drew a flat silver crucifix, which had been resting against the words: *Thou shalt not be afraid for the terror by night . . . nor for the pestilence that walketh in darkness.*

The huntsman kissed the crucifix and put it about his neck, beneath his shirt.

"Approach," said the Witch Queen, "and I will instruct you in what to say."

Presently, the huntsman entered the garden, as the stars were burning up in the sky. He strode to where Bianca stood under a stunted dwarf tree, and he kneeled down.

"Princess," he said. "Pardon me, but I must give you ill tidings."

"Give them then," said the girl, toying with the long stem of a wan, night-growing flower which she had plucked.

"Your stepmother, that accursed, jealous witch, means to have you slain. There is no help for it but you must fly the palace this very night. If you permit, I will guide you to the forest. There are those who will care for you until it may be safe for you to return."

Bianca watched him, but gently, trustingly.

"I will go with you, then," she said.

They went by a secret way out of the garden, through a passage under the ground, through a tangled orchard, by a broken road between great overgrown hedges.

Night was a pulse of deep, flickering blue when they came to the forest. The branches of the forest overlapped and intertwined like leading in a window, and the sky gleamed dimly through like panes of blue-colored glass.

"I am weary," sighed Bianca. "May I rest a moment?"

"By all means," said the huntsman. "In the clearing there, foxes come to play by night. Look in that direction, and you will see them."

"How clever you are," said Bianca. "And how handsome."

She sat on the turf, and gazed at the clearing.

The huntsman drew his knife silently and concealed it in the folds of his cloak. He stopped above the maiden.

"What are you whispering?" demanded the huntsman, laying his hand on her wood-black hair.

"Only a rhyme my mother taught me."

The huntsman seized her by the hair and swung her about so her white throat was before him, stretched ready for the knife. But he did not strike, for there in his hand he held the dark golden locks of the Witch Queen, and her face laughed up at him and she flung her arms about him, laughing.

"Good man, sweet man, it was only a test of you. Am I not a witch? And do you not love me?"

The huntsman trembled, for he did love her, and she was pressed so close her heart seemed to beat within his own body.

"Put away the knife. Throw away the silly crucifix. We have no need of these things. The King is not one half the man you are."

And the huntsman obeyed her, throwing the knife and the crucifix far off among the roots of the trees. He gripped her to him, and she buried her face in his neck, and the pain of her kiss was the last thing he felt in this world.

The sky was black now. The forest was blacker. No foxes played in the clearing. The moon rose and made white lace through the boughs, and through the backs of the huntsman's empty eyes. Bianca wiped her mouth on a dead flower.

"Seven asleep, seven awake," said Bianca. "Wood to wood. Blood to blood. Thee to me."

There came a sound like seven huge rendings, distant by the length of several trees, a broken road, an orchard, an underground passage. Then a sound like seven huge single footfalls. Nearer. And nearer.

Hop, hop, hop, hop. Hop, hop, hop.

In the orchard, seven black shudderings.

On the broken road, between the high hedges, seven black creepings.

Brush crackled, branches snapped.

Through the forest, into the clearing, pushed seven warped, misshapen, hunched-over, stunted things. Woody-black mossy fur, woody-black bald masks. Eyes like glittering cracks, mouths like moist caverns. Lichen beards. Fingers of twiggy gristle. Grinning. Kneeling. Faces pressed to the earth.

"Welcome," said Bianca.

The Witch Queen stood before a window of glass like diluted wine. She looked at the magic mirror.

"Mirror. Whom do you see?"

"I see you, mistress. I see a man in the forest. He went hunting, but not for deer. His eyes are open, but he is dead. I see all in the land. But one."

The Witch Queen pressed her palms to her ears.

Outside the window the garden lay, empty of its seven black and stunted dwarf trees.

"Bianca," said the Queen.

The windows had been draped and gave no light. The light spilled from a shallow vessel, light in a sheaf, like the pastel wheat. It glowed upon four swords that pointed east and west, that pointed north and south.

Four winds had burst through the chamber, and three arch-winds. Cool fires had risen, and parched oceans, and the gray-silver powders of Time.

The hands of the Witch Queen floated like folded leaves on the air, and through dry lips the Witch Queen chanted.

"Pater omnipotens, mittere digneris sanctum Angelum tuum de Infernis."

The light faded, and grew brighter.

There, between the hilts of the four swords, stood the Angel Lucefiel, somberly gilded, his face in shadow, his golden wings spread and blazing at his back.

"Since you have called me, I know your desire. It is a comfortless wish. You ask for pain."

"You speak of pain, Lord Lucefiel, who suffer the most merciless pain of all. Worse than the nails in the feet and wrists. Worse than the thorns and the bitter cup and the blade in the side. To be called upon for evil's sake, which I do not, comprehending your true nature, son of God, brother of The Son."

"You recognize me, then. I will grant what you ask."

And Lucefiel (by some named Satan, Rex Mundi, but nevertheless the left hand, the sinister hand of God's design) wrenched lightning from the ether and cast it at the Witch Queen.

It caught her in the breast. She fell.

The sheaf of light towered and lit the golden eyes of the Angel, which were terrible, yet luminous with compassion, as the swords shattered and he vanished.

The Witch Queen pulled herself from the floor of the chamber, no longer beautiful, a withered, slobbering hag.

Into the core of the forest, even at noon, the sun never shone. Flowers propagated in the grass, but they were colorless. Above, the black-green roof hung down nets of thick, green twilight through which albino butterflies and moths feverishly drizzled. The trunks of the trees were smooth as the stalks of underwater weeds. Bats flew in the daytime, and birds who believed themselves to be bats.

There was a sepulcher, dripped with moss. The bones had been rolled out, had rolled around the feet of seven twisted dwarf trees. They looked like trees. Sometimes they moved. Sometimes something like an eye glittered, or a tooth, in the wet shadows.

In the shade of the sepulcher door sat Bianca, combing her hair.

A lurch of motion disturbed the thick twilight.

The seven trees turned their heads.

A hag emerged from the forest. She was crook-backed and her head was poked forward, predatory, withered, and almost hairless, like a vulture's.

"Here we are at last," grated the hag, in a vulture's voice.

She came closer, and cranked herself down on her knees, and bowed her face into the turf and the colorless flowers.

Bianca sat and gazed at her. The hag lifted herself. Her teeth were yellow palings.

"I bring you the homage of witches, and three gifts," said the hag.

"Why should you do that?"

"Such a quick child, and only fourteen years. Why? Because we fear you. I bring you gifts to curry favor."

Bianca laughed. "Show me."

The hag made a pass in the green air. She held a silken cord worked curiously with plaited human hair.

"Here is a girdle which will protect you from the devices of priests, from crucifix and chalice and the accursed holy water. In it are knotted the tresses of a virgin, and of a woman no better than she should be, and of a woman dead. And here—" a second pass and a comb was in her hand, lacquered blue over green "—a comb from the deep sea, a mermaid's trinket, to charm and subdue. Part your locks with this, and the scent of ocean will fill men's nostrils and the rhythm of the tides their ears, the tides that bind men like chains. Last," added the hag, "that old symbol of wickedness, the scarlet fruit of Eve, the apple red as blood. Bite, and the understanding of sin, which the serpent boasted of, will be made known to you." And the hag made her last pass in the air and extended the apple, with the girdle and the comb, toward Bianca.

Bianca glanced at the seven stunted trees.

"I like her gifts, but I do not quite trust her."

The bald masks peered from their shaggy beardings. Eyelets glinted. Twiggy claws clacked.

"All the same," said Bianca. "I will let her tie the girdle on me, and comb my hair herself."

The hag obeyed, simpering. Like a toad she waddled to Bianca. She tied on the girdle. She parted the ebony hair. Sparks sizzled, white from the girdle, peacock's eye from the comb.

"And now, hag, take a little bite of the apple."

"It will be my pride," said the hag, "to tell my sisters I shared this fruit with you." And the hag bit into the apple, and mumbled the bite noisily, and swallowed, smacking her lips.

Then Bianca took the apple and bit into it.

Bianca screamed—and choked.

She jumped to her feet. Her hair whirled about her like a storm cloud. Her face turned blue, then slate, then white again. She lay on the pallid flowers, neither stirring nor breathing.

The seven dwarf trees rattled their limbs and their bear-shaggy heads, to no avail. Without Bianca's art they could not hop. They strained their claws and ripped at the hag's sparse hair and her mantle. She fled between them. She fled into the sunlit acres of the forest, along the broken road, through the orchard, into a hidden passage.

The hag reentered the palace by the hidden way, and the Queen's chamber by a hidden stair. She was bent almost double. She held her ribs. With one skinny hand she opened the ivory case of the magic mirror.

"*Speculum, speculum. Dei gratia. Whom do you see?*"

"I see you, mistress. And all in the land. And I see a coffin."

"Whose corpse lies in the coffin?"

"That I cannot see. It must be Bianca."

The hag, who had been the beautiful Witch Queen, sank into her tall chair before the window of pale, cucumber green and dark white glass. Her drugs and potions waited, ready to reverse the dreadful conjuring of age the Angel Lucefiel had placed on her, but she did not touch them yet.

The apple had contained a fragment of the flesh of Christ, the sacred wafer, the Eucharist.

The Witch Queen drew her Bible to her and opened it randomly.

And read, with fear, the word: *Resurcat.*

It appeared like glass, the coffin, milky glass. It had formed this way. A thin white smoke had risen from the skin of Bianca. She smoked as a fire smokes when a drop of quenching water falls on it. The piece of Eucharist had stuck in her throat. The Eucharist, quenching water to her fire, caused her to smoke.

Then the cold dews of night gathered, and the colder atmospheres of midnight. The smoke of Bianca's quenching froze about her.

Frost formed in exquisite silver scrollwork all over the block of misty ice that contained Bianca.

Bianca's frigid heart could not warm the ice. Nor the sunless, green twilight of the day.

You could just see her, stretched in the coffin, through the glass. How lovely she looked, Bianca. Black as ebony, white as snow, red as blood.

The trees hung over the coffin. Years passed. The trees sprawled about the coffin, cradling it in their arms. Their eyes wept fungus and green resin. Green amber drops hardened like jewels in the coffin of glass.

"Who is that lying under the trees?" the Prince asked, as he rode into the clearing.

He seemed to bring a golden moon with him, shining about his golden head, on the golden armor and the cloak of white satin blazoned with gold and blood and ink and sapphire. The white horse trod on the colorless flowers, but the flowers sprang up again when the hoofs had passed. A shield hung from the saddlebow, a strange shield. From one side it had a lion's face, but from the other, a lamb's face.

The trees groaned, and their heads split on huge mouths.

"Is this Bianca's coffin?" asked the Prince.

"Leave her with us," said the seven trees. They hauled at their roots. The ground shivered. The coffin of ice-glass gave a great jolt, and a crack bisected it. Bianca coughed.

The jolt had precipitated the piece of Eucharist from her throat.

Into a thousand shards the coffin shattered, and Bianca sat up. She stared at the Prince, and she smiled.

"Welcome, beloved," said Bianca.

She got to her feet, and shook out her hair, and began to walk toward the Prince on the pale horse.

But she seemed to walk into a shadow, into a purple room, then into a crimson room whose emanations lanced her like knives.

Next she walked into a yellow room where she heard the sound of crying, which tore her ears. All her body seemed stripped away; she was a beating heart. The beats of her heart became two wings. She flew. She was a raven, then an owl. She flew into a sparkling pane. It scorched her white. Snow white. She was a dove.

She settled on the shoulder of the Prince and hid her head under her wing. She had no longer anything black about her, and nothing red.

"Begin again now, Bianca," said the Prince. He raised her from his shoulder. On his wrist there was a mark. It was like a star. Once a nail had been driven in there.

Bianca flew away, up through the roof of the forest. She flew in at a delicate wine window. She was in the palace. She was seven years old.

The Witch Queen, her new mother, hung a filigree crucifix around her neck.

"Mirror," said the Witch Queen. "Whom do you see?"

16

"I see you, mistress," replied the mirror. "And all in the land. I see Bianca."

Tanith Lee was born in London in 1947. She died peacefully after a long illness in Hastings, East Sussex, in 2015. After grammar school, she worked at a number of jobs, and at age twenty-five had one year at art college. When DAW Books published her novel *The Birthgrave*, she became a professional full-time writer. Publications include approximately ninety novels and collections and well over three hundred short stories. She also wrote for television and radio. Lee won several awards including two World Fantasy awards for short fiction. In 2009 she was made a Grand Master of Horror and honored with the World Fantasy Convention Lifetime Achievement Award in 2013. She was married to the writer/artist John Kaiine.

Gene Wolfe, a true master of the written word, turns a very familiar old tale (or two) into a modern detective story that is both horrific and humorous. You may chuckle or be creeped out. Or both.

"In The House of Gingerbread," when first published, was nominated for a World Fantasy Award.

In The House of Gingerbread

Gene Wolfe

The woodcutter came up the walk, and the ornate old house watched him through venetian-blinded eyes. He wore a red-brown tweed suit; his unmarked car was at the curb. The house felt his feet on its porch, his quick knock at its door. It wondered how he had driven along the path through the trees. The witch would split his bones to get the marrow; it would tell the witch.

It rang its bell.

Tina Heim opened the door, keeping it on the chain but more or less expecting a neighbor with coleslaw. She had heard you were supposed to bring chicken soup for Death; here it seemed to be slaw, though someone had brought Waldorf salad for Jerry.

"I'm Lieutenant Price," the woodcutter said, unsmiling. He held out a badge in a black leather case. "You're Mrs. Heim? I'd like to talk to you."

She began, "Have the children—"

"I'd like to talk to you," he repeated. "It might be nicer if we did it in the house and sitting down."

"All right." She unhooked the chain and opened the door.

He stepped inside. "You were busy in the kitchen." She had not seen him glance at her apron, but apparently he had. "I was making gingerbread men for school lunches," she explained. "I like to put a few cookies in their lunches every day."

He nodded, still unsmiling. "Smells good. We can talk in there, and you can watch them so they don't burn."

"They're out already, it only takes a few minutes in the microwave. Can you—" It was too late; he had slipped by her and was out of sight. She hurried through the dark foyer and shadowy dining room, and found him sitting on a dinette chair in her kitchen. "Can you just barge into someone's home this way?"

He shook his head. "You know, I didn't think you could bake in a microwave oven."

"It's hard to get cakes to rise, but nice for cookies." She wavered between hospitality and anger, and decided on the former. It seemed safer, and she could always get angry later. "Would you care for one?"

He nodded.

"And some coffee? Or we have milk if you'd prefer that."

"Coffee will be okay," he told her. "No, Mrs. Heim, we can't just barge into somebody's house; we have to get a search warrant. But once you let us in, you can't stop us from going wherever we want to. I could go up to your bedroom now, for example, and search your bureau."

"You're not—"

He shook his head. "I was just giving you an example. That's the way the law is, in this state."

She stared down uncomprehendingly at the little mug with the smiley face on its side. It was full of black coffee. She had poured it without thinking, like an automaton. "Do you want cream? Sugar?"

"No, thanks. Sit down, Mrs. Heim."

Tina sat. He had taken the chair she usually used. She took the one across from him, Jerry's chair, positioning it carefully and feeling as though she had gone somewhere for a job interview.

"Now then," he said. He made a steeple of his fingers. It seemed an old man's gesture, though he looked no older than she. This is my house, she thought. *If this is an interview, then I'm interviewing him.* She knew it was not true.

"Mrs. Heim, your husband died last year. In November." She nodded guardedly.

"And the cause of death was—?"

"Lung cancer. It's on the death certificate." The covers of a thousand paperbacks flashed past in her imagination: *Murder on the Orient Express*, *Fletch*, *The Roman Hat Mystery*. "You said you were a lieutenant—are you on the Homicide Squad? My god, I'm in a mystery novel!"

"No," he said again. "This isn't fiction, Mrs. Heim. Just a little inquiry. Your late husband was a heavy smoker?"

She shook her head. "Jerry didn't smoke."

"Maybe he'd been a heavy smoker, and quit?"

"No," she said. "Jerry never smoked at all."

Price nodded as though to himself. "I've read that sidewise smoke gets people sometimes." He sipped his coffee. "Are you a smoker, Mrs. Heim? I didn't see any ashtrays."

"No. No, I don't smoke, Lieutenant. I never have."

"Uh-huh." His right hand left the handle of the smiley mug and went to his shirt pocket. "As it happens I smoke, Mrs. Heim. Would it bother you?"

"Of course not," she lied. The ashtrays for guests were put away in the cabinet. She brought him one.

He got out a cigarette and lit it with a disposable plastic lighter. "I'm trying to quit," he told her. He drew smoke into his lungs. "Was your husband a chemist, Mrs. Heim? Did he work in a chemical plant?"

She shook her head. "Jerry was an attorney." Surely Price knew all this.

"And his age at death was—?"

"Forty-one."

"That's very young for a nonsmoker to die of lung cancer, Mrs. Heim."

"That's what Jerry's doctor said." Not wanting to cry again, Tina poured coffee for herself, adding milk and diet sweetener, stirring until time enough had passed for her to get her feelings once more under control.

When she sat down again he said, "People must have wondered. My wife died about three years ago, and I know I got a lot of questions."

21

She nodded absently, looking at the little plate on the other side of the dinette table. The gingerbread man had lain there, untouched. Now it was gone. She said, "They X-rayed Jerry's lungs, Lieutenant. The X-rays showed cancer. That's what we were told."

"I know," he said.

"But you don't believe Jerry died of cancer?"

He shrugged. "And now your little boy. What was his name?"

Tina tried to keep all emotion from her voice, and felt she succeeded. "It was Alan."

"Just last month. Must have been pretty hard on you."

"It was. Lieutenant, can't we be honest with each other? What are we talking about?"

"All right." He took another sip of coffee. "Anyhow, you've still got two more. A boy and a girl, isn't that right?"

Tina nodded. "Henry and Gail. But Henry and Gail aren't actually mine."

For the first time, he looked surprised. "Why's that?"

"They're stepchildren, that's all. Of course, I love them as if they were my own, or anyway I try to."

"I didn't know that," he told her. "But Alan was—?"

"Our child. Jerry's and mine."

"Your husband had been married before. Divorce?"

"Yes. Jerry got full custody. Rona doesn't—didn't—even have visiting rights."

"Like that," he said.

"Yes, like that, Lieutenant."

"And now that your husband's dead?" Price flicked ashes into the salad plate that had held the gingerbread man.

"I don't know. If Rona tries to take them, I'll go to court; then we'll see. Won't you tell me what this is about?"

He nodded. "It's about insurance, really, Mrs. Heim. Your husband had a large policy."

She nodded guardedly. "They paid."

Price was no longer listening, not to her. "Did Henry or Gail stay home from school, Mrs. Heim? It's only one-thirty."

"No, they won't be back until after three. Do you want to speak to them?"

He shook his head. "I heard footsteps upstairs. A kid's, I thought."

22

"Henry's eighteen, Lieutenant, and Gail's sixteen. Believe me, they don't sound like kids stamping around up there. Do you want to go up and see? You don't need an excuse—so you said."

He ground out his cigarette in the salad plate. "That's right, I don't need an excuse. Alan was poisoned, wasn't he, Mrs. Heim? Lead poisoning?"

She nodded slowly, pretending there was a lovely clay mask on her face, a mask that would be dissolved by tears, broken by any expression. "He ate paint chips, Lieutenant. In his closet there was a place where the old paint was flaking off. We had repainted his room, but not in there. He was only two, and—and—"

"It's okay," he told her. "I've got two kids of my own."

"No, it will never be okay." She tore off a paper towel and stood in a corner, her back to him, blowing her nose and dabbing at her tears. She hoped that when she turned around, he would be gone.

"Feeling better now?" he asked. He had lit another cigarette.

"A little. You know, it's not fair."

"What isn't?"

"Your smoking like that. But you're still alive, and Jerry never smoked, but Jerry's gone."

"I'm trying to quit." He said it mechanically, toying with his cigarette. "Actually, some insurance people pretty much agree with you, Mrs. Heim."

"What do you mean by that?"

"Your husband had a policy with Attica Life, a hundred thousand dollars."

Automatically she shook her head. "Two hundred thousand. That was what they paid."

He inhaled smoke and puffed it from his nostrils. "It was a hundred thousand, but it had a double indemnity provision for cancer. A lot of them do now, because people are so worried about it. Cancer generally means big hospital bills."

This was it. She waited, fists clenched in her lap.

"Not with your Jerry, of course. Or anyway, not so much. He was dead in what? Three weeks?"

"Yes," she said. "Three weeks after he went into the hospital."

"And anyway he had hospitalization insurance, didn't he? With his law firm?"

She nodded.

"And you'd taken out policies on the kids too, and on you, naturally. Twenty-five thousand on each kid, wasn't it?"

"It still is. We have a very good agent, Lieutenant. I'll introduce you."

"It still is on Henry and Gail, right? Twenty-five thousand with double indemnity for accidental death. When little Alan died, that was accidental death. A little kid, a baby, swallows paint chips—they call that accidental poisoning."

"You think I killed him." If only my eyes could blast, she thought, he'd be frying like bacon. He'd be burning in Hell. "You think I killed my husband and my son to get that money, don't you, Lieutenant?" She tried to picture it, his brown suit blazing, his face seared, his hair on fire.

"No," he said. "No, I don't, Mrs. Heim. Not really."

"Then why are you here?"

He ground out the new cigarette beside the last. "Your insurance company's making waves."

He paused, but she said nothing.

"Do you blame them? Two claims, big claims, double indemnity claims, in less than two years."

"I see." She felt drained now; the fire had gone out. "What do you want me to do—take a lie detector test and say that I didn't murder my husband? That I didn't poison Alan? All right, I will."

"I want you to sign something, that's all. This will most likely be the end of it." The hand that had fumbled for his cigarettes was fumbling again, this time in the breast pocket of his tweed jacket. "You can read it if you want to. Or I'll tell you. Either way."

It was fine print on legal-length paper. Her eyes caught the word exhumation. "Tell me," she said.

"This will let them—the Coroner's Office—check out your husband's body. They'll check his lungs, for example, to see if there really was cancer."

Gravediggers working at night, perhaps, men with shovels methodically, stolidly, resurrecting those same lumps of earth. Yes, surely by night. They would not want the funeral parties to see that—Rest in Peace. They would have lights with long, orange cords to help them work, or maybe only battery torches. "Can they do that?" she asked. "Can they actually tell anything?" She remembered the woman in the Bible: *Lord, it has been four days now; surely there will be a stench.* She said, "It's been more than a year, Lieutenant."

He shrugged. "Maybe yes, maybe no. Your husband was embalmed, wasn't he?"

"Yes. Yes, he was."

"Then there's a good chance. It depends on how good a job they did on him, the soil temperature, and how tight the box is. It depends on a lot of things, really, but there's a good chance. Then there are some tests they can always run—like for arsenic or lead. You can look at a body a hundred years later and still find those things."

"I understand. Do you have a pen?"

"Sure," he said. He took it from the same pocket and handed it to her, first pressing the little plastic thing at the top to extend the point. Like a salesman, she thought. He's just like a salesman who's made the sale.

She took the pen and signed, and he smiled and relaxed.

"You know, I didn't think they used those lead-based paints anymore."

"They don't." She pushed the paper back. "This is an old house, and that was old paint. One doctor said it might be from the twenties. Do you want to see it? The closet, I mean, not the paint. I repainted it, so that—"

"So that it couldn't happen to somebody else's kid," he finished for her. "Sure, let's go up and have a look."

As they went up the stair, he said, "From outside I wasn't really sure this was an old house, even if it does have all that fancy millwork. It looks like it might have been built new in the old style, like they do at Disneyworld."

"It was built in eighteen eighty-two," she told him. "We had a contractor paint the exterior; we were doing the interior ourselves."

She led the way down the upstairs hall and opened the door. "I haven't gone in here since I painted the closet. I think it's time I did."

He nodded, looking appreciatively at the walls and the oak moldings. "This was a maid's room, I guess, in the old days."

"No, this has always been the nursery. The maids' rooms were upstairs under the eaves."

She fell silent. Newspapers daubed with dark paint were still spread over the floor. A can stood where she had left it, its interior hard and cracked. The caked brush lay beside it. She began to say, *"I didn't clean up. I suppose it shows."*

Before the first word had left her lips, there was a sound. It was a faint sound, yet in the stillness it seemed unnaturally loud—a scraping and shuffling that might have been a small dog scrambling to its feet, or merely some small, hard object sliding from a collection of similar objects, a baby's rattle leaving the top of a careless pile of toys.

So that in place of what she had intended, Tina said, "There's a child in there!"

"There's something in there," Price conceded. He went to the closet and twisted the old-fashioned china knob, but the door did not open. "It's locked."

"I didn't lock it." Though she had not been conscious of moving them, her right hand had clasped her left arm, her left hand her right arm. It was cold in the nursery, surely colder than it was outside. Had she shut the vent?

"Sure, you locked it," he told her. "It's a very natural thing to do. That's okay, I don't have to see it."

He's looking at the evidence as a favor to me, she thought. Aloud she said, "I don't even have a key, but we've got to get it open. There's a child inside."

"There's something in there. I doubt if it's a kid." He glanced at the keyhole. "Just an old warded lock. Shouldn't be any trouble."

The paint can had a wire handle. He pulled it off, bending it with strong, blunt fingers.

"I suppose you're right—there can't be a child in there. I mean, who would it be?"

He squatted before the keyhole. "You want my guess? You've got a possum in the wall. Or maybe a squirrel. This place doesn't have rats, does it?"

"We've tried to get rid of them. Jerry set traps in the basement—" there was a faint scrabbling from the closet; she spoke more rapidly to cover the sound: "He even bought a ferret and put it down there, but it died. He thought Henry'd killed it."

"Oh?" Price said. The lock squeaked, clicked back, and he rose, smiling. "Probably never been oiled. It was a little stiff."

He twisted the knob again. This time it turned, but the door did not open. "Stuck too. Did you paint the frame?"

She nodded wordlessly.

"Well, you locked it before the paint was dry, Mrs. Heim." He took a big utility knife from the right pocket of his jacket and opened the screwdriver blade.

"Call me Tina," she said. "We don't have to be so formal."

Only a moment before, she had seen him smile for the first time; now he grinned. "Dick," he said. "No Dick Tracy jokes, please. I get enough at the station."

She grinned back. "Okay."

The screwdriver blade slipped between the door and the jamb. He turned the knob again as he pried with the blade, and the door popped open. For an instant it seemed to her that there were eyes near the floor.

He swung the door wide on squealing hinges. "Nothing in here," he said. "Jerry didn't believe in lubrication."

"Yes, he did—he was always oiling things. He said he was no mechanic, but an oil can was half a mechanic."

Price grunted. He had a pen light, its feeble beam playing over the closet walls. "Something's been in here," he said. "It was bigger than a rat; a coon, maybe."

"Let me see," she said. She had been picking up the paint-smeared newspapers and stuffing them into the can. Now she came to the closet to look. There were scratches on the walls, tiny scratches that might have been made by little claws or fingernails. Flakes of plaster and paint lay on the closet floor.

Price snapped off the pen light and glanced at his watch. "I ought to be going. Thanks for signing the permission. I'll phone you and let you know how the tests came out."

She nodded. "I'd appreciate that."

"Okay, I will. What's that book you've got?"

"This?" She held it up. "Just an old children's book. Jerry found it when he was exploring the attic and brought it down for Alan. It was under the newspapers."

She led the way back down the narrow hall. The new, bright paper she and Jerry had hung decked its walls but could not make its way into her mind. When she took her eyes from it, the old, dark paper returned.

Behind her Price said, "Careful on those stairs."

"We were going to get them carpeted," she told him. "Now it hardly seems worth all the trouble. I'm trying to sell the house."

"Yeah, I noticed the sign outside. It's a nice place, but I guess I can't blame you."

"It is *not* a nice place," she muttered; but her words were so soft that only the house heard them. She opened the door.

"Goodbye," he said. "And thanks again, Tina. It was nice meeting you." Solemnly, they shook hands.

She said, "You'll telephone me, Dick?" She knew how it sounded.

"That's a promise."

She watched him as he went down the walk. A step or two before he reached his car, he patted the side pocket of his jacket—not the right-hand pocket, where he had put his knife, but the left one. For the laboratory, she thought to herself. He's taking it to some police lab, to see if it's poisoned.

She did not look down at the book in her hand, but the verses she had read when she lifted the newspapers that had covered it sang in her ears:

"You may run, you may run, just as fast as you can,

But you'll never catch ME," said the gingerbread man.

That evening the house played Little Girl. The essence, the ectoplasm, the soul of the child seeped from the cracked old plaster that had absorbed it when new. Watching television in the family room that had once been the master bedroom, Henry did not hear or see it; yet he stirred plumply, uncomfortably, on the sofa, unable to concentrate on the show or anything else, cursing his teachers, his sister, and his stepmother—hoping the phone would ring, afraid to call anyone and unable to say why he was afraid, angry in his misery and miserable in his rage.

Bent over her schoolbooks upstairs, Gail heard it. Quick steps, light steps, up the hall and down again: *Gioconda is the model of the brilliant young sculptor, Lucia Settala. Although he struggles to resist the fascination that she exercises over him, out of loyalty to his witch, Sylvia, he feels, Gioconda is the true inspiration of his art. During Lucia's illness, Tina arouses Gioconda's fury and is horribly burned by the model and her brother.*

I'll remember *that*, Gail thought. She wanted to be a model herself, like her real mother; someday she would be. She balanced the book on her head and walked about her bedroom, stopping to pose with studied arrogance.

Tina, drying herself in the bathroom, saw it. Steam left it behind as it faded from the mirror: the silhouette of a child with braids, a little girl whose head and shoulders were almost the outline of a steeply pitched roof. Tina wiped the mirror with her towel, watched the phantom reform, then thrust it out of her mind. Jerry should have put a ventilating fan in here, she thought. I'll have to tell him.

She remembered Jerry was dead, but she had known that all along. It was not so much that she had forgotten, as that she had forgotten she herself was still living and that the living cannot communicate with the dead, with the dead who neither return their calls nor answer their letters. She had felt for a moment that though dead Jerry was merely gone, gone to New York or New Orleans or New Mexico, to someplace new to see some client, draft some papers, appear before some Board. Soon she would fly there to join him, in the new place.

He had given her perfumed body powder and a huge puff with which to apply it. She did so now because Jerry had liked it, thinking how long, how very long, it had been since she had used it last.

The steam specter she had been unable to wipe away had disappeared. She recalled its eyes and shuddered. They had been (as she told herself) no more than holes in the steam, two spots where the steam, for whatever reason, would not condense; that made it worse, since if that were the case they were there still, watching her, invisible.

She shivered again. The bathroom seemed cold despite the steam, despite the furnace over which Jerry had worked so hard. She knew she should put on her robe but did not, standing before the mirror instead, examining her powdered breasts, running her hands along her powdered hips. Fat, she was too fat, she had been too fat ever since Alan was born.

Yet, Dick Price had smiled at her; she had seen the way he had looked at her in the nursery, had felt the extra moment for which he held her hand.

"Then it was cancer after all, Lieutenant?" Gail asked a few days later. "Don't stand, please." She crossed the wide, dark living room that had once been the parlor and sat down, very much an adult.

Price nodded, sipping the drink Henry had mixed for him. It was Scotch and water, with too much of the first and not enough of the second; and Price was determined to do no more than taste it.

Henry said, "I didn't think it could go that fast, sir."

"Occasionally it does," Price told him.

Gail shook her head. "She killed Dad, Lieutenant. I'm sure she did. You don't know her—she's a real witch sometimes."

"And you wrote those letters to the insurance company."

Price set his drink on the coffee table.

"What letters?"

Henry grinned. "You shouldn't bite your lip like that, Goony-Bird. Blows your cover."

Price nodded. "Let me give you a tip, Gail. It's better not to tell lies to the police; but if you're going to, you've got to get your timing right and watch your face. Just saying the right words isn't enough."

"Are you—?"

"Besides, a flat lie is better than a sidestep. Try, 'I never wrote any letters, Lieutenant.'"

"They were supposed to be confidential!"

Henry was cleaning his nails with a small screwdriver. "You think confidential means they won't even show them to the police?"

"He's right." Price nodded again. "Naturally they showed them to us. They were in a feminine hand, and there were details only somebody living here would know; so they were written by you or your stepmother. Since they accused her, that left you. Once in a while we get a nut who writes accusing herself, but your stepmother doesn't seem like a nut, and when she signed and dated the exhumation papers for me the writing was different."

"All right, I sent those letters."

The screwdriver had a clip like a pen. Henry replaced it in his shirt pocket. "I helped her with a couple of them. Told her what to say, you know? Are you going to tell her?"

"Do you want me to?" Price asked.

Henry shrugged. "Man, I don't care."

"Then why ask me about it?" Price stood up. "Thanks for the hospitality, kids. Tell Tina I'm sorry I missed her."

Gail rose too. "I'm sure she's just been delayed somewhere, Lieutenant. If you'd like to stay a little longer—"

Price shook his head.

Henry said, "Just one question, sir, if you know. How did Dad get lung cancer?"

"His lungs were full of asbestos fibers. It's something that usually happens only to insulators."

In the kitchen, Tina pictured the furnace—its pipes spreading upward like the branches of a long-dead tree, tape peeling from them like bark, white dust sifting down like rotten wood, falling like snow upon Jerry's violated grave.

It's the gingerbread house, she thought, recalling the grim paper they had painted over in the nursery. It doesn't eat you, you eat it. But it gets you just the same.

She tried to move, to strike the floor with her feet, the wall with her shoulders, to chew the dishtowel Gail had stuffed into her mouth, to scrape away the bright new duct tape Jerry had bought when he was rebuilding the furnace.

None of it worked. The door of the microwave gaped like a hungry mouth. Far away the front door opened and closed. "She Used to Be My Girl" blasted from the stereo in the family room.

Fatly, importantly, Henry came into the kitchen on a wave of rock, carrying an almost-full glass of dark liquid. "Your boyfriend's gone. Could you hear us? I bet you thought he was going to save you." He took a swallow of the liquid—whisky, she could smell it—and set the glass on the drain-board.

Gail followed him. When the door had shut and she could make herself heard, she asked, "Are we going to do it now?"

"Sure, why not?" Henry knelt, scratching at the tape.

"I think it would be better to leave that on."

"I told you, the heat would melt the adhesive. You want to have to swab her face with paint thinner or something when she's dead?" He caught the end of the duct tape and yanked it away. "Besides, she won't yell, she'll talk. I know her."

Tina spit out the dishtowel. It felt as though she had been to the dentist, as though the receptionist would want to set up a new appointment when she got out of the chair.

Gail snatched the damp towel away. "You fixed up the microwave?"

"Sure, Goony-Bird. It wasn't all that hard."

"They'll check it. They'll check it to see what went wrong."

Tina tried to speak, but her mouth was too dry. Words would not come.

"And they'll find, it." Henry grinned. "They'll find a wire that came unsoldered and flipped up so it shorted the safety interlock. Get me an egg out of the fridge."

She knew she should be pleading for her life; yet somehow she could not bring herself to do it. I'm brave, she thought, surprised. This is courage, this silly reluctance. I never knew that.

"See the egg, Stepmother dear?" Gail held it up to show her. "An egg will explode when you put it in a microwave."

She set it inside, and Henry shut the door.

"It'll work now whether it's open or closed, see? Only I've got it closed so we don't get radiation out here." He pressed a button and instinctively backed away.

The bursting of the egg was a dull thud, like an ax biting wood or the fall of a guillotine blade.

"It makes a real mess. We'll leave it on for a while so it gets hard."

Gail asked, "Is the music going to run long enough?"

"Hell, yes."

Tina said, "If you want to go back to Rona, go ahead. I've tried to love you, but nobody's going to stop you."

"We don't want to live with Rona," Henry told her. "We want to get even with you, and we want to be rich."

"You got a hundred thousand for Dad," Gail explained.

"Then all that for the baby."

Henry said, "Another fifty thou."

"So that's a hundred and fifty thousand, and when you're dead, we'll get it. Then there's another fifty on you, double for an accident. We get that too. It comes to a quarter of a million."

The oven buzzed.

"Okay." Henry opened it. "Let's cut her loose." He got the little paring knife from the sink.

"She'll fight," Gail warned him.

"Nothing I can't handle, Goony-Bird. We don't want rope marks when they find her."

The little knife gnawed at the rope behind Tina's back like a rat. After a moment, her lifeless hands dropped free. The rat moved to her ankles.

Gail said, "We'll have to get rid of the rope."

"Sure. Put it in the garbage—the tape too."

A thousand needles pricked Tina's arms. Pain came with them, appearing out of nowhere.

"Okay," Henry said. "Stand up."

He lifted her. There was no strength in her legs, no feeling.

"See, you're cleaning it. Maybe you stick your head in so you can see what you're doing." He thrust her head into the oven. "Then you reach for the cleaner or something, and your arm hits a button."

Someone screamed, shrill and terror-stricken. *I won't*, she told herself. *I won't scream.* She set her lips, clenched her teeth.

The screaming continued. Henry yelled and released her, and she slid to the floor. Flames and thick, black smoke shot from the microwave.

She wanted to laugh. *So Hansel, so little Gretel, cooking a witch is not quite so easy as you thought, nicht wahr?* Henry jerked a cord from the wall. Tina noted with amusement that it was the cord of the electric can-opener.

Gail had filled a pan with water from the sink. She threw it on the microwave and jerked backward as if she had been struck. The flames caught the kitchen curtains, which went up like paper.

On half-numb legs, Tina tried to stand. She staggered and fell. The kitchen cabinets were burning over the microwave, flames racing along dark, varnished wood that had been dry for a century.

The back door burst inward. Henry fled through it howling, his shirt ablaze. Stronger, harder hands lifted her. She thought of Gretel—of Gail—but Gail was beside them, coughing and choking, reeling toward the open doorway.

As though by magic, she was outside. They were all outside, Henry rolling frantically on the grass as Dick beat at the flames with his jacket. Sirens and wolves howled in the distance, while one by one the dark rooms lit with a cheerful glow.

"My house!" she said. She had meant to whisper but found she was almost screaming. "My home! Gone . . . no—I'll always, always remember her, no matter what happens."

Dick glanced toward it. "It doesn't look good, but if you've got something particularly valuable—"

"Don't you dare go back in there! I won't let you."

"My God!" He gripped her arm. "Look!" For an instant (and only an instant) a white face like a child's stared from a gable window; then it was gone, and the flames peered out instead. An instant more and they broke through the roof; the house sighed, a phoenix embracing death and rebirth. Its wooden lace was traced with fire before its walls collapsed and the fire engines arrived.

Later the fire captain asked whether everyone had escaped.

Tina nodded thankfully. "Dick—Lieutenant Price—thought he saw a face at one of the attic windows, but we're all here."

The captain looked sympathetic. "Probably a puff of white smoke—that happens sometimes. You know how it started?"

Suddenly Henry was silent, though he had voiced an unending string of puerile curses while the paramedics treated his burns. Now the string was broken; he watched Tina with terrified eyes. More practical, Gail edged toward the darkness under the trees.

Tina nodded. "But what I want to know is how Dick came just in time to save us. That was like a miracle."

Price shook his head. "No miracle. Or if it was, it was the kind that happens all the time. I'd come at eight, and the kids said you were still out. Somebody I'd like to talk to about a case I'm on lives a couple of blocks from here, so I went over and rang the bell; but there was nobody home. I came back and spotted the fire through a side window as I drove up."

The captain added, "He radioed for us. You say you know how it started, ma'am?"

"My son Henry was cooking something—eggs, wasn't that what you said, Henry?"

Henry's head moved a fraction of an inch. He managed to answer, "Yeah."

"But the oven must have been too hot, because the eggs, or whatever they were, caught fire. The kitchen was full of smoke by the time Gail and I heard him yell and ran in there."

The captain nodded and scribbled something on his clipboard. "Cooking fire. Happens a lot."

"I called Henry my son a moment ago," Tina corrected herself, "and I shouldn't have, Captain. Actually I'm just his stepmother, and Gail's."

"She's the best mother in the whole world!" Henry shouted. "Isn't that right, Goony-Bird?"

Nearly lost among the oaks and towering hemlocks, Gail nodded frantically.

"Henry, you're a dear." Tina bent to kiss his forehead. "I hope those burns don't hurt too much." Gently, she pinched one of his plump cheeks. He's getting fat, she reflected. But I'll have to neuter him soon, or his testicles will spoil the meat. He'll be easier to manage then.

(She smiled, recalling her big, black-handled dressmaker's shears. That would be amusing—but quite impossible, to be sure. What was it that clever man in Texas had done, put some sort of radioactive capsule between his sleeping son's legs?)

Dick said loudly, "And I'm sure Henry's a very good son." She turned to him, still smiling. "You know, Dick, you've never talked much about your own children. How old are they?"

Gene Wolfe was honored with the World Fantasy Award for Life Achievement in 1996. He was inducted by the Science Fiction Hall of Fame in 2007. The Science Fiction and Fantasy Writers of America named him its twenty-ninth Grand Master in December 2012, and he received the Damon Knight Memorial Grand Master Award in 2013. Wolfe has also won three World Fantasy Awards, two Nebulas, six Locus awards, a British Science Fiction Association Award, the August Derleth Award, and the John W. Campbell Award for individual works. The author of *The Fifth Head of Cerberus*, the bestselling The Book of the New Sun tetralogy, as well as—among numerous other novels—*Soldier of the Mist*, *The Knight*, *The Wizard*, and *The Book of the Long Sun*. He is also a prolific writer of distinguished short fiction, which has been collected in many volumes over the last four decades, most recently in *The Best of Gene Wolfe*. His latest novel, *A Borrowed Man*, was published last fall.

Russian folklore and fairy tales possess some characters that are found only in the Slavic tradition; Baba Yaga is one. Her role is multifaceted and neither "good" nor "evil." She eats children, but can be maternal; she is a helper and healer, but can be malevolent. She lives in a house on chicken legs and her mode of transportation is a mortar and pestle. It is no wonder that many modern writers have interpreted her in many ways in numerous fictions. Here, Angela Slatter takes the old story of "Vasilisa the Beautiful" and makes it uniquely her own.

The Bone Mother

Angela Slatter

Baba Yaga sees the child from her window and knows that her daughter is dead. She bashes the pestle against the bottom of the mortar and swears she will not weep. The child is at the gate now, her hand nervously moving in the pocket of her apron. The old woman sits at the window to wait.

Vasilissa stares at the house. It is a tumbledown black dacha, somewhat forlorn in the late spring light. Chickens scratch at the dirt in a desultory fashion. A fence runs around the yard, and the gateposts are festooned with human skulls.

The blond girl shivers. Her stepmother sent her here and her mother, reduced to the tiny doll wiggling in her pocket, seconded the notion. She, however, is not so sure. Ludmilla, her father's second wife, means her harm but she is loath to think her own mother has the same intent.

"Go to Baba Yaga and get us some coals for the fire," Ludmilla told her. Shura, her mother, said she should obey. "Ask Baba Yaga no questions she does not invite."

"Why, Mother, must I go?" Vasilissa had whispered to the twitching wooden doll. The thing had started speaking to her six months ago—five months after her mother's death, and one month after Ludmilla had married her father. She still doubted sometimes that the doll really did speak, but seeking out a priest and telling him the tale would be far worse than a little madness. Thus, she listened to the doll, who had never set her wrong.

"Because she is your grandmother, but she won't treat you any better for that. She has her own rules. Just do as I say and no harm will befall you."

Vasilissa had set out for Baba Yaga's compound. She walked a day and a night and on the evening of the second day she has come to the black dacha. A thundering of hooves splits the air and a torrent of air pushes past her, shoving her to the ground. She is familiar with the occurrence by now—in the mornings a woman in white charges past her, and at midday a fierce female rider in red does the same. Now, at dusk, a black rider takes her turn. She gallops past, through the gate, and disappears up the stairs of the dacha.

The little girl has spent the last hour sitting in the forest, watching the dacha, trying to ignore the tiny voice of the doll. At last the urging becomes too much and Vasilissa rises and drags her feet as she approaches the gate. The skulls glare down at her, eyes glowing red. She passes under their gaze, icy with fear.

Although she has been waiting for it, the child's knock startles Baba Yaga. She drops the pestle and it clunks heavily against the side of the mortar. From the air three sets of disembodied hands appear and she gestures for them to move the mortar back into a dark corner of the room, then she shuffles to the door.

The girl cowers under the Bone Mother's gaze. For the longest moment the old woman says nothing, just looks at the child, trying to see a trace of her own daughter in the youthful features. Vasilissa peers with the same intent, thinking that the eyes set deep in the wrinkled face once looked out from her mother's face. A smile cracks the withered visage.

"What do you want, girl?" Her voice is the sound of the pestle grinding against the mortar. Vasilissa clears her throat.

"Please, grandmother. My stepmother sent me to beg some coals from you. Our fire has gone out." Her feet are rooted to the spot as she stares up at her grandmother. Baba Yaga is tall and very thin, her face is a map of wrinkles, tattooed with age spots; she has a long nose and a surprisingly full mouth. Her hair is long and iron grey, pulled into an untidy plait hanging down her back.

"Stepmother? How long has she reigned?" Her heart trips at the idea of loss, of not knowing how long her daughter has been gone.

"Ludmilla and her daughters came to live with us five months ago," Vasilissa keeps her voice carefully neutral.

"How does she treat you?"

"As a stepmother does."

Baba Yaga grunts and steps aside so Vasilissa can pass into the parlor. The girl looks behind her surreptitiously.

"What, child?" The question is sharp. Vasilissa swallows hard.

"They say your house stands on the legs of giant chickens and moves around and around."

Her grandmother's bemusement is obvious. "Who would believe a stupid thing like that?" She leans down to the child. "When did you ever see a chicken big enough to support a dacha?"

Vasilissa giggles in spite of herself and steps across the threshold into a dim room filled with the smells of things that have lived for a long time. The doll in her pocket shakes.

After supper, Vasilissa watches her grandmother sleep in the big old bed across the room. Her face is less lined in repose but Vasilissa still thinks of each furrow as a journey taken, a map of her grandmother's past and perhaps one of Vasilissa's own future.

Will I look like her? Would my mother have looked like her had she lived? Is it so bad, to have lines to show where and who you have been?

Baba Yaga stirs, snores a little, settles. The little girl snuggles into the small bed she has been given and closes her eyes. Sleep comes quickly and she does not trouble the little doll for the first time in many nights.

They rise before dawn and eat a light breakfast, then Baba Yaga leads Vasilissa into the stable yard.

"Today, you must earn your keep. When I leave, you will clean the yard, clear out the stables, and sweep the floors. When you have finished that, take a quarter of a measure of wheat from my storehouse and pick out of it all the black grains and wild peas you find there. Then cook my supper." She leans down and whispers. "Or you will be my supper!"

The girl giggles, not in the least bit afraid.

"Yes, grandmother. I bid you good day."

"My riders will come, my riders three. First is my glorious dawn, then my bright day, and last my tenebrous night. They cannot harm you, and will answer if you call." Baba Yaga climbs into the mortar, an ungainly scramble, grasps the pestle in her left hand and a long straw broom in her right.

The mortar, responding to her commands, rises in the air with a grinding sound and floats to the opening gate. Baba Yaga uses the pestle to steer and, with the broom, sweeps behind her to cover any trace of her passing. Vasilissa thinks it an extraordinary way to travel, when there are several fine horses peering at her from the stables. She shrugs.

When her grandmother has disappeared from view, Vasilissa pulls the little doll from her pocket. She puts a few crumbs of bread in front of the thing and a spoonful of milk.

"There, my little doll, take it. Eat a little, drink a little, and listen to my grief."

The doll shakes itself as if waking and eats up the morsels with alacrity. Vasilissa speaks once again.

"Today, little doll, I must clean the yard, clear out the stables, and sweep the floors, then separate a quarter measure of wheat from black grains and wild peas. Then I must cook supper. Tell me, little doll, what shall I do?"

"Cook the supper, of course. Leave the rest to me." The tiny thing jumps up and stands on the top step, raising her arms before she fixes the child with painted blue eyes. "Best you don't see this lest you become too old too soon."

Vasilissa bows her head and goes inside the dacha. She prepares her grandmother's supper, never tempted to look outside at the storm of activity the doll creates. Some things are best not known; some wisdoms should not come too soon.

The mortar makes it way through the trees doing surprisingly little damage. Baba Yaga knows her paths and, as she sweeps behind her, she ensures no one can follow her trail, trace her back to the black dacha too easily. Not everyone appreciates her place in the scheme of things.

Baba Yaga is a woman who cannot be bound. She will bear no more children, she will bow to the wishes of no man; she is independent, adrift from the world and its demands. The world, in ceasing to recognize her value, has granted her a freedom unknown to maids and mothers. Only the crone may stand alone. She heals when she can and, when she cannot, ushers others along their path, easing suffering, tempering fear.

The people of the forest know enough to leave signs when she is needed: a red rag tied to a fence or gate post. An offering is left, too, so as not to actually hand anything over to the old woman and risk the catching of old age, which some of them seem to think of as a contagion. She's a last hope to most, too feared to be willingly approached except in desperation. Oftentimes they wait too long. Mourners put such deaths down not to their own inaction, but to malice, to the crone being hungry to take a life, to feed herself on the juices of the living. She is deathless, strange thing that she is, and they assume she must feed off them to maintain this ever-life.

When she does manage to save someone, there is still fear—gratitude becomes a strange, haunted animal, constrained by a niggling unease, an idea, however unreasonable, that the price of her aid is too high. She should, she tells herself over and again, be used to it; inured to the ache it causes her. But she isn't; she suspects she never will be, and she fears for herself if she ever does become numb. Pain tells her she is still just a little human; something less than mortal, but more than a stone. This comforts, sometimes.

Today she saves a child and helps an old woman along the path, all in the same cottage. The child has a fever, easily quelled by a tea of herbs. She hands the child's mother enough of the mixture for two days more. The woman's mother-in-law lies quietly in a shadowed corner, waiting for the last darkness to fall. There is no request for her help with this one, it's as if the old woman is not worth the trouble, not worth an offering to the dark woman who roams the woods.

Baba Yaga sits by the narrow pallet, hands waving the hovering younger woman away. Her nose twitches at the stale smell of the old woman's body. She has not been bathed and she has soiled herself some time today, or the day before. Baba Yaga looks at the younger woman.

"I hope your daughter treats you thus when your time comes. I hope she pays you the same respect, gives you the same dignity at your dying time," she spits and the woman shrinks away to sink against a wall on the far side of the cottage, hoping the curse will somehow slip from her skin, not embed itself in her pores.

Baba Yaga takes the hand of the old woman. The last vestiges of life have collected in her eyes, which shine in the dim room, and she smiles at the dark woman, grateful, for once, without fear. "Bless you, Baba. I beg you to help me pass on."

The deathless one nods and pulls a flask from the folds of her faded dress. She holds it to the lips of her patient, who drinks greedily. The old woman falls back and sighs her last breath.

Who would do this for me? wonders Baba Yaga. *Who would perform these things for me?*

The fact that she is deathless does not make the absence of an answer any less painful. She closes the old woman's eyes and rises, giving a final glance to the woman's daughter-in-law. "Bury her well. I will know if you do not."

The grinding noise of the mortar barely troubles her; she is so deep in thought that she forgets to sweep away the traces of her passing.

The old woman's son returns late that evening. He has been deep in the forest for almost a month and when he left his mother was hale and hearty. Her illness was sudden, occasioned by a summer cold and compounded by her daughter-in-law's neglect. His shock at her loss is acute.

His wife, afraid of Baba Yaga's curse and in full knowledge of her own culpability, seeks a scapegoat. She is desperate to stay her husband's hand, to keep his grief away from her, to keep him from ever thinking she had a hand in his mother's demise.

"It was Baba Yaga. The Bone Mother came and took her." She does not mention that their daughter was ill, nor that Baba Yaga saved the child's life. She lets her husband believe the dark woman took his mother out of spite, to extend her own life. He stays hollow-eyed beside the corpse, sitting the death watch through the dark hours.

In the morning he buries she who gave him life, and when he finishes shoveling earth on top of the still form, he notices the path of broken branches and crushed grass left by Baba Yaga's mortar. Without a word to his wife, he pulls the axe from the block beside the woodpile and sets out.

Vasilissa, exhausted by her labors in the kitchen and anaesthetized by the honey wine her grandmother had let her try, sleeps so soundly that she does not feel Baba Yaga's long-fingered hand slip under her pillow and grasp the little wooden doll. She does not hear the old woman shuffle from the room and shut the door quietly behind her. The child sleeps on, blissfully ignorant.

Baba Yaga, having eased herself into a chair by the fire, props the doll on a small table beside her and watches to see what the thing will do. At first there is nothing, no sign of life, but there is something about the doll that reminds her of a forest creature pretending to be a rock or a log in the face of a predator. She drops crumbs of bread into the small creature's lap and places a thimble of wine beside it. Her eyes gleam over the golden hair, the large blue eyes so like her own, and the full lips that, if her eyes do not deceive her, begin to pout at the extended scrutiny.

"There, my little doll, take it. Eat a little, drink a little, and listen to my grief." She leans forward, certain of herself now. "My daughter ran away with a worthless man and I did not see her again."

"Oh, Mother!" The doll jumps up and stamps its tiny feet, almost upsetting the thimble of wine.

"Ah! I knew it. You're a cunning little bitch, Shura," Baba Yaga sits back, shaking her head. "Not even properly dead."

"Dead enough, it would seem."

"How did you come to this, daughter?"

"My penance for leaving you alone is to watch over my daughter as long as she needs me. In this ridiculous shape. Imagine my surprise when I died and woke up like this. Hoping for heaven or purgatory—at least—and this is what I get." Shura sits heavily and takes a deep draught of wine. "If I didn't know better I'd say you had something to do with it."

"Who's to say I didn't?" Baba Yaga runs a finger down one of the golden curls, seeing for a moment the little girl Shura had been. Willful, selfish, demanding. Leaving her mother when she was ill unto death to go off with a man.

"Was *he* her father? The one you left with?"

"Of course not, Mother. Did you really think *him* the type to stick around?" Shura sighed. "Vasilissa's father would have had your approval. He was a rich merchant, kind and gentle. *Is* a rich merchant if Ludmilla's kept him safe."

Baba Yaga sits back and releases a pent-up breath. "What's she like?"

"Like me, I suppose. She's looking out for her own daughters, but it's at the expense of mine and I don't like that." She looks down at her tiny fingers. "Truth be told, if I could kick her out of my bed and out of my house I would."

"But you can't."

"But I can't, Mother, no. You could, though. Or take Vasilissa into your own." The painted eyes shine as if alive. "You could do that, Mother, look after my beautiful girl."

The old woman's face collapses in on itself, as if her age has suddenly arrived with no warning, like a fat guest walking across a weak threshold. Shura watches as something liquid and silver makes its way down one of the furrows of her mother's face. This is the first time she has faced the devastation she caused. Her wooden heart, kinder than her human one was, twists painfully in her otherwise hollow chest.

"Don't cry, Mama. Please don't cry. Look after my child. Set me free." She regrets the last the moment it leaves her lips. Baba Yaga's eyes snap open, turned to angry obsidian.

"Thinking of yourself to the last." She lifts the doll and holds it in her strong hand. If the doll could breathe, she would struggle for breath. "You want me to take your child so you can rest in peace. Then she can leave me when I need her, just like you did."

She holds the toy high, contemplating throwing it into the fire, stirring up the coals once more and watching the doll be consumed. Shura, sensing the direction of her mother's thoughts, is smart enough to shut up, to lie limp in the claw-like grip, and to hope as hard as she can that her mother's anger is not as strong as her love.

In the end the old woman simply shakes the doll in frustration, rather like a dog worrying a bone. Shura remains silent: she has retreated to her state of wood and varnish to ignore the horror of what her end could have been, of what her life may continue to be.

Baba Yaga does not leave the dacha that day. Vasilissa finds her in the morning, still sitting by the dead fire, motionless as a stone; although she breathes, her hands and face are very cold. She cannot move her grandmother from the chair, nor will the old woman answer her; the Bone Mother merely shifts her stare from the dead fire to the window that overlooks the yard.

Vasilissa brings cold compresses and drips water between Baba Yaga's dry lips, but the old woman does not stir; her eyes have all the animation of glass. Vasilissa, fearful beyond measure, picks Shura up from the floor by the fireplace. The side of the doll lying nearest the fire is slightly burnt. Shura guzzles down the wine Vasilissa gives her first of all, finishing her meal with cake crumbs.

"There my little doll, take it. Eat a little, drink a little, and listen to my grief." Vasilissa takes a deep breath. "I fear my grandmother is dying."

Shura sags, a marionette whose strings have been cut. "She cannot die, but she can become a stone. She did for almost a year after my father left."

"What must I do, little doll? What must I do, my little mother?" To her distress, Vasilissa's mother shrugs and shakes her head. The child flares up. "We must do something! We cannot leave her like this."

"It's her heart that troubles her, not any physical ailment, Vasilissa." Shura's voice fractures. "How do you cure loneliness? How do you ease the pain of singularity? She stands alone. She stands outside."

Vasilissa gives her mother a frustrated shake and sets her on the mantle. She settles herself on Baba Yaga's lap, curling her child's form around her grandmother, wrapping her arms around the thin shoulders, burying her smooth face in the corrugated skin of Baba Yaga's neck. Her voice is soft as she makes her promises.

"Don't leave me, grandmother. I will not leave you. You will not stand alone any longer. Do not become stone." Her voice strengthens. "I love you, grandmother. I will not leave you."

She falls asleep, her promise still on her lips, sticky and sweet like honey. Her dreams, though, are fraught: she sees a man hunting through the woods, following her grandmother's trail, his axe sharp and his temper frayed by grief.

Vasilissa is woken by a noise in the yard. She looks out the window and sees the skulls on the gateposts, their teeth clattering a warning. Beyond them, in among the tree trunks, she can see someone moving, a man, with the late afternoon sun glittering on the edge of his blade. She grabs Shura and rushes to the kitchen, unsure how much time she may have while he stalks around the dacha, trying to learn its defenses.

The little girl makes her offering to the doll and cries:

"There my little doll, take it. Eat a little, drink a little, and listen to my grief. A man comes, his axe sharp and bright. I fear for us all." She takes Shura to the window where they can see him clearly, standing just outside the fence, angry and uncertain.

"The black rider is coming, I can feel the earth shaking beneath her tread. Tell her to cast her darkest night over us and I will deal with this man. Be brave!" Shura exhorts her daughter.

Vasilissa runs through the dacha and throws open the front door. The man is inside the gate. When he sees her, he moves faster: it seems his anger will be spread over anyone he can find. Vasilissa can hear the beat of hooves and she shouts.

"Black rider, black rider, come to my aid! Throw your darkest night upon us!"

Her last glimpse is of the man, tossed about by three sets of disembodied hands, then all goes black, as black as the inside of the deepest cave. She hears Shura's voice rising, chanting, calling upon spells of forgetfulness, of disorientation, to send the man far away, with no memory of the path to this dacha. For a long while all is silent.

Vasilissa waits and waits. She stretches forth and finds the doll lying not far from her hand. She gathers Shura up, holding her in her lap. After a time (she does not know how long), the darkness does not seem so heavy and a torch flares. Baba Yaga stands at the door of the dacha and lights Vasilissa's way inside.

Baba Yaga takes Shura from her granddaughter and rubs a drop of water on the doll's lips, holds cake crumbs out for her.

"There my little doll, take it. Eat a little, drink a little, and listen to my joy." She says quietly. "I will look after your daughter, Shura."

The doll's eyes shine, her painted mouth moving in a smile. "Thank you, mother. My Vasilissa is faithful above all things."

"And when the time comes, Shura, I will let her go," Baba Yaga promises. "As I release you now, daughter. Rest."

Angela Slatter is the author of the Aurealis Award-winning *The Girl with No Hands and Other Tales* and (with Lisa L. Hannett), *The Female Factory. Sourdough and Other Stories* was a World Fantasy Award finalist and *Midnight and Moonshine (again with Hannett)* an Aurealis finalist. She's also authored *Black-Winged Angels* and *The Bitterwood Bible and Other Recountings*. Her short stories have appeared in publications such as *Fantasy*, Nightmare, *Lightspeed, A Book of Horrors, Horrorology*, and Australian, UK and US "best of" anthologies. She is the first Australian to win a British Fantasy Award, holds an MA and a PhD in Creative Writing and was an inaugural Queensland Writers Fellow. Her first novel, *Vigil*, will be released by Jo Fletcher Books in 2016, and its sequel, *Corpselight*, in 2017. A collection of her dark fairy tales, *A Feast of Sorrows*, will be released later this year.

Elizabeth Bear combines what might seem to be some rather disparate elements in "Follow Me Light": a fairy tale with a hint of "The Little Mermaid" (or any story about the inhuman struggling to be human), a difficult but righteous path chosen instead of the sinister, true beauty hidden by an ugly exterior, and, oxymoronically, "Lovecraftian romance."

Follow Me Light

Elizabeth Bear

Pinky Gilman limped. He wore braces on both legs, shining metal and black washable foam spoiling the line of his off-the-rack suits, what line there was to spoil. He heaved himself about on a pair of elbow-cuff crutches. I used to be able to hear him clattering along the tiled, echoing halls of the public defender's offices a dozen doors down.

Pinky's given name was Isaac, but even his clients called him Pinky. He was a fabulously ugly man, lumpy and bald and bristled and pink-scrubbed as a slaughtered hog. He had little fishy walleyes behind spectacles thick enough to serve barbecue on. His skin peeled wherever the sun or the dry desert air touched it.

He was by far the best we had.

The first time I met Pinky was in 1994. He was touring the office as part of his job interview, and Christian Vlatick led him up to me while I was wrestling a five-gallon bottle onto the water cooler. I flinched when he extended his right hand to shake mine with a painful twist intended to keep the crutch from slipping off his arm. The rueful way he cocked his head as I returned his clasp told me he was used to that reaction, but I doubted most people flinched for the reason I did—the shimmer of hot blue lights that flickered through his aura, filling it with brilliance although the aura itself was no color I'd ever seen before—a swampy gray-green, tornado colored.

I must have been staring, because the squat little man glanced down at my shoes, and Chris cleared his throat. "Maria," he said, "This is Isaac Gilman."

"Pinky," Pinky said. His voice . . . oh, la. If he were robbed with regard to his body, that voice was the thing that made up the difference. Oh, my.

"Maria Delprado. Are you the new attorney?"

"I hope so," he said, dry enough delivery that Chris and I both laughed.

His handshake was good: strong, cool, and leathery, at odds with his parboiled countenance. He let go quickly, grasping the handle of his crutch again and shifting his weight to center, blinking behind the glass that distorted his eyes. "Maria," he said. "My favorite name. Do you know what it means?"

"It means *Mary*," I answered. "It means sorrow."

"No," he said. "It means *sea*." He pointed past me with his chin, indicating the still-sloshing bottle atop the water cooler. "They make the women do the heavy lifting here?"

"I like to think I can take care of myself. Where'd you study, Isaac?"

"Pinky," he said, and, "Yale. Four point oh."

I raised both eyebrows at Chris and pushed my glasses up my nose. The Las Vegas public defender's office doesn't get a lot of interest from Yale Law School grads, *summa cum laude*. "And you haven't hired him yet?"

"I wanted your opinion," Chris said without a hint of apology. He glanced at Pinky and offered up a self-deprecating smile. "Maria can spot guilty people. Every time. It's a gift. One of these days we're going to get her made a judge."

"Really?" Pinky's lipless mouth warped itself into a grin, showing the gaps in his short, patchy beard. "Am I guilty, then?"

The lights that followed him glittered, electric blue fireflies in the twilight he wore like a coat. He shifted his weight on his crutches, obviously uncomfortable at standing.

"And what am I guilty of?"

Not teasing, either, or flirtatious. Calm, and curious, as if he really thought maybe I could tell. I squinted at the lights that danced around him—will-o'-the-wisps, spirit lights. The aura itself was dark, but it wasn't the darkness of past violence or dishonesty. It was organic, intrinsic, and I wondered if it had to do with whatever had crippled him. And the firefly lights—

Well, they were something else again. Just looking at them made my fingertips tingle.

"If there are any sins on your conscience," I said carefully, "I think you've made amends."

He blinked again, and I wondered why I wanted to think *blinked fishily* when fishes do not blink. And then he smiled at me, teeth like yellowed pegs in pale, blood-flushed gums. "How on earth do you manage that?"

"I measure the distance between their eyes."

A three-second pause, and then he started to laugh, while Christian, who had heard the joke before, stood aside and rolled his eyes. Pinky shrugged, rise and fall of bulldog shoulders, and I smiled hard, because I knew we were going to be friends.

In November of 1996, I lost my beloved seventeen-year-old cat to renal failure, and Pinky showed up at my door uninvited with a bottle of Maker's Mark and a box of Oreos. We were both half-trashed by the time I spread my cards out on the table between us, a modified Celtic cross. They shimmered when I looked at them; that was the alcohol. The shimmer around Pinky when he stretched his hand out—was not.

"Fear death by water," I said, and touched the Hanged Man's foot, hoping he would know he was supposed to laugh.

His eyes sparkled like scales in the candlelight when he refilled my glass. "It's supposed to be if you don't find the Hanged Man. In any case, I *don't* see a drowned sailor."

"No," I answered. I picked up my glass and bent to look closer. "But there is the three of staves as the significator. Eliot called him the Fisher King." I looked plainly at where his crutches leaned against the arm of his chair. "Not a bad choice, don't you think?"

His face grayed a little, or perhaps that was the alcohol. Foxlights darted around him like startled minnows. "What does he stand for?"

"Virtue tested by the sea." And then I wondered why I'd put it that way. "The sea symbolizes change, conflict, the deep unconscious, the monsters of the Id—"

"I know what the sea means," he said bitterly. His hand darted out and overturned the card, showing the tan back with its key pattern in ivory. He jerked his chin at the spread. "Do you believe in those?"

It had been foolish to pull them out. Foolish to show him, but there was a certain amount of grief and alcohol involved. "It's a game," I said, and swept them all into a pile. "Just a child's game." And then I hesitated, and looked down, and turned the three of staves back over, so it faced the same way as the rest. "It's not the future I see."

In 1997 I took him to bed. I don't know if it was the bottle and a half of Shiraz we celebrated one of our rare victories with, or the deep bittersweet richness of his voice finally eroding my limited virtue, but we were good in the dark. His arms and shoulders, it turned out, were beautiful, after all: powerful and lovely, all out of proportion with the rest of him.

I rolled over, after, and dropped the tissue-wrapped rubber on the nightstand, and heard him sigh. "Thank you," he said, and the awe in that perfect voice was sweeter than the sex had been.

"My pleasure," I said, and meant it, and curled up against him again, watching the firefly lights flicker around his blunt, broad hands as he spoke softly and gestured in the dark, trying to encompass some inexpressible emotion.

Neither one of us was sleepy. He asked me what I saw in Las Vegas. I told him I was from Tucson, and I missed the desert when I was gone. He told me he was from Stonington. When the sun came up, I put my hand into his aura, chasing the flickering lights like a child trying to catch snowflakes on her tongue.

I asked him about the terrible scars low on the backs of his thighs that left his hamstrings weirdly lumped and writhed, unconnected to bone under the skin. I'd thought him crippled from birth. I'd been wrong about so many, many things.

"Gaffing hook," he said. "When I was seventeen. My family were fisherman. Always have been."

"How come you never go home to Connecticut, Isaac?"

For once, he didn't correct me. "Connecticut isn't home."

"You don't have any family?"

Silence, but I saw the dull green denial stain his aura. I breathed in through my nose and tried again.

"Don't you ever miss the ocean?"

He laughed, warm huff of breath against my ear, stirring my hair. "The desert will kill me just as fast as the ocean would, if I ever want it. What's to miss?"

"Why'd you come here?"

"Just felt drawn. It seemed like a safe place to be. Unchanging. I needed to get away from the coast, and Nevada sounded . . . very dry. I have a skin condition. It's worse in wet climates. It's worse near the sea."

"But you came back to the ocean after all. Prehistoric seas. Nevada was all underwater once. There were ichthyosaurs—"

"Underwater. Huh." He stretched against my back, cool and soft. "I guess it's in the blood."

That night I dreamed they chained my wrists with jeweled chains before they crippled me and left me alone in the salt marsh to die. The sun rose as they walked away singing, hunched inhuman shadows glimpsed through a splintered mist that glowed pale as the opals in my manacles.

The mist burned off to show gray earth and greeny brown water, agates and discolored aquamarine. The edges of coarse gray cloth adhered in drying blood on the backs of my thighs, rumpled where they had pulled it up to hamstring me. The chains were cold against my cheeks when I raised my head away from the mud enough to pillow my face on the backs of my hands.

The marsh stank of rot and crushed vegetation, a green miasma so overwhelming the sticky copper of blood could not pierce it. The pain wasn't as much as it should have been; I was slipping into shock as softly as if I slipped under the unrippled water. I hadn't lost enough blood to kill me, but I rather thought I'd prefer a quick, cold sleep and never awakening to starving to death or lying in a pool of my own blood until the scent attracted the thing I had been left in propitiation of.

Somewhere, a frog croaked. It looked like a hot day coming.

I supposed I was going to find out.

His skin scaled in the heat. It was a dry heat, blistering, peeling, chapping lips and bloodying noses. He used to hang me with jewels, opals, tourmalines the color of moss and roses. "Family money," he told me. "Family jewels." He wasn't lying.

I would have seen a lie.

The Mojave hated him. He was chapped and chafed, cracked and dry. He never sweated enough, kept the air conditioner twisted as high as it would go. Skin burns in the heat, in the sun. Peels like a snake's. Aquamarine discolors like smoker's teeth. Pearls go brittle. Opals crack and lose their fire.

He used to go down to the Colorado River at night, across the dam to Willow Beach, on the Arizona side, and swim in the river in the dark. I told him it was crazy. I told him it was dangerous. How could he take care of himself in the Colorado when he couldn't walk without braces and crutches?

He kissed me on the nose and told me it helped his pain. I told him if he drowned, I would never forgive him. He said in the history of the entire world twice over, a Gilman had never once drowned. I called him a cocky, insincere bastard. He stopped telling me where he was going when he went out at night.

When he came back and slept beside me, sometimes I lay against the pillow and watched the follow-me lights flicker around him. Sometimes I slept.

Sometimes I dreamed, also.

I awakened after sunset, when the cool stars prickled out in the darkness. The front of my robe had dried, one long yellow-green stain, and now the fabric under my back and ass was saturated, sticking to my skin. The mud seemed to have worked it loose from the gashes on my legs.

I wasn't dead yet, more's the pity, and now it *hurt*.

I wondered if I could resist the swamp water when thirst set in. Dehydration would kill me faster than hunger. On the other hand, the water might make me sick enough that I'd slip into the relief of fever and pass away, oblivious in delirium. If dysentery was a better way to die than gangrene. Or dehydration.

Or being eaten. If the father of frogs came to collect me as was intended, I wouldn't suffer long.

I whistled across my teeth. A fine dramatic gesture, except it split my cracked lips and I tasted blood. My options seemed simple: lie still and die, or thrash and die. It would be sensible to give myself up with dignity.

I pushed myself onto my elbows and began to crawl toward nothing in particular.

Moonlight laid a patina of silver over the cloudy yellow-green puddles I wormed through and glanced off the rising mist in electric gleams of blue. The exertion warmed me, at least, and loosened my muscles. I stopped shivering after the first half hour. My thighs knotted tight as welded steel around the insult to my tendons. It would have been more convenient if they'd just chopped my damned legs off. At least I wouldn't have had to deal with the frozen limbs dragging behind me as I crawled.

If I had any sense—

If I had any sense at all, I wouldn't be crippled and dying in a swamp. If I had any sense *left*, I would curl up and die.

It sounded pretty good, all right.

I was just debating the most comfortable place when curious blue lights started to flicker at the corners of my vision.

I'm not sure why it was that I decided to follow them.

Pinky gave me a pearl on a silver chain, a baroque multicolored thing swirled glossy and irregular as toffee. He said it had been his mother's. It dangled between my breasts, warm as the stroke of a thumb when I wore it.

Pinky said he'd had a vasectomy, still wore a rubber every time we made love. Talked me into going on the Pill.

"Belt and suspenders," I teased. The garlic on my scampi was enough to make my eyes water, but Pinky never seemed to mind what I ate, no matter how potent it was.

It was one a.m. on a Friday, and we'd crawled out of bed for dinner, finally. We ate seafood at Capozzoli's, because although it was dim in the cluttered red room the food was good and it was open all night. Pinky looked at me out of squinting, amber eyes, so sad, and tore the tentacles off a bit of calamari with his teeth. "Would you want to bring a kid into this world?"

"No," I answered, and told that first lie. "I guess not."

I didn't meet Pinky's brother Esau until after I'd married someone else, left my job to try to have a baby, gotten divorced when it turned out we couldn't, had to come back to pay the bills. Pinky was still there, still part of the program. Still plugging away on the off chance that eventually he'd meet an innocent man, still pretending we were and always had been simply the best of friends. We never had the conversation, but I imagined it a thousand times.

I left you.

You wanted a baby.

It didn't work out.

And now you want to come back? I'm not like you, Maria.

Don't you ever miss the ocean?

No. I never do.

But he had too much pride, and I had too much shame. And once I was Judge Delprado, I only saw him in court anymore.

Esau called me, left a message on my cell, his name, who he was, where he'd be. I didn't know how he got the number. I met him out of curiosity as much as concern, at the old church downtown, the one from the thirties built of irreplaceable history. They made it of stone, to last, and broke up petroglyphs and stalactites to make the rough rock walls beautiful for God.

I hated Esau the first time I laid eyes on him. Esau. There was no mistaking him: same bristles and thinning hair, same spectacularly ugly countenance, fishy and prognathic. Same twilight-green aura, too, but Esau's was stained near his hands and mouth, the color of clotted blood, and no lights flickered near.

Esau stood by one of the petroglyphs, leaned close to discolored red stone marked with a stick figure, meaning man, and the wavy parallel lines that signified the river. Old as time, the Colorado, wearing the bad-lands down, warden and warded of the desert West.

Esau turned and saw me, but I don't think he saw *me*. I think he saw the pearl I wore around my neck.

I gave all the jewels back to Pinky when I left him. Except the pearl. He wouldn't take that back, and to be honest, I was glad. I'm not sure why I wore it to meet Esau, except I hated to take it off.

Esau straightened up, all five foot four of him behind the glower he gave me, and reached out peremptorily to touch the necklace, an odd gesture with the fingers pressed together. Without thinking, I slapped his hand away, and he hissed at me, a rubbery tongue flicking over flesh-less lips.

Then he drew back, two steps, and looked me in the eye. His voice had nothing in common with his face: baritone and beautiful, melodious and carrying. I leaned forward, abruptly entranced. "Shipwrack," he murmured. "Shipwrecks. Dead man's jewels. It's all there for the taking if you just know where to look. Our family's always known."

My hand came up to slap him again, halted as if of its own volition. As if it couldn't push through the sound of his voice. "Were you a treasure hunter once?"

"I never stopped," he said, and tucked my hair behind my ear with the brush of his thumb. I shivered. My hand went down, clenched hard at my side. "When Isaac comes back to New England with me, you're coming too. We can give you children, Maria. Litters of them. Broods. Everything you've ever wanted."

"I'm not going anywhere. Not for . . . Isaac. Not for anyone."

"What makes you think you have any choice? You're part of his price. And we know what you want. We've researched you. It's not too late."

I shuddered, hard, sick, cold. "There's always a choice." The words hurt my lips. I swallowed. Fingernails cut my palms. His hand on my cheek was cool. "What's the rest of his price? If I go willing?"

"Healing. Transformation. Strength. Return to the sea. All the things he should have died for refusing."

"He doesn't miss the sea."

Esau smiled, showing teeth like yellow pegs. "You would almost think, wouldn't you?" There was a long pause, nearly respectful. Then he cleared his throat and said, "Come along."

Unable to stop myself, I followed that beautiful voice.

Most of a moon already hung in the deepening sky, despite the indirect sun still lighting the trail down to Willow Beach. The rocks radiated heat through my sneakers like bricks warmed in an oven. "Pinky said he didn't have any family."

Esau snorted. "He gave it the old college try."

"You were the one who crippled him, weren't you? And left him in the marsh to die."

"How did you know that?"

"He didn't tell me. I dreamed it."

"No," he answered, extending one hand to help me down a tricky slope. "That was Jacob. He doesn't travel."

"Another brother."

"The eldest brother." He yanked my arm and gave me a withering glance when I stumbled. He walked faster, crimson flashes of obfuscation coloring the swampwater light that surrounded him. I trotted to keep up, cursing my treacherous feet. At least my tongue was still my own, and I used it.

"Jacob, Esau, and Isaac Gilman? How . . . original."

"They're proud old New England names. Marshes and Gilmans were among the original settlers." Defensive. "Be silent. You don't need a tongue to make babies, and in a few more words I'll be happy to relieve you of it, mammal bitch."

I opened my mouth; my voice stopped at the back of my throat. I stumbled, and he hauled me to my feet, his rough, cold palm scraped the skin of my wrist over the bones.

We came around a corner of the wash that the trail ran through. Esau stopped short, planting his feet hard. I caught my breath at the power of the silent brown river running at the bottom of the gorge, at the sparkles that hung over it, silver and copper and alive, swarming like fireflies.

And standing on the bank before the current was Pinky—Isaac—braced on his canes, startlingly insouciant for a cripple who'd fought his way down a rocky trail. He craned his head back to get a better look at us and frowned. "Esau. I wish I could say it was a pleasure to see you. I'd hoped you'd joined Jacob at the bottom of the ocean by now."

"Soon," Esau said easily, manhandling me down the last of the slope. He held up the hand that wasn't knotted around my wrist. I blinked twice before I realized the veined, translucent yellow webs between his fingers were a part of him. He grabbed my arm again, handling me like a bag of groceries.

Pinky hitched himself forward to meet us, and for a moment I thought he was going to hit Esau across the face with his crutch. I imagined the sound the aluminum would make when it shattered Esau's cheekbone. *Litters of them. Broods.* Easy to give in and let it happen, yes. But litters of *what*?

"You didn't have to bring Maria into it."

"We can give her what she wants, can't we? With your help or without it. How'd you get the money for school?"

Pinky smiled past me, a grin like a wolf. "There was platinum in those chains. Opals. Pearls big as a dead man's eyeball. Plenty. There's still plenty left."

"So there was. How did you survive?"

"I was guided," he said, and the blue lights flickered around him. Blue lights that were kin to the silver lights swarming over the river. I could imagine them buzzing. Angry, invaded. I turned my head to see Esau's expression, but he only had eyes for Pinky.

Esau couldn't see the lights. He looked at Pinky, and Pinky met the stare with a lifted chin. "Come home, Isaac."

"And let Jacob try to kill me again?"

"He only hurt you because you tried to leave us."

"He left me for the father of frogs in the salt marsh, Esau. And you were there with him when he did—"

"We couldn't just let you walk away." Esau let go of my arm with a command to be still, and stepped toward Pinky with his hands spread wide. There was still light down here, where the canyon was wider and the shadow of the walls didn't yet block the sun. It shone on Esau's balding scalp, on the yolky, veined webs between his fingers, on the aluminum of Pinky's crutches.

"I didn't walk," Pinky said. He turned away, hitching himself around, the beige rubber feet of the crutches braced wide on the rocky soil. He swung himself forward, headed for the river, for the swarming lights. "I crawled."

Esau fell into step beside him. "I don't understand how you haven't . . . changed."

"It's the desert." Pinky paused on a little ledge over the water. Tamed by the dam, the river ran smooth here and still. I could feel its power anyway, old magic that made this land live. "The desert doesn't like change. It keeps me in between."

"That hurts you." Almost in sympathy, as Esau reached out and laid a webbed hand on Pinky's shoulder. Pinky flinched but didn't pull away. I opened my mouth to shout at him, feeling as if my tongue were my own again, and stopped. *Litters.*

Whatever they were, they'd be Pinky's children.

"It does." Pinky fidgeted with the crutches, leaning forward over the river, working his forearms free of the cuffs. His shoulders rippled under the white cloth of his shirt. I wanted to run my palms over them.

"Your legs will heal if you accept the change," Esau offered, softly, his voice carried away over the water. "You'll be strong. You'll regenerate. You'll have the ocean, and you won't hurt anymore, and there's your woman—we'll take her too."

"*Esau.*"

I heard the warning in the tone. The anger. Esau did not. He glanced at me. "Speak, woman. Tell Isaac what you want."

I felt my tongue come unstuck in my mouth, although I still couldn't move my hands. I bit my tongue to keep it still.

Esau sighed, and looked away. "Blood is thicker than water, Isaac. Don't you want a family of your own?"

Yes, I thought. Pinky didn't speak, but I saw the set of his shoulders, and the answer they carried was *no*. Esau must have seen it too, because he raised one hand, the webs translucent and spoiled-looking, and sunlight glittered on the barbed ivory claws that curved from his fingertips, unsheathed like a cat's.

With your help or without it.

But litters of *what?*

I shouted so hard it bent me over. "*Pinky, duck!*"

He didn't. Instead, he *threw* his crutches backward, turned with the momentum of the motion, and grabbed Esau around the waist. Esau squeaked—*shrieked*—and threw his hands up, clawing at Pinky's shoulders and face as the silver and blue and coppery lights flickered and swarmed and swirled around them, but he couldn't match Pinky's massive strength. The lights covered them both, and Esau screamed again, and I strained, lunged, leaned at the invisible chains that held me as still as a posed mannequin.

Pinky just held on and leaned back.

They barely splashed when the Colorado closed over them.

Five minutes after they went under, I managed to wiggle my fingers. Up and down the bank, there was no trace of either of them. I couldn't stand to touch Pinky's crutches.

I left them where they'd fallen.

Esau had left the keys in the car, but when I got there I was shaking too hard to drive. I locked the door and got back out, tightened the laces on my sneakers, and toiled up the ridge until I got to the top. I almost turned my ankle twice when rocks rolled under my foot, but it didn't take long. Red rock and dusty canyons stretched west, a long, gullied slope behind me, the river down there somewhere, close enough to smell but out of sight. I settled myself on a rock, elbows on knees, and looked out over the scarred, raw desert at the horizon and the setting sun.

There's a green flash that's supposed to happen just when the sun slips under the edge of the world. I'd never seen it. I wasn't even sure it existed. But if I watched long enough, I figured I might find out.

There was still a hand span between the sun and the ground, up here. I sat and watched, the hot wind lifting my hair, until the tawny disk of the sun was halfway gone and I heard the rhythmic crunch of someone coming up the path.

I didn't turn. There was no point. He leaned over my shoulder, braced his crutches on either side of me, a presence solid and cool as a moss-covered rock. I tilted my head back against Pinky's chest, his wet shirt dripping on my forehead, eyes, and mouth. Electric blue lights flickered around him, and I couldn't quite make out his features, shadowed as they were against a twilight sky. He released one crutch and laid his hand on my shoulder. His breath brushed my ear like the susurrus of the sea. "Esau said blood is thicker than water," I said, when I didn't mean to say anything.

"Fish blood isn't," Pinky answered, and his hand tightened. I looked away from the reaching shadows of the canyons below and saw his fingers against my skin, pale silhouettes on olive, unwebbed. He slid one under the black strap of my tank top. I didn't protest, despite the dark red, flaking threads that knotted the green smoke around his hands.

"Where is he?"

"Esau? He drowned."

"But—" I craned my neck. "You said Gilmans never drown."

He shrugged against my back. "I guess the river just took a dislike to him. Happens that way sometimes."

A lingering silence, while I framed my next question. "How did you find me?"

"I'll always find you, if you want," he said, his patched beard rough against my neck. "What are you watching?"

"I'm watching the sun go down."

"Come in under this red rock," he misquoted, as the shadow of the ridge opposite slipped across the valley toward us.

"The handful of dust thing seems appropriate—"

Soft laugh, and he kissed my cheek, hesitantly, as if he wasn't sure I would permit it. "I would have thought it'd be 'Fear death by water.'"

The sun went down. I missed the flash again. I turned to him in a twilight indistinguishable from the gloom that hung around his shoulders and brushed the flickering lights away from his face with the back of my hand. "Not that," I answered. "I have no fear of that, my love."

Elizabeth Bear was born on the same day as Frodo and Bilbo Baggins, but in a different year. When coupled with a childhood tendency to read the dictionary for fun, this led her inevitably to penury, intransigence, and the writing of speculative fiction. She is the Hugo, Sturgeon, Locus, and Campbell Award-winning author of twenty-seven novels (her most recent novels are *Karen Memory* and—co-authored with Sarah Monette—*Apprentice of Elves*) and over a hundred short stories. She lives in Massachusetts.

Yoon Ha Lee's story draws from childhood images of the Dragon King Under the Sea and his realm from Korean folklore. Unlike malevolent European dragons—usually associated with fire and devastation—dragons in Korean tradition are mostly benevolent and connected to the quality, flow, and control of water as well as the waves of the sea.

The Coin of Heart's Desire

Yoon Ha Lee

In an empire at the wide sea's boundaries, where the clouds were the color of alabaster and mother-of-pearl, and the winds bore the smells of salt and faraway fruits, the young and old of every caste gathered for their empress's funeral. In life she had gone by the name Beryl-Beneath-the-Storm. Now that she was dead, the court historians were already calling her Weave-the-Storm, for she had been a fearsome naval commander.

The embalmers had anointed Weave-the-Storm in fragrant oils and hidden her face, as was proper, with a mask carved from white jade. In one hand they had placed a small banner sewn with the empire's sword-and-anchor emblem in dark blue; in the other, a sharp, unsheathed knife whose enameled hilt winked white and gold and blue. She had been dressed in heavy silk robes that had only been worn once before, at the last harvest moon festival. The empire's people believed in supplying their ruler well for the life in the sea-to-come, so that she would intercede with the dragon spirits for them.

The empress had left behind a single daughter. She was only thirteen years old, so the old empress's advisors had named her Early-Tern-

Journeying. Tern had a gravity beyond her years. Even at the funeral, dressed in the white-and-gray robes of mourning, she was nearly impassive. If her eyes glistened when the priests chanted their blessings for the road-into-sunset, that was only to be expected.

Before nightfall, the old empress's bier was placed upon a funeral boat painted red to guide her sunward. One priest cut the boat loose while the empress's guard set it ablaze with fire arrows.

Tern's oldest advisor, a sage who had visited many foreign shrines in his youth, turned to her and said over the crackling flames and the lapping water, "You must rest well tonight, my liege. Tomorrow you will hold court before the Twenty-Seven Great Families. They must see in you your mother's commanding presence, for all your tender years."

Tern knew perfectly well, as did he, that no matter how steely her composure, the Great Families would see her as an easy mark. But she merely nodded and retired to the meditation chamber.

She did not sleep that night, although no one would have blamed her if she had. Instead, she thought long and hard about the problem before her. At times, as she inhaled the sweet incense, she wanted desperately to call her mother back from the funeral ship and ask her advice. But the advice her mother had already passed down to her during the years of her life would have to suffice.

Two hours before dawn, she rang a silver bell to summon her servants. "Wake up the chancellor of the exchequer," she said to them. "I need his advice."

The chancellor was not pleased to be roused from his sleep, and even less pleased when Tern explained her intent. "Buy off the Families?" he said. "It's a bad precedent."

"We're not buying them off," Tern said severely. "We are displaying a bounty they cannot hope to equal. They will ask themselves, if the imperial house can afford to give away such treasures, what greater might is it concealing?"

The chancellor grumbled and muttered, but accompanied Tern to the first treasury. The treasury's walls were hung with silk scrolls painted with exquisite landscapes and piled high with illuminated books. The shapes of cranes and playful cats were stamped onto the books' covers in gold leaf. Tiny ivory figurines no larger than a thumbnail were arrayed like vigilant armies, if not for the curious fact that each one had the head of an extinct bird. Swords rested on polished stands, cabochons of opal and aquamarine gleaming from their gold-washed scabbards, their pale tassels decorated with knots sacred to the compass winds. There were crowns of braided wire cradling fossils inscribed with fractured prophecies, some still tangled with the hair of long-dead sovereigns, and twisted ropes of pearls perfectly graduated in size and color, from shimmering white to violet-gray to lustrous black.

"None of these will do," Tern said. "These are quotidian treasures, fit for rewarding captains, but not for impressing the Twenty-Seven Great Families."

The chancellor blanched. "Surely you don't mean—"

But the young empress had swept past him and was heading toward the second treasury. She drew out her heaviest key and opened the doors, which swung with deceptive ease on their hinges. The guards at the door eyed her nervously.

The smell of salt water and kelp was suddenly strong. A dragon's single, heavy-lidded eye opened in the darkness beyond the doors. "Who desires to drown?" asked the dragon spirit in a low, resonant voice. It sounded hopeful. Most people knew better than to disturb the guardian spirit.

"I am Weave-the-Storm's daughter," Tern said. "They call me Early-Tern-Journeying."

The eye slitted. "So you are," the dragon said, less threateningly. "I've never understood your dynasty's need to change names at random intervals. It's dreadfully confusing."

"Does the tradition trouble you?" Tern asked. "It would be difficult to change, but—"

The light from the hallway glinted on the dragon's long teeth. "Don't trouble yourself on my account," it said. Musingly, it added, "It's remarkable how you resemble her around the eyes. Come in, then."

"This is unwise," the chancellor said. "Anything guarded by a dragon is locked away for a reason."

"Treasures hidden forever do no good," Tern said. She entered the treasury, leaving the chancellor behind. The door swung quietly shut behind her.

Despite the dragon's protection, it was difficult to breathe through the dream of ocean, and difficult to move. Even the color of the light was like that of rain and lightning and foam mixed together. The smell of salt grew stronger, interspersed curiously with the fragrance of chrysanthemums. But then, it was better than drowning.

"What brings you here?" asked the dragon, swimming alongside her. Its coils revealed themselves in pearlescent flashes.

"I must select twenty-seven gifts for the Twenty-Seven Great Families to impress them with the dynasty's might," Tern said. "I don't know what to give them."

"Is that all?" the dragon said, sounding disappointed. "There are suits of armor here for woman and man, horse and elephant. Give one to the head of each family—although I presume none of them are elephants—and if they should plot treachery, the ghosts that live in the armor will strike down your enemies. Unless you've invented gunpowder yet? The armor's no good against decent guns. It's so easy to lose track of time while drowsing here."

Tern craned her head to look at the indistinct shapes of skeleton and coral. "Gunpowder?" she asked.

"Don't trouble yourself about it. It's not important. Shall I show you the armor?" The undulating light revealed finely wrought armor paired with demon-faced masks or impressively spiked chamfrons. She could almost see her face, distorted, in the polished breastplates.

"That's no true gift," Tern said, "practical though it is."

The dragon sighed gustily. "An idealist. Well, then. What about this?"

As though they stood to either side of a brook, a flotilla of paper boats bobbed toward them. Tern knelt to examine the boats and half a verse was written on one's sail.

"Go ahead," the dragon said, "unfold it."

She did. "That's almost a poem by Crescent-Sword-Descending," she said: one of the empire's most celebrated admirals, who had turned back the Irrilesh invasion 349 years ago. "But it's less elegant than the version my tutors taught me."

"That's because Crescent was a mediocre poet, for all her victories at sea," the dragon said. "Her empress had one of the court poets discreetly rewrite everything." Its tone of voice implied that it didn't understand this human undertaking, either. "In any case, each of the boats is inscribed with verses by some hero or admiral. If you float them in the sea on the night of a gravid moon, they will grow into fine warships. To restore them to their paper form—useful for avoiding docking fees—recite their verses on a new moon. And they're loyal, if that's a concern. They won't sail against you."

Tern considered it. "It's an impressive gift, but not quite right." She envisioned her subjects warring with each other.

"These, then," the dragon said, knotting and unknotting itself. A cold current rushed through the room, and the boats scattered, vanishing into dark corners.

When the chill abated, twenty-seven fine coats were arrayed before them. Some were sewn with baroque pearls and star sapphires, others embroidered with gold and silver thread. Some had ruffs lined with lace finer than foam, others sleeves decorated with fantastic flowers of wire and stiff dyed silk. One was white and pale blue and silver, like the moon on a snowy night; another was deep orange and decorated with amber in which trapped insects spelled out liturgies in brittle characters; yet another was black fading into smoke-gray at the hems, with several translucent capes fluttering down from the collar like moth wings, each hung with tiny, clapperless glass bells.

"They're marvelous indeed," Tern said. She peered more closely: each coat, however different, had a glittering crest at its breast. "Are those dragons' scales?"

"Indeed they are," the dragon said. "There are dragons of every kind of storm imaginable: ion storms, solar flares, the quantum froth of the emptiest vacuum . . . in any case, have you never wondered what it's like to view the world from a dragon's perspective?"

"Not especially," Tern said. In her daydreams she had roved the imperial gardens, pretending she could understand the language of carp and cat, or could sleep among the mothering branches of the willow; that she could run away. But dutiful child that she was, she had never done so in truth.

"Each year at the Festival of Dragons," the dragon said, "those who wear the coats will have the opportunity to take on a dragon's shape. It's not terribly useful for insurrection, if that's what the expression in your eyes means. But dragons love to dance, and sometimes people so transformed choose never to abandon that dance. At festival's end, whoever stands in a dragon's skin remains in that dragon's skin."

Tern walked among the coats, careful not to touch them even with the hem of her gown. The dragon rippled as it watched her, but forbore comment.

"Yes," she said at last. "This will do." The coats were wondrous, but they offered their wearers an honest choice, or so she hoped.

"What of something for yourself?" the dragon asked.

Some undercurrent in the dragon's tone made her look at it sharply. "It's one thing to use the treasury for a matter of state," she said, "and another to pillage it for my own pleasure."

"You're the empress, aren't you?"

"Which makes it all the more important that I behave responsibly." Tern tilted her chin up to meet the dragon's dispassionate gaze. "The treasury isn't the only reason you're here, is it."

"Ah, so you've figured it out." The dragon's smile showed no teeth. It extended a hand with eight clawed fingers. Dangling from the smallest claw, which was still longer than Tern's hand, was a disc rather like a coin, except it was made of dull green stone with specks in it like blood clots, and the hole drilled through the center was circular rather than a square. The most interesting thing was the snake carved into the surface, with every scale polished and distinct.

"Is it watching me?" Tern asked, disconcerted by the way the snake's eyes were a brighter red than the flecks in the rest of the stone. "What is it called?"

"That is the Coin of Heart's Desire," the dragon said with no particular inflection.

"Nothing with such a name can possibly bring good fortune," she said.

"It never harmed your mother."

Then why had she never heard of it? "In all the transactions I have ever witnessed," Tern said, "a coin must be spent to be used."

The dragon's smile displayed the full length of its jagged teeth. "You're not wrong."

Tern inspected the coin again. She was certain that the snake had changed position. "How many of my ancestors have spent the coin?"

"I lost count," the dragon said. "This business of reign-names and funeral-names makes it difficult to keep track. But some never spent it at all."

"Why isn't it mentioned in the histories?"

The dragon's eyelid dipped. "Because I like to eat historians. Their bones whisper the most delicious secrets."

There was a saying in the empire: never sing before an empty shrine; never dance with ghosts at low tide; never cross jests with a dragon. Tern said slowly, "Yet the empire has prospered, if those historians are to be believed. We can't all have failed this test."

The dragon did not deny that it was, indeed, a test.

Tern looked over her shoulder at the door. Its outline was visible only as an intersection of shadow and murky light. "There's no other way out of this treasury." When the dragon remained silent, she touched the coin with her fingertip. It was warm, as if it had lain in the eye of a hidden sun. She half-expected to feel the rasp of scales as the snake moved again.

The dragon withdrew its hand suddenly. The coin dropped, and Tern caught it reflexively. "I'm afraid not," it said. "But that's not to say that you won't receive some benefit on your way out. The question is, what do you want?"

"What did my mother trade it for?"

"She asked to leave the treasury and never return," the dragon said. "Two days and two nights she spent in here, contemplating her options, and that was what she came up with. She didn't trust the treasury's temptations. Of course, she thought she had been here much longer. Time moves differently underwater, after all."

Tern tried to imagine her mother as a young woman, newly-crowned empress, hazy with sleeplessness and desperate to escape this test. "How long have I been here?" she asked.

"Not long as humans reckon time," the dragon said. Its cheerfulness was not reassuring.

"The gifts for the Twenty-Seven Families," Tern said. "Whatever becomes of me, will they be delivered to the court?"

The dragon waved a hand. "They're yours to dispose of as you see fit. I'm done looking at them, so I don't see why not."

Tern glanced around again. She might be here for a very long time if this went wrong. "I know what I want," she said.

The dragon drifted closer.

Her voice quavered in spite of herself, but she looked the dragon full in the eye. "I don't know what bargain has bound you here all these years, but I want no more of it. Let this coin purchase your freedom."

The dragon was silent for a long time. At last it said, "Dragons are unpredictable allies, you know."

"I will take that chance," Tern said. Was this reckless? Perhaps. But as she saw it, the empresses of her line were as much prisoners as the dragon was. Best to let the dragon pursue its own destiny.

"Someone needs to guard the treasury, you know." The dragon canted its head. "You don't seem to have a spare dragon."

So this was the real price. "I will stay," Tern whispered.

"A determined thief would make mince of you in minutes, you realize."

Tern frowned. "I thought you'd want to leave."

"I do," the dragon said, "but I take my duty seriously. There's only one thing to be done, then. Pass me the coin, will you?"

Not sure whether she was more bemused or bewildered, Tern did so. She felt a curious pang as the coin left her hand.

"The guardian of a dragon's treasure," the dragon said, "should have a dragon's own defenses."

With that, the dragon slipped out of its skin, so subtly that at first Tern did not realize what was happening. Scales sparkled deep blue and kelp-green, piling up in irregular coils around the dragon's legs. The dragon itself took on the shape of a woman perhaps ten years older than Tern. Her black hair drifted around her face; her eyes were brown. Indeed, she could have been one of Tern's people.

"The skin is yours," the dragon said in much the same voice as before, "to use or discard as you please. Don't tell me that I never gave you choices."

"At least wear something," Tern said, appalled at the thought of the dragon surprising the chancellor while not wearing any human clothes.

"Your empire won't thank you for giving it to a dragon to rule," the dragon said, although it did, at least, choose for itself a plain robe of wool.

"You will rule with a dragon's sense of justice," Tern said, "which is more than I can expect from the women and men out there who are hungering after a child's throne." She handed over the keys of her office.

The dragon's smile was respectful. "We'll see." And, pausing at the threshold: "I won't forget you."

The door closed, and Tern was left with the coin and the dragon skin.

It was not until many generations later, when one of the dragon's descendants braved the second treasury, that Tern learned that she had been given a dragon-name. Not a reign-name, for she was done with that, and not a funeral-name, for she was far from dead. The empire she had ceded was now calling her Devourer-of-Bargains. After all this time, she had come around to the dragon's own opinion on this matter. It was a confusing human practice, but she wasn't in any position to argue.

A number of generations after that, when a different empress braved the treasury, Tern asked what had become of the Dragon Empress from so many years ago.

The empress said, "According to the records, she disappeared after a sixty-year reign, leaving only a note that said, 'I'm looking for another coin.'"

The empress was looking wistfully at a particularly lovely beryl set in silver filigree. Eventually she returned her attention to Tern, but she kept glancing back at it. The woman's face looked oddly familiar, but Tern couldn't place it. Probably a trick of her imagination.

The rest of the conversation was fairly predictable, but Tern contemplated the dragon's sense of justice once the empress had gone. Time moved differently underwater, after all. She could wait.

Yoon Ha Lee's debut short fiction collection *Conservation of Shadows* came out in 2013. His first novel, *Ninefox Gambit*, is being published this year. He lives in Louisiana with his family and an extremely lazy cat. Neither the cat nor any family members have yet been eaten by gators.

"The Glass Bottle Trick" resembles, in many aspects, Charles Perrault's "Bluebeard," but it is far more than a cautionary tale about curiosity or the story of a brave woman who rescues herself. Among other things, it is about the monster of internalized racism. When first published, Hopkinson introduced it with: "Eggs are seeds, perfectly white on the outside. Who knows what complexions their inside might reveal when they crack open to germinate and bear fruit."

The Glass Bottle Trick

Nalo Hopkinson

The air was full of storms, but they refused to break. In the wicker rocking chair on the front verandah, Beatrice flexed her bare feet against the wooden slat floor, rocking slowly back and forth. Another sweltering rainy season afternoon. The arid heat felt as though all the oxygen had boiled out of the parched air to hang as looming rain-clouds, waiting.

Oh, but she loved it like this. The hotter the day, the slower she would move, basking. She stretched her arms and legs out to better feel the luxuriant warmth, then guiltily sat up straight again. Samuel would scold if he ever saw her slouching like that. Stuffy Sammy. She smiled fondly, admiring the lacy patterns the sunlight threw on the floor as it filtered through the white gingerbread fretwork that trimmed the roof of their house.

"Anything more today, Mistress Powell? I finish doing the dishes." Gloria had come out of the house and was standing in front of her, wiping her chapped hands on her apron.

Beatrice felt the shyness come over her as it always did when she thought of giving the older woman orders. Gloria was older than Beatrice's mother. "Ah . . . no, I think that's everything, Gloria. . . ."

Gloria quirked an eyebrow, crinkling her face like running a fork through molasses.

Beatrice gave an abortive, shamefaced "huh" of a laugh. Gloria had known from the start, she'd had so many babies of her own. She'd been mad to run to Samuel with the news from since. But yesterday, Beatrice had already decided to tell Samuel. Well, almost decided. She felt irritated, like a child whose tricks have been found out. She swallowed the feeling. "I think you right, Gloria," she said, fighting for some dignity before the older woman. "Maybe . . . maybe I cook him a special meal, feed him up nice, then tell him."

"Well, I say is time and past time you make him know. A pickney is a blessing to a family."

"For true," Beatrice agreed, making her voice sound as certain as she could.

"Later, then, Mistress Powell." Giving herself the afternoon off, not even a by-your-leave, Gloria headed off to the maid's room at the back of the house to change into her street clothes. A few minutes later, she let herself out the garden gate.

"That seems like a tough book for a young lady of such tender years."

"Excuse me?" Beatrice threw a defensive cutting glare at the older man. He'd caught her off guard, though she'd seen his eyes following her ever since she entered the bookstore. "You have something to say to me?" She curled the Gray's Anatomy *possessively into the crook of her arm, price sticker hidden against her body. Two more months of saving before she could afford it.*

He looked shyly at her. "Sorry if I offended, Miss," he said. "My name is Samuel."

Would be handsome, if he'd chill out a bit. Beatrice's wariness thawed a little. Middle of the sun-hot day, and he wearing black wool jacket and pants. His crisp white cotton shirt was buttoned right up, held in place by a tasteful, unimaginative tie. So proper, Jesus. He wasn't that much older than she.

"Is just . . . you're so pretty, and it's the only thing I could think of to say to get you to speak to me."

Beatrice softened more at that, smiled for him and played with the collar of her blouse. He didn't seem too bad, if you could look beyond the stocious, starchy behavior.

Beatrice doubtfully patted the slight swelling of her belly. Four months. She was shy to give Samuel her news, but she was starting to show. Silly to put it off, yes? Today she was going to make her husband very happy; break that thin shell of mourning that still insulated him from her. He never said so, but Beatrice knew that he still thought of the wife he'd lost, and tragically, the one before that. She wished she could make him warm up to life again.

Sunlight was flickering through the leaves of the guava tree in the front yard. Beatrice inhaled the sweet smell of the sun-warmed fruit. The tree's branches hung heavy with the pale yellow globes, smooth and round as eggs. The sun reflected off the two blue bottles suspended in the tree, sending cobalt light dancing through the leaves.

When Beatrice first came to Sammy's house, she'd been puzzled by the two bottles that were jammed onto branches of the guava tree.

"Is just my superstitiousness, darling," he'd told her. "You never heard the old people say that if someone dies, you must put a bottle in a tree to hold their spirit, otherwise it will come back as a duppy and haunt you? A blue bottle. To keep the duppy cool, so it won't come at you in hot anger for being dead."

Beatrice had heard something of the sort, but it was strange to think of her Sammy as a superstitious man. He was too controlled and logical for that. Well, grief makes somebody act in strange ways. Maybe the bottles gave him some comfort, made him feel that he'd kept some essence of his poor wives near him.

"That Samuel is nice. Respectable, hard-working. Not like all them other ragamuffins you always going out with." Mummy picked up the butcher knife and began expertly slicing the goat meat into cubes for the curry.

Beatrice watched the red lumps of flesh part under the knife. Crimson liquid leaked onto the cutting board. She sighed, "But, Mummy, Samuel so boring! Michael and Clifton know how to have fun. All Samuel want to do is go for country drives. Always taking me away from other people."

"You should be studying your books, not having fun," her mother replied crossly.

Beatrice pleaded, "You well know I could do both, Mummy." Her mother just grunted.

Is only truth Beatrice was talking. Plenty men were always courting her, they flocked to her like birds, eager to take her dancing or out for a drink. But somehow she kept her marks up, even though it often meant studying right through the night, her head pounding and belly queasy from hangover while some man snored in the bed beside her. Mummy would kill her if she didn't get straight A's for medical school. "You going have to look after yourself, Beatrice. Man not going do it for you. Them get their little piece of sweetness and then them bruk away."

"Two patty and a King Cola, please." The guy who'd given the order had a broad chest that tapered to a slim waist. Good face to look at, too. Beatrice smiled sweetly at him, made shift to gently brush his palm with her fingertips as she handed him the change.

A bird screeched from the guava tree, a tiny kiskedee, crying angrily, *"Dit, dit, qu'est-ce qu'il dit!"* A small snake was coiled around one of the upper branches, just withdrawing its head from the bird's nest. Its jaws were distended with the egg it had stolen. It swallowed the egg whole, throat bulging hugely with its meal. The bird hovered around the snake's head, giving its pitiful wail of, "Say, say, what's he saying!"

"Get away!" Beatrice shouted at the snake. It looked in the direction of the sound, but didn't back off. The gulping motion of its body as it forced the egg farther down its own throat made Beatrice shudder. Then, oblivious to the fluttering of the parent bird, it arched its head over the nest again. Beatrice pushed herself to her feet and ran into the yard. "Hsst! Shoo! Come away from there!" But the snake took a second egg.

Sammy kept a long pole with a hook at one end leaned against the guava tree for pulling down the fruit. Beatrice grabbed up the pole, started jooking it at the branches as close to the bird and nest as she dared.

"Leave them, you brute! Leave!" The pole connected with some of the boughs. The two bottles in the tree fell to the ground and shattered with a crash. A hot breeze sprang up. The snake slithered away quickly, two eggs bulging in its throat. The bird flew off, sobbing to itself.

Nothing she could do now. When Samuel came home, he would hunt the nasty snake down for her and kill it. She leaned the pole back against the tree.

The light breeze should have brought some coolness, but really it only made the day warmer. Two little dust devils danced briefly around Beatrice. They swirled across the yard, swung up into the air, and dashed themselves to powder against the shuttered window of the third bedroom.

Beatrice got her sandals from the verandah. Sammy wouldn't like it if she stepped on broken glass. She picked up the broom that was leaned against the house and began to sweep up the shards of bottle. She hoped Samuel wouldn't be too angry with her. He wasn't a man to cross, could be as stern as a father if he had a mind to.

That was mostly what she remembered about Daddy, his temper—quick to show and just as quick to go. So was he; had left his family before Beatrice turned five. The one cherished memory she had of him was of being swung back and forth through the air, her two small hands clasped in one big hand of his, her feet held tight in another. Safe. And as he swung her through the air, her daddy had been chanting words from an old-time story:

Yung-Kyung-Pyung, what a pretty basket!
Margaret Powell Alone, what a pretty basket!
Eggie-law, what a pretty basket!

Then he had held her tight to his chest, forcing the air from her lungs in a breathless giggle. The dressing-down Mummy had given him for that game! "You want to drop the child and crack her head open on the hard ground? Ee? Why you can't be more responsible?"

"Responsible?" he'd snapped. "Is who working like dog sunup to sundown to put food in oonuh belly?" He'd set Beatrice down, her feet hitting the ground with a jar. She'd started to cry, but he'd just pushed her towards her mother and stormed out of the room. One more volley in the constant battle between them. After he'd left them Mummy had opened the little food shop in town to make ends meet. In the evenings, Beatrice would rub lotion into her mother's chapped, work-wrinkled hands. "See how that man make us come down in the world?" Mummy would grumble. "Look at what I come to."

Privately, Beatrice thought that maybe all Daddy had needed was a little patience. Mummy was too harsh, much as Beatrice loved her. To please her, Beatrice had studied hard all through high school: physics, chemistry, biology, describing the results of her lab experiments in her copybook in her cramped, resigned handwriting. Her mother greeted every A with a non-committal grunt and anything less with a lecture. Beatrice would smile airily, seal the hurt away, pretend the approval meant nothing to her. She still worked hard, but she kept some time for play of her own. Rounders, netball, and later, boys. All those boys, wanting a chance for a little sweetness with a light-skin browning like her. Beatrice had discovered her appeal quickly.

"Leggo beast . . ." Loose woman. The hissed words came from a knot of girls that slouched past Beatrice as she sat on the library steps, waiting for Clifton to come and pick her up. She willed her ears shut, smothered the sting of the words. But she knew some of those girls. Marguerita, Deborah. They used to be friends of hers. Though she sat up proudly, she found her fingers tugging self-consciously at the hem of her short white skirt. She put the big physics textbook in her lap, where it gave her thighs a little more coverage.

The farting vroom of Clifton's motorcycle interrupted her thoughts. Grinning, he stewed the bike to a dramatic halt in front of her. "Study time done now, darling. Time to play."

He looked good this evening, as he always did. Tight white shirt, jeans that showed off the bulges of his thighs. The crinkle of the thin gold chain at his neck set off his dark brown skin. Beatrice stood, tucked the physics text under her arm, smoothed the skirt over her hips. Clifton's eyes followed the movement of her hands. See, it didn't take much to make people treat you nice. She smiled at him.

Samuel would still show up hopefully every so often to ask her to accompany him on a drive through the country. He was so much older than all her other suitors. And dry? Country drives, Lord! She went out with him a few times; he was so persistent and she couldn't figure out how to tell him no. He didn't seem to get her hints that really she should be studying. Truth to tell, though, she started to find his quiet, undemanding presence soothing. His eggshell-white BMW took the graveled country roads so quietly that she could hear the kiskedee birds in the mango trees, chanting their query: *"Dit, dit, qu'est-ce qu'il dit?"*

One day, Samuel brought her a gift.

"These are for you and your family," he said shyly, handing her a wrinkled paper bag. "I know your mother likes them." Inside were three plump eggplants from his kitchen garden, raised by his own hands. Beatrice took the humble gift out of the bag. The skins of the eggplants had a taut, blue sheen to them. Later she would realize that that was when she'd begun to love Samuel. He was stable, solid, responsible. He would make Mummy and her happy.

Beatrice gave in more to Samuel's diffident wooing. He was cultured and well-spoken. He had been abroad, talked of exotic sports: ice hockey, downhill skiing. He took her to fancy restaurants she'd only heard of, that her other, young, unestablished boyfriends would never have been able to afford, and would probably only have embarrassed her if they had taken her. Samuel had polish. But he was humble, too, like the way he grew his own vegetables, or the self-deprecating tone in which he spoke of himself. He was always punctual, always courteous to her and her mother. Beatrice could count on him for little things, like picking her up after class, or driving her mother to the hairdresser's. With the other men, she always had to be on guard: pouting until they took her somewhere else for dinner, not another free meal in her mother's restaurant, wheedling them into using the condoms. She always had to hold some thing of herself shut away. With Samuel, Beatrice relaxed into trust.

"Beatrice, come! Come quick, nuh!"

Beatrice ran in from the backyard at the sound of her mother's voice. Had something happened to Mummy?

Her mother was sitting at the kitchen table, knife still poised to crack an egg into the bowl for the pound cake she was making to take to the shop. She was staring in open-mouthed delight at Samuel, who was fretfully twisting the long stems on a bouquet of blood-red roses. "Lord, Beatrice; Samuel say he want to marry you!"

Beatrice looked to Sammy for verification. "Samuel," she asked unbelievingly, "what you saying? Is true?"

He nodded yes. "True, Beatrice."

Something gave way in Beatrice's chest, gently as a long-held breath. Her heart had been trapped in glass, and he'd freed it.

They'd been married two months later. Mummy was retired now; Samuel had bought her a little house in the suburbs, and he paid for the maid to come in three times a week. In the excitement of planning for the wedding, Beatrice had let her studying slip. To her dismay she finished her final year of university with barely a C average.

"Never mind, sweetness," Samuel told her. "I didn't like the idea of you studying, anyway. Is for children. You're a big woman now." Mummy had agreed with him too, said she didn't need all that now. She tried to argue with them, but Samuel was very clear about his wishes, and she'd stopped, not wanting anything to cause friction between them just yet. Despite his genteel manner, Samuel had just a bit of a temper. No point in crossing him, it took so little to make him happy, and he was her love, the one man she'd found in whom she could have faith.

Too besides, she was learning how to be the lady of the house, trying to use the right mix of authority and jocularity with Gloria, the maid, and Cleitis, the yardboy who came twice a month to do the mowing and the weeding. Odd to be giving orders to people when she was used to being the one taking orders, in Mummy's shop. It made her feel uncomfortable to tell people to do her work for her. Mummy said she should get used to it, it was her right now.

The sky rumbled with thunder. Still no rain. The warmth of the day was nice, but you could have too much of a good thing. Beatrice opened her mouth, gasping a little, trying to pull more air into her lungs. She was a little short of breath nowadays as the baby pressed on her diaphragm. She knew she could go inside for relief from the heat, but Samuel kept the air-conditioning on high, so cold that they could keep the butter in its dish on the kitchen counter. It never went rancid. Even insects refused to come inside. Sometimes Beatrice felt as though the house were really somewhere else, not the tropics. She had been used to waging constant war against ants and cockroaches, but not in Samuel's house. The cold in it made Beatrice shiver, dried her eyes out until they felt like boiled eggs sitting in their sockets. She went outside as often as possible, even though Samuel didn't like her to spend too much time in the sun. He said he feared that cancer would mar her soft skin, that he didn't want to lose another wife. But Beatrice knew he just didn't want her to get too brown. When the sun touched her, it brought out the sepia and cinnamon in her blood, overpowered the milk and honey, and he could no longer pretend she was white. He loved her skin pale. "Look how you gleam in the moonlight," he'd say to her when he made gentle, almost supplicating love to her at night in the four-poster bed. His hand would slide over her flesh, cup her breasts with an air of reverence. The look in his eyes was so close to worship that it sometimes frightened her. To be loved so much! He would whisper to her, "Beauty. Pale Beauty, to my Beast," then blow a cool breath over the delicate membranes of her ear, making her shiver in delight. For her part, she loved to look at him, his molasses-dark skin, his broad chest, the way the planes of flat muscle slid across it. She imagined tectonic plates shifting in the earth. She loved the bluish-black cast the moonlight lent him. Once, gazing up at him as he loomed above her, body working against and in hers, she had seen the moonlight playing glints of deepest blue in his trim beard.

"Black Beauty," she had joked softly, reaching to pull his face closer for a kiss. At the words, he had lurched up off her to sit on the edge of the bed, pulling a sheet over him to hide his nakedness. Beatrice watched him, confused, feeling their blended sweat cooling along her body.

"Never call me that, please, Beatrice," he said softly. "You don't have to draw attention to my color. I'm not a handsome man, and I know it. Black and ugly as my mother made me."

"But, Samuel . . . !"

"No."

Shadows lay between them on the bed. He wouldn't touch her again that night.

Beatrice sometimes wondered why Samuel hadn't married a white woman. She thought she knew the reason, though. She had seen the way that Samuel behaved around white people. He smiled too broadly, he simpered, he made silly jokes. It pained her to see it, and she could tell from the desperate look in his eyes that it hurt him too. For all his love of creamy white skin, Samuel probably couldn't have brought himself to approach a white woman the way he'd courted her.

The broken glass was in a neat pile under the guava tree. Time to make Samuel's dinner now. She went up the verandah stairs to the front door, stopping to wipe her sandals on the coir mat just outside the door. Samuel hated dust. As she opened the door, she felt another gust of warm wind at her back, blowing past her into the cool house. Quickly, she stepped inside and closed the door, so that the interior would stay as cool as Sammy liked it. The insulated door shut behind her with a hollow sound. It was airtight. None of the windows in the house could be opened. She had asked Samuel, "Why you want to live in a box like this, sweetheart? The fresh air good for you."

"I don't like the heat, Beatrice. I don't like baking like meat in the sun. The sealed windows keep the conditioned air in." She hadn't argued.

She walked through the elegant, formal living room to the kitchen. She found the heavy imported furnishings cold and stuffy, but Samuel liked them.

In the kitchen she set water to boil and hunted a bit—where did Gloria keep it?—until she found the Dutch pot. She put it on the burner to toast the fragrant coriander seeds that would flavor the curry. She put on water to boil, stood staring at the steam rising from the pots. Dinner was going to be special tonight. Curried eggs, Samuel's favorite. The eggs in their cardboard case put Beatrice in mind of a trick she'd learned in physics class, for getting an egg unbroken into a narrow-mouthed bottle. You had to boil the egg hard and peel it, then stand a lit candle in the bottle. If you put the narrow end of the egg into the mouth of the bottle, it made a seal, and when the candle had burnt up all the air in the bottle, the vacuum it created would suck the egg in, whole. Beatrice had been the only one in her class patient enough to make the trick work. Patience was all her husband needed. Poor, mysterious Samuel had lost two wives in this isolated country home. He'd been rattling about in the airless house like the egg in the bottle. He kept to himself. The closest neighbors were miles away, and he didn't even know their names.

She was going to change all that, though. Invite her mother to stay for a while, maybe have a dinner party for the distant neighbors. Before her pregnancy made her too lethargic to do much.

A baby would complete their family. Samuel would be pleased, he would. She remembered him joking that no woman should have to give birth to his ugly black babies, but she would show him how beautiful their children would be, little brown bodies new as the earth after the rain. She would show him how to love himself in them.

It was hot in the kitchen. Perhaps the heat from the stove? Beatrice went out into the living room, wandered through the guest bedroom, the master bedroom, both bathrooms. The whole house was warmer than she'd ever felt it. Then she realized she could hear sounds coming from the outside, the cicadas singing loudly for rain. There was no whisper of cool air through the vents in the house. The air conditioner wasn't running.

Beatrice began to feel worried. Samuel liked it cold. She had planned tonight to be a special night for the two of them, but he wouldn't react well if everything wasn't to his liking. He'd raised his voice at her a few times. Once or twice he had stopped in the middle of an argument, one hand pulled back as if to strike, to take deep breaths, battling for self-control. His dark face would flush almost blue-black as he fought his rage down. Those times she'd stayed out of his way until he was calm again.

What could be wrong with the air conditioner? Maybe it had just come unplugged? Beatrice wasn't even sure where the controls were. Gloria and Samuel took care of everything around the house. She made another circuit through her home, looking for the main controls. Nothing. Puzzled, she went back into the living room. It was becoming thick and close as a womb inside their closed-up home.

There was only one room left to search. The locked third bedroom. Samuel had told her that both his wives had died in there, first one, then the other. He had given her the keys to every room in the house, but requested that she never open that particular door.

"I feel like it's bad luck, love. I know I'm just being superstitious, but I hope I can trust you to honor my wishes in this." She had, not wanting to cause him any anguish. But where else could the control panel be? It was getting so hot!

As she reached into her pocket for the keys she always carried with her, she realized she was still holding a raw egg in her hand. She'd forgotten to put it into the pot when the heat in the house had made her curious. She managed a little smile. The hormones flushing her body were making her so absent-minded Samuel would tease her, until she told him why. Every thing would be all right.

Beatrice put the egg into her other hand, got the keys out of her pocket, opened the door.

A wall of icy, dead air hit her body. It was freezing cold in the room. Her exhaled breath floated away from her in a long, misty curl. Frowning, she took a step inside and her eyes saw before her brain could understand, and when it did, the egg fell from her hands to smash open on the floor at her feet. Two women's bodies lay side by side on the double bed. Frozen mouths gaped open; frozen, gutted bellies, too. A fine sheen of ice crystals glazed their skin, which like her was barely brown, but laved in gelid, rime-covered blood that had solidified ruby red. Beatrice whimpered.

"But Miss," Beatrice asked her teacher, "how the egg going to come back out the bottle again?"

"How do you think, Beatrice? There's only one way; you have to break the bottle."

This was how Samuel punished the ones who had tried to bring his babies into the world, his beautiful black babies. For each woman had had the muscled sac of her womb removed and placed on her belly, hacked open to reveal the purplish mass of her placenta. Beatrice knew that if she were to dissect the thawing tissue, she'd find a tiny fetus in each one. The dead women had been pregnant too.

A movement at her feet caught her eyes. She tore her gaze away from the bodies long enough to glance down. Writhing in the fast-congealing yolk was a pin-feathered embryo. A rooster must have been at Mister Herbert's hens. She put her hands on her belly to still the sympathetic twitching of her womb. Her eyes were drawn back to the horror on the beds. Another whimper escaped her lips.

A sound like a sigh whispered in through the door she'd left open. A current of hot air seared past her cheek, making a plume of fog as it entered the room. The fog split into two, settled over the heads of each woman, began to take on definition. Each misty column had a face, contorted in rage. The faces were those of the bodies on the bed. One of the duppy women leaned over her own corpse. She lapped like a cat at the blood thawing on its breast. She became a little more solid for having drunk of her own life blood. The other duppy stooped to do the same. The two duppy women each had a belly slightly swollen with the pregnancies for which Samuel had killed them. Beatrice had broken the bottles that had confined the duppy wives, their bodies held in stasis because their spirits were trapped. She'd freed them. She'd let them into the house. Now there was nothing to cool their fury. The heat of it was warming the room up quickly.

The duppy wives held their bellies and glared at her, anger flaring hot behind their eyes. Beatrice backed away from the beds. "I didn't know," she said to the wives. "Don't vex with me. I didn't know what it is Samuel do to you."

Was that understanding on their faces, or were they beyond compassion?

"I making baby for him too. Have mercy on the baby, at least?"

Beatrice heard the *snik* of the front door opening. Samuel was home. He would have seen the broken bottles, would feel the warmth of the house. Beatrice felt that initial calm of the prey that realizes it has no choice but to turn and face the beast that is pursuing it. She wondered if Samuel would be able to read the truth hidden in her body, like the egg in the bottle.

"Is not me you should be vex with," she pleaded with the duppy wives. She took a deep breath and spoke the words that broke her heart. "Is . . . is Samuel who do this."

She could hear Samuel moving around in the house, the angry rumbling of his voice like the thunder before the storm. The words were muffled, but she could hear the anger in his tone. She called out, "What you saying, Samuel?"

She stepped out of the meat locker and quietly pulled the door in, but left it open slightly so the duppy wives could come out when they were ready.

Then with a welcoming smile, she went to greet her husband. She would stall him as long as she could from entering the third bedroom. Most of the blood in the wives' bodies would be clotted, but maybe it was only important that it be *warm*. She hoped that enough of it would thaw soon for the duppies to drink until they were fully real.

When they had fed, would they come and save her, or would they take revenge on her, their usurper, as well as on Samuel?

Eggie-Law, what a pretty basket.

Nalo Hopkinson has lived in her native Jamaica, as well as Trinidad, Guyana, and—for the past thirty-five years—in Canada. She is currently a professor of creative writing at the University of California, Riverside, USA. The author of six novels, two short story collections, and a chapbook, Hopkinson is a recipient of the Warner Aspect First Novel Award, the Ontario Arts Council Foundation Award for emerging writers, the John W. Campbell Award for Best New Writer, the Locus Award for Best New Writer, the World Fantasy Award, the Sunburst Award for Canadian Literature of the Fantastic (twice), the Aurora Award, the Gaylactic Spectrum Award, and the Norton Award. Her collection, *Falling in Love With Hominids* (Tachyon Publications) was published last year.

One cannot really say Catherynne M. Valente retells or reinvents "Sleeping Beauty" with "The Maiden Tree." She approaches it from an angle no one else has seen and spins a story: deep and dark and ravishing.

In nineteenth-century horticulture, a maiden-tree is either a tree that has never been cut and thus has a single main stem, or a young tree raised immediately from the seed. Or both. Nowadays it seems to be a more specialized term most often used in reference to fruit trees and the grafting thereof. Perhaps we can see the "rough symbiosis" of this story as a graft of sorts: one that damages rather than repairs; that thwarts rather than grows.

The Maiden-Tree

Catherynne M. Valente

I t is remarkable how like a syringe a spindle can be.

That explains the attraction, of course. A certain kind of sixteen-year-old girl just cannot say no to this sort of thing, and I was just that measure of girl, the one who looks down on the star-caught point of a midnight needle, sticking awkwardly up into the air like some ridiculous miniature of the Alexandrian Lighthouse and breathe: *yes.* The one who impales herself eagerly on that beacon, places the spindle against her sternum when a perfumed forefinger would be more than enough to do the job, and waits, panting, sweating through her corset-boning, for a terrible rose to blossom in her brain.

Well, we were all silly children once.

They could not get it out. I lie here with the thing still jutting out of my chest like an adrenaline shot, still wispy with flax fine as ash. Eventually the skin closed around it, flakes of dried blood blew gently away, and it and I were one, as if we had grown in the same queen's womb, coughed into the world at the same moment, *genius* and child, and I had spent those sixteen years before we were properly introduced chasing it like a dog her own bedraggled tail. My little *lar domestici*, my household god, standing over me for all these years, growing out of me, the skin-soil of my prostration, as swollen with my blood as everything else within these moss-clotted walls.

And these are the thoughts of a sleeping woman as she breathes in and out in a haze no less impenetrable than if it had been opiate-bred; these are the thoughts of a corpse kept roseate by the rough symbiosis of spindle and maiden, a possibility never whispered of in all the biology texts she ever knew, or hinted at by the alchemists who whittled sixteen years away burning spinning wheels to lead and ash.

I have been arranged here as lovingly as the best morticians could manage, my hair treated with gold dust so that it would lose none of its luster, even as it tangled and grew wild across the linen, and the parquet floor, up to the window-frames and dove-bare eaves. My lips were painted with the self-same dyes that blush the seraphs' cheeks in chapel frescoes, and injected with linseed oil so that my kiss would remain both scarlet and soft. My skin was varnished to the perfection of milk-pink virginity, violet petals placed beneath my tongue to keep the breath, no matter how thin it might become, fresh. From scalp to arch, I have been tenderly stroked with peacock-feather brushes dipped in formaldehyde (specially treated so as not to offend the nose of any future visitor, of course). The place where my breast joins the spindle has been daubed with witch-hazel and clover-tincture, cleaned as best as could be managed—all this was done with such love, devotion, even, before the briar sprouted beneath the first tower, and the roses put everyone else to sleep with me.

But they were not prepared, and this has become a tomb with but one living Juliet clutching her nosegay of peonies and chrysanthemums against her clavicle, her back aching on a cold stone slab.

You cannot imagine what has happened here.

My father stood behind me at each of the great bonfires—one at midsummer, one at midwinter, every year since my first. He kept me well away while those wide-spoked wheels were piled up like hecatombs in the courtyard, carted in on peasants' backs and in wheelbarrows, bound up in tablecloths and burlap sacks, dragged behind families in knotted nets. I was transfixed when they blazed and crackled, bright as Halloween, up to the sky in skeins of smoke and fire, sending off clouds of sparks like flax-seeds. The wheels spun the heavens like a length of long, black cloth.

Now you will be safe, he whispered, and stroked my golden hair. *Now nothing can hurt you, and you will be my little girl forever and ever, amen.*

But Father, I could not help but think, *how will they spin without their wheels? There are less of them every year, and everyone is getting holes in their stockings. The sheep will snarl in their pastures, weighted to the mud by unshorn fleece! Folk will clothe themselves in brambles, and the markets will be so silent, so silent!*

Hush, now, he sighed. *Don't think on that. You are safe, that is enough. I have done what was required of me.*

Will they move to the cities? Will they work in the factories under great windows like checkerboards of glass? Will they stitch a thousand breeches an hour, a hundred bonnets a minute?

No, he said, (and oh, his gaze was dead and cold!) *A textile factory is but a spindle with teeth of steel. They, too, will burn before you are a woman grown. Everything, everything, will be ashes but you.*

Oh, I whispered, *I see.*

I see.

And I inclined my head a little, into his great hand.

I remember the blueberries best, I think. How they grew wild beneath my window, and dappled the air with purple.

The roses took them, too.

I lie here, I lie here, and my hands are so carefully tented in prayer, frozen in prayer, but I hear, oh, how I hear, as only the dead can hear. Out of the loamy soil came a little sprig among the fat, dark berries, innocent as oatmeal, and I heard it come wheedling through the earth, sidling up to the stone. They cleared a space for it, watered it with delight, of course, once they ascertained its botanical nature—what could give the sleeping dear sweeter dreams than a rose blooming just here, below her bower?

Nothing, of course.

And it might have been all right, it might really have been nothing but a rose, white or orange or violet, buds sweetly closed up like pursed lips. But it sent out no flowers at all for months, while the gardeners frowned like midwives and buried fish heads in the flowerbed. It grew, upwards and onwards, and it might have been harmless if it had not found its tendrils brushing through my window one night when October was beating the glass in, if it had not crept slowly across the polished floor and grazed—so faintly!—my angelically positioned foot.

It lay against me for a moment, as though it meant only to decorate.

At first I thought it was my mother's voice—and I cannot recall when, in all these years, I recalled that there had been a witch, and a curse, and that curses generally come from witches, who possess more or less female voices of their own. It is so easy for a certain kind of girl to forget the origins of things.

But at first I did not even understand that I was sleeping. I thought it was the natural result of a spindle-syringe, that the lovely warm feeling of *seeping* was what my father had meant to hide from me, the niggardly old fool. I lay back on the bed only because my head felt so hot, so hot, full of sound and the weeping of golden meats, and I could not stand, I could not stand any longer. And when I whispered to no one at all that there were all these red, red roses blooming inside me, I thought I was very clever with my turns of phrase, and would have to remember to write that down when I was quite myself again.

I did not feel as though I was falling, but rather that I had failed to fall. I lay there, and lay there, (and now it has become so much my habit to lie that I consider myself a student of the art, an initiate to its mysteries—no mystic with limbs like branches could outlast me) and there was a moment, just before dawn, when I tried to rouse myself to go down and sit at a table which surely held fried eggs and fine brown sausages speckled with bits of apple-peel, and made the inevitable discovery.

Of course I panicked, and thrashed in my scented bed, and shrieked myself into Bedlam—but none of this sounded outside the echoes of my own skull, and soon after my father—his face so haggard!—resigned and so thin, so thin, set his men to preserving my flesh. I was still screaming when they stopped up my mouth with wax, but they heard nothing, and patted my cheek with a refined sort of pity, as though they knew all along I was a bad girl, and would come to some end or another.

At first I thought it was my mother's voice. But something in the way it vibrated within me—well, a mother whispers in one's ear, does she not?

You are so beautiful, little darling, like light bottled and sold.

The spindle said it, I know that now, the spindle stuck in me like a husband, and it sang me through sleep with all these black psalms.

Beautiful, yes, but you cannot really think anyone is coming. Do you know what happens to a body in a hundred years? Some bourgeois second-son will hack through the briar—such labor is needed in a world without spindles, in the world your father made with his holocaust of spinning wheels, and there will be no shortage of starving, threadbare boys willing to brave the thorns for a chance at the goods in the castle—but not you, little lar familiari; he will be looking for the coats off of your aunties' frozen backs, for the shoes in a dozen closets, for the tableware and the tablecloths—oh, especially the tablecloths! He will be looking for curtains and carpets and scraps of damask, your mother's trousseau, your sister's gowns, as much as he can carry—and he will come upon this little room. He will be almost too revolted to enter; the smell of twelve hundred months of menses will wash the hall in red, (it will hardly be a year before you'll flood the wax stopper there), and then the smell of bed-sweat and bed-sores gone to fester, the smell of formaldehyde having long since conquered its pretty mask of flowers. He will hardly be able to open the door for the press of your grotesquely spiraling toenails. You'll be a stinking, freakish, blood-stuck frog pickled in a jar, and he won't see you but for the gold in your hair, and your long, lovely bridal dress, which will not have been white for decades.

He'll strip you down as though he meant to be your lover after all. He'll take the dress, and the veils, and the sheets off the bed, he'll shave your hair to stubble and clip your nails for swords, and leave you naked and alone to rot in this tower until the next desperate prince comes through the roses and cuts you up for meat.

Please, please be quiet. I never did anything to you. I only wanted the needle, and the rose.

No one is coming for you. I am all you have, and I love you better and more loyally than all the princes in Araby. Who else would have stayed with you all this while?

Please. I want to sleep.

Aristotle said it was impossible. (Do not be surprised—girls with no natural defense against spindles are always classically educated.) He stroked a beard like lambswool after a March rain and assured a gaggle of rosy-testicled boys that one cannot bury a bed and expect a bed-tree to grow from that large and awkward seed.

But.

You can plant a maiden, oh yes, and watch the maiden-tree flower. And the spindle planted me into a bed, and the bed grew with me. And look, oh, look at us now.

I have wept in my sleep and watered it, but I might have saved the moisture. The rose-briar pushed its way into my heel, sinuously, insistently, as if trying to slide in unnoticed. There was a small, innocent popping noise when it pricked the skin, and left its red mark, predictably like a stigmata. It began a slow wind through the complicated bones of my ankle, and I could feel the leaves sliding against the meat of my calf.

Almost immediately, it detonated a blossom, a monstrous, obscene crimson unfolding on the wall like a spider, and the silence of its breathing clambered into my ear. The petals were crushed by a ceiling of skin, but no matter—in a month or two those too will break through, and all my pores will be the roots of roses.

And with this I will tangle you up in me, came the spindle-voice, soft and shattered as a witch who has sold her soul for the magnitude of her spell. The roses came open inside my legs—oh!—the thorns broke through the nails of my toes, and there was red, nothing but red, everywhere.

If you had lived, you would still have had the spindle stuck in you—you cannot really escape it, the bruised fingers and the sheep-sweat smell of wool in your lap. Isn't it better this way? A rose is a rose is a rose is a maiden, maidens are supposed to be roses, and I will make of you a bed for flowers like erupting maidenheads—

Out of my torso the briars came, up around the shaft of the spindle, around my arms like shackles, around my throat, through my hair. I was soil, I was earth, I could not move and my flesh exploded into roses with a perfume like shadows. I screamed; I was silent.

I've saved you, you'll see. I am your spindle; I am your prince; this is my kiss. With this lacerate of flowers, I have taken you out of the world, the blighted, wasted world your beauty has stripped of cloth, the poor, rubbish-strewn landscape that was the country of your birth—it is all gone now, the vineyards and the rolling hills and the corn—

No, no, someone will come and gather me up like a sack of cotton and I will eat blueberries again and drink new milk and you will be nothing but a faint scar between my breasts and he will remark when we are old that it looks something like a star. I will never hear your voice in my bones again, you cannot keep seeding my skin forever—

I can. Whoever said this was a hundred-year sentence and not a whit more? Calendars lie, I lie. I lie inside you no less than a liver or a spleen, I breathe your breath, I rise and fall with your sleeping breast, my needle pulses in you, warm alongside your heart, and this is all there is.

They wound out of the room, splintering the door, down the stair, and it was not some sepulchral perfume that felled the court—no, no, the roses did it, the roses snapped round their calves and whickered a path to their throats. The stems shot past their lips and sent out their petals there like thick cakes, blocking their breath as mine was never blocked, tearing their lungs as mine were never torn. Trails of thin blood trickled out of five hundred mouths, five hundred gasps were stoppered up like water in a jar. The maiden-tree was in its summer, and from its briar-branches hung five hundred bright and bobbing fruits, orange-ladies and lemon-lords, cherry-sculleries and plum-cooks, and an apple-king, and a queen among figs.

I am not for them. I am for you alone.

And they were not prepared, they were not treated with gold and form-aldehyde, their bodies grayed on the vine as bodies will do, and I can smell my mother's skin sodden through with mold, and I can smell my sisters rotting.

There is nothing but briars, briars all around, and throttling roses scouring the stone.

Nonsense, darling. I am here.

Please. I am so tired.

Years later, even the bed sprouted, little tendrils of green wandering out of the rain-saturated wood, seeking out more wetness, and finding all that there is to find here—my skin, my blood, my tears. The room which was ample to hold a maiden while she slept off an overdose has become a clot of green, snarled full of woody branches and tender, new shoots. I am enough to water them all, and the spindle is enough to water me. That is the biology of maidenhood.

And so it was that even the bridal bower became rooted in me, and the pillows were blossoms, and the coverlet was bark, and I was the heartwood, still and hard within. Aristotle, Aristotle, with your beard of briars, there are such secret things at work when a bed becomes a tree. I do not fault you for ignorance.

I have had a long time to think.
    I am sorry about the needle.

Catherynne M. Valente is the *New York Times* bestselling author of over a dozen works of fiction and poetry, including *Palimpsest*, the Orphan's Tales series, *Deathless*, and the crowdfunded phenomenon *The Girl Who Circumnavigated Fairyland in a Ship of Her Own Making*. Her most recent novel is *Radiance*. She is the winner of the Andre Norton, Tiptree, Mythopoeic, Rhysling, Lambda, Locus, and Hugo awards. She has been a finalist for the Nebula and World Fantasy Awards. She lives on an island off the coast of Maine with a small but growing menagerie of beasts, some of which are human.

Attempting to save a loved one from the faeries always takes courage, intelligence, and a strong will. Holly Black's hero is a brave "tailor" who has an almost-magical talent for creating exquisite clothing.

The Coat of Stars

Holly Black

Rafael Santiago hated going home. Home meant his parents making a big fuss and a special dinner and him having to smile and hide all his secret vices, like the cigarettes he had smoked for almost sixteen years now. He hated that they always had the radio blaring salsa and the windows open and that his cousins would come by and try to drag him out to bars. He hated that his mother would tell him how Father Joe had asked after him at Mass. He especially hated the familiarity of it, the memories that each visit stirred up.

For nearly an hour that morning he had stood in front of his dressing table and regarded the wigs and hats and masks—early versions or copies of costumes he'd designed—each item displayed on green glass heads that stood in front of a large, broken mirror. They drooped feathers, paper roses, and crystal dangles, or curved up into coiled, leather horns. He had settled on wearing a white tank-top tucked into bland gray Dockers but when he stood next to all his treasures, he felt unfinished. Clipping on black suspenders, he looked at himself again. That was better, almost a compromise. A fedora, a cane, and a swirl of eyeliner would have finished off the look, but he left it alone.

"What do you think?" he asked the mirror, but it did not answer. He turned to the unpainted plaster face casts resting on a nearby shelf; their hollow eyes told him nothing either.

Rafe tucked his little phone into his front left pocket with his wallet and keys. He would call his father from the train. Glancing at the wall, his gaze rested on one of the sketches of costumes he'd done for a postmodern ballet production of *Hamlet*. An award hung beside it. This sketch was of a faceless woman in a white gown appliquéd with leaves and berries. He remembered how dancers had held the girl up while others pulled on the red ribbons he had had hidden in her sleeves. Yards and yards of red ribbon could come from her wrists. The stage had been swathed in red. The dancers had been covered in red. The whole world had become one dripping gash of ribbon.

The train ride was dull. He felt guilty the green landscapes that blurred outside the window did not stir him. He only loved leaves if they were crafted from velvet.

Rafael's father waited at the station in the same old blue truck he'd had since before Rafe had left Jersey for good. Each trip his father would ask him careful questions about his job, the city, Rafe's apartment. Certain unsaid assumptions were made. His father would tell him about some cousin getting into trouble or, lately, his sister Mary's problems with Marco.

Rafe leaned back in the passenger seat, feeling the heat of the sun wash away the last of the goose bumps on his arms. He had forgotten how cold the air conditioning was on the train. His father's skin, sun-darkened to deep mahogany, made his own seem sickly pale. A string-tied box of crystallized ginger pastries sat at his feet. He always brought something for his parents: a bottle of wine, a tarte Tatin, a jar of truffle oil from Balducci's.

The gifts served as a reminder of the city and that his ticket was round-trip, bought and paid for.

"Mary's getting a divorce," Rafe's father said once he'd pulled out of the parking lot. "She's been staying in your old room. I had to move your sewing stuff."

"How's Marco taking it?" Rafe had already heard about the divorce; his sister had called him a week ago at three in the morning from Cherry

Hill, asking for money so she and her son Victor could take a bus home. She had talked in heaving breaths and he'd guessed she'd been crying. He had wired the money to her from the corner store where he often went for green tea ice cream.

"Not good. He wants to see his son. I told him if he comes around the house again, your cousin's gonna break probation but he's also gonna break that loco sonofabitch's neck."

No one, of course, thought that spindly Rafe could break Marco's neck.

The truck passed people dragging lawn chairs into their front yards for a better view of the coming fireworks. Although it was still many hours until dark, neighbors milled around, drinking lemonade and beer.

In the back of the Santiago house, smoke pillared up from the grill where cousin Gabriel scorched hamburger patties smothered in hot sauce. Mary lay on the blue couch in front of the TV, an ice mask covering her eyes. Rafael walked by as quietly as he could. The house was dark and the radio was turned way down. For once, his greeting was subdued. Only his nephew, Victor, a sparkler twirling in his hand, seemed oblivious to the somber mood.

They ate watermelon so cold that it was better than drinking water; hot dogs and hamburgers off the grill with more hot sauce and tomatoes; rice and beans; corn salad; and ice cream. They drank beer and instant iced tea and the decent tequila that Gabriel had brought. Mary joined them halfway through the meal and Rafe was only half-surprised to see the blue and yellow bruise darkening her jaw. Mostly, he was surprised how much her face, angry and suspicious of pity, reminded him of Lyle.

When Rafe and Lyle were thirteen, they had been best friends. Lyle had lived across town with his grandparents and three sisters in a house far too small for all of them. Lyle's grandmother told the kids terrible stories to keep them from going near the river that ran through the woods behind their yard. There was the one about the phooka, who appeared like a goat with sulfurous yellow eyes and great curling horns and who shat on the blackberries on the first of November. There was the kelpie that swam in the river and wanted to carry off Lyle and his sisters to drown and devour. And there were the trooping faeries that would steal them all away to their underground hills for a hundred years.

Lyle and Rafe snuck out to the woods anyway. They would stretch out on an old, bug-infested mattress and "practice" sex. Lying on his back, Lyle'd showed Rafe how to thrust his penis between Lyle's pressed-together thighs in "pretend" intercourse.

Lyle had forbidden certain conversations. No talk about the practicing, no talk about the bruises on his back and arms, and no talk about his grandfather, ever, at all. Rafe thought about that, about all the conversations he had learned not to have, all the conversations he still avoided.

As fireworks lit up the black sky, Rafe listened to his sister fight with Marco on the phone. He must have been accusing her about getting the money from a lover because he heard his name said over and over. "Rafael sent it," she shouted. "My fucking brother sent it." Finally, she screamed that if he didn't stop threatening her she was going to call the police. She said her cousin was a cop. And it was true; Teo Santiago was a cop. But Teo was also in jail.

When she got off the phone, Rafe said nothing. He didn't want her to think he'd overheard.

She came over any way. "Thanks for everything, you know? The money and all."

He touched the side of her face with the bruise. She looked at the ground but he could see that her eyes had grown wet.

"You're gonna be okay," he said. "You're gonna be happier."

"I know," she said. One of the tears tumbled from her eye and shattered across the toe of his expensive leather shoe, tiny fragments sparkling with reflected light. "I didn't want you to hear all this shit. Your life is always so together."

"Not really," he said, smiling. Mary had seen his apartment only once, when she and Marco had brought Victor up to see *The Lion King*. Rafe had sent her tickets; they were hard to get so he thought that she might want them. They hadn't stayed long in his apartment; the costumes that hung on the walls had frightened Victor.

She smiled too. "Have you ever had a boyfriend this bad?"

Her words hung in the air a moment. It was the first time any of them had ventured a guess. "Worse," he said, "and girlfriends too. I have terrible taste."

Mary sat down next to him on the bench. "Girlfriends too?"

He nodded and lifted a glass of iced tea to his mouth. "When you don't know what you're searching for," he said, "you have to look absolutely everywhere."

The summer that they were fourteen, a guy had gone down on Rafe in one of the public showers at the beach and he gloried in the fact that for the first time he had a story of almost endless interest to Lyle. It was also the summer that they almost ran away.

"I saw grandma's faeries," Lyle had said the week before they were supposed to go. He told Rafe plainly, like he'd spotted a robin outside the window.

"How do you know?" Rafe had been making a list of things they needed to bring. The pen in his hand had stopped writing in the middle of spelling "colored pencils." For a moment, all Rafe felt was resentment that his blowjob story had been trumped.

"They were just the way she said they'd be. Dancing in a circle and they glowed a little, like their skin could reflect the moonlight. One of them looked at me and her face was as beautiful as the stars."

Rafe scowled. "I want to see them too."

"Before we get on the train we'll go down to where I saw them dancing."

Rafe added "peanut butter" to his list. It was the same list he was double-checking six days later, when Lyle's grandmother called. Lyle was dead. He had slit his wrists in a tub of warm water the night before they were supposed to leave forever.

Rafe had stumbled to the viewing, cut off a lock of Lyle's blond hair right in front of his pissed-off family, stumbled to the funeral, and then slept stretched out on the freshly-filled grave. It hadn't made sense. He wouldn't accept it. He wouldn't go home.

Rafe took out his wallet and unfolded the train schedule from the billfold. He had a little time. He was always careful not to miss the last train. He looked at the small onyx and silver ring on his pinkie. It held a secret compartment inside, so well hidden that you could barely see the hinge. When Lyle had given it to him, Rafe's fingers had been so slender that it had fit on his ring finger as easily as the curl of Lyle's hair fit inside of it.

As Rafe rose to kiss his mother and warn his father that he would have to be leaving, Mary thrust open the screen door so hard it banged against the plastic trashcan behind it.

"Where's Victor? Is he inside with you? He's supposed to be in bed."

Rafe shook his head. His mother immediately put down the plate she was drying and walked through the house, still holding the dishrag, calling Victor's name. Mary showed them the empty bed.

Mary stared at Rafe as though he hid her son from her. "He's not here. He's gone."

"Maybe he snuck out to see some friends," Rafe said, but it didn't seem right. Not for a ten-year-old.

"Marco couldn't have come here without us seeing him," Rafe's father protested.

"He's *gone*," Mary repeated , as though that explained everything. She slumped down in one of the kitchen chairs and covered her face with her hands. "You don't know what he might do to that kid. *Madre de Dios*."

Rafe's mother came back in the room and punched numbers into the phone. There was no answer at Marco's apartment. The cousins came in from the back yard. They had mixed opinions on what to do. Some had kids of their own and thought that Mary didn't have the right to keep Victor away from his father. Soon everyone in the kitchen was shouting. Rafe got up and went to the window, looking out into the dark backyard. Kids made up their own games and wound up straying farther than they meant to.

"Victor!" he called, walking across the lawn. "Victor!"

But he wasn't there, and when Rafe walked out to the street, he could not find the boy along the hot asphalt length. Although it was night, the sky was bright with a full moon and clouds enough to reflect the city lights.

A car slowed as it came down the street. It sped away once it was past the house and Rafe let out the breath he didn't even realize that he had held. He had never considered his brother-in-law crazy, just bored and maybe a little resentful that he had a wife and a kid. But then, Lyle's grandfather had seemed normal too.

Rafe thought about the train schedule in his pocket and the unfinished sketches on his desk. The last train would be along soon and if he wasn't there to meet it, he would have to spend the night with his memories. There was nothing he could do here. In the city, he could call around and find her the number of a good lawyer—a lawyer that Marco couldn't afford. That was the best thing, he thought. He headed back to the house, his shoes clicking like beetles on the pavement.

His oldest cousin had come out to talk to him in the graveyard the night after Lyle's funeral. It had clearly creeped Teo to find his little cousin sleeping in the cemetery.

"He's gone." Teo had squatted down in his blue policeman uniform. He sounded a little impatient and very awkward.

"The faeries took him," Rafe had said. "They stole him away to Faeryland and left something else in his place."

"Then he's still not in this graveyard." Teo had pulled on Rafe's arm and Rafe had finally stood.

"If I hadn't touched him," Rafe had said, so softly that maybe Teo didn't hear.

It didn't matter. Even if Teo had heard, he probably would have pretended he hadn't.

This time when Rafe walked out of the house, he heard the distant fireworks and twirled his father's keys around his first finger. He hadn't taken the truck without permission in years.

The stick and clutch were hard to time and the engine grunted and groaned, but when he made it to the highway, he flicked on the radio and stayed in fifth gear the whole way to Cherry Hill. Marco's house was easy to find. The lights were on in every room and the blue flicker of the television lit up the front steps.

Rafe parked around a corner and walked up to the window of the guest bedroom. When he was thirteen, he had snuck into Lyle's house lots of times. Lyle had slept on a pull-out mattress in the living room because his sisters shared the second bedroom. The trick involved waiting until the television was off and everyone else had gone to bed. Rafe excelled at waiting.

When the house finally went silent and dark, Rafe pushed the window. It was unlocked. He slid it up as far as he could and pulled himself inside.

Victor turned over sleepily and opened his eyes. They went wide.

Rafe froze and waited for him to scream, but his nephew didn't move.

"It's your uncle," Rafe said softly. "From *The Lion King*. From New York." He sat down on the carpet. Someone had once told him that being lower was less threatening.

Victor didn't speak.

"Your mom sent me to pick you up."

The mention of his mother seemed to give him the courage to say: "Why didn't you come to the door?"

"Your dad would kick my ass," Rafe said. "I'm not crazy."

Victor half-smiled.

"I could drive you back," Rafe said. He took his cell phone out of his pocket and put it on the comforter by Victor. "You can call your mom and she'll tell you I'm okay. Not a stranger."

The boy climbed out of bed and Rafe stuffed it with pillows that formed a small boy-shape under the blankets.

"What are you doing?" the boy asked as he punched the numbers into the tiny phone.

"I'm making a pretend you that can stay here and keep on sleeping." The words echoed for a long moment before Rafe remembered that he and Victor had to get moving.

On the drive back, Rafe told Victor a story that his mother had told him and Mary when they were little, about a king who fed a louse so well on royal blood that it swelled up so large that it no longer fit in the palace. The king had the louse slaughtered and its hide tanned to make a coat for his daughter, the princess, and told all her suitors that they had to guess what kind of skin she wore before their proposal could be accepted.

Victor liked the part of the story where Rafe pretended to hop like a flea and bite his nephew. Rafe liked all fairy tales with tailors in them.

"Come inside," his mother said. "You should have told us you were going to take the car. I needed to go to the store and get some—"

She stopped, seeing Victor behind Rafael.

Rafe's father stood up from the couch as they came in. Rafe tossed the keys and his father caught them.

"Tough guy." His father grinned. "I hope you hit him."

"Are you kidding? And hurt this delicate hand?" Rafe asked, holding it up as for inspection.

He was surprised by his father's laugh.

For the first time in almost fifteen years, Rafe spent the night. Stretching out on the lumpy couch, he turned the onyx ring again and again on his finger.

Then, for the first time in more than ten years, he thumbed open the hidden compartment, ready to see Lyle's golden hair. Crumbled leaves fell onto his chest instead.

Leaves. Not hair. Hair lasted; it should be there. Victorian mourning ornaments braided with the hair of the long-dead survived decades. Rafe had seen such a brooch on the scarf of a well-known playwright. The hair was dulled by time, perhaps, but it had hardly turned to leaves.

He thought of the lump of bedclothes that had looked like Victor at first glance. A "pretend me," Victor had said. But Lyle's corpse wasn't pretend. He had seen it. He had cut off a lock of its hair.

Rafe ran his fingers through the crushed leaves on his chest.

Hope swelled inside of him, despite the senselessness of it. He didn't like to think about Faeryland lurking just over a hill or beneath a shallow river, as distant as a memory. But if he could believe that he could pass unscathed from the world of the city into the world of the suburban ghetto and back again, then couldn't he go further? Why couldn't he cross into the world of shining people with faces like stars that were the root of all his costumes?

Marco had stolen Victor; but Rafe had stolen Victor back. Until that moment, Rafe hadn't considered he could steal Lyle back from Faeryland.

Rafe kicked off the afghan.

At the entrance to the woods, Rafe stopped and lit a cigarette. His feet knew the way to the river by heart.

The mattress was filthier than he remembered, smeared with dirt and damp with dew. He sat, unthinking, and whispered Lyle's name. The forest was quiet and the thought of faeries seemed a little silly. Still, he felt close to Lyle here.

"I went to New York, just like we planned," Rafe said, his hand stroking over the blades of grass as though they were hairs on a pelt. "I got a job in a theatrical rental place, full of these antiqued candelabras and musty old velvet curtains. Now I make stage clothes. I don't ever have to come back here again."

He rested his head against the mattress, inhaled mold and leaves and earth. His face felt heavy, as though already sore with tears. "Do you remember Mary? Her husband hits her. I bet he hits my nephew too, but she wouldn't say." His eyes burned with unexpected tears. The guilt that twisted his gut was fresh and raw as it had been the day Lyle died. "I never knew why you did it. Why you had to die instead of come away with me. You never said either."

"Lyle," he sighed, and his voice trailed off. He wasn't sure what he'd been about to say. "I just wish you were here, Lyle. I wish you were here to talk to."

Rafe pressed his mouth to the mattress and closed his eyes for a moment before he rose and brushed the dirt off his slacks.

He would just ask Mary what happened with Marco. If Victor was all right. If they wanted to live with him for a while. He would tell his parents that he slept with men. There would be no more secrets, no more assumptions. There was nothing he could do for Lyle now, but there was still something he could do for his nephew. He could say all the things he'd left unsaid and hope that others would too.

As Rafe stood, lights sprung up from nothing, like matches catching in the dark.

Around him, in the woods, faeries danced in a circle. They were bright and seemed almost weightless, hair flying behind them like smoke behind a sparkler. Among them, Rafe thought he saw a kid, so absorbed in dancing that he did not hear Rafe gasp or shout. He started forward, hand outstretched. At the center of the circle, a woman in a gown of green smiled a cold and terrible smile before the whole company disappeared.

Rafe felt his heart beat hard against his chest. He was frightened as he had not been at fourteen, when magical things seemed like they could be ordinary and ordinary things were almost magical.

On the way home, Rafe thought of all the other fairy tales he knew about tailors. He thought of the faerie woman's plain green gown and about desire. When he got to the house, he pulled his sewing machine out of the closet and set it up on the kitchen table. Then he began to rummage through all the cloth and trims, beads and fringe. He found crushed panne velvet that looked like liquid gold and sewed it into a frockcoat studded with bright buttons and appliquéd with blue flames that lapped up the sleeves. It was one of the most beautiful things he had ever made. He fell asleep cradling it and woke to his mother setting a cup of espresso mixed with condensed milk in front of him. He drank the coffee in one slug.

It was easy to make a few phone calls and a few promises, change around meetings and explain to his bewildered parents that he needed to work from their kitchen for a day or two. Of course Clio would feed his cats. Of course his client understood that Rafe was working through a design problem. Of course the presentation could be rescheduled for the following Friday. Of course. Of course.

His mother patted his shoulder. "You work too hard."

He nodded, because it was easier than telling her he wasn't really working.

"But you make beautiful things. You sew like your great-grandmother. I told you how people came from miles around to get their wedding dresses made by her."

He smiled up at her and thought of all the gifts he had brought at the holidays—cashmere gloves and leather coats and bottles of perfume. He had never sewn a single thing for her. Making gifts had seemed cheap, like he was giving her a child's misshapen vase or a card colored with crayons. But the elegant, meaningless presents he had sent were cold, revealing nothing about him and even less about her. Imagining her in a silk dress the color of papayas—one he might sew himself—filled him with shame.

He slept most of the day in the shadowed dark of his parent's bed with the shades drawn and the door closed. The buzz of cartoons in the background and the smell of cooking oil made him feel like a small child again. When he woke it was dark outside. His clothes had been cleaned and were folded at the foot of the bed. He put the golden coat on over them and walked to the river.

There, he smoked cigarette after cigarette, dropping the filters into the water, listening for the hiss as the river smothered the flame and drowned the paper. Finally, the faeries came, dancing their endless dance, with the cold faerie woman sitting in the middle.

The woman saw him and walked through the circle. Her eyes were green as moss and, as she got close, he saw that her hair flowed behind her as though she were swimming through water or like ribbons whipped in a fierce wind. Where she stepped, tiny flowers bloomed.

"Your coat is beautiful. It glows like the sun," the faery said, reaching out to touch the fabric.

"I would give it to you," said Rafe. "Just let me have Lyle."

A smile twisted her mouth. "I will let you spend tonight with him. If he remembers you, he is free to go. Will that price suit?"

Rafe nodded and removed the coat.

The faery woman caught Lyle's hand as he spun past, pulling him out of the dance. He was laughing, still, as his bare feet touched the moss outside the circle and he aged. His chest grew broader, he became taller, his hair lengthened, and fine lines appeared around his mouth and eyes. He was no longer a teenager.

"Leaving us, even for a time, has a price," the faery woman said. Standing on her toes, she bent Lyle's head to her lips. His eyelids drooped and she steered him to the moldering mattress. He never even looked in Rafe's direction; he just sank down into sleep.

"Lyle," Rafe said, dropping down beside him, smoothing the tangle of hair back from his face. There were braids in it that knotted up with twigs and leaves and cords of thorny vines. A smudge of dirt highlighted one cheekbone. Leaves blew over him, but he did not stir.

"Lyle," Rafe said again. Rafe was reminded of how Lyle's body had lain in the casket at the funeral, of how Lyle's skin had been pale and bluish as skim milk and smelled faintly of chemicals, of how his fingers were threaded together across his chest so tightly that when Rafe tried to take his hand, it was stiff as a mannequin's. Even now, the memory of that other, dead Lyle seemed more real than the one that slept beside him like a cursed prince in a fairy tale.

"Please wake up," Rafe said. "Please. Wake up and tell me this is real."

Lyle did not stir. Beneath the lids, his eyes moved as if he saw another landscape.

Rafe shook him and then struck him, hard, across the face. "Get up," he shouted. He tugged on Lyle's arm and Lyle's body rolled toward him.

Standing, he tried to lift Lyle, but he was used to only the weight of bolts of cloth. He settled for dragging him toward the street where Rafe could flag down a car or call for help. He pulled with both his hands, staining Lyle's shirt and face with grass, and scratching his side on a fallen branch. Rafe dropped his hand and bent over him in the quiet dark.

"It's too far," Rafe said. "Far too far."

He stretched out beside Lyle, pillowing his friend's head against his chest and resting on his own arm.

When Rafe woke, Lyle no longer lay beside him, but the faery woman stood over the mattress. She wore the coat of fire and, in the light of the newly risen sun, she shone so brightly that Rafe had to shade his eyes with his hand. She laughed and her laugh sounded like ice cracking on a frozen lake.

"You cheated me," Rafe said. "You made him sleep."

"He heard you in his dreams," said the faery woman. "He preferred to remain dreaming."

Rafe stood and brushed off his pants, but his jaw clenched so tightly that his teeth hurt.

"Come with me," the faery said. "Join the dance. You are only jealous that you were left behind. Let that go. You can be forever young and you can make beautiful costumes forevermore. We will appreciate them as no mortal does and we will adore you."

Rafe inhaled the leaf-mold and earth smells. Where Lyle had rested, a golden hair remained. He thought of his father laughing at his jokes, his mother admiring his sewing, his sister caring enough to ask him about boy friends even in the middle of a crisis. Rafe wound the hair around his finger so tightly that it striped his skin white and red. "No," he told her.

His mother was sitting in her robe in the kitchen. She got up when Rafe came in.

"Where are you going? You are like a possessed man." She touched his hand and her skin felt so hot that he pulled back in surprise.

"You're freezing! You have been at his grave."

It was easier for Rafe to nod than explain.

"There is a story about a woman who mourned too long and the specter of her lover rose up and dragged her down into death with him."

He nodded again, thinking of the faery woman, of being dragged into the dance, of Lyle sleeping like death.

She sighed exaggeratedly and made him a coffee. Rafe had already set up the sewing machine by the time she put the mug beside him.

That day he made a coat of silver silk, pleated at the hips and embroidered with a tangle of thorny branches and lapels of downy white fur. He knew it was one of the most beautiful things he had ever made.

"Who are you sewing that for?" Mary asked when she came in. "It's gorgeous."

He rubbed his eyes and gave her a tired smile. "It's supposed to be the payment a mortal tailor used to win back a lover from Faeryland."

"I haven't heard of that story," his sister said. "Will it be a musical?"

"I don't know yet," said Rafe. "I don't think the cast can sing."

His mother frowned and called Mary over to chop up a summer squash.

"I want you and Victor to come live with me," Rafe said as his sister turned away from him.

"Your place is too small," Rafe's mother told him.

She had never seen his apartment. "We could move, then. Go to Queens. Brooklyn."

"You won't want a little boy running around. And Mary has the cousins here. She should stay with us. Besides, the city is dangerous."

"Marco is dangerous," Rafe said voice rising. "Why don't you let Mary make up her own mind?"

Rafe's mother muttered under her breath as she chopped, Rafe sighed and bit his tongue and Mary gave him a sisterly roll of the eyes. It occurred to him that that had been the most normal conversation he had had with his mother in years.

All day he worked on the coat and that night Rafe, wearing the silvery coat, went back to the woods and the river.

The dancers were there as before and when Rafe got close, the faery woman left the circle of dancers.

"Your coat is as lovely as the moon. Will you agree to the same terms?"

Rafe thought of objecting, but he also thought of the faery woman's kiss and that he might be able to change the course of events. It would be better if he caught her off-guard. He shouldered off his coat. "I agree."

As before, the faery woman pulled Lyle from the dance.

"Lyle!" Rafe said, starting toward him before the faery could touch his brow with her lips.

Lyle turned to him and his lips parted as though he were searching for a name to go with a distant memory, as if Lyle didn't recall him after all.

The faery woman kissed him then and Lyle staggered drowsily to the mattress. His drooping eyelashes nearly hid the gaze he gave Rafe. His mouth moved, but no sound escaped him and then he subsided into sleep.

That night Rafe tried a different way of rousing Lyle. He pressed his mouth to Lyle's slack lips, to his forehead as the faery woman had done. He kissed the hollow of Lyle's throat, where the beat of his heart thrummed against his skin. He ran his hands over the Lyle's chest. He touched his lips to the smooth, unscarred expanse of Lyle's wrists. Again and again, he kissed Lyle, but it was as terrible as kissing a corpse.

Before he slept, Rafe took the onyx and silver ring off his own pinkie, pulled out a strand of black hair from his own head and coiled it inside the hollow of the poison ring. Then he pushed the ring onto Lyle's pinkie.

"Remember me. Please remember me," Rafe said. "I can't remember myself unless you remember me."

But Lyle did not stir and Rafe woke alone on the mattress. He made his way home in the thin light of dawn.

That day he sewed a coat from velvet as black as the night sky. He stitched tiny black crystals onto it and embroidered it with black roses, thicker at the hem and then thinning as they climbed. At the cuffs and neck, ripped ruffles of thin smoky purples and deep reds reminded him of sunsets. Across the back, he sewed on silver beads for stars. Stars like the faery woman's eyes. It was the most beautiful thing Raphael had ever created. He knew he would never make its equal.

"Where do you get your ideas from?" his father asked as he shuffled out to the kitchen for an evening cup of decaf. "I've never been much of a creative person."

Rafe opened his mouth to say that he got his ideas from everywhere, from things he'd seen and dreamed and felt, but then he thought of the other thing his father said. "You made that bumper for the old car out of wood," Rafe said. "That was pretty creative."

Rafe's father grinned and added milk to his cup.

That night Rafe donned the shimmering coat and walked to the woods.

The faerie woman waited for him. She sucked in her breath at the sight of the magnificent coat.

"I must have it," she said. "You shall have him as before."

Rafael nodded. Tonight if he could not rouse Lyle, he would have to say goodbye. Perhaps this was the life Lyle had chosen—a life of dancing and youth and painless memory—and he was wrong to try and take him away from it. But he wanted to spend one more night beside Lyle.

She brought Lyle to him and he knelt on the mattress. The faerie woman bent to kiss his forehead, but at the last moment, Lyle turned his head and the kiss fell on his hair.

Scowling, she rose.

Lyle blinked as though awakening from a long sleep, then touched the onyx ring on his finger. He turned toward Rafe and smiled tentatively.

"Lyle?" Rafe asked. "Do you remember me?"

"Rafael?" Lyle asked. He reached a hand toward Rafe's face, fingers skimming just above the skin. Rafe leaned into the heat, butting his head against Lyle's hand and sighing. Time seemed to flow backwards and he felt like he was fourteen again and in love.

"Come, Lyle," said the faery woman sharply.

Lyle rose stiffly, his fingers ruffling Rafe's hair.

"Wait," Rafe said. "He knows who I am. You said he would be free."

"He's as free to come with me as he is to go with you," she said.

Lyle looked down at Rafe. "I dreamed that we went to New York and that we performed in a circus. I danced with the bears and you trained fleas to jump through the eyes of needles."

"I trained fleas?"

"In my dream. You were famous for it." His smile was tentative, uncertain. Maybe he realized that it didn't sound like a great career.

Rafe thought of the story he had told Victor about the princess in her louse-skin coat, about locks of hair and all the things he had managed through the eyes of needles.

The faery woman turned away from them with a scowl, walking back to the fading circle of dancers, becoming insubstantial as smoke.

"It didn't go quite like that." Rafe stood and held out his hand. "I'll tell you what really happened."

Lyle clasped Rafe's fingers tightly, desperately, but his smile was wide and his eyes were bright as stars. "Don't leave anything out."

Holly Black is the author of bestselling contemporary fantasy books for kids and teens. Some of her titles include The Spiderwick Chronicles (with Tony DiTerlizzi), The Modern Faerie Tale series, the Curse Workers series, *Doll Bones*, *The Coldest Girl in Coldtown*, the Magisterium series (with Cassandra Clare) and *The Darkest Part of the Forest*. She has been a finalist for an Eisner Award, and the recipient of the Andre Norton Award, the Mythopoeic Award, and a Newbery Honor. She currently lives in New England with her husband and son in a house with a secret door.

When first considering the content of this volume I knew I wanted to include Kiernan's brilliant and unique science fictional version of "Little Red Riding Hood." The paths of needles and pins appear in early oral tellings of the story; the meaning of them and the choice made is a matter of scholarly debate.

The Road of Needles

Caitlín R. Kiernan

1.

Nix Severn shuts her eyes and takes a very deep breath of the newly-minted air filling Isotainer Four, and she cannot help but note the irony at work. This luxury born of mishap. Certainly, no one on earth has breathed air even half this clean in more than two millennia. The Romans, the Greeks, the ancient Chinese, they all set in motion a fouling of the skies that an Industrial Revolution and the two centuries thereafter would hone into a science of indifference. An art of neglect and denial. Not even the meticulously manufactured atmo of Mars is so pure as each mouthful of the air Nix now breathes. The nitrogen, oxygen—four fingers N2, a thumb of 02—and the so on and so on traces, etcetera, all of it transforming the rise and fall of her chest into a celebration. Oh, happy day for the pulmonary epithelia bathed in this pristine blend. She shuts her eyes and tries to think. But the air has made her giddy. Not drunk, but certainly giddy. It would be easy to drift down to sleep, leaning against the bole of a *Dicksonia antarctica*, sheltered from the misting rainfall by the umbrella of the tree fern's fronds, of this tree and all the others that have sprouted and filled the isotainer in the space of less than seventeen hours. She could be a proper Rip Van Winkle, as the *Blackbird* drifts farther and farther off the lunar-Martian rail line. She could do that fabled narcoleptic one better, pop a few of the phenothiazine capsules in the left hip pouch of her red jumpsuit and never wake up again. The forest would close in around her, and she would feed it. The fungi, insects, the snails and algae, bacteria and tiny vertebrates, all of them would make a banquet of her sleep and then, soon, her death.

. . . and even all our ancient mother lost
was not enough to keep my cheeks, though washed
with dew, from darkening again with tears.
Even the thought of standing makes her tired.

No, she reminds herself—that part of her brain that isn't yet ready to surrender. *It's not the thought of getting to my feet. It's the thought of the five containers remaining between me and the bridge. The thought of the five behind me. That I've only come halfway, and there's the other halfway to go.*

Something soft, weighing hardly anything at all, lands on her cheek. Startled, she opens her eyes and brushes it away. It falls into a nearby clump of moss and gazes up with golden eyes. Its body is a harlequin motley of brilliant yellow and a blue so deep as to be almost black.

A frog.

She's seen images of frogs archived in the lattice, and in reader files, but images cannot compare to contact with one alive and breathing. It touched her cheek, and now it's watching her. If Oma were online, Nix would ask for a more specific identification.

But, of course, if Oma were online, I wouldn't be here, would I?

She wipes the rain from her eyes. The droplets are cool against her skin. On her lips, on her tongue, they're nectar. It's easy to romanticize Paradise when you've only ever known Hell and (on a good day) Purgatory. It's hard not to get sentimental; the mind, giddy from clean air, waxes. Nix blinks up at all the shades of green; she squints into the simulated sunlight shining down between the branches.

The sky flickers, dimming for a moment, then quickly returns to its full 600-watt brilliance. The back-up fuel cells are draining faster than they ought. She ticks off possible explanations: there might be a catalyst leak, dinged up cathodes or anodes, a membrane breach impairing ion-exchange. Or maybe she's just lost track of time. She checks the counter in her left retina, but maybe it's on the fritz again and can't be trusted.

She rubs at her eye, because sometimes that helps. The readout remains the same. The cells have fallen to forty-eight percent maximum capacity.

I haven't lost track of time. The train's burning through the reserves too fast. It doesn't matter why.

All that matters is that she has less time to reach Oma and try to fix this fuck-up.

Nix Severn stands, but it seems to take her almost forever to do so. She leans against the rough bark of the tree fern and tries to make out the straight line of the catwalk leading to the port 'tainers and the decks beyond. Moving over and through the uneven, ever-shifting terrain of the forest is slowing her down, and soon, she knows, soon she'll be forced to abandon it for the cramped maintenance crawls suspended far overhead. She curses herself for not having used them in the first place. But better late than fucking never. They're a straight line to the main AI shaft, and wriggling her way through the empty tubes will help her focus, removing her senses from the Edenic seduction of the terraforming engines' grand wrack-up. If she can just reach the front of this compartment, there will be an access ladder, and cramped or not, the going will surely be easier. She'll quick it double time or better. Nix wipes the rain from her face again, and clambers over the roots of a strangler fig. Once on the slippery, overgrown walkway, she lowers the jumpsuit's visor and quilted silicon hood; the faceplate will efficiently evaporate both the rain and any condensation. She does her best to ignore the forest. She thinks, instead, of making dockside, waiting out quarantine until she's cleared for tumble, earthfall, and of her lover and daughter waiting for her, back in the slums at the edge of the Phoenix shipyards. She keeps walking.

2.

Skycaps launch alone.

Nix closes the antique storybook she found in a curio stall at the Firestone Night Market, and she sets it on the table next to her daughter's bed. The pages are brown and brittle, and minute bits of the paper flake away if she does not handle it with the utmost care (and sometimes when she does). Only twice in Maia's life has she heard a fairy tale read directly from the book. On the first occasion, she was two. And on the second, she was six. It's a long time between lifts and drops, and when you're a mother who's also a runner, your child seems to grow up in jittery stills from a time-lapse. Even with her monthly broadcast allotment, that's how it seems. A moment here, fifteen minutes there, a three-week shore leave, a precious to-and-fro while sailing orbit, the faces and voices trickling through in 22.29 or 3.03 light-minute packages. "Why did she talk to the wolf?" asks Maia. "Why didn't she ignore him?"

Nix looks up to find Shiloh watching from the doorway, backlit by the glow from the hall. She smiles for the silhouette, then looks back to their daughter. The girl's hair is as fine and pale as corn silk. She's fragile, born too early and born sickly, half crippled, half blind. Maia's eyes are the milky green color of jade.

"Yeah," says Shiloh. "Why is that?"

"I imagine *this* wolf was a very charming wolf," replies Nix, brushing her fingers through the child's bangs.

Skycaps launch alone.

Sending out more than one warm body, with everything it'll need to stay alive? Why squander the budget? Not when all you need is someone on hand in case of a catastrophic, systems-wide failure.

So, skycaps launch alone.

"Well, I would never talk to a wolf. If there were still wolves," says Maia.

"Makes me feel better hearing that," says Nix. A couple of strands of Maia's hair come away in her fingers.

"If there were still wolves," Maia says again.

"Of course," Nix says. "That's a given."

Her lips move. She reads from the old, old book: "Good day, Little Red Riding Hood," said he. "Thank you kindly, wolf," answered she.

"Where are you going so early, Little Red Riding Hood?" "To my grand-mother's."

Nix Severn's eyelids flutter, and her lips move. The home-away chamber whispers and hums, manipulating hippocampal and cortical theta rhythms, mining long- and short-term memory, spinning dreams into perceptions far more real than dreams or déjà vu. No outbound leaves the docks without at least one home-away to insure the mental stability of skycaps while they ride the rails.

"You should go to sleep now," Nix tells Maia, but the girl shakes her head.

"I want to hear it again."

"Kiddo, you know it by heart. You could probably recite it word for word."

"She wants to hear you read it, fella," says Shiloh. "I wouldn't mind hearing it again myself, for that matter."

Nix pretends to frown. "Hardly fair, two on one like this." But then she gently turns the pages back to the story's start and begins it over.

The home-away mediates between limbic and the cerebral hemispheres, directing neurotransmitters and receptors, electrochemical activity and cortisol levels.

There was once a sweet little maid . . .

Shiloh kisses her brow. "Still, hell, I don't know how you do it, love. All alone and relying on make-believe."

"It keeps me grounded. You learn the trick, or you wash out fast."

The skycap's best friend! Even better than the real thing! Experience the dream and you might never have to come home.

The merch co-ops count on it.

"You could look for other work than babysitting EOTs," whispers Shiloh. "You've got the training. There's good work you could do in the yards, in assembly or rollout."

"I don't want to have this conversation again."

"But with your experience, Nixie, you could make foreman on the quick."

"And get maybe a quarter the grade, grinding day and night."

"We'd see you so much more. That's all. And it scares me more than you'll ever know, you hurtling out there alone with nothing but make-believe and plug and pray for waking company."

Make haste and start before it gets hot, and walk properly and nicely, and don't run, or you might fall.

"The accidents—"

"—the casts hype them, Shiloh. Half what you hear never happened. You know that. I've told you that, how many times now?"

"Going under and never coming up again."

"The odds of psychosis or a flatline are astronomical."

Shiloh rolls over, turning her back on Nix. Who sighs and shuts her eyes, because she has prep at six for next week's launch, and she's not going to spend the day sleepwalking because of a fight with Shiloh.

. . . and don't run, or you might fall.

The emergency alarm screams bloody goddamn murder, and an adrenaline injection jerks her back aboard the *Blackbird*, back to here and now so violently that she gasps and then screams right back at the alarms. But her eyes are trained to see, even through so sudden a disengage, and Nix is already processing the diagnostics and crisis report streaming past her face before the raggedy hitch releases her.

It's bad this time. It doesn't get much worse.

Oma isn't talking.

"*Good day, Little Red Riding Hood . . .*"

3.

Of course, it *isn't* true that there are no wolves left in the world. Not strictly speaking. Only that, so far as zoologists can tell, they are extinct in the wild. They were declared so more than forty years ago, all across the globe, all thirty-nine or so subspecies. But Maia has a terrible phobia of wolves, despite the fact "Little Red Riding Hood" is her favorite bedtime story. Perhaps it's her favorite *because* she's afraid of wolves. Anyway, Shiloh and I told her that there were no more wolves when she became convinced a wolf was living under her bed, and she refused to sleep without the light on. We suspect she knows, perfectly well, that we're lying. We suspect she's humoring us, playing along with our lie. She's smart, curious, and has access to every bit of information on the lattice, which includes, I'd think, everything about wolves that's ever been written down.

I have seen wolves. Living wolves.

There are a handful remaining in captivity. I saw a pair when I was younger, still in my twenties. My mother was still alive, and we visited the bio in Chicago. We spent almost an entire day inside the arboretum, strolling the meticulously manicured, tree-lined pathways. Here and there, we'd come upon an animal or two, even a couple of small herds—a few varieties of antelope, deer, and so forth— kept inside invisible enclosures by the shock chips implanted in their spines. Late in the afternoon, we came upon the wolves, at the end of a cul-de-sac located in a portion of the bio designed to replicate the aspen and conifer forests that once grew along the Yellowstone River out west. I recall that from a plaque placed somewhere on the trail. There was an owl, an eagle, rabbits, a stuffed bison, and at the very end of the cul-de-sac, the pair of wolves. Of course, they weren't purebloods, but hybrids. Both were watered-down with German shepherd genes, or husky genes, or whatever.

There was a bench there beneath the aspen and pine and spruce cultivars, and my mother and I sat a while watching the wolves. Though I know that the staff of the park was surely taking the best possible care of those precious specimens, both were somewhat thin. Not emaciated, but thin. "Ribsy," my mother said, which I thought was a strange word. One I'd never before heard. Maybe it had been popular when she was young.

"They look like ordinary dogs to me," she said.

They didn't, though. Despite the fact that these animals had never lived outside pens of one sort or another, there was about them an unmistakable wildness. I can't fully explain what I mean by that. But it was there. I recognized it most in their amber eyes. A certain feral desperation. They restlessly paced their enclosure; it was exhausting, just watching them. Watching them set my nerves on edge, though my mother hardly seemed to notice. After her remark, how the wolves seemed to her no different than regular dogs, she lost interest and winked on her Soft-See. She had an eyeball conversation with someone from her office, and I watched the wolves. And the wolves watched me.

I imagined there was hatred in their amber eyes.

I imagined that they stared out at me, instinctually comprehending the role that my race had played in the destruction of theirs.

We were here first, they said without speaking, without uttering a sound.

It wasn't only desperation in their eyes; it was anger, spite, and a promise of stillborn retribution that the wolves knew would never come.

Ten times a million years before you, we feasted on your foremothers.

And, in that moment, I was as frightened as any small and defenseless beast, cowering in shadows, as still as still can be in hope it would go unnoticed as amber eyes and hungry jaws prowled the woods.

I have wondered if my eyes replied, I know. I know, but have mercy.

That day, I do not believe there was any mercy in the eyes of the wolves.

You cannot even survive yourselves, said the glittering amber eyes. Ask yourself for charity.

And I have wondered if a mother can pass on dread to her child.

4.

Nix Severn reaches the ladder leading up to the crawlspace, only to find it engulfed in a tangle of thick vines that have begun to pull the lock-bolts free of the 'tainer wall. She stands in waist-high philodendrons and bracken, glaring up at the damaged ladder. Briefly, she considers attempting the climb anyway, but is fairly sure her weight would only finish what the vines have begun, and the resulting fall could leave her with injuries severe enough that she'd be rendered incapable of reaching Oma's core in time. Or at all.

She curses and wraps her right hand around a bundle of the vines, tugging at them forcefully; the ladder groans ominously, creaks, and leans out a few more centimeters from the wall. She releases the vines and turns towards the round hatchway leading to Three and the next vegetation-clogged segment of the *Blackbird*. The status report she received when she awoke inside the home-away, what little there was of it, left no room for doubt that all the terraforming engines had switched on simultaneously and that every one of the containment sys banks had failed in a rapid cascade, rolling backwards, stem to stern. She steps over a log so rotten and encrusted with mushrooms and moss that it could have laid there for years, not hours. A few steps farther and she reaches the hatch's keypad, but her hands are shaking, and it takes three tries to get the security code right; a fourth failure would have triggered lock-down. The diaphragm whirs, clicks, and the rusty steel iris spirals open in a hiss of steam. Nix mutters a thankful, silent prayer to no god she actually believes because, so far, none of the wiring permitting access to the short connecting corridors has been affected.

Nix steps through the aperture, and the hatch promptly spirals shut behind her, which means the proximity sensors are also still functional. The corridor is free of any traces of plant or animal life, and she lingers there several seconds before taking the three, four, five more steps to the next keypad and punching in the next access code. The entrance to Iso-tainer Three obeys the command, and forest swallows her again.

If anything, the situation in Three is worse than that in Four. Her red gloves have to rip away an intertwining wall of creepers and narrow branches, and then she must scale the massive roots of more strangler figs before she can make any forward progress whatsoever. But soon enough she encounters yet another barrier, in the form of a small pond, maybe five meters across, stretching from one side of the hull to the other. The water is tannin stained, murky, and half obscured beneath an emerald algal scum, so there's no telling how deep it might be. The forest floor is quite a bit higher than that of the 'tainer, so the pool could be deep enough she'd have to swim. And Nix Severn never learned to swim.

She's sweating. The readout on her visor informs her that the ambient temperature has risen to 30.55°C, and she pushes back the hood. For now, there's no rain falling in Three, so there's only her own sweat to wipe from her eyes and forehead. She kneels and brushes a hand across the pond, sending ripples rolling towards the opposite shore.

Behind her, a twig snaps, and there's a woman's voice. Nix doesn't stand, or even turn to see. Between the shock of so abruptly popping from the dream-away sleep, her subsequent exertion and fear, and the effects of whatever toxic pollen and spores might be wafting through the air, she's been expecting delirium.

"The water is wide, and I can't cross over," the voice sings sweetly. "Neither have I wings to fly."

"That isn't you, is it, Oma?"

"No, dear," the voice replies, and it's not so sweet anymore; it's taken on a gruff edge. "It isn't Oma. The night presses in all about us, and your grandmother is sleeping."

There's nothing sapient aboard but me and Oma, which means I'm hallucinating.

"Good day, Little Red Riding Hood," says the voice, and never mind her racing heart, Nix has to laugh.

"Fuck you," she says, only cursing her subconscious self, and stands, wiping wet fingers on her jumpsuit.

"Where are you going so early, Little Red Riding Hood?"

"Is that really the best I could come up with?" Nix asks, turning now, because how could she not look behind her, sooner or later. She discovers that there is someone standing there; someone or something. Which word applies could be debated. Or rather, she thinks, there is my delusion of another presence here with me. It's nothing more than that. It's nothing that can actually speak or snap a twig underfoot, excepting in my mind.

In my terror, I have made a monster.

"I know you," Nix whispers. The figure standing between her and the hatchway back to Four has Shiloh's kindly hazel-brown eyes, and even though the similarity ends there, about the whole being there is a nagging familiarity.

"Do you?" it asks. It or she. "Yes, I believe that you do. I believe that you have known me a very, very long while. Whither so early, Little Red Riding Hood?"

"I've never seen you."

"Haven't you? As a child, didn't you once catch me peering in your bedroom window? Didn't you glimpse me lurking in an alley? Didn't you visit me at the bio that day? Don't I live beneath your daughter's bed and in your dreams?"

And now Nix does reach into her left hip pouch for the antipsychotics there. She takes a single step backwards and her boot comes down in the warm, stagnant pool, sinking in up to the ankle. The splash seems very loud, louder than the atonal symphony of dragonflies buzzing in her ears. She wants to look away from the someone or something she only imagines there before her, a creature more canine than human, an abomination that might have been created in an illicit sub rosa recombinant-outcross lab back on earth. A commission for a wealthy collector, for a private menagerie of designer freaks. Were the creature real. Which it isn't.

Nix tries to open the Mylar med packet, but it slips through her fingers and vanishes in the underbrush. The thing licks its muzzle with a mottled blue-black tongue, and Shiloh's eyes sparkle from its face.

"Are you going across the stones or the thorns?" it asks.

"Excuse me?" Nix croaks, her throat parched, her mouth gone cottony. *Why did I answer it. Why am I speaking with it at all?*

It scowls.

"Don't play dumb, Nix."

It knows my name.

It only knows my name because I know my name.

"Which *path* are you taking? The one of needles or the one of pins?"

"I couldn't reach the crawls," she hears herself say, as though the words are reaching her ears from a great distance. "I tried, but the ladder was broken."

"Then you are on the Road of Needles," the creature replies, curling back its dark lips in a parody of a smile and revealing far too many sharp yellow teeth. "You surprise me, Petit Chaperon rouge. I am so rarely ever surprised."

Enough . . .

My ship is dying all around me, and that's enough, I will not fucking see this. I will not waste my time conversing with my id.

Nix Severn turns away, turning much too quickly and much too carelessly, almost falling face first into the pool. It no longer matters to her how deep the water might be or what might be lurking below the surface. She stumbles ahead, sending out sprays of the tea-colored water with every step she takes. They sparkle like gems beneath the artificial sun. The mud sucks at her feet, and soon she's in up to her chest. *But even drowning would be better, she assures herself. Even drowning would be better.*

5.

Nix has been at Shackleton Relay for almost a week, and it will be almost another week before a shuttle ferries her to the CTV *Blackbird*, waiting in dockside orbit. The cafeteria lights are too bright, like almost everything else in the station, but at least the food is decent. That's a popular myth among the techs and co-op officers who never actually spend time at Shackleton, that the food is all but inedible. Truthfully, it's better than most of what she got growing up. She listens while another EOT sitter talks, and she pokes at her bowl of udon, snow peas, and tofu with a pair of blue plastic chopsticks.

"I prefer straight-up freight runs," Marshall Choudhury says around a mouthful of noodles. "But terras, they're not as hinky as some of the caps make them out to be. You get redundant safeguards out the anus."

"Far as I'm concerned," she replies, "cargo is cargo. Jaunts are jaunts."

Marshall sets down his own bowl, lays his chopsticks on the counter beside it.

"Right," he says. "You'll get no kinda donnybrook here. None at all. Just my pref, that's it. Less hassle hauling hardware and whatnot, less coddling the payload. More free for dream-away."

Nix shrugs and chews a pea pod, swallows, and tells him, "Fella, here on my end, the chips are chips, however I may earn them. I'm just happy to have the work."

"Speaking of which . . ." Marshall says, then trails off.

"That your concern now, Choudhury, my personal life?"

"Just one fella's consideration for a comrade's, all."

"Well, as you've asked, Shiloh is still nagging me about hooking something in the yards." She sets her bowl down and stares at the broth in the bottom. "Like she didn't know when I married her, like she didn't know before Maia, that I was EOT and had no intent or interest in ever working anything other than offworld."

"Lost a wife over it," he says, as if Nix doesn't know already. "She gave me the final notice and all, right, but fuck it. Fuck it. She doesn't know the void. Couldn't know what she was asking a runner to give up. Gets wiggled into a fella's blood, don't ever get out again."

Marshall has an ugly scar across the left side of his face, courtesy of a coolant blowout a few years back and the ensuing frostbite. Nix tries to look at him, without letting her eyes linger on the scar, but that's always a challenge. A wonder he didn't lose that eye. He would have, if his goggles had cracked.

"Don't know if that's the why with me." She says. "Can't say. Obviously, I do miss them when I'm out. Sometimes, miss 'em like hell."

"But that doesn't stop you flying, doesn't turn you to the yards."

"Sometimes, fuck, I wish it would."

"She gonna walk?" he asks.

"I try not think about that, and I especially try not to think about that just before outbound. Jesus."

Marshall picks up his bowl and chopsticks, then fishes for a morsel of tofu.

"One day not too far, the cooperatives gonna replace us with autos," he sighs, and pops the white cube into his mouth. "So, gotta judge our sacrifices against the raw inevitabilities."

"Union scare talk," Nix scoffs, though she knows he's probably right. Too many ways to save expenses by completely, finally, eliminating a human crew. *A wonder it hasn't happened before now*, she thinks.

"Maybe you ought to consider cutting your losses, that's all."

"Fella, you only *just* now told me how much choice we don't have, once the life digs in and it's all we know. Make up your damn mind."

"You gonna finish that?" he asks and points at her bowl.

She shakes her head and slides it across the counter to him. Thinking about Maia and Shiloh, her appetite has evaporated.

"Anyway, point is, no need to fret on a terra run, no more than anything else."

"Never said I was fretting. It's not even my first."

"No, but that was not my point, fella," Marshall slurps at the broth left in the bottom of her white bowl, which is the same unrelenting white as the counter, their seats, the ceiling and walls, the lighting. When he's done, he wipes his mouth on a sleeve and says, "Maybe it's best EOTs stay lone. Avoid the entire mess, start to finish."

She frowns and jabs a chopstick at him. "Isn't it rough enough already without coming back from the black and lonely without anyone waiting to greet us?"

"There are other comforts," he says.

"No wonder she left you, you indifferent fuck."

Marshall massages his temples, then changes the subject. For all his faults, he's pretty good at sensing thin ice beneath his feet. "It's your first time to the Kasei though, that's true, yeah?"

"That's true, yeah."

"You can and will and no doubt already have done worse than the Kasei 'tats."

"I hear good things," she says, but her mind's elsewhere, and she's hoping Marshall grows tired of talking soon so she can get back to her quarters and pop a few pinks for six or seven hour's worth of sleep.

"Down on the north end of Cattarinetta Boulevard—in Scarlet Quad—there's a brothel. Probably the best on the whole rock. I happen to know the proprietress."

Nix isn't so much an angel she's above the consolation of whores when away from Shiloh. All those months pile up. The months between docks, the interminable Phobos reroutes, the weeks of red dust and colonist hardscrabble.

"Her name's Paddy," he continues, "and you just tell her you're a high fella to Marshall Mason Choudhury, and she'll see you're treated extra right. Not those half-starved farm girls. She'll set you up with the pinnacle merch."

"That's kind of you," and she stands. "I'll do that."

"Not a trouble," he says and waves a hand dismissively. "And look, as I said, don't you fret over the cargo. Terra's no different than aluminum and pharmaceuticals."

"It's *not* my first goddamn terra run. How many times I have to—"

But she's thinking, *Then why the extra seven-percent hazard commission, if terras are the same as all the rest?* Nix would never ask such a question aloud, anymore than she can avoid asking it of herself.

"Your Oma, she'll—"

"Fella, I'll see you later," she says, and walks quickly towards the cafeteria door before he can get another word or ten out. Sometimes, she'd lay good money that the solitudes are beginning to gnaw at the man's sanity. That sort of shit happens all too often. The glare in the corridor leading back to the housing module isn't quite as bright as the lights in the cafeteria, so at least she has that much to be grateful for.

6.

Muddy, sweat-soaked, insect-bitten and insect-stung, eyes and lungs and nostrils smarting from the hundreds of millions of gametophytes she breathed during her arduous passage through each infested isotainer, arms and legs weak, stomach rolling, breathless, Nix Severn has finally arrived at the bottom of the deep shaft leading down to Oma's dormant CPU. The bzou has kept up with her the entire, torturous way. Though she didn't realize that it was a bzou until halfway through the second 'tainer. Sentient viruses are so rare that the odds of Oma's crash having triggered the creation (or been triggered by) bzou has a probability risk approaching zero, at most a negligent threat to any transport. But here it is, and the hallucination isn't a hallucination.

An hour ago, she finally had the presence of mind to scan the thing, and it bears the distinctive signatures, the unmistakable byte sequence of a cavity-stealth strategy.

"A good quarter of an hour's walk further in the forest, under yon three large oaks. There stands her house. Further beneath are the nut trees, which you will see there," it said when the scan was done. "Red Hood! Just look! There are such pretty flowers here! Why don't you look round at them all? Methinks you don't even hear how delightfully the birds are singing! You are as dull as if you were going to school, and yet it is so cheerful in the forest!"

Oma knows Nix's psych profile, which means the bzou knows Nix's psyche.

Nix pushes back the jumpsuit's quilted hood and visor again— she'd had to lower it to help protect against a minor helium leak near the shaft's rim—and tries to concentrate and figure out precisely what has gone wrong. Oma is quiet, dark, dead. The holo is off, so she'll have to rely on her knowledge of the manual interface, the toggles and pressure pads, horizontal and vertical sliders, spinners, dials, knife switches . . . all without access to Oma's guidance. She's been trained for this, yes, but AI diagnostics and repair has never been her strong suit.

The bzou is crouched near her, Shiloh's stolen eyes tracking her every move.

"Who's there?" it asks.

"I'm not playing this game anymore," Nix mutters, and begins tripping the instruments that ought to initiate a hard reboot. "I'm done with you. Fifteen more minutes, you'll be wiped. For all I know, this was sabotage."

"Who's there, skycap?" the bzou says again.

Nix pulls down on one of the knife switches, and nothing happens.

"Push on the door," advises the bzou. "It's blocked by a pail of water."

Nix pulls the next switch, a multi-boot resort—she's being stupid, so tired and rattled that she's skipping stages—which should rouse the unresponsive Oma when almost all else fails. The core doesn't reply. Here are her worst fears beginning to play themselves out. Maybe it was a full-on panic, a crash that will require triple-caste post-mortem debugging to reverse, which means dry dock, which would mean she is utterly fucking fucked. No way in hell she can hand pilot the *Blackbird* back onto the rails, and this far off course an eject would only mean slow suffocation or hypothermia or starvation.

Nix speaks to the bzou without looking at it. She takes a tiny turnscrew from the kit strapped to her rebreather (which she hasn't needed to use, and it's been nothing but dead weight she hasn't dared abandon, just in case).

Maybe she *isn't* through playing the game, after all. She takes a deep breath, winds the driver to a 2.4 mm. mortorq bit, and keeps her eyes on the panel. She doesn't need to see the bzou to converse with it.

"All right," she says. "Let's assume you have a retract sequence, that you're a benign propagation."

"Only press the latch," it says. "I am so weak, I can't get out of bed."

"Fine. Grandmother, I've come such a very long way to visit you." Nix imagines herself reading aloud to Maia, imagines Maia's rapt attention and Shiloh in the doorway.

"Shut the door well, my little lamb. Put your basket on the table, and then take off your frock and come and lie down by me. You shall rest a little."

Shut the door. Shut the door and rest a little . . .

Partial head crash, foreign-reaction safe mode. Voluntary coma.

Nix nods and opens one of the memory trays, then pulls a yellow bus card, replacing it with a spare from the console's supply rack. Somewhere deep inside Oma's brain, there's the very faintest of hums.

"It's a code," Nix says to herself.

And if I can get the order of questions right, if I can keep the bzou from getting suspicious and rogueing up . . .

A drop of sweat drips from her brow, stinging her right eye, but she ignores it. "Now, Grandmother, now please listen."

"I'm all ears, child."

"And what big ears you have."

"All the better to hear you with."

"Right . . . of course," and Nix opens a second tray, slicing into Oma's comms, yanking two fried transmit-receive bus cards. She hasn't been able to talk to Phobos. She's been deaf all this fucking time. The CPU hums more loudly, and a hexagonal arrangement of startup OLEDs flash to life.

One down.

"Grandmother, what big eyes you have."

"All the better to see you with, Rotkäppchen."

Right. Fuck you, wolf. Fuck you and your goddamn road of stones and needles. Nix runs reset on all of Oma's optic servos and outboards. She's rewarded with the dull thud and subsequent discordant chime of a reboot.

"What big teeth I have," Nix says, and now she does turn towards the bzou, and as Oma wakes up, the virus begins to sketch out, fading in incremental bursts of distorts and static. "All the better to eat you with."

"Have I found you now, old rascal?" the virus manages between bursts of white noise. "Long have I been looking for you."

The bzou had been meant as a distress call from Oma, sent out in the last nanoseconds before the crash. "I'm sorry, Oma," Nix says, turning back to the computer. "The forest, the terra . . . I should have figured it out sooner." She leans forward and kisses the console. And when she looks back at the spot where the bzou had been crouched, there's no sign of it whatsoever, but there's Maia, holding the storybook. . . .

Caitlín R. Kiernan is a two-time recipient of both the World Fantasy and Bram Stoker awards, and the *New York Times* has declared her "one of our essential writers of dark fiction." Her recent novels include *The Red Tree* and *The Drowning Girl: A Memoir,* and, to date, her short stories have been collected in twelve volumes, including *Tales of Pain and Wonder, A is for Alien, The Ammonite Violin & Others,* and the World Fantasy Award-winning *The Ape's Wife and Other Stories.* Her thirteenth, fourteenth, and fifteenth collections—*Beneath an Oil Dark Sea: The Best of Caitlín R. Kiernan (Volume 2)* and *Cambrian Tales* for Subterranean Press and *Houses Under the Sea: Mythos Tales* for Centipede Press—were published last year. Her next novel will be *Interstate Love Song,* based on "Interstate Love Long (Murder Ballad [#]8)." She lives in Providence, Rhode Island.

Hans Christian Andersen's "The Snow Queen" has long been one of his most acclaimed tales. And, with the animated blockbuster/franchise Frozen *based very loosely on it, the story might now be considered his most popular. Kelly Link recasts Andersen's child characters—Gerda and Kay—as adults to reconsider "fairy-tale romance" and the inequitable tribulations of its traditional female protagonists. "Travels with the Snow Queen" won the James Tiptree, Jr. Award for works of science fiction or fantasy that expand or explore one's understanding of gender.*

Travels with the Snow Queen

Kelly Link

P art of you is always traveling faster, always traveling ahead. Even when you are moving, it is never fast enough to satisfy that part of you. You enter the walls of the city early in the evening when the cobblestones are a mottled pink with reflected light, and cold beneath the slap of your bare, bloody feet. You ask the man who is guarding the gate to recommend a place to stay the night, and even as you are falling into the bed at the inn, the bed, which is piled high with quilts and scented with lavender, perhaps alone, perhaps with another traveler, perhaps with the guardsman who had such brown eyes, and a mustache that curled up on either side of his nose like two waxed black laces, even as this guardsman, whose name you didn't ask calls out a name in his sleep that is not your name, you are dreaming about the road again. When you sleep, you dream about the long white distances that still lie before you. When you wake up, the guardsman is back at his post, and the place between your legs aches pleasantly, your legs sore as if you had continued walking all night in your sleep. While you were sleeping, your feet have healed again. You were careful not to kiss the guardsman on the lips, so it doesn't really count, does it.

Your destination is North. The map that you are using is a mirror. You are always pulling the bits out of your bare feet, the pieces of the map that broke off and fell on the ground as the Snow Queen flew overhead in her sleigh. Where you are, where you are coming from, it is impossible to read a map made of paper. If it were that easy then everyone would be a traveler. You have heard of other travelers whose maps are breadcrumbs, whose maps are stones, whose maps are the four winds, whose maps are yellow bricks laid one after the other. You read your map with your foot, and behind you somewhere there must be another traveler whose map is the bloody footprints that you are leaving behind you.

There is a map of fine white scars on the soles of your feet that tells you where you have been. When you are pulling the shards of the Snow Queen's looking-glass out of your feet, you remind yourself, you tell yourself to imagine how it felt when Kay's eyes, Kay's heart were pierced by shards of the same mirror. Sometimes it is safer to read maps with your feet.

Ladies. Has it ever occurred to you that fairy tales aren't easy on the feet?

So this is the story so far. You grew up, you fell in love with the boy next door, Kay, the one with blue eyes who brought you bird feathers and roses, the one who was so good at puzzles. You thought he loved you—maybe he thought he did, too. His mouth tasted so sweet, it tasted like love, and his fingers were so kind, they pricked like love on your skin, but three years and exactly two days after you moved in with him, you were having drinks out on the patio. You weren't exactly fighting, and you can't remember what he had done that had made you so angry, but you threw your glass at him. There was a noise like the sky shattering.

The cuff of his trousers got splashed. There were little fragments of glass everywhere. "Don't move," you said. You weren't wearing shoes.

He raised his hand up to his face. "I think there's something in my eye," he said.

138

His eye was fine, of course, there wasn't a thing in it, but later that night when he was undressing for bed, there were little bits of glass like grains of sugar, dusting his clothes. When you brushed your hand against his chest, something pricked your finger and left a smear of blood against his heart.

The next day it was snowing and he went out for a pack of cigarettes and never came back. You sat on the patio drinking something warm and alcoholic, with nutmeg in it, and the snow fell on your shoulders. You were wearing a short-sleeved T-shirt; you were pretending that you weren't cold, and that your lover would be back soon. You put your finger on the ground and then stuck it in your mouth. The snow looked like sugar, but it tasted like nothing at all.

The man at the corner store said that he saw your lover get into a long white sleigh. There was a beautiful woman in it, and it was pulled by thirty white geese. "Oh, her," you said, as if you weren't surprised. You went home and looked in the wardrobe for that cloak that belonged to your great-grandmother. You were thinking about going after him. You remembered that the cloak was woolen and warm, and a beautiful red—a traveler's cloak. But when you pulled it out, it smelled like wet dog and the lining was ragged, as if something had chewed on it. It smelled like bad luck: it made you sneeze, and so you put it back. You waited for a while longer.

Two months went by, and Kay didn't come back, and finally you left and locked the door of your house behind you. You were going to travel for love, without shoes, or cloak, or common sense. This is one of the things a woman can do when her lover leaves her. It's hard on the feet perhaps, but staying at home is hard on the heart, and you weren't quite ready to give him up yet. You told yourself that the woman in the sleigh must have put a spell on him, and he was probably already missing you. Besides, there are some questions you want to ask him, some true things you want to tell him. This is what you told yourself.

The snow was soft and cool on your feet, and then you found the trail of glass, the map.

After three weeks of hard traveling, you came to the city.

No, really, think about it. Think about the little mermaid, who traded in her tail for love, got two legs and two feet, and every step was like walking on knives. And where did it get her? That's a rhetorical question, of course. Then there's the girl who put on the beautiful red dancing shoes. The woodsman had to chop her feet off with an axe.

There are Cinderella's two stepsisters, who cut off their own toes, and Snow White's stepmother, who danced to death in red-hot iron slippers. The Goose Girl's maid got rolled down a hill in a barrel studded with nails. Travel is hard on the single woman. There was this one woman who walked east of the sun and then west of the moon, looking for her lover, who had left her because she spilled tallow on his nightshirt. She wore out at least one pair of perfectly good iron shoes before she found him. Take our word for it, he wasn't worth it. What do you think happened when she forgot to put the fabric softener in the dryer? Laundry is hard, travel is harder. You deserve a vacation, but of course you're a little wary. You've read the fairy tales. We've been there, we know.

That's why we here at Snow Queen Tours have put together a luxurious but affordable package for you, guaranteed to be easy on the feet and on the budget. See the world by goosedrawn sleigh, experience the archetypal forest, the winter wonderland; chat with real live talking animals (please don't feed them). Our accommodations are three-star: sleep on comfortable, guaranteed pea-free box-spring mattresses; eat meals prepared by world-class chefs. Our tour guides are friendly, knowledgeable, well-traveled, trained by the Snow Queen herself. They know first aid, how to live off the land; they speak three languages fluently.

Special discount for older sisters, stepsisters, stepmothers, wicked witches, crones, hags, princesses who have kissed frogs without realizing what they were getting into, etc.

You leave the city and you walk all day beside a stream that is as soft and silky as blue fur. You wish that your map was water, and not broken glass. At midday you stop and bathe your feet in a shallow place and the ribbons of red blood curl into the blue water.

Eventually you come to a wall of briars, so wide and high that you can't see any way around it. You reach out to touch a rose, and prick your finger. You suppose that you could walk around, but your feet tell you that the map leads directly through the briar wall, and you can't stray from the path that has been laid out for you. Remember what happened to the little girl, your great-grandmother, in her red woolen cape. Maps protect their travelers, but only if the travelers obey the dictates of their maps. This is what you have been told.

Perched in the briars above your head is a raven, black and sleek as the curlicued moustache of the guardsman. The raven looks at you and you look back at it. "I'm looking for someone," you say. "A boy named Kay."

The raven opens its big beak and says, "He doesn't love you, you know."

You shrug. You've never liked talking animals. Once your lover gave you a talking cat, but it ran away and secretly you were glad. "I have a few things I want to say to him, that's all." You have, in fact, been keeping a list of all the things you are going to say to him. "Besides, I wanted to see the world, be a tourist for a while."

"That's fine for some," the raven says. Then he relents. "If you'd like to come in, then come in. The princess just married the boy with the boots that squeaked on the marble floor."

"That's fine for some," you say. Kay's boots squeak; you wonder how he met the princess, if he is the one that she just married, how the raven knows that he doesn't love you, what this princess has that you don't have, besides a white sleigh pulled by thirty geese, an impenetrable wall of briars, and maybe a castle. She's probably just some bimbo.

"The Princess Briar Rose is a very wise princess," the raven says, "but she's the laziest girl in the world. Once she went to sleep for a hundred days and no one could wake her up, although they put one hundred peas under her mattress, one each morning."

This, of course, is the proper and respectful way of waking up princesses. Sometimes Kay used to wake you up by dribbling cold water on your feet. Sometimes he woke you up by whistling.

"On the one hundredth day," the raven says, "she woke up all by herself and told her council of twelve fairy godmothers that she supposed it was time she got married. So they stuck up posters, and princes and youngest sons came from all over the kingdom."

When the cat ran away, Kay put up flyers around the neighborhood. You wonder if you should have put up flyers for Kay. "Briar Rose wanted a clever husband, but it tired her dreadfully to sit and listen to the young men give speeches and talk about how rich and sexy and smart they were. She fell asleep and stayed asleep until the young man with the squeaky boots came in. It was his boots that woke her up.

"It was love at first sight. Instead of trying to impress her with everything he knew and everything he had seen, he declared that he had come all this way to hear Briar Rose talk about her dreams. He'd been studying in Vienna with a famous Doctor, and was deeply interested in dreams."

Kay used to tell you his dreams every morning. They were long and complicated and if he thought you weren't listening to him, he'd sulk. You never remember your dreams. "Other peoples' dreams are never very interesting," you tell the raven.

The raven cocks its head. It flies down and lands on the grass at your feet. "Wanna bet?" it says. Behind the raven you notice a little green door recessed in the briar wall. You could have sworn that it wasn't there a minute ago.

The raven leads you through the green door, and across a long green lawn towards a two-story castle that is the same pink as the briar roses. You think this is kind of tacky, but exactly what you would expect from someone named after a flower. "I had this dream once," the raven says, "that my teeth were falling out. They just crumbled into pieces in my mouth. And then I woke up, and realized that ravens don't have teeth."

You follow the raven inside the palace, and up a long, twisty staircase. The stairs are stone, worn and smoothed away, like old thick silk. Slivers of glass glister on the pink stone, catching the light of the candles on the wall. As you go up, you see that you are part of a great gray rushing crowd. Fantastic creatures, flat and thin as smoke, race up the stairs, men and women and snaky things with bright eyes. They nod to you as they slip past. "Who are they?" you ask the raven.

"Dreams," the raven says, hopping awkwardly from step to step. "The Princess's dreams, come to pay their respects to her new husband. Of course they're too fine to speak to the likes of us."

But you think that some of them look familiar. They have a familiar smell, like a pillow that your lover's head has rested upon.

At the top of the staircase is a wooden door with a silver keyhole. The dreams pour steadily through the keyhole, and under the bottom of the door, and when you open it, the sweet stink and cloud of dreams are so thick in the Princess's bedroom that you can barely breathe. Some people might mistake the scent of the Princess's dreams for the scent of sex; then again, some people mistake sex for love.

You see a bed big enough for a giant, with four tall oak trees for bedposts. You climb up the ladder that rests against the side of the bed to see the Princess's sleeping husband. As you lean over, a goose feather flies up and tickles your nose. You brush it away, and dislodge several seedy-looking dreams. Briar Rose rolls over and laughs in her sleep, but the man beside her wakes up. "Who is it?" he says. "What do you want?"

He isn't Kay. He doesn't look a thing like Kay. "You're not Kay," you tell the man in the Princess's bed.

"Who the fuck is Kay?" he says, so you explain it all to him, feeling horribly embarrassed. The raven is looking pleased with itself, the way your talking cat used to look, before it ran away. You glare at the raven. You glare at the man who is not Kay.

After you've finished, you say that something is wrong, because your map clearly indicates that Kay has been here, in this bed. Your feet are leaving bloody marks on the sheets, and you pick a sliver of glass off the foot of the bed, so everyone can see that you're not lying. Princess Briar Rose sits up in bed, her long pinkish-brown hair tumbled down over her shoulders. "He's not in love with you," she says, yawning.

"So he was here, in this bed, you're the icy slut in the sleigh at the corner store, you're not even bothering to deny it," you say.

She shrugs her pink-white shoulders. "Four, five months ago, he came through, I woke up," she says. "He was a nice guy, okay in bed. She was a real bitch, though."

"Who was?" you ask.

Briar Rose finally notices that her new husband is glaring at her. "What can I say?" she says, and shrugs. "I have a thing for guys in squeaky boots."

"Who was a bitch?" you ask again.

"The Snow Queen," she says, "the slut in the sleigh."

This is the list you carry in your pocket, of the things you plan to say to Kay, when you find him, if you find him:

1. I'm sorry that I forgot to water your ferns while you were away that time.
2. When you said that I reminded you of your mother, was that a good thing?
3. I never really liked your friends all that much.
4. None of my friends ever really liked you.
5. Do you remember when the cat ran away, and I cried and cried and made you put up posters, and she never came back? I wasn't

crying because she didn't come back. I was crying because I'd taken her to the woods, and I was scared she'd come back and tell you what I'd done, but I guess a wolf got her, or something. She never liked me anyway.

6. I never liked your mother.
7. After you left, I didn't water your plants on purpose. They're all dead.
8. Goodbye.
9. Were you ever really in love with me?
10. Was I good in bed, or just average?
11. What exactly did you mean, when you said that it was fine that I had put on a little weight, that you thought I was even more beautiful, that I should go ahead and eat as much as I wanted, but when I weighed myself on the bathroom scale, I was exactly the same weight as before, I hadn't gained a single pound?
12. So all those times, I'm being honest here, every single time, and anyway I don't care if you don't believe me, I faked every orgasm you ever thought I had. Women can do that, you know. You never made me come, not even once.
13. So maybe I'm an idiot, but I used to be in love with you.
14. I slept with some guy, I didn't mean to, it just kind of happened. Is that how it was with you? Not that I'm making any apologies, or that I'd accept yours, I just want to know.
15. My feet hurt, and it's all your fault.
16. I mean it this time, goodbye.

The Princess Briar Rose isn't a bimbo after all, even if she does have a silly name and a pink castle. You admire her dedication to the art and practice of sleep. By now you are growing sick and tired of traveling, and would like nothing better than to curl up in a big featherbed for one hundred days, or maybe even one hundred years, but she offers to loan you her carriage, and when you explain that you have to walk, she sends you off with a troop of armed guards. They will escort you through the forest, which is full of thieves and wolves and princes on quests, lurking about. The guards politely pretend that they don't notice the trail of blood that you are leaving behind. They probably think it's some sort of female thing.

It is after sunset, and you aren't even half a mile into the forest, which is dark and scary and full of noises, when bandits ambush your escort, and slaughter them all. The bandit queen, who is grizzled and gray, with a nose like an old pickle, yells delightedly at the sight of you. "You're a nice plump one for my supper!" she says, and draws her long knife out of the stomach of one of the dead guards. She is just about to slit your throat, as you stand there, politely pretending not to notice the blood that is pooling around the bodies of the dead guards, that is now obliterating the bloody tracks of your feet, the knife that is at your throat, when a girl about your own age jumps onto the robber queen's back, pulling at the robber queen's braided hair as if it were reins.

There is a certain family resemblance between the robber queen and the girl who right now has her knees locked around the robber queen's throat. "I don't want you to kill her," the girl says, and you realize that she means you, that you were about to die a minute ago, that travel is much more dangerous than you had ever imagined. You add an item of complaint to the list of things that you plan to tell Kay, if you find him.

The girl has half-throttled the robber queen, who has fallen to her knees, gasping for breath. "She can be my sister," the girl says insistently. "You promised I could have a sister and I want her. Besides, her feet are bleeding."

The robber queen drops her knife, and the girl drops back onto the ground, kissing her mother's hairy gray cheek. "Very well, very well," the robber queen grumbles, and the girl grabs your hand, pulling you farther and faster into the woods, until you are running and stumbling, her hand hot around yours.

You have lost all sense of direction; your feet are no longer set upon your map. You should be afraid, but instead you are strangely exhilarated. Your feet don't hurt anymore, and although you don't know where you are going, for the very first time you are moving fast enough, you are almost flying, your feet are skimming over the night-black forest floor as if it were the smooth, flat surface of a lake, and your feet were two white birds. "Where are we going?" you ask the robber girl.

"We're here," she says, and stops so suddenly that you almost fall over. You are in a clearing, and the full moon is hanging overhead. You can see the robber girl better now, under the light of the moon. She looks like one of the bad girls who loiter under the street lamp by the corner shop, the ones who used to whistle at Kay. She wears black leatherette boots laced up to her thighs, and a black, ribbed T-shirt and grape-colored plastic shorts with matching suspenders. Her nails are painted black, and bitten down to the quick. She leads you to a tumbledown stone keep, which is as black inside as her fingernail polish, and smells strongly of dirty straw and animals.

"Are you a princess?" she asks you. "What are you doing in my mother's forest? Don't be afraid. I won't let my mother eat you."

You explain to her that you are not a princess, what you are doing, about the map, who you are looking for, what he did to you, or maybe it was what he didn't do. When you finish, the robber girl puts her arms around you and squeezes you roughly. "You poor thing! But what a silly way to travel!" she says. She shakes her head and makes you sit down on the stone floor of the keep and show her your feet. You explain that they always heal, that really your feet are quite tough, but she takes off her leatherette boots and gives them to you.

The floor of the keep is dotted with indistinct, motionless forms. One snarls in its sleep, and you realize that they are dogs. The robber girl is sitting between four slender columns, and when the dog snarls, the thing shifts restlessly, lowering its branchy head. It is a hobbled reindeer. "Well go on, see if they fit," the robber girl says, pulling out her knife. She drags it along the stone floor to make sparks. "What are you going to do when you find him?"

"Sometimes I'd like to cut off his head," you say. The robber girl grins, and thumps the hilt of her knife against the reindeer's chest.

The robber girl's feet are just a little bigger, but the boots are still warm from her feet. You explain that you can't wear the boots, or else you won't know where you are going. "Nonsense!" the robber girl says rudely.

You ask if she knows a better way to find Kay, and she says that if you are still determined to go looking for him, even though he obviously doesn't love you, and he isn't worth a bit of trouble, then the thing to do is to find the Snow Queen. "This is Bae. Bae, you mangy old, useless old thing," she says. "Do you know where the Snow Queen lives?"

The reindeer replies in a low, hopeless voice that he doesn't know, but he is sure that his old mother does. The robber girl slaps his flank. "Then you'll take her to your mother," she says. "And mind that you don't dawdle on the way."

She turns to you and gives you a smacking wet kiss on the lips and says, "Keep the shoes, they look much nicer on you than they did on me.

And don't let me hear that you've been walking on glass again." She gives the reindeer a speculative look. "You know, Bae, I almost think I'm going to miss you."

You step into the cradle of her hands, and she swings you over the reindeer's bony back. Then she saws through the hobble with her knife, and yells "Ho!" waking up the dogs.

You knot your fingers into Bae's mane, and bounce up as he stumbles into a fast trot. The dogs follow for a distance, snapping at his hooves, but soon you have outdistanced them, moving so fast that the wind peels your lips back in an involuntary grimace. You almost miss the feel of glass beneath your feet. By morning, you are out of the forest again, and Bae's hooves are churning up white clouds of snow.

Sometimes you think there must be an easier way to do this. Sometimes it seems to be getting easier all on its own. Now you have boots and a reindeer, but you still aren't happy. Sometimes you wish that you'd stayed at home. You're sick and tired of traveling towards the happily ever after, whenever the fuck that is—you'd like the happily right now. Thank you very much.

When you breathe out, you can see the fine mist of your breath and the breath of the reindeer floating before you, until the wind tears it away. Bae runs on.

The snow flies up, and the air seems to grow thicker and thicker. As Bae runs, you feel that the white air is being rent by your passage, like heavy cloth. When you turn around and look behind you, you can see the path shaped to your joined form, woman and reindeer, like a hall stretching back to infinity. You see that there is more than one sort of map, that some forms of travel are indeed easier. "Give me a kiss," Bae says. The wind whips his words back to you. You can almost see the shape of them hanging in the heavy air.

"I'm not really a reindeer," he says. "I'm an enchanted prince."

You politely decline, pointing out that you haven't known him that long, and besides, for traveling purposes, a reindeer is better than a prince.

"He doesn't love you," Bae says. "And you could stand to lose a few pounds. My back is killing me."

You are sick and tired of talking animals, as well as travel. They never say anything that you didn't already know. You think of the talking cat that Kay gave you, the one that would always come to you, secretly, and looking very pleased with itself, to inform you when Kay's fingers smelled of some other woman. You couldn't stand to see him pet it, his fingers stroking its white fur, the cat lying on its side and purring wildly, "There, darling, that's perfect, don't stop," his fingers on its belly, its tail wreathing and lashing, its pointy little tongue sticking out at you. "Shut up," you say to Bae.

He subsides into an offended silence. His long brown fur is rimed with frost, and you can feel the tears that the wind pulls from your eyes turning to ice on your cheeks. The only part of you that is warm are your feet, snug in the robber girl's boots. "It's just a little farther," Bae says, when you have been traveling for what feels like hours. "And then we're home."

You cross another corridor in the white air, and he swerves to follow it, crying out gladly, "We are near the old woman of Lapmark's house, my mother's house."

"How do you know?" you ask.

"I recognize the shape that she leaves behind her," Bae says. "Look!"

You look and see that the corridor of air you are following is formed like a short, stout, petticoated woman. It swings out at the waist like a bell.

"How long does it last?"

"As long as the air is heavy and dense," he says, "we burrow tunnels through the air like worms, but then the wind will come along and erase where we have been."

The woman-tunnel ends at a low red door. Bae lowers his head and knocks his antlers against it, scraping off the paint. The old woman of Lapmark opens the door, and you clamber stiffly off Bae's back. There is much rejoicing as mother recognizes son, although he is much changed from how he had been.

The old woman of Lapmark is stooped and fat as a grub. She fixes you a cup of tea, while Bae explains that you are looking for the Snow Queen's palace.

"You've not far to go now," his mother tells you. "Only a few hundred miles and past the house of the woman of Finmany. She'll tell you how to go—let me write a letter explaining everything to her. And don't forget to mention to her that I'll be coming for tea tomorrow; she'll change you back then, Bae, if you ask her nicely."

The woman of Lapmark has no paper, so she writes the letter on a piece of dried cod, flat as a dinner plate. Then you are off again. Sometimes you sleep as Bae runs on, and sometimes you aren't sure if you are asleep or waking. Great balls of greenish light roll cracking across the sky above you. At times it seems as if Bae is flying alongside the lights, chatting to them like old friends. At last you come to the house of the woman of Finmany, and you knock on her chimney, because she has no door.

Why, you may wonder, are there so many old women living out here? Is this a retirement community? One might not be remarkable, two is certainly more than enough, but as you look around, you can see little heaps of snow, lines of smoke rising from them. You have to be careful where you put your foot, or you might come through someone's roof. Maybe they came here for the quiet, or because they like ice fishing, or maybe they just like snow.

It is steamy and damp in the house, and you have to climb down the chimney, past the roaring fire, to get inside. Bae leaps down the chimney, hooves first, scattering coals everywhere. The Finmany woman is smaller and rounder than the woman of Lapmark. She looks to you like a lump of pudding with black currant eyes. She wears only a greasy old slip, and an apron that has written on it, "If you can't stand the heat, stay out of my kitchen."

She recognizes Bae even faster than his mother had, because, as it turns out, she was the one who turned him into a reindeer for teasing her about her weight. Bae apologizes, insincerely, you think, but the Finmany woman says she will see what she can do about turning him back again. She isn't entirely hopeful. It seems that a kiss is the preferred method of transformation. You don't offer to kiss him, because you know what that kind of thing leads to.

The Finmany woman reads the piece of dried cod by the light of her cooking fire, and then she throws the fish into her cooking pot. Bae tells her about Kay and the Snow Queen, and about your feet, because your lips have frozen together on the last leg of the journey, and you can't speak a word.

"You're so clever and strong," the reindeer says to the Finmany woman. You can almost hear him add *and fat* under his breath. "You can tie up all the winds in the world with a bit of thread. I've seen you hurling the lightning bolts down from the hills as if they were feathers. Can't you give her the strength of ten men, so that she can fight the Snow Queen and win Kay back?"

"The strength of ten men?" the Finmany woman says. "A lot of good that would do! And besides, he doesn't love her."

Bae smirks at you, as if to say, I told you so. If your lips weren't frozen, you'd tell him that she isn't saying anything that you don't already know. "Now!" the Finmany woman says, "take her up on your back one last time, and put her down again by the bush with the red berries. That marks the edge of the Snow Queen's garden; don't stay there gossiping, but come straight back. You were a handsome boy—I'll make you twice as good-looking as you were before. We'll put up flyers, see if we can get someone to come and kiss you."

"As for you, missy," she says. "Tell the Snow Queen now that we have Bae back, that we'll be over at the Palace next Tuesday for bridge. Just as soon as he has hands to hold the cards."

She puts you on Bae's back again, giving you such a warm kiss that your lips unfreeze, and you can speak again. "The woman of Lapmark is coming for tea tomorrow," you tell her. The Finmany woman lifts Bae, and you upon his back, in her strong, fat arms, giving you a gentle push up the chimney.

Good morning, ladies, it's nice to have you on the premiere Snow Queen Tour. I hope that you all had a good night's sleep, because today we're going to be traveling quite some distance. I hope that everyone brought a comfortable pair of walking shoes. Let's have a head count, make sure that everyone on the list is here, and then we'll have introductions. My name is Gerda, and I'm looking forward to getting to know all of you.

Here you are at last, standing before the Snow Queen's palace, the palace of the woman who enchanted your lover and then stole him away in her long white sleigh. You aren't quite sure what you are going to say to her, or to him. When you check your pocket, you discover that your list has disappeared. You have most of it memorized, but you think maybe you will wait and see, before you say anything. Part of you would like to turn around and leave before the Snow Queen finds you, before Kay sees you. You are afraid that you will burst out crying or even worse, that he will know that you walked barefoot on broken glass across half the continent, just to find out why he left you.

The front door is open, so you don't bother knocking, you just walk right in. It isn't that large a palace, really. It is about the size of your own house and even reminds you of your own house, except that the furniture, Danish modern, is carved out of blue-green ice—as are the walls and everything else. It's a slippery place and you're glad that you are wearing the robber girl's boots. You have to admit that the Snow Queen is a meticulous housekeeper, much tidier than you ever were. You can't find the Snow Queen and you can't find Kay, but in every room there are white geese who, you are in equal parts relieved and surprised to discover, don't utter a single word.

"Gerda!" Kay is sitting at a table, fitting the pieces of a puzzle together. When he stands up, he knocks several pieces of the puzzle off the table, and they fall to the floor and shatter into even smaller fragments. You both kneel down, picking them up. The table is blue, the puzzle pieces are blue, Kay is blue, which is why you didn't see him when you first came into the room. The geese brush up against you, soft and white as cats.

"What took you so long?" Kay says. "Where in the world did you get those ridiculous boots?" You stare at him in disbelief.

"I walked barefoot on broken glass across half a continent to get here," you say. But at least you don't burst into tears. "A robber girl gave them to me."

Kay snorts. His blue nostrils flare. "Sweetie, they're hideous."

"Why are you blue?" you ask.

"I'm under an enchantment," he says. "The Snow Queen kissed me. Besides, I thought blue was your favorite color."

Your favorite color has always been yellow. You wonder if the Snow Queen kissed him all over, if he is blue all over. All the visible portions of his body are blue. "If you kiss me," he says, "you break the spell and I can come home with you. If you break the spell, I'll be in love with you again."

You refrain from asking if he was in love with you when he kissed the Snow Queen. Pardon me, you think, when *she* kissed him. "What is that puzzle you're working on?" you ask.

"Oh, that," he says. "That's the other way to break the spell. If I can put it together, but the other way is easier. Not to mention more fun. Don't you want to kiss me?"

You look at his blue lips, at his blue face. You try to remember if you liked his kisses. "Do you remember the white cat?" you say. "It didn't exactly run away. I took it to the woods and left it there."

"We can get another one," he says.

"I took it to the woods because it was telling me things."

"We don't have to get a talking cat," Kay says. "Besides, why did you walk barefoot across half a continent of broken glass if you aren't going to kiss me and break the spell?" His blue face is sulky.

"Maybe I just wanted to see the world," you tell him. "Meet interesting people."

The geese are brushing up against your ankles. You stroke their white feathers and the geese snap, but gently, at your fingers. "You had better hurry up and decide if you want to kiss me or not," Kay says. "Because she's home."

When you turn around, there she is, smiling at you like you are exactly the person that she was hoping to see.

"Oh come on," Kay says. "Give me a break, lady. Sure it was nice, but you don't want me hanging around this icebox forever, any more than I want to be here. Let Gerda kiss me, we'll go home and live happily ever after. There's supposed to be a happy ending."

"I like your boots," the Snow Queen says.

"You're beautiful," you tell her.

"I don't believe this," Kay says. He thumps his blue fist on the blue table, sending blue puzzle pieces flying through the air. Pieces lie like nuggets of sky-colored glass on the white backs of the geese. A piece of the table has splintered off, and you wonder if he is going to have to put the table back together as well.

"Do you love him?"

You look at the Snow Queen when she says this and then you look at Kay. "Sorry," you tell him. You hold out your hand in case he's willing to shake it.

"Sorry!" he says. "You're sorry! What good does that do me?"

152

"So what happens now?" you ask the Snow Queen.

"Up to you," she says. "Maybe you're sick of traveling. Are you?"

"I don't know," you say. "I think I'm finally beginning to get the hang of it."

"In that case," says the Snow Queen, "I may have a business proposal for you."

"Hey!" Kay says. "What about me? Isn't someone going to kiss me?"

You help him collect a few puzzle pieces. "Will you at least do this much for me?" he asks. "For old time's sake. Will you spread the word, tell a few single princesses that I'm stuck up here? I'd like to get out of here sometime in the next century. Thanks. I'd really appreciate it. You know, we had a really nice time, I think I remember that."

The robber girl's boots cover the scars on your feet. When you look at these scars, you can see the outline of the journey you made. Sometimes mirrors are maps, and sometimes maps are mirrors. Sometimes scars tell a story, and maybe someday you will tell this story to a lover. The soles of your feet are stories—hidden in the black boots, they shine like mirrors. If you were to take your boots off, you would see reflected in one foot-mirror the Princess Briar Rose as she sets off on her honeymoon, in her enormous four-poster bed, which now has wheels and is pulled by twenty white horses.

It's nice to see women exploring alternative means of travel.

In the other foot-mirror, almost close enough to touch, you could see the robber girl whose boots you are wearing. She is setting off to find Bae, to give him a kiss and bring him home again. You wouldn't presume to give her any advice, but you do hope that she has found another pair of good sturdy boots.

Someday, someone will probably make their way to the Snow Queen's palace, and kiss Kay's cold blue lips. She might even manage a happily ever after for a while.

You are standing in your black laced boots, and the Snow Queen's white geese mutter and stream and sidle up against you. You are beginning to understand some of what they are saying. They grumble about the weight of the sleigh, the weather, your hesitant jerks at their reins. But they are good-natured grumbles. You tell the geese that your feet are maps *and* your feet are mirrors. But you tell them that you have to keep in mind that they are also useful for walking around on. They are perfectly good feet.

Kelly Link is the author of the collections *Stranger Things Happen, Magic for Beginners, Pretty Monsters,* and *Get in Trouble.* Her short stories have been published in *The Magazine of Fantasy & Science Fiction, The Best American Short Stories,* and *Prize Stories: The O. Henry Awards.* She has received a Hugo Award and two Nebula, two World Fantasy, and two Locus Awards as well as a grant from the National Endowment for the Arts. She and Gavin J. Grant have co-edited a number of anthologies, including multiple volumes of *The Year's Best Fantasy and Horror* and, for young adults, *Steampunk!* and *Monstrous Affections.* She is the co-founder of Small Beer Press and co-edits the occasional zine *Lady Churchill's Rosebud Wristlet.* She lives with her husband and daughter in Northampton, Massachusetts.

Karen Joy Fowler admired the sort of heroism she read of in Hans Christian Andersen's "The Wild Swans": "Instead of swordplay and dragon-slaying, it celebrated silent, unselfish endurance." The Andersen tale also literalized the concept of the "divided self." Fowler's lovely re-telling/extension of the story plays beautifully on both these themes.

Half Way People
Karen Joy Fowler

Thunder, wind, and waves. You in your cradle. You've never heard these noises before and they are making you cry.

Here, child. Let me wrap you in a blanket and my arms, take you to the big chair by the fire, and tell you a story. My father's too old and deaf to hear and you too young to understand. If you were older or he younger, I couldn't tell it, this story so dangerous that tomorrow, I must forget it entirely and make up another.

But a story never told is also a danger, particularly to the people in it. So here, tonight, while I remember.

It starts with a girl named Maura, which is my name, too.

In the winter, Maura lives by the sea. In the summer, she doesn't. In the summer, she and her father rent two shabby rooms inland and she walks every morning to the coast, where she spends the day washing and changing bedding, sweeping the sand off the floors, scouring and dusting. She does this for many summer visitors, including the ones who live in her house. Her father works at a big hotel on the point. He wears a blue uniform, opens the heavy front door for guests and closes it behind them. At night, Maura and her father walk on tired feet back to their rooms. Sometimes it's hard for Maura to remember that this was ever different.

But when she was little, she lived by the sea in all seasons. It was a lonely coast then, a place of rocky cliffs, forests, wild winds, and beaches of coarse sand. Maura could play from morning to night and never see another person, only gulls and dolphins and seals. Her father was a fisherman.

Then a doctor who lived in the capital began to recommend the sea air to his wealthy patients. A businessman built the hotel and shipped in finer sand. Pleasure boats with colored sails filled the fishing berths. The coast became fashionable, though nothing could be done about the winds.

One day the landlord came to tell Maura's father that he'd rented out their home to a wealthy friend. It was just for two weeks and for so much money, he could only say yes. The landlord said it would happen this once, and they could move right back when the two weeks were over.

But the next year he took it for the entire summer and then for every summer after that. The winter rent was also raised.

Maura's mother was still alive then. Maura's mother loved their house by the ocean. The inland summers made her pale and thin. She sat for hours at the window watching the sky for the southward migrations, the turn of the season. Sometimes she cried and couldn't say why.

Even when winter came, she was unhappy. She felt the lingering presence of the summer guests, their sorrows and troubles as chilled spaces she passed through in the halls and doorways. When she sat in her chair, the back of her neck was always cold; her fingers fretted and she couldn't stay still.

But Maura liked the bits of clues the summer people left behind—a strange spoon in a drawer, a half-eaten jar of jam on a shelf, the ashes of papers in the fireplace. She made up stories from them of different lives in different places. Lives worthy of stories.

The summer people brought gossip from the court and tales from even farther away. A woman had grown a pumpkin as big as a carriage in her garden, hollowed it out, and slept there, which for some reason couldn't be allowed so now there was a law against sleeping in pumpkins. A new country had been found where the people had hair all over their bodies and ran about on their hands and feet like dogs, but were very musical. A child had been born in the east who could look at anyone and know how they would die, which frightened his neighbors so much, they'd killed him, as he'd always known they would. A new island had risen in the south, made of something too solid to be water and too liquid to be earth. The king had a son.

The summer Maura turned nine years old, her mother was all bone and eyes and bloody coughing. One night, her mother came to her bed and kissed her. "Keep warm," she whispered, in a voice so soft Maura was never certain she hadn't dreamed it. Then Maura's mother walked from the boarding house in her nightgown and was never seen again. Now it was Maura's father who grew thin and pale.

One year later, he returned from the beach in great excitement. He'd heard her mother's voice in the surf. She'd said she was happy now, repeated it in every wave. He began to tell Maura bedtime stories in which her mother lived in underwater palaces and ate off golden clam-shells. Sometimes in these stories her mother was a fish. Sometimes a seal. Sometimes a woman. He watched Maura closely for signs of her mother's afflictions. But Maura was her father's daughter, able to travel in her mind and stay put in her body.

Years passed. One summer day, a group of young men arrived while Maura was still cleaning the seaside house. They stepped into the kitchen, threw their bags onto the floor, and raced each other down to the water. Maura didn't know that one had stayed behind until he spoke. "Which is your room?" he asked her. He had hair the color of sand.

She took him to her bedroom with its whitewashed walls, feather-filled pillows, window of buckled glass. He put his arms around her, breath in her ear. "I'll be in your bed tonight," he said. And then he released her and she left, her blood passing though her veins so quickly, she was never sure which she had wanted more, to be held or let go.

More years. The capital became a place where books and heretics were burned. The king died and his son became king, but he was a young king and it was really the archbishop who ruled. The pleasure-loving summer people said little about this or anything else. Even on the coast, they feared the archbishop's spies.

A man Maura might have married wed a summer girl instead. Maura's father grew old and hard of hearing, though if you looked him straight in the face when you spoke, he understood you well enough. If Maura minded seeing her former suitor walking along the cliffs with his wife and children, if her father minded no longer being able to hear her mother's voice in the waves, they never said so to each other.

The hotel had let her father go at the end of the last summer. They were very sorry, they told Maura, since he'd worked there so long. But guests had been complaining that they had to shout to make him hear, and he seemed with age to have sunk into a general confusion. Addled, they said.

Without his earnings, Maura and her father wouldn't make the winter rent. They had this one more winter and then would never live by the sea again. It was another thing they didn't say to each other. Possibly her father didn't know.

One morning, Maura realized that she was older than her mother had been on the night she'd disappeared. She realized that it had been many years since anyone had wondered aloud in her presence why such a pretty young girl wasn't married.

To shake off the sadness of these thoughts, she went for a walk along the cliffs. The wind was bitter and whipped the ends of her hair against her cheeks so hard they stung. She was about to go back, when she saw a man wrapped in a great black cape. He stood without moving, staring down at the water and the rocks. He was so close to the cliff edge, Maura was afraid he meant to jump.

There now, child. This is the wrong time to go to sleep. Maura is about to fall in love.

Maura walked toward the man, carefully so as not to startle him. She reached out to touch him, then took hold of his arm through the thick cape. He didn't respond. When she turned him from the cliff, his eyes were empty, his face like glass. He was younger than she'd thought. He was many years younger than she.

"Come away from the edge," she told him and still he gave no sign of hearing, but allowed himself to be led, step by slow step, back to the house.

"Where did he come from?" her father asked. "How long will he stay? What is his name?" and then turned to address those same questions to the man himself. There was no answer.

Maura took the man's cape from him. One of his arms was an arm. The other was a wing of white feathers.

Someday, little one, you'll come to me with a wounded bird. It can't fly, you'll say, because it's too little or someone threw a stone or a cat mauled it. We'll bring it inside and put it in a warm corner, make a nest of old towels. We'll feed it with our hands and protect it, if we can, if it lives, until it's strong enough to leave us. As we do this, you'll be thinking of the bird, but I'll be thinking of how Maura once did all those things for a wounded man with a single wing.

Her father went to his room. Soon Maura heard him snoring. She made the young man tea and a bed by the fire. That first night, he couldn't stop shaking. He shook so hard Maura could hear his upper teeth banging against his lower. He shivered and sweated until she lay down beside him, put her arms about him, and calmed him with stories, some of them true, about her mother, her life, the people who'd stayed in this house and drowsed through summer mornings in this room.

She felt the tension leave his body. As he slept, he turned onto his side, curled against her. His wing spread across her shoulder, her breasts. She listened all night, sometimes awake and sometimes in dreams, to his breathing. No woman in the world could sleep a night under that wing and not wake up in love.

He recovered slowly from his fevers and sweats. When he was strong enough, he found ways to make himself useful, though he seemed to know nothing about those tasks that keep a house running. One of the panes in the kitchen window had slipped its channel. If the wind blew east off the ocean, the kitchen smelled of salt and sang like a bell. Maura's father couldn't hear it, so he hadn't fixed it. Maura showed the young man how to true it up, his one hand soft between her two.

Soon her father had forgotten how recently he'd arrived and began to call him *my son* and *your brother*. His name, he told Maura, was Sewell. "I wanted to call him Dillon," her father said. "But your mother insisted on Sewell."

Sewell remembered nothing of his life before, believing himself to be, as he'd been told, the old man's son. He had such beautiful manners. He made Maura feel cared for, attended to in a way she'd never been before.

He treated her with all the tenderness a boy could give his sister. Maura told herself it was enough.

She worried about the summer that was coming. Sewell fit into their winter life. She saw no place for him in summer. She was outside, putting laundry on the line, when a shadow passed over her, a great flock of white birds headed towards the sea. She heard them calling, the low-pitched, sonorous sound of horns. Sewell ran from the house, his face turned up, his wing open and beating like a heart. He remained there until the birds had vanished over the water. Then he turned to Maura. She saw his eyes and knew that he'd come back into himself. She could see it was a sorrowful place to be.

But he said nothing and neither did she, until that night, after her father had gone to bed. "What's your name?" she asked.

He was silent awhile. "You've both been so kind to me," he said finally. "I never imagined such kindness at the hands of strangers. I'd like to keep the name you gave me."

"Can the spell be broken?" Maura asked then, and he looked at her in confusion. She gestured to his wing.

"This?" he said, raising it. "This *is* the spell broken."

A log in the fire collapsed with a sound like a hiss. "You've heard of the king's marriage? To the witch-queen?" he asked.

Maura knew only that the king had married.

"It happened this way," he said, and told her how his sister had woven shirts of nettles and how the archbishop had accused her of witchcraft, and the people sent her to the fire. How the king, her husband, said he loved her, but did nothing to save her, and it was her brothers, all of them swans, who encircled her until she broke the spell, and they were men again, all except for his single wing.

So now she was wife to a king who would have let her burn, and queen of those who'd sent her to the fire. These were her people, this her life. There was little in it that he'd call love. "My brothers don't mind the way I do," he said. "They're not as close to her. We were the youngest together, she and I."

He said that his brothers had settled easily enough into life at court. He was the only one whose heart remained divided. "A halfway heart, unhappy to stay, unhappy to go," he said, "a heart like your mother's." This took Maura by surprise. She'd thought he'd slept through her stories about her mother. Her breath grew thin and quick. He must also remember then how she'd slept beside him.

He said that in his dreams, he still flew. It hurt to wake in the morning, find himself with nothing but his clumsy feet. And at the change of seasons, the longing to be in the air, to be on the move was so intense, it overtook him. Maybe that was because the curse had never been completely lifted. Maybe it was because of the wing.

"You won't be staying then," Maura said. She said this carefully, no shaking in her voice. Staying in the house by the sea had long been the thing Maura most wanted. She would still have a mother if they'd only been able to stay in the house by the sea.

"There's a woman I've loved all my life," he answered. "We quarreled when I left; I can't leave it like that. We don't choose whom we love," he told Maura, so gently that she knew he knew. If she wasn't to be loved in return, she would have liked not to be pitied for it. She got neither of these wishes. "But people have this advantage over swans, to put their unwise loves aside and love another. Not me. I'm too much swan for that."

He left the next morning. "Good-bye, father," he said, kissing the old man. "I'm off to find my fortune." He kissed Maura. "Thanks for your kindness and your stories. You've the gift of contentment," he said, and as soon as he named it, he took it from her.

We come now to the final act. Keep your eyes shut tight, little one. The fire inside is dying and the wind outside. As I rock you, monsters are moving in the deep.

Maura's heart froze in her chest. Summertime came and she said good-bye to the seaside house and felt nothing. The landlord had sold it. He went straight to the bars to drink to his good fortune. "For more than it's worth," he told everyone, a few cups in. "Triple its worth," a few cups later.

The new owners took possession in the night. They kept to themselves, which made the curious locals more curious. A family of men, the baker told Maura. He'd seen them down at the docks. They asked more questions than they'd answer. They were looking for sailors off a ship called *The Faucon Dieu*. No one knew why they'd come or how long they'd stay, but they had the seaside house guarded as if it were a fort. Or a prison. You couldn't take the road past without one or another of them stopping you.

Gossip arrived from the capital—the queen's youngest brother had been banished and the queen, who loved him, was sick from it. She'd been sent into seclusion until her health and spirits returned. Maura overheard this in a kitchen as she was cleaning. There was more, but the sound of the ocean had filled Maura's ears and she couldn't hear the rest. Her heart shivered and her hands shook.

That night she couldn't sleep. She got up, and like her mother before her, walked out the door in her nightgown. She walked the long distance to the sea, skirting the seaside house. The moonlight was a road on the water. She could imagine walking on it as, perhaps, her mother had done. Instead she climbed to the cliff where she'd first seen Sewell. And there he stood again, just as she remembered, wrapped in his cape. She called to him, her breath catching so his name was a stutter. The man in the cape turned and he resembled Sewell strongly, but he had two arms and all of Maura's years. "I'm sorry," she said. "I thought you were someone else."

"Is it Maura?" he asked and the voice was very like Sewell's voice. He walked toward her. "I meant to call on you," he said, "to thank you for your kindness to my brother."

The night wasn't cold, but Maura's nightgown was thin. The man took off his cape, put it around her shoulders as if she were a princess. It had been a long time since a man had treated her with such care. Sewell had been the last. But Sewell had been wrong about one thing. She would never trade her unwise love for another, even if offered by someone with Sewell's same gentleness and sorrow. "Is he here?" Maura asked.

He'd been exiled, the man said, and the penalty for helping him was death. But they'd had warning. He'd run for the coast, with the arch-bishop's men hard behind him, to a foreign ship where his brothers had arranged passage only hours before it became illegal to do so. The ship was to take him across the sea to the country where they'd lived as children. He was to send a pigeon to let them know he'd arrived, but no pigeon had come. "My sister, the queen," the man said, "has suffered from the not-knowing. We all have."

Then, just yesterday, for the price of a whiskey, a middle brother had gotten a story from a sailor at the docks. It was a story the sailor had heard recently in another harbor, not a story he'd lived. There was no way to know how much of it was true.

In this story there was a ship whose name the sailor didn't remember, becalmed in a sea he couldn't name. The food ran out and the crew lost their wits. There was a passenger on this ship, a man with a deformity, a wing where his arm should be. The crew decided he was the cause of their

164

misfortunes. They'd seized him from his bed, dragged him up on deck, taken bets on how long he'd stay afloat. "Fly away," they told him as they threw him overboard. "Fly away, little bird."

And he did.

As he fell, his arm had become a second wing. For just one moment he'd been an angel. And then a moment later, a swan. He'd circled the ship three times and vanished into the horizon. "My brother had seen the face of the mob before," the man said, "and it made him regret being human. If he's a swan again, he's glad."

Maura closed her eyes. She pushed the picture of Sewell the angel, Sewell the swan away, made him a tiny figure in the distant sky. "Why was he exiled?" she asked.

"An unnatural intimacy with the queen. No proof, mind you. The king is a good man, but the archbishop calls the tune. And he's always hated our poor sister. Eager to believe the most vile gossip," said the man. "Our poor sister. Queen of a people who would have burned her and warmed their hands at the fire. Married to a man who'd let them."

"He said you didn't mind that," Maura told him.

"He was wrong."

The man walked Maura back to her rooms, his cape still around her. He said he'd see her again, but summer ended and winter came with no word. The weather turned bitter. Maura was bitter, too. She could taste her bitterness in the food she ate, the air she breathed.

Her father couldn't understand why they were still in their rented rooms. "Do we go home today?" he asked every morning and often more than once. September became October. November became December. January became February.

Then late one night, Sewell's brother knocked at Maura's window. It was iced shut; she heard a crack when she forced it open. "We leave in the morning," the man said. "I'm here to say good-bye. And to beg you and your father to go to the house as soon as you wake tomorrow, without speaking to anyone. We thank you for the use of it, but it was always yours."

He was gone before Maura could find the thing that she should say; thank you or good-bye or please don't go.

In the morning, she and her father did as directed. The coast was wrapped in a fog that grew thicker the farther they walked. As they neared the house, they saw shadows, the shapes of men in the mist. Ten men, clustered together around a smaller, slighter figure. The eldest brother waved Maura past him toward the house. Her father went to speak to him. Maura went inside.

Sometimes summer guests left cups and sometimes hairpins. These guests had left a letter, a cradle, and a baby.

The letter said: *My brother told me you could be trusted with this child. I give him to you. My brother told me you would make up a story explaining how you've come to own this house and have this child, a story so good that people would believe it. This child's life depends on you doing so. No one must ever know he exists. The truth is a danger none of us would survive.*

Burn this letter, is how it ended. There was no signature. The writing was a woman's.

Maura lifted the baby. She loosened the blanket in which he was wrapped. A boy. Two arms. Ten fingers. She wrapped him up again, rested her cheek on the curve of his scalp. He smelled of soap. And very faintly, beneath that, Maura smelled the sea. "This child will stay put," Maura said aloud, as if she had the power to cast such a spell.

No child should have a mother with a frozen heart. Maura's cracked and opened. All the love that she would someday have for this child was already there, inside her heart, waiting for him. But she couldn't feel one thing and not another. She found herself weeping, half joyful, half undone with grief. Good-bye to her mother in her castle underwater. Good-bye to the summer life of drudgery and rented rooms. Good-bye to Sewell in his castle in the air.

Her father came into the house. "They gave me money," he said wonderingly. His arms were full. Ten leather pouches. "So much money."

When you've heard more of the old stories, little one, you'll see that the usual return on a kindness to a stranger is three wishes. The usual wishes are for a fine house, fortune, and love. Maura was where she'd never thought to be, at the very center of one of the old stories, with a prince in her arms.

"Oh!" Her father saw the baby. He reached out and the pouches of money spilled to the floor. He stepped on them without noticing. "Oh!" He took the swaddled child from her. He, too, was crying. "I dreamed that Sewell was a grown man and left us," he said. "But now I wake and he's a baby. How wonderful to be at the beginning of his life with us instead of the end. Maura! How wonderful life is."

Karen Joy Fowler is the author of six novels and three short story collections. Her novel *The Jane Austen Book Club* spent thirteen weeks on the *New York Times* bestseller list and was a *New York Times Notable Book*. Fowler's short story collection *Black Glass* won the World Fantasy Award in 1999, and her collection *What I Didn't See* won the World Fantasy Award in 2011. Her 2014 novel *We Are All Completely Beside Ourselves* was honored with the PEN/Faulkner Award. Fowler and her husband, who have two grown children and five grandchildren, live in Santa Cruz, California.

Margo Lanagan retells and expands "The Tinderbox" by Hans Christian Andersen (which was, in turn, his retelling of a Scandinavian folk tale.) Andersen's story of a poor soldier who finds his fortune with the help of a few sparks from flint and steel and some magic dogs is less bleak than many he wrote. But Lanagan's soldier is savage and his story as dark and brutal as war; he flicks a Bic and gets what he wants—no matter how ugly it may be.

Catastrophic Disruption
of the Head

Margo Lanagan

Who believes in his own death? I've seen how men stop being, how people that you spoke to and traded with slump to bleeding and lie still, and never rise again. I have my own shiny scars, now; I've a head full of stories that goat-men will never believe. And I can tell you: with everyone dying around you, still you can remain unharmed. Some boss-soldier will pull you out roughly at the end, while the machines in the air fling fire down on the enemy, halting the chatter of their guns—at last, at last!—when nothing on the ground would quiet it. I always thought I would be one of those lucky ones, and it turns out that I am. The men who go home as stories on others' lips? They fell in front of me, next to me; I could have been dead just as instantly, or maimed worse than dead. I steeled myself before every fight, and shat myself. But still another part of me stayed serene, didn't it. And was justified in that, wasn't it, for here I am: all in one piece, wealthy, powerful, safe, and on the point of becoming king.

I have the king by the neck. I push my pistol into his mouth, and he gags. He does not know how to fight, hasn't the first clue. He smells nice, expensive. I swing him out from me. I blow out the back of his head. All sound goes out of the world.

I went to the war because elsewhere was glamorous to me. Men had passed through the mountains, one or two of them every year of my life, speaking of what they had come from, and where they were going. All those events and places showed me, with their color and their mystery and their crowdedness, how simple an existence I had here with my people—and how confined, though the sky was broad above us, though we walked the hills and mountains freely with our flocks. The fathers drank up their words, the mothers hurried to feed them, and silently watched and listened. I wanted to bring news home and be the feted man and the respected, the one explaining, not the one all eyes and questions among the goats and children.

I went for the adventure and the cleverness of these men's lives and the scheming. I wanted to live in those stories they told. The boss-soldiers and all their equipment and belongings and weapons and information, and all the other people grasping after those things—I wanted to play them off against each other as these men said they did, and gather the money and food and toys that fell between. One of those silvery capsules, that opened like a seed-case and twinkled and tinkled, that you used for talking to your contact in the hills or among the bosses—I wanted one of those.

There was also the game of the fighting itself. A man might lose that game, they told us, at any moment, and in the least dignified manner, toileting in a ditch, or putting food on his plate at the barracks, or having at a whore in the tents nearby. (There were lots of whores, they told the fathers; every woman was a whore there; some of them did not even take your money, but went with you for the sheer love of whoring.) But look, here was this stranger whole and healthy among us, and all he had was that scar on his arm, smooth and harmless, for all his stories of a head rolling into his lap, and of men up dancing one moment, and stilled forever the next. He was here, eating our food and laughing. The others were only words; they might be stories and no more, boasting and no more. I watched my father and uncles, and some could believe our visitor and some could not, that he had seen so many deaths, and so vivid.

"You are different," whispers the princess, almost crouched there, looking up at me. *"You were gentle and kind before. What has happened? What has changed?"*

I was standing in a wasteland, very cold. An old woman lay dead, blown backwards off the stump she'd been sitting on; the pistol that had taken her face off was in my hand—mine, that the bosses had given me to fight with, that I was smuggling home. My wrist hummed from the shot, my fingertips tingled.

I still had some swagger in me, from the stuff my drugs-man had given me, my going-home gift, his farewell spliff to me, with good powder in it, that I had half-smoked as I walked here. I lifted the pistol and sniffed the tip, and the smoke stung in my nostrils. Then the hand with the pistol fell to my side, and I was only cold and mystified. An explosion will do that, wake you up from whatever drug is running your mind, dismiss whatever dream, and sharply.

I put the pistol back in my belt. What had she done, the old biddy, to annoy me so? I went around the stump and looked at her. She was only disgusting the way old women are always disgusting, with a layer of filth on her such as war always leaves. She had no weapon; she could not have been dangerous to me in any way. Her face was clean and bright between her dirt-black hands—not like a face, of course, but clean red tissue, clean white bone-shards. I was annoyed with myself, mildly, for not leaving her alive so that she could tell me what all this was about. I glared at her facelessness, watching in case the drug should make her dead face speak, mouthless as she was. But she only lay, looking blankly, redly at the sky.

She lied to you, my memory hissed at me.

Ah, yes, that was why I'd shot her. *You make no sense, old woman,* I'd said. Sick of looking at her ugliness, I'd turned cruel, from having been milder before, even kind—from doing the old rag-and-bone a favor! *Here I stand,* I said, *with Yankee dollars spilling over my feet. Here you sit, over a cellar full of treasures, enough to set you up in palaces and feed and clothe you queenly the rest of your days. Yet all you can bring yourself to want is this old thing, factory made, one of millions, well used already.*

I'd turned the Bic this way and that in the sunlight. It was like opening a sack of rice at a homeless camp; I had her full attention, however uncaring she tried to seem.

Children of this country, of this war, will sell you these Bics for a packet-meal—they feed a whole family with one man's ration. In desperate times, two rows of chocolate is all it costs you. Their doddering grandfather will sell you the fluid for a twist of tobacco. Or you can buy a Bic entirely new and full from such shops as are left—caves in the rubble, banged-together stalls set up on the bulldozed streets. A new one will light first go; you won't have to shake it and swear, or click it some magic number of times. Soldiers are rich men in war. All our needs are met, and our pay is laid on extra. There is no need for us to go shooting people, not for cheap cigarette-lighters—cheap and pink and lady-sized.

Yes, but it is mine, she had lied on at me. *It was given to me by my son, that went off to war just like you, and got himself killed for his motherland. It has its hold on me that way. Quite worthless to any other person, it is.*

In the hunch of her and the lick of her lips, the thing was of very great worth indeed.

Tell me the truth, old woman. I had pushed aside my coat. *I have a gun here that makes people tell things true. I have used it many times. What is this Bic to you? or I'll take your head off.*

She looked at my pistol, in its well-worn sheath. She stuck out her chin, fixed again on the lighter. *Give it to me!* she said. If she'd begged, if she'd wept, I might have, but her anger set mine off; that was her mistake.

I lean over the king and push the door-button on the remote. The queen's men burst in, all pistols and posturing like men in a movie.

It was dark under there, and it smelled like dirt and death-rot. I didn't want to let the rope go.

Only the big archways are safe, she'd said. *Stand under them and all will be well, but step either side and you must use my pinny or the dogs will eat you alive.* I could see no archway; all was black.

I could *hear* a dog, though, panting out the foul air. The sound was all around, at both my ears equally. I knew dogs, good dogs; but no dog had ever stood higher than my knee. From the sound, this one could take my whole head in its mouth.

Which way should I go? How far? I put out my hands, with the biddy's apron between them. I was a fool to believe her; what was this scrap of cloth against such a beast? I made the kissing noise you make to a dog. *Pup? Pup?* I said.

His eyes came alight, reddish—at the far end of him, praise God. Oh, he was enormous! His tail twitched on the floor in front of me, and the sparse gray fur on it sprouted higher than my waist. He lifted his head—bigger than the whole house my family lived in, it was. He looked down at me over the scabby ridges of his rib-cage. Vermin hopped in the beams of his red eyes. His whole starveling face crinkled in a grin. With a gust of butchery breath he was up on his spindly shanks. He lowered his head to me full of lights and teeth, tightening the air with his growl.

A farther dog woke with a bark, and a yet farther one. They set this one off, and I only just got the apron up in time, between me and the noise and the snapping teeth. That silenced him. His long claws skittered on the chamber's stone floor. He paced, and turned and paced again, growling deep and constant. His lip was caught high on his teeth; his red eyes glared and churned. The hackles stuck up like teeth along his back.

Turning my face aside I forced myself and the apron forward at him. Oh, look—an archway there, just as the old woman said. White light from the next chamber jumped and swerved in it.

The dog's red eyes were as big as those discs the bosses carry their movies on. They looked blind, but he saw me, he saw me; I *felt* his gaze on me, the way you feel a sniper's, in your spine—and his ill-will, only just held back. I pushed the cloth at his nostrils. Rotten-sour breath gusted underneath at me.

But he shrank as the old woman had told me he would, nose and paws and the rest of him; his eyes shone brighter, narrowing to torch-beams. Now I was wrapping not much more than a pup, and a miserable wreck he was, hardly any fur, and his skin all sores and scratches.

I picked him up and carried him to the white-flashing archway, kicking aside coins; they were scattered all over the floor, and heaped up against the red-lit walls. Among them lay bones of dog, bird, sheep, and some of person—old bones, well gnawed, and not a scrap of meat on any of them.

I stepped under the archway and dropped the mangy dog back into his room. He exploded out of himself, into himself, horribly huge and sudden, hating me for what I'd done. But I was safe here; that old witch had known what she was talking about. I turned and pushed the apron at the next dog.

He was a mess of white light, white teeth, snapping madly at the other opening. He smelled of clean hot metal. He shrank to almost an ordinary fighting dog, lean, smooth-haired, strong, with jaws that could break your leg-bone if he took you. His eyes were still magic, though, glaring blind, bulging white. His heavy paws, scrabbling, pushed paper-scraps forward; he cringed in the storm of paper he'd stirred up when he'd been a giant and flinging himself about. As I wrapped him, some of the papers settled near his head: American dollars. *Big* dollars, three-numbered. Oh these, *these* I could carry, these I could use.

For now, though, I lifted the dog. Much heavier he was, than the starving one. I slipped and slid across the drifts of money to the next archway. Beyond it the third dog raged at me, a barking fire-storm. I threw the white dog back behind me, then raised the apron and stepped up to the orange glare, shouting at the flame-dog to settle; I couldn't even hear my own voice.

He shrank in size, but not in power or strangeness. His coat seethed about him, thick with waving gold wires; his tongue was a sprout of fire and white-hot arrow-tips lined his jaws. His eyes, half-exploded from his head, were two ponds of lava, rimmed with the flame pouring from their sockets—clearly they could not see, but my bowels knew he was there behind them, waiting for his chance to cool his teeth in me, to set me alight.

I wrapped my magic cloth around him, picked him up and shone his eye-light about. The scrabbles and shouting from the other dogs behind me bounced off the smooth floor, lost themselves in the rough walls arching over. Where was the treasure the old biddy had promised me in this chamber, the richest of all the three?

The dog burned and panted under my arm. I walked all around, prodding parts of the walls in case they should spill jewels at me or open into treasure-rooms. I reached into cavities hoping to feel bars of gold, giant diamonds—I hardly knew what.

All I found was the lighter the old biddy had asked me to fetch, the pink plastic Bic, lady-sized. And an envelope. Inside was a letter in boss-writing, and attached to that was a rectangle of plastic, with a picture of a foreign girl on it, showing most of her breasts and all of her stomach and legs as she stood in the sea-edge, laughing out of the picture at me.

Someone was playing a joke on me, insulting my God and our women instead of delivering me the treasure I'd been promised.

I turned the thing over, rubbed the gold-painted lettering that stood up out of the plastic. Rubbish. Still, there were all those Yankee dollars, no? Plenty there for my needs. I pocketed the Bic and put the rubbish back in the hole in the wall. I crossed swiftly to the archway, turned in its safety and shook the dog out of the cloth. Its eyes flared wide, and its roar was part voice, part flame. I showed it my back. I'd met real fire, that choked and cooked people—this fairy-fire held no fear for me.

Back in the white dog's chamber, I stuffed my pack as full as I could, every pocket of it, with the dollars. It was *heavy*! It and the white fighting dog were almost more than I could manage. But I took them through and into the red-lit carrion-cave, and I subdued the mangy dog there. I carried him across to where rope-end dangled in its root-lined niche, and I pulled the loop down around the bulk of the money on my back, and the dog still in my arms, and hooked it under myself.

There came a shout from above. Praise God, she had not run off and left me.

Yes! I cried. *Bring me up!*

When she had me well off the floor, I cast the red-eyed dog out of the apron-cloth. He dropped; he ballooned out full-sized, long-shanked. He looked me in the eye, with his lip curled and his breath fit to wither the skin right off my face. I flapped the apron at him. *Boo,* I said. *There. Get down.* The other two dogs bayed deep below. Had they made such a noise at the beginning, I never would have gone down.

And then I was out the top of the tree-trunk and swinging from the branch, slower now than I'd swung before, being so much heavier. The old woman stood there, holding me and my burden aloft, the rope coiling beside her. She was stronger than I would have believed possible.

"Do you have it?" She beamed up at me.

"Oh, I have it, don't worry. But get me down from here before I give you it. I would not trust you as far as I could throw you."

And she laughed, properly witch-like, and stepped in to secure the rope against the tree.

She is not the first virgin I've had, my little queen, but she fights the hardest and is the most satisfying, having never in her worst dreams imagined this could happen to her. I have her every which way, and she urges me on with her screams, with her weeping, with her small fists and her torn mouth and her eyes now wide, now tight-closed squeezing out tears. The indignities I put her through, the unqueenly positions I force her into, force her to stay in, excite me again as soon as I am spent. She fills up the air with her pleading, her horror, her powerless pretty rage, for as long as she still has the spirit.

I left the old woman where she lay, and I took her treasure with me, her little Bic. I walked another day, and then a truck came by and picked me up and took me to the next big town. I found a bank, and had no difficulty storing my monies away in it. There I learned what I had lost when I put the sexy-card back in the cave wall, for the bank-man gave me just such a one, only plainer. The card was the key to my money, he said. I should show the card to whoever was selling to me, and through the magic of computers the money would flow straight out of the bank to that person, without me having to touch it.

"Where is a good hotel?" I asked him, when we were done. "And where can I find good shopping, like Armani and Rolex?" These names I had heard argued over, as we crouched in foxholes and behind walls wait ing for orders; I had seen them in the boss-magazines, between the pages of the women some men tortured themselves with wanting, during the many boredoms of the army.

The bank-man came out with me onto the street and waved me up a taxi. I didn't even have to tell the driver where to go. I sat in the back seat and smiled at my good fortune. The driver eyed me in the mirror.

"Watch the road," I said. "You'll be in big trouble if I get hurt."

"Sir," he said.

At the hotel I found that I was already vouched for; the bank had telephoned them to say I was coming and to treat me well.

"First," I said, "I will have a hot bath, a meal, and some hours' sleep. I've traveled a long way. Then I will need clothes, and this uniform to be burned. And introductions. Other rich men. Rich women, too; beautiful women. I'm sure you know the kind of thing I mean."

When I was stuffing my pack full of dollars underground, I could not imagine ever finding a use for so much money. But then began my new life. A long, bright dream it was, of laughing friends, and devil women in their devil clothes, and wonderful drugs, and new objects and belongings conjured by money as if by wizardry, and I enjoyed it all and thoroughly. Money lifts and floats you, above cold weather and hunger and war, above filth, above having to think and plan—if any problem comes at you, you throw a little money at it and it is gone, and everyone smiles and bows and thanks you for your patronage.

That is, until your plastic dies. *Then* I understood truly what treasure I'd rejected when I left that card in the third cave. There was no more money behind my card; that other card, with the near-naked woman on it, behind *that* had been an endless supply; *that* card would never have died. I had to sell my apartment and rent a cheaper place. Piece by piece I sold all the ornaments and furniture I'd accumulated, to pay my rent. But even the worth of those expensive objects ran out, and I let the electricity and the gas go, and then I found myself paying my last purseful for a month's rent in not much more than an attic, and scrounging for food.

I sat one night on the floor at my attic window, hungry and glum, with no work but herding and soldiering to turn my fortunes around with. I went through my last things, my last belongings left in a nylon backpack too shabby to sell. I pulled out an envelope, with a crest on it, of a hotel—ah, it was those scraps from the first day I had come to this town, with all my money in my pack. These were the bits and pieces that the chamber-boy had saved from the pockets of my soldiering-clothes. *Shall I throw these away, sir?* he'd said to me. *No*, I told him. *Keep them to remind me how little I had before today. How my fortunes changed.*

"Ha!" I laid the half-spliff on my knee. A grain fell out of the tip. That had been a good spliff, I remembered, well-laced with the fighting-powder that made you a hero, that took away all your fear.

"And you!" I took out the pink lighter, still fingerprinted with the mud of that blasted countryside.

"Ha!" One last half-spliff would make this all bearable. A few hours, I would have, when nothing mattered, not this house, not this hunger, not my own uselessness and the stains on my memory from what I had done as a rich man, and before that as a soldier. And then, once it was done . . . well, I would just have to beggar and burgle my way home, wouldn't I, and take up with the goats again. But why think of that now? I scooped the grain back into the spliff and twisted the end closed. I flicked the lighter.

Some huge thing, rough, scabby, crushed me to the wall. I gasped a breath of sweet-rotten air and near fainted. Then the thing adjusted itself, and I was free, and could see, and it was that great gray spindly dog from the underground cave, turning and turning on himself in the tiny space of my attic, sweeping the beams of his red movie-disc eyes about, at me, at my fate and circumstances.

I stared at the lighter in my hand. A long, realizing sound came out of me. So the lighter was the key to the dogs! You flicked it, they came. And see how he lowered his head and his tail in front of me, and looked away from my stare. He was mine, in my power! I didn't need some old apron-of-a-witch to wrap him in and tame him.

Sweat prickled out on me, cold. I'd nearly left this Bic with the old biddy, in her dead hand, for a joke! Some other soldier, some civilian scavenger, some child, might have picked it up and got this power! I'd been going to fling it far out into the mud-land around us, just to laugh while she scrabbled after it. I'd been going to walk away laughing, my pack stuffed with the money I'd brought up from below, and the old girl with nothing.

I looked around the red-lit attic, and out the window at the patched and crowded roofs across the way, dimming with evening. I need never shiver here again; I need never see these broken chimneys or these bent antennae. Now I *enjoyed* the tweaking of the hunger pangs in my belly, because I was about to banish them forever, just as soon as I summoned that hot golden dog with his never-dying money-card.

I clicked the lighter three times.

And so it all began again, the dream, the floating, the powders and good weed, the friends. They laughed again at my stories of how I had come here from such a nowhere. For a time there my family and our goats had lost their fascination, but now they enthralled these prosperous people again, as travelers' tales had once bewitched me around the home fires.

I catch the queen by the shoulders. One of her men dives for his gun. I shoot him; his eye spouts; he falls dead. The queen gives a tiny shriek.

I heard about the princess from the man who fitted out my yacht. He had just come from the tricky job of making lounges for the girl's prison tower, which was all circular rooms.

"Prison?" I said. "The king keeps his daughter in a prison?"

"You haven't heard of this?' he laughed. "He keeps her under lock and key, always has. He's a funny chap. He had her stars done, her chart or whatever, right when she was born, and the chart said she'd marry a soldier. So he keeps her locked up so's this soldier won't get to her. She only meets people her parents choose."

Oh, does she? I thought, even as I laughed and shook my head with the yacht-man.

That night when I was alone and had smoked a spliff, I had the golden dog bring her. She arrived asleep, his back a broad bed for her, his fire damped down for her comfort. He laid the girl on the couch nearest the fire.

She curled up there, belonging as I've never belonged in these apartments, delicate, royal, at peace. She was like a carved thing I'd just purchased, a figurine. She was beautiful, certainly, but not effortfully so, as were most women I had met since I came into my wealth. It was hard to say how much of her beauty came from the fact that I knew she was a princess; her royalty seemed to glow in her skin, to be woven into her clothing, every stitch and seam of it considered and made fit. Her little foot, out the bottom of the nightdress, was the neatest, palest, least walked-upon foot I had ever seen since the newborn feet of my brothers and sisters. It was a foot meant for an entirely different purpose from my own, from most feet of the world.

Even in my new, clean clothes, like a man's in a magazine, I felt myself to be filth crouched beside this creature. These hands had done work, these eyes had seen things that she could never conceive of; this memory was a rubbish-heap of horrors and indignities. It was one thing to be rich; it was quite another to be born into it, to be royal from a long line of royalty, to have never lived anything but the palace life.

The princess woke with the tiniest of starts. Up and back from me she sat, and she took in the room, and me.

Have you kidnapped me? she said, and swallowed a laugh.

Look at your eyes, I said, but her whole face was the thing, bright awake, and curious, and not disgusted by me.

Perhaps your name? she said gently. Her nightwear was modest in covering her neck-to-ankle, but warmth rushed through me to see her breasts so clearly outlined inside the thin cloth.

I made myself meet her eyes. *Can I serve you somehow? Are you hungry? Thirsty?*

How can I be? said the princess, and blinked. *I am asleep and dreaming. Or stoned. It smells very strongly of weed in here. Where was I before?*

I brought a tray of pretty foods from the feast the golden dog had readied. I sat beside her and poured us both some of the cordial. I handed it to her in the frail stemmed glass, raised mine to her and drank.

I shouldn't touch it, she whispered. *I am in a story; it will put me under some spell.*

Then I am magicked too, I said, and raised again the glass I'd sipped from, pretending to be alarmed that half was gone.

She laughed, a small sweet sound—she had very well-kept teeth, just like the magazine women, the poster-women—then she drank.

Now, tell me, what is all this? I said of the tray. *These little things here— they must be fruit by their shape, no? But why are they so small?*

She ate one, and it clearly pleased her. *Who is your chef?* she said, with a kind of frown of pleasure.

He is a secret, I said, for I could hardly tell her that a dog had made this feast.

Of course. She took another of the little fruits, and ate it, and held her fingers ready to lick, a delicate spread fan.

She touched her fingers to a napkin, then put the tray aside. She knelt beside me, and leaned through the perfume of herself, which was light and clean and spoke only quietly of her wealth. *Who are you?* she said, and she put her lips to mine, and held them there a little, her eyes closing, then opening surprised. *Do you not want to kiss me?*

I sit with my fellows in the briefing-room at the barracks. Up on the movie screen, foreign actors are locked together by their lips. Boss-soldiers groan and hoot in the seats in front of us. We giggle at the screen and at the men. "And they call us 'tribals,'" says my friend Kadir, who later will be blown to pieces before my eyes. "Look at how wild they are, what animals! They cannot control themselves."

The princess was poised to be dismayed or embarrassed. *Oh, I do want to,* I said, *but how is it done?* For, except for my mother in my childhood, I had never kissed a woman—even here in my rich-man life—in a way that was not somehow a violence upon her.

So handsome, and you don't already know? But she taught me. She was gentle, but forceful; she pressed herself to me, pushed me (with her little weight!) down onto the couch cushions. I was embarrassed that she must feel my desire, but she did not seem to mind, or perhaps she did not know enough to notice. She crushed her breasts against me, her belly and thighs. And the kissing—I had to breathe through my nose, for she would not stop, and there was no room for my breath with all her little lively tongue, and her hair falling and sliding everywhere, and eventually I dared to put my hands to her rounded bottom and pull her harder against me, and closed my eyes against the consequences.

Hush, she said over me at one point, rising off me, her hair making a slithering tent around our heads and shoulders, all dark gold. Her breasts hung forward in the elaborate frontage of the nightgown—I was astonished by their closeness; I covered them with my hands in a kind of swoon.

I told her what I was, in the night, over some more of that beautiful insubstantial food. I told her about the old woman, and the dogs; I showed her the Bic. *That is all I am*, I said. *Lucky. Lucky to have lived, lucky to have come into this fortune, lucky to have you before me. I am not noble and I have no right to anything.*

Oh, she said, *but it is all luck, don't you see?* And she knelt up and held my face as a child does, to make you listen. *My own family's wealth, it came about from the favors of one king and one bishop, back in the fourteenth century. You learn all the other, all the speaking and manners and how to behave with people lower than yourself; it can be learned by goatherds and by soldiers just as it can by the farmers my family once were, the loyal servants.*

She kissed me. *Certainly you look noble*, she whispered and smiled. *You are my prince, be sure of that.*

She dazzled me with what she was, and had, and said, and what she was free from knowing. But I would have loved her just for her body and its closeness, how pale she was, and soft, and intact, and for her face, perfect above that perfection, gazing on me enchanted. She was like the foods she fancied, beautiful nothingness, a froth of luxury above the hard, real business of the world, which was the machinery of war and missiles, the flying darts and the blown dust and smoke, the shudder in your guts as the bosses brought in the air support, and saved you yet again from becoming a thing like these others, pieces of bleeding litter tossed aside from the action, their part in the game ended.

With the muzzle of the pistol, I push aside the queen's earring—a dangling flower or star, made of sparkling diamonds, a royal heirloom. I press the tip in below her ear, fire, and drop her to the carpet. It's all coming back to me, the efficiency. "Bring me the prince!" I cry.

The women of the bosses' world, they are foul beautiful creatures. They are devils that light a fire in the loins of decent men. One picture is all you need, and such a picture can be found on any boss-soldier's wall in the barracks; my first time in such a place, all my fellows around me were torn as I was between feasting their eyes on the shapes and colors taped to the walls, and uttering damnation on the bosses' souls, and laughing—for it was ridiculous, wasn't it, such behavior? The taping itself was unmanly, a weakness—but the posturing of the picture-girls, I hardly knew how to regard that. I had never seen *faces* so naked, let alone the out-thrusting-ness of the rest of their bodies. I was embarrassed for them, and for the boss-men who looked upon these women, and longed for them—even as the women did their evil work on me, and woke my longings too.

We covered our embarrassment by pulling the pictures down, tearing one, but only a little, and by accident. We put them in the bin, where they were even less dignified, upside down making their faces to themselves, of ecstasy and scorn, or animal abandon. We looked around in relief, the walls bare except for family pictures now. Someone opened a bedside cupboard and found those magazines they have. Around the group of us they went, and we yelped and laughed and pursed our mouths over them, and some tried to whistle as the bosses whistled; I did not touch one at all, not a single page, but I saw enough to disgust and enliven me both for a long time to come.

Someone raised his head, and we all listened. Engines. "Land Rover! They are coming!" And we scrambled to put the things back, made clumsy by our laughter and our fear.

"This is the best one! Take this one with us!"

"Straighten them! Straighten them in the cupboard, like we found them!"

I remember as we ran away, and I laughed and hurried with the rest, another part of me was dazed and stilled by what I had seen, and could not laugh at all. Those women would show themselves, *all* of themselves, parts you had never seen, and did not want to—or did you?—to any man, any; they would let themselves be put in a picture and taped up on a wall for any man's eyes. I was stunned and aroused; I felt so dirtied that I would never be clean, never the man I had been before I saw what I had seen.

And now I was worse, myself, even than those bosses. I lived, I knew, an unclean life. I did not keep my body pure, for marriage or any other end, but only polluted myself and wasted my good seed on wanton women, only poisoned myself with spliffs and powders and liquors.

It is very confusing when you can do anything. You settle for following the urge that is strongest, and call up food perhaps. Then this woman smiles at you, so you do what a man must do; then another man insults you, so you pursue his humiliation. While you wait for a grander plan to emerge in your head, a thousand small choices make up your life, none of them honorable.

It is much easier to take the right path when you only have two to choose from. Easiest of all is when you are under orders, or under fire; when one choice means death, you can make up your mind in a flash.

These things, about the women and my impurity, I would not tell anyone at home. This was why my family stayed away from the greater, the outer world; this was why we hid in the mountains. We could live a good life there, a clean life.

Buzzz. I go to the wall and press the button to see out. Three men stand at the door downstairs. They wear suits, old-fashioned but not in a dowdy way. *You thought you had run ahead of us*, say the steep white collars, the strangely-fastened cuffs, and the fit, the cut of those clothes; even a goat-boy can hear it. *But our power is sunk deep, spread wide, and knotted tight into the fabric of all things.*

The closest one takes off his sunglasses. He calls me by my army name. I fall back a little from the screen. "Who are you and what do you want?"

"We must ask you some questions, in the name of His Majesty the King," he says. He's well fed, the spokesman, and pleased with himself, the way boss-soldiers are, the higher ranks who can fly away back to Boss-Land if things get too rough for them.

"I've nothing to say to any king," I say into the grille. How is he onto me so quickly? Does *he* have magic dogs as well?

"I have to advise you that we are authorized to use force."

I move the camera up to see beyond them. Their car gleams in the apartment's turning circle, with the royal crest on the door. Six soldiers—spick and span, well armed, no packs to weigh them down if they need to run—are lining up alert and out of place on the gravel. Behind them squats an armored vehicle, a prison on wheels.

I pull the sights back down to the ones at the door. I wish I had wired those marble steps the way the enemy used to. I itch for a button to press, to turn them to smoke and shreds. But there are plenty more behind them. By the look of all that, they know they're up against more than one man.

I buzz them in to the lobby. In the bedroom, I take the pistol from my bedside drawer. In the sitting-room lie the remains of the feast, the spilled throw-rug that the princess wrapped herself in as she talked and talked last night. I pick up the Bic and click it twice. "Tidy this up," I say into the bomb-blast of silver, and he picks up the mess in his teeth and tosses it away, and goggles at me for more orders. He could deal with this whole situation by himself if I told him. But I'm not a lazy man, or a coward.

The queen's men knock at the apartment door. I get into position—it feels good, that my body still knows how. "Shrink down, over there," I say to the silver dog. The light from his eyes pulses white around the walls.

Three clicks. "Fetch me the king!" I shout before the gold dog has time to properly explode into being, and they arrive together, the trapped man jerking and exclaiming in the dog's jaws. He wears a nice blue suit, nice shoes, all bespoke, as a king's clothes should be.

The knocking comes again, and louder. The dog stands the king gently on the carpet. I take the man in hand—not roughly, just so he knows who's running this show. "Sit with your friend," I say to the dog, and it shrinks and withdraws to the window, its flame-fur seething. The air is strong with their spice and hot metal, but it won't overpower me; I'm cold and clever and I know what to do.

I lean over the king and push the door-button on the remote. The queen's suits burst in, all pistols and posturing. Then they see me; they aren't so pleased with themselves then. They scramble to stop. The dogs stir by the window and the scent tumbles off them, so strong you can almost see it rippling across the air.

"You can drop those," I say. The men put up their hands and kick their guns forward.

I have the king by the neck. I push my pistol into his mouth, and he gags. He doesn't know how to fight, hasn't the first clue. He smells nice, expensive.

"Maybe he can ask me those questions himself, no?" I shout past his ear at the two suits left. I swing him around to where he will not mess me up so much. "Bring me the queen!" I shout to the golden dog, and blow out the back of the king's head. The noise is terrific; the deafness from it wads my ears.

The queen arrives stiff with fear between the dog's teeth. Her summery dress is printed with carefree flowers. Her skin is as creamy as her daughter's; her body is lean and light and has never done a day's proper work. I catch her to me by the shoulders. One of the guards dives for his gun. I shoot him in the eye. The queen gives a tiny shriek and shakes against me.

The dogs' light flashes in the men's wide eyes. "Please!" mouths their captain. "Let her go. Let her go."

I can feel the queen's voice, in her neck and chest, but her lips are not moving. She's trying to twist, trying to see what's left of the king.

"What are you saying, Your Majesty?" I shake her, keeping my eyes on her men. "Are you giving your blessing, upon your daughter's marriage? Perhaps you should! Perhaps I should make you! No?" My voice hurts in my throat, but I only hear it faintly.

I take her out from the side, quickly so as not to give her goons more chances. I drop her to the carpet. It's all coming back to me, the efficiency.

"The prince!" I command, and there he is, flung on the floor naked except for black socks, his wet man wilting as he scrambles up to face me. I could laugh, and tease him and play with him, but I'm not in that mood. He's just an obstacle to me, the king's only other heir. My gaze fixes on the guards, I push my pistol up under his jaw and I fire. The silent air smells of gun smoke and burnt bone.

"Get these toy-boys out of here," I shout to the dogs, even more painfully, even more faintly. "Put the royals back, just the way they are. In their palace, or their townhouse, or their brothel, or wherever you found them. My carpet, and my clothes here—get the stains off them. Don't leave a single clue behind. Then go down and clear the garden, and the streets, of all those men and traffic."

It's not nice to watch the dogs at work, picking up the live men and the dead bodies both, and flinging them like so many rags, away to nothing. The filthy dog, the scabbed one—why must *he* be the one to lick up the blood from the carpet, from the white leather of the couch? Will he lick me clean too? But my clothes, my hands, are spatter-free already; my fingertips smell of the spiciness of the golden dog, not the carrion tongue of the mangy one.

Then they're gone. Everything's gone that doesn't belong here. The carpet and couch are as white as when I chose them from the catalogue; the room is spacious again without the dogs.

I open the balcony windows to let out the smells of death and dog. Screams come up from the street, and a single short burst of gunfire. A soldier flies up past me, his machine-gun separating from his hands. They go up to dots in the sky, and neither falls back down.

By the time I reach the balcony railing, all is gone from below except people fleeing from what they've seen. The city lies in the bright morning, humming with its many lives and vehicles. I spit on its peacefulness. Their king is dead, and their prince. Soon they'll be ruled by a goatherd, all those suits and uniforms below me, all those bank-men and party-boys and groveling shop-owners. Everyone from the highest dignitary to the lowliest beggar will be at my disposal, subject to my whim.

I stride back into the apartment, which is stuffed fat with the dogs. They shrink and fawn on me, and shine their eyes about.

"I want the princess!" I say to the golden one and he grins and hangs out his crimson tongue. "Dress her in wedding finery, with the queen's crown on her head. Bring me the king-crown, and the right clothes, too, for such an occasion. A priest! Rings! Witnesses! Whatever papers and people are needed to make me king!"

Which they do, and through everyone's confusion and my girl's delight—for she thinks she's dreaming me still, and the news hasn't yet reached her that she is orphaned—the business is transacted, and all the names are signed to all the documents that require them.

But the instant the crown is placed on my head, my rage, which was clean and pure and unquestioning while I reached for this goal, falters. Why should I want to rule these people, who know nothing either of war or of mountains, these spoiled fat people bowing down to me only because they know I hold their livelihoods—their very lives!—in my hands, these soft-living men, these whore-women, who would never survive the cold, thin air of my home, who would cringe and gag at the thought of killing their own food?

"Get them out of here," I say to the golden dog. "And all this nonsense. Only leave the princess—the queen, I should say. Her Majesty."

And the title is bitter on my tongue, so lately did I use it for her mother. King, queen, prince and people, all are despicable to me. I understand for the first time that the war I fought in, which goes on without me, is being fought entirely to keep this wealth safe, this river of luxury flowing, these chefs making their glistening fresh food, these walls intact and the tribals busy outside them, these lawns untrampled by jealous mobs come to tear down the palaces.

And she's despicable too, who was my princess and dazzled me so last night. Smiling at our solitude, she walks towards me in that shameful dress, presenting her breasts to me in their silken tray, the cloth sewn close about her waist to better show how she swells above and below, for all to see, as those dignitaries saw just now, my wife on open display like an American celebrity woman in a movie, like a porn queen in a sexy-mag.

I claw the crown from my head and fling it away from me. I unfasten the great gold-encrusted king-cape and push it off; it suffocates me, crushes me. My girl watches, shocked, as I tear off the sash and brooches and the foolish shirt—truly tear some of it, for the shirt-fastenings are so ancient and odd, it cannot be removed undamaged without a servant's help.

Down to only the trousers, I'm a more honest man; I can see, I can *be*, my true self better. I take off the fine buckled shoes and throw them hard at the valuable vases across the sitting room. The vases tip and burst apart against each other, and the pieces scatter themselves in the dogs' fur as they lie there intertwined, grinning and goggling, taking up half the room.

The princess—the queen—is half-crouched, caught mid-laugh, mid-cringe, clutching the ruffles about her knees and looking up at me. "You are different," she says, her child-face insulting, accusing, above the cream-lit cleft between her breasts. "You were gentle and kind before," she whispers. "What has happened? What has changed?"

I kick aside the king-clothes. 'Now you,' I say, and I reach for the crown on her head.

My mother stirs the pot as if nothing exists but this food, none of us chil-dren tumbling on the floor fighting, none of the men talking and taking their tea around the table. The food smells good, bread baking, meat stewing with onions.

It is a tiny world. The men talk of the larger, outer one, but they know nothing. They know goats, and mountains, but there is so much more that they can't imagine, that they will never see.

I shower. I wash off the blood and the scents of the princess, the bottled one and the others, more natural, of her fear above and of her flower below that I plucked—that I *tore*, more truthfully, from its roots. I gulp down shower-water, lather my hair enormously, soap up and scrub hard the rest of me. Can I ever be properly clean again? And once I am, what then? There seems to be nothing else to do, once you're king, once you've treated your queen so. I could kill her, could I not? I could be king alone, without her eyes on me always, fearful and accusing. I could do that; I've got the dogs. I could do anything. (I lather my sore man-parts—they feel defiled, though she was my wife and untouched by any other man—or so she claimed, in her terror.)

I rinse and rinse, and turn off the hissing water, dry myself and step out into the bedroom. There I dress in clean clothes, several lay-ers, Gore-Tex the outermost. I stuff my ski-cap and gloves in my jacket pockets, my pistol to show my father that my tale is true. I go into my office, never used, and take from the filing drawers my identifications, my discharge papers—all I have left of my life before this, all I have left of myself.

Out on the blood-smeared couch, my wife-girl lies unconscious or asleep, indecent in the last position I forced on her. She's not frightened any more, at least, not for the moment. I throw the ruined ruffled thing, the wedding-dress, to one side, and spread a blanket over her, covering all but her face. I didn't have to do any of what I did. I might have treated her gently; I might have made a proper marriage with her; we might have been king and queen together, dignified and kind to each other, ruling our peoples together, the three giant dogs at our backs. We could have stopped the war; we could have sorted out this country; we could have done anything. Remember her fragrance, when it was just that light bottle-perfume? Remember her face, unmarked and laughing, just an hour or so ago as she married you?

I stand up, away from what I did to her. The fur-slump in the corner rises and becomes the starving gray, the white bull-baiter, the dragon-dog with its flame-coat flickering around it, its eyes fireworking out of its golden mask face.

"I want you to do one last thing for me." I pull on my ski-cap. The dogs whirl their eyes and spill their odours on me.

I bend and put the pink Bic in the princess's hand. Her whole body gives a start, making me jump, but she doesn't wake up.

I pull on my gloves, heart thumping. "Send me to my family's country," I say to the dogs. "I don't care which one of you."

Whichever dog does it, it's extremely strong, but it uses none of that strength to hurt me.

The whole country's below me, the war *there*, the mountains *there*, the city flying away back *there*. I see for an instant how the dogs travel so fast: the instants themselves adjust around them, make way for them, squashing down, stretching out, whichever way is needed for the shape and mission of the dog.

Then I am stumbling in the snow, staggering alongside a wall of snowy rocks. Above me, against the snow-blown sky, the faint lines of Flatnose Peak on the south side, and Great Rain on the north, curve down to meet and become the pass through to my home.

The magic goes out of things with a snap like a passing bullet's. No giant dog warms or scents the air. No brilliant eye lights up the mountainside. My spine and gut are empty of the thrill of power, of danger. I'm here where I used to imagine myself when we were under fire with everything burning and bleeding around me, everyone dying. Snow blows like knife-slashes across my face; the rocky path veers off into the blizzard ahead; the wind is tricky and bent on upending me, tumbling me down the slope. It's dangerous, but not the wild, will-of-God kind of dangerous that war is; all I have to do to survive here is give my whole mind and body to the walking. I remember this walking; I embrace it. The war, the city, the princess, all the technology and money I had, the people I knew—these all become things I once dreamed, as I fight my frozen way up the rocks, and through the weather.

"I should like to meet them," she says to me in the dream, in my dream of last night when she loved me. She sits hugging her knees, unsmiling, perhaps too tired to be playful or pretend anything.

"I have talked too much of myself," I apologize.

"It's natural," she says steadily to me, "to miss your homeland."

I edge around the last narrow section of the path. There are the goats, penned into their cave; they jostle and cry out at the sight of a person, at the smells of the outside world on me, of soap and new clothing.

In the wall next to the pen, the window-shutter slides aside from a face, from a shout. The door smacks open and my mother runs out, ahead of my stumbling father; my brothers and sisters overtake them. My grandfather comes to the doorway; the littler sisters catch me around the waist and my parents throw themselves on me, weeping, laughing. We all stagger and fall. The soft snow catches us. The goats bray and thrash in their pen with the excitement.

"You should have sent word!" my mother shouts over all the questions, holding me tight by the cheeks. 'I would have prepared such a feast!'

"I didn't know I was coming," I shout back. "Until the very last moment. There wasn't time to let you know."

"Come! Come inside, for tea and bread at least!"

Laughing, they haul me up. "How you've all grown!" I punch my littlest brother on the arm. He returns the punch to my thigh and I pretend to stagger. "I think you broke the bone!" And they laugh as if I'm the funniest man in the world.

We tumble into the house. "Wait," I say to Grandfather, as he goes to close the door.

I look out into the storm, to the south and west. Which dog will the princess send? The gray one, I think; I hope she doesn't waste the gold on tearing me limb from limb. And when will he come? How long do I have? She might lie hours yet insensible.

"Shut that door! Let's warm the place up again!" Every sound behind me is new again, but reminds me of the thousand times I've heard it before: the dragging of the bench to the table, the soft rattle of boiling water into a tea-bowl, the chatter of children.

"You will have seen some things, my son," says my father too heartily—he's in awe of me, coming from the world as I do. He doesn't know me any more. "Sit down and tell us them."

"Not all, though, not all." My mother puts her hands over the ears of the nearest sister, who shakes her off annoyed. "Only what is suitable for women and girl-folk."

So I sit, and sip the tea and soak the bread of home, and begin my story.

Margo Lanagan has published five collections of short fiction (*White Time, Black Juice, Red Spikes, Yellowcake,* and *Cracklescape*) and two novels, *Tender Morsels* and *The Brides of Rollrock Island.* She has won four World Fantasy Awards. *Zeroes,* the first novel of a young adult trilogy co-written with Scott Westerfeld and Deborah Biancotti, was published last fall; the second of the series will be published this fall. Lanagan lives in Sydney, Australia.

Peter Christen Asbjørnsen and Jørgen Moe collected "Tatterhood"—a tale of a beautiful twin and an ugly twin—in Norway. Although similar stories are rare elsewhere, they are common in Norway and Iceland. Shveta Thakrar sets her version in the much warmer climate and far more exotic setting of ancient India. In the original story the happy ending includes the "ugly" sister's transformation into a traditionally beautiful woman. Thakrar's conclusion differs in a way that adds even more depth to this tale of familial bonds and human relationships.

Lavanya and Deepika

Shveta Thakrar

Once upon a time, in a land radiant with stars and redolent of sandalwood, where peacocks breakfasted on dreams salty with the residue of slumber, a rani mourned. On the surface, the rani had everything: a kingdom to care for, fine jewels to wear in her long black hair, silken saris threaded through with silver and gold, and a garden of roses and jasmine to rival that of Lord Indra in his celestial realm. When she rode atop her warrior elephant, her subjects bowed before her in awe and love. But one thing remained out of reach—an heir. She longed for a small, smiling face to call her own.

Gulabi Rani consulted midwives, healers schooled in the art of Ayurveda, and magicians. Knowing better than to refuse a monarch, they plied her with charms and salves, medications and horoscopes. She ate the roots and leaves of the shatavari plant as they recommended and drank creamy buttermilk while fastidiously avoiding the color black. Yet her belly stayed flat. At last the healers admitted that, without a husband, there was no hope.

But the rani did not want a husband. Nor did she suffer from a lack of hope. After dismissing the healers and her servants both, she readied a place in the garden. If no one else could help her, she would find the answer herself. Surrounded by her beloved roses, garnet and pink and ivory, Gulabi meditated for weeks on end.

One morning, before even the rooster had crowed, Gulabi opened her eyes and arose. She stretched, allowing the blood to flood back through her stiff body, and strolled down, down, down to the banks of the Sarasvati, whose holy waters flowed clear and bright like liquid diamond.

As she had known he would be, a figure waited there, a yaksha from a neighboring forest. He wore a dhoti around his midsection, and a black-and-red turban wound about his head. "Namaste, rani," he said. "I have heard your calls of distress."

Gulabi placed her palms together in greeting. "Namashkaar. I am honored by your presence."

The nature spirit uncapped an amethyst bottle in the shape of a lotus and beckoned her to come closer. Bending over the bottle, Gulabi inhaled deeply. The fragrance was wonderful, as though all the gardens of the world had been crushed into the crystal blossom. She sighed and reached for it.

"If you wish for a child, you must rub this oil over your womb," the yaksha said, holding the lotus glass aloft. "Use only so much as is necessary to coat the surface and not a drop more."

Willing as the rani might have been, she was also wise. "Ah, but nothing comes without a price. What is yours?"

A grin peered from beneath the yaksha's mustache. "What is it you offer?"

The rani brought forth from the folds of her sari a container of turmeric, an anklet of ruby-encrusted gold, and a single fire-orange rose from her garden. The yaksha studied each of them in turn.

"Would you give me all your roses?" he asked. "Would you give me your garden?"

Gulabi trembled at the thought. The garden where she strolled when seeking solace? The garden filled with the roses for which she was named?

Yet what good were her roses when she had no one to share them with? She bowed her head. "Yes."

"Patience," said the yaksha, amused. "You are too eager in your dealings. But I see your heart is pure and your desire true."

Gulabi thought many things but shrewdly held her tongue.

"I will accept your gifts," continued the yaksha, "and give you one of my own." A pair of blue-and-white chappals appeared in Gulabi's hand.

194

They were just large enough for a baby's fragile feet. "You must save these shoes for your child. I ask nothing else."

"Why?" The question leaped from the rani's lips. How she yearned to say yes, to accept the yaksha's bargain, but she had to know her child would not live to rue her choice.

"Enough. I grow weary." The yaksha sealed the bottle. "Yes or no?"

"Yes," Gulabi said, extending her empty hand. "Give me the oil."

Resting on a mirrored cushion in the company of her ladies-in-waiting, the rani lovingly kneaded the oil into her belly. She sang songs to the child to come as she did, ballads of trouble and triumph. Each circle of her fingers tingled with pleasure, each note rang of delight, as if the oil were seeping into her veins and filling her with its flowery essence. The air in her sun-soaked chamber smelled like a butterfly's paradise.

When she was finished, half the bottle remained. Gulabi was a practical woman with no use for waste. She considered the yaksha's words from this angle and that but concluded a second massage could only magnify her joy. So she performed one.

Soon after sunset, amidst the throes of birthing, Gulabi screamed. In response, the baby emerged.

A gasp escaped the midwife as she received the infant. A moment later, Gulabi, too, gaped at the washed and swaddled baby laid in her arms. It was a girl, which did not surprise her, but the girl was red! Not the red of a newborn taking her first breath, not the scarlet of spilled blood, but a rich, dark crimson, as though she had leached the hue from Gulabi's favorite roses. Under the flickering lamplight, the baby's face gleamed, fresh and dewy like petals, and her hair shone greener than grass.

Gulabi ran a tentative finger along the girl's tender arm. Something pricked her, and she jerked back in pain. "My child has thorns! My child is crimson!" Her heart ached, but she could not deny the truth. "My child . . . my child is a rose."

She did not know what to think but that the yaksha had tricked her.

Her ladies-in-waiting, although curious, kept to the corners while Gulabi gazed down at the tiny girl. The baby did not cry, simply returning her mother's stare with inquisitive eyes. Deep brown eyes, Gulabi was pleased to see, like her own. Her pulse quieted as her heart opened. Perhaps there had been no trick, after all.

"Bring the chappals," she commanded, and her personal attendant ran to do so. Once the sandals were at hand, Gulabi reached into the blanket and placed the right chappal on the baby's right foot. The toes were minuscule, miraculous, with nails like seashells.

When she moved to put the left chappal on, the baby shrieked, her face screwing up and her eyes squeezing out tears. "Sister," she insisted. "Sister, sister!"

The rani paused, confused. Whatever could her daughter mean?

As if to answer, the contractions commenced once more, and another girl joined the first, this one with fine skin the brown of tilled earth, thickly lashed cinnamon eyes, and a cap of fluffy black hair. The midwife sighed with relief as she handed the charming child to Gulabi.

The brown baby caught sight of the rose baby and smiled. "Sister," she said.

Beaming, the rose girl pointed to the brown girl's right foot, and beaming in turn, Gulabi placed the second chappal there. She would have to commission matches for each girl, but for now, this would do.

The time came for Gulabi Rani to name her precious daughters. "Lavanya for grace and Deepika for light," she proclaimed, her voice fierce yet fond. "Let no one say otherwise." She cuddled her daughters, rose and brown, grace and light, close. Together, they began to explore the ways of the world.

The sisters grew up, always together, always playing, as twins are wont to do. Few in the palace were fond of Lavanya, with her garnet-tinted skin and hair like spring leaves, fearing her to be a demon or some other foul spawn. Those who dared lay a hand on her bare flesh risked the cruel prick of thorns hungry for blood. A much-beloved perfume drifted from the girl, captivating those who smelled it, but also enchanting bees and beetles, aphids and earwigs, and many other things the courtiers found less than desirable. Though the kingdom treasured its rani, it could not love her crimson daughter.

The ladies-in-waiting and nurses did their best to avoid the odd girl, going so far as to lock her away in her rooms on the rare occasions they found her alone. Out of sight was out of mind, they said, and a good thing, too. For Deepika, however, they had endless treats and trinkets, offers to brush and braid her hair, and pleas for her to sing, as hers was the sweet voice of the nightingale.

But the sisters refused to be separated even a moment. The strange story of their birth, the chappals that kept pace with their growing feet, their interest in nature and stories—these things bound them to each other more securely than any rope.

Lavanya did not mind the isolation so much. Indeed, she quite liked her peculiar skin, for butterflies spoke to her as they would to no other, in the soft, luscious language of nectar, and she could pluck her thorns as she needed them. Why should she be lonely, when she had Deepika for a companion?

Deepika adored her rose sister in the way the moon adores the sun, finding favors and festivities to mean little when they went unshared. Everything she received, she divided in two; it was the way of things. What use were playmates who did not understand this?

And so they lived for years, learning their lessons, watching their mother the rani rule, and advancing their arts. Lavanya wandered the grounds, gossiping with the roses and evading the petulant gardeners. Yet when she played the bansuri, a flute carved of bamboo, both the plants and their caretakers paused to listen. Deepika took up archery and embroidery. Her arm was strong and her aim true, and her nimble fingers animated the fine needlework images until the fabric thrummed with their tales.

One evening, over a banquet of roasted fowl and spiced vegetables, Gulabi entertained a rani and a raja from another kingdom. They sat in the marble dining chamber discussing matters of politics and economy as Deepika ate her fill of the birds she had hunted, and Lavanya sipped at water from a golden cup. She also ran her fingers through a small dish of rich black soil, a delicious dessert to her earlier meal of sunlight.

But Lavanya could not enjoy it. She did not like the visitors, the knowing way they smiled at Deepika, the boisterousness with which they talked and laughed. It rankled her, though she could not say why.

She looked at Deepika, who scooped thick saffron curd with the spoon of her hand. Her lips parted, then pursed as the raja spoke.

"So you see, Gulabi Rani," he said, his teeth tearing into a fleshy leg of pheasant, "clearly it is in the best interests of all to join our children in marriage."

The words, uttered so casually, so naturally, brought the entire court to silence. Lavanya reached for Deepika's hand just as it found hers. A scratchy sensation stole over her body, the familiar feel of eyes that assessed and quickly dismissed her in favor of her sister.

Of course it would be Deepika. The visitors wanted her for their son as though she were a bauble to be bought and sold. Lavanya glared at them, and the thorns in her arms bristled. How dare they?

"Yes, Deepika would be a fine match for our Vibhas," the visiting rani agreed, ignoring, or perhaps enjoying, the hush that blanketed the hall. "Such a beautiful girl. She would, of course, have to give up the hunting."

Deepika's fingernails dug into Lavanya's palm. Lavanya wished she could do the same to the raja and rani. They were not the first to ask after her sister's hand in marriage, but they were certainly the most presumptuous.

"Your proposal brings honor to our family, but I am afraid I must decline," Gulabi said firmly, having recovered her wits. "My daughters are far too young for such considerations. A few years from now, possibly." She smiled. "However, I have heard you are fond of roses."

She began to talk of her gardens, offering her guests a tour, but though they nodded, raw greed still glittered in their eyes. Lavanya knew this would not be the end of their attempt to buy Deepika and the land she represented. The worry on Deepika's and Gulabi's faces told her they knew it, too.

Why, oh, why had her mother forbidden her to use her thorns on troublemakers like these?

The tiger's roar came in the night, echoing through the empty halls, horrible, hateful, hungry. It stained the sky scarlet with the promise of running blood. Terrified cries and shouts rang out in its wake.

Lavanya, torn from the sweet touch of sleep, raced into the corridor. Deepika met her there, bow and quiver on her back and embroidery thread in her waistband. The sisters followed the sound of their mother's voice to the entrance of the throne room.

"I will never give you my daughter!" Gulabi said, her voice quiet, still, dangerous like a crow's appraisal of its next meal as she confronted the visiting raja and rani. She gripped her sword with both hands.

Lavanya and Deepika

"The offer of marriage was an act of charity," the raja said in the tone of one who believes himself far more clever than his audience. "After all, who else would take a fatherless child with a monster for a sister? But if you insist on defying us, we shall just take what we came for and go on our way." He swept his arm across the expanse of the throne room. "Where are they?"

Deepika scowled, and Lavanya bared her teeth. If only he could see them!

"Be reasonable," the rani said to Gulabi. Beneath its veil of compassion, her look was sly. "Do you really wish for the tiger to kill all your people? That is surely not the just ruler of whom they sing songs, is it?"

When Gulabi did not respond, the visiting rani took the raja's arm. "Let us give her a last chance to consider our offer. There is still time to call off the beast before many suffer."

"We will await your decision in our rooms," pronounced the raja, and they left.

Lavanya yanked Deepika behind a statue of the goddess Lakshmi as the visitors approached. Once it was safe, the sisters hurried to their mother.

Tears trickled down Gulabi's face, one on each cheek, and thickened into sparkling gems. "Take the chappals and flee," she said, every word hard and heavy as a boulder. "A tiger is on the loose, and behind him an army. I must convince them to stay their hands."

"But why?" Lavanya demanded. "Surely they do not think our land worth killing for."

"We are all that stands between them and their empire. They have already conquered our neighbors and allies," Gulabi said, her eyebrows knitted in anger. "But even that is not enough. They have come, more than anything, for your chappals."

Lavanya regarded her feet. When properly paired, the yaksha's gift lent the wearer the swiftness of a divine chariot. If the raja and rani were to obtain the chappals, nothing but their own avarice would be able to catch them. Wicked mirth bubbled in the rose girl's throat. "Such a shame, then, that they must go away disappointed!"

"I will distract them," Gulabi said, "so you can escape. Go deep into the forest, and hide there. But beware the tiger!"

Deepika said nothing, yet swords danced in her stare. One hand toyed with the bow on her shoulder, and Lavanya caught the crafty movement of her mouth. Her sister had a plan.

Gulabi seized the jewels from her cheeks and bound them about the girls' necks, the teardrop pendants glistening with her grief. She clasped her daughters briefly, far too briefly, to her breast. "Because I cannot be with you, these stones will remind you of me."

Then, her steps reluctant and silent, she took them through a secret passage marked with sigils and out of the palace. Pressing kisses to their foreheads and a torch into Lavanya's hand, she motioned them away. "Always stay together. Now go!"

"I will stop him," Deepika told her sister, confident. She nocked an imaginary arrow. "I will shoot him down. No one threatens our mother, and no one calls you a monster."

Lavanya swung the bansuri that hung at her side. "And I will help," she pledged.

Hand in hand, the sisters ventured into the forest. Deepika held up one hand. "Listen," she said, "it is far too still. No hooting of owls, no chirping of crickets, no buzzing of mosquitoes." She sniffed the air. "The tiger is close. Come, we must follow."

It was not long before Deepika halted beneath a pine tree and gestured toward Lavanya's bansuri. Lavanya put the instrument to her lips and began to play, a melody both of challenge and of wonders untold. She could see neither tooth nor tail of the tiger, but if he were nearby, he would not be able to resist her song.

A massive shape bloomed in the light of the torch, all arrogant yellow eyes, ebony-striped silver fur, and claws sharp as scimitars. The tiger padded in circles around the sisters, slowly, purposefully, once, twice, then three times. "Who dares to summon me so?"

Lavanya smiled. "I do." At her side, Deepika pulled back the bowstring.

The tiger opened his jaw wide and roared, the sound hunger itself. "A mere rose? I will crack your neck and drink your blood like rosewater!" He swiped a paw in Deepika's direction, knocking her into a bed of muddy leaves.

Lavanya concealed her rage and the thorn she had plucked from her arm. After all, one must tread carefully with tigers. "Tiger," she lamented, "what sorrow is this, that such a brave beast as you should be reduced to such a state?"

The tiger glowered. "What do you mean, foolish flower? Reduced to what state?"

"How they mourn!" Lavanya cried, sliding the thorn behind her back. "It is on the lips of every person, every serpent, every beast. They say you have fallen, that you carry out the bidding of a mere human! Worse, of two humans. O king of the jungle, how can this be?"

"I undertake no one's bidding but my own!" The tiger tossed his majestic head, but the gesture lacked its customary pride.

"Yet they told us, the rani and the raja, that they sent you to attack our realm," Deepika said, brushing the residue of the forest floor from her sari. She slung the bow over her shoulder and strung an arrow. "They claim they have found your price."

"Tiger," gasped Lavanya, clutching her chest, "could it be true? Are you . . . a *tame* tiger?"

With a growl, the tiger pounced. "Insolent child! I go where I wish!"

Deepika leaped in front of Lavanya and let fly her arrow. The missile rushed toward the tiger, who narrowly dodged it, and thudded into the trunk of a tree. Furious, the tiger charged, batting Deepika to the earth once more before turning to Lavanya.

Lavanya darted behind him, dashing through the trees to hold his attention. When he spun around, jumping through the air, she brandished the thorn she had stretched into a deadly spear. Just before the head pierced his throat, the tiger froze.

"Sister, lend me your thread," Lavanya said. Deepika threw the spool of embroidery thread over the tiger's head, where it expanded into a blue-and-green-and-purple bridle. Snarling, he tried to shake it loose, but his distress only drew it tighter.

The girls climbed onto his back, and Deepika took hold of the reins. "Tiger," said Lavanya, "take us to the land beyond the mountains, where the raja and rani live."

The tiger sneered, yet it was a powerless sound. With a magical bit in his mouth and a spear at his throat, what choice did he have but to obey?

Their star-colored mount bore Lavanya and Deepika much further than they had ever been, past winding rivers, over snow-capped mountains, around bamboo-strewn forests, through villages large and small, and finally, many moons later, into the arid desert realm of their enemy. "I have brought you where you wished to go. Now free me!"

"Soon, tiger," Lavanya said. Her thirst had grown potent, causing her hair to wilt and her skin to slough off like crimson petals, but she willed herself to wait. They neared the dawn fortress, a magnificent pink-and-orange structure with towers and turrets, carvings and cupolas, pillars and pavilions. In the center of the gate, an open doorway tall enough for even a daitya arched to a point far above them. It was clear a proud people dwelled within.

The tiger halted before the opening. "I can go no farther," he announced. "Release me." The sisters' feet had barely touched the ground before the tiger's own scampered away. In the shadow cast by his absence, the rose girl felt smaller than a snail without a shell. How would they ever find their way in this place that extended almost to both ends of the horizon?

Lavanya and Deepika entered the fortress. Rather than the guards they expected, they were greeted by a lively blend of perspiration, incense, spices, produce, and perfumes. Before them pulsed a bazaar teeming with supplicants, nobles, and sages, people selling wares, people buying wares, people hurrying from one place to another. Voices rose and fell in a chaotic chorus of agreement, debate, and all things between, and the speakers' clothes glowed like a galaxy, ranging from grey to the green of raw mangoes.

The massive market square dwarfed Gulabi's entire palace, making a plaything of it in Lavanya's memories. She ran her fingertips over the wall inlaid with many-hued marble flowers and gold, her breath catching at the beauty.

"Look," Deepika whispered, indicating the scene before them. Exhaustion had engraved itself like a script on the faces of the people, in the slump of their shoulders, exhaustion and misery that could not be masked by their fine clothing. Lavanya did not know what to make of it, but her thorns bristled. These were the people who had attacked her land, others' lands. Why were they not gloating over their conquest?

A secluded fountain shaped like a lily stole those and all other thoughts from her mind. Her eyes saw only the inviting spray, her ears heard only the water's splash on the marble as she leaned forward. Cool liquid trickled past her parched lips until her belly brimmed and her skin sang. Oh, how satisfying the crisp, clear flavor of clay on her tongue; how splendid the soft wetness on her toes!

Eventually she withdrew, sated, and stumbled over a small boy with a tattered blue cap and bright brown eyes. Grinning, he flaunted a filthy string knotted with glass bangles. "Red, green, yellow, pink," he called, "whatever you like, I have it!"

Lavanya opened her mouth to refuse, but the words shriveled before the boy's grime-splattered rags. Untying the end of her sari, she removed two golden coins. "Here," she said. "Take these."

The boy grabbed the coins and tucked them out of sight. His mouth turned up in a curve of pleasure, which he promptly smothered into a sober line. "That will buy you half a bangle."

"Do not lie to me," Lavanya scolded. "For the price I paid, you should give me ten, no, twenty, times the bangles you have." But she contented herself with two, one yellow for Deepika and one red for herself.

The bargain completed, the boy scurried away, and Lavanya offered the yellow bangle to her sister. Deepika did not take it. Indeed, Deepika was no longer there.

Lavanya whirled around in alarm. The hem of Deepika's sari winked violet before vanishing around a corner, as though tempting Lavanya to give chase. She did.

Rounding the bend, she spied the ragtag band of boys and girls that had captured Deepika and was now conveying her down a pillared hallway, through a vast courtyard, and into an open-air royal audience. Deepika punched and kicked, whipping her head from side to side, all to no avail.

"Here," the eldest girl said, striding toward the throne. "We have brought you your sister. Now give us our reward!"

Lavanya crept closer. What game was this?

"That is not my sister," the man on the throne replied, his mustache well groomed and his turban dearer than all their garments combined. No beggar was this, but a prince. "My sister is lost to me."

"She hunts, she is strong, she is good enough," the girl countered, unconcerned. "Pay us! You may sulk in the shadows, but we need to eat."

"Bring our parents home," a familiar voice added. "While your parents wage their war, we are left alone." It was the boy with the bangles, the boy who had duped Lavanya. The thorn spear shuddered in her grasp.

"Enough!" said the prince, producing a small purse. "I will compensate you for your trouble, but more I cannot do."

"They took our parents!" The children ambushed him, a murderous, desperate mob of arms and legs and teeth.

Lavanya flung her spear into the bedlam. The blood-covered children fled, leaving the spear to clang off a cage of bone. At its heart sat Deepika, within reach but also far beyond it. Though Lavanya beat her fists against the bars of bone, she could not free her sister. "Release her!"

The prince stood, bruised and battered, and stopped her onslaught. "Brave one," he said, his face forlorn, "this cage was meant for me. If I take her out, they will put me in. I am sorry, but you must go."

"She is my sister," said Lavanya staunchly. "Until she is liberated, I will never leave."

Deepika thrust her chappal through the bars of the cage. "No! Take this and run. I will not see you harmed."

"Never," Lavanya said, giving back the sandal. "When they return, I will be here."

She played her bansuri to while away the time, the sound swirling into the cage like light, and Deepika accompanied her, singing of stories yet to be. Were it not for the bars of bone and the presence of the prince, they might have been home.

From his throne, the prince observed the rose woman and her warrior sister. Doubt darkened his brow. "Such loyalty, such devotion. Truly it is no less than Falguni and I shared." He arose and approached the cage, a bone key in his hand.

Drawn to the song, a crowd had gathered in the courtyard. "My mother was taken!" one person shouted. "My husband!" said another. "My grandfather." "My aunt." "My cousin." "My brother." Despair dripped from their words, despair hardened by wrath. "All conscripted for your parents' abomination of an army, while you, princeling, did nothing."

"If you will not help us," cried an old woman all in white, "we will kill you."

Before the prince could speak, the swarm raised its arsenal, axes and maces, swords and slingshots. Lavanya set down her bansuri. "Peace! We are here to help."

"We are the children of Gulabi Rani," Deepika called from the cage. "We are on your side."

"Go on," said the old woman.

"Hear me!" the prince decreed, lifting his chin and unlocking the cage of bone. "We will bring your families home. It is Vibhas who swears this."

Distrustful mouths grumbled and groused. "Why should we believe you?" demanded the old woman. "You would not listen before."

"I was wrong to lose myself in my loss and neglect my people," Vibhas said. He blinked to clear the lingering clouds of gloom from his vision before guiding Deepika from the cage. "Falguni would be anything but pleased."

"Life must continue, prince," agreed the old woman. "We have all lost someone, we all grieve, yet we endure."

Bowing, Vibhas removed his arm ring and offered it to her in tribute.

In turn, Deepika removed her necklace, and Lavanya unfastened her own. Together, they held them forth. "Accept these as a symbol of our promise. We shall free your families as we free our own."

The throng lowered its weapons, while the boy with the bangles cupped his hands for the pendants. "Go, then," he said. "We will be waiting."

Lavanya and Deepika departed the dawn fortress, Vibhas in tow. As they passed beyond the sandstone walls, a roar mighty as the monsoon rain reverberated around them. Seconds later, the tiger lunged.

Lavanya pushed Vibhas from the tiger's path, though a claw still scratched him, while Deepika fired an arrow at the tiger's heart. Farther, farther, farther went the tip in search of its target, burying itself to the fletching. But would it be far enough?

The tiger bellowed, raking at the arrow, at himself, yet there was no blood, no rending of skin. He lowered his teeth into Deepika's leg, then abruptly released her. She bit her lip but did not scream even as blood spurted from the wound.

Lavanya ran to Deepika, pulling her to safety and cradling her bloody limb. Having torn his shirt into strips, Vibhas bandaged Deepika's leg, then his own arm. As they watched, wary, the madness melted from the tiger's eyes, and the whiskers from his cheeks. His silvery body dissolved into a regal figure, tall, sturdy, and two-legged. A princess.

Lavanya stared. A princess! How could that be?

The princess tugged the shaft from her chest, snapped it in two, and dropped the pieces to the ground. She paid no mind to the tear in her emerald choli, instead studying Deepika as intently as an astronomer observing the stars. Lavanya held her breath as Deepika raised her head and mirrored the probing gaze. Minutes passed before white teeth flashed bright in the light of the lanterns, the half-moon of one mouth framing the challenge, the other accepting it.

Still deep in their private dialogue, they advanced, nearer, ever nearer. Then the princess noticed Vibhas. "Brother!" She bounded away from Deepika and into his open arms, embracing him tightly.

"Falguni," sobbed the staring prince, "is it really you?"

"Yes, me and no other." The princess broke free, laughter shining in her eyes and ringing from her lips.

Vibhas offered an arm to Deepika. "You broke the curse," he said amidst a cascade of tears. "If not for you, Falguni would have spent the rest of her days as a tiger and lost to me. In thanks, I would marry you."

Lavanya stood aside, a prisoner of war: sweet delight for her sister battled in her heart with the knowledge bitter as karela that again, she was not wanted.

Deepika glanced from the princess to the prince, from the prince to the princess. She knew the prince's gratitude for the obligation it was, just as she noted the sword in the princess's hand and saw the strength it revealed. She nodded, certain.

"I choose the princess," Deepika said, weaving her arm through Falguni's equally muscular one. Falguni smiled the secretive smile of a tigress about to spring and led Deepika to one side.

Vibhas joined Lavanya under the archway. "I am glad she did not choose me," he confided, "for she is not the one I desire."

Lavanya frowned, fearing to believe.

"Nor do I believe my sister will be so easily claimed. She, too, enjoys the hunt," Vibhas continued. "When my parents began amassing the lands of their neighbors, their most trusted advisor tried to dissuade them. But they cared only for their empire, forcing the most robust of their subjects into their army while the rest starved. And so the advisor, also a magician, cursed my sister in the hope that they would reconsider."

"But they did not," Lavanya said, completing the tale.

"No," said the prince, his eyes dim with dismay. "Indeed, they were glad for another weapon in their armory."

His pain reminded Lavanya of her mother and the long months they had been separated. Her melancholy increased with the memory of the gardens. On a whim, she asked, "Do I not hold the most splendid rose?"

"You do," the prince agreed, the enchantment turning his gaze to glass. And it was true; she now clasped a blossom the color of her own strange skin.

Lavanya caressed the slim stem. "Do I not need to return to my own mother?"

"You do," the prince said, dreamily repeating her thoughts. "Daughters belong with their mothers." The chappals at Lavanya's crimson feet blazed blue then, a brilliant, restless blue.

"Do you find me ugly?" the rose woman wondered sadly, stroking Vibhas's cheek with the petals. "All think my sister is beautiful, thus the one to love."

"She is beautiful, that is true," Vibhas said, wrapping his hand around hers, the hand that held the bloom. The thorns of her arm did not prick him as he drew close, or if they did, he did not seem to mind. Perhaps they had shattered the spell, for his eyes were clear, his words his own. "But you see, she is not a rose."

Lavanya donned the chappals and linked hands with the others. Leading their chain, she sprinted toward the horizon, fleet of foot, faster even than the wind itself. They visited villages and cities and settlements to herald the end of the war and scatter the seeds of harmony. Then, weary of heart and of body, they hastened home to rest among the roses of Gulabi's garden.

The rani had dispatched with the unwelcome visitors, who had proven no match for her swordplay, and deposited them in the palace dungeon. Vibhas touched Gulabi's feet in apology for the crimes of his parents. Tears rolling down her face, she touched his forehead in forgiveness.

At Falguni's command, the ragged remnants of the army dispersed, impatient to return to the lands they called home. At Vibhas's command, each soldier carried a rose from Gulabi as a sign of goodwill.

Deepika introduced Falguni as schooled in the sword, both curved and straight. "It was I who freed her."

"It was I who allowed myself to be freed," Falguni stated, not one to relinquish her tigress's proud bearing for even a moment. She addressed Gulabi. "The people of the dawn fortress will need a ruler, now that my parents are no longer fit to be such. With your blessing, I would return there in the company of your daughter."

Lavanya imagined Deepika a rani amid the pink-and-orange walls, hunting beside Falguni and crooning victory songs to the stars above. "With your blessing, Vibhas and I will remain here with you," she said, moving closer to her mother.

Gulabi clapped her hands together in approval and in joy. As one, they kicked off their shoes and danced in celebration of the weddings to come, of the freedom they had won, of the rose-loving rani's reunion with her daring daughters.

Seeing this, the courtiers and servants, all the inhabitants of the kingdom, for that matter, forgot their cares, forgot their fears of Lavanya, forgot everything but the chance for merrymaking. The royal musicians struck up a fine tune, and the royal chefs served up a fine feast. As it often does, food led to drink, drink led to song, and song led to laughter that sounded in the air until even the roses swayed blithely on their thorny stems.

Some say a yaksha with a red-and-black turban wound about his head slipped out from behind a banyan tree that day, stealthy as a snake in the grass, to snatch up the chappals, and never were they seen again in that place.

Shveta Thakrar is a writer of South Asian-flavored fantasy, social justice activist, and part-time nagini. She draws on her heritage, her experience growing up with two cultures, and her love of myth to spin stories about spider silk and shadows, magic and marauders, and courageous girls illuminated by dancing rainbow flames. Her short fiction and poetry appear in the *Kaleidoscope* anthology and *Uncanny, Faerie, Strange Horizons*, and *Mythic Delirium* magazines. When not hard at work writing, Shveta makes things out of glitter and paper and felt, devours books, daydreams, draws, bakes sweet treats, travels, and occasionally even practices her harp.

When Theodora Goss writes a fairy tale, she usually grounds the highly fantastic with a least one form of reality. Her fictional, somewhat Eastern European country of Sylvania (which appears in another story she's authored) seems both familiar and exotic. And, although there are no particular wonder tales that parallel or inform "Princess Lucinda and the Hound of the Moon," one feels as if there are.

Princess Lucinda and the Hound of the Moon

Theodora Goss

When the Queen learned that she could not have a child, she cried for three days. She cried in the clinic in Switzerland, on the shoulder of the doctor, an expert on women's complaints, leaving tear stains on his white coat. She cried on the train through Austria, while the Alps slipped past the window of her compartment, their white peaks covered with snow. She cried when the children from the Primary School met her at the station, bringing her bouquets of snowdrops, the first of the season. And after the French teacher presented her with the bouquets, and the children sang the Sylvanian national anthem, their breaths forming a mist on the cold air—she cried especially then.

"It doesn't matter, Margarethe," said King Karel. "My nephew Radomir will make a fine king. Look at how well he's doing at the Primary School. Look at how much he likes building bridges, and if any country needs bridges, it's Sylvania." For the Danube and its tributaries ran through the country, so that wherever you went in Sylvania was over a river, or perhaps two.

And then Queen Margarethe stopped crying, because it was time to greet the French ambassador, and she was after all the youngest daughter of the King of Greece. She had been trained to restrain her emotions, at least at state functions. And the blue satin of her dress would stain.

But that night, when the French ambassador was discussing business with the bankers of Sylvania, and her other guests were discussing French innovations in art (for although Sylvania was a small country, it had a fashionable court) or losing at cards in a cloud of cigarette smoke, the Queen walked out to the terrace.

It was a cold night, and she pulled the blue satin wrap more closely about her shoulders. The full moon above her was wearing a wrap of gray clouds. In its light, she walked down the steps of the terrace, between the topiaries designed by Radomir IV, boxwood swans swimming in a pool of grass, a boxwood stag running from overgrown boxwood hounds. She shivered because her wrap was not particularly warm, but walked on through the rose garden, which was a tangle of canes. She did not want to go back to the castle, or face her guests.

She reached the croquet lawn, beyond which began the forest that surrounded Karelstad, where croquet balls were routinely lost during tournaments between the ministers and the ladies-in-waiting. Suddenly, she heard laughter. She looked around, frightened, and said, "Is anyone there?"

No one answered. But under a chestnut tree that would be covered with white flowers in spring, she saw a basket. She knelt beside it, although the frost on the grass would stain her dress more certainly than tears, and saw a child. It was so young that the laugh she had heard might have been its first, and it waved its fist, either at the moon above or at the Queen, whose face looked like a second moon in the darkness.

She lifted the child from its basket. Surely it must be cold, left out on a night like this, when winter still covered Sylvania. Surely whoever had left it here did not deserve a child. She picked it up, with the blanket it was wrapped in, and carried it over the croquet lawn, through the rose garden, between the boxwood swans and the boxwood stag, up the terrace steps, to the castle.

"Surely she has a mother," said the King. "I know this has been difficult for you, Margarethe, but we can't just keep her."

"If you could send the Chamberlain out for diapers," said the Queen. "And tell Countess Agata to warm a bottle."

"We'll have to advertise in the Karelstad Gazette. And when her mother replies, we'll have to return her."

"Look," said the Queen, holding the child up to the window, for the cook had scattered cake crumbs on the terrace, and pigeons were battling over them. "Look, embroidered on the corner of her blanket. It must be her name: Lucinda."

No one answered the advertisement, although it ran for four weeks, with a description of the child and where she had been found. And when the King himself went to look beneath the chestnut tree, even the basket was gone.

Princess Lucinda was an ordinary child. She liked to read books, not the sort that princesses were supposed to like, but books about airplanes, and mountain climbing, and birds. She liked to play with her dolls, so long as she could make parachutes for them and toss them down from the branches of the chestnut tree. The Queen was afraid that someday Lucinda would fall, but she could not stop her from climbing trees, or putting breadcrumbs on her windowsill for the pigeons, or dropping various objects, including the King's scepter, out of the palace window, to see if they would fly.

Lucinda also liked the gardener's daughter, Bertila, who could climb trees, although not so well as the Princess. She did not like receptions, or formal dresses, or narrow shoes, and she particularly disliked Jaromila, her lady-in-waiting and Countess Agata's daughter.

But there were two unusual things about Princess Lucinda. Although her hair was brown, it had a silver sheen, and in summer it became so pale that it seemed purely silver. And the Princess walked in her sleep. When the doctor noticed that it happened only on moonlit nights, the Queen ordered shutters to be placed on Lucinda's windows, and moonlight was never allowed into her room.

For the Princess' sixteenth birthday, the Queen planned a party. Of course she did not know when the Princess had been born, so she chose a day in summer, when the roses would be at their best and her guests could smoke on the terrace.

Everyone of importance in Sylvania was invited, from the Prime Minister to the French teacher at the Primary School. (Education was considered important in Sylvania, and King Karel had said on several occasions that education would determine Sylvania's success in the new century.) The Queen hired an orchestra that had been the fashion that winter in Prague, although she confessed to the Chamberlain that she could not understand modern music. And Prince Radomir came home from Oxford.

"They ought to be engaged," said the Queen at breakfast. "Look at what an attractive couple they make, and what good friends they are already." Princess Lucinda and Prince Radomir were walking below the morning room windows, along the terrace. The Queen might have been less optimistic if she had known that they were discussing airplane engines. "And then she would be Queen."

She looked steadily at the King, and raised her eyebrows.

"But I can't help it, Margarethe," said King Karel, moving his scrambled eggs nervously around on his plate with a fork. "When the first King Karel was crowned by the Pope himself, he decreed that the throne must always pass to a male heir."

"Then it's about time that women got the vote," said the Queen, and drank her coffee. Which was usually how she left it. King Karel imagined suffragettes crashing through the castle windows and writing "Votes for Women" on the portraits of Radomir IV and his queen, Olga.

"How can you not like him?" asked Bertila later, as she and Lucinda sat on the grass, beneath the chestnut tree.

"Oh, I like him well enough," said Lucinda. "But I don't want to marry him. And I'd make a terrible queen. You should have seen me yesterday, during all those speeches. My shoes were hurting so badly that I kept shifting from foot to foot, and Mother kept raising her eyebrows at me. You don't know how frightening it is, when she raises her eyebrows. It makes me feel like going to live in the dungeon. But I don't want to stand for hours shaking hands with ambassadors, or listen to speeches, even if they are in my honor. I want—"

What did she want? That was the problem, really. She did not know.

"But he's so handsome, with those long eyelashes, and you know he's smart." Bertila lay back on the grass and stared at the chestnut leaves.

"Then you should marry him yourself. Honestly, I don't know what's gotten into you lately. You used to be so sensible, and now you're worse than Jaromila."

"Beast. As though a prince could marry a gardener's daughter." Bertila threw a chestnut, rejected by a squirrel the previous autumn because a worm had eaten through its center, at the Princess.

"Ouch. Stop it, or I'll start throwing them back at you. And not only do I have more chestnuts, I have much better aim. But seriously, Bertie, you'd make a better queen than I would. You're so beautifully patient and polite. And since you're already in love with his eyelashes ..."

"There you are," said Jaromila. "Lying in the dirt as usual, and talking with servants." She tapped one shoe, as pointed and uncomfortable as fashion demanded, on the grass.

"You're not wanted here," said Lucinda.

"But you're wanted at the reception, half an hour ago."

"You see?" said Lucinda to Bertila, in dismay. "You'd make a much better queen than I would!"

"And she'd be just as entitled to it," said Jaromila. She had also seen Lucinda walking with Radomir on the terrace, but she had reacted quite differently than the Queen. She could not tell you the length of Radomir's eyelashes, but she knew that one day he would be king.

"What do you mean?" asked Lucinda.

"Yes, what do you mean?" asked Bertila. She was usually patient, just as Lucinda had said, but today she would have liked to pull Jaromila's hair.

"Well, it's time someone told you," said Jaromila, shifting her feet, because it was difficult to stand on the grass, and because she was nervous. "But you can't tell anyone it was me." From the day the Princess had been found, Queen Margarethe had implied that Lucinda was her own child, born in Switzerland. No one at court had dared to question the Queen, and the Chamberlain and Countess Agata liked their positions too well to contradict her. But Jaromila had heard them discussing it one night, over glasses of sherry. If anyone found out that Jaromila had told the Princess, she would be sent to her grandmother's house in Dobromir, which had no electric lights or telephone, not even a phonograph.

"Told what?" asked Lucinda. "You'd better tell me quickly. I have a whole pile of chestnuts, and you can't run in those shoes."

"That you're not a princess at all. You were found in a basket under this chestnut tree, like a peasant's child."

That afternoon, the Queen had to tell Lucinda three times not to fidget in front of the French ambassador.

As soon as the reception was over, Lucinda ran up to her room and lay on her bed, staring up at the ceiling. Who was she, if she was not the Princess Lucinda? After a while, she got up and took off the dress she had worn to the reception, which had been itching all afternoon. She put on her pajamas. But she could not sleep. For the first time in her life, she opened the shutters on her bedroom windows and looked out. There was the moon, as full as a silver Kroner, casting the shadows of boxwood swans and hounds on the lawn.

In her slippers, she crept down the stairs and out the French doors to the terrace. She walked between the topiaries and the rose bushes, over the croquet lawn, to edge of the forest. There, she lay on the grass and stared up at the moon, through the branches of the chestnut tree. "Who am I?" she asked. It seemed to smile at her, but gave no answer.

Lucinda woke shivering, with dew on her pajamas. She had to sneak back into the castle without being seen by the footmen, who were already preparing for the party.

Jaromila had forgotten to set out the dress she was supposed to wear, a white dress the Queen had chosen, with a train she would probably trip over on the stairs. With a sigh, Lucinda opened the door of her dressing room and started looking through the dresses that hung there, all the dresses she had worn since her christening, for although Lucinda did not care about dresses, Queen Margarethe cared a great deal.

That was why she missed the excitement.

Jaromila had been afraid to go to the Princess' room that morning. Lucinda would certainly tell the Queen what she had said, and when the Queen found out—Jaromila remembered Dobromir. So she stayed in the ballroom, where Queen Margarethe was preparing for the party by changing her mind several times about who should sit where. Countess Agata was writing place cards, and the footmen were setting out the glasses for champagne.

King Karel, still in his slippers, wandered into the ballroom and said, "Margarethe, have you seen my crown? I thought I left it next to my bureau—"

That was when the shaking started. The ballroom shook as though the earth were opening beneath it. Jaromila, who was standing by the French doors, clutched at the curtains to stay upright. The Queen fell on

Countess Agata's lap, which made a relatively comfortable cushion. The King, less fortunate, stumbled into the footmen, who toppled like dominoes. Most of the champagne glasses crashed to the floor.

A voice resounded through the ballroom. "Bring me the Princess Lucinda!"

The King, recovering his breath, said, "Whatever was that?"

Prince Radomir ran into the room and said, "Was it an earthquake?"

One of the footmen, who had fallen by the French doors, said, "By Saint Benedek, that's the biggest dog I've ever seen."

The King went to the French doors, leaving Prince Radomir to pick up the Queen and the Countess. There, on the terrace, stood a hound, as white as milk and as large as a pony.

"Bring me the Princess Lucinda!" he said again, in a voice like thunder. Then he shook himself, and the ballroom shook with him, so the King had to hold on to a curtain, like Jaromila, to stay upright. The remaining champagne glasses crashed to the floor, and the footmen fell down again in a heap.

Nothing in King Karel's training had prepared him for an enormous hound on his terrace, a hound who evidently had the ability to shake his castle to its foundations (his training having focused on international diplomacy and the Viennese waltz). But he was a practical man. So he said, from behind the curtain, "Who are you, and what do you want with the Princess?"

"I am the Hound of the Moon. If you don't bring me the Princess Lucinda, I will bite the head off the statue of King Karel in front of the cathedral, and the steeple off the cathedral itself, and the turrets off the castle. And if I'm still hungry, I'll bite the roofs off all the houses in Karelstad—"

"Here she is, here is the Princess Lucinda!" said the Queen, pushing Jaromila out the French doors. Jaromila, surprised and frightened, screamed. The Countess, who has leaning on Radomir, also screamed and fainted.

But the hound grabbed Jaromila by the sash around her waist, leaped from the terrace and landed among the topiaries, then leaped through the rose garden and over the forest, into the clouds.

Lucinda never noticed. When the castle had shaken, all the dresses on the shelves of the dressing room had fallen on top of her, along with most of the shoes, and when she had crawled out from beneath them, she imagined that she had somehow shaken them down herself. And still the dress for the ball was nowhere to be found.

The hound dropped Jaromila on the floor of a cave whose walls were covered with crystals.

The first thing she said when she had regained her breath was, "I'm not the Princess Lucinda."

"We shall see," said the hound. "Get up, whoever you are, and take a seat."

At the center of the cave, arranged around a table, Jaromila saw three chairs. The first was an obvious example of Opulentism, which had been introduced at the Exposition Universelle in Paris. Its arms were carved to resemble griffins, with garnets for eyes, and it was elaborately gilded. The second was a chair any Sylvanian farmer could have carved on a winter night as he sat by his fireside. The third was simply a stool of white wood.

Surely he didn't expect her to sit on that. And as for the second chair, she wasn't a peasant. Jaromila sat in the first chair, on its cushion of crimson velvet, and put her arms on the griffins.

"Can I offer you something to drink?" asked the hound.

On the table, she saw three cups. The first was certainly gold, and probably Lalique. The others were unimportant, a silver cup like those common in Dobromir, which had a silver mine, and a cup of horn that a shepherd might have drunk from. Of course she would drink from the first. She took a careful sip. The wine it contained, as red as the griffins' eyes, gave her courage.

"I'm not the Princess Lucinda. You will take me home at once!"

"As you wish," said the hound. "But the journey might be cold. Can I offer you a coat?"

In his mouth he held three coats. The first was a crimson brocade embroidered with gold thread, which she had seen just that week in a catalog from Worth's. That was the coat she would wear, not the plain green wool, or the dingy white thing that the hound must have drooled on.

But as soon as she reached to take it, the hound opened his mouth, dropped the coats, and once again grabbed her sash. And then they were off, over the forests of Sylvania, over Karelstad and the croquet lawn, to the castle terrace.

The King was still trying to soothe the Queen, who was crying, "What have I done?" Prince Radomir was waving smelling salts under the Countess' nose. The footmen were trying to sweep up the shattered glasses.

Upstairs, Lucinda had finally found her dress. It was in the Queen's own dressing room, behind an ermine cape. She sighed with relief. Now at last she could go to the party.

Just as the hound landed, Jaromila's sash ripped, and she dropped to the terrace.

"Bring me the Princess Lucinda!" said the hound. "If you don't bring me the Princess, I will drink up the fountain in front of King Karel's statue, and the pond by the Secondary School that the children skate on, and the river Morek, whose waters run through all the faucets of Karelstad. And if I'm still thirsty, I'll drink up the Danube itself—"

"I am the Princess Lucinda," said a voice from the garden. Bertila walked up the terrace steps. She had woken early to see the preparations for the party, and had been watching all this time from behind the topiary stag.

"Isn't that the gardener's daughter?" asked Prince Radomir. But at that moment the Queen screamed (it seemed her turn), and nobody heard him.

Under ordinary circumstances, no one would have mistaken Bertila for a princess. Her dresses were often patched, and because her mother had died when she was born, she sewed on the patches herself, so they were usually crooked. But today all the servants not needed for the party had been given a holiday, and she was wearing an old dress of Lucinda's. Lucinda had been allowed to give it away because it had torn on a tree branch. Bertila had mended it (with the wrong color thread), but the rip was toward the back, so she hoped it would not be noticed.

"Climb on my back then," said the hound, and climb she did. She twisted her fingers into the hair at his neck, and held on as well as she could when he leaped from the terrace over the forests of Sylvania.

"Mama!" cried Jaromila, at which the Countess revived. But the Queen went into hysterics. And that was when Lucinda finally came down the stairs, holding her train, and stared about her, at the footmen sweeping the floor and the sobbing Queen.

"What in the world is going on?" she asked. King Karel tried to tell her, as did the Queen in broken sobs, and even the Countess, who clutched Prince Radomir's arm so hard that he could not answer. Jaromila tried to powder her nose in the mirror, because after all Prince Radomir was present.

"Radomir?" said Lucinda. And then Radomir explained about the hound and Bertila's deception.

"Well," said Lucinda, when the explanation was over. She turned to the King and Queen. "I think it's time you told me everything."

Bertila looked about the cave.

"Will you take a seat?" asked the hound.

"Thank you," said Bertila. Which chair should she choose? Or rather, which chair would Lucinda choose, since she must convince the hound? She had read Lucinda's copy of the Brothers Grimm, which Lucinda had left on the croquet lawn. This was surely a test. Her hands were shaking, and she could scarcely believe that she had spoken in the garden. But here she was, and the deception must continue. Whatever danger Lucinda was in, she must try to save her friend.

Surely Lucinda would never choose a chair so gaudy as the gold one. And a stool did not seem appropriate for a princess. But the wooden chair looked like the one her father had carved for her mother. Lucinda had sat in it often, when she came to the gardener's cottage. The wood had been sanded smooth by a careful hand, and ivy leaves had been painted over the arms and back. That was a chair fit for a princess of Sylvania. She sat down.

"Would you care for something to drink?" asked the hound.

"Thank you," said Bertila. "I really am thirsty."

Lucinda would make fun of the gold cup, and the cup of white horn was like the stool, too plain. But the silver cup, with the snowdrops in enamel, might have been made by the silversmiths of Dobromir, who were the finest in Sylvania. It was a cup fit for the Pope himself. She paused before taking a sip, but surely the hound would not hurt her. He had treated her well so far. The cup was filled with a delicate cider, which smelled like peaches.

"Thank you," she said. "And now I think I'm ready." Although she did not know what she was ready for.

"Very well," said the hound. "You must choose a coat for the journey."

Lucinda would never wear the crimson brocade. But the coat of green wool, with its silver buttons and tasseled hood, looked warm and regal enough for a princess. There was another coat beneath, but it looked tattered and worn.

"I'll wear this one," said Bertila.

"You're not the Princess Lucinda," said the hound.

Bertila stood silently, twisting the coat in her hands. "No" she said finally. "I'm sorry. I hope you don't blame me."

"It was brave of you," said the hound. "But you must return to the castle."

When he landed on the terrace with Bertila, Lucinda was waiting.

"You don't have to threaten anyone this time, or break any glasses," she said. "I'm Princess Lucinda, and I'm ready to go with you."

The Queen was sent to bed with a dose of laudanum. The King cancelled the invitations for the party. Countess Agata had a lunch of poached eggs with the Chamberlain and asked what the monarchy was coming to. Jaromila tried to find Prince Radomir. But he was sitting under the chestnut tree with Bertila, asking if she was all right, and if she was sure. Bertila was blushing and admiring his eyelashes.

"Will you take a seat?" asked the hound.

"What a strange stool," said Lucinda. She had never read the Brothers Grimm, although Bertila had handed her the book with a reproachful glance. "The wood seems to glow. I wonder where it comes from?"

"From the mountains of the moon," said the hound. "Down the slopes of those mountains flow rivers, and on the banks of those rivers grow willow trees, with leaves as white as paper. When the wind blows, they whisper secrets about what is past and what is to come. This stool is made from the wood of those willow trees."

"This is where I'll sit," said Lucinda.

"Can I offer you something to drink?" asked the hound.

"What a curious cup," said Lucinda, picking up the cup of horn. "It's so delicate that the light shines right through it."

"On the slopes of the mountains of the moon," said the hound, "wander herds of sheep, whose wool is as soft and white as thistledown. This cup is carved from the horn of a ram who roamed those mountains for a hundred years."

Lucinda drank from the cup. The water in it was cold, and tasted of snow.

"And now," said the hound, "you must choose a coat for our journey."

"Where are we going?" asked Lucinda. "Oh, how lovely!" She held up a coat that had been lying beneath the coats of crimson brocade and green wool. "Why, it's covered with feathers!"

"The rivers of the moon flow into lakes," said the hound, "and on those lakes live flocks of herons. They build their nests beneath the willow branches, and line them with feathers. There, they lay their eggs and raise their children through the summer. When winter comes, they return to Africa, leaving their nests behind. This coat is made from the feathers of those herons. As for your question, Princess—to meet your mother."

"My mother?" said Lucinda, sitting abruptly back down on the stool. "Oh, I don't know. I mean, until yesterday I thought Queen Margarethe— what is my mother like? Do you think she'll like me?"

The hound seemed to smile, or at least showed his teeth. "She's my mother also. I'm your brother, Lucinda, although we have different fathers. Mine was Sirius, the Dog Star. Yours was a science teacher at the Secondary School."

"And my mother—our mother?" asked Lucinda.

"Our mother is the Moon, and she's the one who sent me for you. Put on your coat, Lucinda. Its feathers will warm you in the darkness we must pass through. Now climb on my back. Mother is eager to see you, and we have waited long enough."

As though in a dream, for nothing in her life, not even the books on airplanes and mountain climbing, had prepared her for such an event, Lucinda put on the coat of white feathers and climbed on the back of the hound. He leaped to the edge of the cave, and then into the sky itself. She was surrounded at first by clouds, and then by stars. All the stars were visible to her, and the Pleiades waved to her as she flew past, calling out, "She's been waiting for you, Lucinda!" Sirius barked and wagged his tail, and the hound barked back. Then they were landing in a valley covered with grass as white as a handkerchief, by a lake whose waters shone like silver.

"Lucinda! Is that really you?"

The woman standing by the side of the lake had silver hair so long that it swept the grasses at her feet, but her face looked not much older than Lucinda's. She seemed at once very young and very old, and at the moment very anxious.

"It is," said the hound. "Go on," he said to Lucinda, nudging her with his nose. "Don't you want to meet her?"

Lucinda walked forward, awkwardly. "It's nice to meet you . . ."

"Oh, my dear," said the Moon, laughing and taking Lucinda in her arms, "I'm so happy to have found you at last!"

The Moon lived in a stone house surrounded by a garden of white roses. A white cat sat on the windowsill, watching Lucinda with eyes like silver Kroners.

"The soup will be ready in a moment," said the Moon. "I find that the journey between the earth and my home always makes me hungry."

"Do you travel to the earth?" asked Lucinda.

The Moon laughed again. Her laughter sounded like a silver bell, clear and sweet. "You would not have been born, otherwise! In a shed at the back of the house live my bats. Whenever I want to travel to the earth, I harness them and they pull me through the darkness. Perhaps later you'll help me feed them. They like the nectar of my roses. Here, blow on this if you think it's too hot."

She put a bowl of soup in front of Lucinda. It was the color of milk but smelled like chicken, and Lucinda suddenly realized that she had forgotten to eat breakfast.

"Tell me about that," said Lucinda. "I mean, how I was born. If you don't mind," she added. There was so much she wanted to know. How did one ask a mother one had just met?

"Well," said the Moon, sitting down at the table and clasping her hands. "Your father's name was Havel Kronborg. When he was a child, he would lie at night in his father's fields, in Dobromir, and look at the stars. But even then, I think, he loved me better than any of them. How glad I was when he received a scholarship to study astronomy in Berlin! And how proud when his first paper was published in a scientific journal. It was about me, of course, about my mountains and lakes. But when his father died, the farm had to be sold to pay the mortgage, so he worked as a science teacher at the Secondary School. Each night he wandered on the slopes of the mountains about Karelstad, observing the stars. And one night, I met him in the forest.

"How well I remember those months. I could only visit him when the moon was dark—even for love, I could not neglect my work. But each month that we met, our child—that was you, Lucinda—was closer to being born, and his book, *Observations on the Topography of the Moon*, closer to being completed.

"When you were born, I wrapped you in a blanket I had woven from the wool of my sheep, and laid you in a basket of willow branches. Your brother slept beside you and guarded you, and all the stars sang you lullabies."

"Was it this blanket?" asked Lucinda. Out of her pocket she pulled a blanket as fine as silk, which the King had given her in the course of his explanation. Her name was embroidered on one corner. She had been carrying it with her since, but had almost forgotten it. How far away Karelstad seemed, and the Queen, and her life as a princess.

The Moon reached out to touch it, and her eyes filled with silver tears. "Your father asked me to leave you with him for a month. How could I refuse? But I told him to set you in the moonlight every night, so I could see you. One night, while he was gathering mushrooms in the forest for a botany lesson, he placed your basket beneath a tree. I watched you lying there, laughing up at me. But suddenly a cloud came between us, and when it had passed, you were gone.

"You can't imagine his grief. He searched all that night through the forest around the castle. When the gardener found him in the morning, he was coughing, and could not speak. The doctor told him he had caught pneumonia. He died a week later. I found the basket by his bedside. It's the only thing I've had of yours, all these years."

Silver tears trickled down her cheeks. She wiped them away with the blanket.

Lucinda reached out her hand, not knowing what to say. The Moon took it in her own, and smiled through her tears. "But now we've found each other. How like him you look, so practical and solemn. I searched the world for years, but never saw you until last night, lying beneath the tree where he had left you. I knew who you were at once, although you've grown so tall. Will you walk with me, Lucinda? I want to show you the country where you were born."

The strangest thing about being on the moon was how familiar it seemed. Lucinda learned to feed the bats, gathering white roses from the garden, tying them together in bundles, and hanging them upside down from the rafters where the bats slept through the night, while the moon was shining. She learned to call the sheep that roamed the mountains, and to comb their fleece. The Moon spun the long hairs caught in the comb on a spinning wheel that sang as it whirled. She learned to gather branches from the willow trees and weave them into baskets, like the one the Moon had shown her, saying, "This is where you slept, as a child."

Sometimes, after the night's work was done, she would sit with the Moon beside the lake, watching the herons teach their children to fly. They would talk about Lucinda's childhood in Karelstad, or the Moon's childhood, long ago, and the things she had seen, when elephants roamed through Sylvania, and the Romans built their roads through its forests, and Morek drove out the Romans, claiming its fertile valleys for his tribe, and Karel I raised an army of farmers and merchants, and drove out the Turks. Then they would lie on the grass and look at the stars dancing above them.

"Their dances were ancient before I was born," said the Moon. "Look at Alcyone! She always wears diamonds in her hair. And Sirius capering among them. We were in love, when I was young. But we each had our work to do, and it could not last. Ah, here is your brother."

The white hound lay next to Lucinda. She put her arm around him, and the three of them watched the stars in their ancient dances.

One day, the Moon showed Lucinda her observatory, on a slope above the lake. "This is where I watch what happens on the earth," she said.

Lucinda put her eye to the telescope. "I can see the castle at Karelstad."

"That was where I last looked," said the Moon. "Since you've been here, I've had no wish to look at the earth. It reminds me of the years before I found you."

"There's Bertila, walking in the garden with Radomir. I can see Jaromila. She's looking in her mirror. And King Karel is talking to the French ambassador. Why do they look so sad? Well, except Jaromila. And there's the Queen. Why, she seems to be crying. And I've never seen her wearing a black dress. Oh!" said Lucinda. "Is it me? Do they think I'm dead?"

The Moon looked at her sadly.

"I'm so sorry," said Lucinda. "It's just—I grew up with them all. And Queen Margarethe was my mother. I mean, I thought she was."

"She was, my dear," said the Moon. "She was the best mother she could be, and so I forgive her, although she has caused me much grief. I knew that eventually you'd want to return to the earth. It's where your father belonged, and you belong there also. But you will come to visit me, won't you?"

"Of course I will, Mother," said Lucinda.

That night, while the moon was shining, they harnessed the bats. Lucinda put on her coat of heron feathers, and took the reigns.

"Before you go," said the Moon, "I have something to give you. This is the book your father wrote. I've kept it for many years, but I would like you to have it. After all, I have my memories of him." For a moment, she held Lucinda, then said to the bats, "Fly swiftly!"

The bats lifted Lucinda above the white roses in the garden, and above the stone house. The Moon called, "Goodbye, my dear," and then she was flying over the mountains of the moon and toward the earth, which lay wrapped in darkness.

She landed on the castle terrace, just as the sun was rising over the forest around Karelstad. Lucinda released the reigns, then ran into the castle and up the stairs, to the Queen's bedroom.

Queen Margarethe was sitting by the window. She had not slept all night, and her eyes were red with weeping. She thought she must be dreaming when she saw Lucinda enter the room and say, "Good morning, Mother."

Lucinda's sixteenth birthday party took place a month late, but was perhaps all the merrier. The orchestra from Prague played, the champagne flowed freely, and the footmen danced with each other in the hall. Under a glittering chandelier, the French ambassador asked Jaromila to marry him, and on the terrace, beneath a full moon, Radomir asked Bertila the same question.

When Lucinda went to her room that night, her head spinning from champagne and her feet aching from the narrow shoes, she found a white stool on which sat a white cup. In the cup was a silver necklace. From it hung a moonstone, which glowed like the moon itself, and next to the cup was a card on which was written, in silver ink, "Happy Birthday, my dear."

The next morning, Lucinda went to the graveyard behind the cathedral. There, by the grave of a forgotten science teacher, she laid a bouquet of white roses.

Observations on the Topography of the Moon received an enthusiastic reception among astronomers in London, Paris, and New York, and was widely quoted in the scientific journals. It was eventually included in the Secondary School curriculum, and the author's portrait appeared on the two Zlata stamp.

After her husband's death, Jaromila opened a couture house in Paris and became famous as the inventor of the stiletto heel. When Radomir finished his degree in engineering, King Karel retired. He and Queen Margarethe lived to a contented old age in the country. King Radomir and Queen Bertila guided Sylvania through two world wars. Karelstad eventually became a center of international banking, where even the streets were said to be paved with Kroners. They sat together listening to the radio on the night Lucinda won the Nobel prize for her theories on astrophysics.

But no one, except the white hound that was occasionally seen wandering around the garden of her house in Dobromir, ever found out that she had been the first person on the moon.

Theodora Goss's publications include the short story collection *In the Forest of Forgetting; Interfictions*, a short story anthology coedited with Delia Sherman; *Voices from Fairyland*, a poetry anthology with critical essays and a selection of her own poems; *The Thorn and the Blossom*, a novella in a two-sided accordion format; and the poetry collection *Songs for Ophelia*. She has been a finalist for the Nebula, Crawford, Locus, Seiun, and Mythopoeic Awards, and on the Tiptree Award Honor List. Her short story "Singing of Mount Abora" won the World Fantasy Award. She teaches literature and writing at Boston University and in the Stonecoast MFA Program. Her first novel will be published in 2017.

"Dozois captures the voice of the fairy tale perfectly," Jeffrey Ford has written of "Fairy Tale." Ford also notes Dozois "grabbed" fairy tales conventions "roughly by the collar, smacked them around, and kicked them squarely in the ass. [The story] subjects the style, structure, and intent of the fairy tale to a Hobbesian wake-up call. With great precision and artifice Dozois tantalizes us by promising the fulfillment of our deepest expectations of this form and then one by one undercuts them by prying open the usually hermetically sealed world of fantasy and letting reality slither in."

I couldn't come close to saying it as well.

Fairy Tale

Gardner Dozois

I t wasn't a village, as is sometimes said these days, when we've forgotten just how small the old world was. In those days, long ago in a world now vanished with barely a trace left behind, a village was four or five houses and their outbuildings. A *large* village was maybe ten or fifteen houses at a crossroad, and perhaps an inn or *gasthaus*.

No, it was a town, even a moderately large one, on the banks of a sluggish brown river, the capital of a small province in a small country, lost and nearly forgotten—even then—in the immensity of the Central European steppes that stretch endlessly from the Barents Sea to the Black, and from the Urals to France. The nearest electric light was in Prague, hundreds of miles away. Even gaslighting was newfangled and marvelous here, although there were a few rich homes on the High Street that had it. Only the King and the Mayor and a few of the most prosperous merchants had indoor toilets.

The Romans had been here once, and as you followed the only road across the empty steppe toward town, you would pass the broken white marble pillars they had left behind them, as well as a vine-overgrown fane where, in another story, you might have ventured forth at night to view for yourself the strange lights that local legends say haunt the spot, and perhaps, your heart in your throat, glimpsed the misty shapes of ancient pagan gods as they flitted among the ruined columns ... but this isn't that kind of story.

Further in, the road would cut across wide fields of wheat being worked by stooped-over peasants, bent double with their butts in the air, moving forward a step at a time with a sort of swaying, shuffling motion as they weeded, sweeping their arms back and forth over the ground like searching trunks, making them look like some strange herd of small double-trunked elephants, or those men who wear their heads below their navels. The bushes are decorated with crucified rabbits, tarry black blood matting their fur, teeth bared in death agony, a warning to their still-living brethren to stay away from the crops.

As the road fell down out of the fields and turned into the High Street of the town, you would see old peasant women, dressed all in black from head to foot, spilling buckets of water over the stone steps of the tall narrow houses on either side of the narrow street, and then scrubbing the steps with stiff-bristled brooms. Occasionally, as you passed, one or another of the old peasant women would straighten up and stare unwinkingly at you with opaque agate eyes, like a black and ancient bird.

At the foot of the High Street, you would see a castle looming above the river, small by the standards of more prosperous countries elsewhere in Europe, but large enough to have dominated the tactical landscape in the days before gunpowder and cannon made all such places obsolete. It's a grim enough pile, and, in another story, cruel vampire lords would live there—but this isn't that kind of story either. Instead of vampires, the King lived there, or lived there for a few months each year, anyway, as he graciously moved his court from province to province, spreading the considerable financial burden of supporting it around.

He was what was called "a good King," which meant that he didn't oppress the peasants any more than he was traditionally allowed to, and occasionally even distributed some small largess to them when he was able, on the ancient principal, sound husbandry, that you get more work out of your animals when they're moderately well-fed and therefore reasonably healthy. So he was a good King, or a good-enough King, at any rate. But in many a dimly lit kitchen or bistro or backroom bar, the old men of the town huddled around their potbellied stoves at night and warmed their hands, or tried to, and muttered fearfully about what might happen when the Old King died, and his son and heir took over.

But as this isn't really a story of palace intrigue, either, or only partially so, you must move on to a large but somewhat shabby-gentile house, one that has seen better days, in a shady street on the very outskirts of town, the kind of neighborhood that will be swallowed by the expanding town and replaced by rows of worker's flats in thirty years or so. That girl there, sullenly and rather uselessly scrubbing down the flagstones in the small courtyard, is the one we're interested in.

For the kind of story this *is*, is a fairy tale. Sort of.

There are some things they don't tell you, of course, even in the Grimm's version, let alone the Disney.

For one thing, no one ever called her "Cinderella," although occasionally they called her much worse. Her name was Eleanor, an easy-enough name to use, and no one ever really paid enough attention to her to bother to come up with a nickname for her, even a cruel and taunting one. Most of the time, no one paid enough attention to her even to taunt her.

There *was* a stepmother, although whether she was evil or not depended on your point of view. These were hard times in a hard age, when even the relatively well-to-do lived not far from hunger and privation, and if she chose to take care of her own children first in preference to her dead husband's child, well, there were many who would not blame her for that. In fact, many would instead compliment her on her generosity in giving her husband's by-blow a place in her home and at her heath when no law of Man or God required her to do so, or to lift a finger to insure the child's survival. Many *did* so complement her, and the stepmother would lift her eyes piously to Heaven, and throw her hands in the air, and mutter modest demurements.

For one of the things that they never tell you, a missing piece that helps make sense of the whole situation, is that Cinderella was a bastard. Yes, her father had doted on her, lavishing love and affection on her, had taken her into his house and raised her from a babe, but he had never married Eleanor's mother, who had died in childbirth, and he himself had died after marrying the Evil Stepmother but *before* making a will that would have legally enforced some kind of legacy or endowment for his bastard daughter.

Today, of course, she would sue, and there'd be court-battles and DNA-testing, and appearances with lots of shouting on daytime talk-shows, and probably she would eventually win a slice of the pie. In those days, in that part of the world, she had no recourse under the law—or anywhere else, since the Church shunned those born in sin.

So the stepmother really *was* being quite generous in continuing to supply Eleanor's room and board rather than throwing her out of the house to freeze and starve in the street. That she didn't as well provide much in the way of warmth of familial affection, being icy and remote to Eleanor—the visible and undeniable evidence of her late husband's love for another woman—on those rare occasions when she deigned to notice her at all, is probably not surprising, and to really expect her to feel otherwise is perhaps more than could be asked. She had problems of her own, after all, and had already gone a long mile further than she needed to just by continuing to feed the child in the first place.

There were stepsisters too, children of a previous marriage (a marriage where the husband had *also* died young . . . but before you're tempted to cast the stepmother in a Black Widow scenario, keep in mind that in those days, in that place, dying young was not an especially rare phenomenon), but they were not particularly evil either—although they didn't much like Eleanor, and let it show. However, they were no more cruel and vindictive—but no less, either—than most young girls forced into the company of someone they didn't much like, someone of fallen status whom their mother didn't much like either and made no particular effort to protect. Someone who, truth be told, had probably lorded it over *them*, just a little bit, when she was her father's favorite and they were the new girls in the household.

Neither were the stepsisters particularly ugly; this is something that came in with Disney, who always equates ugliness with evil. They were, in fact, quite acceptably attractive by the standards of their day.

Although it is true that when Eleanor was around, they tended to dim in her presence, in male eyes at least, as bright bulbs can be dimmed by a brighter one.

Eleanor *was* beautiful, of course. We have to give her that much if the rest of the story is going to make any sense. Like her stepsisters, she had been brought up as a child of the relatively prosperous merchant class, which ensured that she had been well-enough nourished as a babe to have grown up with good teeth and glossy hair and strong, straight bones—unlike the peasants, who were often afflicted with rickets and other vitamin-deficiency diseases.

No doubt she had breasts and legs, like other young women, but whether her breasts were large or small, whether her legs were long or squat, is impossible to tell at this distant point in time.

We can tell from the story, though, that she was considered to be striking, and perhaps a bit unusual; so, since no one knows what she really looked like, let's cater to the tastes of our own time and say that she was tall and coltish, with long lovely legs and small—but not *too* small—breasts, a contrast to many around her upon whom a diet consisting largely of potatoes and coarse black bread had imposed a dumpier sort of physique.

Since this tale is set in that part of Central Europe that had changed hands dozens of times in the past few hundred years and was destined to change hands again a few times more before the century was out, with every wave of raping-and-pillaging Romans, Celts, Goths, Huns, Russians, Mongols, and Turks scrambling the gene-pool a bit further, let's also say that she had red hair and green eyes and a pale complexion, a rare but possible combination, given the presence of Russian and Celtic DNA in the genetic stew. That should make her sufficiently distinctive. (It's possible, of course, that she *really* looked like a female Russian weight-lifter, complete with faint mustache, or like a walking potato, and you're welcome to picture her that way instead if you'd like—but if so, you must grant at least that she was a striking and *charismatic* weight-lifter or potato, one who had had men sniffing around her from the time she started to grow hair in places other than her head.)

In truth, like most "beautiful" women, who often are not really even pretty if you can catch them on those rare occasions when their faces are in repose, her allure was based in large part on her charisma and *élan*, and a personality that, to date, at least, remained vital and intense in spite of a life that increasingly tried to grind her down.

Eleanor didn't wait on the others to the degree shown in the Disney version, of course—this was a hard society, and everyone had to work, including the stepmother and the two stepsisters. Much of the cost of maintaining the house (which was not a working farm, regardless of what the stories tell you, too close to the center of town, although they may have kept a few chickens) was defrayed by revenues from land that Eleanor's father had owned elsewhere, but those revenues had slowly declined since the father's death, and in order to keep a tenuous foot-hold on the middle-class, they had been forced to take in seamstress work, which occupied all of them for several hours a day.

It's true, though, that since her father died, two years before, and since revenues had declined enough to preclude keeping servants, that much of the rest of the work of maintaining the household had fallen on Eleanor's shoulders, in addition to her seamstress chores.

She found it bitterly hard, as would you; in fact, spoiled by modernity, we'd find it even more onerous than she did, and suffer even more keenly. Housework was hard physical labor in those days, especially in the backward hinterlands of Central Europe, where even the (from our perspective) minimal household conveniences that might be available to a rich family in London would not arrive for a long lifetime, or maybe two. Housework was brutal and unrelenting labor, stretching from dawn until well after dusk, the equivalent in its demands on someone's reserves of strength and endurance of working on a road-gang or in a coal mine; it was the main reason, along with the demands and dangers of childbirth, why women wore out so fast and died so young. Not for nothing did the phrase "Slaving over a hot stove" come into existence; doing laundry was even worse, a task so demanding—pounding the clothes, twisting them dry, starting over again—that it was rarely tackled more than once a week even in households where there were several women to divide the work up amongst them; and scrubbing, inside or out, was done on your knees in any and all weathers, with a stiff-bristled brush and raw potash soap that stung your nostrils and blistered your hands.

Of course, every *other* woman in this society, except for the very richest, had to deal with these kind of labors as well, so there was nothing unique about Eleanor's lot, or any reason to feel sorry for her *in particular*, as the stories sometimes seem to invite us to do . . . the subtext pretty obviously being that she is an aristocrat-in-hiding, or at least a member of the prosperous upper class, being forced to do the work of a *peasant*. Think of that! Being made to work just like a common, ordinary girl! As if she wasn't any better than anyone else! (Oddly enough, this reaction of indignation usually comes from people who have to work for a living every day *themselves*, not from whatever millionaires or members of the peerage might be lurking in the audience.)

In fact, though, Eleanor had also been spoiled, not by modernity but by her father, sheltered by his money from most of the chores even a child of the merchant class would usually have had to become inured to . . . so perhaps she did feel it more keenly than most women of her day would have. Her father had also spoiled her in other ways, though, more significant ways, teaching her to read (something still frowned upon, if no longer actively forbidden by law), teaching her to love books and learning, teaching her to dream. Teaching her to be *ambitious*—but ambitious for what purpose? She had a good mind, and her father had given her the beginnings of a decent education, but what was she supposed to *do* with it? Further formal schooling was out of the question, even if there had been money for it—that was for men. All the professions were for men as well. There was nothing she could do, no way her life could change. She was doomed to stay here in this once-loved house she had come to hate, working like a slave day and night for people she didn't even like, much less consider to be family, until her youth and strength and beauty drained away like water spilled in the street, and she woke up one day to find herself spavined and old.

She could feel this doom closing in around her like a black cloud, making every day a little more hopeless and bitter and grim. She could feel herself dying, a little bit every day, her mind dulling, her strength and resiliency waning.

Somehow, she had to get *out* of here.

But there was no way out. . . .

After several months of this bleak circle, she decided at last that there was only one possible way to escape: she would trade sex for a better life—or at least a more comfortable one.

It was a choice that untold thousands of young women—and not a few men—had made before her, and that thousands more would make after her. She'd looked her situation over with cold-eyed clarity, and realized that she had no commodity to offer that anyone would ever value except for youth, beauty, and virginity—and that none of them were going to last long. A few more years of constant grinding toil would take care of the youth and beauty, and sooner or later one of the men who had been circling her with increasing persistence would corner her in the stables or behind a market stall or in an alley somewhere and rape her, and that would be the end of her virginity (a valuable commodity ever since syphilis had started to ravage Europe a few centuries back) as well. If he got her pregnant, she'd be stuck here forever.

Young as she was, she was not unaware of the trick that her body could be made to do when she huddled alone in the darkness on her cot at night, biting a dish-cloth to keep anyone from hearing the sounds that she couldn't stop herself from making, and she was not so hard-headed as to be immune to thoughts of love and romance and marriage. In fact, she'd exchanged hot glances, longing words, and one quick delicious kiss with Casimir, a big, lumbering, sweet-natured boy who worked in the glass foundry a street away. She was pretty sure that she could win his heart, perhaps even get him to marry her—but what good would that do? Even if they could somehow scrape up enough money to live on, she'd still be stuck in this stifling provincial town, living much the same kind of life she was living now. And then the children would start coming, one a year until she wore out and died. . . .

No, love and marriage were not going to save her. Sex was going to have to do that. She'd have to trade her body to someone rich enough to take her out of here, out of this life, perhaps even, if things worked out for the best, out of this town altogether.

Eleanor's religious upbringing had not perhaps been the strictest possible, her father tending towards clandestine secularism, but of course, she still had some qualms about the idea of selling herself in this fashion. Still, she had heard the women talking at the well or in the marketplace or even in the church when no man was around to hear, and it didn't sound all that difficult. Lay on your back, open your legs, let him grunt on top of you for five minutes while you stared at the ceiling. A lot less difficult than scrubbing the floor until your fingers bleed.

But if she was going to sell herself, she was damned if she wasn't going to get the best price possible.

Eleanor prided herself on her clear-eyed logic and hardheaded rationality, but here's where her plan began to be tinged by a deep vein of pastel romanticism that she wouldn't even have admitted to herself that she possessed.

She had no intention of becoming a common whore, if whore she must be. Even a town of this size had a few such, and the life they led was nothing to envy or emulate. No, she would set her sights higher.

Why not set them as high as they would go?

The Prince. She had seen him go by in a parade once, the year before, up on a prancing roan stallion, tall and handsome, his plumed hat nodding, the silver fastenings on his uniform gleaming in the sun. She'd even had hot dreams about him, those nights when his ghost rather than Casimir's had visited her in her bed.

She was realistic enough to know that marriage was out of the question. Princes didn't marry commoners, even those from families with a lot more money than her own. It was just never going to happen. That was so ingrained in her worldview that she never entertained the possibility that the Prince would marry her, even as the remotest fantasy.

Princes did *fuck* commoners, though, that happened all the time, and always had. And if they liked them well enough, sometimes they *kept* them. Being a royal mistress didn't sound so bad; since she had no choice, she'd settle for that.

All she had to do was get him to want her.

Why not? He was a man, wasn't he? Every other man she knew pursued her and tried to grope her or worse when there was nobody else around, even men three times her age. Maybe a Prince would be no different.

And if for some reason the Prince *didn't* like her, she thought, with a flash of the practical shrewdness that was so typical of her, the palace would be full of other rich men. *Somebody* would want her.

There was a Ball at the palace every weekend when the King and his court were in residency during the summer months. Her family was not rich enough for any of them to be invited to these affairs, nor ever had been, even at their most prosperous. But she would get in *some*how.

Well, we all know what comes next, of course. The dress made in secret, although there were no birds or mice to help her. Nor did she need any—she was, after all, a seamstress. There were no Fairy Godmothers either, no pumpkins turned to coaches, no magically conjured horses. She slipped out of the house while her stepmother, a woman who had been embittered and disappointed by life, was slowly drinking herself sodden with her nightly regimen of alternating glasses of *tisane* and brandy, and walked all the way through town to the river, the night air like velvet around her, the blood pounding in her throat, the castle slowly rising higher and higher above the houses, blazing with lights, as she drew near.

Somehow, she got inside. Who knows how? Maybe the guards were reluctant to stop a beautiful and well-dressed young woman who moved with easy confidence. Maybe she walked in with a group of other partygoers. Maybe the guards were all drunk, and she just walked by them.

Maybe there were no guards, in this sleepy backwater in a time without a major war brewing. Maybe there were guards, but they just didn't care.

However she did it, she got in, and it was everything she'd ever dreamed of.

It *was* glamorous. Give them their due; the aristocracy has always known how to do glamorous.

Although the grim Gothic tower with its battlements and crenellations and murder-holes still loomed darkly up behind, this part of the castle had been modernized and made into a palace instead. In the Grand Ballroom, there were floor-to-ceiling windows that overlooked the whole sweep of the town, which was stretched out below like a diorama on a tabletop, there were balconies and tapestried alcoves with richly embroidered Oriental hangings, there were flowers everywhere, and a polished marble floor that seemed to stretch on forever, shimmering in the light of a thousand candles like a lake of mist lit by moonlight. Out on the marble floor, people in vivid, multi-colored clothes twirled around like butterflies caught in a whirlwind, while music filled all the air, thick and rich and hot as blood, and made the nerves jump under the skin.

It *was* glamorous, as long as you didn't get too close to the privies (it was a warm summer night, after all). This would bother you, though, more than it bothered Eleanor, who was already used to an everyday level of stink that would have turned the stomachs of most moderns.

Cranking her charm to its highest setting, palms damp, she swallowed her fear and mingled.

She didn't really fool anyone, of course. She was a good seamstress, but the materials she'd had to work with were nowhere near fine enough for court fashion. But it didn't matter much. She was beautiful, and charming, and vivacious, and still had enough of the remnants of society manners learned before her family fell on harder times to get by—although she wasn't fooling anybody there, either. No matter. She was an exotic amusement, someone new in over-familiar court circles where everyone had worked through all possible permutations of their relationships with everyone else long before. They'd have tired of her within days, of course, but by then she might well have found some rich young gentleman willing to take her on as a toy, and perhaps even keep her for a while . . . so her plan might actually have worked, if she'd been willing to settle for someone less exalted.

But then the Prince crossed the floor, and stood at the edge of the ring of preening young men who now surrounded her, and their eyes met, and his first grew round with surprise, and then slowly grew hot.

He strode forward, the crowd of lesser men melting away before him, and held out his hand, imperiously commanding her to dance, all the while his eyes smoldered at her. She'd never seen anyone so handsome.

Eleanor took his hand and they spun away, and for a second, gliding across the softly gleaming marble floor, moving with him with the music all around them, it seemed like the perfect culmination of every fairy tale she'd ever read.

Then he yanked her roughly aside into one of the curtained alcoves, tugging the hangings shut behind them. There was a divan in there, and an oil-lamp, and a small table with a nearly empty bottle of brandy on it. The air was thick and foul, with a strong reek of pungent animal musk to it, like the den of a panther or a bear, and the divan was rumpled and stained.

Startled, she started to speak, but the Prince waved her brusquely to silence. For a long moment, the Prince stared at her, coldly, sneeringly, contemptuously, almost as if he hated her. His heavy, handsome face was harsh and cruel, cold as winter ice in spite of the heat that burned in his small hard eyes. He was visciously drunk, his face flushed, swaying where he stood, and he reeked of brandy and sweat and old semen, a streak of which still glistened on his pants from some previous encounter earlier in the evening. He made a wet, gloating noise, like a greedy child smacking its lips, and swept Eleanor crushingly into his arms.

All at once, he was kissing her brutally, biting her lips, forcing his tongue into her mouth, his breath like death, the taste of him sour and rancid and bitter. He grabbed her breasts, squeezing them savagely with his powerful hands, mashing and twisting them, so that sudden blinding pain shot through her.

Then he was forcing her down onto the divan, bearing her down under his crushing weight, tearing at her clothes, forcing a knee roughly between her legs, prying them open.

If she'd been as hardheaded and practical as she thought she was, she would have laid back and let him force himself on her, endured his grunting and thrusting and battering either in silence or with as much of a simulation of passionate enjoyment as she could muster, let him contemptuously wipe his dick on her afterward and then tell him how witty that was. But as he bore her down, smothering her under his weight and stench, bruising her flesh with his vise-like fingers, all her buried romanticism came rushing to the surface—it wasn't supposed to be like this!—and as she heard her dress and undergarments rip under his tearing hands and felt the night air on her suddenly exposed breasts, she fought herself free with a sudden burst of panicked strength, and clawed the Prince's face.

They both leaped to their feet. The Prince stared at her in astonishment for a moment, three deep claw marks on his cheek dripping vivid red blood, and then came for her again, murder rather than sex on his mind this time.

Eleanor had been attacked before—once by a stable hand and once by a greengrocer in a lane behind the market at dusk—and she knew what to do.

She kicked the Prince hard in the crotch, putting her weight and the strength of her powerful young legs into it, and the Prince mewed and folded and fell, wrapping himself into a tight ball on the floor, for the instant too shocked by pain even to scream.

Eleanor's practicality returned with a rush. She was moments away from being arrested, and probably jailed for the rest of her life, certainly for many years. Maybe they'd even execute her. What the Prince had tried to do to her wouldn't matter, she knew. No one would care. All that would count was what *she* had done to *him*.

She gathered her ruined dress around her, hiding her breasts as well as she could, and fled the alcove. Straight across the Grand Ballroom and out of the palace, as fast as she could go without actually running, as voices began to rise in the distance behind her, and the palace clock chimed midnight.

You know the rest, or you think that you do.

The next day, the Prince did begin searching obsessively for her, but it was for revenge, not for love; the three red weals across his handsome face filled him with a rage that momentarily eclipsed even drinking and screwing, his usual preoccupations, and goaded him to furious action.

Fortunately for Eleanor, she had been wise enough not to use her real name, or her full name, at least, with those she'd talked with at the Ball, and as she was not a regular in court circles, nobody knew where to find her.

That was where the famous slipper came in. Yes, there was a slipper, but it was an ordinary one, not one made of glass. "Glass" is a mistranslation of the French word used by Perrault; what he really said was "fur." It wasn't fur either. For that matter, it wasn't really a slipper. It was an ordinary dress shoe of the type appropriate to that time and place.

But it *had* slipped off Eleanor's foot while she struggled with the Prince in the alcove, and it *was* infused with her scent. By mid-afternoon the next day, the secret police were using teams of keen-nosed hunting dogs, following her scent on the slipper, to try to track her through the streets to her home.

There was, of course, no nonsense about trying the slipper on the feet of every woman in the kingdom. Nor did Eleanor's stepsisters cut bits of their own feet off in order to try to get them to fit into the slipper, as some versions of this story would have it. Nor did flocks of angry birds fly down and peck out their eyes and bite off their noses (a scene Disney inexplicably missed somehow), as in other versions.

In fact, except for a glimpse of her stepmother lying down in a darkened room with a wet cloth over her eyes, seen when Eleanor sneaked cautiously into the house late the previous evening, Eleanor never saw her stepmother or her stepsisters again.

The Prince had his hunt organized and moving by noon, pretty early for a Prince, especially a mammothly hung-over one, which shows you how serious he was about revenge. Fortunately for Eleanor, *she* was used to rising at the crack of dawn, so she got the jump on him.

In fact, she hadn't slept at all that night, but had spent the night with plans and preparations. She didn't know about the slipper-sniffing dogs, of course, but she knew that this was a small enough town that the Prince could find her eventually if he wanted to badly enough, and she was shrewd enough to guess that he would.

So by the time the sky was lightening in the east, and the birds were twittering in the branches of the trees in the wet gray dawn (perhaps arguing about whether pecking out the eyes of Eleanor's stepsisters was *really* a good use of their time), Eleanor was out the door with a coarse burlap sack in which she'd secreted a few hunks of bread and cheese, and what was left of her father's silver service, which usually resided in a locked highboy—the key for which was kept somewhere that Eleanor wasn't supposed to know about.

Her next stop was to intercept Casimir on his way to the glass foundry and talk faster and more earnestly than she ever had in her life, for she'd

{}

suddenly realized that although she still wanted to get *out*, she didn't want to go without *him*.

What she said to convince him, we'll never know. Perhaps he wasn't all that difficult to convince; having no family and only minimal prospects, he had little to lose here himself. Perhaps he'd wanted to run away with her all along, but was too shy to ask.

Whatever she said, it worked. He slipped back into his room to retrieve from under a loose floorboard a small amount of money he'd been able to save—perhaps against the day he could convince Eleanor to marry him—and then they were off.

By now, everybody in town knew about the slipper and the hunt for the Mystery Girl, and you could already hear the hounds baying in the distance.

They escaped from town by hiding in a dung cart—Eleanor's idea, to kill her scent.

After scrubbing in a fast-moving stream, while she shyly hid her breasts from him and he pretended not to look, they set off on foot across the countryside, walking the back roads to avoid pursuit, hitching rides in market-bound farmer's carts, later catching a narrow-gauge train that started and stopped, stopped and started, sometimes, for no apparent reason, sitting motionless for hours at tiny deserted stations where weeds grew up through the tracks and dogs slept on their backs on the empty sun-drenched platforms, all four legs in the air. In this manner, they inched their way across Europe, slowly running through Casimir's small store of cash, living on black bread, stale cheese, and sour red wine.

In Hamburg, they sold Eleanor's father's silver to buy passage on a ship going to the United States, and some crudely forged identity papers. Before they were allowed aboard with their questionable papers, Eleanor had to blow the harbormaster, kneeling before him on the rough plank floor of his office, splinters digging into her knees, while he jammed his thick dirty cock that smelled like a dead lizard into her mouth, and she tried not to gag.

Casimir never found out; there were some of the harbormaster's companions who would have preferred for *him* to pay their unofficial passage fee rather than her, and Casimir, still being a boy in many ways, would have indignantly refused, and they would have been caught and maybe killed. She considered it a small enough price to pay for getting a chance at a new life in a new world, and rarely thought about it thereafter. She figured that Casimir had nothing to complain about, as when she did come to his bed, after they had been safely married in the New World, she came to it as a virgin, and they had the bloody sheet to prove it (just as well, too—Casimir was a good man, and a sweet-natured one, but he *was* a man of his time, after all, and couldn't be expected to be *too* liberal about things).

They made their way eventually to Chicago, where work for seam-stresses and glaziers could be had, and where they had forty-five tumul-tuous years together, sometimes happy, sometimes not, until one bitter winter afternoon, carrying a pane of glass through the sooty city snow, Casimir's heart broke in his chest.

Eleanor lived another twenty years, and died on a cot in the kitchen near the stove (in the last few days, she'd refused to be taken upstairs to the bedroom), surrounded by children and grandchildren, and by the homey smells of cooked food, wood smoke, and the sharper smells of potash and lye, all of which she now found oddly comforting, although she'd hated them when she was young. She regretted nothing that she'd ever done in her life, and, except for a few moments at the very end when her body took over and struggled uselessly to breathe, her passing was as easy as any human being's has ever been.

After the Old King died, the Prince only got to reign for a few years before the monarchy was overthrown by civil war. The Prince and the rest of the royal family and most of the nobility were executed, kind or cruel, innocent or corrupt. The winning side fell in its turn, some decades later, and eventually a military junta, run by a local Strongman, took over.

Years later, Eleanor's grandson was in command of a column of tanks that entered and conquered the town, since one of the Strongman's suc-cessors had allied himself with the Axis.

Later that night, Eleanor's grandson climbed up to the ruins of the royal castle, mostly destroyed in an earlier battle, and looked out over the remains of the floor of the Grand Ballroom, open now to the night sky, weeds growing up through cracks in the once brilliantly polished marble that still gleamed dully in the moonlight, and wondered why he felt a moment of drifting melancholy, a twinge of sorrow that quickly dissipated, like waking from a sad dream that fades even as you try to remember it, and is gone.

Gardner Dozois is the founding editor of *The Year's Best Science Fiction* anthologies (1984–present) and was editor of *Asimov's Science Fiction* magazine (1984–2004), garnering fifteen Hugo Awards and thirty-two Locus Awards for editing. He has edited more than one hundred anthologies not including the (so-far) thirty-three volumes of *The Year's Best*. As a writer, he's authored more than fifty short stories and twice won the Nebula Award for Best Short Story. He was inducted into the Science Fiction Hall of Fame in 2011.

"The Queen Who Could Not Walk" has no basis in any particular fairy tale, but like many older stories it has a king, a queen, a wise beggar woman, and a journey to understanding and forgiveness that plucks on the heartstrings.

The Queen Who Could Not Walk

Peter S. Beagle

F ar Away And Long Ago is a real country, older and more enduring than any bound by degrees and hours and minutes on a map.
For a time there lived a king and queen there no worse than most
kings and queens, and probably a little better. These two ruled their subjects kindly enough, considering that they rarely saw any of them, except
for the servants who assured the king and queen that they were better
rulers than the ruled deserved. When they rode abroad on their semi-
annual passages, the streets were lined with ranks of cheering people
who waved their caps, if they owned any, and threw flowers, if they could
afford them, and kisses if they could not. And the affection and loyalty displayed was reasonably genuine, for the people knew well how
much worse things could be, and often had been, and were thus grateful.
Part of their tenderness for the queen undoubtedly stemmed from the
well-known fact that she was crippled, her legs stricken useless from the
very day of her wedding. Her affliction caused her no pain—indeed, her

health otherwise was remarkably vigorous—but no doctor was ever able to provide cause or cure, nor could any wisewoman mumble and chant her way through the mystery, however many chickens she slaughtered. So the queen sat all day on her padded throne, or reclined gracefully on a specially built divan; she was carried everywhere within the palace and its great crystal-roofed gardens by the king himself; and, of course, traveled in a closed sedan chair whenever she went outside. Everything was done for her comfort that might be done, and if sometimes that constant awareness was an ache in itself, she kept it close and never let it show. For she had been raised properly, and she knew how queens properly dealt with aches.

It says a good deal for the king that it never occurred to him to reject his wife, to return her to her family as damaged goods, as many advised him. On the contrary, he had both sense and wit enough to treat her altogether as his partner and companion in all matters: ruling in sorrow at times, and in discomfort always, but ruling. And, as has been said, they were at least better than the average run of those who had come before them.

Now it is to this day a curious aspect of the governance of that realm that kings and queens are not born to royalty, but selected in earliest childhood, and at a certain mirror point in life—a time never known until it arrives, until certain priests have cast their bones and consulted uncharted stars—he or she must step down, exchanging jeweled crown and stately robes for loincloth and begging-bowl, and go out into the world far beyond the sheltered world they have known since first being raised up. None were encouraged to linger in their old surroundings, and few ever did, but drifted away silently along every curve of the round earth. Once in a great while, word would come of a lost king being worshipped as a holy man in some spiny mountain village, or rumor might whisper of a former queen achieving rural renown as a cook in a village inn. But in the main they simply wandered off into absence without protest or complaint. Some were quickly forgotten; others—for good or ill—never were.

When the end came for this particular king, announced for his ears alone by a wizened, sour-faced old priest with a lisp, he grieved deeply to leave his wife to the mercy of time and her ruined legs. But he had prepared as well as he could, hiring, at great expense, the finest deviser he could seek out to design a chair with wheels for her, a sort of mobile throne: the first ever seen, as it happens, in the land of Far Away And Long Ago, where all moves slowly. The king disliked the result, as he had known he would, having always taken great delight in carrying the queen in his arms himself wherever in the palace she desired to go. But the queen in fact was quite pleased, and played with her new wheelchair like a child, rolling and spinning and turning in circles. And when she did notice the sadness in her husband's eyes as he looked on, she said to him quickly, "But you will always have to push me, you know. I cannot make this thing go very far by myself." And the king smiled and nodded, and kissed her, and said nothing.

He also spoke privately to a servingman he trusted, and whom he knew to be fond of the queen, asking him to look after her in his place when he should be gone forever. The man promised to do all that one of his lowly status could do to aid and comfort a royal personage, and allowed himself the liberty of rejecting the handsome payment that the king offered him. "My services are not for sale, Majesty," he rebuked the king gently. "The strength of my arms and my back is for sale. My friendship is not." And the king was much shamed by this, and asked his pardon.

When the king left, quietly, in the night, so as not to awaken the queen to grief quite so soon, she was inconsolable as she had not been since she lost the use of her legs. The servingman was too wise to attempt to comfort her—which would not have been his place, in any event—but he did what he knew how to do, keeping palace officials and family members alike graciously and dexterously away from her until she felt herself at least a little recovered and able to deal with such matters. For she must now be queen in full measure, reigning alone, with no guide, and no true knowledge of those she governed. She could only do her best, he counseled her, as he and her many other servants did.

And so she lived, ruling as she imagined her husband would have done—*Where could he be now? Sleeping cold in what hayfield? Begging his evening meal along what road?*—until her own time of stars and runes and farseeing priests came. She was aged then, though not as old as many had been who obediently cast aside power and took up holy homelessness. Her servant—old himself now, but long ascended to the highest rank in her household—fiercely pleaded her case for unique consideration, on the grounds of her disability; but the gods were the gods, implacable as ever. The only mercy allotted her was permission to take her special chair along with her into the wild. It was the last service her old friend could perform; she never saw him again.

There she sat, day after day: one old woman among the throng of beggars, hawkers and petitioners who crowded the courtyard of the palace that had for so long, and so recently, been her home and her life. It was the hot season, and she suffered greatly; but to wheel herself back into the blessed shade of a god's statue meant making herself less visible to those passersby who wished to gain merit by placing coins in pleading hands. Most would have offered alms gladly to one who had lately been their ruler; but few of those had ever seen her face, and fewer still recognized her in her dusty rags. She went thirsty most days, and hungry many a night; and still she sat on alone on her wheeled throne.

Then the rains came. Within a day they had driven half the courtyard swarm to cover; within two they had beaten down all lowering growth and battered every leaf off the ornamental trees that ringed the palace. In three days the cracked and withered earth, soaked beyond absorbing, had become a hungry, gummy marsh, sucking boots and sandals off their wearers' feet, and making it impossible for the wheels of the old queen's chair to turn at all. Prisoned on her throne, her begging-bowl full only of water, her condition more hopeless than that of the lowest beggar in her former realm, she bowed lower and lower beneath the pitiless lash of the rain, and waited to die.

She never really remembered the beggar woman coming to her, though sometimes she thought she recalled a voice out of the wind and rain, and rough, strong hands over hers on the arms of the wheelchair. But when she opened her eyes fully it was to the steamy, pungent warmth of a cowshed, and the hands were drying her face and hair and body as they stripped her few scraps of clothing from her starving body and lifted her out of her chair to set her down, curled like a child, against a warm, breathing flank and cover her with straw, piles and piles of straw. She fell asleep with the soft, comforting murmur that cows make to their newborns in her ears, and she did not wake until the storm had passed and sunlight was shining in her eyes through the chinks in the shed walls.

The beggar woman was sitting on a hay bale, knees drawn up to her chest, greedily munching a fruit in its skin. Her voice, when she saw the queen reaching feebly for her chair, was as rough as her hands. "Lie still—you haven't the strength of a blind kitten. Show some sense now, and lie still!"

The queen could not tell the woman's age. Her brown face and bare arms were streaked with dried mud, and her hair was so dirty and tangled that it was impossible to be sure of what color it was. As for her dress, it was little better than the queen's rags, and she wore no shoes at all. She finished the fruit, tossed away the core with a grunt of disgust, hopped down from the hay bale and rummaged to find a bucket lying loose in one of the stalls. With this in hand she addressed herself to the cow who had kept the queen warm and alive all night, and quickly returned with new milk all but spilling over the bucket's rim. "You'll have to sit up and lap it as it stands. This inn's well enough for bed, but it's not much for breakfast."

The beggar woman strolled close to look at the wheelchair, propped against the stall door. "A pretty thing," she remarked, "but not much good without a dog or a goat to pull it, I'd think. Or maybe—" and here she turned and smiled sardonically at the exhausted and bewildered queen "—some poor fool to push it? Drink your milk while it's warm, best thing for you." She scraped with a dirty forefinger at the mud caking the chair's wheels. It fell away in long lakes and wrinkled clods. "Pretty, though, I'll say that . . ."

The queen drank as much as she could manage of the sweet milk, and only then found the strength to ask, "Who are you?"

The beggar woman shrugged. "No one you'd know." But the queen had fallen back to sleep, and the beggar woman put more straw over her; then picked up the begging-bowl, fallen to the dirt floor, and studied it thoughtfully for some time. "Pretty," she said again, and left the shed with the bowl under her arm.

The queen drowsed out the rest of the day under the straw, waking only to sip more of the milk and sleep again. Waking at last, warm and hungry, she saw the beggar woman crouched nearby, sorting through loaves of bread, entire rounds of cheese, sacks of dried lentils and peas, two bottles of wine, and even a packet of salt fish. When she saw that the queen was awake and watching her, she smiled proudly—the queen noticed that several of her lower teeth were gone—gesturing grandly over her treasure. "There's money, too," she announced, jingling coins in her hand. "All enough to see us on our way, I should think."

"On our way to where?" the queen asked dazedly. "And where is my bowl? You have saved my life, and I must beg for both of us now—it is the least I can do to repay you. If you will help me into my chair . . ."

The beggar woman laughed as harshly as she seemed to do every-thing else. "We'll neither of us need be seeking alms for a while now, my fine lady; how on earth did you come by a begging-bowl lined with silver?" Not waiting for an answer, she went on, "Well, we're not bound off anywhere tonight—nor tomorrow, either, until you get some strength into you. But winter's coming on, and there's too many sparrows pecking for crumbs around a palace, if you take my meaning. We'll do better in the hill country, where folk see fewer of our kind." She peered sharply at the queen then, out of shrewd, quick dark eyes. "Not but what it'll take wiser than I to ponder what your kind *is*. But you're some somebody, any-way, with your silver-lined bowl and that bloody chair that I'll be forever pushing and pulling out of every rut, I've no doubt. And maybe that . . . that *air* of yours will pay for itself along the way. Here—" she handed the queen a torn-off heel of bread and a chunk of cheese to go with it. "Eat and sleep for a few days, until the roads are dry. Eat and sleep."

The queen took her at her word, doing nothing for three days but dozing and waking, nibbling this or that of the beggar woman's bounty, and turning back to the deep comfort of the cow's warmly receptive side. In the night, vaguely roused by her companion's snoring a few feet from her, she tried hard to think about her lost life and her lost husband . . . but even he seemed as distant as though he had never been anything but a story that she had told herself in her childhood. She dreamed often during those days and nights, and while some of the dreams were sad, and some were frightening, in all of them she walked, as she had walked before her wedding day. But in those dreams she was always alone.

The beggar woman herself came and went as she chose: always cheer-ful, in her odd, half-mocking way, most often unwashed, sometimes with food or a few coins and sometimes not; but frequently, as the queen's vision cleared, bearing bruises on her legs and arms, or even on her face. When the queen pressed her for an explanation, she would either turn the question aside with a snort and a gesture, or say simply, "Minor dis-agreement." From somewhere she procured a sailor's needle and thread in order to mend the queen's torn and fouled clothes as best she could. Being no seamstress, she pricked her fingers often and swore interest-ingly each time; but she kept at the work with a gruff patience that belied the perennial half-derisive air with which she otherwise tended the queen. She spent a good deal of time squatting by the chair, cleaning the mud off the wheels and adding soft rags and feathers to the cushion

that padded the seat. Now and then she would look up to growl wonderingly, "Tell me again who made this bloody ridiculous thing for you? He
must have taken you for a monkey—you need two sets of hands and a
tail just to steer."

"It was my husband who had it made," the queen answered her. "He
wanted me to have at least that much control over my life when he should
be . . . when he must take up his new way." She had long been too old to
weep, but her eyes still ached where the tears would have been.

"And you lost your legs on your wedding day?" The beggar woman
cackled, rudely and raucously. "That must have been a bridal night indeed."

"Indeed," the queen said quietly, and the beggar woman laughed
again.

One morning the queen woke to sunlight, and saw that the cowshed doors stood open and small birds were flying in and out. The beggar
woman was busily arranging their food supplies for travel, doing it with
astonishing inventiveness. Sacks of varying sizes were slung around a rod
at the back of the wheelchair; other pouches and packages were bundled
in wherever there was any secure space for them; and somehow there was
still room for the queen, when the beggar woman lifted her in strong,
skinny arms and deposited her on the cushioned seat with an exasperated
grunt of "Sitting on it half your life didn't make it any smaller, I'll tell you
that." But she took firm hold of the chair's handles and guided them out
of the cowshed, where they both paused to take a long last look toward
the storm-washed palace glinting in the sun. The beggars were returning,
their wheedling voices audible from the cowshed as they crowded close,
quarrelling savagely over the handful of alms distributed every morning.
The beggar woman's voice was oddly gentle for a moment as she said,
"I was born there. Just behind that horse trough, in a mud puddle." Her
usual hoarse chuckle displaced any wistfulness. "At least my mam told me
it was mud."

The queen said, "I was born on the steps of the palace. The pains overtook my mother there."

She did not mention that her mother, a wealthy merchant's wife, had
come out with her attendants and nurses to enjoy a last breath of free air
before her confinement. The beggar woman looked at her with something
like a new respect. "Aye, well, you know then. That would be where you
get that hoity-toity style, no doubt of it. Didn't make you much good at it,
though, did it? I watched you out there, you know—watched you for some

little while—and you'd have thought you'd never begged in your life." She laughed again, rooting in one ear with a broken-nailed forefinger. "Well, time we started. It's a long way to the hills, and it'll be longer pushing my lady's bloody carriage and pair." She gripped the chair handles and thrust her weight forward. "Sit *still*, now!"

As the wheelchair jolted over ruts and naked tree roots, the queen asked the beggar woman, "Why did you save me, there, in the rain? I am nothing to you—why now are you making yourself responsible for my life?"

The beggar woman seemed to ponder the question quite seriously, scratching her frowsy head and wrinkling her invariably smudged nose. She said finally, "Just never saw anyone drown sitting up before. So stupid, I took it for a sign." And the queen laughed for the first time in a very long while.

They covered very little distance that first day, despite the fact that the roads were fairly level, with few deep holes, and no obstacles that the wheelchair could not be guided around. The hills, glistening cool invitation on the horizon, yet drew no closer, and the beggar woman was only able to cozen a few morsels of bread and honey out of a wary farmer eating his lunch beside the road. But the night was warm, and the queen slept well in a bed of soft grasses arranged for her by the beggar woman, who grumbled constantly as she did so. "You needn't think we'll be going on like this, my lady, just because you're too lazy to walk. Come a time, there will, when I'll be the one lounging in this idiot contraption, while you wheeze your guts out pushing me uphill. Tomorrow, next day, I'll be sitting there before you're even awake, just waiting my turn. Fair's fair, and it's a long way yet to the hills."

She said that often—*it's a long way yet to the hills*—even when they were deep among them, with the winding roads becoming steeper and rougher every day, and every other breath she panted was a curse as she toiled to keep the wheelchair from slipping back down a stony trail at her, or from running away with the helpless queen when the path suddenly dropped off. But for all her oaths and weary threats, she pushed the cumbersome chair and its usually terrified passenger further on and further up into country where cows grazed precariously on slanting rooftops, and gardens grew on carved terraces designed to take advantage of every single foot of ground. The hill people, as the beggar woman had foretold, indeed showed more generosity to strange travelers than city folk had done; but all the same, they proved just as anxious to see them on their way, rarely allowing them to rest so much as a night in their barns or cellars. Only during a storm—and not always then—were they likely to be granted shelter; and the queen, who already knew how to be grateful for the dumb kindness of a cow, came to appreciate dry firewood and a daughter's outworn clothes. Once a blacksmith repaired a broken wheel of the chair, and asked nothing for his labor; once a fisherman went out of his way to point out a safer road than the bandit-plagued one they were traveling. The queen learned to accept whatever strange gifts came their way with the courtesy she would have shown an ambassador from a greater kingdom, and to give back what she could—a smile—with her whole full heart.

It became more difficult every day for her to remember palace beds and palace meals, servants—except for the one, out of so many—and grand festivals in honor of neighboring rulers; even such tiny joys as reading poetry aloud to her husband the king, or being carried by him through the palace grounds on a cool blue evening. Whenever she realized that she had forever lost one or another such cherished moment, then she would mourn bitterly, while the beggar woman mocked her. "And what are you grizzling for this time? A man, was it?— some sturdy rogue, liked the notion of a woman who could never run away from him? Sit up and stop mewling—it's a long way yet to the hills."

She herself appeared stringy-muscled and tireless, which the queen knew was not so. Almost every night, she could hear the deep whine in her companion's splintering breath as they lay by each other on cold ground or a stable's gritty floor, after another day of stubbornly wrestling the battered wheelchair still further on toward . . . toward what hills, what goal?

For that the beggar woman had some definite objective beyond seeking more generous almsgivers, the queen had long ceased doubting. They were bound *somewhere*, if it cost the beggar woman the last strength in her body, which the queen could see happening in the frighteningly wide eyes that seemed to sink deeper into the thinning face day by day; feel in the raw hands that forced the chair onward. If guilt and sympathy could have brought her up out of her chair, the beggar woman would indeed have been riding in her place; as it was, the best she could do was to urge her to lie up for a day, two days, in some cave or—better—an abandoned barn, which she angrily refused to do. "Maybe you've some martyr's notion of dying in the filthy rain, as you began, but I surely don't. Winter's coming round again, and we'll go to earth when we reach our earth. Hold your peace, therefore—and stop squirming so when I pick you up." And the skinny, trembling arms raised her, and the chapped and bleeding hands eased her once more into the chair with the old surprising dexterity, determined gentleness, and the equally familiar snarling "O bloody woman, didn't anyone at least teach you to hold your head up? Sit straight, blast you!" The blanket tucked so precisely around her was, at the last, the only one they had.

There came a morning, as the queen had known it must come, when it was nearly noon before the beggar woman—she who usually demanded that they be on the road by sunrise—was able to struggle to her feet, snatch up whatever scraps were left over from last night's dinner of scraps, and then at last grip the wheelchair handles. There had been soft rain in the night; the midday air was no warmer than dawn had been, and the queen clenched her teeth to keep them from chattering. But the beggar woman stepped out bravely for all of that, grumbling inaudibly as she lunged the chair along muddy paths and through heaps of dankly clinging leaves. It was not until she was endeavoring to guide it over the mild rise of a tree root that she went down slowly, cluttering and half-turning like a leaf herself. She attempted to rise, and could not, and did not try again.

The queen had never been able to afford to take any action without considering the consequences; so she never knew where she discovered the courage to twist and hurl herself out of her chair in complete thoughtlessness, falling hard enough beside the beggar woman that for a moment she could not breathe. For long minutes the two of them lay very still together, then the queen scrabbled herself into a sitting position, and pulled the poor bruised head onto her thigh.

Only when the beggar woman opened her eyes did the queen fully realize how old she was. It was not a matter of lines never observed before, or of another missing tooth or two, or hair that seemed suddenly to have become grayer and thinner than when they had stopped the night before; but layers of ancient grief and rage and weariness, all laid down one atop another, like geological strata. The beggar woman's words sounded like stones in her throat, but they came clearly to the queen's ears. She said, "A long way to the hills. At last it is all to end in the hills."

"Nonsense," the queen said with a firmness she wished with all her heart to feel. "There is a village within a mile—you told me so yourself

And with these words she screamed, because feeling had begun to return to her legs, and with it pain such as she had never known in all her life. The agony crept steadily upward from her feet, long since bare, and she screamed "Make it stop! *O, gods, make it stop!*" while the beggar woman wept and coughed and cried out, calling a name the queen did not know; and so they rocked and moaned together, scattering the dank leaves.

But finally the queen's new legs hurt her less and less, and the pain seemed to low into the wobbly strength of a fawn. She stood up for the first time since her wedding day—promptly fell down—then stood again, swaying, feeling herself thin as rain. She said, "It is your turn to ride," and stooped to lift the beggar woman into the wheelchair. But the other shook her head weakly, and the queen stepped back, still cautious on her feet. Staring down, she saw the beggar woman's face seemingly growing younger, as happens sometimes when death is close, the rumples of a life smoothed away like a bedsheet. The queen said again, "Please. You must ride now."

"I have done all things that I must do," replied the beggar woman. "All but one."

Then the queen dropped on her knees beside her, as she could not have done only minutes before, and she pleaded, "I would have died but for you. Not merely in the rain, that first day, but in every way, from the inside out. Wherever we have journeyed, you have sheltered me, you have gone without that I might have, gone cold that I might sleep warm. What you did to me you have atoned for again and again, and I have gladly forgiven you . . . no, we have forgiven each other, we two old women." She stroked the beggar woman's dirty cheek and kissed her forehead, saying, "Come—the village is close enough that I can carry you. Never mind the poor old chair, we'll not need it any more. I would be proud to carry you."

"*No*," whispered the beggar woman as the queen began to lift her where she lay. "*No*—too long a way . . . I thought if I brought you . . . if you forgave, my power . . . but curses come high, and it is too long, too long to the hills . . ." But there was no resistance in her; nor breath, either, when the queen stood up with the body in her arms that was almost weightless, even when she freed one hand to close the beggar woman's eyes. She said no farewell, neither made any prayer, but she stood so for a long time.

If there had not been rain, the queen would never have been able to claw out a grave with her bare hands. Even so, it took her most of the day before she felt it deep enough to protect the beggar woman's body from weather and animals. She marked the grave with the wheelchair, promising silently to return with a stone once the ground had settled. Then she wiped her hands on the cleanest of her rags, and started on alone, still on trembling fawn's legs.

On the outskirts of the village she met an old man gathering firewood. She knew him, but he did not know her; and she realized from his wondrously sweet faraway smile that he never would. But he clucked pityingly at her bleeding hands, and she helped him arrange the broken branches more comfortably in the three slings he bore on his back, and she carried all she could herself, and so they walked on together. He took her hand trustingly, and smiled again when she called him by a name that he did not recognize. And the queen rested her head gently against his white head, and they went on.

Thanks to classic works such as *The Last Unicorn, Tamsin,* and *The Innkeeper's Song,* **Peter S. Beagle** is acknowledged as a fantasy icon. He was honored with the World Fantasy Award for Life Achievement in 2011. The recipient of the Hugo, Nebula, Locus, and Mythopoeic Fantasy Awards, Beagle has written numerous teleplays and screenplays including the animated versions of *The Lord of the Rings* and *The Last Unicorn,* plus the fan-favorite "Sarek" episode of *Star Trek: The Next Generation.* His most recent novel is *Sweet Lightning,* a baseball fantasy.

The narrator, a young storyteller, seems to make up her own fairy tales as well as knowing other stories—like that of an Erlking—from her mother. For all its resemblance to a known tale you cannot quite place, "Lebkuchen" is a modern story from a modern storyteller. Perhaps "Lebkuchen" resonates because it deals with a complex response most of us must experience at some point in life.

Lebkuchen

Priya Sharma

Skating passes the afternoons. I circle the lake, around and around, carving lines in the ice. The blades of my skates make a slicing sound with each turn. I like the world this way. *Just here, just now.* Frozen lake and frozen sky, barricaded by trees. The crows form a line on a branch to watch me, folding themselves up to keep warm.

I tell them the story of the ice maiden. She was a village girl who drowned herself for the love of a shepherd's son, long ago. The galloping winter encased her in ice. It was too dangerous to cut her body free, so her family planned a vigil on the bank until the thaw. The Erlking, a frozen monarch himself, rode past and saw her lying there. He placed a perfect kiss upon her icy lips as he claimed her for his bride. I imagine her face beneath my feet, pale and perfect in her crystal coffin.

My tale telling is interrupted. Villagers come with noisy chatter that scatters the crows. They've seen me now, so I won't leave, even though they don't like me. Not anymore. I'm fast but they're faster. The girls catch up with me.

"Look at her. She's disgusting."

"She smells. She never washes."

"Her hair's filthy."

They go on like this for a while, circling me and calling to one another.

"It's your fault." The storekeeper's daughter is bold. She's the only one that dares to address me. She smells of clean nightgowns and her mother's kisses. Her hair is golden beneath her fur cap. "It's your fault that it's always winter."

I don't care. Winter is happiness. It's Mother making Lebkuchen and sewing by the fire. It's her, jumping up and clapping her hands when Father comes home. It's her bedtime tales of changelings, lost travelers and the Erlking's adventures.

The girls leave but not before I've plucked a hair from my denouncer's coat. None of them notice. I put this piece of spun sunshine in my pocket.

The boys linger. They knock me down. I'm sprawled before them, my skirt tangled around my knees. I feel dizzy when I sit up, realizing that I've cut my head and bled upon the ice. Red stains white. These boys are wolves in human skin. They've scented fear. One tries to kiss me. I can taste the cheese he had for lunch and smell the sourness of his sweat. I rake at his eyes with my nails and call down every curse I've learnt. They don't know that the words are empty without the charms to make them real. They're still laughing but they're not so sure anymore. They're thinking of what their pretty friend said about me causing the lingering winter. They're wondering what my mother might have taught me.

"Leave her alone!"

I hear the sure *swish swish* sound of Peter's approach as he comes to save me from my would-be ravishers. He's flushed, a circle of pink on his cheeks, which only serves to heighten the blue of his eyes.

The boys are even more unsure now. Every one of them is a coward. Peter, even outnumbered, will not be cowed. He's tall, with the strength needed of a farmer's son.

The storekeeper's daughter makes eyes at him. I've seen her glance over to see if he's watching her.

She's welcome to him.

"Leave her be." Peter speaks with authority.

"She's crazy."

"She's a witch!"

Witch. A term used for women who dare to be wise.

"She's no such thing, are you, Lebkuchen?"

Someone snickers. I'm furious Peter thinks he has the right to use my pet name because I followed him about when I was small.

"I am," I turn on him too, "and I'll make sure that each of you grow a tail by morning."

"You're hurt," he reaches out to touch my head. Then to the boys, "What did you do to her?"

I turn and skate away. The crows gather again, lovers of drama that they are.

"Lebkuchen!" Peter calls after me, torn between wanting to follow me and chastising my tormenters. "Wait!"

I walk home. The forest keeps me company. I listen as the trees whisper to one another. They're as vain as people. Today their boughs are adorned with icicles. Jack Frost's fingers. I touch one and it snaps off. A clean, certain sound.

I can see home. Snow heaped along the sills. My mother's skates are strung up in one window, a single unlit candle in the other. Garlands, made of mistletoe and holly, decorate the windows and the door. Poisoned berries and the spiked leaves are a defense against trolls. One in particular. His hands are strong enough to crush rocks. His eyes are pyres. He comes marching out of the woods without warning, right up to the door.

It's getting colder. I wish I'd brought my hat. Snow starts to fall. It smothers the world into silence. I put out my hands and let snowflakes pile up on my palms. They are gentle at first but then come faster and faster. There are flakes caught in my eyelashes.

Home.

Mother looks up. Her books are strewn across the table, open at different pages. So many, all mixed up. Lexicons and manuals. Almanacs and tomes of forecasting tables. Spell books and recipe books. Runes scribbled in the margins of a book on animal husbandry. I put them back on the shelf.

"The other children hate me."

She nods as if this is only to be expected. I sit at her knee, head on her lap. She doesn't complain that I'm too old for this. I ask her to press her handkerchief against my bleeding scalp.

"How did you make me?" I ask.

She looks through the window at the cold outside. Her skin is the shade of shrouds.

"I don't recall."

"Shall I tell you? It was like this," I begin, "you made me from snow."

"Snow," she repeats. "Snow baby."

"Yes. From the first snowfall of a new moon. You gathered each flake before they touched the ground. When you had enough, you shaped me and lit me with the new moon's light."

"Stop this!"

The troll has come down from his great hall, carved deep into the mountain. He carries an axe whose sharp edge has slain many trees.

Except he's no troll. It's Father. He fills the doorframe, stoops to enter, but he's just a man. I can hear his dogs scampering around outside, happy to be free of their harness.

Father's well armed, not just with an axe but with a talisman, so no garland can keep him out. I curse this amulet. Mother made it as a gift, to keep him safe from sorcery, even her own. *Proof of love,* she said. *Let no one ever claim I bewitched him.*

Seeing Mother has put him in a rage. She looks as she ever did, except for the blankness of her face. He storms about, shouting and smashing crockery. I see the house through his eyes. There's no hot meal ready for him. Chicken bones and mouse droppings litter the floor. Dust on Mother's mantle and mirror. Dirty clothes, abandoned where I dropped them.

"I'm tired of this." He slumps down in a chair. My father's temper blows in and out. "It has to stop."

Mother blinks. Father gets up and takes her by the wrist, pulling her to her feet. I'm knocked to the floor. The threadbare rug doesn't cushion my fall.

Father pulls her to the door and opens it. The cold air whips in a flurry of snow as he drags her out into the dark. I fly at him and bite his arm. He raises a hand against me. I crouch, teeth bared, waiting for the fist to fall.

It doesn't come. He picks me up by the scruff as if handling a pup and throws me back inside.

Next morning. Father's gone. So's Mother. I lie in bed listening to the creaking trees trying to shed their load of snow. Listening to the single bell of the village church. The wind carrying the calls of the great wolf that outwits the hunters' guns. To the sound of ships, far off in the north, crashing on the rocks.

Hunger gets me up. Father never leaves the cupboard bare. I lift the pail lid and sniff. Fresh milk. Yellow butter in a dish. A slab of meat, marbled with waxy fat. He always leaves wood. Logs stacked by the hearth. I touch each one, thankful for the gift made by the trees. I stroke the places where the axe bit deep into the wood.

There's a saying here. *You're never alone if you have a fire.*

I open Mother's books.

Mother smiles. I tell her I'm cold and ask for a blanket. She looks around until she finds one in the linen chest, where the mice now nest. I tell her to spread it over my knees and kiss my head.

"Mother, how did you make me?"

"I'm not sure." Her skin has a fevered glow.

"Shall I tell you?"

"Please."

"I'm a fire baby. You made me from the fire's heart, where the flames aren't red or yellow but white. Fire that has its own light."

"Fire baby."

Mother stares at me, her marvelous creation.

I go out in the afternoon. I'd rather stay at home but there's something I have to do. The cold greets me when I step outside, tugging at the seams of my clothes and finding its way in. I've lost my gloves, so my hands are cold. Frost bites my fingertips.

As I leave I put a cup of milk by the door. It's for the gods. Not the gods of fire, the sun, the trees but small gods, which I loved best. God of nails, of spoons and of twine. Gods of the mundane, who should be worshipped every day. Gods woven into the warp and weft.

I pass the heap of snow on the hill above the house. I don't look at it. I won't look at it. I walk with care, fearing a fall. My wind has frozen my bones and made them brittle. The ruts in the track are filled with ice and sparkling snow which cracks and crunches underfoot. The only sound in my glittering kingdom.

I've made the golden hair into a charm. I learnt how to do this from Mother's books. I knotted it around a piece of deer hide, a strip of fish skin and a crow's feather. The hide ensures her heart is always hunted. Fish scale so that she'll be taken by currents rather than making her own fate. The feather so she'll never feel settled. I fix this charm to the dead tree at the crossroads using a rusted nail. This way she'll never feel alive.

Let the storekeeper's daughter look at Peter all she wants.

Father's sled is outside when I get home. I didn't expect him back so soon. The unhitched dogs flop in piles, pink tongues lolling. The cold shows me their breath.

He sits in Mother's chair, rocking. He stops when he sees me. Frowns. Everyone thinks him handsome, but his hair and beard are too long. Thinness makes him look ill.

"This can't go on."

I look around. He's swept the floor. I can smell the broth bubbling in the pot.

Mother's not here.

I read out instructions from Mother's cookbook and she follows them. I watch her stir the melting honey and molasses in the pan. The sifted flour looks like a snowdrift in the bowl. She adds spices. Ginger. Cinnamon. Nutmeg. It's the smell of *winter* and *Mother*. I want to cry.

"How did you make me?"

She pauses.

"I forget."

"Shall I remind you?"

"Oh, yes." She looks like I've offered her a treat. Her skin is the color of withering leaves.

"It was like this. You made me from flour, ground by a firstborn's hands, mixed with spices and the same firstborn's tears. You added honey and molasses with a few flakes of salt so I wouldn't be too sweet. You lit me with candle light."

She looks at her hands.

"I'm your baby. Your Lebkuchen."

Lebkuchen. *Bread of life.*

Lebkuchen

The door opens. Father, again. He hangs up his coat. Mother gets up when she sees him. She knows what's expected of her now. He wasn't always so keen to be rid of her. I remember that once he seized her in his arms and kissed her cheeks, her lips. His bewildered happiness was short-lived. Mother's mouth didn't move. Her face stayed smooth. Father backed away, confused. He spat on the floor, like he'd just eaten something bitter. He cursed and clipped my ear, thinking it was done to trick him out of childish spite.

"You don't have to go," I tell Mother.

Father shakes his head at me. I run to her instead, crying and clinging. Father's hands fall on my shoulders and he prises me away. I wait for a shaking.

"Hush, Lebkuchen, hush." His arms enfold me. "You know she has to go."

Mother doesn't need a second telling. She opens the door. The world outside is white. As she walks out, I notice she's not wearing any shoes. Father clutches me tighter and kisses the top of my head. Snow mother. Fire mother. Lebkuchen mother. The farther she is from me, the less substantial she becomes. She gets fainter and fainter until she's no more than a column of flour and spice dust, whipped away by the wind. The snow is streaked with sticky sweetness for the dogs to lick.

"Lebkuchen, just like your mother, with her gifts and face and books. You forget you're also mine. No more of this now. You're breaking my heart."

He wipes my face. I notice that he's trimmed his hair and beard. He fetches the comb and tugs at my knots and tangles. I sit quiet.

"Tsk, Lebkuchen, you're too old to be carrying on like this. We've both been through a trial and you when you were neither woman nor child. I've stayed away too often. No more. And you'll come with me whenever I need to be gone long."

We finish making the Lebkuchen together and eat some in silence.

"Put your coat on."

I shake my head. I know what he's doing.

"Lebkuchen, you can't ignore it anymore. Come and pay your respects."

It's already warmer outside. The icicles are dripping water and light. We go up on the hill. The snow covering her grave is melting. *Beloved Wife. Beloved Mother.*

"She wouldn't want to see you like this. It's all right for you to love other people," he nudges my side with his elbow, "even me."

269

I turn my wet face away.

"You can't shut the world out. And don't shut yourself in. If hurt can't find you, love can't either."

There's a waterfall of words inside me. I'm scared they might wash me away.

"People forget how things were once winter's over," is all I can say.

"We won't forget," he says. "We'll remind each other."

Spring is sudden. Everything buds and blooms. Life bursts from the ground as if it's been asleep too long. I go to the dead tree and retrieve the charm. I unknot the deer hide, the fish skin and the feather. I reverse the words and burn the charm upon a fire made from branches of the dead tree. The storekeeper's daughter is not my friend. Or my enemy.

I walk to the farm, beyond the village church. Flesh of fields revealed now the snow has gone. I see Peter with another boy, leading a dappled mare. Peter's eyes are the color of summer skies. His hair is heavy wheat.

The storekeeper's daughter makes eyes at him.

"Peter."

I step onto the track to stop him. His name is a charm. It burns my mouth.

His friend looks at me like I might bite. I growl at him.

"I made this for you."

I take the talisman from my pocket and hold it out to Peter. It'll ensure that he'll never be enthralled, glamoured, or seduced by any spell. It'll protect him from fevers and be his luck-bringer. All this, even if he's happiest when the storekeeper's daughter looks his way.

"Don't take anything from her." His friend puts a hand on Peter's arm.

"She won't hurt me."

"You don't believe in magic?" I can't help but ask.

"No, but I believe in you."

Peter takes the amulet and ties it around his neck. We nod at one another but don't smile. My mother's love was all exclamations and declarations. I love more like my father, I think. In a quieter, but not lesser way.

I turn and go. It's time for home. I have honey and molasses to melt. Flour and spices to sift into a bowl. Father's out, fishing on the lake. It won't be long before he's home.

Priya Sharma is a doctor who lives in the UK. Her original short stories have appeared in several magazines including *Black Static*, *Interzone*, *Albedo One*, and *On Spec* as well as anthologies *Nightmare Carnival* and *Once Upon a Time: New Fairy Tales*. Some have been reprinted in *The Best Dark Fantasy and Horror* and *The Year's Best Horror*.

During the 1950s, Warren Roberts discovered more than nine hundred versions of this type of tale—"the kind and unkind girl"—in a multitude of countries. Neil Gaiman's modern-day version of "Diamonds and Toads" is darker than the old tale. First written to accompany a staged photograph, if seen with that image, the ending takes on a single unambiguous meaning. Without it (or its description), you may find another interpretation altogether.

Diamonds and Pearls:
A Fairy Tale

Neil Gaiman

Once upon the olden times, when the trees walked and the stars danced, there was a girl whose mother died, and a new mother came and married her father, bringing her own daughter with her.

Soon enough the father followed his first wife to the grave, leaving his daughter behind him.

The new mother did not like the girl and treated her badly, always favoring her own daughter, who was indolent and rude. One day, her stepmother gave the girl, who was only eighteen, twenty dollars to buy her drugs. "Don't stop on the way," she said.

So the girl took the twenty-dollar bill, and put an apple into her purse, for the way was long, and she walked out of the house and down to the end of the street, where the wrong side of town began.

She saw a dog tied to a lamppost, panting and uncomfortable in the heat, and the girl said, "Poor thing." She gave it water.

The elevator was out of service. The elevator there was always out of service. Halfway up the stairs she saw a hooker, with a swollen face, who stared up at her with yellow eyes. "Here," said the girl. She gave the hooker the apple.

She went up to the dealer's floor and she knocked on the door three times. The dealer opened the door and stared at her and said nothing. She showed him the twenty-dollar bill.

Then she said, "Look at the state of this place," and she bustled in.

"Don't you ever clean up in here? Where are your cleaning supplies?" The dealer shrugged. Then he pointed to a closet. The girl opened it and found a broom and a rag. She filled the bathroom sink with water and she began to clean the place.

When the rooms were cleaner, the girl said, "Give me the stuff for my mother."

He went into the bedroom, came back with a plastic bag. The girl pocketed the bag and walked down the stairs.

"Lady," said the hooker. "The apple was good. But I'm hurting real bad. You got anything?"

The girl said, "It's for my mother."

"Please?"

"You poor thing."

The girl hesitated, then she gave her the packet. "I'm sure my stepmother will understand," she said.

She left the building. As she passed, the dog said, "You shine like a diamond, girl."

She got home. Her mother was waiting in the front room. "Where is it?" she demanded.

"I'm sorry," said the girl. Diamonds dropped from her lips, rattled across the floor.

Her stepmother hit her.

"Ow!" said the girl, a ruby red cry of pain, and a ruby fell from her mouth.

Her stepmother fell to her knees, picked up the jewels. "Pretty," she said. "Did you steal them?"

The girl shook her head, scared to speak.

"Do you have any more in there?"

The girl shook her head, mouth tightly closed.

The stepmother took the girl's tender arm between her finger and her thumb and pinched as hard as she could, squeezed until the tears glistened in the girl's eyes, but she said nothing. So her step-mother locked the girl in her windowless bedroom, so she could not get away.

The woman took the diamonds and the ruby to Al's Pawn and Gun, on the corner, where Al gave her five hundred dollars no questions asked.

Then she sent her other daughter off to buy drugs for her.

The girl was selfish. She saw the dog panting in the sun, and, once she was certain that it was chained up and could not follow, she kicked at it. She pushed past the hooker on the stair. She reached the dealer's apartment and knocked on the door. He looked at her, and she handed him the twenty without speaking. On her way back down, the hooker on the stair said, "Please . . . ?" but the girl did not even slow.

"Bitch!" called the hooker.

"Snake," said the dog, when she passed it on the sidewalk.

Back home, the girl took out the drugs, then opened her mouth to say, "Here," to her mother. A small frog, brightly colored, slipped from her lips. It leapt from her arm to the wall, where it hung and stared at them unblinking.

"Oh my god," said the girl. "That's just disgusting." Five more colored tree frogs, and one small red, black, and yellow-banded snake.

"Black against red," said the girl. "Is that poisonous?" (Three more tree frogs, a cane toad, a small, blind white snake, and a baby iguana.) She backed away from them.

Her mother, who was not afraid of snakes or of anything, kicked at the banded snake, which bit her leg. The woman screamed and flailed, and her daughter also began to scream, a long loud scream that fell from her lips as a healthy adult python.

The girl, the first girl, whose name was Amanda, heard the screams and then the silence but she could do nothing to find out what was happening.

She knocked on the door. No one opened it. No one said anything. The only sounds she could hear were rustlings, as if of something huge and legless slipping across the carpet.

When Amanda got hungry, too hungry for words, she began to speak.

"Thou still unravish'd bride of quietness," she began. "Thou foster child of Silence and slow Time . . ."

She spoke, although the words were choking her.

"Beauty is truth, truth beauty,—that is all ye know on earth, and all ye need to know . . ." A final sapphire clicked across the wooden floor of Amanda's closet room.

The silence was absolute.

Neil Gaiman is a *New York Times* bestselling author of more than twenty books for adults and children, including the novels *Neverwhere*, *Stardust*, *American Gods*, *Anansi Boys*, *Coraline*, and *The Graveyard Book*; and the Sandman series of graphic novels. *The Ocean at the End of the Lane* is his most recent novel for adults. His latest collection of short fiction, *Trigger Warning*, and *The View from the Cheap Seats: A Collection of Introductions, Essays, and Assorted Writings* were published last year. He is the recipient of numerous literary honors, including the Locus and Hugo Awards and the Newbery and Carnegie Medals. Born and raised in England, Gaiman now lives in a house in some woods somewhere in New York State.

Arthurian fiction can sometimes be considered "legend"—if it has somewhat "believable" qualities and at least the perception of historicity—but when Merlin and his wizardry are part of the story, we are in the realm of the wonder tale. Here we have a delightfully alternative version of a historically quite unmagical queen made fantastical because Merlin enters her world.

The Queen
and the Cambion

Richard Bowes

1.

"Silly Billy, the Sailor King," some called King William IV of Great Britain. But never, of course, to his royal face. Then it was always "Yes, sire," and "As your majesty wishes!"

Because certain adults responsible for her care didn't watch their words in front of a child, the king's young niece and heir to his throne heard such things said. It angered her.

Princess Victoria liked her uncle and knew that King William IV always treated her as nicely as a boozy, confused former sea captain of a monarch could be expected to, and much of the time rather better.

Often when she greeted him, he would lean forward, slip a secret gift into her hands, and whisper something like, "Discovered this in the late king your grandfather's desk at Windsor."

These generally were small items, trinkets, jewels, mementos, long-ago tributes from minor potentates that he'd found in the huge half-used royal palaces, stuck in his pocket, and as often as not remembered to give to his niece.

The one she found most fascinating was a piece of very ancient parchment that someone had pressed under glass hundreds of years before. This came into her possession one day when she was twelve as King William passed Victoria and her governess on his way to the royal coach.

His Britannic Majesty paused and said in her ear, "It's a spell, little cub. Put your paw in mine."

Victoria felt something in her hand and slipped it into a pouch under her cloak while the Sailor King lurched by as though he was walking the quarterdeck of a ship in rough water. "Every ruler of this island has had it and many of us have invoked it," he mumbled while climbing the carriage steps.

She followed him. "To use in times of great danger to Britain?" she whispered.

He leaned out the window. "Or on a day of doldrums and no wind in the sails," he roared as if she was up in a crow's nest, his face red as semi-rare roast beef. "You'll be the monarch and damn all who'd say you no."

Victoria didn't take the gift from under her cloak until she was quite alone in the library of the dark and dreary palace at Kensington. It was where she lived under the intense care of her mother the widowed Duchess of Kent, a German lady, and Sir John Conroy, a handsome enough Irish army officer of good family.

The duchess had appointed Conroy comptroller of her household. Between them they tried to make sure the princess had no independence at all. Victoria really only got out of their sight when King Billy summoned her to the Royal Court.

Nobody at Kensington ever used the library. She went to the far end of that long room lined with portraits of the obscure daughters and younger sons of various British kings, many with their plump consorts and empty-eyed children. Victoria pushed aside a full-length curtain and in the waning daylight looked at the page.

She deciphered a bit of the script and discovered words in Latin that she knew. She saw the name Arturus, which made her gasp. Other words just seemed to be a collection of letters.

Then for fear that someone was coming she hid it away behind a shelf full of books of sermons by long-dead clergymen. It was where she kept some other secret possessions, for she was allowed very little privacy.

She knew the pronunciation for the Latin. By copying several of the other words and showing them to her language tutor, she discovered they were Welsh.

Her music teacher, born in Wales, taught her some pronunciation but became too curious about a few of the words she showed him. Victoria then sought out the old stable master who spoke the language, including some of the ancient tongue, and could read and write a bit.

He was honored and kept her secret when the princess practiced with him. One evening when she had learned all the words and her guardians were busy, Victoria went to the library, took out the page, and slowly read it aloud.

She wasn't quite finished when a silver light shone on the dusty shelves and paintings. Before her was a mountaintop with the sun shining through clouds. In the air, heading her way, sailed a man who rode the wind as another might a horse.

In his hand was a black staff topped with a dragon's head. His gray cloak and robes showed the golden moon in all its phases. His white hair and beard whipped about as the wind brought him to the mountaintop.

At the moment he alighted he noticed Victoria. A look of such vexation came over his face that she stumbled on the words and couldn't immediately repeat them. He and the mountaintop faded from her sight. She, however, remembered what she'd seen.

Victoria was no scholar. But the library at Kensington Palace did contain certain old volumes and she read all she could find about Arthur and especially about Merlin.

An observant child like Victoria knew John Conroy was more than the duchess's comptroller. She understood it was his idea to keep her isolated and to have her every move watched. From an early age she knew why.

She heard her uncle tell someone in confidence but with a voice that could carry over wind, waves, and cannon fire, "The mad old man, my father, King George that was, had a coach load and more of us sons. But in the event, only my brother Kent before he died produced an heir, fair, square, and legitimate. So the little girl over there stands to inherit the crown when I go under."

If the king did "go under" before she was eighteen, Victoria knew, her mother would be regent. The Duchess of Kent would control her daughter and the Royal Court, and Conroy would control the duchess.

In the winter before her eighteenth birthday, five years after he gave her the spell, King William became very ill. But even in sickness, he remembered what the duchess and Conroy were up to. And though his condition was grave, he resolutely refused to die.

On May 24, 1837, Victoria would become eighteen. On May 22 the king was in a coma and the duchess and her comptroller had a plan.

From a window of the library at Kensington Palace Victoria saw carriages drive up through a mid-spring drizzle, saw figures in black emerge. She recognized men Conroy knew: several hungry attorneys, a minor cabinet minister, a rural justice, the secretary of a bishop who believed he should have been an archbishop. They gathered in Conroy's offices downstairs.

Because the servants were loyal, the princess knew that a document had been prepared in which Victoria would cite her own youth and foolishness and beg that her mother (and her mother's "wise advisor") be regent until she was twenty-one.

Even those who admired Victoria would not have said the princess was brilliant, but neither was she dull or naïve. She knew how much damage the conspirators would be able to do in three years of regency. She might never become free. All they needed was her signature.

Understanding what was afoot, Victoria went to the shelf where the manuscript page was hidden. She wondered if she was entitled to do this before she was actually the monarch and if the old wizard would be as angry as the last time.

Victoria heard footsteps on the stairs. She looked at the pictures of her obscure and forgotten ancestors all exiled to the library and made her choice.

The door at the other end of the library opened. The duchess and Conroy entered with half a dozen very solemn men.

"My dearest daughter, we have been trying to decide how best to protect you," said her mother.

By the light of three candles Victoria stood firm and recited the Latin, rolled out the Welsh syllables the way she'd been taught.

Duchess and accomplice exchanged glances. Madness was commonplace in the British dynasty. George III had been so mad that a regent had been appointed.

They started toward Victoria, then stopped and stared. She turned and saw what they did—a great stone hall lit by shafts of sun through tall windows. The light fell on figures including a big man crowned and sitting on a throne.

Victoria saw again the tall figure in robes adorned with golden moons in all their phases. In his hand was the black staff topped with a dragon's head. This time his hair and beard were iron gray, not white. He shot the king a look of intense irritation. The king avoided his stare and seemed a bit amused.

Merlin strode out of the court at Camelot and the royal hall vanished behind him. Under his breath he muttered, "A curse upon the day I was so addled as to make any oath to serve at the beck and call of every halfwit or lunatic who planted a royal behind on the throne of Britain."

Then he realized who had summoned him to this dim and dusty place, and his face softened just a bit. Not a monarch yet to judge by her attire. But soon enough she would be.

Victoria gestured toward the people gaping at him. Merlin was accustomed to those who tried to seize power using bloody axes, not pieces of paper. But a wizard understands the cooing of the dove, the howl of the wolf, and the usurper's greed.

He leveled his staff and blue flames leaped forth.

The documents Conroy held caught fire, and he dropped them. The red wig on one attorney and the ruffled cuffs of the bishop's secretary also ignited. Since none of them would ever admit to having been there none would ever have to describe how they fled, the men snuffing out flames, barely pausing to let the duchess go first.

When they were gone, Merlin erased the fire with a casual wave. Easy enough, he thought. Nothing like Hastings or the Battle of Britain. Shortly he'd be back in Camelot giving the king a piece of his mind.

"Lord Merlin . . ." the young princess began, "We thank you."

A wizard understands a bee and a queen equally. And both can understand a wizard. Merlin spoke and she heard the word "Majesty" in her head. He dropped to one knee and kissed her hand. For young Victoria this was their first meeting. For Merlin it was not.

Time was a path that crossed itself again and again and memory could be prophecy. Later in her life, earlier in his, this queen would summon him.

He had a certain affection for her. But in his lifetime he'd already served all four of the Richards, five or six of the Henrys, the first Elizabeth, the ever-tiresome Ethelred, Saxon Harold, Norman William, and a dozen others.

He waited for her to dismiss him. But Victoria said in a rush of words, "I read that you are a cambion born of Princess Gwenddydd by the incubus Albercanix. She became a nun after your birth." The princess was enthralled.

Merlin met her gaze, gave the quick smile a busy adult has for a child. One trick that always distracted monarchs was to show how they came to have power over such a one as he.

The wizard waved his hand and Victoria saw the scene after Mount Badon, the great victory which made Arthur king of Britain. That day Merlin ensorcelled seven Saxon wizards, Arthur slew seven Saxon kings, and may well have saved his sorcerer's life.

For this princess Merlin mostly hid the gore away. He showed her Arthur and himself younger, flushed with victory and many cups of celebratory mead as in gratitude the wizard granted the king any wish within his power to give.

"Neither of us knew much law so it wasn't well thought out," he explained, and showed himself swearing an oath to come forevermore to the aid of any monarch of Britain who summoned him. "But my time is precious and must not be wasted," he told her.

Even this mild version left Victoria round-eyed with wonder, as was Merlin's intent. For certain monarchs his message could be so clear and terrifying that Richard III had gone to his death on Bosworth Field and Charles I had let his head be whacked off without trying to summon him.

For a moment wizard and princess listened and smiled at the sounds downstairs of carriages fleeing into the night.

He bowed, asked if there was anything more she desired. When she could think of nothing he bowed once more, stepped backward through the bookshelves and the wall of Kensington Palace.

She watched as the great hall of the castle with its knights and king appeared and swallowed up Merlin.

2.

"I am ruled by our young queen and happily so, as is every man of fair mind in this land," said Lord Melbourne, Queen Victoria's first prime minister.

And for a brief time that was true.

Melbourne could be a bit of a wizard, producing parliamentary majorities out of nothing, or making them disappear without a trace. A few years into young Victoria's reign, gossip held she was in the palm of his hand.

In fact she found him charming, but with her mother left behind at Kensington Palace and John Conroy exiled to the Continent, the head-strong young queen was led by no one.

The dusty castles and palaces in London and Windsor were lately the haunts of drunken and sometimes-deranged kings. She opened them up and gathered visiting European princes and her own young equerries and ladies-in-waiting for late-night feasts and dances.

Then Lord Melbourne explained to her that the people of Britain were unhappy with their monarch. "The time has come," he said, "for you to find a husband, produce an heir, and ensure stability. The choice of a groom will be yours, an opportunity and a peril. Like every marriage."

Victoria's first reaction was anger. But she knew that few women of any rank got to choose their husbands. Her choices were wide. The eligible princes of Europe paraded through Buckingham Palace and Windsor Castle.

Victoria and the Grand Duke Alexander of Russia danced the wild mazurka. Young equerries of her staff had her picture on lockets next to their hearts in the hope that she might decide to marry into her nobility and select one of them.

The nation was fascinated with its legendary past and so was its queen. She dreamed of sending the candidates on quests, having them do great deeds. But she knew that wasn't possible.

Victoria's resentment of the task made her unable to decide among the candidates. Naturally, everyone grew impatient—the potential grooms, the government, and the people of England.

As the situation worsened, the queen considered invoking Merlin, but she felt intimidated. Then Melbourne himself said the future of Britain hung on her decision. She thought this surely was a moment to summon the wizard.

One evening in her private chambers she drew out the parchment and ran through the invocation. Immediately the light of the oil lamps in her room was drowned by sunlight shining on ocean waves, pouring through windows of clearest glass into a room blue as the sea around it.

Despite his robes with the golden moon in all its phases, it took her a few moments to recognize the tall figure with dark hair and beard standing over a giant tortoise that rested on an oaken table.

Victoria watched fascinated as he stopped what he was doing and said good-bye effusively but quickly to a figure with liquid green eyes and saucy silver back flippers. The Sea King's Daughter and her palace disappeared as he strode into Victoria's private drawing room.

Merlin in the full flush of his wizardry had just murmured, "Gryphons and Guilfoils, marjoram and unicorn mange, the heart of Diana's own rabbit soaked in the blood of hummingbirds from the Emperor's gardens in far Cathay . . ."

Then he'd felt the summons, turned, seen Victoria, and lost track of the spell he was working. But a summons when it came had to be obeyed.

It could originate at any point in the long history of Britain's monarchy from the Battle of Badon on. And each caught him at a moment in his life when he was deep into weaving magic and casting spells. At his most powerful he was at his most vulnerable.

He stepped out of a place where each drinking cup had a name and every chair an ancestry into a room with walls covered by images of flowers and pictures of bloodless people. The floor was choked with furniture and every single surface was covered with myriad small objects.

Merlin had encountered Victoria when he was just a youth and she was middle-aged. That meeting would, of course, not have happened to her yet.

Now in her private apartments at Windsor Palace he knelt before Victoria, whose expression was full of curiosity about the tortoise, the palace, the creature with the flippers, and him.

But what she said was, "I brought you here because my prime minister and my people have decided I must marry for the good of Britain. I need your help to make the right decision."

And he told her as patiently as he could, "In the palace of the Sea King's Daughter, as an act of charity I was working a spell to restore the zest of life to an ancient tortoise. It houses within itself the soul of

Archimedes, the great mage of legendary times. This is the sort of favor I hope someone might someday perform if I ever needed it.

"It was all about to come together: ingredients at hand, incantation memorized, pentagrams and quarter-circles drawn, the tortoise staring up with hope in its eyes."

She sat amazed by this and by the man, dark-bearded and thirty years younger than when she'd seen him a few years before.

Victoria dreamed of turning her kingdom into a kind of Camelot, a land of castles, enchanted woods, knights in armor, and maidens under sleeping spells floating down rivers. She looked at Merlin now and thought of how perfectly he would fit into such a world.

Merlin understood. He was young, vain, and used to being wanted. He found himself liking her, but memories of the complications and quarrels after an extended tumble with Elizabeth I reminded him how unwise such liaisons could be.

His interest at that moment was getting back as quickly as possible to the life he'd had to leave.

Victoria watched him stand at the floor-length windows and stare out into the night. When he gestured, one window blew open.

Any wizard is a performer and Merlin intended to bedazzle her. He held out his right arm, candlelight danced, and a bird appeared. The shadow of a raptor rested on his wrist and seemed to flicker like a flame.

Merlin had summoned a questing spirit, the ghost of the Lord of Hawks. He whistled a single note and it became solid, all angry, unblinking eyes and savage beak.

The wizard filled a clear crystal bowl with water and said, "Your majesty, give me the name of a suitor."

She named the Grand Duke Alexander of Russia. Merlin held the hawk near the bowl which was so clear that the water seemed to float in air. He whispered the grand duke's name and looked at the surface of the water. On it he saw Alexander's fate, a winter scene with blood on the snow. An anarchist had hurled the bomb that tore the Tsar apart.

Merlin knew Victoria was not a vicious soul. If she saw this particular piece of the future it would be hard for her to keep it a secret from the Tsar-to-be.

And it was best not to upset the balance of the world. Undoing that would require more magic than he had.

So he looked at the young queen and shook his head—this one was not suitable. She looked but he had already cleared away the image.

"Who is your majesty's next suitor?"

Victoria spoke the name, Merlin relayed it to his medium, and the image of a mildly retarded prince of Savoy floated in the bowl. He shook his head, she looked relieved, and they ran through some more European royalty.

Merlin knew the man he was looking for, the one she actually had married.

He'd seen pictures galore at that time in her future and his past when he'd been summoned by this queen.

She stared at Merlin as she smiled and said, "Lord Alfred Paget." This was the most dashing of her young courtiers. A royal equerry of excellent family, he made no secret of his romantic love for his queen.

She in turn was charmed and more than a bit taken with Paget. He would be her choice if she decided to marry one not of royal birth.

But Merlin knew that wasn't the name he was looking for. When an image floated on the water, it actually made Merlin grin. He let Victoria see the once dashing Paget fat, self-satisfied, and seventy years old.

"Oh dear. This will not do!" she said with a horrified expression. Then she and the wizard laughed.

This search for a husband was far more pleasant than much of what he did in service to the Badon oath. Merlin had seen an unfaithful royal princess killed in Paris by flashing lights and a willful, runaway machine. He had visited a distant time when the king of Britain was not much more than a picture that moved.

Victoria gave the name and title of Albert, Prince of Saxe-Coburg and Gotha. A glance at the face floating on the water was all Merlin needed. This was the one he'd been waiting for.

Albert would die long before Victoria did and she would mourn him for the rest of her life. A hardier husband might be in order. But Albert was the one she was destined to marry and that was how it would be.

The image floating in the bowl was flattering. Merlin invited the queen to look, indicated his approval, and congratulated her.

His task done, Merlin prepared to leave. Victoria realized this and looked stricken.

Anyone, be they human or cambion, enjoys being found attractive. And to have won the heart of a queen was better still. Merlin bowed deeply to the monarch and wished her great happiness in her marriage.

As he strode out of her presence, Victoria saw the tortoise that contained the soul of Archimedes and the sun dancing on the waves outside the palace and the lovely daughter of the one who rules the tides.

The queen noted every detail and wondered if her kingdom could ever contain anything so beautiful. She wrote a letter to Prince Albert of Saxe-Coburg and Gotha as she thought of Merlin.

3.

"Twenty-five years into her reign, her majesty has abandoned her responsibilities."

"Since poor Prince Albert died, I hear she wears nothing but mourning clothes . . ."

"The processes of government demand the public presence of a monarch."

". . . and talks to the trees at Windsor Palace, like her daft grandfather did . . ."

"No one in her royal household, her government, and especially her family dares to broach the subject to her."

". . . curtsies to them trees as well, I got told."

Isolated as a monarch is, Victoria heard the nonsense her people were saying. She knew they said she talked to her late husband as she walked the halls of Buckingham Palace and Windsor Castle, of Balmoral in Scotland and Osborne House on the Isle of Wight.

And here they were right, sometimes she did. More than anything else, what she had lost with the death of the man to whom she'd been married for twenty years was the one person in Britain who could speak to her as an equal. She still spoke to him, but there was no reply. She felt utterly alone.

At Osborne House after a day with little warmth in the sun she stood at a window with a wind coming in from the sea and thought of Merlin.

Indeed with its graceful Italianate lines, fountains, and views of the water, Osborne was Victoria's attempt to evoke the glimpses she'd caught of the palace of the Sea King's Daughter. She envied that royal family as she did no other.

In the years of her marriage she had sometimes remembered the handsome wizard of their last meeting and always with a pang of guilt. It almost felt as if she had betrayed the marriage. In her widowhood, though, she thought about him more often.

That evening at Osborne, Victoria demanded she be completely alone in her private apartments. The queen debated with herself as to whether this was a time of danger to the crown or, as her uncle had said, a day of doldrums and no wind in the sails.

Victoria finally decided it was a good deal of both. She took the glass-bound page out of its hiding place and read the summons aloud. Immediately she saw half-naked people in savage garb looking up at a huge picture that moved. It showed some kind of carriage without horses racing down a dark, smooth road.

As monarch of a forward-looking nation, the queen had been shown zoetropes and magic lanterns. This appeared far more like real life, except that it moved too fast. Her royal train was always an express and its engine could attain speeds of almost fifty miles an hour. But that was as nothing to what this machine seemed to do.

A man, who looked familiar, like a distant cousin perhaps, sat in it smiling. "In this driver's seat everyone is a king," he said.

The queen couldn't know that she'd just had a glimpse of a distant successor.

In the year 2159 King Henry X had on a permanent loop in his offices what he called "My Agincourt." The great triumph of his reign was being named spokesperson for Chang'an/Ford/Honda, the world's mightiest automaker.

Victoria saw that the people who had been looking up at the image were now frozen, staring at a figure running straight toward her.

This one had long dark hair but no sign of a beard, was tall but not quite as tall as the Merlin she remembered. He looked very young. Instead of robes he wore what Victoria identified as some form of men's underclothes, a thing about which she made a point of knowing nothing. As he stepped into her room she saw emblazoned on the shirt the lion and the unicorn, the royal crest, directly over his heart.

Victoria had sons and she placed this boy as sixteen at most. She stared at him and said, "You're just a child. Who are you? Where are your proper clothes? And how did you get here?"

Merlin, after a moment of surprise, looked this small woman in black directly in the eyes, which none had done since Albert. Victoria heard him say,

"I am Merlin, the cambion of Albercanix and Gwenddydd. I was apprenticed to Galapas, the Hermit of the Crystal Cave, a disagreeable old tyrant. "One morning, running through my spells, I found myself summoned by Henry X, king of Britain. I was working a great magic on his courtiers when you called me here."

He glanced down at the soft clothes and shoes which still puzzled him. "And this is the livery of that king." He seemed confused.

When the young wizard first arrived in 2159, King Henry peered at him over a glass and said, "Not what I expected. Just curious as to whether this old piece of parchment actually worked—needed something to remind myself and others of the old mystique of royalty. Perhaps you could turn a few advertising people into mice. It'll teach them to respect me and the monarchy in its last days."

Victoria saw in this confused, gangling lad the man she'd encountered. The queen realized that King Arthur and the Badon Oath were well in his future and that he didn't understand what had happened to him. It occurred to her that the child of a demon and a princess who became a nun might be as separate and alone as she was.

"Your attire simply won't do," she said.

Merlin discovered that unlike King Henry this monarch was greatly respected. All the servants deferred to her and some courtiers were even afraid.

The queen had a trusted footman and pageboy dress this stranger in clothes her sons had outgrown. Merlin hated the infinite buttons and hooks, the itching flannel and stiff boots.

Victoria passed him off as a young visiting kinsman, "From the Anhalt-Latvia cousins."

Merlin remembered King Henry, so full of strange potions and drinks he sometimes had trouble standing and often couldn't remember who Merlin was.

The young wizard had tried not to show how bedazzled he was by the magic of that court, lights that came and went with the wave of a hand, cold air that seeped out of walls to cool a kingdom where it was always hot outdoors, unseen musicians who beat drums, sang, played harps of incredible variety through the day and night without tiring.

The king's entourage was so amazed by Merlin's spells of invisibility and the way he could turn them into frogs and back into courtiers that they lost any interest in their monarch and flocked around him.

They persuaded Merlin to surrender his own rough robes and gave him shorts, T-shirts, and soft shoes like everyone else in the kingdom. He had never worn clothes with legs or felt fabric as light.

All he knew for certain was that he didn't want to return to the Crystal Cave and the Hermit. He spent some amazing days and light-filled nights in the court of 2159.

Victoria, everyone agreed, seemed more cheerful since the appearance of her strange relative. The two of them took walks together and he showed her nixies riding in on the morning waves and sprites dancing by moonlight. He turned her pug dog into a trained bear and turned it back again.

Merlin didn't understand this world in which palaces and castles all looked utterly indefensible, ruins had been built just to be ruins, and the queen's knights seemed an unlikely band of warriors without a missing eye or gouged-out nose among them.

On their walks Victoria sometimes ran on about wanting to create a court full of art and poetry like King Arthur at Camelot. It amazed her that he understood none of this. So she told him the bits and pieces she had learned over the years about the Badon Oath and Arthur's kingdom. The young mage was fascinated.

Once she made Merlin sit through a chamber music concert and talked afterward about "The melodies of the wonderful Herr Mendelssohn to whom I could listen forever." He told her about the court of her descendent Henry X where invisible musicians played all day and all night.

He could have told her more about the future of her kingdom, but out of respect and even affection he never much mentioned her descendant. Never described seeing King Henry in a false crown, armor, and broadsword quaff "Royal English Ale" from a horn cup and signify his approval. Never said how he'd sampled the ale and found it so vile he spat it out. When he finished that endorsement, the king had turned and seen the shocked expression on young Merlin's face. He said, "I'm the last, you know. I'm preserved in so many formats that they'll never need another king for their ads. I've no children that I know of and no one is interested in succeeding me. I'm sorry I let you see all this." He started to cry great drunken tears.

Merlin walked away as quickly as he could. He strode into the room where his majesty's greatest promotional moments played on a screen.

He didn't know where he was going but he headed for a door and the blazing-hot outdoors.

When some of his majesty's courtiers tried to stop him he froze them in place with a spell. At that moment of his magic Victoria's summons rescued him.

For that and her stories he would always be grateful. But he was young, male, and a wizard and this was a queen's court with many young women attached to it.

Merlin had a fine rumpus of a rendezvous in a linen closet with an apprentice maid of the wardrobe and another more leisurely meeting with a young lady-in-waiting in her chamber.

Spells to blank the memories of passersby didn't quite dispel the stories. The queen steadfastly refused to hear this gossip.

But she understood how keeping him there was as unnatural as imprisoning a wild animal. She ordered certain clothing to be made. One day Merlin returned to his rooms and found on the bed robes and a cloak with the moon in all its phases and fine leather boots like the ones her majesty had noticed older Merlins wearing.

The youth had never seen anything so splendid. He changed and went to her private rooms where she was waiting. "Sir Merlin, you have fulfilled and more the tasks for which you were summoned," she said and he saw how hard this was for her. "You are dismissed with our thanks and the certainty we will meet again."

Merlin bowed low. And before the royal tears came, or his own could start, he found himself hurtling backward through the centuries to the hermit Galapas and the Crystal Cave.

Merlin didn't linger there but immediately set out across Wales, finding within himself the magic to cover miles in minutes. One story Victoria had told was of a king trying to build a castle before his enemies were upon him.

Each day the walls would be raised and each night they would be thrown down. All were in despair until a bold youth in a cloak of moons appeared. He tamed two dragons that fought every night in the caves below the castle and made the walls collapse. Merlin knew he was that youth.

4.

"Queen Victoria," a commentator said at her Golden Jubilee, "inherited a Britain linked by stagecoach and reigned in a Britain that ran on rails. She ruled over a quarter of the globe and a quarter of its people."

At Balmoral Castle in the Highlands late in her reign the queen went into high mourning because a gamekeeper, John Brown, had died.

"Mrs. Brown mourns dead husband," was how a scurrilous underground London sheet put it.

In fact, Brown, belligerent, hard-drinking, and rude to every person at court except her majesty, was the only one on Earth who spoke to her as one human being to another.

He died unmourned by anyone but the queen. But she mourned him extravagantly. Memorial plaques were installed; statuettes were manufactured.

He was gone but the court's relief was short-lived. To commemorate becoming Empress of India, Victoria imported servants from the subcontinent. Among them was Abdul Karim who taught her a few words of Hindi. For this the queen called him "the Munshi" or teacher and appointed him her private secretary.

Soon the Munshi was brought along to state occasions, allowed to handle secret government reports, introduced to foreign dignitaries. He engaged in minor intrigue and told her majesty nasty stories about his fellow servants. The entire court wished the simple, straightforward Mr. Brown was back. Victoria's children, many well into middle age, found the Munshi appalling. The government worried about its state secrets.

"Indian cobra in queen's parlor," the slander sheets proclaimed.

The queen would hear nothing against him. But she knew he wasn't what she wanted.

"Oh the cruelty of young women and the folly of old men," Merlin cried as he paced the floor in the tower of glass that was his prison cell.

Nimue the enchantress who beguiled his declining years had turned against him, used the skills he'd taught her to imprison him.

When he was a boy, Queen Victoria had told him about King Uther Pendragon, whose castle walls collapsed each night. Solving that, young Merlin won the confidence of Pendragon. The birth of the king's son Arthur, hiding the infant from usurpers, the sword in the stone, the kingdom of Britain, and all the rest had followed from that.

But Victoria never told Merlin about Nimue. She thought it too sad.

"Sired by an incubus, baptized in church, tamer of dragons, advisor to kings, I am a cambion turned into a cuckold," he wailed.

Most of his magic had deserted him. He hadn't even enough to free himself. Still he did little spells, turned visiting moths into butterflies, made his slippers disappear and reappear. Merlin knew he had a reason for doing this but couldn't always remember what it was.

Then one morning while making magic he found himself whisked from the tower and summoned to a room crammed full of tartan pillows and with claymore swords hung on the walls as decoration. Music played in the next room and an old lady in black looked at him kindly.

The slump of his shoulders, the unsteadiness of his stance, led the Queen of England, the Empress of India, to rise and lead him over to sit on the divan next to her.

"That music you hear is a string quartet playing a reduction of Herr Mendelssohn's 'Scottish Symphony,'" she said. "Musicians are on call throughout my waking hours. You told me long ago this was how things were arranged at the Royal Court in 2159."

It was a brisk day and they drank mulled wine. "The sovereign of Britain requires a wizard to attend Her," she said, "for a period of time which She shall determine."

Merlin realized he was rescued. And when the Munshi walked into the room unannounced, the Wizard stood to his full height. Seeing a white-bearded man with flashing eyes and sparks darting from his hands, the Munshi fled.

Everyone at Balmoral marveled at the day her majesty put aside her secretary and gave orders that he was not to approach her. All wondered if someone else had taken his place but no evidence of that could ever be found.

People talked about the eccentricities of Queen Victoria's last years: the seat next to hers that she insisted always be kept empty in carriages, railroad cars, at state dinners, the rooms next to hers that must never be entered.

At times the queen would send all the ladies and servants away from her chambers and not let them in until next morning.

Some at court hinted that all this had shaded over into madness and attributed it to heredity. Most thought it was just old age, harmless and in its way charmingly human.

In fact a few members of her court did see things out of the corners of their eyes. Merlin could conjure invisibility but his concentration was no longer perfect.

Her majesty walking over the gorse at Balmoral in twilight, on the shore on a misty day at Osborne, in the corridors of Windsor Castle would suddenly be accompanied by a cloaked figure with a white beard and long white hair.

When the viewer looked again he would have disappeared.

She talked to Merlin about their prior meetings and how she cherished each of them. The wizard would once have sneered at the picturesque ruins and the undefendable faux castles that dotted the landscape near any royal residence. Now he understood they had been built in tribute to the sage who'd saved the young princess, the handsome magician who had helped choose her husband, the quicksilver youth of her widowhood.

When she finally became very ill at Windsor, Queen Victoria had ruled for more than sixty years. Merlin remembered that this was the time when she would die.

He stayed with her, put in her mind the things he knew she found pleasing, summoned up music only she could hear. He wondered if, when she was gone, he would be returned to Nimue and the tower.

"She assumed the throne in the era of Sir Walter Scott and her reign has lasted into the century of Mr. H. G. Wells," the *Times* of London said.

In the last days when her family came to see her, Victoria had the glass with the parchment inside it under her covers. Merlin stood in a corner and was visible only to the queen.

When her son who would be Edward VII appeared, Merlin shook his head.

This man would never summon him. It was the same with her grandson who would be George V.

A great-grandchild, a younger son who stammered, was brought in with his brothers. Merlin nodded: this one would summon him to London decades later when hellfire fell from the skies.

The boy was called back after he and his brothers had left, was given the parchment, and shown how to hide it.

"You are my last and only friend," Victoria told Merlin. He held her hands when she died and felt grief for the first time in his life. But he wasn't returned to his glass prison.

Uninvited, invisible, utterly alone at the funeral, he followed the caisson that bore the coffin through the streets of Windsor, carried the only friend he'd ever had to the Royal Mausoleum at Frogmore.

"We say of certain people, 'She was a woman of her time,'" an orator proclaimed. "But of how many can it be said that the span of their years, the time in which they lived, will be named for them?"

"A bit of her is inside each one of us," said a woman watching the cortege.

"And that I suppose is what a legend is."

In the winter twilight with snow on the ground, Merlin stood outside the mausoleum. "I don't want to transfer my mind and soul to another human or beast, and I won't risk using that magic and getting summoned. There's no other monarch I wish to serve."

He remembered the Hermit of the Crystal Cave. Old Galapas hadn't been much of a teacher, but Merlin had learned the Wizard's Last Spell from him.

It was simple enough and he hadn't forgotten. Merlin invoked it and those who had lingered in the winter dusk saw for a moment a figure with white hair and beard, wearing robes with the moon in all its phases.

The old wizard waved a wand, shimmered for a moment, then appeared to shatter. In the growing dark what seemed like tiny stars flew over the mausoleum, over Windsor, over Britain and all the world.

Richard Bowes has published six novels, four story collections, and seventy-five short stories. His work has appeared on a couple of dozen award short lists, and he has won two World Fantasy, a Lambda, Million Writers, and IHG Awards. Recent stories have appeared in Ellen Datlow's *The Doll Collection*, *The Magazine of Science Fiction & Fantasy*, *Farrago's Wainscot*, *Uncanny*, *Tor.com*, *XIII*, *Interfictions*, *Best Gay Stories 2015*, *The Year's Best Dark Fantasy and Horror 2015*, *The Time Traveller's Almanac*, and *In the Shadow of the Towers*.

Jane Yolen, the prolific author of scores of modern fairy tales, tells a clever story about a wise slave and an equally astute djinn. In pre-Islamic Arabian folklore, djinn (or jinn) are a race of supernatural beings who could be called through magic to perform desired tasks. The familiar "genie" in a bottle/lamp icon comes primarily from the tale of Aladdin collected in The Book of 1001 Nights. *Although it is a genuine Middle Eastern folk tale, "Aladdin" was not included in the original Arabic versions of* The Nights. *Antoine Galland—whose* Les Mille et une nuits, contes arabes traduits en français *was the first European translation—included the story and six others not in the Arabic manuscript after hearing them told by a Syrian Maronite monk, Hanna Diab.*

Memoirs of a Bottle Djinn

Jane Yolen

The sea was as dark as old blood, not the wine color poets sing of. In the early evening it seemed to stain the sand. As usual this time of year the air was heavy, ill-omened. I walked out onto the beach below my master's house, whenever I could slip away unnoticed, though it was a dangerous practice. Still, it was one necessary to my well-being. I had been a sailor for many more years than I had been a slave. And the smell of the salt air was not a luxury for me but a necessity.

If a seabird had washed up dead at my feet, its belly would have contained black worms and other evil auguries, so dark and lowering was the sky. So I wondered little at the bottle that the sea had deposited before me, certain it contained noxious fumes at best, the legacy of its long cradling in such a salty womb.

In my country poets sing the praises of wine and gift its color to the water along the shores of Hellas, and I can think of no finer hymn. But in this land they believe their prophet forbade them strong drink. They are a sober race who reward themselves in heaven even as they deny themselves on earth. It is a system of which I do not approve, but then I am a Greek by birth and a heathen by inclination despite my master's long importuning. It is only by chance that I have not yet lost an eye, an ear, or a hand to my master's unforgiving code. He finds me amusing, but it has been seven years since I have had a drink.

I stared at the bottle. If I had any luck at all, the bottle had fallen from a foreign ship and its contents would still be potable. But then, if I had any luck at all, I would not be a slave in Araby, a Greek sailor washed up on these shores the same as the bottle at my feet. My father, who was a cynic like his father before him, left me with a cynic's name—Antithias— a wry heart, and an acid tongue, none proper legacies for a slave.

But as blind Homer wrote, "Few sons are like their father; many are worse." I guessed that the wine, if drinkable, would come from an inferior year. And with that thought, I bent to pick it up.

The glass was a cloudy green, like the sea after a violent storm. Like the storm that had wrecked my ship and cast me onto a slaver's shore. There were darker flecks along the bottom, a sediment that surely foretold an undrinkable wine. I let the bottle warm between my palms.

Since the glass was too dark to let me see more, I waited past my first desire and was well into my second, letting it rise up in me like the heat of passion. The body has its own memories, though I must be frank: passion, like wine, was simply a fragrance remembered. Slaves are not lent the services of houri nor was one my age and race useful for breeding. It had only been by feigning impotence that I had kept that part of my anatomy intact—another of my master's unforgiving laws. Even in the dark of night, alone on my pallet, I forwent the pleasures of the hand for there were spies everywhere in his house and the eunuchs were a notably gossipy lot. Little but a slave's tongue lauding morality stood between gossip and scandal, stood between me and the knife. Besides, the women of Araby tempted me little. They were like the bottle in my hand—beautiful and empty. A wind blowing across the mouth of each could make them sing but the tunes were worth little. I liked my women like my wine—full-bodied and tanged with history, bringing a man into poetry. So I had put my passion into work these past seven years, slave's work though it was. Blind Homer had it right, as usual: "Labor conquers all things." Even old lusts for women and wine.

Philosophy did not conquer movement, however, and my hand found the cork of the bottle before I could stay it. With one swift movement I had plucked the stopper out. A thin strand of smoke rose into the air. A very bad year indeed, I thought, as the cork crumbled in my hand.

Up and up and up the smoky rope ascended and I, bottle in hand, could not move, such was my disappointment. Even my father's cynicism and his father's before him had not prepared me for such a sudden loss of all hope. My mind, a moment before full of anticipation and philosophy, was now in blackest despair. I found myself without will, reliving in my mind the moment of my capture and the first bleak days of my enslavement.

That is why it was several minutes before I realized that the smoke had begun to assume a recognizable shape above the bottle's gaping mouth: long, sensuous legs glimpsed through diaphanous trousers; a waist my hands could easily span; breasts beneath a short embroidered cotton vest as round as ripe pomegranates; and a face . . . the face was smoke and air. I remembered suddenly a girl in the port of Alexandria who sold fruit from a basket and gave me a smile. She was the last girl who had smiled upon me when I was a free man and I, not knowing the future, had ignored her, so intent was I on my work. My eyes clouded over at the memory, and when they were clear again, I saw that same smile imprinted upon the face of the djinn.

"I am what you would have me be, master," her low voice called down to me.

I reached up a hand to help her step to earth, but my hand went through hers, mortal flesh through smoky air. It was then, I think, that I really believed she was what I guessed her to be.

She smiled. "What is your wish, master?"

I took the time to smile back. "How many wishes do I get?" She shook her head but still she smiled, that Alexandrian smile, all lips without a hint of teeth. But there was a dimple in her left cheek. "One, my master, for you drew the cork but once."

"And if I draw it again?"

"The cork is gone." This time her teeth showed as did a second dimple, on the right.

I sighed and looked at the crumbled mess in my hand, then sprinkled the cork like seed upon the sand. "Just one."

"Does a slave need more?" she asked in that same low voice.

"You mean that I should ask for my freedom?" I laughed and sat down on the sand. The little waves that outrun the big ones tickled my feet, for I had come out barefoot. I looked across the water. "Free to be

301

a sailor again at my age? Free to let the sun peel the skin from my back, free to heave my guts over the stern in a blinding rain, free to wreck once more upon a slaver's shore?"

She drifted down beside me and, though her smoky hand could not hold mine, I felt a breeze across my palm that could have been her touch. I could see through her to the cockleshells and white stones pocking the sand.

"Free to make love to Alexandrian women," she said. "Free to drink strong wine."

"Free to have regrets in the morning either way," I replied. Then I laughed.

She laughed back. "What about the freedom to indulge in a dinner of roast partridge in lemons and eggplant? What about hard-boiled eggs sprinkled with vermilion? What about cinnamon tripes?" It was the meal my master had just had.

"Rich food like rich women gives me heartburn," I said.

"The freedom to fill your pockets with coins?" Looking away from her, over the clotted sea, I whispered to myself, "'Accursed thirst for gold! What dost thou not compel mortals to do,'" a line from the *Aeneid*.

"Virgil was a wise man," she said quietly. "For a Roman!" Then she laughed.

I turned to look at her closely for the first time. A woman who knows Virgil, be she djinn or mortal, was a woman to behold. Though her body was still composed of that shifting, smoky air, the features on her face now held steady. She no longer looked like the Alexandrian girl, but had a far more sophisticated beauty. Lined with kohl, her eyes were gray as smoke and her hair the same color. There were shadows along her cheeks that emphasized the bone and faint smile lines crinkling the skin at each corner of her generous mouth. She was not as young as she had first appeared, but then I am not so young myself.

"Ah, Antithias," she said, smiling at me, "even djinns age, though corked up in a bottle slows down the process immeasurably."

I spoke Homer's words to her then: "In youth and beauty, wisdom is but rare." I added in my own cynic's way, "If ever."

"You think me wise, then?" she asked, then laughed and her laughter was like the tinkling of camel bells. "But a gaudy parrot is surely as wise, reciting another's words as his own."

"I know no parrots who hold Virgil and Homer in their mouths," I said, gazing at her not with longing but with a kind of wonder. "No djinn either."

"You know many?"

"Parrots, yes; djinn, no. You are my first."

"Then you are lucky, indeed, Greek, that you called up one of the worshippers of Allah and not one of the followers of Iblis."

I nodded. "Lucky, indeed."

"So, to your wish, master," she said.

"You call me master, I who am a slave," I said. "Do *you* not want the freedom you keep offering me? Freedom from the confining green bottle, freedom from granting wishes to any *master* who draws the cork?"

She brushed her silvery hair back from her forehead with a delicate hand. "You do not understand the nature of the djinn," she said. "You do not understand the nature of the bottle."

"I understand rank," I said. "On the sea I was between the captain and the rowers. In that house," and I gestured with my head to the palace behind me, "I am below my master and above the kitchen staff. Where are you?"

Her brow furrowed as she thought. "If I work my wonders for centuries, I might at last attain a higher position within the djinn," she said.

It was my turn to smile. "Rank is a game," I said. "It may be conferred by birth, by accident, or by design. But rank does not honor the man. The man honors the rank."

"You are a philosopher," she said, her eyes lightening.

"I am a Greek," I answered. "It is the same thing." She laughed again, holding her palm over her mouth coquettishly. I could no longer see straight through her though an occasional piece of driftwood appeared like a delicate tattoo on her skin.

"Perhaps we both need a wish," I said, shifting my weight. One of my feet touched hers and I could feel a slight jolt, as if lightning had run between us. Such things happen occasionally on the open sea.

"Alas, I cannot wish, myself," she said in a whisper. "I can only grant wishes."

I looked at her lovely face washed with its sudden sadness and whispered back, "Then I give my wish to you." She looked directly into my eyes and I could see her eyes turn golden in the dusty light, I could at the same time somehow see beyond them, not into the sand or water, but to a different place, a place of whirlwinds and smokeless fire.

303

"Then, Antithias, you will have wasted a wish," she said.

Shifting her gaze slightly, she looked behind me, her eyes opening wide in warning. As she spoke, her body seemed to melt into the air and suddenly there was a great white bird before me, beating its feathered pinions against my body before taking off towards the sky.

"Where are you going?" I cried.

"To the Valley of Abqar," the bird called. "To the home of my people. I will wait there for your wish, Greek. But hurry. I see both your past and your future closing in behind you." I turned and, pouring down the stone steps of my master's house, were a half-dozen guards and one shrilling eunuch pointing his flabby hand in my direction. They came towards me screaming, though what they were saying I was never to know for their scimitars were raised and my Arabic deserts me in moments of sheer terror.

I think I screamed; I am not sure. But I spun around again towards the sea and saw the bird winging away into a halo of light.

"Take me with you," I cried. "I desire no freedom but by your side."

The bird shuddered as it flew, then banked sharply, and headed back towards me, calling, "Is that your wish, master?" A scimitar descended.

"That is my wish," I cried, as the blade bit into my throat.

We have lived now for centuries within the green bottle and Zarifa was right, I had not understood its nature. Inside is an entire world, infinite and ever-changing. The smell of the salt air blows through that world and we dwell in a house that sometimes overlooks the ocean and sometimes overlooks the desert sands.

Zarifa, my love, is as mutable, neither young nor old, neither soft nor hard. She knows the songs of blind Homer and the poet Virgil as well as the poems of the warlords of ayyām al-'Arab. She can sing in languages that are long dead.

And she loves me beyond my wishing, or so she says, and I must believe it for she would not lie to me. She loves me though I have no great beauty, my body bearing a sailor's scars and a slave's scar and this curious blood necklace where the scimitar left its mark. She loves me, she says, for my cynic's wit and my noble heart, that I would have given my wish to her.

So we live together in our ever-changing world. I read now in six tongues beside Greek and Arabic, and have learned to paint and sew. My paintings are in the Persian style, but I embroider like a Norman queen. We learn from the centuries, you see, and we taste the world anew each time the cork is drawn.

So there, my master, I have fulfilled your curious wish, speaking my story to you alone. It seems a queer waste of your one piece of luck, but then most men waste their wishes. And if you are a poet and a storyteller, as you say, of the lineage of blind Homer and the rest, but one who has been blocked from telling more tales, then perhaps my history can speed you on your way again. I shall pick up one of your old books my master, now that we have a day and a night in this new world. Do you have a favorite I should try—or should I just go to a bookseller and trust my luck? In the last few centuries it has been remarkably good you see.

Jane Yolen, author of over two hundred short stories and over 350 books, is often called the Hans Christian Andersen of America—though she wonders (not entirely idly) whether she should really be called the "Hans Jewish Andersen of America." She has been named both Grand Master of the World Fantasy Convention and Grand Master of the Science Fiction Poetry Association. She has won two Nebulas for her short stories, and a bunch of other awards, including six honorary doctorates. One of her awards, the Skylark, given by the New England Science Fiction Association, set her good coat on fire, a warning about faunching after shiny things that she has not forgotten.

"The Mussel Eater" is a reimagining of a Maori tale, "Pania of the Reef." There are various versions of the story, but none are told as deliciously as Cade's nor are the consequences of curiosity and desire quite so consuming.

The Mussel Eater

Octavia Cade

The Pania is sitting in a rock pool, grooming. Karitoki can't help but be fascinated—Pania usually stay in their packs, out beyond the harbour and away from town. Even living by the ocean as he does, he has never been so close to one before.

"I was curious," she says, when he asks her. She has seen him eyeing her, seen him moving closer, and holds out one of her hands. It is stronger than his, and the nails are pointed. "Are you curious, too?"

Her hair feels like seaweed—air-dried, stiff with salt, and so matted with sand from the shallows he can hardly get his fingers through it. "Let me," says the Pania, reaching with her razor nails, but he pushes her hands away and undoes the strands himself, unknotting, untangling, easing the way with sweet water and ignoring her moue, half-disgusted, at the freshness of it.

"You smell like the sea," says Karitoki.

"What else would I smell like?" she says, and beneath the salt and the brine and the under-tang of shellfish is a faint, sweet odor of rot, of mussels left too long on the beach and under the sun, of the torn fragments left by seabirds, breaking open calcium carbonate and leaving fleshy feet to spoil. When he is done with her hair, he sits back and watches her coat herself with oil.

"The water's cold," she says. "It helps to keeps the heat in." And she went on insulating herself, applying fish oil to her legs, her feet, oil glossing over the bare hint of scales. Karitoki has seen this before, on a boat travelling along the coast: Pania on the rocks, sunning themselves and basting until their bodies gleamed and their flesh was bright against the waves. He and the other young men would watch them from the deck, fascinated by their plump shine, the flash of bone and breast. And beneath all fascination would be the longing to swim with them as the seals swam, around their fins and nuzzling up to the sturdy fish-scent of them, all danger and teeth and ruthless purpose. But Karitoki is not a seal, and so his swimming is perilous. Pania are guardians but they are not his; they exist to dote on dolphins, on whales and seals and ocean mammals and they have little tolerance for threats. Karitoki is no threat, he wishes no harm—but he has never been near enough to prove this and the Pania, oiling herself before him, is now so very close. His fingers itch to touch her. He wants to show that he is friendly, that he can be trusted.

The Pania lets him help in return for the mussels he has dug up out of sand, and Karitoki's hands shake as he wets his palms, makes them slick and slippery. The oil is strong, pungent. He will smell of fish for days. "Do you always use this?" he says, and his hands are warm on the Pania's collarbones, the sharp protuberances of shoulder blades.

"What else should I use?" she says. "What else is there that smells so wonderful?" And Karitoki, who makes his living with mussels, who breathes in the redolent, wine-scented steam of their braising but who prefers that scent on his plate and not on his women, is briefly silent.

"I can bring you something that smells better," he says.

He brings orange oil to the ocean, boiled out of pith from the Northland orchards and fragrant. When he smooths it onto the Pania's legs, onto her webbed feet, she smells of groves and distilleries and he laps at her skin until he feels scales on his tongue. She'll only allow it for so long—the oil is thin and stinging, and when it's left on too long it makes her itch. She washes it off in salt water while he digs for mussels on the beach. Just a few, barely enough, but they share them out between them.

The Pania eats hers raw, but Karitoki steams his in a pan over a driftwood fire, steams them with oranges and fennel until they're plump and sweet. He offers some to her, but though her teeth gleam at him like bone spears she doesn't eat cooked food. Instead, she winds the fennel through her hair and uses an orange as club, to smash the little crabs in their rock pools so she can suck out their insides.

He walks her back out to sea, and tries to look like he's enjoying it. The Pania had laughed when he'd left his sandals on, snickered through her fingers and looked at him with cheerful mockery, so he'd shrugged them off and tried to move as if he didn't care what he stepped on.

"You can't feel the bottom if your feet are all tied up like that," she says, and the sandy bottom squelches beneath his toes. He can see her give a little shimmy with each step, to embed her feet further in, to luxuriate in sensation.

"It's not the sand I'm worried about," he says, squeamish. Karitoki digs for mussels but he's seen the long-liners, seen what the paddle crabs do to their lures, stripping the lines in minutes while the fish swim away unbaited. And he's played in the water himself, enough to be pinched and nipped to bleeding as the crabs cover the bottom like cobblestones.

"Think yourself lucky," says the Pania, wallowing, the water hip deep now and enough for her to swim in so she does, her body slick and undulating beside him, her thighs thick as his waist, plump and gleaming with fat. Even when she had walked beside him she had not been worried— the crabs could sense a Pania, and scuttled away from the webbed feet, the fin-fringed legs, the quick clawed hands and gleaming teeth.

When a crab catches hold of Karitoki's foot he swears, just a little and under his breath at that, and the Pania is under the water before he can blink, snatching his foot and the crab both, and if he gets his foot back before he's overbalanced back into the water, it's only because the crab lets go after the Pania has bitten through its shell. He hears the crunching, underwater as it is, and when the Pania surfaces water is streaming down her and she's spitting out shell in fragments.

"Teeth are better than oranges," she says.

There is crabmeat caught in her gums. Her teeth shine like broken glass in her mouth, but not the glass that washes up on the beach as pebbles, worn smooth by the ocean, opaque. They shine like sharks' teeth, and if Karitoki thought to check his foot for bleeding he thinks better of it now. Instead, he shifts his weight forward a fraction, buries his pinched flesh in the sand behind him, and stays very, very still. Pieces of crab are floating in the water around him. Too small for the Pania, but he knows they would attract gulls if the situation were different. But gulls, like crabs, know a Pania when they see one, and have no wish to be stuffed, feathers and beak and eggy salt flesh, into that gaping maw. Karitoki knows she could do it—snatch a bird from its dive and devour it, bones and all, as easily as she consumed the crab.

The Pania gleams her sharp teeth at him. "*Much* better than oranges," she says.

Karitoki brings olive oil to the ocean, a pressed pale liquid that glimmers green on the Pania and makes her skin shimmer. It spills down her in viscous waves, over her shoulders and down her arms in slow currents, making her skin shine bright in the sun. The Pania cups oil in her hands, smells the trees and the fruit and the warm wood echo of it, and she spills it over Karitoki in turn, spreads it down his back, working it into muscles and keeping her nails away.

It takes damp sand to scrub it all off, to make her smell of fish again, and while she does Karitoki cuts up mussels into chunks, binds them with egg and flour and onions and fries them in oil. The Pania squirms closer in the sand, fascinated with the bubble and spit, but when Karitoki turns the fritters in their pan she is splashed by the spatter, just a little, and retreats to the sea, hissing, will not let him cool her burns with oil. When he turns to make a second batch he sees the bowl is gone, and the Pania is out of reach, finger-licking and scooping the raw mix into balls in her hands. She swallows them whole and sends the bowl floating back, while Karitoki eats his fritters with oil-stained hands, with lemon and pepper.

They spend their time in rock pools, mostly. The Pania can come ashore if she wishes, but she loves the salt water too well to leave it, and Karitoki can only bear it so long before his skin starts to pucker and shrivel. Instead, he sits on the rocks and dangles his feet in the water, compares his own pink flesh to hers, glossy and finned and well muscled for swimming, the expanded chest, the extra capacity for lungs and breath.

"You could come just for an afternoon," says Karitoki. "We wouldn't ever be out of sight of shore." He's kept quiet, mostly, about the time he spends on the beach, the time he spends not digging mussels, but even if they are hidden by rocks it is not a private place and people talk, are suspicious with him. His brothers don't believe he's made a friend. "How much have you got to talk about?" they ask, not willing to grasp that he's not interested in talking, not really. If only they'd see the Pania close up, he thinks. It's one thing for adolescents to stare from a distance, to gaze upon the plump sweet flesh of the pack and swallow down their desire, but having the curves under his own hands, feeling the slick of oil and inhaling the harsh fish scent of it is something else entirely. They don't believe his stories, don't believe that a Pania would allow him so close. They'd change their minds if he were to take her hand and bring her to them, but instead they look at his picnic basket and saucepan with skepticism. "Why would you bother?" they ask. "Even if you wanted to risk getting up close, you know they won't eat anything but raw."

"If I could only persuade her to try," says Karitoki. He knows how mussels taste, is bound to them by position as well as preference, for the mussel beds are a family occupation and there was never any other career for him. Knows, too, dozens of recipes, hundreds of them; knows what appeals to those who like sweet flavours and those who like sour, those who like grapes with their food and those who'd rather have their shellfish soaked in ale. "Perhaps if she tried, she could see that it wasn't all bad," he says.

"You're trying to make her follow you home," says his oldest brother. "To make her leave the pods, leave them to fend for themselves. Good luck! You'll need a better bait than cooked mussels to turn a Pania's head."

Karitoki does not give up. He returns the next day, brings butter to the ocean and braises mussels for her; sautés them in the butter with garlic, leaves them to simmer in wine and a few fragrant strands of saffron. Karitoki offers her some of the sauvignon when he is done, the bottle only half-empty after braising. "This is what keeps me warm," he says, and if that is the truth it is not all of it, for wine can bring a warm body in more ways than one and Karitoki has used it before for seduction. But when the Pania tastes it, brings the bottle to her mouth, her teeth close on the glass and bite it off, and if he did not snatch it from her she would have cut herself on the edges. Dragging the bottle away, he spills some on her by accident.

She laps it up, screws up her face. "It's so sour," she says. "I don't like it." She prefers the butter, likes the way the little pats of it sit in her hands and soften until she can work it into her skin, between the wet fish creases of her. The butter, he thinks, is worst of all. She no longer smells purely of fish—she is rancid fish, now, and there are small lumps left on her flesh where the butter hasn't yet sunk in.

But the Pania is happy, sniffs herself in constant fascination. "It's like fat," she says. "Like the blubber on the seals, or the whales." She wears it as if it were perfume as well as warmth, and Karitoki eats upwind of her.

He has smelt blubber before. When he was younger, still a child but almost grown, a southern right whale had stranded itself on the beach, stranded in the middle of the night. The Pania had grouped offshore of it, wailing, and he could not remember now if he had seen his Pania wailing with them, but he had remembered the smell. The whale had died before the town could refloat it, had lain for some days upon the beach while awaiting its disposal. Karitoki remembered the sweet scent of salt rot, the way it had clung to his clothes when he went to visit, to watch it waste before blessings and the ceremonial *karakia*, before the body was taken away for stripping and science.

"What will happen to the meat?" Karitoki had asked. "Is it given to the Pania?"

"They'd no more eat it than you would," he was told.

"Of course we wouldn't," says the Pania, when her butter-skin brings him back out of memories and he asks her of her diet. There are many reasons. "We like our food better cold," she says, as if it's been sitting on the beach under sunlight for all hours of the day, as if she cannot eat at midnight, eat in the early hours of the morning when the flesh has chilled out of sunlight. "We prefer not to eat carrion," she says, as if they all don't eat it, Pania and human both, when the fishing boats come back to harbor

The Mussel Eater

and the catch is shared out between them. "Don't you think it would taste terrible?" she says, as if the meat, rich and dark and oily, would not give her calories for days, would not be tender between the bright carnivorous teeth of her. "We hear them singing, sometimes," she says, and this is the part Karitoki would like to believe, because if it were true it speaks of loyalty, and he has worked so hard to earn hers and he would like to think that he could keep it.

"There is our duty, also," says the Pania, a guardian to the last. "And some things just taste better." She does not eye him as she says this, which would have given him a thrill, of sorts, but stares at the ocean. Karitoki wants to know if she is remembering tastes which are beyond him, but he cannot bring himself to ask. Better, perhaps, if he does not know.

Karitoki brings coconut oil to the ocean. He cooks mussels for the Pania, cooks them with lemongrass and lime, with chili and palm sugar and coconut milk. The Pania is not interested, not remotely, but she is delighted with the fish sauce he adds in careful drops, steals the bottle from him and sucks the sauce gently from it while he sucks sugar from his fingers.

She is not interested in sweetness, he learns. The flavor is unwelcome on her tongue, and she will not let him kiss her while he tastes of palm. Even the scent on his breath disturbs her, and he must keep his mouth shut, breath through his nose, while he spreads the oil down her back. She permits this only because other Pania, in other regions, have told her of coconuts, how they float in the ocean and can be bitten through when nothing but soft fish is available and their jaws are bored with tiny bones.

"I would like to see a coconut," says the Pania, knowing her home waters are too far south for her desires. Karitoki would bring her one, but when he opens his mouth to offer she wrinkles her nose and slinks back into the water, her own self stinking of oil and sauce.

He does bring her a coconut, and she has never been so animated. He leaves mussels smoking on the beach, and there is not the slightest flutter of mockery as he wears his sandals into the harbor waters. She is too intent for that—scudding the nut across the waves, tossing it up and down, chasing it through the ocean like prey. She throws it to him in games of catch and Karitoki pretends to clumsiness, misses where

313

otherwise he would not, for she is strong in the water and can propel the coconut like cannonballs.

He does not have to pretend long. The Pania's delighted cries call her kin. Some of the pack ventures into the harbor, and they are better gamesters than he is even if he were paying attention, and with the wet wall of flesh about him he is not. Pania brush up against him, playful, undulating, brushing him with their fins and their fingers, dunking down under the water and bringing up crabs to eat. They twist off the crab legs and offer them to him, giggle behind their hands at his small white teeth, at how he has to suck the meat from the claws instead of crunching them whole.

Pania bring dolphins with them, their fins slicing through the water, and they too are playing with the coconut. Karitoki is stupefied with pleasure, almost, with the flesh and the fins and the frisson of it all, so stunned with sensuality that when the coconut comes his way again he never even sees the throw. When the nut hits him it draws blood, the skin split and seeping.

Instantly the mood is changed. Some of the dolphins have calves with them, and Pania exist to be protective. Blood in the water about their charges raises every lethal instinct in them and they are now less nymph than shark, circling Karitoki and drawing him away from the pod, out to deeper waters where he is less maneuverable than they, and far less swift.

"It's all right," he says, hands held above the water and the sea floor falling off beneath him, and the water squeezing his lungs to panic and breathlessness. "It was an accident. I don't want them. It's all right!"

The Pania—his Pania—is there as well, circling him closer than all the rest. Her teeth are all on show, and she does not take her eyes off him. None of them take their eyes off him.

"I like cooked food, remember?" he says, reaching out to her in desperation. "*Cooked*, not raw. I'm not here to hunt your dolphins."

You were the only one I wanted to hunt, he thinks. *You were the only one I wanted to gobble up.*

"This is my blood, not theirs," he says, at the last, and the salt water has not yet sealed the wound. He has his hands over it, pressing down, but red still trickles into the water and the Pania moves closer. It is his blood but it is warm, and in the ocean warm blood is the purview of pods, of whales and dolphins and seals. Of the creatures the Pania are sworn to protect, to nurture above all else. "It's not theirs!" Karitoki says again, desperate now, for the Pania are not creatures of subtlety and his blood in the water is not *his* blood. It is *only* blood, and he is the outsider.

"Warm," croons the Pania. Her eyes are black and flat, shark eyes. "*Warm.*"

And then she is on him, and her hair and her flesh smell of smoke and salt and the great white bones of her jaw are opening towards him, nuzzling into his thighs and his side and the thick, fleshy column of his neck, and Karitoki feels her whole body against him. She is cool, cool like the ocean under thermocline, and the oil has washed off her and the heat has washed out. He realizes, then, in the thin space between shock and screaming and the hard, hydra impact of her sisters, that all his dreams are sea foam. There's no place for her in Napier town, and she'll never sit with him in the art deco blocks of cafes along Marine Parade and eat her mussels with a spoon, with saffron and spices and sauvignon. He can't cover her up with butter and oranges, can't make of her anything other than Pania, a guardian and predator in one.

There are mussels smoking on the beach. He had put them in raw, left the heat and the smoke to open them up while he swam with the Pania and her coconut. He would have made a sauce of parsley and Pernod and tarragon, with the remnants of mussel oil for garnish.

He knows, as her teeth sink into his shoulder, into the raw, massed, mussel-fed flesh of him, that the Pania would never have eaten it.

Octavia Cade is a New Zealand writer who has just finished her PhD in science communication. She kept sane in grad school by baking, hiking, and writing science fiction and fantasy stories. Her short fiction has appeared in Strange Horizons, *Apex Magazine*, and *The Book Smugglers*, among others.

Steve Duffy portrays his ursine characters anthropomorphically, but not as fully human surrogates. In his version of "Goldilocks and the Three Bears" the furry trio encounters prejudice and hatred in their attempt to assimilate into 1958 upper-middle-class suburbia. Allegories are well and good, but bruins are not humans and with a story like this, that is wise to remember.

Bears: A Fairy Tale of 1958

Steve Duffy

They tried so hard, the bear family; really they did. They'd known from the get-go there'd be difficulties, the relocation would have its problems. It's always worst for the first new family that moves in to a fancy-schmancy neighborhood. But they understood the importance of fitting in. They'd told themselves, they'd said to each other: well, if we just keep our heads down, try to get along, then you know, maybe folks will meet us halfway. You can't expect them to change their ways overnight just to suit us. We need to work at it, be ambassadors. Be a credit to the species, hold our heads up high. So that's just what they did—they put everything they had into it, but it still wasn't enough. That was the hard part.

From the very first—when the slick realtor had showed them round the house in that faux-friendly, glad-handing way—they'd had misgivings. Mama Bear hated how he looked at her, the way he hardly even bothered to disguise his frequent glances at her heavy low-slung pelvis—as if he could see right through the summery, ill-fitting dress she'd worn specially for the occasion. She felt shamed and exposed, felt all the indignity of the collar and muzzle, the tug of his hand on the chain.

"Get a load of those features," he'd said, leaning in the kitchen doorway, tilting his hat back on his head the better to watch her as she tried
to make sense of convection oven, E-Z-Kleen range hood, griddle, rotis-
serie. "Just makes you hungry as a hunter, doesn't it?" He was chewing a
stick of gum he hadn't bothered to remove since they'd arrived. She could
see it now as he worked it between his teeth. It reminded her of a plump
gray maggot, the kind you'd find beneath a chunk of dead wood.

Later, in the front room, her heart had felt as heavy as the sleep of
hibernation, watching Papa Bear as he nodded his great dense head
gravely and earnestly, narrowing his tiny eyes in a show of acumen while
Mr. Traynor skimmed over the various clauses of the contract, flicking
through the papers haphazardly, not even pretending to explain. When
the realtor's pen was extended he grappled it determinedly between his
callused pads and made his mark. She never forgot the way he looked
when glancing up from the contract, proud of the step he'd just taken
and yet filled with unassuagable doubts. "That's fine, that's fine," said Jack
Traynor, cramming everything into his inside jacket pocket and backing
out the door. "You folks are making the right decision, that's for sure." He
couldn't wait to get out of there and bank their check.

The first night after the move she could hardly sleep. Midnight came
and went, and one a.m., and she was still at the window, gazing over the
way at the fine landscaped gardens of their neighbors. Goodness, but
those monkey-puzzle trees in the Lockes' arboretum would be so hard to
climb . . . she stopped herself. For shame. She'd already disgraced herself
in front of the Lockes, earlier in the day.

Baby had been sent off to play while the grown-ups emptied the furniture van. He'd gone exploring, and a few hours later, after much hol-
lering and head-scratching, she'd found him over in the garden of their
nearest neighbors—the Lockes, a charming couple, simply exquisite.
They had trees all round the side of the house, Scotch pines, trained willows and those amazing monkey-puzzles, and Baby was in his element,
as was all too clear. When she finally tracked him down under the pines
he'd just finished Number Two, and was diligently scratching soil over
his adorably undersized leaving. "You mind that now," she'd exclaimed,
snatching him up—and pausing, entirely out of habit, to check Baby's
scat. Good, firm texture; he'd always been a healthy tot, and they hoped
he'd thrive in such a good area. Without giving it a second thought,
Mama leaned down and sniffed deeply, assessing in an instant the state

of her son's digestion: some nibs of corn there still, and a sticky, slightly tarry residue—

"Can we help you?" Several degrees north of glacial. Hurriedly, with a little snort of surprise, Mama straightened up. There they were: tall handsome Kenny Locke who was something in advertising, and his wife Mimi, picture-perfect in what looked like real honest-to-goodness Balenciaga. She was so exquisitely turned out, Mama Bear just couldn't believe it; one hand poised hip-high like a model from the glossy magazines, the other hovering at her mouth, where she worried between perfect pearly teeth the tip of her kidskin glove.

Mama introduced herself, held out a paw before catching herself and restricting the movement to a hey-neighbor wave. "And this is Baby," she explained shyly, hoisting him up from off her hip.

"Yes well, it seems Baby's already made himself known," said Mimi Locke, with the merest glance at the discreet plug of infant dung there on the close-mown grass beneath her tree. "If in future you could . . ." She left the sentence unfinished: it was difficult to say whether this was out of distaste for the subject of the conversation, or for its object.

Mama Bear couldn't apologize fast enough or long enough. In the midst of her explanations she scooped up the offending scrap of ordure, then became hyper-aware of it and held it behind her back, then when she turned to lope back across the lawn she didn't know what to do with it . . . it was all too shaming for words. Most shaming of all, behind her back she heard them, Mimi and Kenny Locke, their murmurs as she retreated:

"Well, I guess it's true what they say about bears, Meem," and his rich confident voice sank to a whisper in his wife's petite ear, rising only at the end of the gag: ". . . but they'll sure shit in the woods." Mimi's tinkling laughter stung like the shards of a flawed crystal glass that shatters in the hand. Later that first evening, upstairs in the bedroom of their new house, Mama Bear cried herself to sleep with that laughter still sounding in her ears.

In the morning there was garbage thrown all over their new lawn, and someone had written in straggly weedkiller letters across the grass GO HOME BRUINS.

After that, how could they ever really feel at home? Each day was sure to bring some fresh humiliation, a new chance to look down at the tightrope and see the void beneath. For Mama, maybe the final straw had been that disastrous afternoon tea at the Minafers. As the ladies of Scotsford chattered and smiled, Mama Bear had perched on the sofa as if on a hotplate, answering questions in strangled monosyllables while contriving to break a modest yet on the whole representative cross-section of her hostess's best china. "I believe your husband is in show business, Mrs.—ah . . .?" someone had said—the well-meaning yet essentially dimwitted Missy Scrivener—as she bent, blushing to her burning muzzle, to pick up the pieces.

"Why yes, he's with the circus," she'd replied, struggling to her feet. It was nothing to be ashamed of. Papa was one of the best-paid performers in his field: he drew down thirty grand a year with Krafft's, and they'd hibernated in Florida each year now since '53. How many of these high-toned muckamucks could afford to keep a beach house on the Keys? And yet somewhere behind her back she heard laughter, unsuccessfully smothered.

She swung round, eyeing the rest of the room suspiciously. She saw nothing in the whey-pale powdered faces she could recognize; no hint of fellow-feeling, no shred of empathy. Weren't these people supposed to understand money? Then why couldn't they see it was neutral, after all? Bob Minchin sold limousines to people at his Lincoln dealership downtown. Papa Bear rolled atop his log for them in the big top. Who was to say which one of them ought to have bragging rights over the other?

"Oh, now, let me take those," urged the hostess Mindy Minafer, trying to retrieve the broken cups and plates from her clumsy guest. The sudden movement up close drew an involuntary grunt from Mama Bear—you couldn't even call it a growl, not really. And the way her claws caught Mindy: that was purely accident. Mindy ought to have known better than to have her hands in there. The hush that fell across the airy sunstruck drawing room was none the less petrified for that.

Soon afterwards, people began making their excuses, drifting away in ones and twos until there was only Mama Bear, bidding a bandaged and thin-lipped Mindy goodbye in the miserable expectation this would turn out to be her first, last and only invite to a Scotsford soiree. Which turned out to be true.

After that, Mama mostly stayed home, wishing she could be a wife like any other, wishing she had that role at least to fulfill. She dreamed of how it would feel to be one of those cool, classy WASPish brides you saw on TV: to wait each evening with a freshly mixed Martini against her high-powered hubby's return. But of course Papa didn't have a regular nine-to-five: work claimed him Easter till Halloween, the everlasting circuit, life on the road. Nothing for it but to hold her head high, and try to carry on the best she could.

Trips out to the shops—though soon enough she grew sick of negotiating the narrow aisles of the supermarket, overturning pyramids of canned goods and toilet tissue at each incautious turn. Walks with her son out to the park, watching from the shade of the plane trees as the rest of the youngsters played shirts-versus-skins baseball. Trying to explain to Baby as he pleaded with her, puzzled, asking why he couldn't take a turn at bat. In the end whole afternoons and evenings with the blinds drawn, just watching TV, Western shows and daytime soaps and old romantic movies; the hearings of the Senate committee on Ursine Integration, half-a-dozen wrinkled-up old white men barely managing to stay awake while so-called experts pontificated on the kind of problems she faced every day and they would never know, not ever.

When one bright day in June Papa turned up out of the blue, Mama Bear was in her dressing-gown still, though it was half-past three in the afternoon. She hurried out to the sidewalk as his taxi pulled away, but his first words weren't for her.

"I lay out good money for that gardener, goddamit," he rumbled, scowling at the scutch grass and wild scallions growing though the unwatered lawn, patchwork turf still evident where the burned-in slur had been removed. Mama tried to explain—the neighbors encouraged their dogs to make dirty on the grass when she wasn't watching, and anyway the gardener they'd hired hardly ever showed these days—but he waved it away with an angry paw. "Working my ass off so this place can look like some damn pauper shack when I get home . . ." He lurched off inside the house, Mama Bear hurrying after. Across the way, curtains twitched.

All that evening he was mute, unapproachable. Finally Mama Bear came right out and asked the question.

"No . . . no, Mama, everything is not all right," he said heavily. He squinted through his glass of bourbon, the lamplight reflecting yellow in his baleful eye. "Everything is going pretty much to shit, if you really want to know."

Mama Bear flinched, as always, at the word. "Honey!"

"Honey's all dried up," he said, tipping back the whole tumbler full of bourbon in a single blink-inducing draught. "Nothing left but the ol' ca-ca now. The ol' poopy-doop."

"Don't talk that way," she told him, scared a little, not wanting to hear what else he might say. "Oh, you don't know how much I've been looking forward to having you home, Papa, even if it is only for a week—"

"It isn't a week's leave," he said, heavily. He rose to his feet, staggered a little, made for the corner bar to replenish his glass. Without turning to face her, he said: "It's mandatory leave. *Indefinite* mandatory leave."

"I don't understand . . . ?" Mama tried to face him, look into his eyes, to find out what it might mean, all of it. Papa pushed past her, not roughly but not tenderly either, shambled back to the sofa, collapsed as if he'd taken a tranquilizer dart to the flank.

"I blew it, Mama." Staring at the ceiling, where cobwebs hung from the chandelier. "Matinee performance in Schenectady. I was waiting to go on . . . I just turned round and walked right out the big top. Couldn't go on. Just . . . couldn't."

"Honey? What?"

Papa Bear held a paw up as if to forestall her; let it fall. "I just *couldn't*."

She felt she should understand without having to ask, felt ashamed because she didn't. "Was it . . . did someone say something? Did you get into a fight again?"

"I just . . ." For the longest time he tried to say it. Not even another slug of bourbon could loosen his tongue. "Ah, what the hell. You don't understand."

Now the tears came, she couldn't help it. "I want you to help me understand!" Wanted him to hold her, to say, it's all right, it's gonna be okay. Instead he sat back, stared at the ceiling, said as if to no one:

"You'll never know what it cost me, to do that every day. To go through with that whole . . . that whole charade."

"They pay you good!" She was sobbing openly now. "The best!"

"They make me jump through hoops," he said, more in resignation than in bitterness. "They make me jump through their goddamn hoops, each and every day, and there's not one goddamn thing I can do about it, because they own me. Bought and paid for."

"They don't own you! They pay you a wage! A *good* wage!"

"They own my ass, Mama." Correcting her heavily. "They want me to do handstands—I do handstands. End of story. And one day—one

322

day . . ." He was searching for a form of words to make it more compre-
hensible to her, or perhaps to himself. "This one afternoon in Schenectady, I was checking out the apparatus—the log, the hoops, the podiums,
all set up in the middle of the ring—and I just said the hell with it. You
know?" He drained his tumbler, set it down with a crack on the glass
tabletop. "The hell with it. Walked. Lay on the bunk in my goddamn
caravan, stayed there till the boss came knocking." For the first time he
met her eyes, blinking owlishly as one who emerges into bright sunlight
from the back of a deep dark cave. "And here I am. Indefinite mandatory
leave." He snorted mirthlessly, got up to pour himself another bourbon.

Mama Bear tried to make sense of it all. "You've been overdoing
things—working too hard . . ."

"I've been doing what I do," said her husband bleakly into the middle
distance, one paw on the bottle, the other bracing himself against the
cocktail bar. "I've been dancing to their tune. All my life, Mama. Now the
music's stopped, and there isn't a chair left for me to sit in."

And so their dream move to Scotsford turned all the way nightmare, and
there was nothing anyone could do about it. For the remainder of that evening Mama Bear alternately cried and pleaded, while Papa drank steadily
and without appreciable effect, till all of a sudden he let out an enormous
roar and sent the glass-top table flying against the farther wall. After that
she ran crying up to bed, tiptoed down hours after in the predawn gray to
find her husband collapsed on the couch, breathing stertorously through
his wide open mouth. Looking down at him she didn't know what to
think—what to feel, even. She didn't know whether she wanted things to
be the way they'd been before, or what she wanted. Just not this.

The weather turned hot and humid in the weeks that followed, those
enervating dog days of summer when the only sounds across suburbia's
lazy lawns are the hissing of sprinklers and the elastic crack of tennis ball
on catgut. When French windows are wedged permanently open, and ice
clinks welcomingly in pitchers of cool iced tea and daiquiris fetched out
to poolside. Inside the dream homes, sweltering Negro staff polished and
cleaned and laundered, while life moved out on to the decks and patios.
Recumbent in its thousand sweet suntraps, Scotsford stretched out in the
heat, grew blasé and lethargic, tilted its face to the sweltering rays and
adjusted its sunglasses.

In the house of the bears, things were different. No French window was left ajar against the heat, and all the blinds were drawn in the daytime. No one came in or out of the house: the cleaner, Hortense, had long since been let go, along with the gardener, Booker T. The only person who seemed to be let in still was the delivery boy from Biddle's Market. Pressed on the details by Missy Scrivener, the Biddle's boy would only say that things were kinda gloomy inside, and they mostly left his money laid out ready on the kitchen table.

Yes, and through the crack in the kitchen door Mama Bear would watch the kid come in, glance nervously around, leave the boxes on the table, grab his cash and scoot. She told herself she watched to make sure he left the groceries and was off on his way with no shenanigans, didn't steal or poke his nose in where it wasn't wanted . . . but a part of her she couldn't really get to, let alone acknowledge, probably watched him because he was the only thing worth watching in all that gloomy house. The only creature moving at the noon.

More and more Papa was sleeping through the hot hours, midday till six. When he rose, he'd mostly just lie on his bed, staring at the ceiling; only when the sun was slipping down behind the roof of the Lockes' house would he even consider stirring. One evening Mama Bear heard a fearsome crash from out back: running to the French windows she saw Papa sprawled amidst the wreck of the swing set on the lawn. The tube-aluminum frame of the garden furniture was all wrenched out of shape, bowed and bent beneath his helpless bulk. Papa, she thought, though it was dusk already and getting hard to see, was crying. That evening in bed, desperate to restore what she could of his dignity and self-esteem, she presented herself to him. After a brief humiliating interlude of strain and poke he rolled away, as if from the failure of some trick he'd learned once for a special performance, but long since forgotten how to do properly.

After that, they mostly kept out of each other's way. Papa hit the bottle with increasing frequency, and Mama began to find herself doing odd little things around the house, things she couldn't always have consciously explained but which just felt right. She sent Baby out to the woods to gather dry leaves and twigs, which she strewed throughout the rooms. She found herself one day dragging her claws through the jazzy patterned wallpaper, leaving a crosshatched pattern of parallel score-marks clean down to the plaster underneath. Once, she came to as if from a stupor to find herself squatting to stool in the darkest corner of the dining room.

With no air blowing through, the house began to smell old and musty, like the back of a deep hibernation cave. Papa's empties were mounting up around the study, and it reeked of stale booze in there— if failure were to have a scent, it would surely be the sour stink that lingers round a sticky flyblown liquor bottle. Mama's occasional indiscretions, mimicked eagerly by Baby now, lent an earthy tainted smell to the dining room, and drew flies in the hundreds in their own right. Those doors were kept shut; other rooms they wandered through in a kind of desultory fretfulness, as if looking for something but unable to remember quite what it was. Curling up for a while, fast asleep in the fever heat, forgetting in the instant of their waking what they'd just that second dreamed. Passing each other without a word, without a touch.

For the most part the bears ate alone now, each one wandering through to the kitchen and raiding the refrigerator or the pantry shelves. One day—one afternoon of pregnant rumbling thunder in the far-off hills—Mama went to the Westinghouse and found it empty. Only condiments and rancid month-old butter, was all. She stared into the chilly glowing void for what must have been a long while, till the buzz of the refrigerator motor kicking in woke her with a little start from her stupor.

Dully she hunted through the cupboards, found nothing that spoke to her rumbling slavering hunger. There was a packet of porridge oats, which she tried dry and spat out. Tipping the contents into a saucepan, she added water and watched while the mess bubbled up on the greasy crusted stove. The smell drew the rest of the family, and in their various stages of wakefulness they all sat around the table and waited for the porridge to boil.

Finally it was ready. Mama dolloped the gray goop into large Tupperware mixing bowls and placed them on the table. Baby took the bowl in both hands and lapped eagerly at its contents, only to recoil in shock and pain. "Too hot!" he squeaked. The dropped bowl skittered around on the tabletop, coming to rest in a glutinous blob of spilled porridge. Mama winced internally—she'd meant to check the temperature. She'd meant to order food; she'd meant to do a lot of things, one way and another. She was so forgetful nowadays . . .

Impervious to scalds, Papa tasted his portion and spat it on to the floor. "Needs sweetening," he grumbled. "Don't we have any damn sugar in this house?"

Mama was fairly sure they hadn't—in fact, she vividly recalled pouring the best part of a packet down her maw, crusting her muzzle with sweet granules as she tore apart what was left of the bag with her rough tongue—but she went through the motions of looking anyway. "Okay, that's it," ordered Papa. "In the car, now."

And so the whole family piled into the station wagon, which Papa proceeded to drive all herky-jerky down to the store. Cars threw on the brakes and honked horns as Papa shot one intersection after another, jumped a red light downtown, made a huge and illegal U-turn across the flower-bedded midway on Main to park up outside Biddle's.

Inside, Mama hurried timorously down the aisles in Papa's snarling wake, wincing as he swept the entire contents of the honey shelf into his cart with a swipe of his paw. At the checkout there was another contretemps, when the girl at the register wanted to see some ID for the roughly scrawled check he'd presented. "You see the check?" he growled. "You see the *name* on the check?"

"Um, that's, er, Bear, yes I do, sir," confirmed the nervous teenager.

Papa Bear loosened his collar, pushed back his trilby, and thrust his face to within an inch of the checkout girl's. She recoiled, tipping over her castor-wheeled stool. "Well, here's my ID, then," he said, and barged his shopping cart on through and out to the car. Scalded by shame, Mama backed away, trying to keep up with her husband while apologizing to the gathering knot of Biddle's staff.

And so, after another death-defying chariot ride through the downtown, they came once more to a squealing halt in their own driveway, demolishing a flowerbed and knocking over their own mailbox in the process. Laden down with honeypots, they staggered the few yards from car to front door, left ajar in the haste of their departure. In the houses and gardens of their neighbors, this excursion had not gone unnoticed. As the front door banged shut after the bears, a murmur of adverse comment blew up and down the avenue like a dry harsh Santa Ana.

Inside, Papa was heading for the kitchen when he came to a sudden halt. Head up, he sniffed the stale hot air. "Honey?" asked Mama Bear, bumping in to him from behind.

"Nah . . ." He shrugged, and carried on into the kitchen. Where they both stopped and gaped.

The porridge had been flung all over the walls and ceilings. Great globs of it dripped down to the spattered floor; over by the back door, Baby's little dish, still stuck with its gloopy contents, slid slowly down the wall like a Tupperware snail.

Mama let out a single barking sob. Papa, meanwhile, pushed past her into the dining room, rumbling "What the . . .?"

In the dining room there was nothing; nothing, except the certain knowledge that some uninvited guest had passed that way not minutes before. Call it a spoor: every animal leaves some kind of track, after all. Following his nose, Papa hurried through to the living room.

Pushing aside the room dividers, he yelped in harsh surprise. All of the cushions on all of the chairs lay ripped apart, like so many chickens torn by the fox. Feathers fell through the air still, settling on the leaf-strewn carpet, the denuded chairs; settling on the triangular-bladed kitchen knife that had doubtless done the damage. The knife from their very own kitchen, part of a set. When everything had been perfect, back in the beginning.

The trail was so fresh, though, it drew Papa on with hardly time for a glance at the damage. Onwards, up the stairs to Baby's room. At the turn of the landing, he stopped and waited for Mama to catch up. With a jerk of his huge heavy head he indicated the door to their son's room. Together they moved towards it.

And there she was: the culprit, the interloper, the crafty assassin of hearth and home. Picture perfect, Shirley Temple in ribbons and curls, the Locke girl, little Goldie Locke, caught mid-bounce on Baby's mussed-up bed.

It was Mama who moved first of all, though she hardly knew she was doing it: a lunge forward and the beginnings of a roar, and then she got wedged in between Papa and the doorframe, luckily for little Goldie, maybe. But even a doorway full of angry bear didn't seem to shake the Locke girl's composure. She completed the bounce by landing on her little keister, shook her hair from her eyes and regarded the bears with the haughty self-possession of a born aristocrat.

"What . . . what . . ." Mama couldn't even get the words out; Papa was still mute in the grip of some complicated emotion. It was left to Baby, pushing in between their legs, to ask the obvious, indeed the necessary question: "What are you doing on my bed?"

"You left the front door wiiide open." A lisping singsong, befitting her gingham and curls. "Stupid bears."

All three of the bears were shocked into silence. It was as if, after all the whispering campaigns and sly talk exchanged behind their backs, Scotsford was finally showing its hand.

"Stupid bruins," Goldie Locke continued happily. "Stupid, stupid bruins. You smell."

Mama opened her mouth, and shut it again.

"You do so!" The little girl answered the thought, rather than the unspoken words. "You do ca-ca in the dining room! Where you eat your dinner!"

Mama looked round at her husband. He was staring, not at the girl but at her. Hastily he looked away, as did she.

"Stinky, stinky bruins . . ." An extemporized schoolyard rhyme, complete with mocking rise and fall. "And you got leaves and branches everywhere round the house! And old bottles! And *ca-ca*! You're like . . . *tramps*!"

The three bears shrank together.

"My mummy said all bruins smell, so I came inside to see. And you *do* smell." The vindication made her giggle, and she lifted a hand to her mouth. Politely, as she'd been taught by her mother. "You're stinky. Stinky poo-poo." And then it was simply too funny for words, and she laughed at them, right to their faces.

Recovering from her laughing jag, hiccupping a little, the little girl regarded the bears. "I wanna go home now," she said. "It smells in here." She got up from the bed. The bears made no move.

Goldie Locke frowned. "You get out of the way," she told them. "Stinky bears. Go on now! Or I'll tell my daddy."

Still the bears did not move. They stood as one and looked at her.

"My daddy says you should all be in a *zoo*!" The Zee word. At his mother's side, little Baby burst into tears. Slowly, without taking her eyes off the girlchild, Mama lowered a paw to the top of his head.

"He says you get money by tricks, and you stink, and you belong in a zoo. I don't wanna stay here, it's stinky and I feel sick to my tummy." She glared at them in unconcealed disgust. "You let me go past, you hear?"

What did they feel, Mama, Papa, Baby? What stirred in the thick gamy meat of their hearts as the little blond girl mocked them and insulted them? What might their reaction have been, had they only found it in their nature to react?

Impatiently, Goldie Locke stamped one perfect sandaled foot on the unvacuumed carpet, lifting a little puff of dust. "Get *back!*" she ordered, with a shrillness that brooked no contradiction. Every ringmaster's whip that ever cracked, in that command; every lick from the licking stick.

As if by magic, the three bears shuffled back a pace. With all the confidence in the world, little Goldie Locke stepped towards them.

Later that evening, on the piney hillside above Scotsford, Papa Bear paused for breath near the top of the ridge. He'd been carrying Baby on his shoulders, and now he set him down on the sandy ground while he waited for Mama to catch them up.

Hampered by the . . . well, by the hamper she was carrying, plus the sundry bags and coats and what-nots, Mama lumbered after them up the hill. Her dress was torn from pushing through the bushes back down in the valley, but it had been necessary—very much necessary—that their departure go unobserved. Hence the unconventional route through the back garden.

Puffing a little, she finally caught up with the boys in the little clearing near the hilltop. Gratefully she let go her various burdens, just in time for Baby to come barreling straight into them as he forward-rolled over to greet her. Everything was sent flying, and a good half of the stuff went rolling off down the hill. She made only the most perfunctory attempts to retrieve it. Instead, she gathered up her son and turned to her husband, watching for his response.

Papa was staring back down the hill at the town they'd left behind. Scotsford lay bathed in the super-radiant glow of a nuclear sunset: across the hushed and lovely suburb pools winked blue, patio barbecues wafted savory smells into the evening air, porch lights glittered against the gathering dusk. From up on the hill you could no longer hear the vague hum of conversations, the hi-fis playing Mantovani; you couldn't feel the taut thin lines of tension that lay behind it all, like guy ropes braced to hold the big top high.

The big bear looked down at the houses of the humans for the longest time, till the sun was finally down behind the farther hillside. Ruminatively he ran a claw under his collar and tie, ripped them away almost without thinking. Ditched the trilby. And then, with a perfect spontaneity that made Mama Bear forget for a moment all the trials and tribulations down the weeks and months and years—forget the horrors they'd left back in the Scotsford house, even—he pitched seven perfect roll-overs, and stood triumphant at the end, stood tall and proud and bearlike once again. Mama barked her approval, and Baby mimicked his papa; they romped and sported in the clearing, all of them, tearing up the rich loam and pine needles underfoot, cloaking themselves with the stink of nature once more. And then, as the nightbirds cried and the huge yellow moon rose up ahead of them, they lumbered off one by one into the forest and were gone.

Steve Duffy has written/coauthored five collections of weird short stories. *Tragic Life Stories*, *The Five Quarters*, *The Night Comes On* (all from Ash-Tree Press), and his most recent, *The Moment of Panic* (PS Publishing). His work also appears in a number of anthologies published in the UK and the US. He won the International Horror Guild Award for Best Short Story, was shortlisted for a World Fantasy Award in 2009, and again in 2012.

Charles de Lint invented Newford, a place where myth and magic spill into the "real" modern world; peopled it with the likes of Jilly Coppercorn, Sophie Etoile, Christy Riddell, and many others, all the while crafting stories that weave in and out of it and its environs. If ever there were a place where dreams want to be real, or can even slip into reality, it would be Newford. It's a natural place for wonder stories.

The Moon Is Drowning While I Sleep

Charles de Lint

If you keep your mind sufficiently open,
people will throw a lot of rubbish into it.
—William A. Orton

1

Once upon a time there was what there was, and if nothing had happened there would be nothing to tell.

2

It was my father who told me that dreams want to be real. When you start to wake up, he said, they hang on and try to slip out into the waking world when you don't notice. Very strong dreams, he added, can almost do it; they can last for almost half a day, but not much longer.

I asked him if any ever made it. If any of the people our subconscious minds toss up and make real while we're sleeping had ever actually stolen out into this world from the dream world.

He knew of at least one that had, he said.

He had that kind of lost look in his eyes that made me think of my mother. He always looked like that when he talked about her, which wasn't often.

Who was it? I asked, hoping he'd dole out another little tidbit about my mother. Is it someone I know?

But he only shook his head. Not really, he told me. It happened a long time ago—before you were born. But I often wondered, he added almost to himself, what did she dream of?

That was a long time ago and I don't know if he ever found out. If he did, he never told me. But lately I've been wondering about it. I think maybe they don't dream. I think that if they do, they get pulled back into the dream world.

And if we're not careful, I think they can pull us back with them.

3

"I've been having the strangest dreams," Sophie Etoile said, more as an observation than a conversational opener.

She and Jilly Coppercorn had been enjoying a companionable silence while they sat on the stone river wall in the old part of Lower Crowsea's Market. The wall is by a small public courtyard, surrounded on three sides by old three-story brick and stone town houses, peaked with mansard roofs, dormer windows thrusting from the walls like hooded eyes with heavy brows. The buildings date back over a hundred years, leaning against each other like old friends too tired to talk, just taking comfort from each other's presence.

The cobblestoned streets that web out from the courtyard are narrow, too tight a fit for a car, even the small imported makes. They twist and turn, winding in and around the buildings more like back alleys than thoroughfares. If you have any sort of familiarity with the area you can maze your way by those lanes to find still smaller courtyards, hidden and private, and, deeper still, secret gardens.

There are more cats in Old Market than anywhere else in New-ford and the air smells different. Though it sits just a few blocks west of some of the city's principal thoroughfares, you can hardly hear the traffic, and you can't smell it at all. No exhaust, no refuse, no dead air. Old Market always seems to smell of fresh bread baking, cabbage soups, frying fish, roses and those tart, sharp-tasting apples that make the best strudels.

Sophie and Jilly were bookended by stairs going down to the Kick-aha River on either side of them. The streetlamp behind them put a glow on their hair, haloing each with a nimbus of light. Jilly's hair was darker, all loose tangled curls; Sophie's was soft auburn, hanging in ringlets.

In the half-dark beyond the lamp's murky light, their small figures could almost be taken for each other, but when the light touched their features, Jilly could be seen to have the quick, clever features of a Rack-ham pixie, while Sophie's were softer, as though rendered by Rossetti or Burne-Jones. Though similarly dressed with paint-stained smocks over loose T-shirts and baggy cotton pants, Sophie still managed to look tidy, while Jilly could never seem to help a slight tendency toward scruffiness. She was the only one of the two with paint in her hair.

"What sort of dreams?" Jilly asked her friend.

It was almost four o'clock in the morning. The narrow streets of Old Market lay empty and still about them, except for the odd prowling cat, and cats can be like the hint of a whisper when they want, ghosting and silent, invisible presences. The two women had been working at Sophie's studio on a joint painting, a collaboration that was going to combine Jilly's precise, delicate work with Sophie's current penchant for bright flaring colors and loosely rendered figures. Neither was sure the experiment would work, but they'd been enjoying themselves immensely, so it really didn't matter.

"Well, they're sort of serial," Sophie said. "You know, where you keep dreaming about the same place, the same people, the same events, except each night you're a little further along in the story."

Jilly gave her an envious look. "I've always wanted to have that kind of dream. Christy's had them. I think he told me that it's called lucid dreaming."

"They're anything but lucid," Sophie said. "If you ask me, they're downright strange."

"No, no. It just means that you know you're dreaming, when you're dreaming, and have some kind of control over what happens in the dream."

Sophie laughed. "I wish."

4

I'm wearing a long pleated skirt and one of those white cotton peasant blouses that's cut way too low in the bodice. I don't know why. I hate that kind of bodice. I keep feeling like I'm going to fall out whenever I bend over. Definitely designed by a man. Wendy likes to wear that kind of thing from time to time, but it's not for me.

Nor is going barefoot. Especially not here. I'm standing on a path, but it's muddy underfoot, all squishy between my toes. It's sort of nice in some ways, but I keep getting the feeling that something's going to sidle up to me, under the mud, and brush against my foot, so I don't want to move, but I don't want to just stand here, either.

Everywhere I look it's all marsh. Low flat fens, with just the odd crack willow or alder trailing raggedy vines the way you see Spanish moss in pictures of the Everglades, but this definitely isn't Florida. It feels more Englishy, if that makes sense.

I know if I step off the path I'll be in muck up to my knees.

I can see a dim kind of light off in the distance, way off the path. I'm attracted to it, the way any light in the darkness seems to call out, welcoming you, but I don't want to brave the deeper mud or the pools of still water that glimmer in the starlight.

It's all mud and reeds, cattails, bulrushes and swamp grass and I just want to be back home in bed, but I can't wake up. There's a funny smell in the air, a mix of things rotting and stagnant water. I feel like there's something horrible in the shadows under those strange, over-hung trees—especially the willows, the tall sharp leaves of sedge and water plantain growing thick around their trunks. It's like there are eyes watching me from all sides, dark misshapen heads floating frog-like in the water, only the eyes showing, staring. Quicks and bogles and dark things.

I hear something move in the tangle bulrushes and bur reeds just a few feet away. My heart's in my throat, but I move a little closer to see that it's only a bird caught in some kind of net.

Hush, I tell it and move closer.

336

The bird gets frantic when I put my hand on the netting. It starts to peck at my fingers, but I keep talking softly to it until it finally settles down. The net's a mess of knots and tangles, and I can't work too quickly because I don't want to hurt the bird.

You should leave him be, a voice says, and I turn to find an old woman standing on the path beside me. I don't know where she came from. Every time I lift one of my feet it makes this creepy sucking sound, but I never even heard her approach.

She looks like the wizened old crone in that painting Jilly did for Geordie when he got onto this kick of learning fiddle tunes with the word "hag" in the title: "The Hag in the Kiln."

"Old Hag You Have Killed Me."

"The Hag With the Money" and god knows how many more.

Just like in the painting, she's wizened and small and bent over and . . . dry. Like kindling, like the pages of an old book. Like she's almost all used up. Hair thin, body thinner. But then you look into her eyes and they're so alive it makes you feel a little dizzy.

Helping such as he will only bring you grief, she says.

I tell her that I can't just leave it.

She looks at me for a long moment, then shrugs. So be it, she says.

I wait a moment, but she doesn't seem to have anything else to say, so I go back to freeing the bird. But now, where a moment ago the netting was a hopeless tangle, it just seems to unknot itself as soon as I lay my hand on it. I'm careful when I put my fingers around the bird and pull it free. I get it out of the tangle and then toss it up in the air. It circles above me, once, twice, three times, cawing. Then it flies away.

It's not safe here, the old lady says then.

I'd forgotten all about her. I get back onto the path, my legs smeared with smelly, dark mud.

What do you mean? I ask her.

When the Moon still walked the sky, she says, why it was safe then. The dark things didn't like her light and fair fell over themselves to get away when she shone. But they're bold now, tricked and trapped her, they have, and no one's safe. Not you, not me. Best we were away.

Trapped her? I repeat like an echo. The moon?

She nods.

Where?

She points to the light I saw earlier, far out in the fens.

They've drowned her under the Black Snag, she says. I will show you.

She takes my hand before I realize what she's doing and pulls me through the rushes and reeds, the mud squishing awfully under my bare feet, but it doesn't seem to bother her at all. She stops when we're at the edge of some open water.

Watch now, she says.

She takes something from the pocket of her apron and tosses it into the water. It's a small stone, a pebble or something, and it enters the water without a sound, without making a ripple. Then the water starts to glow and a picture forms in the dim flickering light. It's as if we have a bird's-eye view of the fens for a moment, then the focus comes in sharp on the edge of a big still pool, sentried by a huge dead willow. I don't know how I know it, because the light's still poor, but the mud's black around its shore. It almost swallows the pale, wan glow coming up from out of the water.

Drowning, the old woman says. The moon is drowning.

I look down at the image that's formed on the surface and I see a woman floating there. Her hair's all spread out from her, drifting in the water like lily roots. There's a great big stone on top of her torso so she's only visible from the breasts up. Her shoulders are slightly sloped, neck slender, with a swan's curve, but not so long. Her face is in repose, as though she's sleeping, but she's under water, so I know she's dead.

She looks like me.

I turn to the old woman, but before I can say anything, there's movement all around us. Shadows pull away from trees, rise from the stagnant pools, change from vague blotches of darkness into moving shapes, limbed and headed, pale eyes glowing with menace. The old woman pulls me back onto the path.

Wake quick! she cries.

She pinches my arm—hard, sharp. It really hurts. And then I'm sitting up in my bed.

5

"And did you have a bruise on your arm from where she pinched you?" Jilly asked.

Sophie shook her head and smiled. Trust Jilly. Who else was always looking for the magic in a situation?

"Of course not," she said. "It was just a dream."

"But . . ."

"Wait," Sophie said. "There's more."

Something suddenly hopped onto the wall between them and they both started, until they realized it was only a cat.

"Silly puss," Sophie said as it walked toward her and began to butt its head against her arm. She gave it a pat.

6

The next night I'm standing by my window, looking out at the street, when I hear movement behind me. I turn and it isn't my apartment any more. It looks like the inside of an old barn, heaped up with straw in a big, tidy pile against one wall. There's a lit lantern swinging from a low rafter beam, a dusty but pleasant smell in the air, a cow or maybe a horse making some kind of nickering sound in a stall at the far end.

And there's a guy standing there in the lantern light, a half dozen feet away from me, not doing anything, just looking at me. He's drop-down gorgeous. Not too thin, not too muscle-bound. A friendly, open face with a wide smile and eyes to kill for—long moody lashes, and the eyes are the color of violets. His hair's thick and dark, long in the back with a cowlick hanging down over his brow that I just want to reach out and brush back.

I'm sorry, he says. I didn't mean to startle you.

That's okay, I tell him.

And it is. I think maybe I'm already getting used to all the to-and-froing.

He smiles. My name's Jeck Crow, he says.

I don't know why, but all of a sudden I'm feeling a little weak in the knees. Ah, who am I kidding? I know why.

What are you doing here? he asks.

I tell him I was standing in my apartment, looking for the moon, but then I remembered that I'd just seen the last quarter a few nights ago and I wouldn't be able to see it tonight.

He nods. She's drowning, he says, and then I remember the old woman from last night.

I look out the window and see the fens are out there. It's dark and creepy and I can't see the distant glow of the woman drowned in the pool from here the way I could last night. I shiver and Jeck comes over all concerned. He's picked up a blanket that was hanging from one of the support beams and lays it across my shoulders. He leaves his arm there, to keep it in place, and I don't mind. I just sort of lean into him, like we've always been together. It's weird. I'm feeling drowsy and safe and incredibly aroused, all at the same time.

He looks out the window with me, his hip against mine, the press of his arm on my shoulder a comfortable weight, his body radiating heat.

It used to be, he says, that she would walk every night until she grew so weak that her light was almost failing. Then she would leave the world to go to another, into Faerie, it's said, or at least to a place where the darkness doesn't hide quicks and bogles, and there she would rejuvenate herself for her return. We would have three nights of darkness, when evil owned the night, but then we'd see the glow of her lantern approaching and the haunts would flee her light and we could visit with one another again when the day's work was done.

He leans his head against mine, his voice going dreamy.

I remember my mam saying once, how the Moon lived another life in those three days. How time moves differently in Faerie so that what was a day for us, might be a month for her in that place. He pauses, then adds, I wonder if they miss her in that other world.

I don't know what to say. But then I realize it's not the kind of conversation in which I have to say anything.

He turns to me, head lowering until we're looking straight into each other's eyes. I get lost in the violet, and suddenly I'm in his arms and we're kissing. He guides me, step by sweet step, backward toward that heap of straw. We've got the blanket under us and this time I'm glad I'm wearing the long skirt and peasant blouse again, because they come off so easily.

His hands and his mouth are so gentle and they're all over me like moth wings brushing my skin. I don't know how to describe what he's doing to me. It isn't anything that other lovers haven't done to me before, but the way Jeck does it has me glowing, my skin all warm and tingling with this deep, slow burn starting up between my legs and just firing up along every one of my nerve ends.

I can hear myself making moaning sounds and then he's inside me, his breathing heavy in my ear. All I can feel and smell is him. My hips are grinding against his and we're synced into perfect rhythm, and then I wake up in my own bed and I'm all tangled up in the sheets with my hand between my legs, fingertip right on the spot, moving back and forth and back and forth . . .

7

Sophie fell silent. "Steamy," Jilly said after a moment.

Sophie gave a little bit of an embarrassed laugh. "You're telling me. I get a little squirmy just thinking about it. And that night—I was still so fired up when I woke that I couldn't think straight. I just went ahead and finished and then lay there afterward, completely spent. I couldn't even move."

"You know a guy named Jack Crow, don't you?" Jilly asked.

"Yeah, he's the one who's got that tattoo parlor down on Palm Street. I went out with him a couple of times, but—" Sophie shrugged "—you know. Things just didn't work out."

"That's right. You told me that all he ever wanted to do was to give you tattoos."

Sophie shook her head, remembering. "In private places so only he and I would know they were there. Boy."

The cat had fallen asleep, body sprawled out on Sophie's lap, head pressed tight against her stomach. A deep resonant purr rose up from him. Sophie hoped he didn't have fleas.

"But the guy in my dream was nothing like Jack," she said. "And besides, his name was Jeck."

"What kind of a name is that?"

"A dream name."

"So did you see him again—the next night?"

Sophie shook her head. "Though not from lack of interest on my part."

8

The third night I find myself in this one-room cottage out of a fairy tale. You know, there's dried herbs hanging everywhere, a big hearth considering the size of the place, with black iron pots and a kettle sitting on the hearthstones, thick hand-woven rugs underfoot, a small tidy little bed in one corner, a cloak hanging by the door, a rough set of a table and two chairs by a shuttered window.

The old lady is sitting on one of the chairs.

There you are, she says. I looked for you to come last night, but I couldn't find you.

I was with Jeck, I say, and then she frowns, but she doesn't say anything.

Do you know him? I ask.

Too well.

Is there something wrong with him?

I'm feeling a little flushed, just talking about him. So far as I'm concerned, there's nothing wrong with him at all. He's not trustworthy, the old lady finally says.

I shake my head. He seems to be just as upset about the drowned lady as you are. He told me all about her—how she used to go into Faerie.

She never went into Faerie.

Well then, where did she go?

The old lady shakes her head. Crows talk too much, she says, and I can't tell if she means the birds or a whole bunch of Jecks. Thinking about the latter gives me goosebumps. I can barely stay clearheaded around Jeck; a whole crowd of him would probably overload my circuits and leave me lying on the floor like a little pool of jelly.

I don't tell the old lady any of this. Jeck inspired confidences, as much as sensuality; she does neither.

Will you help us? she says instead.

I sit down at the table with her and ask, Help with what?

The Moon, she says.

I shake my head. I don't understand. You mean the drowned lady in the pool?

Drowned, the old lady says, but not dead. Not yet.

I start to argue the point, but then realize where I am. It's a dream and anything can happen, right? It needs you to break the bogles' spell, the old lady goes on.

Me? But—

Tomorrow night, go to sleep with a stone in your mouth and a hazel twig in your hands. Now mayhap, you'll find yourself back here, mayhap with your crow, but guard you don't say a word, not one word. Go out into the fen until you find a coffin, and on that coffin a candle, and then look sideways and you'll see that you're in the place I showed you yesternight.

She falls silent.

And then what am I supposed to do? I ask.

What needs to be done.

But—

I'm tired, she says.

She waves her hand at me and I'm back in my own bed again.

9

"And so?" Jilly asked. "Did you do it?"

"Would you have?"

"In a moment," Jilly said. She sidled closer along the wall until she was right beside Sophie and peered into her friend's face. "Oh, don't tell me you didn't do it. Don't tell me that's the whole story."

"The whole thing just seemed silly," Sophie said.

"Oh, please!"

"Well, it did. It was all too oblique and riddlish. I know it was just a dream, so that it didn't have to make sense, but there was so much of a coherence to a lot of it that when it did get incomprehensible, it just didn't seem ... oh, I don't know. Didn't seem fair, I suppose."

"But you *did* do it?"

Sophie finally relented.

"Yes," she said.

10

I go to bed with a small, smooth stone in my mouth and have the hardest time getting to sleep because I'm sure I'm going to swallow it during the night and choke. And I have the hazel twig as well, though I don't know what help either of them is going to be.

Hazel twig to ward you from quicks and bogles, I hear Jeck say. And the stone to remind you of your own world, of the difference between waking and dream, else you might find yourself sharing the Moon's fate.

We're standing on a sort of grassy knoll, an island of semisolid ground, but the footing's still spongy. I start to say hello, but he puts his finger to his lips.

She's old, is Granny Weather, he says, and cranky, too, but there's more magic in one of her toenails than most of us will find in a lifetime.

I never really thought about his voice before. It's like velvet, soft and smooth, but not effeminate. It's too resonant for that.

He puts his hands on my shoulders and I feel like melting. I close my eyes, lift my face to his, but he turns me around until I'm facing away from him. He cups his hands around my breasts and kisses me on the nape of my neck. I lean back against him, but he lifts his mouth to my ear.

You must go, he says softly, his breath tickling the inside of my ear. Into the fens.

I pull free from his embrace and face him. I start to say, Why me? Why do I have to go alone? But before I can get a word out he has his hand across my mouth.

Trust Granny Weather, he says. And trust me. This is something only you can do. Whether you do it or not is your choice. But if you mean to try tonight, you mustn't speak. You must go out into the fens and find her. They will tempt you and torment you, but you must ignore them, else they'll have you drowning too, under the Black Snag.

I look at him and I know he can see the need I have for him, because in his eyes I can see the same need for me reflected in their violet depths.

I will wait for you, he says. If I can.

I don't like the sound of that. I don't like the sound of any of it, but I tell myself again, it's just a dream, so I finally nod. I start to turn away, but he catches hold of me for a last moment and kisses me. There's a hot rush of tongues touching, arms tight around each other, before he finally steps back.

I love the strength of you, he says.

I don't want to go, I want to change the rules of the dream. But I get this feeling that if I do, if I change one thing, everything'll change, and maybe he won't even exist in whatever comes along to replace it. So I lift my hand and run it along the side of his face. I take a long last drink of those deep violet eyes that just want to swallow me, then I get brave and turn away again.

And this time I go into the fens.

I'm nervous, but I guess that goes without saying. I look back but I can't see Jeck anymore. I can just feel I'm being watched, and it's not by him. I clutch my little hazel twig tighter, roll the stone around from one side of my mouth to the other, and keep going.

It's not easy. I have to test each step to make sure I'm not just going to sink away forever into the muck. I start thinking of what you hear about dreams, how if you die in a dream, you die for real, that's why you always wake up just in time. Except for those people who die in their sleep, I guess.

I don't know how long I'm slogging through the muck. My arms and legs have dozens of little nicks and cuts—you never think of how sharp the edge of a reed can be until your skin slides across one. It's like a paper cut, sharp and quick, and it stings like hell. I don't suppose all the muck's doing the cuts much good either. The only thing I can be happy about is that there aren't any bugs.

Actually, there doesn't seem to be the sense of anything living at all in the fens, just me, on my own. But I know I'm not alone. It's like a word sitting on the tip of your tongue. I can't see or hear or sense anything, but I'm being watched.

I think of Jeck and Granny Weather, of what they say the darkness hides. Quicks and bogles and haunts.

After a while I almost forget what I'm doing out here.

I'm just stumbling along with a feeling of dread hanging over me that won't go away. Bogbean and water mint leaves feel like cold, wet fingers sliding along my legs. I hear the occasional flutter of wings, and sometimes a deep kind of sighing moan, but I never see anything.

I'm just about played out when suddenly I come upon this tall rock under the biggest crack willow I've seen so far. The tree's dead, drooping leafless branches into the still water at a slant, the mud's all black underfoot, the marsh is, if anything, even quieter here, expectant almost, and I get the feeling like something—somethings are closing in all around me.

I start to walk across the dark mud to the other side of the rock until I hit a certain vantage point. I stop when I can see that it's shaped like a big strange coffin, and I remember what Granny Weather told me. I look for the candle and see a tiny light flickering at the very top of the black stone, right where it's pushed up and snagged among the dangling branches of the dead willow. It's no brighter than a firefly's glow, but it burns steady.

I do what Granny Weather told me and look around myself using my peripheral vision. I don't see anything at first, but as I slowly turn toward the water, I catch just a hint of a glow. I stop and then I wonder what to do. Is it still going to be there if I turn to face it?

Eventually, I move sideways toward it, always keeping it in the corner of my eye. The closer I get, the brighter it starts to glow, until I'm standing hip deep in the cold water, the mud sucking at my feet, and it's all around me, this dim eerie glowing. I look down into the water and I see my own face reflected back at me, but then I realize that it's not me I'm seeing, it's the drowned woman, the moon, trapped under the stone.

I stick my hazel twig down the bodice of my blouse and reach into the water. I have to bend down, the dark water licking at my shoulders and chin and smelling something awful, but I finally touch the woman's shoulder. Her skin's warm against my fingers, and for some reason that makes me feel braver. I get a grip with one hand on her shoulder, then the other, and give a pull.

Nothing budges.

I try some more, moving a little deeper into the water. Finally I plunge my head under and get a really good hold, but she simply won't move. The rock's got her pressed down tight, and the willow's got the rock snagged, and dream or no dream, I'm not some kind of superwoman. I'm only so strong and I have to breathe.

I come up spluttering and choking on the foul water.

And then I hear the laughter.

I look up and there's these things all around the edge of the pool. Quicks and bogles and small monsters. All eyes and teeth and spindly black limbs and crooked hands with too many joints to the fingers. The tree is full of crows and their cawing adds to the mocking hubbub of sound.

First got one, now got two, a pair of voices chant. Boil her up in a tiddy stew.

I'm starting to shiver—not just because I'm scared, which I am, but because the water's so damn cold. The haunts just keep on laughing and making up these creepy little rhymes that mostly have to do with little stews and barbecues. And then suddenly, they all fall silent and these three figures come swinging down from the willow's boughs.

I don't know where they came from, they're just there all of a sudden. These aren't haunts, nor quicks nor bogles. They're men and they look all too familiar.

Ask for anything, one of them says, and it will be yours.

It's Jeck, I realize. Jeck talking to me, except the voice doesn't sound right. But it looks just like him. All three look like him.

I remember Granny Weather telling me that Jeck was untrustworthy, but then Jeck told me to trust her. And to trust him. Looking at these three Jecks, I don't know what to think anymore. My head starts to hurt and I just wish I could wake up.

You need only tell us what it is you want, one of the Jecks says, and we will give it to you. There should be no enmity between us. The woman is drowned. She is dead. You have come too late. There is nothing you can do for her now. But you can do something for yourself. Let us gift you with your heart's desire.

My heart's desire, I think.

I tell myself, again, it's just a dream, but I can't help the way I start thinking about what I'd ask for if I could really have anything I wanted, anything at all.

I look down into the water at the drowned woman and I think about my dad. He never liked to talk about my mother. It's like she was just a dream, he said once.

And maybe she was, I find myself thinking as my gaze goes down into the water and I study the features of the drowned woman who looks so much like me. Maybe she was the Moon in this world and she came to ours to rejuvenate, but when it was time for her to go back, she didn't want to leave because she loved me and dad too much. Except she didn't have a choice.

So when she returned, she was weaker, instead of stronger like she was supposed to be, because she was so sad. And that's how the quicks and the bogles trapped her.

I laugh then. What I'm making up, as I stand here waist deep in smelly dream water, is the classic abandoned child's scenario. They always figure that there was just a mix-up, that one day their real parents are going to show up and take them away to some place where everything's magical and loving and perfect.

I used to feel real guilty about my mother leaving us—that's something else that happens when you're just a kid in that kind of a situation. You just automatically feel guilty when something bad happens, like it's got to be your fault. But I got older. I learned to deal with it. I learned that I was a good person, that it hadn't been my fault, that my dad was a good person, too, and it wasn't his fault either.

I'd still like to know why my mother left us, but I came to understand that whatever the reasons were for her going, they had to do with her, not with us. Just like I know this is only a dream and the drowned woman might look like me, but that's just something I'm projecting onto her. I want her to be my mother. I want her having abandoned me and dad not to have been her fault either. I want to come to her rescue and bring us all back together again.

Except it isn't going to happen. Pretend and real just don't mix.

But it's tempting all the same. It's tempting to let it all play out. I know the haunts just want me to talk so that they can trap me as well, that they wouldn't follow through on any promise they made, but this is my dream. I can make them keep to their promise. All I have to do is say what I want.

And then I understand that it's all real after all. Not real in the sense that I can be physically harmed in this place, but real in that if I make a selfish choice, even if it's just in a dream, I'll still have to live with the fact of it when I wake up. It doesn't matter that I'm dreaming, I'll still have done it.

What the bogles are offering is my heart's desire, if I just leave the Moon to drown. But if I do that, I'm responsible for her death. She might not be real, but it doesn't change anything at all. It'll still mean that I'm willing to let someone die, just so I can have my own way.

I suck on the stone and move it back and forth from one cheek to the other. I reach down into my wet bodice and pluck out the hazel twig from where it got pushed down between my breasts. I lift a hand to my hair and brush it back from my face and then I look at those sham copies of my Jeck Crow and I smile at them.

My dream, I think. What I say goes.

I don't know if it's going to work, but I'm fed up with having everyone else decide what happens in my dream. I turn to the stone and I put my hands on it, the hazel twig sticking out between the fingers of my right hand, and I give the stone a shove. There's this great big outcry among the quicks and bogles and haunts as the stone starts to topple over. I look down at the drowned woman and I see her eyes open, I see her smile, but then there's too much light and I'm blinded.

When my vision finally clears, I'm alone by the pool. There's a big, fat, full moon hanging in the sky, making the fens almost as bright as day. They've all fled, the monsters, the quicks and bogles and things. The dead willow's still full of crows, but as soon as I look up, they lift from the tree in an explosion of dark wings, a circling murder, cawing and crying, until they finally go away. The stone's lying on its side, half in the water, half out.

And I'm still dreaming.

I'm standing here, up to my waist in the smelly water, with a hazel twig in my hand and a stone in my mouth, and I stare up at that big full moon until it seems I can feel her light just singing through my veins. For a moment it's like being back in the barn with Jeck, I'm just on fire, but it's a different kind of fire, it burns away the darknesses that have gotten lodged in me over the years, just like they get lodged in everybody, and just for that moment, I'm solid light, innocent and newborn, a burning Midsummer fire in the shape of a woman.

And then I wake up, back home again.

I lie there in my bed and look out the window, but it's still the dark of the moon in our world. The streets are quiet outside, there's a hush over the whole city, and I'm lying here with a hazel twig in my hand, a stone in my mouth, pushed up into one cheek, and a warm, burning glow deep inside.

I sit up and spit the stone out into my hand. I walk over to the window. I'm not in some magical dream now; I'm in the real world. I know the lighted moon glows with light borrowed from the sun. That she's still out there in the dark of the moon, we just can't see her tonight because the earth is between her and the sun.

Or maybe she's gone into some other world, to replenish her lantern before she begins her nightly trek across the sky once more.

I feel like I've learned something, but I'm not sure what. I'm not sure what any of it means.

11

"How can you say that?" Jilly said. "God, Sophie, it's so obvious. She really was your mother and you really did save her. As for Jeck, he was the bird you rescued in your first dream. Jeck Crow—don't you get it? One of the bad guys, only you won him over with an act of kindness. It all makes perfect sense."

Sophie slowly shook her head. "I suppose I'd like to believe that, too," she said, "but what we want and what really is aren't always the same thing."

"But what about Jeck? He'll be waiting for you. And Granny Weather? They both knew you were the Moon's daughter all along. It all means something."

Sophie sighed. She stroked the sleeping cat on her lap, imagining for a moment that it was the soft dark curls of a crow that could be a man, in a land that only existed in her dreams.

"I guess," she said, "it means I need a new boyfriend."

12

Jilly's a real sweetheart, and I love her dearly, but she's naive in some ways. Or maybe it's just that she wants to play the ingénue. She's always so ready to believe anything that anyone tells her, so long as it's magical.

Well, I believe in magic, too, but it's the magic that can turn a caterpillar into a butterfly, the natural wonder and beauty of the world that's all around me. I can't believe in some dreamland being real. I can't believe what Jilly now insists is true: that I've got faerie blood, because I'm the daughter of the Moon.

Though I have to admit that I'd like to.

I never do get to sleep that night. I prowl around the apartment, drinking coffee to keep me awake. I'm afraid to go to sleep, afraid I'll dream and that it'll all be real.

Or maybe that it won't.

When it starts to get light, I take a long cold shower, because I've been thinking about Jeck again. I guess if my making the wrong decision in a dream would've had ramifications in the waking world, then there's no reason that a rampaging libido shouldn't carry over as well.

I get dressed in some old clothes I haven't worn in years, just to try to recapture a more innocent time. White blouse, faded jeans, and hightops with this smoking jacket overtop that used to belong to my dad. It's made of burgundy velvet with black satin lapels. A black hat, with a flat top and a bit of a curl to its brim, completes the picture.

I look in the mirror, and I feel like I'm auditioning to be a stage magician's assistant, but I don't much care.

As soon as the hour gets civilized, I head over to Christy Riddell's house. I'm knocking on his door at nine o'clock, but when he comes to let me in, he's all sleepy-eyed and disheveled and I realize that I should've given him another couple of hours. Too late for that now.

I just come right out with it. I tell him that Jilly said he knew all about lucid dreaming and what I want to know is, is any of it real—the place you dream of, the people you meet there?

He stands there in the doorway, blinking like an owl, but I guess he's used to stranger things, because after a moment he leans against the doorjamb and asks me what I know about consensual reality.

It's where everything that we see around us only exists because we all agree it does, I say.

Well, maybe it's the same in a dream, he replies. If everyone in the dream agrees that what's around them is real, then why shouldn't it be?

I want to ask him about what my dad had to say about dreams trying to escape into the waking world, but I decide I've already pushed my luck.

Thanks, I say.

He gives me a funny look. That's it? he asks.

I'll explain it some other time, I tell him.

Please do, he says without a whole lot of enthusiasm, then goes back inside.

When I get home, I go and lie down on the old sofa that's out on my balcony. I close my eyes. I'm still not so sure about any of this, but I figure it can't hurt to see if Jeck and I can't find ourselves one of those happily-ever-afters with which fairy tales usually end. Who knows? Maybe I really am the daughter of the Moon. If not here, then someplace.

Charles de Lint is a full-time writer and musician who makes his home in Ottawa, Canada. This renowned author of more than seventy adult, young adult, and children's books has won the World Fantasy, Aurora, Sunburst, and White Pine Awards, among others. *Modern Library*'s Top 100 Books of the 20th Century poll, voted on by readers, put eight of de Lint's books among the top 100. De Lint is also a poet, artist, songwriter, performer, and folklorist. He writes a monthly book-review column for *The Magazine of Fantasy & Science Fiction*.

Veronica Schanoes uses a fairy-tale framework to tell the tragic story of Nancy Spungen. Best known for her relationship with punk rocker Sid Vicious of the Sex Pistols, Spungen was a troubled little girl who really never grew up. Like Nancy, the fictional Lily's chances for a traditionally happy ending are slim because she is plagued with inner agony and mental pain. Schnanoes wrote this unflinching story because she was angry with how "coffee-table histories of punk seem to have no problem demonizing" Spungen—"a dead, mentally ill, teenage girl."

Rats

Veronica Schanoes

What I am about to tell you is a fairy tale and so it is constantly repeating. Little Red Riding Hood is always setting off through the forest to visit her granny. Cinderella is always trying on a glass slipper. Just so, this story is constantly re-enacting itself. Otherwise, Cinderella becomes just another tired old queen with a palace full of pretty dresses, abusing the servants when the fireplaces haven't been properly cleaned, embroiled in a love-hate relationship with the paparazzi. Beauty and Beast become yet another wealthy, good-looking couple. They are only themselves in the story and so they only exist in the story. We know Little Red Riding Hood only as the girl in the red cloak carrying her basket through the forest. Who is she during the dog days of summer? How can we pick her out of the mob of little girls in bathing suits and jellies running through the sprinkler in Tompkins Square Park? Is she the one who has cut her foot open on the broken beer bottle? Or is she the one with the translucent green water gun?

Just so, you will know these characters by their story. As with all fairy tales, even new ones, you may well recognize the story. The shape of it will feel right. This feeling is a lie. All stories are lies, because stories have beginnings, middles, and endings, narrative arcs in which the end is the fitting and only mate for the beginning—yes, that's right, we think upon closing the book. Yes, that's the way. Yes, it had to happen like that. Yes.

But life is not like that—there is no narrative causality, there is no foreshadowing, no narrative tone or subtly tuned metaphor to warn us about what is coming. And when somebody dies it is not tragic, not inevitably brought on as fitting end, not a fabulous disaster. It is stupid. And it hurts. It's not all right, Mommy! sobbed a little girl in the playground who had skinned her knee, whose mother was patting her and lying to her, telling her that it was all right. It's not all right, it hurts! she said. I was there. I heard her say it. She was right.

But this is a fairy tale and so it is a lie, perhaps one that makes the stupidity hurt a little less, or perhaps a little more. You must not expect it to be realistic. Now read on . . .

Once upon a time.

Once upon a time, there was a man and a woman, young and very much in love, living in the suburbs of Philadelphia. Now, they very much enjoyed living in the suburbs and unlike me and perhaps you as well they did not at all regret their distance from the graffiti and traffic, the pulsing hot energy, the concrete harmonic wave reaction of the city. But happy as they were with each other and their home, there was one source of pain and emptiness that seemed to grow every time they looked into each others' eyes, and that was because they were childless. The house was quiet and always remained neat as a shot of bourbon. Neither husband nor wife ever had to stay at home nursing a child through a flu—neither of them ever knew what the current bug going around was. They never stayed up having serious discussions about orthodonture or the rising cost of college tuition, and because of this, their hearts ached.

"Oh," said the woman. "If only we had a child to love, who would kiss us and smile, and burn with youth as we fade into old age."

"Oh," the man would reply. "If only we had a child to love, who would laugh and dance, and remember our stories and family long after we can no longer."

And so they passed their days. Together they knelt as they visited the oracles of doctors' offices; together they left sacrifices and offerings at the altars of fertility clinics. And still from sun-up to sundown, they saw their faces reflected only in the mirrors of their quiet house, and those faces were growing older and sadder with each glance.

One day, though, as the woman was driving back from the super-market with the trunk of the station wagon, bought when they were first married and filled with dewy hope for a family, laden with unnaturally bright, unhealthily glossy fruits, vegetables, and even meat, she felt a certain quickening in her womb as she drove over a pothole, and she knew by the bruised strawberries she unpacked from the car that at last their prayers were answered and she was pregnant. When she told her husband he was as delighted as she and they went to great lengths to ensure the health and future happiness of their baby.

But even as the woman visited doctors, she and her husband knew the four shadows were lurking behind, waiting, and would come whether invited or not, so finally they invited the four to visit them. It was a lovely Saturday morning and the woman served homemade rugelach while the four shadows bestowed gifts on the child growing in her mother's womb.

"She will have an ear for music," said the first, putting two raspberry rugelach into its mouth at once.

"She will be brave and adventurous," said the second, stuffing three or four chocolate rugelach into its pockets to eat later.

But the third was not so kindly inclined—if you know this story, you know that there is always one. But contrary to what you may have heard, it was invited just as much as the others were, because while pain and evil cannot be kept out, they cannot come in without consent. In any case, there is always one. This is the way the story goes.

"She shall be beautiful and bold—adventurous and have a passion for music and all that," said the third. "But my gift to your child is pain. This child shall suffer and she will not understand why; she will be in pain and there will be no rest for her; she will suffer and suffer and she will always be alone in her suffering, world without end." The third scowled and threw a piece of raisin rugelach across the room. Some people are like that. Shadows too. The rugelach fell into a potted plant.

Sometimes cruelty cannot help itself, even when it has been placated with an invitation and excellent homemade pastry, and then what can you do?

You can do this: you can turn for help to the fourth shadow, who is not strong enough to break the evil spell—it never is, you know; if it were, there would be no story—but it can, perhaps, amend it.

So as the man and woman sat in shock, but perhaps not as much shock as they might have been had they never heard the story themselves, the fourth approached the woman, who had crossed her hands protectively over her womb.

"Now, my dear," it began, spraying crumbs from the six apricot rugelach it was eating. "Uncross your hands—it looks ill-bred and it does no good, you know. What's done is done, and I cannot undo it: you must bite the bullet and play the cards you're dealt. My gift is this: your daughter, on her seventeenth birthday, will prick herself on a needle and find a—a respite, you might say—and after she has done that, she will be able to rest, and eventually she will be wakened by a kiss, a lover's kiss, and she will never be lonely again."

And the soon-to-be parents had to be content with that.

After the woman gave birth to her daughter she studied the baby anxiously for signs of suffering, but the baby just lay, small, limp, and sweating in her arms, with a cap of black fuzz like velvet covering her head. She didn't cry, and hadn't, even when the doctor had smacked her, partially out of genuine concern for this quiet, unresponsive, barely baby, and partially out of habit, and partially because he liked to hit babies. She just lay in her mother's arms with her eyes squeezed shut, looking so white and soft that her mother named her Lily.

Lily could not tolerate her mother's milk—she could nurse only a little while before vomiting. She kept her eyes shut all day, as if even a little light burned her painfully. After she was home for a few days, she began to cry, and then she cried continuously and loudly, no matter how recently she had been fed or changed. She could only sleep for an hour at a time and she screamed otherwise, as though she were trying to drown out some other more distressing noise.

One afternoon, when Lily was a toddler, her mother lay her down for a nap and after ten or fifteen minutes dropped the baby-raising book she was reading in a panic. Lily's crying had stopped suddenly, and when her mother looked into her room, there was Lily smashing her own head against the wall, over and over, with a look of relief on her two-year-old face. When her mother rushed to stop her, she started screaming again, and she screamed all the while her mother was washing the blood off the wall.

She had night terrors and terrors in the bright sunshine and very few friends. She continued to hit her head against the wall. She tried to hit herself with a hammer and when she was prevented from doing so she lay about her, smashing her mother's hand. When her mother went to the emergency room to have her hand set and put in a cast the nurses clucked their tongues and told each other what a monster her husband must be.

When she got home she found Lily curled in a ball under the dining-room table, gibbering with fear of rats, of which there were none, and she would allow only her mother to speak to her.

Lily did love music. She snuck out of the house late at night and got rides into the city to see bands play, and she loved her father's recordings of Bach and Chopin as well. Back when she was three or four, Chopin had been the only thing that could get her to lie down and sleep. Chopin and phenobarbital. She wrote long reviews of new records for her school paper which were cut for reasons of space. As she got older, she got better and better at forcing the burning gnawing rats under her skin on the people around her. But she still felt alone because they could just walk away from her but she could not rip her way out of her skin her brain her breath although she tried so hard, more than once, but her mother caught her, put her back together, sewed her up, every single time but not once could she clean Lily so well that she didn't feel the corrosion and corruption sliding through her veins, her lymph nodes, her brain, so that she didn't feel the rats burrowing through her body.

Lily ran away to New York City when she was sixteen and a half and in what her parents loathed, she found a kind of peace, in the neon lights and phantasmagoric graffiti that blotted out what was in her eyes and especially in the loud noises and the hard fast beats coming from CBGB that drowned out the rats clawing through her brain much better than her own screaming ever had, it was like banging her head against the wall from the inside. She knew there was something wrong with her—she talked to other people who loved the bands she saw because the fast and loud, young and snotty sound wired them, jolted them full of electricity and sparks, but Lily just sped naturally and all she wanted was to make it stop.

On her seventeenth birthday, Lily went home with a skinny man who played bass and shot heroin. Lily watched him cook the powder in some water over his lighter and stuck her arm out. "Show me how," she told him.

"You have easy veins," he told her, because her veins were large and close to the surface of her skin, fat and filled with rats. They showed with shimmering clarity, veiled only by the fleshy paper of her lily-white skin.

He shot her up and just after the needle came away from her skin— it stopped. It really stopped, not just the rat-pain that she knew about, but the black tarpits of her thinking and feeling—they stopped too. It stopped, and God, it felt so good and free that she didn't mind the puking, it even felt fine, because everything else had stopped, and she could finally get some sleep, some real sleep.

The next morning she woke up and felt like shit again. And it was worse, because for a while she'd felt fine. Just fine.

We should all get to feel just fine sometimes.

So Lily found some kind of respite on a needle's tip and the marks it left were less obvious than the old dull hard scars on her wrists that she rubbed raw when she needed a fix. She worked as a stripper, using feathers, black gloves, and fetish boots to hide all kinds of scars, and sometimes in a midtown brothel. So she was often flush, and if she was still a holy terror, a mindfuck and a half, now she was flush, and had some calmer periods and a social circle, even if they did sometimes ignore her. She wrote pieces on music for underground papers, and once every two weeks her mother came to visit and bought her groceries and took her out to lunch and apologized when she threw cutlery at waiters and worried and worried over how thin Lily was becoming.

You can't stay high all the time, but you can try.

Lily knew she was getting thin. She would stare in the mirror and not see herself, and when she could put the rats to sleep she wasn't quite sure who she was or how she would know who she was.

Who are you? asked the caterpillar, drawing on his hookah. Keep your temper.

The rats were eating her from the inside out and she was dissolving, she was real only under her mother's eyes—the power of her mother's gaze held her bones together even as her ligaments and skin slowly liquified, dissipating in a soft-focus movie dissolve.

Dissolve.

Fade in. We are in London with Lily, far enough away from her mother that she could dissolve entirely. Lily had heard that there was something happening in London, something that could shut down the banging slamming violence in her skull even better than the noise at CBs, some kind of annihilation.

There was.

Look at Lily at the Roxy, if you can recognize her. Can you find her? She is in the bathroom, shooting herself up with heroin and water from the toilet. She is out front sitting by the stage, sitting on the stage, sitting at the bar, throwing herself against the wall so violently that she breaks her own nose. The rats are still following her, snapping and snarling at anybody who comes near, and when nobody comes near, they turn on themselves, begin to eat themselves, gnaw on their own soft bellies.

Can you recognize Lily? When her face and form began to dissolve in the mirror, she panicked and knew she had to take some drastic action before she blinked and found only a mass of rats where her reflection should be, a feeding frenzy. In London the colors were bright like the sun when you have a hangover, so bright it hurt to look at them. The clothing was made to be noticed, to cause people to shrink back and flinch away. Lily wanted to look like that. She bleached her hair from chestnut brown to white blonde and left dark roots showing. She back-combed it so a frizzy mess stood out around her head like a halo: Saint Lily, Our Lady of the Rats. She drew large black circles around both eyes, coloring them in carefully. She outlined her lips even more carefully, and the shine on them is blinding. Her black clothing was covered in bright chrome like a 1950s car.

She was visible then. She could see herself when she looked in the mirror, bright and blonde, outlined in black. Covered in rats.

Her mother thought she looked like a corpse.

Everyone can see her now, everyone who matters, anyway. She is out and about and she is sleeping with the young man playing bass, well, posing with the bass, on stage. He is wearing tight black jeans, no shirt, and a gold lamé jacket. He is a year older than her. Neither of them is out of their teens. They are children. Despite everything, their skin looks new and shiny.

She had been frightened of him the first time they met. Now she was visible but that came with a certain price as well. Usually the rats kept everyone at arm's length if that close, so that no matter how desperately she threw herself at people they shied away. They knew enough to be frightened by the rats, even if they couldn't see them, even if they didn't know they were there. They told themselves, told each other that they avoided her because she was nasty, the most horrible person in the world, a liar, a selfish bitch, and she was, she knew she was, but really they were afraid of the rats.

But the rats stood aside when Chris came near. They drew back at his approach, casting their eyes down and to the side as if embarrassed by their own abated ferocity. There was something familiar about him, but

Lily was too confused by the rats' unusual behavior to think much about what it was. Chris was slight with skin so pale that Lily longed to bruise him and watch the spreading purple, skin that had sharp lines etched into it by smoke and sleeplessness, and zits all over his face. One of them was infected. When he spoke she could barely understand him, his voice was so deep and the vowels so impenetrable.

When she shot him up he said it was his first time but she knew better from the way he brought his sweet blue veins up so that they almost floated above the surface of his sheer skin. When they fucked later that night she could tell that it was his first time.

Lily didn't have much curiosity left—it hurt too much to be awake and she tried to dull herself as much as possible. But while they were kissing for the first time she felt a chill that startled her into wakening and she looked over his shoulder and saw what was so familiar about her Chris (she knew he was hers and she his now). Over his shoulder she saw his rats—just a few, younger than hers, but growing and mating and soon the two of them would be locked together, breaking skin with needles and teeth, surrounded by flocks of rats that could no longer be distinguished or separated out, just a sea of lashing tails and sharp teeth and clutching claws. But she wouldn't be alone, he would see them too, and he wouldn't be alone, she would see them too, their children, their parents, their rats.

Do you recognize this story yet? Perhaps you've seen the T-shirts on every summer camp kid on St. Mark's Place as they fantasize about desperation and hope that self-destruction holds some kind of romance.

Do you recognize this story yet? Perhaps you've read bits of interviews here and there: she was nauseating, she was the most horrible person in the world, she was a curse, a dark plague sent to London on purpose to destroy us, she turned him into a sex slave, she destroyed him, say the middle-aged men and occasional women who look back twenty-five years at a schizophrenic teenage girl with a personality disorder shooting junk—because here and now we still haven't figured out a way to make that kind of illness bearable, who'd wanted to die since she was ten because she hurt so much, and what they see is a frenzied harpy. She destroyed him.

And her? What about her?

Can we not weep for her?

Look again at those photographs and home movies and look at how young they were. Shiny. Not old enough ever to have worried about lines on her face, or knees that ached with the damp, or white hairs—every ache and twinge is a fucking blessing and don't you forget it.

Do you recognize this story yet?

Don't you already know what happens next?

Kiss kiss kiss fun fun lies. Yes oh yes we're having fun. I'm so happy!

Kiss kiss kiss fight fight fight. He hit her and she wore sunglasses at night. She trashed his mother's apartment. He left her and turned back at the train station. He was running by the time he got back to the squat they had been sharing—he had a vision of Lily sprawled on the floor dying—not alone, please, anything but alone. He lifted her head up onto his lap; her heart was beating still but her lips were turning blue. His mum had been a nurse and he knew how to make her breathe again.

Kiss.

On tour with the band, away from Lily, he became a spitting wire, destroying rooms, grabbing pretty girls from the audience, shitting all over them, smashing himself against any edge he could find, carving his skin so that he became a pustule of snot and blood and shit and cum where oh where was his Lily Lily I love you.

The band broke up. He could fuck up but he couldn't play. They moved to New York and bopped around Alphabet City. They tried methadone and they need so much they stopped bothering and anyway methadone only stopped the craving for heroin; it didn't give her any respite. When they were flush they spent money like it was going out of style, on smack, on make-up, on clothing, on presents for each other.

She bought him a knife.

If there is a knife in the story, somebody will have to get stabbed by the end.

Lily knows that she can't stand much more of this, much more of herself, much more of her jonesing, much more of the endless days trapped in a gray room in a gray city, and even though it's all gray the city still hurts her eyes it's a kind of neon gray. The effort it takes just to open her eyes in the morning (afternoon), just to get dressed is too much and if she could feel desire any more, if she could want anything, all she would want would be to stop fighting, stop moving, to sink back and let herself blur and dissolve under warm blankets.

But the smack-sickness shakes her down and she has to move.

Even her rats are weak, she can see. They are staggering and puking. Sometimes they half-heartedly bite one another. She wants to die, but her Chris takes too good care of her, except when he hits her, for that to happen.

When they were curled up together under the covers back in London which is already acquiring the coloring of a home in her quietly bleeding memory, Lily had asked Chris how much he loved her. More than air, he said. More than smack. Would you douse yourself in gasoline and set yourself on fire if I needed you to? she asked. Yes, he said. Would you set me on fire if I needed you to? she asked. Not that, he said. I love you, I couldn't live without you, don't, don't, don't leave me alone. Not that. Anything but alone.

The regular chant of lovers.

If I needed you to? she pressed. Wouldn't you do it if I needed you to? He couldn't. He wouldn't.

Then you don't really love me at all, she told him, if you don't love me enough to help me when I need it.

So he had to say yes. And he had to promise.

Now, in piercing gray New York City she puts the knife in his hand and reminds him of his promise. He pushes her away. No. But he doesn't drop the knife. Perhaps he's forgotten to. She reminds him again and somehow she finds energy and drive she hasn't had in months to scream and berate and plead in a voice like fingernails on a blackboard. She hits him with his bass and scratches at his sores. A man keeps his promises, she tells him. A real man isn't scared of blood.

She winds up shaking and crying to herself on the bathroom floor when Chris comes in, takes her head on his lap and stabs her in the gut, wrenching the knife up towards her breasts. he goes on stabbing and sawing and stroking her forehead until she stops breathing.

The last things she sees are the expression of blank, loving concern on his face and the rats swarming in as her blood spreads across the bathroom tiles.

He watches the rats gnaw on the soft flesh of her stomach and crawl through her body in triumph until finally he watches them lie down and die, exposing their little bellies to the ceiling. The next morning, he remembers nothing.

The police find him sitting bolt upright in bed, staring straight ahead, with the knife next to him. They take Lily away in a body bag. No more kisses.

He is dying now, he thinks. Her absence is slowly draining his blood away. His rats are all dead and their corpses appear everywhere he looks.

You know the rest of the story. He dies a month later of an overdose procured for him by his mother. Why are you still reading? What are you waiting for? The kiss? But he kissed her already, don't you remember? And she woke up, and afterwards she was never alone.

They were children, you know. And there still are children in pain and they continue to die and for the people who love them that is not romantic. Their parents and friends don't know what is going to happen ahead of time. They have no narrator. When these children die all that is left is a blank, an absence, and friends and parents lose the ability see in color. The future takes on a different shape and they go into shock, staring into space for hours. They walk out into traffic and they don't see the trucks, don't hear the horns. A mist lifts and they find that they have pinned the messenger to the wall by his throat. They find themselves calling out names on streets in the dead of night. Walking up the block becomes too hard and they turn back. They can't hear the doctor's voice.

Death is not romantic; it is not exciting; it is no poignant closure and it has no narrative causality. There are even now teenagers—children—slicing themselves and collapsing their veins and refusing to eat because the alternative is worse, and their deaths will not be a story. Instead there will be an empty place in the future where their lives would have been. Death has no narrative arc and no dignity, and now you can silkscreen these two kids' pictures on your fucking T-shirt.

Veronica Schanoes is a writer and scholar living in New York City. Her fiction has most recently appeared on *Tor.com* and in *The Doll Collection,* edited by Ellen Datlow, and *Queen Victoria's Book of Spells,* edited by Ellen Datlow and Terri Windling. She is an Associate Professor in the Department of English at Queens College-CUNY, and her first book, a monograph about feminist revisions of fairy tales called *Fairy Tales, Myth, and Psychoanalytic Theory: Feminism and Retelling the Tale* appeared from Ashgate Publishing in 2014.

L. Frank Baum's The Wonderful Wizard of Oz *was the first truly American fantasy for children. Numerous sequels, plays and musicals, film and television shows, and a myriad of Oz-related products have, in the years since its publication in 1901, grown from Baum's initial book. By keeping some of the magic found in older fairy tales and combining it with the reality of early twentieth-century middle America, Baum devised a story that became a beloved classic.*

As inescapable as a Kansas cyclone, "reality" TV shows are part of the twenty-first century culture. Rachel Swirsky introduces the concept to Oz—the granting of a wish is the contest's prize—but it's not the only game in the Emerald City: a rebellion is brewing.

Beyond the Naked Eye

Rachel Swirsky

WISH.

The letters are chipped from emerald. Serifs sparkle. They hover in midair like insects with faceted carapaces. Their shadows fall, rich and dark, over a haze of yellow, which as the view widens becomes distinguishable as part of a brick and then as part of a road, which itself becomes a winding yellow ribbon that crosses verdant farmland.

Ten contestants. One boon from the Wizard.

Whose wish will come true?

We all watch in our crystal globes. Blue-tinted ones sit on rough tables in Munchkin Country. Red-tinted ones float beside Quadlings. Green-tinted ones are held aloft in the lacquered fingernails of Emerald Citizens.

Convex glass distorts our view. We see wide, but we do not see deep.

After revealing the rich lands of Oz, the view soars upward until it shows nothing but sky. A silver swing drops down. It's shaped like a crescent moon. Glinda, the Good Witch of the South, perches on it. She wears a drop-waisted, sleeveless gown. Sparkling white fabric falls in loose folds to just above her ankles.

Her voice is as sweet as honeydew.

"We're down to our four finalists. They've worked together to make it down the road of yellow brick. They've almost made it to the Emerald City. What will happen next? Only one can win. Will it be Lion, Tin Man, Scarecrow, or Dorothy?"

She raises her finger to her lips, telling a secret to everyone watching. "Remember, in Oz, wishes really do come true."

Those of us who fancy ourselves members of the City's intellectual elite gather in fashionable bathhouses to watch the show. This season, it is unthinkable not to wear hats during social gatherings, even when otherwise nude. This makes for awkward bathhouse situations. We hold ourselves stiffly, craning our necks to keep silk and felt dry.

Despite our collective ridiculousness, we still feel entitled to laugh at Glinda's dramatic pronouncements, and at the overblown challenges she puts to the contestants.

"Bread and circuses," we call it.

Some are of the opinion that it's all propaganda. "The Wizard wants to rub everyone's noses in how powerful he is," they remark.

"Not possible," others argue. "He's not that stupid. He could grant all of those people's wishes if he wanted to. He's losing public sympathy by the day." Smugly they tap the sides of their noses. "Someone's making this to show him up."

The two camps argue back and forth. Periodically, wild passion overcomes someone's good sense, and they gesticulate wildly, splashing everyone with emerald-hued water.

In the end we all agree on one thing: bread and circuses.

Effective bread and circuses, though. Everyone watches. Even us.

I keep quiet during the evenings at the bathhouse. I prefer to watch and listen. Few people know the name Kristol Kristoff, and I prefer it that way.

I'm a jeweler.

I have a loupe that I inherited from my great-grandfather. It magnifies everything by ten times.

Sometimes I find it frustrating to look at the mundane, unmagnified world. There are so many blemishes that one can't see with the naked eye. It's impractical to evaluate everything by what's superficially visible. If I had my preference, the ubiquitous Emerald City glasses would come with jeweler's loupes attached.

Working in the Emerald City, I perform most of my work on emeralds, which are actually a form of beryl green due to the intrusion of other minerals, usually chromium. Most emeralds are included—which means that they contain a relatively high proportion of other minerals—and also fragile. This makes them both motley and transitory.

The Emerald City is the same. Like any city, it's composed of a variety of minerals. It contains inclusions of Munchkins, Gillikins, Winkies, and Quadlings. An emerald would not be green without inclusions; a city would not be a city without immigrants.

An emerald will crack under high pressure. The Emerald City will do the same. Introduce a famine, ignite a fire, depose a leader. Stones or cities will shatter.

It's happened before.

The show began with the image of a farmhouse whirling through a tornado. It crashed to the ground in an explosion of dirt and debris. Slowly the wind blew the detritus away, revealing what lay below.

Two skinny, old legs poked out from beneath the farmhouse. Two wrinkled, old feet wore two shiny silver slippers.

"Congratulations, Dorothy!" Glinda beamed. "You've killed the Wicked Witch of the East and won the first challenge!"

She removed the shoes from the corpse and presented them to the little girl.

"These silver slippers will give you an advantage in later elimination rounds," Glinda said.

Smiling, Dorothy put on the shoes. She didn't seem to care that they'd just been taken from a dead woman.

In the Emerald City, we wear green, which is regrettable for my complexion.

Still, I am fortunate enough to own a very fine silk cloak, clasped with a very fine emerald cloak pin, both of which I inherited from my grandfather. While the former is threadbare, few people notice such things, as few people are used to looking at the world with a jeweler's eye for detail. It makes me seem much richer than I am, which is useful from time to time, such as when I visit the Palace.

A maid in a short frilly uniform, all white thighs and rouged knees, greeted me when I arrived. She threw her arms around my neck with overwhelming familiarity.

"Mister Kristoff!" she exclaimed.

When I paused to take a second look, I noticed with embarrassment that she was not actually a maid at all, but Lady Flashgleam Sparkle in costume.

"Why in the name of Lurline are you dressed like that?" I asked.

Flashgleam scanned for witnesses. "Not here. Come on."

She took my hand—so forward!—and pulled me across the threshold into one of the Palace's many emerald-accented parlors. As she led me briskly through corridors lined with gems and mirrors, I expected someone to stop us and ask Flashgleam why she was in costume, but apparently no one pays heed to maids who are escorting visitors.

We reached her rooms. She closed the door behind us and then went to her windows—which overlooked a courtyard where gardeners grew green orchids, green roses, and green hydrangeas—and swept the velvet curtains closed.

Flashgleam Sparkle is the only remaining scion of the house Sparkle, which had once sent its noble sons and daughters to attend the courts of Ozma III through Ozma XVI. Now that the line of the Ozmas has been broken, and the Wizard sits in their stead, most of the old noble families have departed the Emerald City for country estates.

Flashgleam, as the sole Sparkle heir, remained in the City of Emeralds, surrounded by the remnants of her family's glory. Last year, after she had the family's townhouse closed, declaring it too large for a single person, the Wizard offered her accommodations in his Palace as suited a person with her venerable lineage.

This was all according to plan.

While two people of our relative stations would not normally have interacted, Flashgleam had been my client for a number of years. Whenever she received gifts of jewelry—for instance, from suitors—she had the habit of commissioning me to craft facsimiles with which she could replace the original ornaments. Subsequently, she sold the genuine jewels through black market connections. It is always important—she says—for a woman to have unexpected reservoirs of cash.

My discretion in helping her create such forgeries had encouraged her to invite me into her secret cabal.

It has, I must say, made my life considerably more interesting than it was before.

Flashgleam arrayed herself on a divan. She crossed her legs, exposing white thigh with the casual disregard of dignity that only women of high station can afford. She said, "When I'm wearing this uniform, I can poke around anywhere."

I asked, "What did you find?"

"The pot of treasure," she said with a broadening smile. "We were right about everything. He's a charlatan."

When the show began, there were ten individual contestants. First thing, Glinda split them into teams. Team Dorothy (so named because she'd won the first challenge) approached the City from Munchkin Country. A group of three approached from Quadling Country and another three-entity group approached from Gillikin.

None started in Winkie Country due to the embargo against the Wicked Witch of the West.

The Quadling Team was the first to be eliminated. Their team leader, a lanky Quadling boy, lost a wrestling match with a Fighting Tree. After that, Dairy Belle, the animated butter pat, couldn't figure out how to do a glamour shoot reflecting her unique Quadling heritage, not least because she melted under the spotlights.

At first it seemed as though Pulp, who was one of the famous living paper dolls fashioned by Mrs. Cuttenclip, might make it on her own. She folded herself into a paper airplane and caught a passing wind. It would have carried her to the Emerald City much faster than the other teams could manage, but alas, the wind blew her into a river, where she turned into mulch and was swept downstream.

Initially, the viewers—the cynical bathhouse crowd among them—were in it to watch blood and teeth. The Kalidah challenge mustered a great deal of excitement. The bathhouses echoed with ladies' screams as the monsters' ursine bodies lumbered into view. Even I admit having felt a tremor when the light flashed across their bared tiger-teeth.

If it hadn't been for the first interview with Dorothy, perhaps the show would never have been anything more than a blood sport.

Glinda began the interview during a quiet moment. Dorothy sat under a peach tree in the evening light, her dog, Toto, running circles around her feet. Glinda knelt so that she was eye-to-eye with the child. She asked, "What do you wish for?"

Dorothy looked up. Breeze stirred her wheat-blonde curls.

"I just want to go home," she said.

"Don't you like Oz?" asked Glinda.

Dorothy's hand flew to her mouth. Her cheeks flushed with embarrassment. "Oh! I should mind my manners! Of course I like Oz. It's a beautiful place!"

"So why not stay?"

Dorothy's cornflower eyes cut shyly away. She smoothed her pinafore. "Kansas is . . . well, it may be boring, but it's home. You have to go back home. It's where you belong."

A drop glittered in her eye.

She murmured, "And Aunt Em must miss me terribly."

In the bathhouse, the intellectuals snorted derisively. "Sentimental manipulation," they called it.

Even so, Dorothy's words had taken what had been a silly amusement—no more significant than any game of cards—and transformed it into something that could tug at any of us.

We all remembered being children. We all remembered wanting to go home.

I am reasonably certain that Flashgleam Sparkle is the mastermind behind WISH.

I have not asked, and she has not volunteered the information. Still, the Good Witch of the South is reputed to be sympathetic to her cause, although the affiliations of witches are ever fickle.

More to the point, while Flashgleam and I avoided the subject of the show's derivation, we *had* discussed how well it suits her agenda.

If the Wizard was indeed a fraud—as we had long suspected—then the show would present him a terrible dilemma.

Once WISH became popular—an instantaneous phenomenon—he couldn't shut it down without revealing not only that he wasn't the architect behind it, but also that he had so little control of what was going on in his own territory that he hadn't been able to identify and halt such a large, rebellious magical undertaking before it began.

If he let the show run, he found himself tangled in yet another dilemma—he couldn't refuse to grant an audience to the winner unless he was willing to show himself as both incompetent *and* heartless. Yet, if he was a fraud, he couldn't admit the winner without being exposed as unable to grant their wish.

So far the Wizard had appeared to be biding his time, plotting his strategy as he allowed the competition to unfold. Flashgleam believed that he would eventually find a way to cut himself free of the dilemma; fraud or not, the Wizard was not stupid.

However, she also believed that the show would cause turmoil behind the throne. Frantic and furious, the Wizard would interrogate his staff, searching for his betrayer, disturbing the loyalties he'd so carefully built. During his reign, he'd quelled nascent rebellions with the mere threat of magic. Flashgleam hoped that disorder in his administration would give her the finger-holds she needed to pry the Wizard loose from his throne.

All this hinged, of course, on the thesis that he was actually a fraud.

"It's all done with gears," Flashgleam said. She smoothed the ruffled maid's collar over her bosom. "And pulleys and levers and . . . I don't know, I'm not a machinist. But it's all machines."

"The Wizard?" I asked.

"His audience chamber," she corrected. "There's a curtain drawn in front of it. But behind, it's all machines. There's something like a projector focused on the emerald throne. I think he's using photographic stills to create illusions."

"That's why everyone reports seeing different things in the throne room," I said.

"Right!" She raised her hands in excitement. Her fingers shone with the convincing forgeries of rings her lovers had gifted her. "Flames, and bats, and women carved from wood. They're photographs. Manipulations."

"So this is proof."

"Proof," she agreed. "Finally."

I was no watchmaker, but as a jeweler, I had more experience than most with the intricacies of machinery. "If you can give me fifteen minutes or so with the machines, I can figure out how to disrupt them."

Flashgleam looked up, a slight frown on her face. "Hmm?"

"He'll be able to repair them eventually, of course."

"Oh." Flashgleam laughed indulgently. "Always thinking like a craftsman, aren't you? You'd solve everything with a chisel if you could." She leaned forward. "Chaos is well and good, but assassinations are simpler."

I shouldn't have been taken aback, but I was. I had allowed myself to be lulled by the fact that Flashgleam Sparkle had, so far, limited herself to subterfuge. I'd hoped that we might expose the Wizard as a hapless marionette and let the Emerald Citizens themselves demand regime change without any need for cloaks and daggers.

"You're going to kill the Wizard?" I asked.

"We needed to know if he was a fraud. He is. He has no magic. He won't see us coming." She shook her head. "But no, I'm not going to kill the Wizard."

I knew what she was going to say next. I knew, but I still was unhappy when the words came from her lips.

"You are."

When Glinda caught him alone, the Lion giggled nervously.

"I think I want to win. I mean, I wouldn't be here if I didn't, right?" His amber eyes darted back and forth. "But then, thinking about it, if I had courage then I'd want to fight, right? And fighting ... anything could happen. There could be, like, a bear. And he'd run at me, and I'd, like, snarl back, because I'd be brave, and he'd probably chew my ears off."

His tail twitched.

"Is that what I'm competing for? A chance to, you know, have a bear chew my ears off?"

He rested his head on his paws. His downturned muzzle looked mournful despite his massive teeth.

"But I want to win. Of course I do. Uh. Courage. Give it to me. Yeah."
Hesitantly, he swiped his paw through the air.
"Rawr."

Despite a strong early showing, the Team Gillikin fizzled midway.

Another child was heading that team, a twelve-year-old from Up Town with purple skin and telescoping limbs. She traveled with a nymph from the Gillikin fog banks and a melancholy man from the Flathead Mountains who carried his brain in a jug.

In the Forest of the Winged Monkeys, they were kidnapped by the location's simian namesakes. One hundred feet into the air, the Flathead panicked and dropped his jug. At two hundred feet, a rising wind dispersed the mist maiden into the clouds.

Only the little girl survived; when the Monkeys lifted her into the air, she telescoped her legs so that no matter how high they took her, she was always touching the ground.

Though saddened by the loss of her companions, she was able to travel much more quickly without worrying about how they'd keep up. She telescoped her legs out as far as they would go and bounded by leagues.

Not far from the border, she glimpsed a pair of telescoping green legs doing the same. Upon investigation, they turned out to belong to a young green boy, who was off to seek his fortune in Quadling Country. Their conversation further revealed that they were both odd-colored, telescoping children born to tan, fixed-length parents, and—more importantly—that they enjoyed each other's company.

The girl revealed that her wish had been to find someone else like her. As it had been fulfilled, she left the competition and telescoped into the clouds with her new green friend.

The first time that Lady Sparkle broached the subject of revolution with me, she was wearing a woolen traveling cloak, as if she planned to leave the City. A petite fascinator fashioned from feathers and silk left her head almost shockingly bare.

She handed me a pair of jade hair sticks and watched my hands as I examined the carvings I'd need to replicate in order to make convincing facsimiles.

Rachel Swirsky

She ordinarily made pleasant small talk, which was unusual for someone of her status. For weeks I'd been noticing that her superficially inane
conversation was in fact driving at something. She'd been feeling out my
politics, I was sure, though I didn't know to what end.

That day, however, she made a direct assay. "I've heard stories about
your grandfather, you know."

I made a noncommittal noise and squinted at the hair sticks. The
kinds of stories that aristocrats told about my grandfather were not my
favorite subject of conversation.

She pressed me on it. "He was the royal jeweler, wasn't he?"

Matter-of-factly I said, "He was."

She gestured at my little shop with its dusty shelves and poor lighting. "So how did you end up here?"

I shrugged. Though I refused to meet her eye, I could feel her glance
on me.

"You're not untalented," she continued. "In fact, you're very talented
indeed."

With a sigh I looked up, still holding the jeweler's loupe to my eye.
Flashgleam Sparkle is a pretty woman, but under magnification, she
looked all powder and artifice: a woman made of paint.

"You've heard stories about my grandfather," I said. "So why don't you
tell me?"

Her dimples deepened, as if she was merely trying out a piece of juicy
gossip, but her tone remained serious. "He was caught in a plot to over-
throw Ozma the Sixteenth."

"That's right."

Her smile broadened. She lifted her glasses away from her face. I
barely contained my gasp—I was a man of the world, but still, a woman
like her baring her eyes while alone with a man?

"He imbued her diadem with a sleeping spell," Flashgleam continued.

I allowed myself a raised brow. "That part isn't common knowledge."

"I'm not a common woman."

She leaned toward me, placing her hands on my desk. Her eye loomed
giant in my jeweler's loupe, an aristocratic shade of deep river-green.

"I think you're more like him than you let on," Flashgleam said. "Am
I right?"

When I said nothing, she reached into the purse hung on her sash
and pulled out a handful of sparkling green chips.

"I can offer incentive," she said.

As I looked into her palm, I struggled to maintain my equanimity.

"They're genuine," she said, answering my unspoken question. "Lurline emeralds."

Lurline emeralds were the most valuable gem in all of Oz. They'd been created when Lurline made fairyland, and they were imbued with her magic. My grandfather had worked with them when he was a jeweler for the court. None were supposed to exist outside of the Ozmas' treasury.

Exercising my steeliest will, I waved my hand in refusal. "If I help you, I will do it out of conviction. Not avarice."

The rest of our conversation is easy to imagine, but I'll add one corroborating detail:

When Flashgleam Sparkle left my shop that afternoon wearing her woolen traveling cloak, neither I nor anyone else in the City saw her for several days. It wasn't long after she returned that all the globes in the City lit up with those sparkling emerald serifs.

WISH.

There are many people in the Emerald City who are discontented with the Wizard.

Some are Ozma purists, waiting for the return of Ozma XVII. Others note his fascistic tendencies: public punishments, harsh curfews, a large and well-armored imperial guard.

Where the Ozmas had always delegated policy-making to the Witches of the Realms, the Wizard insisted on deciding all matters without regard for local hierarchies. Against his advisors' warnings, he'd implemented the embargo against the Wicked Witch of the West, ostensibly motivated by concern for the Winkie people, but it was well-known that the actual dispute was about the Wizard's attempts to control the provinces.

Flashgleam Sparkle dislikes the Wizard because, unlike the Ozmas, he declines to be controlled by the nobility. She finds herself cut loose from the power she'd always assumed would be hers by right of inheritance.

I myself dislike the Wizard for much the same reason that I expect my grandfather disliked Ozma XVI. My family has served monarchs as their jewelers for generations. We've always paid attention to their flaws. The Wizard doesn't really care about the people. Ozma XVI didn't either.

Maybe Flashgleam Sparkle will.

"I'm a bit different from the others," the Tin Man told Glinda when it was his turn with her. "The Scarecrow never had a brain. The Lion never had any courage. I used to have a heart."

He rapped his knuckles against the side of his head. The sound echoed in his empty skull. "I don't have a brain anymore either, but what I miss is my heart."

The illusion of emotion clouded his eyes, something complicated and delicate like wistfulness or regret.

"I don't have blood anymore, so I won't need my heart to pump," he said. "All I need to do is feel. More deeply and more complexly than I ever did. Every minute. Every hour. I want to understand what it feels like to hate and love and laugh at something at the same time. I want to feel the poignant pain of looking at something beautiful and knowing it's going to die. I want to feel everything. Everything."

His fingers grasped the air, trying to hold on to something that wasn't there, a gesture that could easily have been mistaken for passion.

His hand drifted back to his side.

"If I win, of course," he added softly.

Last night's poppy challenge was a bit silly. Make the best bouquet you can in ten minutes. But oops, there's a twist. The bouquet was only a decoy. The real challenge was to get out of the poppy field before falling asleep.

The Tin Man and the Scarecrow, having no circulatory systems, were immune to poppy pollen, which everyone agreed was unfair. They carried Dorothy out of the poppy field when she fell asleep, but the Lion was too heavy for them to bring along.

It looked as though the Lion was out until the Tin Man accidentally rescued the Queen of the Field Mice, earning a challenge advantage. The Queen of the Field Mice promised him a favor, which he immediately spent by asking her tiny, squeaking subjects to drag the Lion out of the poppy field.

A lady sitting near me gestured angrily at her emerald globe. "That doesn't even make sense!"

Her hat was wide-brimmed with dense feathers, and her anger had caused her to gesture with such passion that she was in danger of losing her headgear to the water.

"It does seem a bit silly," agreed a friend of hers who was wearing a rather more sensible cloche.

"*Deus ex mus!*" shouted a mustachioed gentleman.

"Stupid strategy," someone else muttered. "They should have ditched Dorothy and the Lion and taken a ticket to the top two."

"But they made a pact!" cried the lady again. "You wouldn't leave behind a sweet girl like that, would you?"

"Bread and circuses, my dear fellows, bread and circuses," said a man near the middle of the pool. He wore a homburg and a stern expression, reminding us that, as intellectuals, we were there to analyze, not involve ourselves in drama.

In our globes we saw the field mice returning. Squeaking, they emerged from the field of flowers, each harnessed with fine thread to a wagon.

Atop the wagon, the Cowardly Lion lay, drowsing, an upturned scarlet poppy capping his nose. He woke with a sneeze that sent the poppy tumbling.

"Oh!" he exclaimed. "What happened? Is there a monster? Don't let it eat me!"

His eyes were so round with fear that even the man in the homburg laughed.

After watching my fellow Emerald intellectuals discuss the poppy challenge, I learned two things. First, that I am strangely reassured to find that even the most jaded of my fellow Citizens can still feel tenderly for a lost child. Second, that the contestants had finally made their way to the emerald gates, and whatever was going to happen was going to happen soon.

I learned to cut gems while sitting—as the saying goes—at my grandfather's knee. Literally on his knee, in my case; I needed the boost so I could see his worktable. I watched his face as often as I watched his hands. He squinted while he worked. His nostrils flared with concentration.

He was an unmade man by then, cast down from courtly heights to the small corner where my shop still resides. His days of working with Lurline emeralds were long past, but his unmatched work brought many aristocrats to him anyway, toting their unset sapphires and their rubies of unknown provenance.

Ozma herself had spared his life. With a yawn and a tinkling laugh, she'd said, "Oz must preserve beautiful things!"

Still, she let her witches weave chains around my grandfather's ankles so that he could not leave his allotted rooms.

When customers came in, he'd sweep me off of his knee and hand me a spare loupe. He'd push the loupe against my eye and then lean down, speaking quietly, so that no one could hear him. "Watch for the imperfections. There are imperfections everywhere. Never trust anyone who pretends to be flawless."

Glinda finds the Scarecrow in the chamber on the outskirts of the royal sector that he's been given for the night. He trips over the loose straw in his feet as he escorts her in and lands with a thump on the floor.

A concerned expression flashes across Glinda's face. The Scarecrow waves it away.

"If I had a fit every time I did something stupid, I'd spend all day stomping around."

He's a good-natured fellow, the Scarecrow, quick to mock himself, which I'd guess he'd have to be with those guilelessly painted eyes and that swaying, straw-stuffed gait.

Glinda asks him why he wishes he had a brain. "That's a good question!" he exclaims. "I don't know why I think I want to think since I don't have a brain to think I want to think with. But I'd like to think anyway. At least I think so. You think?"

He sits on the bed and leans against the emerald headboard. At his feet, there's a pair of complimentary emerald-encrusted slippers, which must be awful to wear.

"I was only born the day before yesterday," the Scarecrow says, "so maybe my opinion doesn't count. But it's awfully pretty, isn't it?"

Glinda turns to see what he's looking at. It's sunset blazing through the window, reds and golds and violets refracting through the City's crystalline towers.

The Scarecrow's voice is lower when he continues. "I want a brain, but I think if I get one, I'll be sad that my friends couldn't get what they want, too. Is that what thinking gets you? Understanding that a sweet thing can be bitter, too?"

He looks sadly at Glinda.

"Maybe that's not right. You'd know better than I do. You have a brain."

Tonight. Whatever is going to happen will happen tonight.

Everyone in Flashgleam's rebellion wears a watch that I have calibrated. When the tick tells me to, I depart the bathhouse—where everyone is still watching Glinda and the Scarecrow—and head into the corridor.

The City is a labyrinthine place, built as a single creation. It's not like the towns out in Gillikin Country, where one house is distinct from the next. In the City, towers share walls and are connected by archways. Central towers look down on courtyards; those on the outskirts look out over Oz. The royal spire rises above all others, gazing imperially downward.

I work my way along jeweled corridors. Few people are out; most of the population is congregated in bathhouses and parlors. Those that aren't walk swiftly, hunched over handheld globes.

I wear my grandfather's cloak anyway. For disguise. For confidence.

The corridors grow increasingly ornate as I near the royal sector. Gold embellishes the archways. Statues of the Ozmas (their nameplates removed by the new regime) pose gracefully in niches. The hundred passages that wind through the City's outskirts converge into a few main arteries.

From behind me I hear a page trumpeting. Footsteps echo. Bad luck for me. The royal pages have chosen to escort the contestants down this corridor.

I shrink against the wall. It's best they don't see me. I don't want to be delayed.

Still, I admit, I'm fascinated to watch the finalists pass. The Tin Man walks first, each movement clanking. The Scarecrow follows, his straw fingers wrapped around those of the little girl. The Tin Man and Scarecrow look more wary than hopeful. Perhaps they are concerned that there will be another challenge waiting, or perhaps they are wondering whether everything that's happened is a trick. The Tin Man tightens his fingers around his axe, and the Scarecrow clutches the little girl's hand, both of them protecting her as best they know how.

Dorothy dances delightedly down the hall, exclaiming over the jewels and statues, without a hint of fright in her eyes.

The Cowardly Lion slinks after them, belly low to the ground.

How cruel it seems that none of them will get their wish.

What would I wish for?

What would I tell Glinda if she were sitting beside me, the fabric of her gown pooling around her knees?

I'd tell her, I think, that I wish everyone had a jeweler's loupe.

I wish that everyone would try to see things as they really are.

I wish that everyone would understand that glamour is often deceit.

I wish that everyone would realize that when you know a flaw is there, you can figure out how to work with it, how to cut around it, how to make the gem glow despite the cracks. Everyone should know how to make the most beautiful objects they can out of things that aren't perfect.

Because nothing is perfect.

Eight anterooms branch off of the Wizard's audience chamber. We meet in the one Flashgleam described. Today she's more suitably attired, wearing a high-waisted gown with a narrow skirt draped in tiers. Her head is bare except for a single peacock feather pinned over one ear.

She's deep in conversation with the other conspirators. There are perhaps half a dozen; it's difficult for me to distinguish one from the next as they are all cloaked and in the shadows.

I stand quietly aside until Flashgleam notices my presence. She claps me familiarly on the shoulder. She means to compliment, I think, but her touch is uncomfortable.

From within her cloak, she withdraws an enormous emerald that's been carved into a spike. The wickedly sharp tip glints even in this dark room. She offers it, blunt end first.

"Symbols," she says, "It's all about symbols. The City itself is purging him. The emeralds themselves are rising up."

The spike is cool in my palm. A real emerald would be too fragile to wield as a weapon—this one must be enchanted. It must be a Lurline emerald, purloined from Ozma's treasury. To think that anyone could steal such an enormous jewel is startling, but if anyone can, it's Lady Sparkle.

"You're the perfect one to do this." Her voice is soft and charismatic and urgent. "The avatar of emerald."

Perhaps it's the magic of the emerald in my palm that blunts my tongue. "And this way no one noble has to dirty their hands."

"No, of course that's not why," she assures me rapidly. Despite her shocked tone, we both know she's lying.

I wish I had my jeweler's loupe today, but all I have are my eyes. Lady Sparkle's skin is smooth. Her lips are beautifully rounded. There's not a blemish on her cheek, not a discoloration on her costume, not a barbule out of place in the peacock feather behind her ear.

At normal magnification she's flawless.

Jewelers are trained to cut gems, not break them, but in training for the first, one must inevitably learn the second.

A chisel, misplaced, will transform a jewel that was once worth Ozma's ransom into something worthless and fractured.

You can crack a gem in two. You can shatter it. You can do many things that a jeweler ought not to.

A jeweler understands the vulnerability of stone.

The other conspirators rush around at whatever business Flashgleam has assigned them. They pay me no attention.

I recognize one of them now that she's thrown off her cloak. It's Glinda, wearing a white robe with a starched collar. She stands at the entrance to the audience chamber, holding back the velvet curtain that separates us from where the Wizard is receiving Dorothy and her fellows. She only holds it open a fraction, but it still seems a silly risk to me.

Not, apparently, to Flashgleam, who moves to join her. She peers over Glinda's shoulder and gestures to me.

A risk it may be, but I might as well. If the Wizard finds us now, it will make little difference whether I'm at the forefront or standing back.

"There it is," Flashgleam whispers to me, pointing. "The throne with the screen on it. Do you see?"

"He's a clever old bastard," Glinda says. Surprisingly, despite her harsh words, her voice is as honeydew as ever.

"Shh," says Flashgleam.

She points again, this time indicating the contestants who are entering the chamber. The Tin Man stands at the forefront, axe in hand, protecting the other three.

Lights flash through the audience chamber. Flashgleam points to the spots on the ceiling where concealed bulbs are shining down magenta and cerulean.

Suddenly the throne seems to ignite. A Ball of Fire rages without consuming anything. In a shower of sparks, it disappears and becomes a lovely Lady and then a snarling Beast. Finally it settles in the form of an enormous Head with blood-hued skin and faceted eyes.

"What do you want of the Wizard?" it booms.

Timorously each contestant states his or her wish.

The Head answers, "I will grant your favors."

The contestants rejoice. The Head interrupts.

His roar cuts into their celebration. "If you meet my condition!"

They fall silent.

"You must kill the Wicked Witch of the West!"

Dorothy stammers. Glinda shakes her head. "Clever old bastard," she repeats, "Taking advantage of the show. He's given them his own challenge."

"Doesn't matter now," Flashgleam answers.

Glinda drops the curtain. It sways back into place. She departs the anteroom on her own mission.

The conspirators' voices rise as they enter the final throes of their plans.

Flashgleam's fingertips brush mine. "We're almost ready. Don't worry about anything. He'll be incapacitated. He won't be able to hurt you."

I look toward the curtain.

"What are you going to do about Dorothy?" I ask.

Flashgleam blinks. Her brow draws down. "What do you mean?"

"Dorothy. How are you going to get her home?"

"That's not what we should be worried about now."

I push past her and tear the curtain aside. The contestants in the audience chamber don't notice the noise. The Tin Man looks poised to attack the throne. The Lion's low growl fills the room.

Dorothy sniffles into her apron. The Scarecrow wraps his arms around her shoulders, and she turns into the embrace. Tears leave glistening marks on her cheeks. I lose my breath.

Even the most jaded Citizen of Oz feels tenderly toward a child who has lost her home.

I round on Flashgleam. Angrily I repeat, "What are you going to do for Dorothy?"

She's still staring at me as if my words make no sense. She gives some calculated, reassuring answer, but I don't even hear her. The spike is cold in my hand. Lurline emerald.

All my life I've been the one who held the loupe to my eye, who strove to see beyond the superficial. All my life I've been the one who looked for imperfections.

All my life I've been a fool. All my life I've looked for the flaws in what stands before me, not for the flaws in my own thoughts.

It's foolish to hope for a ruler who will be benevolent and just. Ozma XVI, the Wizard, Lady Flashgleam Sparkle—they're all the same. No monarch is ever going to care more about the people than they do about themselves.

I rush forward. Lady Sparkle exclaims, "They're not ready yet!"

I push past her. Everyone looks up as I enter the audience chamber. Even the Wizard's giant avatar regards me with surprise clouding his faceted eyes.

Lurline emerald can break through a man's sternum. It can break through anything.

The Emerald City is named for the emerald from which it was carved. It's held together by magic that keeps it from shattering, but the magic in a Lurline emerald is stronger than any other enchantment.

I pass the Wizard's hidden niche without a glance. Nearby, a place in the wall shines with a translucence I've learned indicates a weak point in the rock.

I'm a jeweler. I know the vulnerability of stone.

There's a horrible noise as I drive the spike into the wall. A crack appears. Slowly it branches toward the floor, casting its roots into the ground. The tower shudders.

Lady Flashgleam rushes toward me, but she stops when she sees the fracture. She staggers backward. For once, even her seemingly perfect lips are stunned into silence.

The magic will die slowly. There will be plenty of time for everyone to get out.

But the Palace will splinter. The Palace will fall.

Its collapse will resonate throughout the Emerald City, of course. The City is all built from one piece. One can't extricate the Palace from the City without consequence, just as one can't depose a ruler without pain.

But I know this City. The highest spire is the weakest. The rest may tremble, but it won't collapse.

We won't collapse.

I push between the Tin Man and the Scarecrow. They've intuited that I'm on their side. They let me pass.

I take Dorothy's hand and lead her and her friends out of the audience chamber and down into the City. I don't know if I can grant her wish. I don't know if I can grant any of them their wishes. It's a flawed world we live in, and not everyone can get what he or she wants. But at least I won't forget her. At least I won't cast her aside while I search for power.

Even the most jaded Emerald Citizen can feel for a child who's lost her home.

Rachel Swirsky holds an MFA from the Iowa Writers Workshop. She has twice won the Nebula Award, and been nominated for the Hugo, the World Fantasy Award, and the Locus Award, among others. Her second collection, *How the World Became Quiet: Myths of the Past, Present, and Future* was published by Subterranean Press in 2013. Her father's favorite movie is *The Wizard of Oz*, which is probably why that story looms large in her childhood. Also, her older brothers once tried to convince her that the garage was full of flying monkeys.

Hulijing *(Chinese)*, kitsune *(Japanese)*, kumiho *(Korean): there are differences, but all are shapeshifting fox spirits. They are most often portrayed as changing into beautiful women. Neither good nor evil, they are often seductive and dangerous tricksters, and there are love stories about fox-girls and young human men.*

As steampunkish modern technology intrudes into the world of Ken Liu's tale and the power of magic weakens—not a good situation for a hulijing. *But there's always a possibility that old magic can be replaced by new.*

Good Hunting

Ken Liu

Night. Half moon. An occasional hoot from an owl.

The merchant and his wife and all the servants had been sent away. The large house was eerily quiet.

Father and I crouched behind the scholar's rock in the courtyard. Through the rock's many holes I could see the bedroom window of the merchant's son.

"Oh, Tsiao-jung, my sweet Tsiao-jung . . ."

The young man's feverish groans were pitiful. Half-delirious, he was tied to his bed for his own good, but Father had left a window open so that his plaintive cries could be carried by the breeze far over the rice paddies.

"Do you think she really will come?" I whispered. Today was my thirteenth birthday, and this was my first hunt.

"She will," Father said. "A *hulijing* cannot resist the cries of the man she has bewitched."

"Like how the Butterfly Lovers cannot resist each other?" I thought back to the folk opera troupe that had come through our village last fall.

"Not quite," Father said. But he seemed to have trouble explaining why. "Just know that it's not the same."

I nodded, not sure I understood. But I remembered how the merchant and his wife had come to Father to ask for his help.

"How shameful!" the merchant had muttered. "He's not even nineteen. How could he have read so many sages' books and still fall under the spell of such a creature?"

"There's no shame in being entranced by the beauty and wiles of a hulijing,*"* *Father had said. "Even the great scholar Wong Lai once spent three nights in the company of one, and he took first place at the Imperial Examinations. Your son just needs a little help."*

"You must save him," the merchant's wife had said, bowing like a chicken pecking at rice. "If this gets out, the matchmakers won't touch him at all."

A *hulijing* was a demon who stole hearts. I shuddered, worried if I would have the courage to face one.

Father put a warm hand on my shoulder, and I felt calmer. In his hand was Swallow Tail, a sword that had first been forged by our ancestor, General Lau Yip, thirteen generations ago. The sword was charged with hundreds of Daoist blessings and had drunk the blood of countless demons.

A passing cloud obscured the moon for a moment, throwing everything into darkness.

When the moon emerged again, I almost cried out.

There, in the courtyard, was the most beautiful lady I had ever seen.

She had on a flowing white silk dress with billowing sleeves and a wide, silvery belt. Her face was pale as snow, and her hair dark as coal, draping past her waist. I thought she looked like the paintings of great beauties from the Tang Dynasty the opera troupe had hung around their stage.

She turned slowly to survey everything around her, her eyes glistening in the moonlight like two shimmering pools.

I was surprised to see how sad she looked. Suddenly, I felt sorry for her and wanted more than anything else to make her smile.

The light touch of my father's hand against the back of my neck jolted me out of my mesmerized state. He had warned me about the power of the *hulijing*. My face hot and my heart hammering, I averted my eyes from the demon's face and focused on her stance.

The merchant's servants had been patrolling the courtyard every night this week with dogs to keep her away from her victim. But now the courtyard was empty. She stood still, hesitating, suspecting a trap.

"Tsiao-jung! Have you come for me?" The son's feverish voice grew louder.

The lady turned and walked—no, glided, so smooth were her movements—towards the bedroom door.

Father jumped out from behind the rock and rushed at her with Swallow Tail.

She dodged out of the way as though she had eyes on the back of her head. Unable to stop, my father thrust the sword into the thick wooden door with a dull thunk. He pulled but could not free the weapon immediately.

The lady glanced at him, turned, and headed for the courtyard gate.

"Don't just stand there, Liang!" Father called. "She's getting away!"

I ran at her, dragging my clay pot filled with dog piss. It was my job to splash her with it so that she could not transform into her fox form and escape.

She turned to me and smiled. "You're a very brave boy." A scent, like jasmine blooming in spring rain, surrounded me. Her voice was like sweet, cold lotus paste, and I wanted to hear her talk forever. The clay pot dangled from my hand, forgotten.

"Now!" Father shouted. He had pulled the sword free.

I bit my lip in frustration. *How could I become a demon hunter if I was so easily enticed?* I lifted off the cover and emptied the clay pot at her retreating figure, but the insane thought that I shouldn't dirty her white dress caused my hands to shake, and my aim was wide. Only a small amount of dog piss got onto her.

But it was enough. She howled, and the sound, like a dog's but so much wilder, caused the hairs on the back of my neck to stand up. She turned and snarled, showing two rows of sharp, white teeth, and I stumbled back.

I had doused her while she was in the midst of her transformation. Her face was thus frozen halfway between a woman's and a fox's, with a hairless snout and raised, triangular ears that twitched angrily. Her hands had turned into paws, tipped with sharp claws that she swiped at me.

She could no longer speak, but her eyes conveyed her venomous thoughts without trouble.

Father rushed by me, his sword raised for a killing blow. The *huli-jing* turned around and slammed into the courtyard gate, smashing it open, and disappeared through the broken door.

Father chased after her without even a glance back at me. Ashamed, I followed.

The *hulijing* was swift of foot, and her silvery tail seemed to leave a glittering trail across the fields. But her incompletely transformed body maintained a human's posture, incapable of running as fast as she could have on four legs.

Father and I saw her dodging into the abandoned temple about a *li* outside the village.

"Go around the temple," Father said, trying to catch his breath. "I will go through the front door. If she tries to flee through the back door, you know what to do."

The back of the temple was overgrown with weeds and the wall half-collapsed. As I came around, I saw a white flash darting through the rubble.

Determined to redeem myself in my father's eyes, I swallowed my fear and ran after it without hesitation. After a few quick turns, I had the thing cornered in one of the monks' cells.

I was about to pour the remaining dog piss on it when I realized that the animal was much smaller than the *hulijing* we had been chasing. It was a small white fox, about the size of a puppy.

I set the clay pot on the ground and lunged.

The fox squirmed under me. It was surprisingly strong for such a small animal. I struggled to hold it down. As we fought, the fur between my fingers seemed to become as slippery as skin, and the body elongated, expanded, grew. I had to use my whole body to wrestle it to the ground.

Suddenly, I realized that my hands and arms were wrapped around the nude body of a young girl about my age.

I cried out and jumped back. The girl stood up slowly, picked up a silk robe from behind a pile of straw, put it on, and gazed at me haughtily.

A growl came from the main hall some distance away, followed by the sound of a heavy sword crashing into a table. Then another growl, and the sound of my father's curses.

The girl and I stared at each other. She was even prettier than the opera singer that I couldn't stop thinking about last year.

"Why are you after us?" she asked. "We did nothing to you."

"Your mother bewitched the merchant's son," I said. "We have to save him."

"*Bewitched? He's* the one who wouldn't leave *her* alone."

I was taken aback. "What are you talking about?"

"One night about a month ago, the merchant's son stumbled upon my mother, caught in a chicken farmer's trap. She had to transform into her human form to escape, and as soon as he saw her, he became infatuated.

"She liked her freedom and didn't want anything to do with him. But once a man has set his heart on a *hulijing*, she cannot help hearing him no matter how far apart they are. All that moaning and crying he did drove her to distraction, and she had to go see him every night just to keep him quiet."

This was not what I learned from Father.

"She lures innocent scholars and draws on their life essence to feed her evil magic! Look how sick the merchant's son is!"

"He's sick because that useless doctor gave him poison that was supposed to make him forget about my mother. My mother is the one who's kept him alive with her nightly visits. And stop using the word *lure*. A man can fall in love with a *hulijing* just like he can with any human woman."

I didn't know what to say, so I said the first thing that came to mind. "I just know it's not the same."

She smirked. "Not the same? I saw how you looked at me before I put on my robe."

I blushed. "Brazen demon!" I picked up the clay pot. She remained where she was, a mocking smile on her face. Eventually, I put the pot back down.

The fight in the main hall grew noisier, and suddenly, there was a loud crash, followed by a triumphant shout from Father and a long, piercing scream from the woman.

There was no smirk on the girl's face now, only rage turning slowly to shock. Her eyes had lost their lively luster; they looked dead.

Another grunt from Father. The scream ended abruptly.

"Liang! Liang! It's over. Where are you?"

Tears rolled down the girl's face.

"Search the temple," my Father's voice continued. "She may have pups here. We have to kill them too."

The girl tensed.

"Liang, have you found anything?" The voice was coming closer.

"Nothing," I said, locking eyes with her. "I didn't find anything."

She turned around and silently ran out of the cell. A moment later, I saw a small white fox jump over the broken back wall and disappear into the night.

It was *Qingming*, the Festival of the Dead. Father and I went to sweep Mother's grave and to bring her food and drink to comfort her in the afterlife.

"I'd like to stay here for a while," I said. Father nodded and left for home.

I whispered an apology to my mother, packed up the chicken we had brought for her, and walked the three *li* to the other side of the hill, to the abandoned temple.

I found Yan kneeling in the main hall, near the place where my father had killed her mother five years ago. She now wore her hair up in a bun, in the style of a young woman who had had her *jijili*, the ceremony that meant she was no longer a girl. We'd been meeting every *Qingming*, every *Chongyang*, every *Yulan*, every New Year's, occasions when families were supposed to be together.

"I brought you this," I said, and handed her the steamed chicken.

"Thank you." And she carefully tore off a leg and bit into it daintily. Yan had explained to me that the *hulijing* chose to live near human villages because they liked to have human things in their lives: conversation, beautiful clothes, poetry and stories, and, occasionally, the love of a worthy, kind man.

But the *hulijing* remained hunters who felt most free in their fox form. After what happened to her mother, Yan stayed away from chicken coops, but she still missed their taste.

"How's hunting?" I asked.

"Not so great," she said. "There are few Hundred-Year Salamanders and Six-Toed Rabbits. I can't ever seem to get enough to eat." She bit off another piece of chicken, chewed, and swallowed. "I'm having trouble transforming too."

"It's hard for you to keep this shape?"

"No." She put the rest of the chicken on the ground and whispered a prayer to her mother.

392

"I mean it's getting harder for me to return to my true form," she continued, "to hunt. Some nights I can't do it at all. How's hunting for you?"

"Not so great either. There don't seem to be as many snake spirits or angry ghosts as a few years ago. Even hauntings by suicides with unfinished business are down. And we haven't had a proper jumping corpse in months. Father is worried about money."

We also hadn't had to deal with a *hulijing* in years. Maybe Yan had warned them all away. Truth be told, I was relieved. I didn't relish the prospect of having to tell my father that he was wrong about something. He was already very irritable, anxious that he was losing the respect of the villagers now that his knowledge and skill didn't seem to be needed as much.

"Ever think that maybe the jumping corpses are also misunderstood?" she asked. "Like me and my mother?"

She laughed as she saw my face. "Just kidding!"

It was strange, what Yan and I shared. She wasn't exactly a friend. More like someone who you couldn't help being drawn to because you shared the knowledge of how the world didn't work the way you had been told.

She looked at the chicken bits she had left for her mother. "I think magic is being drained out of this land."

I had suspected that something was wrong, but didn't want to voice my suspicion out loud, which would make it real.

"What do you think is causing it?"

Instead of answering, Yan perked up her ears and listened intently. Then she got up, grabbed my hand, and pulled until we were behind the buddha in the main hall.

"Wha—"

She held up her finger against my lips. So close to her, I finally noticed her scent. It was like her mother's, floral and sweet, but also bright, like blankets dried in the sun. I felt my face grow warm.

A moment later, I heard a group of men making their way into the temple. Slowly, I inched my head out from behind the buddha so I could see.

It was a hot day, and the men were seeking some shade from the noon sun. Two men set down a cane sedan chair, and the passenger who stepped off was a foreigner, with curly yellow hair and pale skin. Other men in the group carried tripods, levels, bronze tubes, and open trunks full of strange equipment.

"Most Honored Mister Thompson." A man dressed like a mandarin came up to the foreigner. The way he kept on bowing and smiling and bouncing his head up and down reminded me of a kicked dog begging for favors. "Please have a rest and drink some cold tea. It is hard for the men to be working on the day when they're supposed to visit the graves of their families, and they need to take a little time to pray lest they anger the gods and spirits. But I promise we'll work hard afterwards and finish the survey on time."

"The trouble with you Chinese is your endless superstition," the foreigner said. He had a strange accent, but I could understand him just fine. "Remember, the Hong Kong-Tientsin Railroad is a priority for Great Britain. If I don't get as far as Botou Village by sunset, I'll be docking all of your wages."

I had heard rumors that the Manchu Emperor had lost a war and been forced to give up all kinds of concessions, one of which involved paying to help the foreigners build a road of iron. But it had all seemed so fantastical that I didn't pay much attention.

The mandarin nodded enthusiastically. "Most Honored Mister Thompson is right in every way. But might I trouble your gracious ear with a suggestion?"

The weary Englishman waved impatiently.

"Some of the local villagers are worried about the proposed path of the railroad. You see, they think the tracks that have already been laid are blocking off veins of *qi* in the earth. It's bad *feng shui*."

"What are you talking about?"

"It is kind of like how a man breathes," the mandarin said, huffing a few times to make sure the Englishman understood. "The land has channels along rivers, hills, ancient roads that carry the energy of *qi*. It's what gives the villages prosperity and maintains the rare animals and local spirits and household gods. Could you consider shifting the line of the tracks a little, to follow the *feng shui* masters' suggestions?"

Thompson rolled his eyes. "That is the most ridiculous thing I've yet heard. You want me to deviate from the most efficient path for our railroad because you think your idols would be angry?"

The mandarin looked pained. "Well, in the places where the tracks have already been laid, many bad things are happening: people losing money, animals dying, household gods not responding to prayers. The Buddhist and Daoist monks all agree that it's the railroad."

Thompson strode over to the buddha and looked at it appraisingly. I ducked back behind the statue and squeezed Yan's hand. We held our breaths, hoping that we wouldn't be discovered.

"Does this one still have any power?" Thompson asked.

"The temple hasn't been able to maintain a contingent of monks for many years," the mandarin said. "But this buddha is still well respected. I hear villagers say that prayers to him are often answered."

Then I heard a loud crash and a collective gasp from the men in the main hall.

"I've just broken the hands off of this god of yours with my cane," Thompson said. "As you can see, I have not been struck by lightning or suffered any other calamity. Indeed, now we know that it is only an idol made of mud stuffed with straw and covered in cheap paint. This is why you people lost the war to Britain. You worship statues of mud when you should be thinking about building roads from iron and weapons from steel."

There was no more talk about changing the path of the railroad.

After the men were gone, Yan and I stepped out from behind the statue. We gazed at the broken hands of the buddha for a while.

"The world's changing," Yan said. "Hong Kong, iron roads, foreigners with wires that carry speech and machines that belch smoke. More and more, storytellers in the teahouses speak of these wonders. I think that's why the old magic is leaving. A more powerful kind of magic has come."

She kept her voice unemotional and cool, like a placid pool of water in autumn, but her words rang true. I thought about my father's attempts to keep up a cheerful mien as fewer and fewer customers came to us. I wondered if the time I spent learning the chants and the sword dance moves were wasted.

"What will you do?" I asked, thinking about her, alone in the hills and unable to find the food that sustained her magic.

"There's only one thing I *can* do." Her voice broke for a second and became defiant, like a pebble tossed into the pool.

But then she looked at me, and her composure returned.

"The only thing *we* can do. Learn to survive."

The railroad soon became a familiar part of the landscape: the black locomotive huffing through the green rice paddies, puffing steam and pulling a long train behind it, like a dragon coming down from the distant, hazy, blue mountains. For a while, it was a wondrous sight, with children marveling at it, running alongside the tracks to keep up.

But the soot from the locomotive chimneys killed the rice in the fields closest to the tracks, and two children playing on the tracks, too frightened to move, were killed one afternoon. After that, the train ceased to fascinate.

People stopped coming to Father and me to ask for our services. They either went to the Christian missionary or the new teacher who said he'd studied in San Francisco. Young men in the village began to leave for Hong Kong or Canton, moved by rumors of bright lights and well-paying work. Fields lay fallow. The village itself seemed to consist only of the too-old and too-young, and their mood one of resignation. Men from distant provinces came to inquire about buying land for cheap.

Father spent his days sitting in the front room, Swallow Tail over his knee, staring out the door from dawn to dusk, as though he himself had turned into a statue.

Every day, as I returned home from the fields, I would see the glint of hope in Father's eyes briefly flare up.

"Did anyone speak of needing our help?" he would ask.

"No," I would say, trying to keep my tone light. "But I'm sure there will be a jumping corpse soon. It's been too long."

I would not look at my father as I spoke because I did not want to look as hope faded from his eyes.

Then, one day, I found Father hanging from the heavy beam in his bedroom. As I let his body down, my heart numb, I thought that he was not unlike those he had hunted all his life: they were all sustained by an old magic that had left and would not return, and they did not know how to survive without it.

Swallow Tail felt dull and heavy in my hand. I had always thought I would be a demon hunter, but how could I when there were no more demons, no more spirits? All the Daoist blessings in the sword could not save my father's sinking heart. And if I stuck around, perhaps my heart would grow heavy and yearn to be still too.

I hadn't seen Yan since that day six years ago, when we hid from the railroad surveyors at the temple. But her words came back to me now.

Learn to survive.
I packed a bag and bought a train ticket to Hong Kong.

The Sikh guard checked my papers and waved me through the security gate.

I paused to let my gaze follow the tracks going up the steep side of the mountain. It seemed less like a railroad track than a ladder straight up to heaven. This was the funicular railway, the tram line to the top of Victoria Peak, where the masters of Hong Kong lived and the Chinese were forbidden to stay.

But the Chinese were good enough to shovel coal into the boilers and grease the gears.

Steam rose around me as I ducked into the engine room. After five years, I knew the rhythmic rumbling of the pistons and the staccato grinding of the gears as well as I knew my own breath and heartbeat. There was a kind of music to their orderly cacophony that moved me, like the clashing of cymbals and gongs at the start of a folk opera. I checked the pressure, applied sealant on the gaskets, tightened the flanges, replaced the worn-down gears in the backup cable assembly. I lost myself in the work, which was hard and satisfying.

By the end of my shift, it was dark. I stepped outside the engine room and saw a full moon in the sky as another tram filled with passengers was pulled up the side of the mountain, powered by my engine.

"Don't let the Chinese ghosts get you," a woman with bright blond hair said in the tram, and her companions laughed.

It was the night of *Yulan*, I realized, the Ghost Festival. *I should get something for my father, maybe pick up some paper money at Mongkok.*

"How can you be done for the day when we still want you?" a man's voice came to me.

"Girls like you shouldn't tease," another man said, and laughed.

I looked in the direction of the voices and saw a Chinese woman standing in the shadows just outside the tram station. Her tight western-style cheongsam and the garish makeup told me her profession. Two Englishmen blocked her path. One tried to put his arms around her, and she backed out of the way.

"Please. I'm very tired," she said in English. "Maybe next time."

"Now, don't be stupid," the first man said, his voice hardening. "This isn't a discussion. Come along now and do what you're supposed to."

I walked up to them. "Hey."

The men turned around and looked at me.

"What seems to be the problem?"

"None of your business."

"Well, I think it *is* my business," I said, "seeing as how you're talking to my sister."

I doubt either of them believed me. But five years of wrangling heavy machinery had given me a muscular frame, and they took a look at my face and hands, grimy with engine grease, and probably decided that it wasn't worth it to get into a public tussle with a lowly Chinese engineer.

The two men stepped away to get in line for the Peak Tram, muttering curses.

"Thank you," she said.

"It's been a long time," I said, looking at her. I swallowed the *you look good*. She didn't. She looked tired and thin and brittle. And the pungent perfume she wore assaulted my nose.

But I did not think of her harshly. Judging was the luxury of those who did not need to survive.

"It's the night of the Ghost Festival," she said. "I didn't want to work any more. I wanted to think about my mother."

"Why don't we go get some offerings together?" I asked.

We took the ferry over to Kowloon, and the breeze over the water revived her a bit. She wet a towel with the hot water from the teapot on the ferry and wiped off her makeup. I caught a faint trace of her natural scent, fresh and lovely as always.

"You look good," I said, and meant it.

On the streets of Kowloon, we bought pastries and fruits and cold dumplings and a steamed chicken and incense and paper money, and caught up on each other's lives.

"How's hunting?" I asked. We both laughed.

"I miss being a fox," she said. She nibbled on a chicken wing absentmindedly. "One day, shortly after that last time we talked, I felt the last bit of magic leave me. I could no longer transform."

"I'm sorry," I said, unable to offer anything else.

"My mother taught me to like human things: food, clothes, folk opera, old stories. But she was never dependent on them. When she wanted, she could always turn into her true form and hunt. But now, in this form, what can I do? I don't have claws. I don't have sharp teeth. I can't even run very fast. All I have is my beauty, the same thing that your father and you killed my mother for. So now I live by the very thing that you once falsely accused my mother of doing: I *lure* men for money."

"My father is dead, too."

Hearing this seemed to drain some of the bitterness out of her. "What happened?"

"He felt the magic leave us, much as you. He couldn't bear it."

"I'm sorry." And I knew that she didn't know what else to say either.

"You told me once that the only thing we can do is to survive. I have to thank you for that. It probably saved my life."

"Then we're even," she said, smiling. "But let us not speak of ourselves any more. Tonight is reserved for the ghosts."

We went down to the harbor and placed our food next to the water, inviting all the ghosts we had loved to come and dine. Then we lit the incense and burned the paper money in a bucket.

She watched bits of burnt paper being carried into the sky by the heat from the flames. They disappeared among the stars. "Do you think the gates to the underworld still open for the ghosts tonight, now that there is no magic left?"

I hesitated. When I was young I had been trained to hear the scratching of a ghost's fingers against a paper window, to distinguish the voice of a spirit from the wind. But now I was used to enduring the thunderous pounding of pistons and the deafening hiss of high-pressured steam rushing through valves. I could no longer claim to be attuned to that vanished world of my childhood.

"I don't know," I said. "I suppose it's the same with ghosts as with people. Some will figure out how to survive in a world diminished by iron roads and steam whistles, some will not."

"But will any of them thrive?" she asked.

She could still surprise me.

"I mean," she continued, "are you happy? Are you happy to keep an engine running all day, yourself like another cog? What do you dream of?"

I couldn't remember any dreams. I had let myself become entranced by the movement of gears and levers, to let my mind grow to fit the gaps between the ceaseless clanging of metal on metal. It was a way to not have to think about my father, about a land that had lost so much.

"I dream of hunting in this jungle of metal and asphalt," she said. "I dream of my true form leaping from beam to ledge to terrace to roof, until I am at the top of this island, until I can growl in the faces of all the men who believe they can own me."

As I watched, her eyes, brightly lit for a moment, dimmed.

"In this new age of steam and electricity, in this great metropolis, except for those who live on the Peak, is anyone still in their true form?" she asked.

We sat together by the harbor and burned paper money all night, waiting for a sign that the ghosts were still with us.

Life in Hong Kong could be a strange experience: from day to day, things never seemed to change much. But if you compared things over a few years, it was almost like you lived in a different world.

By my thirtieth birthday, new designs for steam engines required less coal and delivered more power. They grew smaller and smaller. The streets filled with automatic rickshaws and horseless carriages, and most people who could afford them had machines that kept the air cool in houses and the food cold in boxes in the kitchen—all powered by steam.

I went into stores and endured the ire of the clerks as I studied the components of new display models. I devoured every book on the principle and operation of the steam engine I could find. I tried to apply those principles to improve the machines I was in charge of: trying out new firing cycles, testing new kinds of lubricants for the pistons, adjusting the gear ratios. I found a measure of satisfaction in the way I came to understand the magic of the machines.

One morning, as I repaired a broken governor—a delicate bit of work—two pairs of polished shoes stopped on the platform above me.

I looked up. Two men looked down at me.

"This is the one," said my shift supervisor.

The other man, dressed in a crisp suit, looked skeptical. "Are you the man who came up with the idea of using a larger flywheel for the old engine?"

I nodded. I took pride in the way I could squeeze more power out of my machines than dreamed of by their designers.

"You did not steal the idea from an Englishman?" his tone was severe.

I blinked. A moment of confusion was followed by a rush of anger. "No," I said, trying to keep my voice calm. I ducked back under the machine to continue my work.

"He is clever," my shift supervisor said, "for a Chinaman. He can be taught."

"I suppose we might as well try," said the other man. "It will certainly be cheaper than hiring a real engineer from England."

Mr. Alexander Findlay Smith, owner of the Peak Tram and an avid engineer himself, had seen an opportunity. He foresaw that the path of technological progress would lead inevitably to the use of steam power to operate automata: mechanical arms and legs that would eventually replace the Chinese coolies and servants.

I was selected to serve Mr. Findlay Smith in his new venture.

I learned to repair clockwork, to design intricate systems of gears and devise ingenious uses for levers. I studied how to plate metal with chrome and how to shape brass into smooth curves. I invented ways to connect the world of hardened and ruggedized clockwork to the world of miniaturized and regulated piston and clean steam. Once the automata were finished, we connected them to the latest analytic engines shipped from Britain and fed them with tape punched with dense holes in Babbage-Lovelace code.

It had taken a decade of hard work. But now mechanical arms served drinks in the bars along Central and machine hands fashioned shoes and clothes in factories in the New Territories. In the mansions up on the Peak, I heard—though I'd never seen—that automatic sweepers and mops I designed roamed the halls discreetly, bumping into walls gently as they cleaned the floors like mechanical elves puffing out bits of white steam. The expats could finally live their lives in this tropical paradise free of reminders of the presence of the Chinese.

I was thirty-five when she showed up at my door again, like a memory from long ago.

I pulled her into my tiny flat, looked around to be sure no one was following her, and closed the door.

"How's hunting?" I asked. It was a bad attempt at a joke, and she laughed weakly.

Photographs of her had been in all the papers. It was the biggest scandal in the colony: not so much because the Governor's son was keeping a Chinese mistress—it was expected that he would—but because the mistress had managed to steal a large sum of money from him and then disappear. Everyone tittered while the police turned the city upside down, looking for her.

"I can hide you for tonight," I said. Then I waited, the unspoken second half of my sentence hanging between us.

She sat down in the only chair in the room, the dim light bulb casting dark shadows on her face. She looked gaunt and exhausted. "Ah, now you're judging me."

"I have a good job I want to keep," I said. "Mr. Findlay Smith trusts me."

She bent down and began to pull up her dress.

"Don't," I said, and turned my face away. I could not bear to watch her try to ply her trade with me.

"Look," she said. There was no seduction in her voice. "Liang, look at me."

I turned and gasped.

Her legs, what I could see of them, were made of shiny chrome. I bent down to look closer: the cylindrical joints at the knees were lathed with precision, the pneumatic actuators along the thighs moved in complete silence, the feet were exquisitely molded and shaped, the surfaces smooth and flowing. These were the most beautiful mechanical legs I had ever seen.

"He had me drugged," she said. "When I woke up, my legs were gone and replaced by these. The pain was excruciating. He explained to me that he had a secret: he liked machines more than flesh, couldn't get hard with a regular woman."

I had heard of such men. In a city filled with chrome and brass and clanging and hissing, desires became confused.

I focused on the way light moved along the gleaming curves of her calves so that I didn't have to look into her face.

"I had a choice: let him keep on changing me to suit him, or he could remove the legs and throw me out on the street. Who would believe a legless Chinese whore? I wanted to survive. So I swallowed the pain and let him continue."

She stood up and removed the rest of her dress and her evening gloves. I took in her chrome torso, slatted around the waist to allow articulation and movement; her sinuous arms, constructed from curved plates sliding over each other like obscene armor; her hands, shaped from delicate metal mesh, with dark steel fingers tipped with jewels where the finger-nails would be.

"He spared no expense. Every piece of me is built with the best crafts-manship and attached to my body by the best surgeons—there are many who want to experiment, despite the law, with how the body could be animated by electricity, nerves replaced by wires. They always spoke only to him, as if I was already only a machine.

"Then, one night, he hurt me and I struck back in desperation. He fell like he was made of straw. I realized, suddenly, how much strength I had in my metal arms. I had let him do all this to me, to replace me part by part, mourning my loss all the while without understanding what I had gained. A terrible thing had been done to me, but I could also be *terrible*.

"I choked him until he fainted, and then I took all the money I could find and left.

"So I come to you, Liang. Will you help me?"

I stepped up and embraced her. "We'll find some way to reverse this. There must be doctors—"

"No," she interrupted me. "That's not what I want."

It took us almost a whole year to complete the task. Yan's money helped, but some things money couldn't buy, especially skill and knowledge.

My flat became a workshop. We spent every evening and all of Sun-days working: shaping metal, polishing gears, reattaching wires.

Her face was the hardest. It was still flesh.

I pored over books of anatomy and took casts of her face with plaster of Paris. I broke my cheekbones and cut my face so that I could stagger into surgeons' offices and learn from them how to repair these injuries. I bought expensive jeweled masks and took them apart, learning the deli-cate art of shaping metal to take on the shape of a face.

Finally, it was time.

Through the window, the moon threw a pale white parallelogram on the floor. Yan stood in the middle of it, moving her head about, trying out her new face.

Hundreds of miniature pneumatic actuators were hidden under the smooth chrome skin, each of which could be controlled independently, allowing her to adopt any expression. But her eyes were still the same, and they shone in the moonlight with excitement.

"Are you ready?" I asked.

She nodded.

I handed her a bowl, filled with the purest anthracite coal, ground into a fine powder. It smelled of burnt wood, of the heart of the earth. She poured it into her mouth and swallowed. I could hear the fire in the miniature boiler in her torso grow hotter as the pressure of the steam built up. I took a step back.

She lifted her head to the moon and howled: it was a howl made by steam passing through brass piping, and yet it reminded me of that wild howl long ago, when I first heard the call of a *hulijing*.

Then she crouched to the floor. Gears grinding, pistons pumping, curved metal plates sliding over each other—the noises grew louder as she began to transform.

She had drawn the first glimmers of her idea with ink on paper. Then she had refined it, through hundreds of iterations until she was satisfied. I could see traces of her mother in it, but also something harder, something new.

Working from her idea, I had designed the delicate folds in the chrome skin and the intricate joints in the metal skeleton. I had put together every hinge, assembled every gear, soldered every wire, welded every seam, oiled every actuator. I had taken her apart and put her back together.

Yet, it was a marvel to see everything working. In front of my eyes, she folded and unfolded like a silvery origami construction, until finally, a chrome fox as beautiful and deadly as the oldest legends stood before me.

She padded around the flat, testing out her sleek new form, trying out her stealthy new movements. Her limbs gleamed in the moonlight, and her tail, made of delicate silver wires as fine as lace, left a trail of light in the dim flat.

She turned and walked—no, glided—towards me, a glorious hunter, an ancient vision coming alive. I took a deep breath and smelled fire and smoke, engine oil and polished metal, the scent of power.

"Thank you," she said, and leaned in as I put my arms around her true form. The steam engine inside her had warmed her cold metal body, and it felt warm and alive.

"Can you feel it?" she asked.

I shivered. I knew what she meant. The old magic was back but changed: not fur and flesh, but metal and fire.

"I will find others like me," she said, "and bring them to you. Together, we will set them free."

Once, I was a demon hunter. Now, I am one of them.

I opened the door, Swallow Tail in my hand. It was only an old and heavy sword, rusty, but still perfectly capable of striking down anyone who might be lying in wait.

No one was.

Yan leapt out like a bolt of lightning. Stealthily, gracefully, she darted into the streets of Hong Kong, free, feral, a *hulijing* built for this new age.

. . . once a man has set his heart on a hulijing, *she cannot help hearing him no matter how far apart they are . . .*

"Good hunting," I whispered.

She howled in the distance, and I watched a puff of steam rise into the air as she disappeared.

I imagined her running along the tracks of the funicular railway, a tireless engine racing up, and up, towards the top of Victoria Peak, towards a future as full of magic as the past.

Ken Liu's fiction has appeared in *The Magazine of Fantasy & Science Fiction, Asimov's, Analog, Strange Horizons, Lightspeed,* and *Clarkesworld,* among other places. He is a winner of the Nebula, Hugo, and World Fantasy awards. His debut novel, *The Grace of Kings,* the first in a fantasy series, was published by Saga Press in April 2015. A collection of his short stories, *The Paper Menagerie and Other Stories,* appeared in March 2016. Liu has worked as a programmer and as a lawyer (two professions he finds "surprisingly similar"). He lives near Boston with his family.

This is not a story based on "Red Riding Hood" so much as a story about what happened after the Red's encounter with the wolf . . . and also what happened a long time before. Still, it might be fitting to quote Sandra Beckett in Recycling Little Red Riding Hood: *"No folk or fairy tale has been so relentlessly reinterpreted, recontextualized, and retold over the centuries as* Little Red Riding Hood."

By the Moon's Good Grace

Kirstyn McDermott

It be all I can do to keep still in me bed, waiting in the dark for the snoring to start up on the other side of the curtain, that snuffling death-rattle of his I been hearing most of me life, and when it does come I gotta wait some more till I be sure me Mam be sleeping sound as well. She been giving me the side-eye since we come back damp and wretched from the woods, me stepfather carrying his story the way he sees fit to show it and me with me mouth pinned shut, not knowing what to do with the words even if I could lay tongue to the right ones. Not me story to tell, he says, not me place to bring such frightful tidings to me own Mam, specially when I don't see the proper shape of them.

I can still feel where his fingers dug into me arms, shaking sense into me; the bruises'll bloom with first light.

Waiting, waiting, while the crimson thread knotted round me breastbone thickens and twists, becomes a cord, becomes a rope, becomes a cable like them what pull Old Yag's punt across the river, and so it drags on me, tugging till I can't bear it one breath more and throw off the blankets. Quiet, mindful of the creak and tattle of the floorboards, I make me way to the door and grab me cloak from its hanging hook. So soft, this fine woolen weave me Granmama must've bartered more'n a few good hens over, more again to have it dyed red, red as a castle rose, and her stitching be finer still.

The thirteenth moon of your thirteenth year, my girl; a milestone to be well marked.

Me eyes prickle and I rub at them, angry and sad and scared all at once, but I push the whole mess down, throw the hood over me head and slip from the cottage into the night.

Full-bellied Moon shines the way but I don't need her, don't need nothing but me own bare feet that know this winding woodland path better'n any paved or cart-runneled road, me feet and the pull of the thread that draws me on sure as any compass. Running till the breath catches cold in me throat, ducking each low branch and leaping over roots that hump and thrust from the dirt, running till me toe catches on some unseen thing, some stone or twig that sends me sprawling. I break the fall with me hands, palms scraping raw along the ground but better that than another bump on the head, and I roll panting onto me back to see I've landed in the same little clearing where I seen the wolf this afternoon.

Where it seen me.

Those sharp amber eyes fixing on mine as it stepped from the trees, paw by careful paw. I were frozen, breathless, but outta wonder more'n fear, standing motionless as it circled towards me, muzzling the air. Were it the basket in me hand that caught its nose, the cloth-wrapped salted pork tucked in beside the apple scrumpy and fresh-baked bread? If I tossed the meat to the ground for toothsome jaws to chomp over, would I be allowed to go on me way?

The wolf come so close I might've touched it, might've bent and run me fingers through that thick grey pelt to feel the softness of its fur, the heat of its skin. Me own skin itched with the longing of it.

As it stared at me, yellow eyes clever like no beast's should have a right to be, a trembling welled up inside me, a great shivery warmth that filled me chest and belly and legs, and I swear that when that hot, pink tongue licked over the back of me hand it be like the Goddess Moon herself reached down through the clouds to touch me. Me knees buckled and I crumpled to the ground like poor wooden Judy with her strings cut off.

The wolf growled.

I lowered the hood of me cloak and lifted up me face, thinking that this weren't no bad kind of death if it be the time for it. But the beast stared past me, back into the forest the way I'd come with me Mam's last words an echo in me ears—*straight to Granmama's, you mind me; this ain't no day for flower-plucking.* Thunder rumbled in that pale throat and its hackles spiked stiffer'n any tomcat's. Then, just as sudden as it showed itself, the wolf turned and loped off into the trees. The forest round me kept still, kept hushed, like it be holding its breath but I didn't stay to see what it might be expecting. Only gathered up me cloak like I be doing now and scrambled to me feet, bidding me traitor legs to come to their senses.

Wolf-clearing or no, this ain't where I meant to be stopping tonight. The thread, it keeps on tugging and a'tugging, and I got no answer but to let it run me all the way to me Granmama's house. Even then, hunched over with me hands braced on me knees, trying not to retch up me dinner amid all the huffing and a'puffing, I still feel the pull of it. Only when I find me way down to the old mill pond does it let up some, does it let me stop and fall down beside the water which be still and smooth as a Lord's window pane.

Now I know why I been led here.

Stop your shrieking, girl, he yelled at me this afternoon, axe dripping blood onto the floorboards. *It were nought but a damned wolf about to have your throat out, and you standing there mouth open like a bullfrog catching flies. Now hush up and lend me a hand.*

He wouldn't listen. Wouldn't stop to hear about Granmama, or what happened—what I *thought* had happened—before he busted through the door all fury and fright. And me not able to find the proper words neither, so he just kept yelling at me to shut me gob and help him, and when I didn't—when I *couldn't*—he pushed me away. Pushed me hard. Me foot slipped in something, maybe the blood, most likely the blood, and I remember falling with me fingers grabbing at the air, and I remember nothing else.

Till he be shaking me and slapping at me cheeks. His clothes were wet. The wolf be gone, the floorboards smeared pink in his hurry to clean up. *You say nothing to your Mam,* he told me. *You know how she be about the bloody wolves, she'd have me hide us quick as spit.*

But Granmama—

Your Granmama ain't come back yet; Lord know where she's taken herself off to.

The wolf—

You think your Mam wants to hear your lunatic ravings? That wolf ain't touched your Granmama, I cut open its belly meself. All you gotta tell her, it be stalking you and I come by and scared it off. You hear me? His face all scrunched up and ugly with anger, maybe a little bit of fear as well, so I just nodded and let him help me stand. I felt woozy and when I touched the back of me head, I found me a swelling and some crusted blood. It come away in dry black crumbs under me fingernails.

His own hands were clean. Freshly scrubbed.

The Moon throws her reflection onto the surface of the pond, so clear and perfect it might be her own twin sister rising in greeting. I take off me cloak and fold it neatly on the grass. Me white cotton nightgown be torn now, dirty round the hem, and I can hear me Mam already, sighing and tutting as she tells me to fetch her sewing basket. I take it off as well, place it on top of the cloak. Me skin prickles with gooseflesh and I rub at me arms, teeth chattering.

The crimson thread tugs, gently.

Water, cold as snowmelt, laps at me ankles, calves, thighs. Before long me foot bumps against something solid, something soft, and I reach down with both hands, shivering as the water splashes round me. I grab a chunk of fur, wet and thick, and pull. The body barely budges, so I crouch down to brace meself then pull even harder, grunting through me clenched teeth as I try to drag it back to the shore. It takes a good long time and clumps of fur keep coming away in me hands, dumping me on me arse more than once. Each time I swear a bit louder, then find me a new grip and keep on going.

It be only in the shallows, with the wolf lolling on its back and those pale front legs bent awkward in the air, that I see all the rocks stuffed into her belly. I swear again, thinking that the Moon, she might've told me. The Moon, or her water-logged sister, now broken into so many silvery splinters.

Nothing for it but to kneel down, reach me way into the beast and roll out stone after stone. Most of them be slippery with moss and slide easily enough in me hands. There be a couple caught stubborn 'neath her ribs and the dull crack of bone makes me wince as I wrench them free.

Emptied out, it still be a strain, but there be enough useless weight gone now for me to pull her up outta the water and on to the grass.

"You a heavy bitch," I tell the dead wolf, then I lay me weary self down beside her and stare at the Moon.

I don't remember even closing me eyes, but I must've done cause the next thing I know I be waking up to a warm tongue licking at me cheek. I let out a cry and roll away, scrabble to me knees to find meself face to furry face with the same yellow-eyed beast from the woods this afternoon.

Me teeth be all achatter from the cold and me skin be prickled as a plucked hen's.

The wolf tilts its head to one side. If it had lips, it might be smiling.

"Wh-what you after?" I ask, getting to me feet proper. Beside me, the dead wolf I dragged outta the pond lies still. Its hollowed belly gapes in the moonlight and I swallow, feeling sick to see it.

The other wolf, the wolf with the too-clever eyes, nuzzles at me hand. It takes me wrist in its mouth, all gentle like a mother cat moving her kittens, and tugs. Fangs press into me skin but don't break it. The wolf tugs again, then lets me go. It trots a few paces away towards me Granmama's house before stopping to look back over its shoulder, head cocked. Its eyes glitter in the moonlight. I grab me cloak from where I left it near the edge of the water and wrap it round me shoulders, the wool soft and warm on me shivery skin. Then I bundle me tattered nightgown up close to me chest and run after the wolf.

By the time I reach the front door, the beast has lifted the latch with its too-clever paws and slipped inside.

Behind me, there come a spat of barking noises, ratchety as an old sinner's cough. I turn round and see maybe seven or eight big grey wolves all jostling and asnuffling round the dead one down by the mill pond. One of them nudges the body with its nose, licks at lifeless jowls that won't ever lick back. Another sits on its haunches and shows its silvery throat to the moon. That howl be full of hurt and helplessness. It sinks into me bones. Into me blood. Me heart beats with it.

Wiping at me eyes, I push into me Granmama's house and shut the door on the night and all its wolves.

Excepting one.

Which I do me best to ignore as I busy meself lighting a fire in the grate. I still be chilled from me swim and me hands shake as I shape the kindling. Sneaking a sidelong glance, I see the wolf sniffing over the stain on the floor. It makes a kind of whine, a kind of growl, and scratches at the wooden boards. The fire takes and I use the bellows to build the flames till they big enough to keep spitting and acrackling on their own. Then I sit back and pull me cloak tighter round meself, pull the hood up over me head. Outside, another howl splits the night. If I be still, if I hold me breath, I can feel the echo of its song in me heart.

The too-clever wolf finds the basket I left behind on the sideboard this afternoon. The hunk of salted pork disappears between its jaws in three quick bites. Now it looks to me, amber eyes bright, and for a moment I wonder if it means to fill its belly with girl flesh after all. If it maybe just wanted me all warmed up first.

"Do what you gonna do," I says. "Only do it quick."

But the wolf just closes its eyes and dips its head and then—

And then—

Smarter folks'n me might find the proper words for how it happens, but they not here to see it.

The arch and crack of a furry spine, the stretch and pull of slender legs.

Paws spreading and splaying into feet and into hands, ten fingers and ten toes all neatly nailed if you pay no mind to the dirt and grit lodged under them.

That long snout pushing back somehow, pushing in, the whole head bulging and breaking and putting itself back together in ways that seems like it gotta *hurt*, but the wolf, it makes no sound at all, even as fur melts away to smooth skin like frost meeting the winter sun.

In me mind, I see me Granmama again. *Don't be frightened, my girl,* she says this afternoon, *you watch now, and you see.* I remember how her dressing gown puddled to the floor. I remember how I screamed at the shock of it.

Me face burns with shame.

Maybe now I *should* look away, but the only naked woman I ever glimpsed before be me Mam with her soft curves and dimples, belly all skin and wrinkles after me baby brother come wailing into the world, and the woman squatting here before me be a different creature. Her legs be hairy and lean and muscled and I can see the rise and judder of her

412

ribs with each panting breath. Her shoulder blades stick out like stunted wings and, between them, a line of coarse dark hair grows right down the middle of her back to disappear into the crack of her arse. She smells like sweat and earth and something else besides. Something musky and wolfish that sticks in me throat and makes me cough.

The woman looks up. Pushes the tangle of long, brown hair outta her eyes and makes her mouth into a shape kinda like a smile, kinda like a snarl. Maybe she outta practice.

"Don't be scared," she says. Her voice be rough, like tearing cotton. Maybe she outta practice with that as well.

"What there be to scare me?" I ask, bold as I can. "You lost those nasty old fangs of yours."

The woman blinks. Then she throws back her head and laughs, a great howling bellow that makes me shiver, makes me flinch. A sudden yearning bubbles up inside me, a feeling like seeing some fine court lady in pearls and a pretty dress and wondering how me own self might look in such a getup, or watching the miller's oldest son heave round sacks of flour at market and thinking how it might be to lick the fresh dusting of white from his cheeks.

I want to laugh like the wolf-woman laughs. I want to howl down a blessing from the Moon.

Instead, I pull me cloak tighter round me shoulders and stick out me chin like me stepfather does when he gets mean and no nonsense. "Granmama were like you," I says. "Weren't she?"

"No." The woman runs a flattened palm over the stain on the floor, slow and gentle. She lifts her hand to her face and sniffs, then licks at her fingers with a bright pink tongue. When she looks back at me, her eyes be all aglitter. "*I* were like *her*." She makes a gruff, throaty sound, not really a growl, not really a sob, as she pushes herself to her feet. Her first couple of steps towards the fire be wobbly as me baby brother's but she soon rights herself. "Been a while since I went on two legs." Where her thighs meet, the hair be dark as the rest of her legs, dark as me Mam's down there as well, but thicker. A corkscrewed tangle of black curls that spread and spike almost up to her belly button.

I turn back to the flames; me face can't get no hotter.

The woman kneels, then tips back me hood and runs a hand through me hair. It still be damp from the mill pond but she be gentle, like me Mam would be. Each time her fingers snag on a knot she stops to work it

413

loose. "You and me have talking to do, Little Red," the woman says in that rough, scratchy voice of hers. "You need to tell me about your Granmama, about what happened here. You need to speak for her, what can't speak for herself no more."

Me stomach clenches. Bile scrapes at the back of me throat. I don't want to remember what happened today. What I seen, or thought I seen. (What I *know* I seen.) Better to keep that all squashed down hard inside me guts so it blackens and rots like cabbage left in the ground and I don't need to think on it no more. Just turn it and till it and seed it over fresh.

"Who *you* be?" I says, jerking free from those gentle hands as I twist round to face her. "Who you be to be pawing at me and asking for me Granmama's story like you got some kinda right to it?"

The woman sits back on her heels. "I gotta right to it," she says, quiet and careful. "Your Granmama were me *mother*, Little Red. I got more right to her story than any soul you care to name."

I don't believe her at first, or I don't wanna believe her. The weight of it be too heavy to hold, too hard to carry. Me Mam had a sister, that be true. A sister who went away before I were even born, who skipped off with some fella what made wicked eyes at her and promised her the whole of the Moon, or so me Mam says. She don't talk too much about it. When she does, her face gets all sorrowful and less *solid* somehow, like you might break it with a breath.

I never wanted a sister, if that be what loving one gets you.

But now I peer at the woman real close, and she pulls that dark mess of hair outta her face, and there be that same quirk in the corner of her mouth that me Mam gets when she be worried about an eggbound hen, or whether the flour might stretch to a last loaf of bread, and I try to picture this woman being plumper in the cheeks, rounder all over like me Mam, and I think maybe I can see it.

"So you me aunt?" I says.

The woman nods. "That I am."

"And you a wolf, too? And me Granmama were a wolf?"

"Not for always, but there were some moons she ran with us." She smiles. "Some *months* even."

And in that smile, me Mam and me Granmama both be shining bright, and me tears start spurting before I can stop them. "She ch-changed," I says. "Needed to sh-show me, she says." The woman reaches out, squeezes me shoulder and the words, they spill from me like beads poured from a pouch. I tell her everything I can remember, not in any kind of order but just as it comes into me head, one big jumble for her to gather up and winnow as she please.

"This axe-man, he be your mother's husband?" she asks after I can speak no more. Her voice has lost its rougher edges; her tongue be steel-tipped.

"He don't mean to kill Granmama; he took her for a wolf—an ordinary wolf, I mean."

Her nostrils flare. "But he did mean to kill this *ordinary wolf?*"

"It were gonna eat me, he thought." Guilt makes a hard, cold lump in me throat; it hurts to swallow round. "Were me own useless screaming that brung him here."

The woman stares at me, head tilted to the side. I can only match her gaze for a moment. "That fire of yours be dying," she says at last, pushing herself up from the floor. "You ain't got the touch for flamework." She rolls her shoulders and rubs at her arms. Her skin be goosepimpled, her nipples chilled to hard, brown nubs. "I forget how it be to be furless."

I poke at the half-burned logs, not really expecting them to catch. Me stomach turns queasy and sullen, like I been gorging on apples filched too early in the season, and me eyes itch from crying. Rocking back and forth, wishing I could wind it all backwards, wind meself right back to this morning and start on over. I wouldn't scream this time, wouldn't say nothing or do nothing but kneel down and wrap me arms round me Granmama's neck and press me face to her soft, wolfish fur.

"Must have big ears, your mother's husband. To have heard you all the way through them woods."

I wipe me nose and look up. The woman has put on me Granmama's nightdress, the one with tiny yellow and blue flowers embroidered round the collar. It stretches across those broad shoulders right enough, but then hangs too big and billowy, missing me Granmama's bosom and hips to shape it proper.

"Ever get to wondering why he be snuffling round so close?" The woman climbs into me Granmama's bed and pulls the blankets up to her sharp and pointed chin. "Why he be following on your heels, Little Red?"

I lay the poker aside and hunker down into me cloak, trying not to think on how he been looking at me diff'rent this past year. Sneaky glances out the sides of his eyes when he supposes I ain't paying him much mind.

Me chest ain't nothing like me Mam's yet, or me Granmama's, but it ain't
dead flat no more neither. And he been looking. A shudder runs up me
spine. With the fire down to embers, the house be getting cold.

"You meaning to sit there all night like some poor senseless cub left
out in the snow?" The woman lifts up one side of the bedclothes. "Plenty
room for your scrawny behind."

I half expect her to take me in her long, strong arms and cuddle me,
the way me Mam used to do when I be sick or fever-ridden, or when I
woke up in the night from dreams I didn't wanna remember. Or maybe
it be more of a wish, cause when she rolls over instead, her back curv-
ing away in a bony arc, I feel so sad and hollow I nearly start crying all
over again.

"What those wolves be doing?" I ask after a time. "Down where I
pulled Granmama from the pond?"

"Won't be there no more," she says. "They'll have taken her, those
what can make themselves hands for hauling. Rest of the pack be guarding their passage."

"Where to?"

"We got our own ways to farewell the dead. Our own places to honour them."

I think on the little churchyard in our village and the vicar with
his black robes. Me Mam's never had much patience for preaching or
church learning and he frowns at us whenever we cross paths at market
or along the road. She just smiles and nods and sometimes, if her arms
ain't full of sewing or vegetables or me baby brother, she even curtsies.
Always be polite to that man, she tells me. *Ain't nothing in that fat little
book of his'll teach you more'n what me or your Granmama can, but he thinks
it gives him power. Let him think it, him and other men like him, and you go
on your way knowing better.*

"Shouldn't you be there?" I whisper. "With the other wolves, saying
goodbye to your Mam?"

"I should," the woman says. "Yet here I be with you, Little Red."

"That ain't me name," I tell her.

"Maybe it be your wolf name," she says.

I take a careful breath then inch across the bed till I be pressed tight
against her back, the two of us snug as roosting hens. She makes a soft
sort of growling sound but don't move or shove me away, and so I risk
laying me arm across her hip. Her rich, earthy scent be strange and strong,

but it don't hide the smell of rosewater from me Granmama's nightdress, not wholly, and so I sniff deep and deeper still, pulling the both of them into me, me Granmama and me new gruff aunt whose words catch in me heart like a fishhook.

Maybe it be your wolf name.

We be about halfway home when me aunt stops sudden and grabs me by the arm. She sticks her nose in the air and sniffs hard, then closes her eyes and keeps very still, like she be trying to catch some faint or distant noise. All I can hear be the birds squawking out their morning songs, and I be about to walk on when she drags me off the path and behind a thatch of prickle-bush.

"Do not move," she whispers. "Do not speak."

Frightened, I do as I be told.

After only a moment or two, there come the sounds of footsteps, the strides long and sure. Peering through the dense leaves, I see enough to know him, that axe swinging sharp in his hand as he heads back the way we come. Back towards me Granmama's house. I hold me breath and look down. Me aunt be clutching me hand tight and I notice a smear of jam on the cuff of her sleeve. Strawberry or raspberry or maybe even boysenberry—she were up with the sun, opening every jar of preserves in the larder and spreading them thick on chunks of bread from the loaf me Mam baked.

I forget the marvel of such food; wolves have no tongue for sweet.

If we hadn't left when we did—

If I weren't so keen to get home to me Mam who must be worried near outta her wits—

If we still be there, scoffing down jam and trying to find some smock and kirtle that fit me aunt better'n old flour sacks, while the front door burst open and he come storming in—

I bite down on me lip, not wanting to think on it.

"That him?" me aunt asks after he be far outta earshot. "That your mother's husband?"

I nod, and she makes a low growling noise then pulls me to me feet. We move quicker now, not stopping for breath till we reach the cottage and find me Mam out front with me baby brother stuck on her hip, tipping out breakfast scraps for the chickens. She sees us too and her face come over all changeable, like she surprised and angry and excited all at once and don't know what she should be feeling most.

Then she drops the scrap bucket and marches across the yard. "Take him," she says, thrusting me brother into me arms. "Now get inside and keep your ears to yourself."

I start to explain, start to apologise, but she just roars at me to *get your arse inside right now*, and so I go as fast as I can manage it, what with a newly squawling brat trying to kick and wriggle his way free of me grip. I don't think I ever seen me Mam furious enough to be trembling.

I plop me brother down in his cradle and scout round for the bit of leather he likes to gnaw on, but me Mam probably has it in her apron pocket. No matter, even I can tell it ain't his teeth that be bothering him this moment. "Shhh," I says, finding his rag dolly stuffed down the side of the bedding. "Shhh," I says again, waving it in his face. "She weren't yelling at you; it be me she mad at."

I leave the dolly on his chest and scurry over to the window for a peek. They both still out there in the front yard, me Mam with her back to the cottage so I can't see her face, and me aunt stooped a little, her hands moving in a quick, urgent language all their own. No one be yelling no more, excepting me baby brother who don't seem to have no use for his dolly today, so I can't hear a word of it through the window. But I keep watching as me aunt reaches out for me Mam and me Mam shrugs off her touch like it belongs to some beggar woman, as fingers point and heads shake with anger and then with sorrow, as me Mam finally steps forward and sags into me aunt's chest and their arms wrap round each other's waists and they both crumple to the ground like they got not a single leg bone between them.

Me aunt looks up over the hitch and shake of me Mam's shoulders, looks up and stares me straight in the eye, and all of a sudden I feel like a thief caught with some treasure I ain't got no right to be holding.

I lurch away from the window and go back to me baby brother. I waggle his dolly about and pull me face into silly shapes and blow farting noises through me lips till he starts to giggle. He reaches out with his pudgy little hands and I let him grab me finger. I even let him suck on it a little. "You not too bad," I tell him, tickling his tummy with me other hand. "For a stinky little goblin."

We be sitting like there that when the cottage door opens and me Mam and me aunt come in, both of them with eyes swollen from crying.

"Boil some water, Little Red," me aunt says. "Strong talking gonna need strong tea."

Me aunt drips four slow spoonfuls of honey into her cup and stirs it counterclockwise. "Our family always been wolves, long back as can we remember. We always been wolves and we always been secret, till time come it needful to tell. This secret be the most important one you ever gonna keep."

I fasten an imaginary button over me mouth. "I won't tell a soul, I promise."

"This ain't no game," me aunt snarls. "Swear it on your life, swear it on your *mother's* life—for it might come to that, up to the end."

Startled tears prick at me eyes. Me Mam reaches across the table to lay a hand over her sister's. "Don't scare the girl, Rachel. She been through enough already." She turns back to me and her face be so kind I just wanna curl up in her lap and have her stroke me hair, like she used to do when I be littler. "But you need to understand," she says. "You never talk to no one about this who ain't wolf. No matter if you think they your best friend in the whole world, or if they even more to you than that, you don't say a word, mind me?"

"Then why *she* telling *us?*" Me voice be too loud, but that be the only way to stop it breaking. "We ain't no wolves to carry her secrets for her."

Me aunt snorts, her cup clattering onto its saucer. "You told me this child be bright."

"Bright as the Moon," me Mam says with a glare. Then she takes me hand in hers and I feel the roughness of her skin and the hard little callouses from all her sewing, and I want time to stop and whatever be coming to stop with it. But time pays no mind to such useless prayers as mine, and me Mam, she keeps on talking.

"I *am* a wolf," she says. "Like me sister and me own mam, though I ain't worn the fur since long before you be born. And you a wolf too, me girl, and now you come to the age for changing and for choosing what kinda wolf you gonna be. There be fur and there be skin and there be those what live betwixt, like your Granmama kept herself. There no wrong way to be a wolf, mind me, but no easy way neither."

Me aunt takes me by the chin, lifts me face so there ain't nothing to do but look her dead in the eye. "You search inside yourself and think on how you been feeling since your bloods come, the itch of being stuck all the time in your own skin, your jaw aching like it want nothing more'n to rip and to rend. Think on how you felt last night, seeing the Moon swollen up in the sky, hearing your kin howling for her comfort, and you know me and your Mam be speaking the truth."

She lets me go and I slump back into me chair. Under the table, me toes curl and clench. "How I come to be a wolf then, if I don't get bit by one?"

"Peasant superstition!" Me aunt's laugh be bitter as old ale.

"You a wolf because you born a wolf," me Mam says, and sighs. "Rachel, we doing this all wrong."

"You expect us to do it right? Were our mother kept all the stories, this be her job."

"Well, she not here no more!" She thumps her fist on the table. In his crib, me baby brother starts crying again. "Goddess preserve us," me Mam mutters, getting up to soothe him. She brings him back in her arms and unfastens her bodice, pushes a nipple into his grizzly mouth till he latches on and begins to suck like her milk gonna dry up any moment.

"Be Jacob a wolf too?" I ask.

"No," me Mam says. "This little tyke be just a boy, through and through. He gonna grow up a man and never know nothing of wolves save to stay outta their way."

"Like his father?" me aunt says, low and dangerous.

"You let that alone," me Mam snaps. "That ain't for right now." Her voice sounds strained, tired, but there be steel running through it. I keep perfectly still, fingernails digging welts into me palms as the two of them glower at each other across the table. Cause I see it now, the wolf curled up inside me Mam all these years, hibernating behind her plump cheeks and pretty smile. I see it sleeping, and I don't want it to stir.

"Well then," me aunt says finally. "We start over. We start at the beginning."

And so she explains again, about our family, about the wolves and their secrets. Me Mam chips in now and then, to add a bit more or to put the words another way when she sees me getting confused, but mostly she just sits, nursing me baby brother and letting me aunt shape the story to her own way of telling. I learn how most wolves, once they get to changing, run in fur near all their lives, how they make families with wolves of the woods—them that won't never know skin—and how they be treated no different by their natural brethren, never hunted down or driven away, never shunned or scorned or had violence done to them for what they happen to be. I learn how if a she-wolf gets herself with cub while running in fur, then those cubs will always be natural wolves no matter the father, and how if she likewise be skin-walking and find herself a man, then her children be just the same as him, like me own brother who ain't never gonna feel the howl of wolf-blood in his veins.

And how if she change her shape while her belly be heavy, then there won't be no cubs, nor baby neither.

Only when two wolves lay together in their skins, do a moon-baby get conceived, and only if the she-wolf keep herself a woman all those months of growing, do a new beast get born what will come to know both worlds as well, or as little, as it wishes.

"Wolves like us," me aunt says, "they be rare."

I turn to me Mam. "Then me Pa, he be a wolf too? Like you?"

She always told me he were a hunter. She told me he got stuck out in a blizzard the very first winter after I be born, that he caught chill and died. Now she nods. "A wolf what couldn't bear to walk on two legs from moon to moon, a wolf what went back to run in the woods."

A sharp pain stabs between me ribs. "He didn't wanna be me Pa?"

"He didn't wanna be a *man*," me Mam says. "There be a world of difference in those two things, though you too young to see it. He did love you, girl, and he might've stayed if I pressed him to it, but it would've been a misery to us both. I never took to the fur so much; he were a lost thing without it."

"But might he still be living?" I ask. "And might I meet him, as a wolf?"

Me Mam looks to me aunt, who shakes her head. "He don't run in our woods no more, not for years, nor any we keep treaty with. Might be dead, might be living, but you ain't ever likely to find out, Little Red."

I don't know why I feel so sunk. I ain't had a father growing up and this only means I still ain't got one, and there should be no difference in it, and yet, and yet. Seems it be one thing to think me Pa dead all me life, and another to know he shot off and left me behind. I wonder if he ever come back some moonlit nights to take a peek through the window at me sleeping, furless face.

If he ever wishes he could wind back time and make his choice over again.

"You go with Rachel tonight," me Mam says, and I jolt forward, realising she been talking a whole bunch more besides. "She might not have all your Granmama's stories down perfect, but she got more'n enough to guide you through your change."

"Tonight?"

"The last rising of the full Moon," me aunt says, sounding impatient. "You gonna run with me and mine this month, we see how you take to four paws."

It all be rushing on me so fast, I ain't got no way to keep up. "But Mam, I thought *you* would—"

"It been so long, I probably forgot how to change *meself*, let alone show you how to go about it."

"Don't listen to your mother," me aunt says. "Once you learn the trick of it, ain't nothing you ever gonna leave aside—no matter how motheaten and raggedy your fur be getting."

"Maybe so," me Mam says with a frown that don't quite manage to hide the smile underneath it. "But I can't be leaving our little Jacob behind now, can I?"

As I look at me baby brother, asleep on her breast with his golden curls all aglow in the sun, there come this great hot seething from deep in me guts, a rolling and a roiling heat like I never know before. If not for him, we could all three of us leave this stupid shack, me Mam and me aunt and me; we could wear our finest fur and moon-sharp fangs and chase each other's tails through the trees. If not for this mewling brat, this pathetic creature so soft and pink and helpless I could rip open its belly with less effort than it be to—

Me aunt slaps me cheek and I round on her, snarling—

And she slaps me again, harder, and then she has me by the jaw, her fingers digging into me flesh like they not gonna stop till they find bone. "Never," she growls. "Jacob may not be wolf, but he still your brother and we never turn on kin. *Never*. You bare teeth at that child again, you gonna have more'n a slap or two coming for you."

She lets me go and I can't help it, I start sobbing worse'n me baby brother ever done in his life. And I try to tell me Mam how sorry I am, how I didn't mean it, how I don't even know where it sprung from, that murderous heat so sudden and fierce, but she just shushes me and squeezes me hand. "You have to go with Rachel," she says. "This be your change coming on you, and it ain't good for none us to be holding it back longer'n we already done. You can be any kinda wolf you choose but you need to learn the ways of it first, and me sister be your best teacher for that."

I nod, staring down at the tabletop. I don't wanna look at me aunt, don't want her to see the shame in me eyes, don't wanna face the disappointment in hers. "Now then, Little Red," she says, ruffling me hair. "Wolves don't sulk, we—"

As she turns her head towards the cottage door, I hear it, the tread of boots up the front path, their heavy scrape on the stoop. Then the door opens and me stepfather come inside, axe still in hand, mouth falling open with no small measure of surprise.

"How long you been here?" he shouts at me. "I been out in the woods all morning, searching. Your Mam worried herself sick when she see your empty bed."

Before I can find a lie to pin to me tongue, me Mam pushes herself up from her chair. "Only thing I worry about now, Stefan, be your great hullaballoo waking your son, just as I coax him to sleeping." She makes her careful way over to the crib to lay me baby brother down, touching her husband's cheek as she passes. "Girl took herself off for a early walk, but she home now, and safe, and that be all that matters."

He stares at me, eyes all dark and narrow as they take in the night-gown I still be wearing, before turning his sneer on me aunt. "And who might this fine lady be, gracing our humble home with her presence so unexpected?"

"You ain't never met me sister, Rachel," me Mam says, hurrying back to stand by his side. Me aunt got a face on her like she ready to open his throat with her teeth.

"Your sister," he says. "Rachel." He put his arm round me Mam's waist.

"She gonna take our girl off our hands for a bit. Give us some time to ourselves."

" Who gonna help you round here then, you and the wee one?"

Me Mam laughs, slaps him gentle on the shoulder. "She only be gone for a month; I been on me own with a babe longer'n that before your grumpy self even come into the picture. Now sit and I'll put your lunch out."

He grunts and slips his arm from her waist, hefts his axe in both hands. "Ain't got time for sitting, what with half the day gone chasing after girls what never been lost in the first place." And so, while me Mam rushes about fixing bread and meat and his favourite red onion relish, putting it all in a sack along with a bottle of scrumpy, he just stands there, running a thumbnail over his blade and glancing up every now and then at me aunt who don't offer up even a single word by way of conversation.

Only after he leaves, does she get to her feet and stalk over to me Mam. "You'll keep that man in your house, knowing the blood he got on his hands?"

"It be *his* house and, I told you, this ain't the time for talking on it."

Me aunt don't say nothing to that, but the muscles in her jaw tighten and twitch like it be all they can do to keep her mouth shut. Me Mam, she quiet now too but when I go over and take her hand, she lace her fingers through mine so hard it hurts.

"Wolves never turn on kin," I says to me aunt, me voice sounding stronger'n I feel.

She tilts her head, her lips twisting to a grim smile before she turns her back on the both of us. "You just make sure'n get to your Granmama's by sundown, Little Red," she says, pausing at the cottage door. "Us *wolves*, we got business with the Moon tonight."

I wrap both hands round the mug of water me aunt gives me and gulp the whole of it down in three hard swallows.

"Gonna be thirsty after," she says. "Specially the first time. Your mother, she don't tell you nothing about this?"

I shrug. "She says, better I come here with an empty head than one full of second-best shadows."

"Me sister still got *some* wolf-sense left to her, then."

It be cold in me Granmama's house without the fire burning, so even though me aunt strips down to her goosepimpled skin, she lets me keep me cloak draped over me bare shoulders, long as the hood be down and collar unbuttoned so me wolf self be able to slip out under it. Anything else just gonna tangle or tear the seams, she tells me, and me Mam got better to do with her days than stitch up after me.

"This gonna come natural, I promise." Me aunt crouches on the floor beside me. "You made for this, Little Red; you be wolf as much as you be woman." She smiles. "Now, you tell it back to me, the story of the Moon, in words of your own so I know you got it fixed in your noggin."

"Long as the Moon be full," I says, "she let us choose our shape, be it fur or skin. And time, that don't matter none, only that day-shifting be harder, so for now I best to call on her when she riding through the sky, not when she moving down 'neath the earth. Which means three nights each month and, later, when I be better at the ways of me changing, the two days between them, and that be all."

"Cause what gonna happen when the Moon starts to wane?"

"Whatever shape I be, fur or skin, that be the shape I keep till her belly swell up round again."

Her long fingers ruffle me hair. "Good little wolf. Now we ready."

At that, me throat cinches tight, and I croak out the one question I been too scared to ask till now. "Will it hurt?"

"Not enough to make trouble," me aunts says, and then she tells me to shut me eyes and think again on how it be last night, running barefoot through the woods, not knowing where I be headed, or even why, but running all the same, cause there be something dragging on me, something calling on me, and *the crimson thread*, I whisper, and *yes*, she whisper back, *find it, it belong to you*, and so I think on that, and remember the tug of it on me ribcage, and I reach into meself and there be the thread already laying over me palms, sliding through me fingers, the Moon thrumming through it and thrumming through me, and I pull on it and let it pull on me and feel the loose and stretch of me limbs

as the crimson knot unravels

and me body unravels

and rebuilds

and knows itself a Wolf.

Wolf got no words for being wolf, they useless as cloth and knife when we got fur and fang to keep us warm, keep us fed. Wolf live in the sight and sound of the world, thick in the smell of it. Our tongue be for tasting blood of the hare, flesh of the deer. For licking up the mouth of other wolf, to show we be of the pack and honour it.

I honour me aunt and I honour her mate, for they be top wolf.

Her mate what give me a rabbit, let me tear open the soft fur so the guts steam on the snow, so I know I be of the pack and always welcome.

Wolf time be hunting and sleeping and wrestling with the cubs of me aunt and the other cubs of the pack. It be feasting when we run down our

425

prey and hunger when none be found. It be nosing out scents and knowing what passed here, and when, and if it come back or go on its way. It be casting our howl to the wind and catching some other song thrown back from over the woods.

Wolf watch the men work, watch them stalk with their gun and lay their trap, too lazy to hunt with tooth and claw of their own. Wolf watch and wolf see, and wolf slip back into the trees quiet as the shadow.

Man never know what wolf know, that always be the way of it.

Heart beating, blood rushing, breath frosting.

Earth below to feed us. Moon above to bless us.

And now the Moon grow big again, me aunt nuzzles me snout and nips me haunch. I turn me shoulder, cause I be wolf, and won't be girl not ever again, but she growl and snap and fix me with her yellow eye to remind me of the promise I make.

And a great shame come over me, worse'n not sharing a kill, and I follow me aunt with tail tucked tight all the way back to the den of me grandmama.

Where be the woman-scent of me own Mam, come and gone this very day, and the crimson thread, it tug on me, and me aunt growls again, her clever paw on the latch, and she push us inside before the unravelling truly begin.

Panting and sore, I roll over to find me aunt still in her wolf shape. Though it be dark inside, and I ain't got the sight no more for nighttime, there be enough moonlight shining in the windows to get by. "You ain't changing?" I ask me aunt and she cocks her head in that way I come to understand means it be a stupid question 'neath her dignity to answer. I get to me feet, rub me bare arms. Sweat be turning to frost on me skin, and I feel more naked than ever in me life.

I feel like me fur been stolen from me.

Me aunt makes a sharp, rough bark—*look here; look close*—and I see me cloak folded up neat on the table and, sitting beside it, a basket.

Me useless girl-nose has lost the scent of me Mam, but I know this be her handiwork. There be bread and eggs already boiled in their shells, thick slices of smoked pork, and scrumpy that I gulp straight from its little jug once me aunt turns her nose up at it. Under the cloak, a fresh-washed smock I be quick to throw on, as well as a kirtle and the woollen tights I tore on the fence nail, climbing over when I should've gone round, darned so fine I can barely see the stitches.

I picture me Mam trekking all the way out here in the snow, me baby brother hitched on one hip maybe, just so there be fresh food and warm clothes waiting for when I be done with me change, and I remember how I nearly didn't come back this night at all, how me aunt had to snarl and take me by the scruff, how I didn't spare me Mam no mind when I be wolf.

I think on these things, and they settle in me stomach like stones.

Me aunt, she pads across to the door, nudges it open with her snout.

"Don't leave," I beg. "I ain't ready for you to leave."

She looks back at me and makes a sound something like a bark, something like a whine, before loping off into the night. This ain't goodbye for good, I know that—we be kin, and I always be welcome to run in her pack, whether it be the very next moon, or any number from now—but she be *wolf*, not some tame hound to slaver at me furless heels, and I should know better'n to ask it.

Not one of us be more important'n any other, and me aunt always gonna put the needs of her pack first.

That be the way of it with wolves.

Shivering, I close the door. I be exhausted, tired down to me very bones as me Mam would say it, but if I gonna rest here then I need to light a fire, get some heat into this empty house before the winter chill seeps right into me chest, right into me heart. The cloak me Granmama made be no match for this kinda cold, and I ain't got me cousins to curl up with no more, ain't got their thick wolfish pelts to nuzzle into, let alone a pelt of me own.

Twice, me clumsy fingers drop the tinderbox before I get a spark to take and coax some hopeful flames to dancing, but then, as I push more twigs in between the bigger logs, there come a sly creaking from behind and I swivel round to see the door swinging open once again.

"Thought wild beasts be scared of fire," me stepfather says. He holds his axe in his right hand; the blade glimmers as he steps towards me.

I scrabble to me feet, almost tripping on the hem of me smock. "You got no place to be here," I tell him, edging sideways and trying to get the table between us.

"Saw me the strangest thing while I be out there in the night, waiting and watching. Two wolves come into this house, but only one wolf leave. And now you be here, all on your own." He moves to his left and I dodge in the other direction, but he only be feinting and he grabs me by the arm as I hurtle past, throws me so hard against the wall, me breath gets knocked from me lungs. "Little wolf-girl," he says, pressing himself to me, pushing the head of his axe up under me chin. "That what you be?"

Me eyes blur with tears, and me heart beats so fast I think it gonna burst itself right through me ribcage, but I ain't got it in me to change again so soon, not so drained as I be right now, and so terrified. I bare me teeth at him instead; it be all I can do.

He laughs, a nastier sound as ever I heard. "Think you scare me, little wolf-girl? Already sent one of your kind on her sinful way, reckon I can deal with the grand-pup she made." Lowering the axe, he takes a step back then punches me full in the guts. I slide down the wall to the floor, feeling like I'm gonna vomit. "Not hard to puzzle out, your Granmama gone after I kill that wolf right here in her house, then you off with that filthy woman, night o' the full moon. Your mama always been so protective of the wolves and no wonder, her own mama being one, for how long only the good Lord be knowing, and now her daughter. What I gonna find, little wolf-girl, I slit open your belly? Rabbit fur, chicken feathers? Bones of little children snatched from their beds?"

I start to crawl towards the open door, but he kicks me twice in the side and so I just lie where I be, matching his hateful sneer with a glare of me own.

"Your mama too soft, sending you away with them monsters rather'n do right by her people." His axe swings like a pendulum, counting off the seconds left to me. "But you ain't gonna pollute me family no more, not you nor any like you. Come morning I gonna round up some good men, and we gonna clean them woods of wolves. Have ourselves a righteous burning. But first, I gotta clean me own house."

He spits in me face, his disgust slipping slimy as frogspawn down me cheek and over me lips, but I ain't about to look away. If he gonna kill me, he gonna do it with me eyes full upon him. For I still be *wolf*, and ain't no man foul as this gonna make me cower.

The axe lifts, and time swells, and I suck me last breath from the Moon-blessed world—

—as barrelling through the door there come a great growling fury what knocks me stepfather to the ground like he be nothing more'n a scarecrow. Powerful jaws snap the bones in his wrist even as he tries to swing the axe, and his screaming barely starts before it trickles to gasping and gurgling from a throat torn crimson by sharp and bloody fangs.

This wolf be a stranger to me. It not of me aunt's pack and so, when it starts towards me, I shake me head and plead to be left alone. "You got more'n enough meat already," I tell it.

But then it looks at me, then *she* looks at me, and those pale blue eyes shine so fierce and sorrowful that I flush with shame not to have seen straight off, not to have known. She licks the tears from me cheeks with her pink wolf tongue, and I put me arms round her neck and bury me face in her fur and breathe her in deep as I can.

She smells like wolf, and she smells like me Mam, and there ain't no telling where one nor the other begins.

The Moon be set and the sun not far off rising by the time we done with cleaning and tidying away.

"Jacob gonna wake before we get home, we don't hurry," me Mam says, pulling on me Granmama's winter boots. "He be frightened half to death, no one be there for him." Still, she spares a moment to frown at her fingernails, even though she already scrubbed them twice, and makes me check her face again.

"Ain't not a speck left on you," I promise. "You washed it all clean."

"Maybe one day, that be the truth of it," she mutters, hustling the both of us outta the house.

There still be patches of blood on the snow where we dragged his body, where it lay before the wolves come slinking outta the woods to carry it off. I ain't ever gonna forget the deep, mournful sound of me Mam's howl as she called to her kin, or the way me aunt yelped and bounded about her, excited as cub in its first spring to find her sister wearing the fur at last. But me Mam, she just turned tail back into Granmama's house and by the time I followed her, she already be woman again.

I kick at the biggest stain, hoping to bury it 'neath cleaner snow, but it just spreads itself bigger and me Mam yells at me to keep up. "Little bit of blood don't matter none," she says. "Ain't no one gonna find any piece o' that man, once they be done with him." Her face be tight and hard, her lips pressed to a trembling white line, like she be furious but trying not to show it. I seen her make that face before, when me stepfather come home stinking of ale, or when some fine lady dream up a fault in her stitching and wanna pay less than be promised.

"Sorry, Mam," I says, me voice wheedling with worry. "I ain't meant for him to find out I be wolf."

And then me Mam, she stops dead in her tracks and turns round, grabs me shoulders with both hands like she means to shake the teeth from me head. "You don't got to apologize for this," she says. "You don't got to apologize for what you be, not ever. That man were gonna take your life, girl, just as he took me own Mam's and would've taken mine, he ever found out, no matter that I be the mother of his child, no matter that I loved him." Her words break, and her breath billows in frosty plumes. "Maybe I *still* love him, and maybe I be loving him till the end of me sorry days, for in many ways he were a fine man, and better women than me been known to blind themself to what lie black and rotten 'neath a man's finery. But that be *my* burden to carry, not yours. Not ever yours."

She hugs me close and the crimson thread thickens and tugs, the pull of it gentle as me Mam's hands, and I know it be knotted as tight round her breastbone as it be knotted round mine, that it binds me to her now and always, as it always has done, and there be nothing in the world what could ever see it severed.

Far off in the hills, there come a howl, long and yodeling. Me aunt's maybe, or maybe one of her pack, and I yearn to throw back me head, open me mouth and call back an answer full-throated.

"Would you still love me if I be wolf," I ask me Mam. "If I never be nothing else?"

She smiles, all wistful and strange. "Wolf be simple, don't it? Wolf be an arrow, shooting from where you be to where you *want* to be, without the muddle of a woman's heart to skew the path. Sometimes, wolf be what we need most." She pulls up me hood, presses a kiss to me brow. "Skin or fur, daughter, you be me kin, and I love you for it. By the Moon's good grace, that be nothing you ever need doubt."

Then she takes me hand and we run together, me with me red cloak and her wrapped in me Granmama's forest green, and I feel them all threaded through me, me Mam and me Granmama both, and me aunt as well, those clever yellow eyes watching the wane and wax of Moon, watching and waiting for the night I come to run for a time with her.

Kirstyn McDermott has been working in the darker alleyways of speculative fiction for much of her career and her two novels, *Madigan Mine* and *Perfections*, have each won the Aurealis Award for Best Horror Novel. Her most recent book is *Caution: Contains Small Parts*, a collection of short fiction published by Twelfth Planet Press. When not wearing her writing hat, she produces and co-hosts a literary discussion podcast, *The Writer and the Critic*, which generally keeps her out of trouble. After many years based in Melbourne, Kirstyn now lives in Ballarat and is pursuing a creative PhD at Federation University.

One of the bloodier German folk tales collected by the Brothers Grimm, "The Juniper Tree" tells of a boy who is abused then murdered by his stepmother, chopped into pieces, and cooked into a stew that is devoured by his oblivious father. With some help from his loving stepsister and the magic of his deceased mother, he is turned into a bird and finds his revenge.

Peter Straub's version of the story is both powerful and disturbing, subtle yet graphic. Although not identified, the narrator is Timothy Underhill, a character who appears (most notably) in Straub's novels Koko, The Throat, Lost Boy Lost Girl, *and* In the Nightroom. *Here, we learn how Tim uses the "magic" of the movies to survive devastating trauma as a boy and heal.*

The Juniper Tree

Peter Straub

I t is a schoolyard in my Midwest of empty lots, waving green and brilliant with tiger lilies, of ugly new "ranch" houses set down in rows in glistening clay, of treeless avenues cooking in the sun. Our schoolyard is black asphalt—on June days, patches of the asphalt loosen and stick like gum to the soles of our high-top basketball shoes.

Most of the playground is black empty space from which heat radiates up like the wavery images on the screen of a faulty television set. Tall wire mesh surrounds it. A new boy named Paul is standing beside me.

Though it is now nearly the final month of the semester, Paul came to us, carroty-haired, pale-eyed, too shy to ask even the whereabouts of the lavatory, only six weeks ago. The lessons baffle him, and his Southern accent is a fatal error of style. The popular students broadcast in hushed, giggling whispers the terrible news that Paul "'talks like a nigger." Their voices are *almost* awed—they are conscious of the enormity of what they are saying, of the enormity of its consequences.

Paul is wearing a brilliant red shirt too heavy, too enveloping, for the weather. He and I stand in the shade at the rear of the school, before the cream-colored brick wall in which is placed at eye level a newly broken window of pebbly green glass reinforced with strands of copper wire. At our feet is a little scatter of green, edible-looking pebbles. The pebbles dig into the soles of our shoes, too hard to shatter against the softer asphalt. Paul is singing to me in his slow, lilting voice that he will never have friends in this school. I put my foot down on one of the green candy pebbles and feel it push up, hard as a bullet, against my foot. "Children are so cruel," Paul casually sings. I think of sliding the pebble of broken glass across my throat, slicing myself wide open to let death in.

Paul did not return to school in the fall. His father, who had beaten a man to death down in Mississippi, had been arrested while leaving a movie theater near my house named the Orpheum-Oriental. Paul's father had taken his family to see an Esther Williams movie costarring Fernando Lamas, and when they came out, their mouths raw from salty popcorn, the baby's hands sticky with spilled Coca-Cola, the police were waiting for them. They were Mississippi people, and I think of Paul now, seated at a desk on a floor of an office building in Jackson filled with men like him at desks: his tie perfectly knotted, a good shine on his cordovan shoes, a necessary but unconscious restraint in the set of his mouth.

In those days I used to spend whole days in the Orpheum-Oriental.

I was seven. I held within me the idea of a disappearance like Paul's, of never having to be seen again. Of being an absence, a shadow, a place where something no longer visible used to be.

Before I met that young-old man whose name was "Frank" or "Stan" or "Jimmy," when I sat in the rapture of education before the movies at the Orpheum-Oriental, I watched Alan Ladd and Richard Widmark and Glenn Ford and Dane Clark. *Chicago Deadline.* Martin and Lewis, tangled up in the same parachute in *At War with the Army.* William Boyd and Roy Rogers. Openmouthed, I drank down movies about spies and criminals, wanting the passionate and shadowy ones to fulfill themselves, to gorge themselves on what they needed.

The feverish gaze of Richard Widmark, the anger of Alan Ladd, Berry Kroeger's sneaky eyes, girlish and watchful—vivid, total elegance.

When I was seven, my father walked into the bathroom and saw me looking at my face in the mirror. He slapped me, not with his whole strength, but hard, raging instantly. "What do you think you're looking at?" His hand cocked and ready. "What do you think you see?"

"Nothing," I said.

"Nothing is right."

A carpenter, he worked furiously, already defeated, and never had enough money—as if, permanently beyond reach, some quantity of money existed that would have satisfied him. In the morning he went to the job site hardened like cement into anger he barely knew he had. Sometimes he brought men from the taverns home with him at night. They carried transparent bottles of Miller High Life in paper bags and set them down on the table with a bang that said: Men are here! My mother, who had returned from her secretary's job a few hours earlier, fed my brothers and me, washed the dishes, and put the three of us to bed while the men shouted and laughed in the kitchen.

He was considered an excellent carpenter. He worked slowly, patiently; and I see now that he spent whatever love he had in the rented garage that was his workshop. In his spare time he listened to baseball games on the radio. He had professional, but not personal, vanity, and he thought that a face like mine should not be examined.

Because I saw "Jimmy" in the mirror, I thought my father, too, had seen him.

One Saturday my mother took the twins and me on the ferry across Lake Michigan to Saginaw—the point of the journey was the journey, and at Saginaw the boat docked for twenty minutes before wallowing back out into the lake and returning. With us were women like my mother, her friends, freed by the weekend from their jobs, some of them accompanied by men like my father, with their felt hats and baggy weekend trousers flaring over their weekend shoes. The women wore blood-bright lipstick that printed itself onto their cigarettes and smeared across their front teeth. They laughed a great deal and repeated the words that had made them laugh. "Hot dog," "slippin' 'n' slidin'," "opera singer." Thirty minutes after departure, the men disappeared into the enclosed deck bar; the women, my mother among them, arranged deck chairs into a long oval tied together by laughter, attention, gossip. They waved their cigarettes in the air. My brothers raced around the deck, their shirts flapping, their hair glued to their skulls with sweat—when they squabbled, my mother ordered them into empty deck chairs. I sat on the deck, leaning against the railings, quiet. If someone had asked me: What do you want to do this afternoon, what do you want to do for the rest of your life? I would have said, I want to stay right here, I want to stay here forever.

After a while I stood up and left the women. I went across the deck and stepped through a hatch into the bar. Dark, deeply grained imitation wood covered the walls. The odors of beer and cigarettes and the sound of men's voices filled the enclosed space. About twenty men stood at the bar, talking and gesturing with half-filled glasses. Then one man broke away from the others with a flash of dirty blond hair. I saw his shoulders move, and my scalp tingled and my stomach froze and I thought: Jimmy. "Jimmy." But he turned all the way around, dipping his shoulders in some ecstasy of beer and male company, and I saw that he was a stranger, not "Jimmy," after all.

I was thinking: someday when I am free, when I am out of this body and in some city whose name I do not even know now, I will remember this from beginning to end and then I will be free of it.

The women floated over the empty lake, laughing out clouds of cigarette smoke, the men, too, as boisterous as the children on the sticky asphalt playground with its small green spray of glass like candy.

In those days I knew I was set apart from the rest of my family, an island between my parents and the twins. Those pairs that bracketed me slept in double beds in adjacent rooms at the back of the ground floor of the duplex owned by the blind man who lived above us. My bed, a cot coveted by the twins, stood in their room. An invisible line of great authority divided my territory and possessions from theirs.

This is what happened in the morning in our half of the duplex. My mother got up first—we heard her showering, heard drawers closing, the sounds of bowls and milk being set out on the table. The smell of bacon frying for my father, who banged on the door and called out my brothers' names. "Don't you make me come in there, now!" The noisy, puppyish turmoil of my brothers getting out of bed. All three of us scramble into the bathroom as soon as my father leaves it. The bathroom was steamy, heavy with the odor of shit and the more piercing, almost palpable smell of shaving-lather and amputated whiskers. We all pee into the toilet at the same time. My mother frets and frets, pulling the twins into their clothes so that she can take them down the street to Mrs. Candee, who is given a five-dollar bill every week for taking care of them. I am supposed to be running back and forth on the playground in Summer Play School, supervised by two teenage girls who live a block away from us. (I went to Play School only twice.) After I dress myself in clean underwear and socks and put on my everyday shirt and pants, I come into the kitchen while my father finishes his breakfast. He is eating strips of bacon and golden-brown pieces of toast shiny with butter. A cigarette smolders in the ashtray before him. Everybody else has already left the house. My father and I can hear the blind man banging on the piano in his living room. I sit down before a bowl of cereal. My father looks at me, looks away. Angry at the blind man for banging at the piano this early in the morning, he is sweating already. His cheeks and forehead shine like the golden toast. My father glances at me, knowing he can postpone this no longer, and reaches wearily into his pocket and drops two quarters on the table. The high-school girls charge twenty-five cents a day, and the other quarter is for my lunch. "Don't lose that money," he says as I take the coins. My father dumps coffee into his mouth, puts the cup and his plate into the crowded sink, looks at me again, pats his pockets for his keys, and says, "Close the door behind you." I tell him that I will close the door. He picks up his gray toolbox and his black lunch pail, claps his hat on his head, and goes out, banging his toolbox against the door frame. It leaves a broad gray mark like a smear left by the passing of some angry creature's hide.

Then I am alone in the house. I go back to the bedroom, close the door and push a chair beneath the knob, and read *Blackhawk* and *Henry and Captain Marvel* comic books until at last it is time to go to the theater.

While I read, everything in the house seems alive and dangerous. I can hear the telephone in the hall rattling on its hook, the radio clicking as it tries to turn itself on and talk to me. The dishes stir and rattle in the sink.

At these times all objects, even the heavy chairs and sofa, become their true selves, violent as the fire that fills the sky I cannot see, and races through the secret ways and passages beneath the streets. At these times other people vanish like smoke.

When I pull the chair away from the door, the house immediately goes quiet, like a wild animal feigning sleep. Everything inside and out slips cunningly back into place, the fires bank, men and women reappear on the sidewalks. I must open the door and I do. I walk swiftly through the kitchen and the living room to the front door knowing that if I look too carefully at any one thing, I will wake it up again. My mouth is so dry, my tongue feels fat. "I'm leaving," I say to no one. Everything in the house hears me.

The quarter goes through the slot at the bottom of the window, the ticket leaps from its slot. For a long time, before "Jimmy," I thought that unless you kept your stub unfolded and safe in a shirt pocket, the usher could rush down the aisle in the middle of the movie, seize you, and throw you out. So into the pocket it goes, and I slip through the big doors into the cool, cross the lobby, and pass through a swinging door with a porthole window.

Most of the regular daytime patrons of the Orpheum-Oriental sit in the same seats every day—I am one of those who comes here every day. A small, talkative gathering of bums sits far to the right of the theater, in the rows beneath the sconces fastened like bronze torches to the walls. The bums choose these seats so that they can examine their bits of paper, their "documents," and show them to each other during the movie. Always on their minds is the possibility that they might have lost one of these documents, and they frequently consult the tattered envelopes in which they are kept.

I take the end seat, left side of the central block of seats, just before the broad horizontal middle aisle. There I can stretch out. At other times I sit in the middle of the last row, or the first; sometimes when the balcony is open I go up and sit in its first row. From the first row of the balcony, seeing a movie is like being a bird and flying down into the movie from above. To be alone in the theater is delicious. The curtains hang heavy, red, anticipatory; the mock torches glow on the walls. Swirls of gilt wind through the red paint. On days when I sit near a wall, I reach out toward the red, which seems warm and soft, and find my fingers resting on a chill dampness. The carpet of the Orpheum-Oriental must once have been bottomlessly rich brown; now it is a dark non-color, mottled with the pink and gray smears, like melted Band-Aids, of chewing gum. From about a third of the seats dirty gray wool foams from slashes in the worn plush.

On an ideal day I sit through a cartoon, a travelogue, a sequence of previews, a movie, another cartoon, and another movie before anyone else enters the theater. This whole cycle is as satisfying as a meal. On other mornings, old women in odd hats and young women wearing scarves over their rollers, a few teenage couples, are scattered throughout the theater when I come in. None of these people ever pays attention to anything but the screen and, in the case of the teenagers, each other.

Once, a man in his early twenties, hair like a haystack, sat up in the wide middle aisle when I took my seat. He groaned. Rusty-looking dried blood was spattered over his chin and his dirty white shirt. He groaned again and then got to his hands and knees. The carpet beneath him was spotted with what looked like a thousand red dots. The young man stumbled to his feet and began reeling up the aisle. A bright, depthless pane of sunlight surrounded him before he vanished into it.

At the beginning of July, I told my mother that the high-school girls had increased the hours of the Play School because I wanted to be sure of seeing both features twice before I had to go home. After that I could learn

439

the rhythms of the theater itself, which did not impress themselves upon me all at once but revealed themselves gradually, so that by the middle of the first week, I knew when the bums would begin to move toward the seats beneath the sconces—they usually arrived on Tuesdays and Fridays shortly after eleven o'clock, when the liquor store down the block opened up to provide them with the pints and half-pints that nourished them. By the end of the second week, I knew when the ushers left the interior of the theater to sit on padded benches in the lobby and light up their Luckies and Chesterfields, when the old men and women would begin to appear. By the end of the third week, I felt like the merest part of a great, orderly machine. Before the beginning of the second showing of *Beautiful Hawaii* or *Curiosities Down Under*, I went out to the counter and with my second quarter purchased a box of popcorn or a packet of Good 'N Plenty candy.

In a movie theater nothing is random except the customers and hitches in the machine. Filmstrips break and lights fail; the projectionist gets drunk or falls asleep; and the screen presents a blank yellow face to the stamping, whistling audience. These inconsistencies are summer squalls, forgotten as soon as they have ended.

The occasion for the lights, the projectionist, the boxes of popcorn and packets of candy, the movies, enlarged when seen over and over. The truth gradually came to me that this deepening and widening out, this enlarging, was why movies were shown over and over all day long. The machine revealed itself most surely in the exact, limpid repetitions of the actors' words and gestures as they moved through the story. When Alan Ladd asked "Blackie Franchot," the dying gangster, "Who did it, Blackie?" his voice widened like a river, grew *sandier* with an almost unconcealed tenderness. I had to learn to hear the voice within the speaking voice.

Chicago Deadline was the exploration by a newspaper reporter named "Ed Adams" (Alan Ladd) of the tragedy of a mysterious young woman, "Rosita Jandreau," who had died alone of tuberculosis in a shabby hotel room. The reporter soon learns that she had many names, many identities. She had been in love with an architect, a gangster, a crippled professor, a boxer, a millionaire, and had given a different facet of her being to each of them. Far too predictably, the adult me complains, the obsessed "Ed" falls in love with "Rosita." When I was seven, little was predictable—I had not yet seen *Laura*—and I saw a man driven by the need to understand, which became identical to the need to protect. "Rosita Jandreau" was the embodiment of memory, which was mystery.

Through the sequences of her identities, the various selves shown to brother, boxer, millionaire, gangster, all the others, her memory kept her whole. I saw, twice a day, for two weeks, before and during "Jimmy," the machine deep within the machine. Love and memory were the same.

Both love and memory accommodated us to death. (I did not understand this, but I saw it.) The reporter, Alan Ladd, with his dirty blond hair, his perfect jawline, and brilliant, wounded smile, gave her life by making her memory his own.

"I think you're the only one who ever understood her," Arthur Kennedy—"Rosita's" brother—tells Alan Ladd.

Most of the world demands the kick of sensation, most of the world must gather and spend money, hunt for easier and more temporary forms of love, must feed itself, sell newspapers, destroy the enemy's plots with plots of its own . . .

"I don't know what you want," "Ed Adams" says to the editor of *The Journal*. "You got two murders . . ."

". . . and a mystery woman," I say along with him. His voice is tough and detached, the voice of a wounded man acting. The man beside me laughs. Unlike his normal voice, his laughter is breathless and high pitched. It is the second showing today of *Chicago Deadline*, early afternoon—after the next showing of *At War with the Army* I will have to walk up the aisle and out of the theater. It will be twenty minutes to five, and the sun will still burn high over the cream-colored buildings across wide, empty Sherman Boulevard.

I met the man, or he met me, at the candy counter. He was at first only a tall presence, blond, dressed in dark clothing. I cared nothing for him, he did not matter. He was vague even when he spoke. "Good popcorn." I looked up at him—narrow blue eyes, bad teeth smiling at me. Stubble on his face. I looked away and the uniformed man behind the counter handed me popcorn. "Good for you, I mean. Good stuff in pop-corn—comes right out of the ground. Grows on big plants tall as I am, just like other corn. You know that?'"

When I said nothing, he laughed and spoke to the man behind the counter. "*He* didn't know that the kid thought popcorn grew inside poppers." The counterman turned away. "You come here a lot?" the man asked me.

I put a few kernels of popcorn in my mouth and turned toward him. He was showing me his bad teeth.

"You do," he said. "You come here a lot."

I nodded.

"Every day?"

I nodded again.

"And we tell little fibs at home about what we've been doing all day, don't we?" he asked, and pursed his lips and raised his eyes like a comic butler in a movie. Then his mood shifted and everything about him became serious. He was looking at me, but he did not see me. "You got a favorite actor? I got a favorite actor. Alan Ladd."

And I both saw and understood—that he thought he looked like Alan Ladd. He did, too, at least a little bit. When I saw the resemblance, he seemed like a different person, more glamorous. Glamour surrounded him, as though he were acting, impersonating a shabby young man with stained, irregular teeth.

"The name's Frank," he said, and stuck out his hand. "Shake?"

I took his hand.

"Real good popcorn," he said, and stuck his hand into the box. "Want to hear a secret?"

A secret.

"I was born twice. The first time, I died. It was on an Army base. Everybody *told* me I should have joined the Navy, and everybody was right. So I just had myself get born somewhere else. Hey—the Army's not for everybody, you know?" He grinned down at me. "Now I told you my secret. Let's go in—I'll sit with you. Everybody needs company, and I like you. You look like a good kid."

He followed me back to my seat and sat down beside me. When I quoted the lines along with the actors, he laughed.

Then he said—

Then he leaned toward me and said—

442

He leaned toward me, breathing sour wine over me, and took—
No.

"I was just kidding out there," he said. "Frank ain't my real name. Well, it was my name. Before. See? Frank used to be my name for a while. But now my good friends call me Stan. I like that. Stanley the Steamer. Big Stan. Stan the Man. See? It works real good."

You'll never be a carpenter, he told me. You'll never be anything like that because you got that look. *I* used to have that look, okay? So I know. I know about you just by looking at you.

He said he had been a clerk at Sears; after that he had worked as the custodian for a couple of apartment buildings owned by a guy who used to be a friend of his but was no longer. Then he had been the janitor at the high school where my grade school sent its graduates. "Good old booze got me fired, story of my life," he said. "Tight-ass bitches caught me drinking down in the basement, in a room I used there, and threw me out without a fare-thee-well. Hey, that was my room. My place. The best things in the world can do the worst things to you; you'll find that out someday. And when you go to that school, I hope you'll remember what they done to me there."

These days he was resting. He hung around, he went to the movies.

He said: You got something special in you. Guys like me, we're funny, we can tell.

We sat together through the second feature, Dean Martin and Jerry Lewis, comfortable and laughing. "Those guys are bigger bums than us," he said. I thought of Paul backed up against the school in his enveloping red shirt, imprisoned within his inability to be like anyone around him.

You coming back tomorrow? If I get here, I'll check around for you.

443

Peter Straub

*

Hey. Trust me. I know who you are.

You know that little thing you pee with? Leaning sideways and whispering into my ear. That's the best thing a man's got. Trust me.

The big providential park near our house, two streets past the Orpheum-Oriental, is separated into three different areas. Nearest the wide iron gates on Sherman Boulevard through which we enter was a wading pool divided by a low green hedge, so rubbery it seemed artificial, from a playground with a climbing frame, swings, and a row of seesaws. When I was a child of two and three, I splashed in the warm pool and clung to the chains of the swings, making myself go higher and higher, terror and joy and grim duty so woven together that no one could pull them apart.

Beyond the children's pool and playground was the zoo. My mother walked my brothers and me to the playground and wading pool and sat smoking on a bench while we played; both of my parents took us into the zoo. An elephant extended his trunk to my father's palm and delicately lipped peanuts toward his maw. The giraffe stretched toward the constantly diminishing supply of leaves, ever fewer and higher, above his cage. The lions drowsed on amputated branches and paced behind the bars, staring out not at what was there but at the long, grassy plains imprinted on their memories. I knew the lions had the power not to see us, to look straight through us to Africa. But when they saw you instead of Africa, they looked right into your bones, they saw the blood traveling through your body. The lions were golden brown, patient, green-eyed. They recognized me and could read thoughts. The lions neither liked nor disliked me, they did not miss me during their long weekdays, but they took me into the circle of known beings.

("You shouldn't have looked at me like that," June Havoc ["Leona"] tells "Ed Adams." She does not mean it, not at all.)

Past the zoo and across a narrow park road down which khaki-clothed park attendants pushed barrows heavy with flowers stood a wide, unexpected lawn bordered with flower beds and tall elms—open space

444

hidden like a secret between the caged animals and the elm trees. Only my father brought me to this section of the park. Here he tried to make a baseball player of me.

"Get the bat off your shoulders," he says. "For God's sake, will you try to hit the ball, anyhow?"

When I fail once again to swing at his slow, perfect pitch, he spins around, raises his arm, and theatrically asks everyone in sight, "Whose kid is this, anyway? Can you answer me that?"

He has never asked me about the Play School I am supposed to be attending, and I have never told him about the Orpheum-Oriental— I will never come any closer to talking to him than now, for "Stan," "Stanley the Steamer," has told me things that cannot be true, that must be inventions and fables, part of the world of children wandering lost in the forest, of talking cats and silver boots filled with blood. In this world, dismembered children buried beneath juniper trees can rise and speak, made whole once again. Fables boil with underground explosions and hidden fires, and for this reason, memory rejects them, thrusts them out of its sight, and they must be repeated over and over. I cannot remember "Stan's" face—cannot even be sure I remember what he said. Dean Martin and Jerry Lewis are bums like us. I am certain of only one thing: Tomorrow I am again going to see my newest, scariest, most interesting friend.

"When I was your age," my father says, "I had my heart set on playing pro ball when I grew up. And you're too damned scared or lazy to even take the bat off your shoulder. Kee-rist! I can't stand looking at you anymore.

He turns around and begins to move quickly toward the narrow park road and the zoo, going home, and I run after him. I retrieve the softball when he tosses it into the bushes.

"What the hell do you think you're going to do when you grow up?" my father asks, his eyes still fixed ahead of him. "I wonder what you think life is all *about*. I wouldn't give you a job, I wouldn't trust you around carpenter tools, I wouldn't trust you to blow your nose right—to tell you the truth, I wonder if the hospital mixed up the goddamn babies."

I follow him, dragging the bat with one hand, in the other cradling the softball in the pouch of my mitt.

At dinner my mother asks if Summer Play School is fun, and I say yes. I have already taken from my father's dresser drawer what "Stan" asked me to get for him, and it burns in my pocket as if it were alight. I want to ask: Is it actually true and not a story? Does the worst thing always have to be the true thing? Of course, I cannot ask this. My father does not know about worst things—he sees what he wants to see, or he tries so hard, he thinks he does see it.

"I guess he'll hit a long ball someday. The boy just needs more work on his swing." He tries to smile at me, a boy who will someday learn to hit a long ball. The knife is upended in his fist he is about to smear a pat of butter on his steak. He does not see me at all. My father is not a lion, he cannot make the switch to seeing what is really there in front of him.

Late at night Alan Ladd knelt beside my bed. He was wearing a neat gray suit, and his breath smelled like cloves. "You okay, son?" I nodded. "I just wanted to tell you that I like seeing you out there every day. That means a lot to me."

"Do you remember what I was telling you about?"

And I knew: it was true. He had said those things, and he would repeat them like a fairy tale, and the world was going to change because it would be seen through changed eyes. I felt sick—trapped in the theater as if in a cage.

"You think about what I told you?'"

"Sure," I said.

"That's good. Hey, you know what? I feel like changing seats. You want to change seats too?"

"Where to?"

He tilted his head back, and I knew he wanted to move to the last row.

"Come on. I want to show you something."

We changed seats.

For a long time we sat watching the movie from the last row, nearly alone in the theater. Just after eleven, three of the bums filed in and proceeded to their customary seats on the other side of the theater—a rumpled graybeard I had seen many times before; a fat man with a stubby, squashed face, also familiar; and one of the shaggy, wild-looking young men who hung around the bums until they became indistinguishable from them.

They began passing a flat brown bottle back and forth. After a second I remembered the young man—I had surprised him awake one morning, passed out and spattered with blood, in the middle aisle.

Then I wondered if "Stan" was not the young man I had surprised that morning; they looked as alike as twins, though I knew they were not.

"Want a sip?" "Stan" said, showing me his own pint bottle. "Do you good."

Bravely, feeling privileged and adult, I took the bottle of Thunderbird and raised it to my mouth. I wanted to like it, to share the pleasure of it with "Stan," but it tasted horrible, like garbage, and the little bit I swallowed burned all the way down my throat.

I made a face, and he said, "This stuff's really not so bad. Only one thing in the world can make you feel better than this stuff."

He placed his hand on my thigh and squeezed. "I'm giving you a head start, you know. Just because I liked you the first time I saw you." He leaned over and stared at me. "You believe me? You believe the things I tell you?"

I said I guessed so.

"I got proof. I'll show you it's true. Want to see my proof?" When I said nothing, "Stan" leaned closer to me, inundating me with the stench of Thunderbird. "You know that little thing you pee with? Remember how I told you how it gets real big when you're about thirteen? Remember I told you about how incredible that feels? Well, you have to trust Stan now, because Stan's going to trust you." He put his face right beside my ear. "Then I'll tell you another secret."

He lifted his hand from my thigh and closed it around mine and pulled my hand down onto his crotch. "Feel anything?"

I nodded, but I could not have described what I felt any more than the blind men could describe the elephant.

"Stan" smiled tightly and tugged at his zipper in a way even I could tell was nervous. He reached inside his pants, fumbled, and pulled out a thick, pale club that looked like nothing human. I was so frightened I thought I would throw up, and I looked back up at the screen. Invisible chains held me to my seat.

"See? Now you understand me."

Then he noticed that I was not looking at him. "Kid. Look. I said, look. It's not going to hurt you."

I could not look down at him. I saw nothing.

"Come on. Touch it, see what it feels like."

I shook my head.

"Let me tell you something. I like you a lot. I think the two of us are friends. This thing we're doing, it's unusual to you because this is the first time, but people do this all the time. Your mommy and daddy do it all the time, but they just don't tell you about it. We're pals, aren't we?"

I nodded dumbly. On the screen, Berry Kroeger was telling Alan Ladd, "Drop it, forget it, she's poison."

"Well, this is what friends do when they really like each other, like your mommy and daddy. Look at this thing, will you? Come on."

Did my mommy and daddy like each other? He squeezed my shoulder, and I looked.

Now the thing had folded up into itself and was drooping sideways against the fabric of his trousers. Almost as soon as I looked, it twitched and began to push itself out like the slide of a trombone.

"There," he said. "He likes you, you got him going. Tell me you like him too."

Terror would not let me speak. My brains had turned to powder.

"I know what—let's call him Jimmy. We'll say his name is Jimmy. Now that you've been introduced, say hi to Jimmy."

"Hi, Jimmy," I said, and, despite my terror, could not keep myself from giggling.

"Now go on, touch him."

I slowly extended my hand and put the tips of my fingers on "Jimmy."

"Pet him. Jimmy wants you to pet him."

I tapped my fingertips against "Jimmy" two or three times, and he twitched up another few degrees, as rigid as a surfboard.

"Slide your fingers up and down on him."

If I run, I thought, he'll catch me and kill me. If I don't do what he says, he'll kill me.

I rubbed my fingertips back and forth, moving the thin skin over the veins.

"Can't you imagine Jimmy going in a woman? Now you can see what you'll be like when you're a man. Keep on, but hold him with your whole hand. And give me what I asked you for."

I immediately took my hand from "Jimmy" and pulled my father's clean white handkerchief from my back pocket.

He took the handkerchief with his left hand and with his right guided mine back to "Jimmy." "You're doing really great," he whispered.

In my hand "Jimmy" felt warm and slightly gummy. I could not join my fingers around its width. My head was buzzing. "Is Jimmy your secret?" I was able to say.

"My secret comes later.'"

"Can I stop now?"

"I'll cut you into little pieces if you do," he said, and when I froze, he stroked my hair and whispered, "Hey, can't you tell when a guy's kidding around? I'm really happy with you right now. You're the best kid in the world. You'd want this, too, if you knew how good it felt."

After what seemed an endless time, while Alan Ladd was climbing out of a taxicab, "Stan" abruptly arched his back, grimaced, and whispered, "Look!" His entire body jerked, and too startled to let go, I held "Jimmy" and watched thick, ivory-colored milk spurt and drool almost unendingly onto the handkerchief. An odor utterly foreign but as familiar as the toilet or the lakeshore rose from the thick milk. "Stan" sighed, folded the handkerchief, and pushed the softening "Jimmy" back into his trousers. He leaned over and kissed the top of my head. I think I nearly fainted. I felt lightly, pointlessly dead. I could still feel him pulsing in my palm and fingers.

When it was time for me to go home, he told me his secret his own real name was Jimmy, not Stan. He had been saving his real name until he knew he could trust me.

"Tomorrow," he said, touching my cheek with his fingers. "We'll see each other again tomorrow. But you don't have anything to worry about. I trust you enough to give you my real name. You trusted me not to hurt you, and I didn't. We have to trust each other not to say anything about this, or both you and me'll be in a lot of trouble."

"I won't say anything," I said.

*

I love you.

I love you, yes I do.

Now *we're* a secret, he said, folding the handkerchief into quarters and putting it back in my pocket. A lot of love has to be secret. Especially when a boy and a man are getting to know each other and learning how to make each other happy and be good, loving friends—not many people can understand that, so the friendship has to be protected. When you walk out of here, he said, you have to forget that this happened. Otherwise people will try to hurt us both.

Afterward I remembered only the confusion of *Chicago Deadline*, how the story had abruptly surged forward, skipping over whole characters and entire scenes, how for long stretches the actors had moved their lips without speaking. I could see Alan Ladd stepping out of the taxicab, looking straight through the screen into my eyes, knowing me.

My mother said that I looked pale, and my father said that I didn't get enough exercise. The twins looked up from their plates, then went back to spooning macaroni and cheese into their mouths. "Were you ever in Chicago?" I asked my father, who asked what was it to me. "Did you ever meet a movie actor?" I asked, and he said, "This kid must have a fever." The twins giggled.

Alan Ladd and Donna Reed came into my bedroom together late that night, moving with brisk, cool theatricality, and kneeled down beside my cot. They smiled at me. Their voices were very soothing. I saw you missed a few things today, Alan said. Nothing to worry about. I'll take care of you.

I know, I said, I'm your number-one fan.

Then the door cracked open, and my mother put her head inside the room. Alan and Donna smiled and stood up to let her pass between them and the cot. I missed them the second they stepped back. "Still awake?"

I nodded. "Are you feeling all right, honey?" I nodded again, afraid that Alan and Donna would leave if she stayed too long. "I have a surprise for you," she said. "The Saturday after this, I'm taking you and the twins all the way across Lake Michigan on the ferry. There's a whole bunch of us. It'll be a lot of fun." Good, that's nice, I'll like that.

"I thought about you all last night and all this morning."

When I came into the lobby, he was leaning forward on one of the padded benches where the ushers sat and smoked, his elbows on his knees and his chin in his hand, watching the door. The metal tip of a flat bottle protruded from his side pocket. Beside him was a package rolled up in brown paper. He winked at me, jerked his head toward the door into the theater, stood up, and went inside in an elaborate charade of not being with me. I knew he would be just inside the door, sitting in the middle of the last row, waiting for me. I gave my ticket to the bored usher, who tore it in half and handed over the stub. I knew exactly what had happened yesterday, just as if I had never forgotten any of it, and my insides began shaking. All the colors of the lobby, the red and the shabby gilt, seemed much brighter than I remembered them. I could smell the popcorn in the case and the oily butter heating in the machine. My legs moved me over a mile of sizzling brown carpet and past the candy counter.

Jimmy's hair gleamed in the empty, darkening theater. When I took the seat next to him, he ruffled my hair and grinned down and said he had been thinking about me all night and all morning. The package in brown paper was a sandwich he'd brought for my lunch—a kid had to eat more than popcorn.

The lights went all the way down as the series of curtains opened over the screen. Loud music, beginning in the middle of a note, suddenly jumped from the speakers, and the Tom and Jerry cartoon "Bull Dozing" began. When I leaned back, Jimmy put his arm around me. I felt sweaty and cold at the same time, and my insides were still shaking. I suddenly realized that part of me was glad to be in this place, and I shocked myself with the knowledge that all morning I had been looking forward to this moment as much as I had been dreading it.

"You want your sandwich now? It's liver sausage, because that's my personal favorite." I said no thanks, I'd wait until the first movie was over. Okay, he said, just as long as you eat it. Then he said, look at me. His face was right above mine, and he looked like Alan Ladd's twin brother. You have to know something, he said. You're the best kid I ever met. Ever. The man squeezed me up against his chest and into a dizzying funk of sweat and dirt and wine, along with a trace (imagined?) of that other, more animal odor that had come from him yesterday. Then he released me.

You want me to play with your little "Jimmy" today?

No.

Too small, anyhow, he said with a laugh. He was in perfect good humor.

Bet you wish it was the same size as mine.

That wish terrified me, and I shook my head.

Today we're just going to watch the movies together, he said. I'm not greedy.

Except for when one of the ushers came up the aisle, we sat like that all day, his arm around my shoulders, the back of my neck resting in the hollow of his elbow. When the credits for *At War with the Army* rolled up the screen, I felt as though I had fallen asleep and missed everything. I couldn't believe that it was time to go home. Jimmy tightened his arm around me and in a voice full of amusement said *Touch me*. I looked up into his face. Go on, he said, I want you to do that little thing for me. I prodded his fly with my index finger. "Jimmy" wobbled under the pressure of my fingers, seeming as long as my arm, and for a second of absolute wretchedness I saw the other children running up and down the school playground behind the girls from the next block.

"Go on," he said.

Trust me, he said, investing "Jimmy" with an identity more concentrated, more focused, than his own. "Jimmy" wanted "to talk," "to speak his piece," "was hungry," "was dying for a kiss." All these words meant the same thing. *Trust me:* I trust you, so you must trust me. Have I ever hurt you? No. Didn't I give you a sandwich? Yes. Don't I love you? You know I won't tell your parents what you do—as long as you keep coming here, I won't tell your parents anything because I won't *have* to, see? And you love me, too, don't you?

There. You see how much I love you?

I dreamed that I lived underground in a wooden room. I dreamed that my parents roamed the upper world, calling out my name and weeping because the animals had captured and eaten me. I dreamed that I was buried beneath a juniper tree, and the cut-off pieces of my body called out to each other and wept because they were separate. I dreamed that I ran down a dark forest path toward my parents, and when I finally reached the small clearing where they sat before a bright fire, my mother was Donna and Alan was my father. I dreamed that I could remember everything that was happening to me, every second of it, and that when the teacher called on me in class, when my mother came into my room at night, when the policeman went past me as I walked down Sherman Boulevard, I had to spill it out. But when I tried to speak, I could not remember what it was that I remembered, *only that there was something to remember*, and so I walked again and again toward my beautiful parents in the clearing, repeating myself like a fable, like the jokes of the women on the ferry.

Don't I love you? Don't I show you, can't you tell, that I love you? *Yes.* Don't you, can't you, love me too?

He stares at me as I stare at the movie. He could see me, the way I could see him, with his eyes closed. He has me memorized. He has stroked my hair, my face, my body into his memory, stroke after stroke, stealing me from myself. Eventually he took me in his mouth and his mouth memorized me, too, and I knew he wanted me to place my hands on that dirty blond head resting so hugely in my lap, but I could not touch his head.

I thought: I have already forgotten this, I want to die, I am dead already, only death can make this not have happened. I thought: I have already forgotten this, I want to die, I am dead already, only death can make this not have happened.

When you grow up, I bet you'll be in the movies and I'll be your number-one fan.

*

By the weekend, those days at the Orpheum-Oriental seemed to have been spent under water; or underground. The spiny anteater, the lyrebird, the kangaroo, the Tasmanian devil, the nun bat, and the frilled lizard were creatures found only in Australia. Australia was the world's smallest continent, its largest island. It was cut off from the Earth's great landmasses. Beautiful girls with blond hair strutted across Australian beaches, and Australian Christmases were hot and sunbaked—everybody went outside and waved at the camera, exchanging presents from lawn chairs. The middle of Australia, its heart and gut, was a desert. Australian boys excelled at sports. Tom Cat loved Jerry Mouse, though he plotted again and again to murder him, and Jerry Mouse loved Tom Cat, though to save his life he had to run so fast he burned a track through the carpet. Jimmy loved me and he would be gone someday, and then I would miss him a lot. Wouldn't I? *Say you'll miss me.*

I'll—

"I'll miss—

I think I'd go crazy without you.

When you're all grown-up, will you remember me?

Each time I walked back out past the usher, tearing in half the tickets of the people just entering, handing them the stubs, every time I pushed open the door and walked out onto the heat-filled sidewalk of Sherman Boulevard and saw the sun on the buildings across the street, I lost my hold on what had happened inside the darkness of the theater. I didn't know what I wanted. I had two murders and a . . . My right hand felt as though I had been holding a smaller child's sticky hand very tightly between my palm and fingers. If I lived in Australia, I would have blond hair like Alan Ladd and run forever across tan beaches on Christmas Day.

I walked through high school in my sleep, reading novels, daydreaming in classes I did not like but earning spuriously good grades; in the middle of my senior year Brown University gave me a full scholarship. Two years later I amazed and disappointed all my old teachers and my parents and my parents' friends by dropping out of school shortly before I would have failed all my courses but English and history, in which I was getting As. I was certain that no one could teach anyone else how to write. I knew exactly what I was going to do, and all I would miss of college was the social life.

For five years I lived inexpensively in Providence, supporting myself by stacking books in the school library and by petty thievery. I wrote when I was not working or listening to the local bands; then I destroyed what I had written and wrote it again. In this way I saw myself to the end of a novel, like walking through a park one way and then walking backward and forward through the same park, over and over, until every nick on every swing, every tawny hair on every lion's hide, had been witnessed and made to gleam or allowed to sink back into the importunate field of details from which it had been lifted. When this novel was rejected by the publisher to whom I sent it, I moved to New York City and began another novel while I rewrote the first all over again at night. During this period an almost impersonal happiness, like the happiness of a stranger, lay beneath everything I did. I wrapped parcels of books at the Strand Bookstore. For a short time, no more than a few months, I lived on Shredded Wheat and peanut butter. When my first book was accepted, I moved from a single room on the Lower East Side into another, larger single room, a "studio apartment," on Ninth Avenue in Chelsea, where I continue to live. My apartment is just large enough for my wooden desk, a convertible couch, two large crowded bookshelves, a shelf of stereo equipment, and dozens of cardboard boxes of records. In this apartment everything has its place and is in it.

My parents have never been to this enclosed, tidy space, though I speak to my father on the phone every two or three months. In the past ten years I have returned to the city where I grew up only once, to visit my mother in the hospital after her stroke. During the four days I stayed in my father's house I slept in my old room, my father upstairs. After the blind man's death my father bought the duplex— on my first night home he told me that we were both successes. Now, when we speak on the telephone, he tells me of the fortunes of the local baseball and basketball teams and respectfully inquires about my progress on "the new book." I think: this is not my father, he is not the same man.

My old cot disappeared long ago, and late at night I lay on the twins' double bed. Like the house as a whole, like everything in my old neighborhood, the bedroom was larger than I remembered it. I brushed the wallpaper with my fingers, then looked up to the ceiling. The image of two men tangled up in the ropes of the same parachute, comically berating each other as they fell, came to me, and I wondered if the image had a place in the novel I was writing, or if it was a gift from the as yet unseen novel that would follow it. I could hear the floor creak as my father paced upstairs in the blind man's former territory. My inner weather changed, and I began brooding about Mei-Mei Levitt, whom fifteen years earlier at Brown I had known as Mei-Mei Cheung.

Divorced, an editor at a paperback firm, she had called to congratulate me after my second novel was favorably reviewed in the *Times*, and on this slim but well-intentioned foundation we began to construct a long and troubled love affair. Back in the surroundings of my childhood, I felt profoundly uneasy, having spent the day beside my mother's hospital bed without knowing if she understood or even recognized me, and I thought of Mei-Mei with sudden longing. I wanted her in my arms, and I yearned for my purposeful, orderly, dreaming adult life in New York. I wanted to call Mei-Mei, but it was past midnight in the Midwest, an hour later in New York, and Mei-Mei, no owl, would have gone to bed hours earlier.

Then I remembered my mother lying stricken in the narrow hospital bed, and suffered a spasm of guilt for thinking about my lover. For a deluded moment I imagined that it was my duty to move back into the house and see if I could bring my mother back to life while I did what I could for my retired father. At that moment I remembered, as I often did, an orange-haired boy enveloped in a red wool shirt. Sweat poured from my forehead, my chest.

Then a terrifying thing happened to me. I tried to get out of bed to go to the bathroom and found that I could not move. My arms and legs were cast in cement; they were lifeless and *would not move*. I thought that I was having a stroke, like my mother. I could not even cry out—my throat, too, was paralyzed. I strained to push myself up off the narrow bed and smelled that someone very near, someone just out of sight or around a corner, was making popcorn and heating butter. Another wave of sweat gouted out of my inert body, turning the sheet and the pillowcase slick and cold.

I saw—as if I were writing it—my seven-year-old self hesitating before the entrance of a theater a few blocks from this house. Hot, flat, yellow sunlight fell over everything, cooking the life from the wide boulevard. I saw myself turn away, felt my stomach churn with the smoke of underground fires, saw myself begin to run. Vomit backed up in my throat. My arms and legs convulsed, and I fell out of bed and managed to crawl out of the room and down the hall to throw up in the toilet behind the closed door of the bathroom.

My age, as I write these words, is forty-three. I have written five novels over a period of nearly twenty years, "only" five, each of them more difficult, harder to write than the one before. To maintain this hobbled pace of a novel every four years, I must sit at my desk at least six hours every day; I must consume hundreds of boxes of typing paper, scores of yellow legal pads, forests of pencils, miles of black ribbon. It is a fierce, voracious activity. Every sentence must be tested three or four ways, made to clear fences like a horse. The purpose of every sentence is to be an arrow into the secret center of the book. To find my way into the secret center I must hold the entire book, every detail and rhythm, in my memory. This comprehensive act of memory is the most crucial task of my life.

My books get flattering reviews, which usually seem to describe other, more linear novels, and they win occasional awards—I am one of those writers whose advances are funded by the torrents of money spun off by bestsellers. Lately I have had the impression that the general perception of me, to the extent that such a thing exists, is that of a hermetic painter inscribing hundreds of tiny, grotesque, fantastical details over every inch of a large canvas. (My books are unfashionably long.) I teach writing at various colleges, give occasional lectures, am modestly enriched by grants. This is enough, more than enough. Now and then I am both dismayed and amused to discover that a young writer I have met at a PEN reception or a workshop regards my life with envy. Envy misses the point completely.

"If you were going to give me one piece of advice," a young woman at a conference asked me, "I mean, *real* advice, not just the obvious stuff about keeping on writing, what would it be? What would you tell me to do?"

I won't tell you, but I'll write it out, I said, and picked up one of the conference flyers and printed a few words on its back. Don't read this until you are out of the room, I said, and watched while she folded the flyer into her bag.

What I had printed on the back of the flyer was: *Go to a lot of movies.*

On the Sunday after the ferry trip I could not hit a single ball in the park. My eyes kept closing, and as soon as my eyelids came down, visions started up like movies—quick, automatic dreams. My arms seemed too heavy to lift. After I had trudged home behind my dispirited father, I collapsed on the sofa and slept straight through to dinner. In a dream a spacious box confined me, and I drew colored pictures of elm trees, the sun, wide fields, mountains, and rivers on its walls. At dinner, loud noises, never scarce around the twins, made me jump. That kid's not right, I swear to you, my father said. When my mother asked if I wanted to go to Play School on Monday, my stomach closed up like a fist. I have to, I said, I'm really fine. I have to go. Sentences rolled from my mouth, meaning nothing, or meaning the wrong thing. For a moment of confusion I thought that I really was going to the playground, and saw black asphalt, deep as a field, where a few children, diminished by perspective, clustered at the far end. I went to bed right after dinner. My mother pulled down the shades, turned off the light, and finally left me alone. From above came the sound, like a beast's approximation of music, of random notes struck on a piano. I knew only that I was scared, not why. The next day I had to go to a certain place, but I could not think where until my fingers recalled the velvety plush of the end seat on the middle aisle. Then black-and-white images, full of intentional menace, came to me from the previews I had seen for two weeks—*The Hitchhiker*, starring Edmund O'Brien. The spiny anteater and nun bat were animals found only in Australia.

I longed for Alan Ladd, "Ed Adams," to walk into the room with his reporter's notebook and pencil, and knew that I had *something to remember* without knowing what it was.

After a long time the twins cascaded into the bedroom, undressed, put on pajamas, brushed their teeth. The front door slammed—my father had gone out to the taverns. In the kitchen, my mother ironed shirts and talked to herself in a familiar, rancorous voice. The twins went to sleep. I heard my mother put away the ironing board and walk down the hall to the living room.

I saw "Ed Adams" calmly walking up and down on the sidewalk outside our house, as handsome as a god in his neat gray suit. "Ed" went all the way to the end of the block, put a cigarette in his mouth, and leaned into a sudden, round flare of brightness before exhaling smoke and walking away. I knew I had fallen asleep only when the front door slammed for the second time that night and woke me up.

In the morning my father struck his fist against the bedroom door and the twins jumped out of bed and began yelling around the bedroom, instantly filled with energy. As in a cartoon, into the bedroom drifted tendrils of the odor of frying bacon. My brothers jostled toward the bathroom. Water rushed into the sink and the toilet bowl, and my mother hurried in, her face tightened down over her cigarette, and began yanking the twins into their clothes. "You made your decision," she said to me, "now I hope you're going to make it to the playground on time." Doors opened, doors slammed shut. My father shouted from the kitchen, and I got out of bed.

Eventually I sat down before the bowl of cereal. My father smoked and did not meet my eyes. The cereal tasted of dead leaves. "You look the way that asshole upstairs plays piano," my father said. He dropped quarters on the table and told me not to lose that money.

After he left, I locked myself in the bedroom. The piano dully resounded overhead like a sound track. I heard the cups and dishes rattle in the sink, the furniture moving by itself, looking for something to hunt down and kill. *Love me, love me*, the radio called from beside a family of brown-and-white porcelain spaniels. I heard some light, whispery thing, a lamp or a magazine, begin to slide around the living room, *I am imagining all this*, I said to myself, and tried to concentrate on a *Blackhawk* comic book. The pictures jigged and melted in their panels. *Love me*, Blackhawk cried out from the cockpit of his fighter as he swooped down to exterminate a nest of yellow, slant-eyed villains. Outside, fire raged beneath the streets, trying to pull the world apart. When I dropped the comic book and closed my eyes, the noises ceased and I could hear the hovering stillness of perfect attention. Even Blackhawk, belted into his airplane within the comic book, was listening to what I was doing.

In thick, hazy sunlight I went down Sherman Boulevard toward the Orpheum-Oriental. Around me the world was motionless, frozen like a frame in a comic strip. After a time I noticed that the cars on the boulevard and the few people on the sidewalk had not actually frozen into place but instead were moving with great slowness. I could see men's legs advancing within their trousers, the knee coming forward to strike the crease, the cuff slowly lifting off the shoe, the shoe drifting up like Tom Cat's paw when he crept toward Jerry Mouse. The warm, patched skin of Sherman Boulevard . . . I thought of walking along Sherman Boulevard forever, moving past the nearly immobile cars and people, past the theater, past the liquor store, through the gates, and past the wading pool and swings, past the elephants and lions reaching out to be fed, past the secret park where my father flailed in a rage of disappointment, past the elms and out the opposite gate, past the big houses on the opposite side of the park, past picture windows and past lawns with bikes and plastic pools, past slanting driveways and basketball hoops, past men getting out of cars, past playgrounds where children raced back and forth on a surface shining black. Then past fields and crowded markets, past high yellow tractors with mud dried like old wool inside the enormous hubs, past wagons piled high with hay, past deep woods where lost children followed trails of bread crumbs to a gingerbread door, past other cities where nobody would see me because nobody knew my name, past everything, past everybody.

At the Orpheum-Oriental, I stopped still. My mouth was dry and my eyes would not focus. Everything around me, so quiet and still a moment earlier, jumped into life as soon as I stopped walking. Horns blared, cars roared down the boulevard. Beneath these sounds I heard the pounding of great machines, and the fires gobbling up oxygen beneath the street. As if I had eaten them from the air, fire and smoke poured into my stomach. Flame slipped up my throat and sealed the back of my mouth. In my mind I saw myself taking the first quarter from my pocket, exchanging it for a ticket, pushing through the door, and moving into the cool air. I saw myself holding out the ticket to be torn in half, going over an endless brown carpet toward the inner door. From the last row of seats on the other side of the inner door, inside the shadowy but not yet dark theater, a shapeless monster whose wet black mouth said *Love me, love me* stretched yearning arms toward me. Shock froze my shoes to the sidewalk, then shoved me firmly in the small of the back, and I was running down the block, unable to scream because I had to clamp my lips against the smoke and fire trying to explode from my mouth.

The rest of that afternoon remains vague. I wandered through the streets, not in the clean, hollow way I had imagined but almost blindly, hot and uncertain. I remember the taste of fire in my mouth and the loudness of my heart. After a time I found myself before the elephant enclosure in the zoo. A newspaper reporter in a neat gray suit passed through the space before me, and I followed him, knowing that he carried a notebook in his pocket, that he had been beaten by gangsters, that he could locate the speaking secret that hid beneath the disconnected and dismembered pieces of the world. He would fire his pistol on an empty chamber and trick evil "Solly Wellman," Berry Kroeger with his girlish, watchful eyes. And when "Solly Wellman" came gloating out of the shadows, the reporter would shoot him dead.

Dead.

Donna Reed smiled down from an upstairs window: Has there ever been a smile like that? Ever? I was in Chicago, and behind a closed door "Blackie Franchot" bled onto a brown carpet. "Solly Wellman," something like "Solly Wellman," called and called to me from the decorated grave where he lay like a secret. The man in the gray suit finally carried his notebook and his gun through a front door, and I saw that I was only a few blocks from home.

Paul leans against the wire fence surrounding the playground, looking out, looking backward. Alan Ladd brushes off "Leona" (June Havoc), for she has no history that matters and exists only in the world of work and pleasure, of cigarettes and cocktail bars. Beneath this world is another, and "Leona's" life is a blind, strenuous denial of that other world.

My mother held her hand to my forehead and declared that I not only had a fever but had been building up to it all week. I was not to go to the playground the next day; I had to spend the day lying down on Mrs. Candee's couch. When she lifted the telephone to call one of the high-school girls, I said not to bother, other kids were gone all the time, and she put down the receiver.

I lay on Mrs. Candee's couch staring up at tile ceiling of her darkened living room. The twins squabbled outside, and maternal, slow-witted Mrs. Candee brought me orange juice. The twins ran toward the sandbox, and Mrs. Candee groaned as she let herself fall into a wobbly lawn chair. The morning newspaper folded beneath the lawn chair said that *The Hitchhiker* and *Double Cross* had begun playing at the Orpheum-Oriental. *Chicago Deadline* had done its work and traveled on. It had broken the world in half and sealed the monster deep within. Nobody but me knew this. Up and down the block, sprinklers whirred, whipping loops of water onto the dry lawns. Men driving slowly up and down the street hung their elbows out of their windows. For a moment free of regret and nearly without emotion of any kind, I understood that I belonged utterly to myself. Like everything else, I had been torn asunder and glued back together with shock, vomit, and orange juice. The knowledge sifted into me that I was all alone. "Stan," "Jimmy," whatever his name was, would never come back to the theater. He would be afraid that I had told my parents and the police, about him. I knew that I had killed him by forgetting him, and then I forgot him again.

The next day I went back to the theater and went through the inner door and saw row after row of empty seats falling toward the curtained screen. I was all alone. The size and the grandeur of the theater surprised me. I went down the long descending aisle and to the last seat, left side, on the broad middle aisle. The next row seemed nearly a playground's distance away. The lights dimmed and the curtains rippled slowly away from the screen. Anticipatory music filled the air, and the first letters appeared on the screen.

What I am, what I do, why I do it. I am simultaneously a man in his early forties, that treacherous time, and a boy of seven before whose bravery I

462

will ever fall short. I live underground in a wooden room and patiently, in joyful concentration, decorate the walls. Before me hangs a large and appallingly complicated vision I must explore and memorize, must witness again and again in order to locate its hidden center. Around me, everything is in its proper place. My typewriter sits on the sturdy table. Beside the typewriter a cigarette smolders, raising a gray stream of smoke. A record revolves on the turntable, and my small apartment is dense with music. ("Bird of Prey Blues," with Coleman Hawkins, Buck Clayton, and Hank Jones.) Beyond my walls and windows is a world toward which I reach with outstretched arms and an ambitious and divided heart. As if "Bird of Prey Blues" has evoked them, the voices of sentences to be written this afternoon, tomorrow, or next month stir and whisper, beginning to speak, and I lean over the typewriter toward them, getting as close as I can.

Peter Straub is the author of nineteen novels, which have been translated into more than twenty languages. They include *Ghost Story*, *Koko*, *Mr. X*, *In the Night Room*, and two collaborations with Stephen King, *The Talisman* and *Black House*. He has written two volumes of poetry and two collections of short fiction, and he edited the Library of America's edition of *H. P. Lovecraft's Tales* and the Library of America's two-volume anthology, *American Fantastic Tales*. He has won the British Fantasy Award, eight Bram Stoker Awards, two International Horror Guild Awards, and three World Fantasy Awards. In 1998, he was named Grand Master at the World Horror Convention. In 2006, he was given the HWA's Life Achievement Award. In 2008, he was given the Barnes & Noble Writers for Writers Award by Poets & Writers. In 2010, he was honored with the World Fantasy Life Achievement Award.

The best-known wonder-tale amphibian is the one in "The Frog Prince." He needs to be kissed by a princess (or sleep on her pillow, etc.) to be transformed back into a human. A Russian variation "Tsarevna Lyagushka" ("The Frog Princess") involves three princes who shoot arrows to find brides. One's projectile is found by a frog who is, of course, a princess in need of a magic makeover. The princes in an Italian version use slings; in a Greek variant they set out singly to find their brides. And so on. The frogs in these stories are all in need of transformation. The following story by Jeff VanderMeer involves a frog and transformations, but it is not the croaker who needs to change.

Greensleeves

Jeff VanderMeer

Outside the Samuel Devonshire Memorial Library that January night, birds froze in mid-air, skidding to emergency touch-downs at O'Hare; children, hauled inside by their parents, were thrown in fireplaces to thaw; iron horses ghosting through the city huffed and puffed, breath breaking on the tracks.

Inside, librarian Mary Colquhoun had her four stories of silence. Silence coated the aisles, the stacks, the desks. No one could shake it off. Mary had cultivated this silence over the years until she knew its every subtlety: the pitch and tone of its soundless echo, the whispery quality of the first floor compared to the musty pomp of the second, the gloom of the fourth. If clean and absolute enough, the silence could conjure up memories, coffee washing over her in sleepy brown waves. The muscles of her forty-five-year-old face would relax, wrinkles smoothing out. She could forget the few hardcore bibliophiles who still perused the pages of such classics as *Green Eggs and Ham*. She could forget that the drifters had pitched camp in a far corner of the second floor. "Shhh . . ." hissed the air ducts. "Hush," sighed the computers. "Quiet," clucked the clocks.

To the right and left of Mary's desk, the stacks rose monolithic; ahead, some hundred-sixty feet down the hall, the glass doors showed a welter of snow, through which Mary could just discern, with the binoculars kept for this purpose, the bright sheen of the road. Snow plows, lights shining, trudged down the street at random intervals. The front automated counter stamped its seal of approval, always burbling to itself. When someone tried to leave without checking out her books, the doors refused to open, jaws set in bulletproof glass.

The second through fourth floors were hunched against the building's sides, leaving the roof open to view three hundred feet above her. Stage lights illuminated a dome of stained glass: an eagle, its wings spread wide against an aqua sky. Under their expanse, Mary sometimes thought she saw smaller birds: finches, sparrows, and warblers. Once a week she placed seed atop the stacks.

Tonight, however, there was only the eagle, a blanket of snow darkening the glass, flakes falling into the library through a hole in its left eye. Although the thermostat read seventy-five degrees, Mary always shivered when she thought of that black hole.

Mary's concentration was broken when she heard the door open, vibrating through the stillness.

She glanced up, but the door was shut and no one in sight. Snuggling into her chair, she opened a book, Edward Whittemore's *Jerusalem Poker*. Usually, she would have played poker with the library staff, but they were all at home, Mary having volunteered for single duty. The library had served as an excellent retreat from two marriages, better almost than a convent, though she had never meant to stay eight years, only long enough to regain her feet. Sometimes, though, thoughts rebounding in her head would escape, breaking the conundrum of silence: *Mary, Mary quite contrary, your garden is dead; books are fine and good, but where, oh where, to rest your weary head?* Strange thoughts, fey and disconnected. They only served to make her remember the past. Once, she knew, she had managed a nightclub, but that had failed along with her husbands. Their faces had faded with the years, until now, they might as well have been stick figures, fingers thin and brittle, but still pointed at her. *You, they told her, you were to blame. We only wanted what was best....* Except, they never really had. So now she cavorted with Lord Byron and vacationed with Don Quixote. A shelver and filer. A bespectacled terror to the children and a patient custodian to the parents.

Then the door did open with a rush of cold air, and Mary looked up. In stepped a multicolored blob. Mary straightened her glasses, bringing the binoculars up to her eyes. She raised her eyebrows. *Oh, this is interesting. Very interesting. No mere bird can compare.*

The creature was a man, the man a jester. The belled cap, the striped velvet-satin tunic, the patched pantaloons, had been colored by an aficionado of urban camouflage: red graffiti rioting against cement and earth tones, the oily sheen of dirty glass. The boots, black and worn, pointed towards the eagle's eye. The air *changed* as he moved, a rising wave of . . . purity? She could not quite put a name to it. On the second floor the drifters broke into a jig.

Now Mary could see his face: a strong jaw, cheekbones ruddy with cold, softened by a well-proportioned nose and eyes which skipped from aisle to counter to shelf like pebbles glancing over water. His mouth curled into a perpetual smile, held in place by lines carved into the skin. The body attached to the face was strong and wiry. Mary's chest constricted and she realized she was hyperventilating. She sucked in deep breaths, tried to relax, hands aflutter. She had fallen in Intense Like.

Mary Colquhoun no longer believed in love at first sight. Both husbands had been hooked that way. No, one did not throw oneself at another human being. One did not exchange glances across crowded rooms and instantly become intimate. *Now I choose more sensible ways*, Mary reassured herself, when in fact she deliberately and with some effort blocked every path. Except one: Intense Like, which could evolve into love, or more probably, mild disdain. The buzz of her former husbands' advice threatened to overwhelm her, but she shook it off. Something deep within her had been rekindled upon seeing this ridiculous jester.

The man stepped up to her desk. Mary put down the binoculars and closed her mouth. Swallowing, she took off her glasses, smiled.

"What can I do for you?"

His grin broadened.

"Well, Miss . . . Mrs. . . . ?"

"Oh. Miss Mary Colquhoun."

"*Miss* Mary Colquhoun, my name is Cedric Greensleeves—professional calling, you understand—and I am searching for my frog."

"Your what?"

"My frog."

"Oh?" she said.

Cedric Greensleeves' chuckle chased away her silence.

"Yes," he said, his tone teasing her. "I work for the . . . the Amazing Mango Brothers Circus, currently touring the Greater Chicago area. I provide entertainment for the children and, sometimes, for lucky parents. My Familiar, so to speak, is a frog. A big one—five feet long and four wide. Stands three feet at the shoulder. Found him myself in the South American rainforests. Very rare. And smart, devious—even Machiavellian—in his intrigues."

"I see," interjected Mary, simply to catch her breath. Her heart still beat fast, but she couldn't shed her skin. She had labeled herself, she realized, the unfamiliar brushed off as petty irritation. She shivered.

On the second floor, the drifters danced to slow rhythms, birthing shadows which left their masters and undulated down to the first floor, over the guard rail.

Cedric glanced up, eyes narrow: the gaze of an ancient man.

"It's the homeless," Mary said. "I let them use the second floor fireplace. It's electric." Her jaw unclenched somewhat.

Cedric nodded. "I know. *And the chosen shall dance.*"

Mary could have sworn she saw fire reflected in his eyes.

"What do you mean?" she asked.

"Nothing." The fire, if she had not imagined it, had vanished.

"Anyway, we were driving past here on our way to the show and the car was caught in a snow drift." He said *car* as if it were a foreign word, a word without meaning. "I opened the door, the frog made a break for it—as if I don't treat him with kid gloves already—and I've been looking for him ever since."

Cedric leaned over Mary's desk, stared at her. His eyes were cinnamon-colored, flecked with gold. "Have you seen him?"

"No. No. I haven't seen your frog. Sorry."

In her mind, a forgotten part of her past said, "Stay, stay and have a nightcap in this silly mausoleum of learning, under the eagle's eye . . ."

A vision of conquest possessed her: a way to re-enter the world triumphant, on the wings of clocks and computers, with this man beside her, perhaps traveling on ghost trains, subduing misfortune through the passage of years, the green hum of television screens. A bustling consumerism, a wonderful new nightclub, perhaps, magic rising from the machinery of the Samuel Devonshire, her husbands swept away, little stick limbs and all.

But the vision faded and she was back inside her skin and she knew the library's special properties were not transferable or exportable, that it simply *was*, like—she guessed—the man who stood before her. Cedric was talking.

"—sure this was the place, but if you do see him, please give me a call." Cedric rummaged through the many pockets on his vest.

"He can giggle and he can sing. 'Greensleeves,' of course. Rather, he can whistle it."

He picked a card from its hiding place and offered it to Mary. As he leaned towards her, the smell of salt spray and sandalwood washed over her. Mary closed her eyes to catch the scents. Cedric's hands touched her, shocking, burning. Vaguely, as if from a tunnel of snow, Mary heard him say, "This *was* the right place, but for now . . . goodbye."

She opened her eyes. Cedric Greensleeves had reached the doors. Mary lunged for the red button that would lock them, but her hand wavered, a terrible thought freezing her. *He knows. He knows I'm hiding. He saw it with his own eyes.* How could she keep anything from those cinnamon eyes? The jester passed into the night, leaving jumbled impressions in her mind and a silence the color of sandalwood.

Mary tried to relax, shoulders untensing, fists flowering into hands. *Giggles and Greensleeves*, she thought, glancing down at the card. A frog with belled cap graced the front. On the back, it read, "Greensleeves and His Magic Frog: Services of Whimsy Available at Typical Prices. Call 777-FROG for details. Or contact the Amazing Mango Brothers Circus. Humor on demand."

Probably a womanizer, she thought, but felt hollow inside as she remembered his eyes, the perpetual smile.

Mary hardly noticed the last bibliophiles shuffle off into the night.

At nine, the clocks dutifully chimed and ate their tongues for another hour. The computers amused themselves by placing obscene phone calls to the CIA, while the heated air ducts wheezed from perpetual sore pipes. An unease had stolen over Mary. The quality of silence had changed once again. It was somehow . . . *green*?!

Slapslapslap! Green swathes swept by her sixth sense, wrapping themselves in her hair, hitting her face like the pages of a wind-blown newspaper. She spluttered, rose from her chair. Damn it! Something was out of synch. Straightening her skirt, she began to walk towards the entrance. A left-behind brat had probably overturned a whole shelf of *Better Homes and Gardens*, spilling this dreadful silence from the second or third floors and down onto her.

Then a sound which was a sound began to rise and Mary stood transfixed, an expression of wonder illuminating her face. For two hundred years, the building that housed the library had played host to other institutions: banks, hotels, synagogues, post offices, but never—never!—had this sound been heard among the balconies and hallways, stacks and marble statues.

The clocks burped and hiccupped in surprise as the sound twisted its way towards the ceiling. A whistle, or brace of whistles intertwined, clear and vibrant, broke Mary's silence, unraveling thread by thread the cloak she had woven for so many years. "Greensleeves'" melody filled the Samuel Devonshire Memorial Library, softly, softly, then louder and deeper, until Mary lost herself in the mournful notes. On the second floor, the drifters halted in mid-step of a Caribbean mamba and bowed to their partners, now sweeping across the floor in synchronized simplicity. Their shadows stayed with them, teaching the steps, before separating to form their own company. No laughter, but the men and women facing each other stared into opposite eyes and felt the thrill of intimacy. The fireplace crackled a counterpoint.

Below, Mary stood entranced, remembering past romances and the possible one which had slipped through her clumsy fingers. Slowly, awkwardly, she began to dance, hands held as if in an invisible partner's grasp. Her high heels slid effortlessly across the floor, her moves more and more elegant as she lost herself to the music.

She spoke to her invisible partner, but the fantasy soon soured. She shoved it away, but it shoved back. It was no use; despite her best efforts, her husbands' stick figure faces took on depth, color, substance. Now both danced with her, silent while she apologized to them: *I'm sorry. I'm sorry. Just, please, please . . .*

Mary stopped dancing. Her shoulders slumped. Why did she always apologize? Why? It always made her feel terrible. She'd done nothing wrong. Angrily, she brushed tears away; the eagle looked on without mercy. She tried to stop crying, failed, and bit on her lip, arms wrapped around her shoulders. *God*, she thought, *what am I doing here?* The eagle, possessing the only eye of divinity in the cavern, did not answer. There was no need. She knew the answer, no matter how she blocked it out with silence. And still "Greensleeves" rose and fell upon her ears, breaking every covenant she had made with herself. The sound, piercing the roof through the eagle's broken eye, emerged into the cold night air to nudge the memories of passersby. Mary whispered the words, eyes shut.

The last note echoed, died away. The whistler giggled. Giggled and broke the spell. Giggled and was answered by a tentative burble from the checkout machine, only too happy to gossip. Mary's eyes blinked open. The frog! The frog *was* here, between the aisles. Her librarian instincts came to the fore. Search and destroy! Find the intruder! Return the intruder to Cedric. . . .

Mary rolled up her sleeves and walked down the nearest row, shoes clicking on the marble floor. She reached the end, was faced by more stacks. A loud, obnoxious giggle sounded to her left. A solid green bullet. An emerald Volkswagen Beetle. A *whump!* and the thing she had seen bowled her over, its skin clammy, its breath damp.

Face red, Mary got up and dusted off her skirt. All thoughts of "Greensleeves" left her. For the first time in several months, Mary Colquhoun was mad. *Either that*, she thought, *or start crying again.* She stomped down the aisles. She came to the end: a wall lined with portraits. No frog. Mary started to turn around when a chorus of voices spoke up.

"He went that-a-way!"

"Divide and Conquer!"

"Up the kazoo with Tyler too!"

"He's heading North by Northwest!"

"Get a net!"

"Get a gun!"

"Get a life . . ."

She stared at the wall. A dozen pairs of eyes stared back from the paintings. Governors and hotel managers, postal generals and noveau riche millionaires. Mary was too mad to be shocked, too wise in the library's ways.

A man with bushy eyebrows and a beard streaked white said, "Ya know, when I was in the army, we smoked 'em out. That worked real good. Take my word for it."

"SHUT UP!!" shouted Mary. The sound rebounded from the walls and almost knocked her off her feet. A hand went to her mouth. A garbled echo sounded: "Sush op . . ."

She, Mary Colquhoun, usually quiet as a dust mouse, had raised her voice, broken her own silence. A ghost of a nightclub owner flickered in her features. She smiled. She laughed. She chortled. Nothing was particularly funny, but she couldn't help herself. She'd call Cedric, tell him his frog was in the library. Grinning, she left the disgruntled portraits still whispering advice.

"Get it in a headlock. Get it in a headlock."

"Make it play Simon Says . . ."

"Promise it ice cream—or orange marmalade; frogs like marmalade."

She turned a corner. The voices faded.

11.

"Satchmo," Mary said, the second floor electric fireplace raging behind her, "I need your help. Please?"

She spoke to the tall, grizzled black man who served as the drifters' unofficial leader. Mary had called Cedric, only to get his answering service and an extra helping of frog giggle.

Although Satchmo had lived on the second floor for almost two years, Mary did not feel comfortable speaking to him. He called himself Satchmo sarcastically because he owned a saxophone, and she had observed him long enough to realize that, if eccentric, he wasn't crazy. But he *was* mute, and that created a special silence in itself. When he had first arrived, Satchmo had greeted her with a notecard that read, WHY ARE YOU SO SAD? Three weeks later, it had been, YOU DON'T TALK MUCH. And still later, WERE YOU A MUTE ONCE? At which point, she had to giggle despite herself.

Gradually, he had revealed himself through the cards: I HATE VEAL. CAT FUR MAKES MY EYES WATER. MY PARENTS DIED WHEN I WAS FIVE. MY HERO IS MARCEL MARCEAU. IS THERE FUZZ IN MY BEARD? Last week the message had been more complex: SOME OF MY ANCESTORS WERE BARBARY PIRATES ON THE WEST AFRICAN COAST. DO I LOOK BLOODTHIRSTY TO YOU?

She did like him, though his questions often tempted her to write back, LEAVE ME ALONE! Satchmo's music stopped her. His saxophone was a curious instrument. It had been hollowed out, keys stripped from it. But he would put the reed to his lips and the silence would ripple, dance with color. No library visitors ever heard him or saw the music, but his fellow drifters could, and so could Mary.

"I need you to help me catch a . . . a rather *large* frog."

Satchmo grinned, revealing uneven yellow teeth. He scribbled a note, handed it to her.

WHY SHOULD I PLAY TOADY TO A FROG?

She frowned. Now was not the time for word games.

"Please, Satchmo. It'll ruin the books, possibly bring down the stacks, and then I'll be in real trouble."

Satchmo's eyes widened.

Scribble.

HOW BIG IS THIS FROG?

She sighed. "Big. Three or four feet at the shoulder."

Behind him, the drifters muttered darkly. They had been interrupted in the middle of a Romanian polka.

Scribble.

WILL YOU ORDER ME BOOKS ON BARBARY PIRATES?

"Anything . . ."

Satchmo motioned for her to wait, and walked over to the other drift-ers. He scribbled something on a card, gave it to a pale, stocky woman.

"He says," she said, "do you want to help this nutso woman catch a frog the size of a large dog or do you want to keep dancing?"

Mary groaned. She had hoped Satchmo would give them no choice. Almost to a man, this particular group of drifters had . . . eccentrici-ties. Behind Satchmo were pretenders to the name of Nixon, Nader, both Shelleys, Thatcher, Kubrick, Marx, Antoinette, and many more. Visitors to the library soon learned to avoid the second floor. But Mary kind of liked it there.

Much to her amazement, after a prolonged huddle, Satchmo walked over and handed her a note that read, WE WILL HELP—EXCEPT FOR THE ONE KNOWN AS MARY SHELLEY. Mary Shelley was a tiny, bird-like woman with a stutter.

"I-I-I tthh-think we shh-should ll-ll-let it go. I-I-I like mon-mon . . . Monsters!"

Thus began the first (and last) Samuel Devonshire Memorial Frog Hunt. While the clocks churned out seconds like organ grinders, the drifters spread across the first floor. Mary watched and coordinated from the second floor. Satchmo played the sax, hoping to entice the beast with swamp-green music. Thatcher tried to set an ambush. Marx formed a collective with a reluctant Marie Antoinette. Nixon built a trap with himself as bait. Kubrick sat in a corner and made psychotic faces. Nader ran around pleading for humane measures. Or at least that's what Mary thought he was doing.

Mary had unleashed a monster—an ineffective monster, for the frog remained At Large. Very large. The portraits were no help either. Insulted, they now screamed abuse at her.

Finally, as the scene below developed into a free dance experiment with Maggie and Marx doing the tango, she heard a giggle. A suspiciously green giggle. From above her. Through an air duct. An air duct leading to the fourth floor. Aha! Aha! She would have to deal with it herself. Alerting the lunatic drifters would only result in losing the element of surprise. Quietly, she backed away from the second floor railing . . .

Mary feared the fourth floor. People disappeared while on it: spinsters or young louts, babies or dogs, it made no difference. At least three, four times a year someone made the trip up . . . and never came down. She had never called the police because the missing person always turned up at some later date . . . but they didn't come down. Why try to understand it?

Besides, it was too late now. She was walking onto the fourth floor, brought by the pre-Civil War elevator, a clanking contraption which belched smoke and drank three cans of oil a week.

She shivered; it was colder here. And so gray. The fourth had once housed rare books, but a fire had finished them and the debris had never been cleared. Scarred book spines poked out from gutted shelves. She could feel a watchful silence, not at all green, as she drew her arms tightly together. Ghosts lived here. Phantom janitors with spectral mops, or perhaps the books themselves would rise, the pages flap-flapping like wings. *Get a grip*, she thought, suppressing the urge to slap herself.

She sped wraith-like through the stacks, headed for the railing which overlooked the first floor. When she reached it and stared down at the dancing drifters, she wondered if she shouldn't have told someone where she was going. The grayness, the silence, unnerved her. The frog wasn't dangerous, was it? Above her, she could see the eagle, spread continent-wide across the dome.

"Frog?" she whispered. "Greensleeves?"

No response. She sighed. The frog would not willingly give itself up. She edged her way along the corridor formed by the railing and the nearest stacks. Alert for movement, she sensed only dust and a faint burnt smell.

Then came a rustle, a twitch, followed by a hearty belch. She caught a hint of green silence, tracked it forward. She crept towards a cubbyhole which jutted out like a balcony. Peering out from behind a column, she saw—

THE FROG! She gasped, but the creature did not hear her. It watched the drifters. The frog was larger than she remembered when it had bolted past her in the first floor stacks: huge, with pouting lips and thick, dark green skin. No wonder it didn't feel the cold. As she watched, it giggled, apparently amused by the drifters' search. (Mary had no idea what made a frog giggle.)

A thought struck her and the hairs on her neck rose. A giggling frog could mean an intelligent frog.

How much do I know about Cedric Greensleeves? she fretted. *Is it really a good idea to jump this frog? Does it bite? Whywhywhy am I doing this?!*

She jumped.

The moment her feet left the ground, time seemed to slow down. She took hours, days, weeks to fall. In those weeks, the frog looked up, saw her, and—eyes wide—spit out whatever it had been chewing. Mary distinctly saw its lips move, form the word *Fuuuccckkk* with excruciating slowness.

She fell across its back legs, grabbed hold. The frog kicked out. Her grip loosened, but she recovered and grappled with it: a blur of thrashing, scrabbling frog muscles. She held on and slapped at the green flesh. But when she tried to squeeze its chest, the beast inflated its throat and, like some beach blow-up toy, increased its surface area 100%. She spat out frog slime.

With a final kick, she landed on her back, the frog atop her, its head too close for comfort. The eyes winked at her, the mouth smiled, and— *whap!*

The blow which lost the battle. A tongue to the forehead. An incredibly tough, wide tongue. It felt like a battering ram. *Whap!* She flailed at it, tried to flop back onto her stomach, but *whap!* failed. She grunted in disgust, punched the frog in the head. It punched back. *Whap!* She fell, but stubbornly latched on to one slippery toe. *Whap!* Her hand fell to the floor. The frog giggled, stepped over her bruised body and, with one last *Whap!* to the belly, hopped from view.

Mary lay there for a long time. It felt better than standing up, going back downstairs, and admitting to Satchmo that, yes, a frog had bested her in fisticuffs. Worse yet, frog saliva beaded her forehead, matted her hair. Two for the frog, zero for the librarian.

Mary glanced up at the glass eagle. It was much prettier up close, the detail of wings and talons almost life-like.

Never mind the frog. It wasn't a fair match. It used kudzu judo on you . . .

A whisper, or perhaps an exhalation of breath. But who had spoken? She sat up, glanced around her. No one. Had she imagined it?

"What's kudzu judo?" she asked, just in case.

A complicated form named after a trailing vine which strangles and smothers forests in the South . . .

"How do you know?"

I read over people's shoulders . . .

A spark of irritation entered her voice. "So who are you, where are you, and what are you doing spying on me?"

A slow, deep chuckle.

Up here, Mary. Look up. Really look.

She looked up at . . . well, at the eagle. It filled her field of vision. Now that she examined it, she could see the burnished brown-amber wings *moving*, second hand slow, but swimming through the glass. *Alive.* She gasped. The azure eye blinked, the talons unclenched. Snow drifted through the vacant hole. She rubbed her eyes, but the stained glass still rippled.

"I'm dreaming," she said. "I'm dreaming."

The chuckle again. It sent the clocks clucking among themselves, scrambled the computers, put a hitch in the drifters' dance.

I've seen you feed the birds which enter through my eye, Mary . . .

In a subdued voice, she said, "You're the eagle? You're alive?"

I woke the morning the meteorite shattered my eye. I had been lost in dreams of sand and heat and sweat. It brought me out of myself, into the world . . .

"But, but," she spluttered, "that's ridiculous!"

How curious . . . Talking portraits are not ridiculous. Frogs the size of baby elephants are not ridiculous, but somehow I am ridiculous. Surely you understand this place is special? You thought so yourself in your daydream of nightclubs and green computers. The only air of reality trickles through my broken eye . . .

"You can read my thoughts?" Mary found this rude, even peepingtommish, but she suppressed the thought when she realized he might eavesdrop.

I read dreams, Mary. The sleeping city keeps me awake with its dreams. So many dreams. During the day, it is worse: childish wish fulfillment, revenge, anxiety, paranoia. It tires me, saps my will. They enter through my eye, never let me rest . . .

"You've watched me all this time?"

Yes, Mary. I have tried for so long to make you hear me. But my voice grows weaker and weaker, and you have never before been close enough to hear it . . .

"Why weaker?" she asked, concerned.

Look once again. Closer still. Truly see . . .

She looked. At first she saw nothing except the movement of his body, but then . . . the glass was moving *around* his wings, encroaching like a cancer. The glass which formed the sky was bleeding into the wings, making them lose their form. The eagle beat his wings to keep them from being pinned down and distorted.

The intact eye sparkled as it watched her, the glass liquid, color changing . . .

I need your help, Mary . . .

"How?" she said, still caught up in the dark vision of cells eaten up—eradicated and replaced with the unhealthy.

You must help release me . . .

A sudden jolt of librarian sense came over Mary. She got up, backed away from the railing.

"What, exactly, do you mean?"

A long, sorrowful sigh.

That's what they all say. All the ones who come here. And then they forget, certain that they dreamed me! Only to dream again at night—of me. What do I mean, Mary? I mean you must release me from the dome . . .

"But won't the roof cave in?" She wrung her hands. "No. No. How could I possibly do it, anyway? I'd need construction workers, city permits. Everyone would think I was crazy. Mad! Ha! I would be mad . . ."

The eye blinked, the wingtips dipped, rose again.

Please, Mary. I have watched over you for so long. I know how much this library means to you, but please, release me. If not soon, then never. The glass shifts and shifts and imprisons me, clips my wings. Ever since I woke, the glass has been closing in on me. I do not want to return to thoughtlessness. Nor can I stand the dreams. Mary . . .

She sympathized, but what could she do? Nothing. If she set him free, the dome would collapse, ruining the upper floors and destroying the first. She would lose both job and library, be kicked out into the world again. With Cedric gone, her bold plans seemed foolish.

"I will think about it," she said, avoiding his eye. "I will tell you when I have decided."

Mary's ever so clumsy legs led her to the elevator. Behind her, a whisper: *Please, Mary. Ask Cedric. Cedric will know what to do . . .*

Downstairs, the drifters, frog, and Cedric were gathered around her desk. Cedric had changed clothes so that now he looked as though he had been painted in greens and blues and browns, camouflage more suitable for a forest. But it fit him. Cedric seemed shorter than before, less magical, but still the cinnamon eyes, flecked with gold, the grin—those were the same and just as alluring. The frog (beast!) sat at Cedric's feet, throat swelling and deflating as it breathed. She noted with grim satisfaction that it seemed tired. She tried to wipe the drool from her collar, only stopping when Cedric stared at her.

"Well," she said, folding her arms. "This is a fine sight. I spend all night searching for that . . . that *toad*. I grapple with it. I ruin my clothes. And here you are, all of you, not one bit of help!"

Cedric winked, then bowed. "Sorry, my lady. You were the one who told me he wasn't here."

My lady . . . her anger washed away. There was a glow about Cedric, a vigor and lightness that touched her heart.

"Well, at least it's over," she said, looking down.

"Indeed," replied Cedric. He turned to Satchmo. "Are you and your fellows ready?"

Ready? Mary thought.

"What is going on?"

Satchmo scribbled a note, an embarrassed look on his face. The note read, WE ARE ALL LEAVING WITH CEDRIC.

"Leaving!"

Cedric nodded. "Yes. The drifters, the frog, and I. They have been waiting a long time, you know. I should have found this place much sooner."

"Leaving," she said again, shocked. "But *why*, Satchmo?! This place is your home . . ." *My home.*

Scribble.

YOUR HOSPITALITY HAS BEEN WELCOME, BUT HUDDLING AROUND AN ELECTRIC FIREPLACE IN A LIBRARY IS NOT LIKE HOME.

For a moment, Mary could think of nothing to say. They were all leaving, taking her dreams with them. Then, from above, she thought she heard a whisper, a slow flutter of wings. A wild hope sprang into her mind.

"Wait," said Mary as Cedric turned towards the door. Cedric stopped.

"What, Mary?"

"The eagle. You can't leave the eagle." *You can't leave* me.

"The eagle? What about the eagle?"

"It's alive and it's trapped," she said, hoping beyond hope that he would stay, that she could make him stay. Or take her along, wherever they might go. "The glass around its wings is killing it. It won't be alive much longer." Did she sound crazy?

Cedric glanced up at the dome, produced an old-fashioned spyglass from a pocket, and squinted through it. Finally, he nodded.

"So it is," he said softly. "So it is. But if I help rescue the eagle, the library will be destroyed. The air of reality will enter and contaminate it. The clocks will just be clocks. The portraits will never speak again. I will never enter here again, Mary. You will have to leave. Do you want to leave, even to save the eagle?"

He stared directly at her as he spoke, the gaze which told her, *I know you. I know everything about you.*

She bowed her head. The eagle had pleaded with her and she, cruelly, had not answered it. Besides, surely Cedric would take her with him now.

"Yes," she said. "Yes, I do."

A shadow passed over Cedric's face.

"Very well," Cedric said. He faced the drifters. "Will you help? We will need good dancers. Very good dancers."

Satchmo scribbled a note.

WHAT IS ANOTHER HOUR OR TWO?

Cedric clapped him on the shoulder.

"Thank you, Satchmo. Everyone, close your eyes. Tightly!"

The drifters closed their eyes. Mary closed her eyes. And when Cedric said to open them—

—they were all on top of the dome and she was freezing. Her shoes had snow on them. She almost fell in surprise. The brisk wind sent them all whirling like tops. Cedric laughed, breath smoking from his mouth. The drifters giggled like children.

"Stomp your feet!" Cedric shouted over the wail of the wind. "Stomp your feet and set this poor bird free!"

It was then—Cedric jumping up and down on the glass, his body silhouetted by skyscrapers, a shadow against the frozen air, Lake Shore Drive threading through him like a glittering necklace—that Mary realized how much of the Faery was in him, and how little in her.

But then Satchmo tumbled by, grabbed her arm, and all thoughts left her head. Together they danced, slowly at first: a waltz to warm up. Soon he pulled out his saxophone and, with one hand around her waist, played it to perfection, a rising cluster of notes that did not waver, that flowed to the gyrations of his hips. She jumped up and down for the joy of it, the cold air slapping her face, making her tingle all over.

Around them, the drifters jostled, pushed, crawled, and boogied. Some stood on their heads while others stomp-stomp-stomped in position. The glass began to shake. The shaking became a self-sustained tremor so that when she stopped dancing for a moment, Mary could feel it. She saw that the dome's far edge had begun to sink inward. Drifters hastily moved towards the center.

And there was Cedric, still on the damaged portion, jumping higher than all of them until his upward pumping arms seemed to embrace the moon. His frog jumped higher still until, at the top of its arch, Mary could not even see it against the stars: just the two amber eyes glowing like far-away planets.

Soon Cedric came over to take Mary's hand. Satchmo drifted away, lost in his music. Together, Cedric and Mary bounded across the dome, through the scattered snow. His hands were warm, almost electric, and she held them tightly.

Some minutes later, the entire dome rumbled and roared beneath them. In mid-dance, glass crumbled under Mary's feet. She screamed, but Cedric yelled, "Don't worry! Keep dancing. Keep dancing." She believed him, believed in the warmth of his hands, the fire in his eyes. *Faery Fire.*

The rumbling intensified as the cracks grew deeper. Still they danced, dancing to their deaths without a care. It was all too much fun.

She could not pinpoint the moment she began to fall. First she weighed 112 pounds, then she was weightless, still holding Cedric's hand. Shards of glass passed them, followed by the almost-animate glass feathers of the eagle's right wing. She glimpsed the eye, the beak, the talons, and then she fell further, faster, and actually laughed, laughed her lungs out in freefall. Something warm and bright welled up inside Mary and she wondered lazily if she had ever been so happy, falling towards the library's floor in Cedric's arms. The marble crept up on them. Around her: arms and legs, more above her. She caught sight of Satchmo's hand holding the saxophone. Everything seemed silent—the flying glass, the eagle as it rose; she could not even hear herself breathe.

At the exact moment vertigo threatened to overwhelm Mary, Cedric snapped his fingers. He released her hand. Suddenly as two-dimensional and truly weightless as a leaf, she drifted towards the floor. The wind played with her, creating new ways for her to move, running fingers through her hair, but protecting her from the glass clouds that stormed across the library's upper level.

Then: something hard against her back. The floor. The spell broke and all 112 pounds of her felt betrayed. She was so heavy, so heavy after being so light. She longed for that sensation again, to fly away. Now the glass crashed—against marble floors, against shelves and chairs, with a thousand crystalline shudders.

Soon Satchmo and Cedric, grinning ear to ear like fools, had reached her side. She ignored them, watched the other drifters—light as snowflakes, as butterflies. No weight. No sensation. Why couldn't life be like that? Simple, with no thinking to it, only motion.

Across the face of the deep, she saw the eagle gliding, gliding. . . . Suddenly she was glad, so glad, that they had freed him. How light he must be.

When Mary finally got to her feet, tingling and bruised, a single glance told her the library would never be the same. Glass had threaded her hair. Glass had barricaded the elevators. Glass had infiltrated the computer's keys, smothering her files. Glass hung from the stacks like belated Christmas decorations. The emergency lights had turned on. Sadly, she realized she could not see the silence, not hear it in any form. Cedric's frog squatted nearby, but she could not sense the familiar green silence. The portraits against the wall were shrouded in darkness. Only faces. Pipes spilled water on the floor; it froze over as she watched. The fire alarm, burglar alarm, and repeat book offender alarm lights were all flashing, meaning they would not be alone for long.

She walked over to the entrance where the drifters had congregated. The frog hopped over with her, jumped onto Cedric's toes.

Cedric extricated himself, took Mary by the arm, and led her out of the drifters' earshot.

"There is no magic here, anymore, Mary," he said. "We must go."

481

"Yes, we must," she said, smiling. She clasped his hand. Gently, he removed it.

"Not you. The drifters, the frog, and I. I'm sorry."

"But . . . but I thought . . ."

"You were wrong. I'm sorry."

"I love you," she said. "I loved being with you on the roof. I want to go with you."

Cedric sighed. "My lady, everyone loves me. It is part of my Glamour, useful when I must travel in this world. I cannot take you with me."

"Why not?" she said petulantly. "You're taking the drifters."

"I can take the drifters because where we are going, no one will judge them. And I can use them. You only came to this library because you hated yourself."

"But I've changed."

"Yes, you have. Satchmo tells me you yelled at the portraits. My frog tells me you almost bested him in a fight. And, just now, you told me you loved me, not caring how I might hurt you." For a moment, his face was creased with wrinkles, the eyes sunk deep into the orbitals. "Don't cry. I must take the others away now. Do not follow us. It would kill you."

She nodded, but could not meet his eyes.

"The police will be here soon. Even my magic cannot cloak us from so many probing eyes."

"Go," she said.

"You saved the eagle, Mary."

She tried to smile. "Yes, I guess I did."

Cedric walked with her to the door. There, Satchmo kissed her hand—and pressed the saxophone into it. He scribbled a note while Mary just stared at him, too surprised to respond.

Keep the saxophone safe. I won't need it anymore. Don't be sad, Mary . . .

She nodded, squeezed his hand, then watched as the drifters followed Cedric out the door.

Halfway down the street, the city enveloped them. But what a city! For a moment, the skin of reality peeled back to reveal twinkling pagodas, streets shiny with silver, crowds of brightly clad folk; and, in the air, strange beasts roamed, not the least of which was the eagle, which flitted between the pagodas with a nightingale's grace.

The vision faded. She was alone. In the cold stone library. Moonlight bled through the shattered dome. Wind blew in her face. Sirens rose over the sounds of tinkling glass. Snow had begun to fall, coating the floor. Slowly, she walked back to her desk, took her purse and *Jerusalem Poker* from the drawers.

A dream. It all felt like a dream. But a hint of cinnamon flecked the air and her hair was still caked with frog spit.

At the door, she stopped, turned off the emergency lights, and looked back for the last time. There, in the gloom, she could just discern the stick-figure phantasms of her husbands, dancing slowly with each other, disintegrating as the moonlight touched them. The sight was almost funny.

It was only when Mary walked onto the street that she remembered the saxophone in her hand. She looked down at it. The hollow, smooth wood felt warm, warmer than her palm. On a whim, she raised it to her lips, unfurled her fingers to play, and blew. . . .

The sound? An echo of an echo: a silence that seemed to remember the past and present simultaneously. It reminded her of pan pipes, of mystery and illusion. A different silence. Not a graceful tune, surely, to prickle only the very edges of her senses, but pure.

And new.

Jeff VanderMeer's most recent fiction is the *New York Times*-bestselling Southern Reach trilogy (*Annihilation, Authority,* and *Acceptance*), all released in 2014. His *Wonderbook,* the world's first fully illustrated, full-color creative writing guide, won the BSFA Award for best nonfiction and has been nominated for a Hugo Award and a Locus Award. A Shirley Jackson Award winner and three-time World Fantasy Award, VanderMeer has been a finalist for the Nebula and Philip K. Dick Awards, among others. His nonfiction appears in the *New York Times,* the *Guardian,* the *Washington Post, Atlantic.com,* and the *Los Angeles Times.* VanderMeer has edited or coedited more than a dozen fiction anthologies, has taught at the Yale Writers' Conference and the Miami International Book Fair, and lectured at MIT and the Library of Congress. He lives in Tallahassee, Florida, with his wife, the noted editor Ann VanderMeer.

"Beauty and the Beast" is one of the more popular fairy tales and it has many variations in fiction—short and long—and other media as well. But other than two 1979 Angela Carter stories in her now-classic The Bloody Chamber, *I cannot recall any other modern short stories of note that precede this 1983 tale by Tanith Lee. Little can be said to preface "Beauty" other than it is science fiction and considers the perception of beauty.*

Beauty

Tanith Lee

His hundred and fifty-first birthday dawned aboard the sleek ship
from Cerulean, high above the white-capped ocean that was the
earth. By nightfall he would be at home, in his beautiful robot-
run house. Beyond the tall windows a landscape of the western hemisphere would fall away, pure with snow, to a frozen glycerin river. Far
from the weather control of the cities, the seasons came and went there
with all the passion and flamboyance of young women. And in the house,
the three young women came and went like the seasons.

Dark slender Lyra with her starry eyes and her music-well-named;
Joya, much darker, ebony-skinned, and angel-eyed, full of laughter—
well-named, too. And the youngest, his only born child, made with a
woman from whom he had long since parted: Estár, with her green-
brown hair the color of the summer oak woods, and her unrested tur-
bulent spirit—ill-named for a distant planet, meaning the same as the
Greek word *psyche*.

It seemed his seed made daughters, either mixed with the particles
of unknown women in crystal tubes, or mingled in a human womb. They
were his heirs; both to his mercantile fortune and to his treasures: of art

and science. He loved each of them, and was loved in turn. But sometimes Estár filled him with a peculiar fear. Her life would never be simple, and perhaps never happy. He did not like to think of her, maybe far from the shelter of the house, the shelter he could give her. In fifty, sixty more years, he might be dead. What then?

Tonight, there was the ceremonial dinner party to welcome him home, and to mark his birthday. A few charming guests would be there, delighting in the golden rooms. There would be the exchange of presents, for, with every birthday, gifts were given as well as received. This time, they had told him those three, laughing, what they wanted. "Natural things!" they had cried. Lyra wished for pearls, real pearls, the kind only to be taken from oysters that had died, neither cultured nor killed for. And Joya had demanded a dress of silk, an old dress made before the ending of the silkworm trade. Estár, he guessed, had subconsciously put them up to it, and when her turn came he had waited, uneasy in some way he could not explain. "A rose," she said, "a grown rose. But something from a hothouse or a city cultivatory won't do."

"In all this snow—" exclaimed Joya.

"I can send to the east," he said.

"No," said Estár, all too quietly. "You must pluck it yourself."

"But then," said Lyra, "he would have to detour from Cerulean. He'll never be home in time for the dinner party to give you such a present."

Estár smiled. "It seems I've posed you a riddle, Papa."

"It seems you have," he said, wincing a little at the title "Papa" which she had adopted from some book. His other daughters called him by his name, graciously, allowing him to be a person, not merely an adjunctive relation. "Well, I'll keep my eyes wide for roses in the snow."

Yet how ominous it had seemed, and not until the ship landed at the huge western terminus did he discover why.

"Mercator Levin? Would you be good enough to step this way?"

The attendant was human, a courteous formality that boded ill.

"Is anything wrong?" he asked. "My cargo?"

"Is quite in order, I assure you. The commissioner wishes to speak with you, on another matter."

Perplexed, he followed, and presently entered the circular office with its panoramic views of the landing fields. Dusk was imminent, and the miles of ground constellated by lights. Far away, little flaming motes, the ships sank slowly down or up.

He was offered wines, teas, coffees, and other social stimulants. He refused them all, his oppression growing. The commissioner, a few years his junior, was patently troubled, and paving the way—to something. At last he leaned back in his chair, folded his hands and said, "Depending on how you see your situation, Mercator Levin, it is my duty to inform you that either a great honor, or a great annoyance, is about to befall your family."

"What can you mean?"

"This, sir, has been placed in our care, for you."

He watched, he looked, he saw, and the control and poise of one and a half centuries deserted him. Risen from a recess in the desk, a slim crystal box stood transparent in the solarized light. A heap of soil lay on the floor of the box. Growing straight up from it was a translucent stem only faintly tinged with color, and leafless. At the head of the stem there blossomed a rose slender as a tulip, its petals a pale and singing green. There were no thorns, or rather only one and that metaphysical, if quite unbearably penetrating.

"I see it is not an honor," said the commissioner, so softly Levin was unsure if he were dealing with a sadist or a man of compassion. In any event, that made no odds. "I'm very sorry, Mercator. But I had no choice. And you, as you know, have none either. As you see, the name and code stamped into the crystal are your own."

"Yes," he said.

"So, if you would be so kind. I am to act as the witness, you understand, of your acceptance."

"But I don't accept," Levin said.

"You know, sir, that failure to comply—"

"I know. I'll do it. But accept? How could I?"

"No." And the commissioner lowered his eyes.

When he was within a foot of the desk and the box, the crystal opened for him. Levin reached in and took the smooth stem of the green rose in his fingers. The roots broke away with a crisp snap, like fresh lettuce, and a sweet aroma filled the air. It was the most disgusting, nauseating scent he had ever smelled.

Homecoming, normally so full of pleasure, was now resonant with dread. He dismissed the snow-car at the edge of the hill, and climbed, as he always did, toward the lovely, sprawling house. Most of it was of one-story construction in deference to the high winds that blew here in winter and often in the spring also, and all weatherproofed in a wonderful plasteel that made its walls seem to catch the prevailing light within themselves, glowing now a soft dull silver like the darkening sky. It had been turned into lace besides by the hundred golden windows—every illuminator was on to welcome him.

Inside, the house was warm and fragrant, old wood, fine synthetics. The robot servants had laid everything ready in his rooms, even to the selection of bedside books and music. His luggage was here ahead of him. He prepared himself, dressed for the party, went down. He had hurried to do so, but without eagerness. The glass of spirit he left untouched.

The main communal room of the house was some forty square meters, summer-heated from the floor, and also by the huge open central fire of natural coals, its suspended chimney like the glass pillar of a hallucination floating just above. How that chimney had fascinated Lyra and Joya as children. Something in its strength and exquisite airy unactuality—

For a while, the scene held in the room. They had not noticed him yet, though they expected him at any second. Lyra was playing the piano in a pool of light. What would it mean to her to be sent away? She was studying with two of the greatest musicians of the age, and already her compositions—three concertos, a symphony, song cycles, sonatas—were phenomenal and unique. She promised so much to herself, to her world. And she was, besides, in love. The young man who stood by the piano, watching her white hands, her face. Levin looked at him with a father's jealousy and a father's pride that the lover of his daughter should be both handsome and good. His amber skin, carven features and dark eyes, the violinist's hands, the talent of his calling—all these were charming and endearing things.

And then, standing listening by the fire, Joya, jet-black on the redness of the coals, no longer fascinated by the chimney, fascinating instead her two admirers, one male and one female. They were her friends, poets, a little eccentric as all Joya's friends turned out to be. It had alarmed him at first. He had feared she would be forced to change. But Joya had not altered, only extending her sunshine to others, giving them a steadiness they lacked, herself losing none. And she was now four months pregnant. She had told him her news the day he left, her eyes bright. It was splendid, enchanting. The thought of her as the mother of children filled him with painful happiness. She did not know who had fathered the child, which would be a son, nor did she care, had not bothered with the tests to discover. He had chided her gently, since the father had every right to know, and Joya had laughed: "Later. For now he's only mine."

And to send Joya away, two lives now—No! No, no.

Seated between the fire and the piano, the other guests were also listening to the music, four contemporaries of Levin's, well-known, stimulating and restful people of experience, and, in one case, genius, and three well-liked others, mutual acquaintances of them all. And there, on the periphery of the group, alone, his third daughter, his born daughter, and he grew cold at the perfection of the omens. The apple tint she used upon her brown hair had been freshly enhanced. Her dress, of the fashion known as Second Renascence, was a pale and singing green. She played with a glass of wine in her left hand, twirling the stem between her fingers. The translucent stem. It was as if she had known. He had heard rumors of such things before. It was ironical, for just now he recalled, of course, that she had almost never been born, her mother's frenetic lifestyle having brought on the preliminaries of a miscarriage—the child had been saved, and had continued to grow inside the woman's womb to a well coordinated seventh-month term. But how nearly—

Estár seemed to feel his eyes on her. She looked about, and, not speaking to anyone, got up and came noiselessly over to him in the doorway. She was tall and slim, and almost a stranger.

"Welcome home, Papa." She did not reach to kiss him as the others did, restrained, perhaps inhibited. He had noticed it with many born children. Those not carried in flesh seemed far easier with the emotional expressions of the flesh, a paradox. "Did you," said Estár, "find my rose?"

He looked at her in devastating sadness.

"At first, I thought I'd have to fail you," he said. "But in the end—look. Here it is."

And he held the green flower out to her in silence.

She gazed at it, and her pale face whitened. She knew it, and if by prescience she had foretold it, then that clearly had not been with her conscious mind. For a long while she did not take the rose, and then she reached out and drew it from his hand. The music was ending in the room. In another moment the others would become aware of his arrival, of this scene at the door.

"Yes," Estár said. "I see it must be me. *They* are your daughters. I'm only your guest."

"Estár," he said. "What are you saying?"

"No," she said. "I'm sorry. I meant only I have nothing to lose, or little—a nice home, a kind father—but they have everything to lose . . . love, children, brilliance—no, it has to be me, doesn't it?"

"I intend to petition," he began, and stopped.

"You know that everyone petitions. And it does no good at all. When do I have to leave?"

"The usual period is a month. Oh Estár—if there were anything at all—"

"You'd do it. I know. You're marvelous, but there are limits. It's not as if I'll never see you again. And, I respect your judgment. I do. To choose me."

The music ended. There was applause and laughter, and then the first cry of his name across the room.

"You fool," he said to his youngest daughter, "don't you know that I chose you—not because I consider you expendable—but because I love you the best?"

"Oh," she said. Her eyes filled with tears, and she lowered her head, not letting him see them.

"That is the decision this thing forces us to," he said. "To sacrifice in blood. Could I ask you the unforgivable thing—not to tell the others until this wretched party is over?"

"Of course," she said. "I'll go to my rooms for a little, ten minutes, perhaps. Then I'll come back, bright as light. Watch me. You'll be proud. Tell them I went to put your—your gift in water."

Levin had been a child five years old when the planet of his birth received its first officially documented visit from the stars. The alien ships fell like a summer snow, a light snow; there were not many. The moon cities, Martian Marsha, and the starry satellite colonies that drifted between, these the aliens by-passed. They came to the home world and presented it with gifts, clean and faultless technologies, shining examples of intellect and industry, from a culture similar to, much advanced on, greatly differing from, the terrestrial. And later, like wise guests not outstaying their welcome, the ships, and most of the persons who came with the ships went away. Their general purpose was oblique if altruistic. The purpose of those who remained less so, more so. At first they were seen in the capacity of prefects. To some extent, Earth had been conquered. Left free, no doubt she must still answer now and then to her benign superiors. But the remaining aliens required neither answers nor menials. It seemed they stayed only because they wished to, in love with Earth, tired of journeying . . . something of this sort. Perfectly tended by their own machineries, setting up their own modest estates far from the cities and the thoroughfares of popular life, they appropriated nothing and intruded not at all. They seemed content merely to be there. It was easy, for the most part, to forget them.

And then, about the time that Levin ended his adult education, around twenty-six or so, the first roses were sent. Immersed in a last fascinating study of something he had now quite forgotten, he missed the event. Only common outcry had alerted him. He remembered ever after the broodingly sinister concern that overcame him. It seemed the aliens in fact had decided to demand one thing. Or rather, they asked, courteously and undeniably. Somehow, without any threat, it was made clear that they could take without asking, that to ask was their good manners. The rose was a gracious summons, and with the first roses an explanation went of what the gracious summons entailed. Despite the outcry, despite petitions, letters, speeches loudly made in the senates and councils of every nation and every ethnic alliance of the world, the summonses were obeyed. There was no other choice. *I will not*, had been replied to, gently, illimitably: *You will.*

Without force, without threat, by unspoken undemonstrated implication only. The Earth was in fee to her friends. Stunned at the first, the only blow, there was, finally, no battle. The battles came later, seventy years later, when the second wave of roses—those alien roses from gardens blooming with the seeds of another planet, roses purple, azure, green— was dashed across humanity's quietude. Some resorted to concealment, then, and some fought. Some simply refused, standing firm; alone. But once again the inexorable pressure, invisibly and indecipherably applied, undid them. Men found themselves in conflict only with other men. The aliens did not attack them or seize from them. But they waited and were felt to be waiting. Roses thrown on fires were found not to burn. Roses flung among garbage were mysteriously returned, all burnished. The aliens made no other demand. The first demand was always enough.

Without their gifts, humanity would not thrive quite as it did. Gradually, persuaded by their own kind, bamboozled, worn out with beating their heads on the hard walls of censure, those who had hidden and fought and stood alone, crumbled, gave in, let go.

And it was a fact, in all the first two waves of the sending of the roses, and in all the sporadic individual sendings that had followed in these fifty years after the two waves, nothing had ever been asked of those who could not spare the payment. It had a kind of mathematical soulless logic, hopelessly unhuman, *in*human.

Always the families to whom the roses went were rich—not prosperous, as almost all were now prosperous—but something extra. Rich, and endowed with friends and kin, abilities of the mind and spirit: consolations for the inevitable loss. The loss of one child. A son, or a daughter, whichever of the household was best suited to be sent, could most easily be spared, was the most likely to find the prospect challenging or acceptable, or, endurable.

He remembered how at twenty-six it had suggested to him immolations to Moloch and to Jupiter, young children given to the god. But that was foolish, of course. They did not, when they went to the alien estates, go there to die, or even to worship, to extend service. They were neither sacrifices nor slaves. They had been seen quite often after, visiting their families, corresponding with them. Their lives continued on those little pieces of alien ground, much as they had always done. They were at liberty to move about the area, the buildings, the surrounding landscapes, at liberty to learn what they wished of the aliens' own world, and all its facets of science and poetry.

There was only discernible in them, those ones who went away, a distancing, and a dreadful sourceless silence, which grew.

The visits to their homes became less. Their communications and videochats ceased. They melted into the alien culture and were gone. The last glimpses of their faces were always burdened and sad, as if against advice they had opened some forbidden door and some terrible secret had overwhelmed them. The bereaved families knew that something had consumed their sons and daughters alive, and not even bones were left for them to bury.

It was feared, though seldom spoken of, that it was natural xenophobia, revulsion, which destroyed and maybe killed the hearts of humanity's children. They had grown with their own kind, and then were sent to dwell with another kind. Their free revisitings of family and friends would only serve to point the differences more terribly between human and alien. The aliens—and this was almost never spoken of—were ugly, were hideous. So much had been learned swiftly, at the very beginning. Out of deference to their new world, out of shame, perhaps, they covered their ugliness with elegant garments, gloves, masking draperies, hoods and visors. Yet, now and then, a sighting—enough. They were like men or women, a little taller, a slender, finely muscled race . . . But their very likeness made their differences the more appalling, their loathsomeness more unbearable. And there were those things which now and then must be revealed, some inches of pelted hairy skin, the gauntleted over-fingered hands, the brilliant eyes empty of white, lensed by their yellow conjunctiva.

These, the senders of roses.

It seemed, without knowing, Levin always had known that one day the obscene sacrifice would be asked of him. To one of these creatures would now travel his youngest daughter Estár, who wore by choice the clothing of reborn history.

While she ordered the packing of her luggage, he wrote letters and prepared recordings of appeal and righteous anger.

Both knew it to be useless.

Somewhere in the house, Joya and Lyra wept.

On the first day of Midwinter, the snow-car stood beside the porch.

"Good-bye," she said.

"I will—" he began.

"I know you'll do everything you can." She looked at her sisters, who were restraining their frightened tears with skill and decorum so that she should not be distressed. "I shall see you in the spring. I'll make sure of that," she said. It was true, no doubt. Joya kissed her. Lyra could not risk the gesture, and only pressed her hand. "Good-bye," Estár said again, and went away.

The snow sprang in two curved wings from the car. In ten seconds it was a quarter of a mile away. The snow fell back. The sound of crying was loud. Levin took his two remaining daughters in his arms and they clung to him. Catching sight of them all in a long mirror, he wryly noted he and they were like a scene from an ancient play—Greek tragedy or Shakespeare: Oedipus and Antigone, Lear with Cordelia lost—*A Winter's Tale*.

He wondered if Estár cried, now that she was in private and unseen.

Tanith Lee

2

Estár had not cried; she was sickened from fear and rage. Neither of these emotions had she expressed, even to herself, beyond the vaguest abstracts. She had always been beset by her feelings, finding no outlet. From the start, she had seen Lyra express herself through music, Joya through communication. But Estár had been born with no creative skills and had learned none. She could speak coherently and seemingly to the point, she could, if required to, write concise and quite interesting letters, essays, and fragments of descriptive poetry. But she could not convey *herself* to others. And *for* herself, what she was aware of, suffered, longed for—these concepts had never come clear. She had no inkling as to what she wanted, and had often upbraided herself for her lack of content and pleasure in the riches fate had brought her, her charming family, the well-ordered beauty of her world. At fifteen, she had considered a voluntary term at Marsha, the Martian colonial belt, but had been dissuaded by physical circumstance. It seemed her lungs, healthy enough for Earth, were not of a type to do well for her in the thin half-built atmosphere of Mars. She had not grieved, she had not wanted to escape to another planet any more than she wanted anything else. There had simply been a small chance that on Mars she might have found a niche for herself, a *raison d'Estár.*

Now, this enforced event affected her in a way that surprised her. What did it matter after all if she were exiled? She was no ornament at home to herself or others and might just as well be placed with the ambiguous aliens. She could feel, surely, no more at a loss with this creature than with her own kind, her own kin.

The fear was instinctive, of course, she did not really question that. But her anger puzzled her. Was it the lack of choice? Or was it only that she had hoped eventually to make a bond between herself and those who loved her, perhaps to find some man or woman, one who would not think her tiresome and unfathomable and who, their novelty palling, she would not come to dislike. And now these dreams were gone. Those who must live with the aliens were finally estranged from all humanity, that was well known. So, she had lost her own chance at becoming human.

It was a day's journey. The car, equipped with all she might conceivably need, gave her hot water and perfumed soap, food, drink, played her music, offered her books and films. The blue-white winter day only

494

gradually deepened into dusk. She raised the opaque blinds of the forward windows and looked where the vehicle was taking her.

They were crossing water, partly frozen. Ahead stood a low mountain. From its conical exaggerated shape, she took it to be man-made, one of the structured stoneworks that here and there augmented the Earth. Soon, they reached a narrow shore, and as the dusk turned gentian, the car began to ascend.

A gentle voice spoke to her from the controls. It seemed that in ten minutes she would have arrived.

There was a tall steel gate at which the snow-car was exchanged for a small vehicle that ran on an aerial cable.

Forty feet above the ground, Estár looked from the window at the mile of cultivated land below, which was a garden. Before the twilight had quite dispersed, she saw a weather control existed, manipulating the seasons. It was autumn by the gate and yellow leaves dripped from the trees. Later, autumn trembled into summer, and heavy foliage swept against the sides of the car. It was completely dark when the journey ended, but as the car settled on its platform, the mild darkness and wild scents of spring came in through its opening doors.

She left the car and was borne down a moving stair, a metal servant flying leisurely before with her luggage. Through wreaths of pale blossom she saw a building, a square containing a glowing orb of roof, and starred by external illuminators.

She reached the ground. Doors bloomed into light and opened.

A lobby, quite large, a larger room beyond. A room of seductive symmetry—she had expected nothing else. There was no reason why it should not be pleasant, even enough like other rooms she had seen as to appear familiar. Yet, too, there was something indefinably strange, a scent, perhaps, or some strain of subsonic noise. It was welcome, the strangeness. To find no alien thing at once could have disturbed her. And maybe such psychology was understood, and catered to.

A luminous bead came to hover in the air like a tame bird.

"Estár Levina," it said, and its voice was like that of a beautiful unearthly child. "I will be your guide. A suite has been prepared for you. Any questions you may wish—"

"Yes," she broke in, affronted by its sweetness, "when shall I meet—with your controller?"

"Whenever you desire, Estár Levina."

"When *I* desire? Suppose I have no desire ever to meet him?"

"If such is to be your need, it will be respected, wherever possible."

"And eventually it will no longer be possible and I shall be briskly escorted into his presence."

The bead shimmered in the air.

"There is no coercion. You are forced to do nothing that does not accord with your sense of autonomy."

"But I'm here against my will," she said flatly.

The bead shimmered, shimmered.

Presently she let it lead her silently across the symmetrical alien room, and into other symmetrical alien rooms.

Because of what the voice-bead had said to her, however, she kept to her allotted apartment, her private garden, for a month.

The suite was beautiful, and furnished with all she might require. She was, she discovered, even permitted access, via her own small console, to the library bank of the house. Anything she could not obtain through her screen, the voice-bead would have brought for her. In her garden, which had been designed in the manner of the Second Renascence, high summer held sway over the slender ten-foot topiary. When darkness fell, alabaster lamps lit themselves softly among the foliage and under the falling tails of water.

She wondered if she was spied on. She acted perversely and theatrically at times in case this might be so. At others she availed herself of much of what the technological dwelling could give her.

Doors whisked open, clothes were constructed and brought, baths run, media deposited as though by invisible hands. It was as if she were waited on by phantoms. The science of Earth had never quite achieved this fastidious level, or had not wanted to. The unseen mechanisms and energies in the air would even turn the pages of printed books for her, if requested.

She sent a message to her father after two days. It read simply: *I am here and all is well.* Even to her the sparseness was disturbing. She added a postscript: *Joya must stop crying over me or her baby will be washed away.*

She wondered, as her mail was sent out, if the alien would read it.

On the tenth day, moodily, she summoned from the library literature and spoken theses on the aliens' culture and their world.

"Curiosity," she said to the walls, "killed the cat."

She knew already, of course, what they most resembled—some species of huge feline, the hair thick as moss on every inch of them save the lips, the nostrils, the eyes, and the private areas of the body. Though perhaps ashamed of their state, they had never hidden descriptions of themselves, only their actual selves, behind the visors and the draperies.

She noted that while there were many three-dimensional stills of their planet, and their deeds there and elsewhere, no moving videos were available, and this perhaps was universally so.

She looked at thin colossal mountain ranges, tiny figures in the foreground, or sporting activities in a blur of dust—the game clear, the figures less so. Tactfully, no stress was laid even here, in their own habitat, on their unpalatable differences. What Earth would see had been vetted. The sky of their planet was blue, like the sky of Earth. And yet utterly alien in some way that was indecipherable. The shape of the clouds, maybe, the depth of the horizon ... Like the impenetrable differences all about her. Not once did she wake from sleep disoriented; thinking herself in her father's house.

The garden appealed to her, however; she took aesthetic comfort from it. She ate out on a broad white terrace under the leaves and the stars in the hot summer night, dishes floating to her hands, wine and coffees into her goblet, her cup, and a rose-petal paper cigarette into her fingers.

Everywhere secrets, everywhere the concealed facts.

"If," she said to the walls. "I am observed, are you enjoying it, O Master?" She liked archaic terms, fashions, music, art, attitudes. They had always solaced her, and sometimes given her weapons against her own culture which she had not seemed to fit. Naturally, inevitably, she did not really feel uneasy here. As she had bitterly foreseen, she was no more un-at-home in the alien's domicile than in her father's.

But why was she here? The ultimate secret. Not a slave, not a pet. She was free as air. As presumably all the others were free. And the answers that had come from the lips and styluses of those others had never offered a satisfactory solution. Nor could she uncover the truth, folded in this privacy. She was growing restless. The fear, the rage, had turned to a fearful angry ache to know—to seek her abductor, confront him, perhaps touch him, talk to him.

Curiosity . . . if by any chance he did not spy on her, did not nightly read reports on her every action from the machines of the house, why then the Cat might be curious too.

"How patient you've been." she congratulated the walls, on the morning of the last day of the month. "Shall! invite you to my garden? Or shall! meet you in yours?" And then she closed her eyes and merely thought, in concise clipped words within her brain: *I will wait for you on the lawn before the house, under all that blossom. At sunset.*

And there at sunset she was, dressed in a version of Earth's fifteenth century, and material developed from Martian dust crystals.

Through the blossoming spring trees the light glittered red upon her dress and on her, and then a shadow came between her and the sun.

She looked up, and an extraordinary sensation filled her eyes, her head, her whole torso. It was not like fear at all, more like some other tremendous emotion. She almost burst into tears.

He was here. He had read her mind. And, since he had been able to do that, it was improbable he had ever merely spied on her at all.

"You admit it," she said. "Despite your respect for my—my privacy—how funny—you admit I have *none!*"

He was taller than she, but not so much taller that she was unprepared for it. She herself was tall. He was covered, as the aliens always covered themselves, totally, entirely. A glint of oblique sun slithered on the darkened faceplate through which he saw her, and through which she could not see him at all. The trousers fit close to his body, and the fabric shone somewhat, distorting, so she could be sure of nothing. There was no chink. The garments adhered. Not a centimeter of body surface showed, only its planes, male and well-formed: familiar, alien—like the rooms, the skies of his world. His hands were cased in gauntlets, a foolish, inadvertent complement to her own apparel. The fingers were long. There were six of them. She had seen a score of images and threedems of such beings.

But what had happened. That was new.

Then he spoke to her, and she realized with a vague shock that some mechanism was at work to distort even his voice so it should not offend her kind.

"That I read your thoughts was not an infringement of your privacy, Estár Levina. Consider. You intended that they should be read. I admit, my mind is sensitive to another mind which signals to it. You signaled very strongly. Almost I might say, with a razor's edge."

"I," said, "am not a telepath."

"I'm receptive to any such intentional signal. Try to believe me when I tell you I don't, at this moment, know what you are thinking. Although I could guess."

His voice had no accent, only the mechanical distortion. And yet it was—charming—in some way that was quite ab-human, quite unacceptable.

They walked awhile in the outer garden in the dusk. Illuminators ignited to reveal vines, orchids, trees—all of another planet, mutating gently among the strands of terrestrial vegetation. Three feet high, a flower like an iris with petals like dark blue flames allowed the moon to climb its stem out of the valley below.

They barely spoke. Now and then she asked a question, and he replied. Then, somewhere among a flood of Earthly sycamores, she suddenly found he was telling her a story, a myth of his own world. She listened, tranced. The weird voice, the twilight, the spring perfume, and the words themselves made a sort of rhapsody. Later that night, alone, she discovered she could not remember the story and was forced to search it out among the intellectual curios of the library bank. Deprived of his voice, the garden, and the dusk, it was a very minor thing, common to many cultures, and patently more than one planet. A quest, a series of tasks. It was the multitude of plants that had prompted the story, that and the rising of a particular star.

When they reentered the house, they went into an upper room, where a dinner was served. And where he also ate and drank. The area of the facial mask which corresponded with his lips incredibly somehow was not there as he raised goblet or fork toward them. And then, as he lowered the utensil, it was there once more, solid and unbreachable as ever. Not once, during these dissolves of seemingly impenetrable matter, did she catch a glimpse of what lay beyond. She stared, and her anger rose like oxygen, filling her, fading.

"I apologize for puzzling you," he said. "The visor is constructed of separable atoms and molecules, a process not yet in use generally on Earth. If this bothers you, I can forgo my meal."

"It bothers me. Don't forgo your meal. Why," she said, "are you able to eat Earth food? Why has this process of separable atoms not been given to Earth?" And, to her astonishment, her own fragile glass dropped from her hand in pieces that never struck the floor.

"Have you been cut?" his distorted voice asked her unemphatically. Estár beheld she had not.

"I wasn't," she said, "holding it tightly enough for that to happen."

"The house is eager to serve you, unused to you, and so misunderstands at times. You perhaps wanted to crush something?"

"I should like," she said, "to return to my father's house."

"At any time, you may do so."

"But I want," she said, "to stay there. I mean that I don't want to come back here."

She waited. He would say she had to come back. Thus, she would have forced him to display his true and brutal omnipotence.

He said, "I'm not reading your mind, I assure you of that. But I can sense instantly whenever you lie."

"Lie? What am I lying about? I said, I want to go home."

"'Home' is a word which has no meaning for you, Estár Levina. This is as much your home as the house of your father."

"This is the house of a beast," she said, daringly. She was very cold, as if winter had abruptly broken in. "A superior, wondrous monster." She sounded calm. "Perhaps I could kill it. What would happen then? A vengeance fleet dispatched from your galaxy to destroy the terrestrial solar system?"

"You would be unable to kill me. My skin is very thick and resilient. The same is true of my internal structure. You could, possibly, cause me considerable pain, but not death."

"No, of course not." She lowered her eyes from the blank shining mask. Her pulse beat from her skull to her soles. She was ashamed of her ineffectual tantrum. "I'm sorry. Sorry for my bad manners, and equally for my inability to murder you. I think I should go back to my own rooms."

"But why?" he said. "My impression is that you would prefer to stay here."

She sat and looked at him hopelessly.

"It's not," he said, "that I disallow your camouflage, but the very nature of camouflage is that it should successfully wed you to your surroundings. You are trying to lie to yourself, and not to me. This is the cause of your failure."

"Why was I brought here?" she said. "Other than to be played with and humiliated." To her surprise and discomfort, she found she was being humorous, and laughed shortly. He did not join in her laughter, but she sensed from him something that was also humorous, receptive. "Is it an experiment in adaptation; in tolerance? To determine how much proximity a human can tolerate to one of us? Or vice versa."

"No."

"Then what?"

There was a pause. Without warning, a torrent of nausea and fear swept over her. Could he read it from her? Her eyes blackened and she put one hand over them. Swiftly, almost choking, she said, "If there is an answer, don't, please don't tell me."

He was silent, and after a few moments she was better. She sipped the cool wine from the new goblet which had swum to her place. Not looking at him at all, she said, "Have I implanted this barrier against knowledge of that type, or have you?"

"Estár," she heard him say, far away across the few yards of the table, "Estár, your race tends sometimes to demand too little or too much of itself. If there's an answer to your question, you will find it in your own time. You are afraid of the idea of the answer, not the answer itself. Wait until the fear goes."

"How can the fear go? You've condemned me to it, keeping me here."

But her words were lies, and now she knew it.

She had spoken more to him in a space of hours than to any of her own kind. She had been relaxed enough in his company almost to allow herself to faint, when, on the two other occasions of her life that she had almost fainted, in company with Levin, or with Lyra, Estár had clung to consciousness in horror, unreasonably terrified to let go.

The alien sat across the table. Not a table knife, not an angle of the room, but was subtly strange in ways she could not place or understand. And he, his ghastly nightmarish ugliness swathed in its disguise . . .

Again with no warning she began to cry. She wept for three minutes in front of him, dimly conscious of some dispassionate compassion that had nothing to do with involvement. Sobbing, she was aware after all he did not read her thoughts. Even the house did not, though it brought her a foam of tissues. After the three minutes she excused herself and left him. And now he did not detain her.

In her rooms, she found her bed blissfully prepared and lay down on it, letting the mechanisms, visible and invisible, undress her. She woke somewhere in the earliest morning and called the bead like a drop of rain and sent it to fetch the story he had told her. She resolved she would not go near him again until he summoned her.

A day passed.

A night.

A day.

She thought about him. She wrote a brief essay on how she analyzed him, his physical aura, his few gestures, his inherent hideousness to which she must always be primed, even unknowingly. The distorted voice that nevertheless was so fascinating.

A night.

She could not sleep. He had not summoned her. She walked in her private garden under the stars and found a green rose growing there, softly lighted by a shallow lamp. She gazed on the glow seeping through the tensed and tender petals. She knew herself enveloped in such a glow, a light penetrating her resistance.

"The electric irresistible charisma," she wrote, "of the thing one has always yearned for. To be known, accepted, and so to be at peace. No longer unique, or shut in, or shut out or alone."

A day.

She planned how she might run away. Escaping the garden, stumbling down the mountain, searching through the wilderness for some post of communications or transport. The plan became a daydream and he found her.

A night.

A day.

That day, she stopped pretending, and suddenly he was in her garden. She did not know how he had arrived, but she stepped between the topiary and he was there. He extended his hand in a formal greeting; gloved, six-fingered, not remotely unwieldy. She took his hand. They spoke. They talked all that day, and some of the night, and he played her music from his world and she did not understand it, but it touched some chord in her, over and over with all of its own fiery chords.

She had never comprehended what she needed of herself. She told him of things she had forgotten she knew. He taught her a board game from his world, and she taught him a game with dots of colored light from Earth.

One morning she woke up singing, singing in her sleep. She learned presently she herself had invented the fragment of melody and the handful of harmonies. She worked on it alone, forgetting she was alone, since the music was with her. She did not tell him about the music until he asked her, and then she played it to him.

She was only ashamed very occasionally, and then it was not a cerebral, rather a hormonal thing. A current of some fluid nervous element would pass through her, and she would recall Levin, Lyra, Joya. Eventually something must happen, for all that happened now was aside from life, unconnected to it.

She knew the alien's name by then. It had no earthly equivalents, and she could not write it, could not even say it; only think it. So she thought it.

She loved him. She had done so from the first moment she had stood with him under the spring trees. She loved him with a sort of welcome, the way diurnal creatures welcome the coming of day.

He must know. If not from her mind, then from the manner in which, on finding him, she would hurry toward him along the garden walks. The way she was when with him. The flowering of her creativity, her happiness.

What ever would become of her?

She sent her family three short noncommittal soothing messages, nothing compared to the bulk of their own.

When the lawns near the house had altered to late summer, it was spring in the world and, as she had promised, Estár went to visit her father.

3

Buds like emerald vapor clouded the boughs of the woods beyond the house. The river rushed beneath, heavy with melted snows. It was a windless day, and her family had come out to meet Estár. Lyra, a dark note of music, smiling, Joya, smiling, both looking at her, carefully, tactfully, assessing how she would prefer to be greeted, not knowing. How could they? Joya was slim again. Her child had been born two weeks ago, a medically forward seven-month baby, healthy and beauteous—they had told her in a recording, the most recent of the ten they had sent her, along with Lyra's letters. . . . Levin was standing by the house door, her father. They all greeted her, in fact, effusively. It was a show, meant to convey what they were afraid to convey with total sincerity.

They went in, talking continuously, telling her everything. Lyra displayed a wonderful chamber work she and Ekosun, her lover, were composing—it was obvious he had been staying with her here, and had gone away out of deference to Estár's return, her need for solitary confinement with her family. Joya's son was brought, looking perfectly edible, the color of molasses, opening on a toothless strawberry mouth and two wide amber eyes. His hair was already thick, the color of corn. "You see," said Joya, "I know the father now, without a single test. This hair—the only good thing about *him*."

"She refuses even to let him know," said Levin.

"Oh, I will. Sometime. But the child will take my name, or yours, if you allow it."

They drank tea and ate cakes. Later there came wine, and later there came dinner. While there was food and drink, news to tell, the baby to marvel at, a new cat to play with—a white cat, with a long gray understripe from tail to chin-tip—a new painting to worship, Lyra's music to be heard—while there was all this, the tension was held at bay, almost unnoticeable. About midnight, there came a lull. The baby was gone, the cat slept, the music was done and the picture had faded beyond the friendly informal candlelight. Estár could plead tiredness and go to bed, but then would come tomorrow.

It must be faced sometime.

"I haven't," she said, "really told you anything about where I've been."

Joya glanced aside. Lyra stared at her bravely.

Levin said, "In fact, you have."

She had, he thought, told them a very great deal. She was strangely different. Not actually in any way he might have feared. Rather, she seemed more sure, quieter, more still, more absorbent, more favorably aware of them than ever in the past. One obvious thing, something that seemed the emblem of it all, the unexpected form of this change in her—her hair. Her hair now was a calm pale brown, untinted, no longer green.

"What have I told you then?" she said, and smiled, not intending to, in case it should be a smile of triumph.

"At least," he said, "that we needn't be afraid for you."

"No. Don't be. I'm really rather happy."

It was Lyra who burst out, unexpectedly, shockingly, with some incoherent protest.

Estár looked at her.

"He's—" she sought a word, selected one, "interesting. His world is interesting. I've started to compose music. Nothing like yours, Lyra, not nearly as complex or as excellent, but it's fulfilling. I like doing it. I shall get better."

"I'm so sorry," said Lyra. "I didn't mean—it's simply—"

"That I shouldn't be happy because the situation is so unacceptable. Yes. But it isn't. I'd never have chosen to go there, because I didn't know what it would entail. But, in fact, it's exactly the sort of life I seem to need. You remember when I meant to go to Marsha? I don't think I would have done as much good there as I'm doing here, for myself. Perhaps I even help him in some way. I suppose they must study us, benignly. Perhaps I'm useful."

"Oh, Estár," Lyra said. She began to cry, begged their pardon and went out of the room, obviously disgusted at her own lack of finesse. Joya rose and explained she was going to look after Lyra. She too went out.

"Oh dear," said Estár.

"It's all right," Levin said. "Don't let it trouble you too much. Over-excitement. First a baby invades us, then you. But go on with what you were saying. What do you do on this mountain?"

He sat and listened as she told him. She seemed able to express herself far better than before, yet even so he was struck by the familiarity rather than the oddness of her life with the alien. Really, she did little there she might not have done here. Yet here she had never done it. He pressed her lightly, not trusting the ice to bear his weight, for details of the being with whom she dwelled. He noticed instantly that, although she had spoken of him freely, indeed very often, in the course of relating other things, she could not seem to speak of him directly with any comfort. There was an embarrassment quite suddenly apparent in her. Her gestures became angular and her sentences dislocated.

Finally, he braced himself. He went to the mahogany cabinet that was five hundred years old, and standing before it pouring a brandy somewhat younger, he said, "Please don't answer this if you'd rather not. But I'm afraid I've always suspected that, despite all genetic, ethnic or social disparity, those they selected to live with them would ultimately become their lovers. Am I right, Estár?"

He stood above the two glasses and waited.

She said. "Nothing of that sort has ever been discussed."

"Do you have reason to think it will be?"

"I don't know . . ."

"I'm not asking out of pure concern, or out of any kind of prurient curiosity. One assumes, judging from what the others have said or indicated, that nobody has ever been raped or coerced. That implies some kind of willingness."

"You're asking me if I'd be willing to be his lover?"

"I'm asking if you are in love with him."

Levin turned with the glasses, and took her the brandy. She accepted and looked at it. Her face, even averted, had altered, and he felt a sort of horror. Written on her quite plainly was that look he had heard described—a deadly sorrow, a drawing inward and away. Then it was gone.

"I don't think I'm ready to consider that," she said.

"What is it," he said, "that gives you a look of such deep pain?"

"Let's talk about something else," she said.

Merchant and diplomat, he turned the conversation at once, wondering if he were wrong to do so. They talked about something else.

It was only much later, when they parted for the night, that he said to her, "Anything I *can* do to help you, you've only to tell me."

And she remembered when he brought the rose and gave it to her, how he had said he loved her the best. She wondered if one always loved, then, what was unlike, incompatible.

"This situation has been rather an astonishment to us all," he added now. She approved of him for that, somehow. She kissed him good night. She was so much easier with him, as if estrangement had made them closer, which it had not.

Two weeks passed, Lyra and Joya laughed and did not cry. There were picnics, boat rides, air trips. Lyra played in live concert, and they went to rejoice in her. Things now seemed facile enough that Ekosun came back to the house, and after that a woman lover of Joya's. They breakfasted and dined in elegant restaurants. There were lazy days too, lying on cushions in the communal rooms listening to music or watching video plays, or reading, or sleeping late, Estár in her old rooms among remembered things that no longer seemed anything to do with her. The green rose of her summons, which would not die but which had something to do with her, had been removed.

It was all like that now. A brightly colored interesting adventure in which she gladly participated, with which she had no link. The very fact that their life captivated her now was because of its—alienness. And her family, too. How she liked and respected them all at once, what affection she felt for them. And for the same reason.

She could not explain it to them, and would be ill advised to do so even if she could. She lied to herself, too, keeping her awareness out of bounds as long as she might. But she sensed the lie. It needed another glass of wine, or another chapter of her book, or a peal of laughter, always something, and then another thing and then another, to hold it off.

At the end of two weeks her pretense was wearing thin and she was exhausted. She found she wanted to cry out at them: I know who you are! You are my dear friends, my dazzling idols—I delight in you, admire you, but I am sometimes uneasy with you. Now I need to rest and I want to go—

Now I want to go home.

And then the other question brushed her, as it must. The house on the mountain was her home because he (she wordlessly expressed his name) was there. And because she loved him. Yet in what way did she love him? As one loved an animal? A friend? A lord? A teacher? A brother? Or in the way Levin had postulated, with a lover's love? And darkness would fall down on her mind and she would close the door on it. It was unthinkable.

When she devised the first tentative move toward departure, there was no argument. They made it easy for her. She saw they had known longer than she that she wanted to leave.

"I almost forgot to give you these. I meant to the first day you came back. They're fawn topaz, just the color your hair is now."

On Joya's smoky palm, the stones shone as if softly alight. "Put your hair back, the way you had it at the concert, and wear them then."

"Thank you," said Estár. "They're lovely."

She reached toward the earrings and found she and her sister were suddenly holding hands with complete naturalness. At once she felt the pulse under Joya's skin, and a strange energy seemed to pass between them, like a healing touch.

They laughed, and Estár said unthinkingly, "But when shall I wear them on the mountain?"

"Wear them for him," said Joya.

"For—"

"For him," said Joya again, very firmly.

"Oh," Estár said, and removed her hand.

"No, none of us have been debating it when you were out of the room," said Joya. "But we do know. Estár, listen to me, there's truly nothing wrong in feeling emotion for this—for him, or even wanting him sexually."

"Oh really, Joya."

"*Listen.* I know you're very innocent. Not ignorant, innocent. And there's nothing wrong in that either. But now—"

"Stop it, Joya." Estár turned away, but the machines packing her bag needed no supervision. She stared helplessly at the walls. Joya would not stop.

"There is only one obstacle. In your case, not culture or species. You know what it is. The way they look. I'm sorry, I'm sorry, Estár. But this is the root of all your trouble, isn't it?"

"How do I know?" She was exasperated.

"There is no way you can know. Unless you've seen him already, without that disguise they wear. Have you?"

Estár said nothing. Her silence, obviously, was eloquent enough.

"Go back then," said Joya, "go back and make him let you see him. Or find some way to see him when he doesn't realize you can. And then you *will* know."

"Perhaps I don't want to know."

"Perhaps not. But you've gone too far."

"You're trying to make me go too far. You don't understand."

"Oh, don't I?"

Estár rounded on her, and furiously saw only openness.

"You might possibly," said Estár, "want to spoil—something—"

"I might. But what does that matter? He—it—whatever the alien is, he's real and living and male and you're committed to him, and until you see him and know if you can bear it, how can you *dare* commit yourself?"

"But they're ugly," Estár said flatly. The words, she found, meant very little.

"Some humans are ugly. They can still be loved, loving."

"Suppose somehow I do see him—and I can't think how I would be able to—and suppose then I can't stand to look at him—"

"Then your feelings will undergo some kind of alternate channeling. But the way you are now is absurd."

"Oh prithee, sweet sister," Estár snarled, "let me be. Or, blameless one, throw thou the first stone."

Joya looked bemused. Then she said, "I did, didn't I? Two of them. You caught them, too."

And went out of the room, leaving the brown topaz earrings in Estár's hand.

It was so simple to return in the end it was like being borne away by a landslide.

All at once she was in a vehicle, the house flowing off behind her to a minuscule dot, and so to nothing. Then she was alone and sat down with her thoughts to consider everything—and abruptly, before she was ready, the conical mountain loomed before her.

There was a ghost of winter frost in the garden by the gate. Further on, the banana-yellow leaves were falling. She had seen many places anachronized by a weather control, yet here it seemed rather wonderful . . . for no reason at all.

The blossom was gone from about the building, but roses had opened everywhere. Alien roses, very tall, the colors of water and sky, not the blood and blush, parchment, pallor, and shadow shades of Earth. She walked through a wheatfield of roses and in at the doors.

She went straight through all the intervening rooms and arrived in the suite the alien called—had given her. There, she looked about her steadfastly. Even now, she was not entirely familiar with the suite, and unfamiliar with large sections of the house and gardenland.

Under such circumstances, it was not possible to recognize this place as her home. Even if, intellectually, she did so.

She wondered where he might be in the house. Surely he would know she had returned. Of course he would know. If she went out into her own garden, perhaps—

A word was spoken. It meant "yes." And although she did not know the word she knew its meaning for it had been spoken inside her head.

She waited, trembling. How close they were, then, if he could speak to her in such a way. She had been probing, seeking for him, her intuitive telepathy now quite strong, and she had touched him, and in turn been touched. There was no sense of intrusion. The word spoken in her head was like a caress, polite and very gentle.

So she went out into her garden, where it was beginning to be autumn now, and where the topiary craned black against the last of the day's sunlight. He stood just beyond the trees, by the stone basin, with the colored fish. A heron made of blue steel balanced forever on the rim, peering downward, but the fish were sophisticated and unafraid of it, since it had never attacked them.

Suppose it was this way with herself? There he stood, swathed, masked, hidden. He had never given her cause to fear him. But was that any reason not to?

He took her hand; she gave her hand. She loved him, and was only frightened after all because he must know it. They began to talk, and soon she no longer cared that she loved him or that he knew.

They discussed much and nothing, and it was all she had needed. She felt every tense string of her body and her brain relaxing. All but one. What Levin, her father, had hinted, what Lyra had shied away from saying and Joya said. Could he perceive and sense this thing in her thoughts?

Probably. And if she asked, in what way would he put her off? And could she ask? And would she ask?

When they dined that evening, high up in the orb of the roof, only the table lit, and the stars thickly clustered over the vanes above, she watched the molecules parting in his visor to accommodate cup or goblet or fork.

Later, when they listened to the music of his planet, she watched his long hands, cloaked in their gauntlets, resting so quiet yet so animate on the arms of a chair they were like sleeping cats.

Cat's eyes. If she saw them would she scream with horror? Yes, for weeks her sleep had been full of dreams of him, incoherent but sexual dreams, dreams of desire. And yet he was a shadow. She dreamed of coupling in the dark, blind, unseeing. She could hate Joya for being so right.

When the music ended, there came the slow turn of his head, and she beheld the graceful power of it, that concealed skull pivoted by that unseen neck. The cloaked hands flexed. The play of muscle ran down his whole body like a wave, and he had risen to his feet, in a miracle of coordinated movement.

"You're very tired, Estár," he said.

"But you know what I want to ask you."

"Perhaps only what you feel you should want to ask."

"To see you. As you are. It must happen, surely, if I live here with you."

"There's no need for it to happen now. Sometimes, with those others like yourself who are the companions of my kind, it only happens after many years. Do you comprehend, Estár? You're not bound to look at me as I am."

"But," she said, "You would allow it?"

"Yes."

She stared at him and said, "When?"

"Not tonight, I think. Tomorrow, then. You recall that I swim in the mornings. The mechanism that waits on you will bring you to my pool. Obviously, I swim without any of this. You can look at me, see me, and after that stay or go away, as you wish."

"Thank you," she said. Her head began to ache and she felt as if some part of her had died, burned out by the terror of what she had just agreed to.

"But you may change your mind," he said. "I won't expect you."

There was no clue in his distorted, expressive voice. She wondered if he, too, was afraid.

She made all the usual preparations for bed and lay down as if tonight were like any other, and did not sleep. And in the morning, she got up and bathed and dressed, as if it were any other morning. And when the machines had washed and brushed her hair, and enhanced her face with pastel cosmetics, she found she could not remember anything of the night or the routines of waking, bathing, dressing or anything at all. All she could remember was the thing to come, the moment when she saw him as he truly was. That moment had already happened to her maybe five thousand times, over and over, as she conjured it, fled from it, returned to it, in her mind.

And therefore, was he aware of all she had pictured? If he had not sensed her thoughts, he must deduce her thoughts.

She drank scalding tea, glad to be burned.

The voice-bead hovered, and she held out her hand. It came to perch on her fingers, something which she liked it to do, a silly affectionate ruse, her pretense, its complicity, that it was somehow creaturally alive.

"Estár, shall I take you to the indoor pool?"

"Yes," she said. "Take me there now."

It was a part of the house she had not been in very much, and then, beyond a blank wall which dissolved as the molecules in his visor had done, a part of the house she had never entered.

His rooms.

They opened one from another. Spare, almost sparse, but supple with subtle color, here and there highlighted by things which, at some other time, she would have paused to examine in fascinated interest—musical instruments from his world, the statue of a strange animal in stranger metal, an open book on whose surfaces be had written by hand in the letters of an alien alphabet.

But then doors drew aside, and the bead glimmered before her out into a rectangular space, open above on the skies of Earth, open at its center on a dense blue water. Plants grew in pots along the edges of the pool, huge alien ferns and small alien trees, all leaning lovingly to the pool which had been minerally treated to resemble the liquids of their home. With a very little effort, Estár might imagine it was his planet she saw before her, and that dark swift shape sheering through the water, just beneath its surface, that shape was the indigenous thing, not the alien thing at all. Indeed, she herself was the alien, at this instant.

And at this instant, the dark shape reached the pool's end, only some ten feet from her.

There came a dazzle across the water as he broke from it. He climbed from the pool and moved between the pots of ferns and trees, and the foliage and the shadow left him, as the water had already done. It was as he had told her. She might see him, unmasked, naked, open-eyed.

She stared at him until she was no longer able to do so. And then she turned and walked quickly away. It was not until she reached the inner rooms that she began to run.

She re-entered the suite he had given her, and stayed there only for an hour before she sent the voice-bead to him with her request. It returned with his answer inside five minutes. This time, there was no telepathic communion. She could not have borne it, and he had recognized as much.

4

"Please don't question me," she said. "Please."

Her family who, not anticipating her arrival on this occasion had not been waiting to meet her—scattered like blown leaves about the room—acquiesced in gracious troubled monosyllables.

They would realize, of course, what must have occurred. If any of them blamed themselves was not apparent. Estár did not consider it, would consider nothing, least of all that she was bound, eventually, to return to the place she had fled.

She went to her apartment in Levin's house, glanced at its known unknown angles and objects, got into the remembered unremembered bed. "Bring me something to make me sleep," she said to the household robots. They brought it to her. She drank the cordial and sank thousands of miles beneath some sea. There were dreams, but they were tangled, distant. Waking for brief moments she could not recall them, only their colors, vague swirlings of noise or query. They did not threaten her. When she woke completely, she had more of the opiate brought, and slept again.

Days and nights passed. Rousing, she would permit the machines to give her other things. She swallowed juices, vitamins, and small fruits. She wandered to the bathroom, immersed herself in scented fluid, dried herself and returned to bed. And slept.

It would have to end, obviously. It was not a means of dying, merely of temporary oblivion, aping the release of death. The machineries maintained her physical equilibrium, she lost five pounds, that was all. No one disturbed her, came to plead or chide. Each morning, a small note or two would be delivered—Joya or Lyra—once or twice Levin. These notes were handwritten and full of quiet solicitude. They were being very kind, very patient. And she was not behaving well, to worry them, to throw her burden upon them secondhand in this way. But she did not care very much about that.

What galvanized her in the end, ousted her from her haven of faked death, was a simple and inevitable thing. Her dreams marshalled themselves and began to assume coherence. She began to dream of him. Of the instant when he had left the water and she had seen him as he was. So they condemned her to relive, over and over again, that instant, just as she had lived it over and over before it had happened. Once the dreams were able to do this to her, naturally, there was no point in sleeping any longer. She must wake up, and find a refuge in the alternative of insomnia.

Seven days had gone by. She emerged from the depths a vampire, eager to feed on each of the other living things in the house, to devour their lives, the world and everything, to cram her mind, her consciousness. Again, they humored her. None of them spoke of what must have caused this, but the strain on them was evident. Estár liked them more each second, and herself less. How could she inflict this on them? She inflicted it. Three days, three nights went by. She did not sleep at any time.

Catching the atmosphere like a germ, Joya's son became fractious. The cat leapt, its fur electric, spitting at shadows. A terrible recurring headache, of which she did not speak but which was plain in her face, began to torment Lyra. Her lover was absent. Estár knew Ekosun would dislike her for consigning her sister to such pain. Finally Joya broke from restraint, and said to her, "I'm sorry. Do you believe that?" Estár ignored the reference, and Joya said, "Levin's in contact with the Mercantile Senate. They have a great deal of power. It may be possible to force the issue." "No one has ever been able to do anything of the sort."

"What would you like me to do?" said Joya. "Throw myself from a great height into the river?"

Estár laughed weakly. She took Joya in her arms. "It wasn't you. I would have had to—you were right. Right, right."

"Yes," said Joya, "I was right. Perhaps one of the most heinous crimes known to humanity."

When Estár courteously excused herself and went away, Joya did not protest. Joya did not feel guilty, only regretful at the consequences of an inevitable act. Clean of conscience, she in turn set no further conflict working in Estár—the guilty are always the most prone to establish complementary guilt, and the most unforgiving thereafter.

And so Estár came to spend more and more time with Joya, but they did not speak of him once.

On the twelfth day Estár fell asleep. She dreamed and saw him, framed by the pool and the foliage of his planet, and she started awake with a cry of loud anger.

It seemed she could never forget the awfulness of the revelation, could not get away from it. And therefore she might as well return to the mountain. Probably he would leave her very much alone. Eventually, it might be possible for her to become reconciled. They might meet again on some level of communication. Eventually. Conceivably. Perhaps.

That evening she spent in one of the communal rooms of her family's house. She tried to repay their sweetness and their distress with her new calm, with gentle laughter, thanking them with these things, her reestablished sense of self, her resignation tinged by intimations of hope, however dull, and by humor coming back like a bright banner.

They drank cold champagne and vodka, and the great fire roared under the transparent column, for like the drinks still the nights were cold. Estár had grown in this house, and now, quite suddenly and unexpectedly, she remembered it. She smiled at her father who had said he loved her the best of his daughters. She knew it was untrue, and yet that he had said it to her had become a precious thing.

There was a movement, a flicker like light. For a moment she thought it came from the fire, or from some mote traveling across the air of the room, the surface of her eye. And then she knew it had moved within her brain. She knew that he had spoken to her, despite the miles between them, and the manner in which she had left him. There were no words at all. It was like a whisper, or the brush of a low breeze across the plateau of her mind. She felt a wonderful slowness fill her, and a silence.

One hour later a message came for her, delivered to the house by a machine only glimpsed in the gusty evening. She opened the synthetic wrapper. She had anticipated, nor was she wrong to have done so. There was one line of writing, which read: *Estár. Tomorrow, come back to the mountain.* And he had signed it with that name she could not read or speak, yet which she knew now as well, maybe better, than her own. She looked a long while at the beautiful unhuman letters.

They watched her, and she said to them, "Tomorrow I am going back to the mountain. To him."

There was again that expression on her face; it had been there, mostly, since she had reentered Levin's house on this last visit. (Visit. She did not belong to them anymore.) The expression of the children of Earth sacrificed to monsters or monstrous gods, given in their earthly perfection to dwell with beasts. That dreadful demoralizing sadness, that devouring fading in the face of the irreparable. And yet there was nothing in her voice, and as she left the room her step was untrammelled and swift. And,

Levin recollected, not wanting to, the story of lemmings rushing in blithe tumult toward the ocean to be drowned.

A peacock-green twilight enclosed the mountain garden and the building. Estár looked at it in wonder; it transformed everything. It seemed to her she was on some other planet, neither her own nor his.

A capsule had given her sleep throughout the journey. Drowsily serene she walked into the building and the voice-bead played about her, as if glad she had returned. They went to her suite and she said, "Where is he?" And opened her door to find him in the room.

She started back. In the blue-green resin of the dusk she saw at once that he was dressed in the garments of his own world, which concealed hardly anything of him.

She turned away and said coldly: "You're not being fair to me."

"It will soon be dark," he said. "If you leave the lamps unlit, you won't see me well. But you have seen me. The pretense is finished." There was no distortion to his voice. She had never really heard him speak before.

She came into the room and sat down beside a window. Beyond the glassy material, the tall topiary waved like seaweed, in the sea of sky. She looked at this and did not look at him.

Yet she saw only him.

The water-sky dazzled as the pool had done, and he stepped out of the sky, the pool, and stood before her as in all her dreams, unmasked, naked, open-eyed. The nature of the pool was such, he was not even wet.

The hirsute pelt which covered his kind was a reality misinterpreted, misexplained. It was most nearly like the fur of a short-haired cat, yet in actuality resembled nothing so much as the nap of velvet. He was black, like her sister Joya, yet the close black nap of fur must be tipped, each single hair, with amber; his color had changed second to second, as the light or dark found him, even as he breathed, from deepest black to sheerest gold. His well-made body was modeled from these two extremes of color, his fine musculature, like that of a statue, inked with ebony shadows, and highlighted by gilding. Where the velvet sheathing faded into pure skin, at the lips; nostrils, eyelids, genitals, the soles of the feet, palms of the hands, the flesh itself was a mingling of the two shades; a somber cinnamon, couth and subtle, sensual in its difference, but not shocking in any visual or aesthetic sense. The inside of his mouth, which he had also contrived to let her see, was a dark golden cave, in which conversely the humanness of the white teeth was in fact itself a shock. While at his loins the velvet flowed into a bearded blackness, long hair like unraveled silk; the same process occurred on the skull, a raying mane of hair; very black, very silken, its edges burning out through amber, ochre, into blandness—the sunburst of a black sun. The nails on his six long fingers, the six toes of his long and arched feet, were the tint of new dark bronze, translucent, bright as flames. His facial features were large and of a contrasting fineness, their sculptured quality at first obscured, save in profile, by the sequential ebb and flare of gold and black, and the domination of the extraordinary eyes. The long cinnamon lids, the thick lashes that were not black but startlingly flaxen—the color of the edges of the occipital hair—these might be mistaken for human. But the eyes themselves could have been made from two highly polished citrines, clear saffron, darkening around the outer lens, almost to the cinnamon shade of the lids, and at the center by curiously blended charcoal stages to the ultimate black of the pupil. Analogously, they were like the eyes of a lion, and perhaps all of him lionlike, maybe, the powerful body, its skin unlike a man's, flawless as a beast's skin so often was, the pale, fire-edged mane. Yet he was neither like a man nor an animal. He was like himself, his kind, and his eyes were their eyes, compelling, radiant of intellect and intelligence even in their strangeness, and even in their beauty. For he was beautiful. Utterly and dreadfully beautiful. Coming to the Earth in the eras of its savagery, he would have been worshipped in terror as a god. He and his would have been forced to hide what they were for fear the true sight of it would burn out the vision of those who looked at them. And possibly this was the reason, still, why they had hidden them-selves, and the reason too for the misunderstanding and the falsehoods. To fear to gaze at their ugliness, that was a safe and sensible premise. To fear their grandeur and their marvel—that smacked of other emotions less wise or good.

And she herself, of course, had run from this very thing. Not his alien hideousness—his beauty, which had withered her. To condescend to give herself to one physically her inferior, that might be acceptable. But not to offer herself to the lightning bolt, the solar flame. She had seen and she had been scorched, humiliated and made nothing, and she had run away, ashamed to love him. And now, ashamed, she had come back, determined to put away all she had felt for him or begun to feel or thought to feel.

Determined to be no more than the companion of his mind, which itself was like a star, but, being an invisible, intangible thing, she might persuade herself to approach.

But now he was here in a room with her, undisguised, in the gracious garments of his own world and the searing glory of his world's race, and she did not know how she could bear to be here with him.

And she wondered if he were pleased by her suffering and her confusion. She wondered why, if he were not, he would not let her go forever. And she pictured such an event and wondered then if, having found him, she *could* live anywhere but here, where she could not live at all.

The sky went slowly out, and they had not spoken any more.

In the densening of the darkness, those distant suns, which for eons had given their light to the Earth, grew large and shining and sure.

When he said her name, she did not start, nor did she turn to him.

"There is something which I must tell you now," he said to her. "Are you prepared to listen?"

"Very well."

"You think that whatever I may say to you must be irrelevant to you, at this moment. That isn't the case."

She was too tired to weep, or to protest, or even to go away.

"I know," he said quietly. "And there's no need for you to do any of these things. Listen, and I shall tell you why not."

As it turned out, they had, after all, a purpose in coming to the Earth, and to that other handful of occupied planets they had visited, the bright ships drifting down, the jewels of their technology and culture given as a gift, the few of their species left behind, males and females, dwellers in isolated mansions, who demanded nothing of their hosts until the first flowering of alien roses, the first tender kidnappings of those worlds' indigenous sons and daughters.

The purpose of it all was never generally revealed. But power, particularly benign power, is easily amalgamated and countenanced. They had got away with everything, always. And Earth was no exception.

They were, by the time their vessels had lifted from the other system, a perfect people, both of the body and the brain; and spiritually they were more nearly perfect than any other they encountered. The compassion of omnipotence was intrinsic to them now, and the generosity of wholeness.

Yet that wholeness, that perfection had had a bizarre, unlooked-for side effect. For they had discovered that totality can, by its very nature, cancel out itself.

They had come to this awareness in the very decades they had come also to know that endless vistas of development lay before them, if not on the physical plane, then certainly on the cerebral and the psychic. They possessed the understanding, as all informed creatures do, that their knowledge was simply at its dawn. There was more for their race to accomplish than was thinkable, and they rejoiced in the genius of their infancy, and looked forward to the limitless horizons—and found that their own road was ended, that they were not to be allowed to proceed. Blessed by unassailable health, longevity, strength, and beauty, their genes had rebelled within them, taking this peak as an absolute and therefore as a terminus.

Within a decade of their planetary years, they became less fertile, and then sterile. Their bodies could not form children, either within a female womb or externally, in an artificial one. Cells met, embraced, and died in that embrace. Those scarcity of embryos that were successfully grown in the crystalline generative placentae lived, in some cases, into the Third Phase, approximate to the fifth month of a human pregnancy—and then they also died, their little translucent corpses floating like broken silver flowers. To save them, a cryogenic program was instituted. Those that lived, on their entry to the Third Phase, were frozen into stasis. The dream persisted that at last there would be found some way to realize their life. But the dream did not come true. And soon even the greatest and most populous cities of that vast and blue-skied planet must report that, in a year twice the length of a year of the Earth, only eight or nine children had been saved to enter even that cold limbo, which now was their only medium of survival.

The injustice of fate was terrible. It was not that they had become effete, or that they were weakened. It was their actual peerlessness which would kill the race. But being what they were, rather than curse God and die, they evolved another dream, and before long pursued it across the galaxies. Their natural faculties had remained vital as their procreative cells had not. They had conceived the notion that some other race might be discovered, sufficiently similar to their own that—while it was unlikely the two types could mingle physically to produce life— in the controlled environment of a breeding tube such a thing might be managed. The first world that offered them scope, in a system far beyond the star of Earth, was receptive and like enough that the first experiments were inaugurated. They failed.

And then, in one long night, somewhere in that planet's eastern hemisphere, a female of that race miscarrying and weeping bitterly at her loss, provided the lamp to lead them to their dream's solution.

With the sound and astounding anatomical science of the mother world, the aliens were able to transfer one of their own children, one of those embryos frozen in cryogenesis for fifty of their colossal years, into the vacated womb.

And, by their science too, this womb, filled and then despoiled, was repaired and sealed, brought in a matter of hours to the prime readiness it had already achieved and thought to abandon.

The mother was monitored and cared for, for at no point was she to be endangered or allowed to suffer. But she thrived, and the transplanted child grew. In term, the approximate ten-month term normal to that planet, it was born, alive and whole. It had come to resemble the host race almost exactly; this was perhaps the first surprise. As it attained adulthood, there was a second surprise. Its essence resembled only the essence of its parental race. It was alien, and it pined away among the people of its womb-mother. Brought back to its true kind, then, and only then, it prospered and was happy and became great. It seemed, against all odds, their own were truly their own. Heredity had told, not in the physical, but in the ego. It appeared the soul of their kind would continue, unstoppable. And the limitless horizons opened again before them, away and away.

By the date in their travels when they reached Earth, their methods were faultless and their means secret and certain. Details had been added, refining details typical of that which the aliens were. The roses were one aspect of such refinements.

Like themselves, the plants of the mother world were incredibly long-lived. Nourished by treated soil and held in a vacuum—as the embryos were held in their vacuum of coldness—such flowers could thrive for half an Earth century, even when uprooted.

Earth had striven with her own bellicosity and won that last battle long before the aliens came. Yet some aggression, and some xenophobic self-protective pride remained. Earth was a planet where the truth of what the aliens intended was to be guarded more stringently than on any other world. A woman miscarrying her child in the fourth or fifth

Beauty

month, admitted to a medical center, and evincing psychological evidence
of trauma—even now it happened. This planet was full of living beings,
a teeming globe prone still to accident and misjudgment. As the woman
lay sedated, the process was accomplished. In the wake of the dead and
banished earthly child, the extra-terrestrial embryo was inserted, and
anchored like a star. Women woke, and burst into tears and tirades of
relief—not knowing they had been duped. Some not even remembering,
for the drugs of the aliens were excellent, that they had ever been close to
miscarrying. A balance was maintained. Some recalled, some did not. A
sinister link would never be established. Only the eager and willing were
ever employed.

There was one other qualification. It was possible to predict logisti-
cally the child's eventual habitat, once born. Since the child would have
to be removed from that habitat in later years, the adoptive family was
chosen with skill. The rich—who indeed tended more often to bear their
children bodily—the liberated, the open-minded, the unlonely. That
there might be tribulation at the ultimate wrenching away was unavoid-
able, but it was avoided or lessened wherever and however feasible.
Nor was a child ever recalled until it had reached a level of prolonged
yearning, blindly and intuitively begging to be rescued from its unfitted
human situation.

Here the roses served.

They in their crystal boxes, the embryos frozen in their crystal wombs.
With every potential child a flower had been partnered. The aura of a life
imbued each rose. It was the aura, then, which relayed the emanations of the
child and the adult the child became. The aura which told, at last, this telepathically sensitive race, when the summons must be sent, the exile rescued.

The green rose now flourishing in her garden here was Estár's own
rose, brought home.

The woman who had carried Estár inside her, due to her careless-
ness, had lost Levin's child, and received the alien unaware. The woman
had needed to bear a child, but not to keep the child. Levin had gladly
claimed what he took to be his own.

Estár, the daughter of her people, not Levin's daughter, not Lyra's
sister or Joya's either, Estár had grown up and grown away, and the
green rose which broadcast her aura began to cry soundlessly, a wild
beacon. So they had released her from her unreal persona, or let her
release herself.

521

And here she was now, turning from the window of stars to the invisible darkness of the room, and to his invisible darkness.

For a long while she said nothing, although she guessed—or telepathically she knew—he waited for her questions. At last one came to her.

"Marsha," she said. "They disqualified me from going there."

"A lie," he said. "It was arranged. In order that your transposition should be easier when it occurred."

"And I—" she said, and hesitated

"And you are of my kind, although you resemble the genera which was your host. This is always the case. I know your true bloodline, your true father and mother, and one day you may meet them. We are related, you and I. In the terminology of this world, distant cousins. There is one other thing."

She could not see him. She did not require to see him with her eyes. She now waited, for the beauty of his voice.

"The individual to whom you are summoned—this isn't a random process. You came to me, as all our kind return, to one with whom you would be entirely compatible. Not only as a companion, but as a lover, a bonded lover—a husband, a wife. You see, Estár, we've learned another marvel. The changes that alter our race in the womb of an alien species, enable us thereafter to make living children together, either bodily or matrically, whichever is the most desired."

Estár touched her finger to the topaz in her left ear.

"And so I love you spontaneously, but without any choice. Because we were chosen to be lovers?"

"Does it offend you?"

"If I were human," she said, "it might offend me. But then."

"And I, of course," he said, "also love you."

"And the way I am—my appearance . . . do you find me ugly?"

"I find you beautiful. Strangely, alienly lovely. That's quite usual. Although for me, very curious, very exciting."

She shut her eyes then, and let him move to her across the dark. And she experienced in her own mind the glorious wonder he felt at the touch of her skin's smoothness like a cool leaf, just as he would experience her delirious joy in the touch of his velvet skin, the note of his dark and golden mouth discovering her own.

Seeing the devouring sadness in her face when she looked at them, unable to reveal her secret, Estár's earthly guardians would fear for her.

They would not realize her sadness was all for them. And when she no longer moved among them, they would regret her, and mourn for her as if she had died. Disbelieving or forgetting that in any form of death, the soul—Psyche, Estár, (well-named)—refinds a freedom and a beauty lost with birth.

Acknowledgments

"The Queen Who Could Not Walk" © 2013 The Avicenna Development Corporation. First publication: *Weird Tales #361*, Summer 2013.

"Follow Me Light" © 2005 Elizabeth Bear. First publication: *SciFiction*, 12 January 2005.

"The Coat of Stars" © 2007 Holly Black. First publication: *So Fey, Queer Fairy Fiction*, ed. Steve Berman (Lethe Press).

"The Queen and the Cambion" © 2012 Richard Bowes. First publication: *The Magazine of Fantasy & Science Fiction*, March-April 2012.

"The Mussel Eater" © 2014 Octavia Cade. First publication: *The Book Smugglers*, 18 November 2014.

"Fairy Tale" © 2003 Gardner Dozois. First publication: *SciFiction*, 15 January 2003.

"Bears: A Fairy Tale of 1958" © 2013 Steve Duffy. First publication: *Little Visible Light*, eds. S. P. Miskowski & Kate Jonez (Omnium Gatherium).

"Halfway People" © 2010 Karen Joy Foweler. First publication: *My Mother She Killed Me, My Father He Ate Me: Forty New Fairy Tales*, eds. Kate Bernheimer & Carmen Giménez Smith (Penguin Books).

"Diamonds and Pearls: A Fairy Story" © 2009 Neil Gaiman. First publication: *Who Killed Amanda Palmer: A Collection of Photographic Evidence*. Neil Gaiman, Kyle Cassidy & Beth Hommel (Eight Foot Books).

"Princess Lucinda and the Hound of the Moon" © 2007 Theodora Goss. First publication: *Realms of Fantasy*, June 2007.

"The Glass Bottle Trick" © 2000 Nalo Hopkinson. First publication: *Whispers from the Cotton Tree Root: Caribbean Fabulist Fiction*, ed. Nalo Hopkinson (Invisible Cities Press).

"The Road of Needles" © 2013 Caitlín R. Kiernan. First publication: *Once Upon A Time: New Fairy Tales*, ed. Paula Guran (Prime Books).

"Catastrophic Disruption of the Head" © 2011 Margo Lanagan. First publication: *The Wilful Eye*, eds. Isobelle Carmody & Nan McNab (Allen & Unwin).

"Beauty" © 1983 Tanith Lee. First publication: *Red as Blood or Tales from the Sisters Grimmer* (DAW Books).

"Red as Blood" © 1979 Tanith Lee. First publication: *The Magazine of Fantasy & Science Fiction*, July 1979.

About the Editor

P aula Guran edits the annual Year's Best Dark Fantasy and Horror series as well as a growing number of other anthologies. She is senior editor for Prime Books and earlier edited the Juno fantasy imprint from its small press inception through its incarnation as an imprint of Pocket Books. In an previous life she produced weekly email newsletter *DarkEcho* (winning two Stokers, an IHG award, and a World Fantasy Award nomination), edited magazine *Horror Garage* (earning another IHG and a second World Fantasy nomination), and has contributed reviews, interviews, and articles to numerous professional publications. It is easy to find her online through paulaguran.com, Twitter, Facebook, and elsewhere. The mother of four, mother-in-law of two, and grandmother of three, Guran lives in Akron, Ohio.